JAN   2021

WITHDRAWN

THE BEST OF MICHAEL MARSHALL SMITH

THE BEST OF MICHAEL MARSHALL SMITH

MICHAEL MARSHALL SMITH

Subterranean Press 2020

The Best of Michael Marshall Smith Copyright © 2020 by Michael Marshall Smith. All rights reserved.

Dust jacket illustration Copyright © 2020 by Stefan Koidl. All rights reserved.

Interior illustrations Copyright © 2020 by Les Edwards. All rights reserved.

Interior design Copyright © 2020 by Desert Isle Design, LLC. All rights reserved.

See pages 563-565 for individual story copyright information.

First Edition

ISBN
978-1-59606-950-3

Subterranean Press
PO Box 190106
Burton, MI 48519

subterraneanpress.com

Manufactured in the United States of America

This is for my readers, with heartfelt thanks,
and especially my first readers—
David Smith, Stephen Jones,
and Paula Grainger

TABLE OF CONTENTS

The Handover 9
Save As… 23
Being Right 37
Hell Hath Enlarged Herself 53
More Tomorrow 79
The Motel Business 111
Dear Alison 125
The Man Who Drew Cats 137
This is Now 155
To Receive is Better 169
They Also Serve 177
The Scariest Thing in the World 197
The Seventeenth Kind 211
What You Make It 231
Not Waving 253
Later 281
Walking Wounded 289
The Gist 307
Author of the Death 339
The Dark Land 353
Different Now 377
The Things He Said 383
The Window of Erich Zann 395
Everything You Need 425
What Happens When You Wake Up in the Night 437
Failure 445
Charms 459
The Burning Woods 471
Shit Happens 509
Always 531
Best Of—Story Notes 539

THE **HANDOVER**

Nobody moved much when he came into the bar. From the way Jack shut the door behind him—quietly, like the door of a cupboard containing old things seldom needed but neatly stored—we could tell he didn't have any news we'd be in a hurry to hear.

There were three guys sipping beer up at the counter. One of them glanced up, gave him a brief nod. That was it.

It was nine thirty by then. There were five other men in the place, each sitting at a different table, nobody talking. Some had books in front of them but I hadn't heard a page turn in a while. I was sitting near the fire and working steadily through a bowl of chili, mitigating it with plenty of crackers. I'd like to say Maggie's chili is the best in the West, but, to be frank, it really isn't. It's probably not even the best in town: even this town, even now. I wasn't hungry, merely eating for something to do. Only alternative would have been drinking, but just a couple will go to my head these days and I didn't want to be drunk. Being drunk has a tendency to make everything run into one long dirge, like being stoned, or living in Iowa. I haven't ever taken a drink on important days, on Thanksgiving, anniversaries or my birthday. Not a one. This evening wasn't any kind of celebration, not by a long chalk, but I didn't want to be drunk for it either.

Jack walked up to the bar, water dripping from his coat onto the floor. He wasn't moving fast, and he looked old and cold and worn through. It was bitter outside and the afternoon had brought a fresh fall of snow. Only a couple of inches, but it was beginning to mount up. Maggie poured a cup of coffee without being asked, set it in front of him. Her coffee isn't too bad, once you've grown accustomed to it. Jack methodically poured five spoons of sugar into the brew, which is one of the ways of getting accustomed to it, and stirred it slowly. The skin on his hand looked delicate and thin, like blue-white tissue paper that had been scrunched into a ball and absently flattened out again. Sixty-eight isn't so old, not these days, not in the general scheme of things. But some nights it can seem ancient, if you're living inside it. Some nights it can feel as if you're still trying to run long after the race is finished. At sixty-four, and the second youngest in the place, I personally felt older than God.

Jack stood for a moment, looking around the room as if memorizing it. The counter itself was battered with generations of use, like everything else. The edges of chairs and tables were worn smooth, the pictures on the walls so varnished with smoke you'd had to have known them for forty years to guess what they showed. We all knew what they showed. The bulbs in the wall fixings were weak and dusty, giving the room a dark and gloomy cast. The sole area of brightness was in the corner, where the jukebox sat. Was a big thing when Pete, my old friend and Maggie's late husband, bought it. But only the lights work these days, and not all of them, and none of us are too bothered about it. Nobody comes into the bar who wouldn't rather sit in peace than hear someone else's choice of music, much too loud. I guess this comes with age, and anyway the 45s in the machine are too old to evoke much more than sadness. The floor was clean, and the bar only smelt slightly of old beer. You want it to smell that way, a little, otherwise it would be like drinking in a church.

Maggie waited until Jack had caught his breath, then asked. Someone had to, I guess, and it was always going to be her. She said: 'No change?'

Jack raised his head, looked at her. 'Course there's a change,' he muttered. 'No-one said she weren't going to change.'

He picked up his coffee and came to sit on the other side of my table. But he didn't catch my eye, so I let him be, and cleared up the rest of my food, rejecting the raw onion garnish in deference to my innards. They

THE HANDOVER

won't stand for that kind of thing any more. It wasn't going to be long before a cost-benefit analysis of the chili itself consigned it to history alongside them.

When I was done I pushed the bowl to one side, burped as quietly as I could, and lit up a Camel. I left the pack on the table so Jack could take one if he had a mind to. He would, sooner or later. The rest of the world may have decided that cigarettes are more dangerous than a nuclear war, but in Eldorado, Montana, a man's still allowed to smoke after his meal if he wants to. What are they going to do: come bust us? The people who make the rules live a long ways from here, and the folk in this town have never been much for caring what State ordinances say.

One of the guys at the bar finished his beer, asked for another. Maggie gave him one, but didn't wait for money. Outside, the wind picked up a little and a door started banging, the sound like an unwelcome visitor knocking to be let out of the cellar. But it was a ways up the street, and you stopped noticing it after a while. It's not an uncommon sound in Eldorado.

Otherwise everyone just held their positions, and eventually Jack helped himself to a cigarette. I struck a match for him, as his fingers seemed numb and awkward. He still hadn't taken his coat off, though with the fire it was pretty warm in the room.

Once he was lit, and he'd stopped coughing, he nodded at me through the smoke. 'How's the chili?'

'Filthy,' I confirmed. 'But warm. Most of it.'

He smiled. He rested his hands on the table, palms down, and looked at them for a while. Liver spots and the shadow of old veins, like a fading map of territories once more uncharted. 'She's getting worse,' he said. 'Going to be tonight. Maybe already.'

I'd guessed as much, but hearing it said still made me feel tired and sad. He hadn't spoken loudly, but everybody else heard too.

It got even quieter, and the tension settled deeper, like a dentist's waiting room where everyone's visiting for the first time in years and has their suspicions about what they're going to hear. Maybe 'tension' isn't the right word. That suggests someone might have felt there was something they could do, that some virile force was being held in abeyance, ready for the sign, the right time. There wasn't going to be any sign. This night had been a while in coming but it had come, like a phone call in the small hours. We knew there wasn't anything to be done.

Maggie pottered around, put on a fresh jug of coffee. I started to stand, meaning to get me a cup, but Jack put his hand on my arm. I sat back, waited for him to speak.

'Wondered if you'd walk with me,' he said.

I looked at him, feeling a dull twinge of dread. 'Already?'

'Only really came back down here to fetch you, if you wanted to go.'

I realized in a kind of way that I was honored. I took my heavy coat from the back of the chair and put it on. A couple heads raised to watch us leave, but most people turned away. Every one of them knew where we were going, the job we were going to do. Maybe you'd expect something to be said, the occasion to be marked in some way: but in all my life, of the things I heard that were worth saying, none of them were actually said in words.

And what could anyone have said?

Outside it was even colder than I expected. I stuffed my hands deep in my pockets and pulled my neck down into my scarf like a turtle. The snow was six inches deep in the street, and I was glad I had my thick boots on. The moon was full above, snow clouds hidden away someplace around a corner, recuperating and getting ready for more. And there would be more, no doubt of that. The winters just keep getting colder and deeper around here, or so my body tells me. The winters are coming into their prime.

Jack started walking up the street, and I fell in beside him. Within seconds my long bones felt like they were slowly being twisted, and the skin on my face like it was made of lead. We walked past the old fronts, all of them dark now. The hardware store, the pharmacy, the tea rooms. Even in light of day the painted signs are too faded to read, and the boardwalk which used to run the length of the street has rotted away to nothing. It happened like a series of paintings. One year it looked fine; then another it was tatty; then finally it was broken down and there was no reason to put it back. Sometimes, when I'd walked up the street in recent years, I would catch myself recalling the way things had once been, working my memory like a tongue worrying

THE HANDOVER

the hole where a tooth had once sat. I could remember standing or sitting outside certain stores, the people who'd owned them, the faces of the people I'd spied from across the way. The times all tended to blend into one, and I could be the young boy running to the drug store on an errand for his mom, or the youth mooning over the younger of two sisters, or a man buying whiskey to blur the night away: switching back and forth in a blink, like one man looking out of three sets of eyes. It was like hearing a piece of music you grew up to, some tune you had in your head day after day until it was as much a part of your life as breathing. It was also a kind of time travel, and for a moment I'd feel as I once had, young and empty of darkness, ready to learn and experience and do. Eager to be shown what the world had in store for me, to conquer and make mistakes.

To love, and lose, and love again. Amen.

Eldorado was founded in 1850 by two miners, Joseph and Ezekiel Clarke: boys who came all the way from New Hampshire with nothing but a pair of horses and a dream. Sounds funny now, calling it a dream, even corny. People don't think of money that way anymore. These days they think it's a right. They stay where they are and try to make it come to them, instead of going off to find it for themselves. The brothers came in search of gold, like so many others. They were late on the trail, and worked through the foothills, finding nothing, or stakes that had already been worked dry, gradually climbing higher and higher into the mountains. They panned the local river and found nothing once more, but then one afternoon came upon the seam—just as they were about to give up and move on, maybe head over to Oregon or California and see if it was paradise like everyone said.

It must have seemed like magic. They found gold. When we were young we all heard the story. A kind of Genesis tale. A little glade, hidden up amidst the mountains at over three thousand feet: and there for the taking, a seam of money, a pocket of dreams.

The brothers stayed, and built themselves a cabin out of the good wood that grew all around. But news travelled fast even in those days, and it wasn't long before they had company. A lot of company. The old mine workings have gone to ruin now but it was a big old construction, I can tell you that. Was a few years when Eldorado was home to over four thousand people, producing five million dollars a year in gold. The town had saloons and boarding houses, a post office and a fistful of gambling rooms, even a grand hotel. Almost all have fallen down now, though until ten years ago people still used the hotel to board their animals in, when it got real cold. Two walls are still more or less there, hidden amongst the trees, though I wouldn't want to stand underneath them for long. I once showed the site to a couple of tourists who came up all this way in a rental car, having noticed the old town sign down the road. They seemed a little disappointed to find there was still people living here, and were soon on their way again.

That was near ten years ago, and no-one's come up to look since, though the sign's still there. It says 'Eldorado, 15 miles', and stands on a turn of the local road from Giles to Covent Fort, though lately I swear the trees around it have been growing faster. Neither Giles nor Covent are much to brag about these days either, and the road between them isn't often used.

If it weren't for that town sign, there would be no way of knowing we were up here at all.

When the gold ran out there was zinc for a while, and a little copper. The gold fever died away but Eldorado continued to prosper for a time. There was a Masonic lodge built, and two banks, and a school house with a clock and a bell—the fanciest building in town, the symbol there was a community here, and that we were living well. I can't even remember where the lodge was now, the banks are gone, and the school closed in 1957. I went to that school, learned most of what I know. Everybody did. It was the place where you turned into a grown-up, one year at a time, back when a year was as long as anyone could imagine, when two seemed like infinity. Probably that was why, for a long time, folks would stop by the abandoned school every now and then, by themselves and on the quiet, and do a little patching up. Wasn't any sense in it, because it wasn't going to reopen, not least because there were no new children—but I know I did it, and Jack too, and Pete before he died. Had to be that others did as well, otherwise it would have fallen down a lot earlier than it did.

Now it's gone, and even on the brightest spring day that patch of the mountain seems awful quiet. I guess you could say that no-one here has learned anything since then. Certainly what you see on television doesn't

THE HANDOVER

seem to have much application to us. I stopped watching a long time ago, and I know I'm not the only one. TVs don't last forever, and there ain't no-one around here knows how to fix them. And anyway they just showed a world that isn't ours, things that we can't buy and wouldn't want to, so what use was it anyway. We've got quite a few books, spread amongst us. That's good enough.

Eventually the copper ran out and though people looked hard and long, there wasn't anything else useful to be found. The gambling dens moved on, in search of people who still had riches to throw away. The boarding houses closed soon afterward, as those who hadn't made Eldorado their home went elsewhere. Plenty people stayed, for a while. My folks did, in the 1920s. Never got to the bottom of why. But anyhow they came, and they stayed, and I followed in their footsteps, I guess, by staying here too. So did some others.

But not enough. And nobody new.

Halfway to the end of Main, Jack and I turned off the road and made our way as best we could up what used to be Fourth Street. I guess it still is, but you'd be hard pressed to find the first three, or the other eight, unless you'd once walked them, and gone visiting on them, or grown up in a house that used to stand on one. Now they've gone to trees and grass, just a few piles of lumber dotted around, like forgotten games of giant pick-up-sticks. You'd think we might have made an effort to keep the houses standing, even after people stopped living in them. But it's not the kind of thing that occurs to you until it's far too late, and then there doesn't seem a great deal of point. Spilt milk, stable door, all of those.

The grade has always been kind of steep on Fourth, and Jack and I found the going hard. Jack had already made the trip once that night, and I let him go in front, following his footprints in the snow. There was another way of getting up to the house, a little less steep, but that involved going past the town's first cemetery, now overgrown, and the notion wasn't even discussed. Ahead of us, a single light shone in one of the upper windows of the Buckley house, which sits alone right at the end, a last stand against the oncoming trees. I felt sick to my stomach, remembering times I'd made the walk before, towards that grand old house hunkered beneath the wall of the mountain. Hundreds of times, but a handful of times in particular. My life often seems that way to me now. So much of it was just landscape I passed through, a long open plain with little to distinguish the miles, or like some indifferent movie that went on for a long, long time.

But then there's something inside me like a satchel, or a little box, where I keep the *real* things. A few smells, and sounds, touches like a faint summer breeze. Some evenings, a couple afternoons and a handful of dawns, when I woke up somewhere I was happy to be, coddled warm with someone and protected from the bright light of day and tomorrow. It's nights I remember most. Some bad, some good. You fall in love at night, and that's also when people die. Even if their last breath is drawn in daylight, by the time you've truly understood what's happened, darkness has come to claim the event as its own. Nights last the longest, without doubt, both at the time and afterwards. They contain multitudes, and don't fade as easily as the sun.

They're there, in my bag, and I'll take them with me when I go.

When we got to the house we stomped the snow off our boots on the porch, and let ourselves in. Over the last few weeks of visiting I had gotten used to the dust, how it overlaid the way the house had used to be. She'd kept it up as well as she could over the years, but now you could almost hear it running down, like the wind dropping after a storm. The downstairs was empty but for Naomi's cat, who was sitting in the middle of the hall, looking at the wall. It glanced up at us as we started on the stairs, then walked slowly away into the darkness of the kitchen.

I knew then that it was already over.

When we reached the upper landing we hesitated outside the doorway to the bedroom, as if feeling we had to be invited in. The interior was lit by candles, an old kerosene lamp by the window. The Doc was sitting on a blanket box at the end of the bed, elbows on his knees. He looked like an old man, tired, waiting for a train to take him home. Not like someone who'd once been the second-fastest runner in town, after me, a boy who could move like the wind. He'd gone away, many years ago. Left town, got trained, spent some years out there in the other places. Half the books in town were his, brought back with him when he returned to Eldorado.

He looked up, beckoned us in with an upward nod of the head. We approached like a pair of children, with short steps and hands down by our

THE HANDOVER

sides. I kept my eyes straight ahead, knowing there'd be a time to look after the words had been said.

Jack rested a hand on the Doc's shoulder. 'She wake at all?'

He shook his head. 'Just died. That's all she did.'

'So that's it,' I said.

The three of us sighed then, all together. Letting out what had once been inside.

The Doc started to speak, faltered. Then tried again. 'Maybe it's not going to happen,' he said, trying for a considered tone, but coming out querulous and afraid. 'After all, how do we know?'

Jack and I shook our heads. Wasn't any use in this line of thought. Nobody knew how we knew. But we knew. We'd known since the children stopped coming.

We walked around on separate sides of the bed, and looked down.

I don't know what Jack was looking at, but I can tell you what I saw. An old woman, face lined, though less so than when I'd seen her in the afternoon of the previous day. Death had levelled the foothills of her suffering, filled in the dried stream beds of age. The coverlet was pulled up to just under her chin, so she looked tucked up nice and warm. The shape beneath the blankets was so thin it barely seemed to be there at all: it could have been just a runkle in the sheets, covering nothing more than cooling air.

Most of all she looked still, like a mountain range seen from the sky.

Wasn't the first time I'd seen someone dead, not nearly. I saw my own parents laid out, inexplicably cold and quiet, and my wife, and many of my friends. There's been a lot of dying hereabouts over the last few years, every passing marked and mourned.

But Naomi looked different.

It's funny how, when you first know someone, it will be the face you notice most of all. The eyes, the mouth, the way they have their hair. Everybody has the same number of limbs, but their face is all their own. Then, over the years, it's as if this part of them leaves their body and goes into your head, crystallizes there. You hardly notice what the years are doing, the way people's actual faces thicken and dim and change. Every now and then something brings you up short, and makes you see the way things have become. Then you lose it again, as quick as it came, and you just see the continuity, the essence behind the face. The person as they were.

I saw Naomi as she and her sister had once been, the two brightest sparks in Eldorado, the girls most likely to make you lose your stride and catch your breath—whether you were fifteen, like them, or so old that your balls barely still had their wits about them. I saw her as the little lady who could shout loudest in the playground, who could give you a Chinese burn you'd remember for days. I saw her as I had when Pete and I used to hike up Fourth with flowers in our hands and our hearts in our throats, when Pete was cautiously dating Naomi, and I was going with her sister Sarah, who was two years younger and much prettier, or so I thought back then.

It's that year that many of the nights I keep in my bag came from, the ones that bring faint memories of music to my head. Sarah and I came to a parting of the ways before Thanksgiving, and she eventually married Jack, had no children but generally seemed content, and died in 1984. Pete and Naomi lasted a couple more months than we had, and then Pete met Maggie and things changed. Five years later, both on rebounds from different people altogether, gloriously grouchy and full of cheap liquor, Naomi and I spent a night walking together through the woods which used to stop on the edge of town. We looked for the stream where the Clarkes first panned, and maybe even found it, and we didn't do anything more than kiss, but that was exciting enough. Then the morning came, and brought its light, and everything was burned away. We'd never have been right for each other anyhow, that was clear, and it wasn't the way it was supposed to be. Of course a decade or two later, when I first started to look back upon my life and read it properly, like a book I should have paid more attention to the first time, I realized that this might have been wrong. When I thought back, it was always Naomi's face that was clearest in my mind, though she'd been Pete's and I'd been Sarah's, and anyhow both of those futures were long in the past and dead and buried half a lifetime ago. By then Naomi was married, and when we met we were polite. Almost as if that current which can pass between any two people, the spark of possibility, however small, had been used up all in that night in the woods, under-used and thrown away, and now we could be nothing but friends. Naomi never had children either, nor Maggie. None of us did.

THE HANDOVER

Even now, when the forest has started to march its way right up Main Street, I can remember that night with her as if I'm still wearing the same clothes and haven't had time to change. Remember also the way the sisters always seemed to glow, all their lives, as if they were running on more powerful batteries than the rest of us, as if whoever stirred their bodies into being had been more practiced at the art.

I loved my wife a great deal, and we had many good years together, but as I get older it's like those middle times were a long game we all played, a long and complex game of indeterminate rules. Those seasons fade, and we return to the playground like tired ghosts coming home after a long walk, and it's how we were then that seems most important. I can't remember much of what happened last year, but I can still picture those girls when we were young. On the boardwalk, in the big old house their father built, around the soda fountain when they were still little and we were all sparkling and young and blessed, a crop of new flowers bursting into life in a field which would always be there.

Almost all of those people are dead now. Distributed amongst the two cemeteries, biding their time, like broken panes in the windows of an old building. A few of the windows are still intact, like me and Jack and Maggie and all, but you have to wonder why. There's nothing to see through us now.

When Jack and I had looked down on Naomi a while, and nothing had changed, we turned from the bed. The Doc had quietly gotten his things together, but didn't look ready to leave just yet.

'There's something me and Bill have to do,' Jack said. 'Only stopped by for the truck. And, well, you know.'

The Doc nodded, not looking at us. He knew what we were going to do. 'I'll stay a while,' he said. Back in '72 there'd been something going on between him and Naomi. He probably didn't realize that we knew. But everybody did. Then after her husband died in '85, oftentimes the Doc had taken his evening meal at the Buckley table. I'd always wondered if it might be me who did that. Didn't work out that way.

'What are we going to do about her cat?' I asked.

'What can anyone do about a cat?' the Doc said, with the ghost of a smile. 'Reckon it'll do pretty much what it wants. I'll feed it, though.'

We shook his hand, not really knowing why, and left the house.

Jack's truck was parked around the side. It wasn't going to be a picnic getting down the hill, but it was too far to walk. We got it started after only a couple of tries, and Jack nosed her carefully out into the ruts of the street.

Fate was kind to us, and we got down to Main without much more than a spot of grief. Turned right, away from the bar, away from what's left of the town.

When we drew level with the other cemetery, Jack slowed to a halt and turned the engine off. We sat with the windows down for a while, smoking and listening. It was mighty cold. Wasn't anything to hear apart from wind up in the mountains, and the rustle of trees bending our way. Beyond the fence, the stones and wooden crosses marched away in ranks into the night. Friends, parents, lovers, children, in their hundreds. A field full of the way things might have been, or had been once, and could never be again. Folks are dead for an awfully long time. The numbers mount up.

Jack turned, looked at me. 'We're sure, aren't we?'

'Yes,' I said. 'We've been outnumbered for a long, long while. After Naomi, there's only fifteen of us left.'

It felt funny, Jack turning to me, wanting to be reassured. I still remembered him as one of the big kids, someone I hoped I might be like one day. And I did grow up to be like him, then older'n he'd once been, and then just old, like him. Everything seemed so different back then, everyone so distinct from one another. Just your haircut can make you a different color, when everyone's only got ten years of experience to count on. Then you get older, and everyone seems the same. Everybody gets whittled away at about the same rate. Like the 1950s, and '60s, and '70s and '80s, times that once seemed so different to each other, but are now just stuff that happened to us once and then went away; like good weather or a stomach ache.

Jack stared straight out the windshield for a while. 'I don't hear anything.'

'May not happen for hours,' I said. 'No way of telling. May not even happen tonight.'

He laughed quietly. 'You don't think so?'

'No,' I admitted. 'It'll happen tonight. It's time.'

THE HANDOVER

I thought then that I might have heard something, out there in the darkness, the first stirring beyond the fence. But if I did, it was quiet, and nothing came of it right then. It was only midnight. There was plenty of darkness left.

Jack nodded slowly. 'Then I guess we might as well get it over with.'

We smiled at each other, briefly, like two boys passing in the school yard. Boys who grew to like each other, but who could never have realized that they'd be sharing such a task, on a far-away night such as this.

Later we'd drive back up into town, park outside Maggie's bar, and sit inside with the others and wait. She was staying open for good that night.

But first we went down the hill, down a rough track to an old road hardly anyone drove any more. We got out of the truck and stood a while, looking down the mountain, at a land as big as Heaven.

And then together we took down the town sign.

SAVE AS...

As soon as I walked out of the hospital I knew what I was going to do. It was 1 am by then, for what little difference that made. Other people's clocks meant nothing. I was on hospital time, crash time, blood time: surprised by how late it was, as if I'd believed what happened must have taken place in some small pocket of horror outside the real world, one where the normal rules of progression and chronology don't apply. Of *course* it must have taken time, for the men and women in white coats to run the stretcher trolleys down the corridors, shouting for crash teams and saline; to cut through my wife's matted clothes and expose wet ruins where only an hour ago all had been smooth and dry; to gently move my son's head so its position in relation to his body was the same as it had always been. All of this took time, as did the eventual slow looks up at me, the silent shakes of the doctors' heads, the many forms I had to sign and all the words I had to listen to.

Then the walk from the emergency room to the outside world, my shoes tapping softly on linoleum as I passed rows of people with bandaged fingers. That took the most time of all.

The air in the car park was cool and moist, freshened by the rain. I could smell the grass which grew in the darkness beyond the lamps' pools of yellow light, and hear in the distance the sound of wet tires on the freeway. Tires which, I hoped, would retain their grip, safely transport the cars' passengers to their homes. Tires which wouldn't fail under a sudden braking to avoid a car which had slewed into their path, hurtling the vehicles together.

I suddenly realized that I had no means of getting home. The remains of the Lexus were presumably by the side of the road where the accident had taken place, or had been carted off to a wrecker's yard. For a moment the problem took up the whole of my mind, unnaturally luminescent: and then I realized both that I could presumably call a cab from reception, and that I didn't really care.

Two orderlies walked across the far side of the lot, faint laughter carrying to me. The smell of smoke in their wake reminded me I was a smoker, and I fumbled a cigarette from the packet in my jacket pocket. The carton was perfectly in shape, the cigarette unbent. One of the very few things Helena and I had ever argued about was my continued inability to resist toying with death in the form of tubes of rolled tobacco. Her arguments were never those of the zealot, merely measured and reasonable. She loved me, and Jack loved me, and she didn't want the two of them to be left alone. The fact that the crash which had crushed her skull had left my cancer sticks unbroken was a joke which she would have liked, and laughed at hard.

For a moment I hesitated. I couldn't decide whether Helena's death meant I should smoke the cigarette or not. Then I lit it and walked back to reception.

If I was going to go through with this, I didn't have much time.

The cab dropped me at the corner of Montague and 31st. I overtipped the driver—who'd had to put up with a sudden crying jag which left me feeling cold and embarrassed—and watched the car swish away down the deserted street. The cross-roads was bleak and exposed; an empty used car lot and burnt-out gas station taking two corners, run-down buildings of untellable purpose squatting kitty corner on the others. It couldn't have been more different from the place where I'd originally gone to visit the Same Again Corporation, an altogether more gleaming street in the heart of the business district. I guessed space was cheaper out here, and maybe they needed a lot of it: though I couldn't really understand why. Data storage is pretty compact these days.

Whatever. The card I'd kept in my wallet was adamant that I should go to the address on Montague in case of emergency, and so I walked quickly down towards 1176. I saw from across the street that a light was on behind the frosted glass of the door, and picked up the pace with relief. It was open, just as the card said it would be.

As I crossed the street a man came out of Same Again, holding a very wet towel. He twisted it round on itself, squeezing as much of the water out of it as he could. It joined the rain already on the sidewalk and disappeared.

When he saw where I was heading he looked up.

'Help you?' he asked, warily. I showed him the card. An unreadable expression crossed his face. 'Go inside,' he said. 'Be right with you.'

The reception area was small but smart. And very quiet. I waited at the desk for a few moments, while the man finished whatever the hell he was doing. I noticed a soft dripping sound. A patch of carpet near one of the walls was damp, and there was a similar spot on the ceiling. I turned to find the man reaching out to me.

'Sorry about that,' he said, but didn't offer any more explanation. 'Okay, can I have that card?'

He took it and went behind the desk, tapped my Customer Number into the terminal there.

'My name's...' I said, but he held up his hand.

'Don't tell me,' he said quickly. 'Not a thing. I assume something pretty major has happened.' He looked at me for a moment, and decided he didn't have to wait for an answer. 'So it's very important that I know as little as possible. How many people have already been involved?'

'Involved?'

'Are aware of whatever event it is that has brought you here.'

'I don't know.' I wasn't sure who counted. The doctors and nurses, presumably, and the people who'd loaded up the ambulance. They'd seen the faces. Others knew that *something* had happened, in that they'd driven past the mess on the freeway, or walked past me as I stood in the parking lot of the hospital. But surely they didn't count, because they had no knowledge of who had been involved, or in what. 'Maybe ten, twelve?'

The man nodded briskly. 'That's containable. Okay, I've processed the order. Go through that door and a technician will take it from there. May I just remind you of the terms of the contract you entered into with Same

Again, most specifically that you are legally bound not to reveal to anyone either that you are a subscriber to our service, or that you have made use of it on this or any other occasion?'

'Fine,' I said. It was illegal. We both knew that, and I was the last person who wanted any trouble.

The door led me into a cavernous dark area where a young woman in a green lab coat waited for me. Without looking directly at my face she indicated that I should follow her. At the end of the room was a chair. I sat in it and sat quietly while she applied conductant gel to my temples and attached the wires.

When she was done she asked if I was comfortable.

I turned my head towards her, clamping my lips tightly together. My teeth were chattering inside my head, the muscles of my jaw and neck spasming. I could barely see her through a haze of grief I knew I could not bear. I nodded.

She loaded up a hypo and injected something into the vein on the back of my hand. I started counting backwards from twenty but made it no further than nine.

I got home about four o'clock that afternoon. After I'd locked the Lexus I stood in the driveway for a moment, savoring a breeze which softened the heat like a ceiling fan in a noisy bar. The weather men kept saying summer was going to burst soon, but they were evidently as full of shit as their genus had always been. Chaos theory may have grooved a lot of people's lives but the guys who stood in front of maps for a living were obviously still at the stage of consulting entrails. It hadn't rained for weeks and didn't look like it was going to start any time soon—and that was good, because in the evening we had friends coming round for a cookout in the back yard.

I let myself into the house and went straight through into the kitchen. Helena was at the table, basting chicken legs, half an eye on an old Tom Hanks film playing on the set in the corner. I noticed with approval that it was an old print, one which hadn't been parallaxed.

'Good movie,' I said.

'Would be,' she replied. 'If you could see what the hell was going on.'

SAVE AS...

I'm against the 'enhancing' of classics: Helena takes the opposite view, as is her wont. We'd had the discussion about a hundred times and as neither of us really cared, we only put ourselves through it for fun. I kissed her on the nose and dunked a stick of celery in the barbecue sauce.

'Dad!' yelped a voice, and I turned in time to catch Jack as he leapt up at me. He looked like he'd been dragged through a hedge sideways by someone who was an internationally-acknowledged expert in the art of interfacing humans and hedges to maximum untidying effect. I raised an eyebrow at Helena, who shrugged.

'How many pairs of hands do you see?' she asked.

I set Jack down, endured him boxing my kneecaps for a while, and then sent him upstairs for a bath—promising I'd come up and talk to him. I knew what he really wanted was to rehearse yet again the names of the kids who'd be coming tonight. He's a sociable kid, much more than I was at his age—but I think I was looking forward to the evening as much as him. The secret of good social events is to only invite people you like having in your life, and not the ones you merely tolerate. Tonight we had my boss—who was actually my best friend—and his wife; a couple of Helena's old girlfriends who were as good a time as anyone could handle; and another old colleague of mine over from England with his family.

I hung with Helena in the kitchen until she tired of me nibbling samples of everything she'd painstakingly arranged on serving plates. She was too tall to box my knee caps and so bit me on the neck instead, a bite which turned into a kiss and became in danger of throwing her cooking schedule out of whack. She shooed me out and I left her to it and went through into the study.

There were screeds of emails to be sent before I could consign the day to history and settle down into the evening and weekend, but most were already drafted and the rest didn't take long. As the software punted them out I rested my chin on my hands and gazed out onto the yard. A trestle table was already set up, stacks of paper plates at the ready. The old cable spool we used as a table when it was just family had been rolled to over by the tree, and bottles of red wine were open and breathing. Beer would be frosting in the fridge, and the fixings for Becky and Janny's drink of choice—Mint Juleps, for chrisake—ready and waiting in the kitchen. I could hear Helena sternly chopping some errant vegetable in the kitchen, and Jack hollering in the bath upstairs.

For a moment I felt perfectly at peace.

I was thirty six, had a wife I'd die for and a happy, intelligent kid; a job I actually enjoyed and more money than we needed; and a house that looked and felt like an advert for The Good Life. So what if that was shmaltzy: it was everything I wanted. After my twenties, a slow-motion train wreck of bad relationships and shitty jobs—and my early thirties, when no-one around me seemed to be able to talk about anything other than houses, marriage or children—my life had finally found its mark. The good things were in place, but with enough perspective to let me exist in the outside world too.

I was a lucky guy, and not too dumb to realize it.

The machine told me I had new mail. I scanned the sender addresses: one from my sister in Europe, and a spam about 'Outstanding business opportunities ($$$$$$)!'. I was mildly surprised to see that there was also one from my own email address—entitled 'Read This!'—but not very. As part of my constant battle to design a kill file which would weed out email invitations to business opportunities of any kind—regardless of the number of suffixed dollar signs—I was often sending test messages to myself. Evidently the new version of the kill file wasn't cutting it. I could tool around with it a little more on Sunday afternoon, maybe aided by a glass of JD. Right now it hardly seemed important.

I told the computer to have a nap and went upstairs to confront the dripping chaos that our bathroom would now be.

John and Julia arrived first, as usual: they were always invited on a 'turn up when you feel like it' basis. Helena was only just out of the shower so Julia went up to chat with her; meanwhile John and I stood in the kitchen with bottles of beer and chewed a variety of rags, him nibbling on Helena's cooking, me trying to rearrange things so she wouldn't notice.

We moved out into the yard when Becky and Janny arrived, and I started the Weber up, supervising the coals with foremanship from Helena at the table. I'd strung a couple of extension speakers out the door from the stereo in the living room, and one of Helena's compilations played quietly in

SAVE AS...

the background: something old, something new, something funky and something blue. Jack sat neatly on a chair at the end of the trestle in his new pants and checked shirt, sipping at a diet coke and waiting for the real fun to begin. Becky chatted with him in the meantime, while Janny reran horror stories of her last relationship: she's working on being the Fran Liebowitz of her generation, and getting there real fast. When everyone round the table erupted as she got to the end of yet another example of why her ex-boyfriend had not been fit to walk the earth, Helena caught my eye, and smiled.

I knew what she meant. *There but for the grace of God*, she was thinking, *could have gone you or I*.

Being funny is cool; being happy is better. I left the coals to themselves for a bit, and went and stood behind Helena with my hand on her shoulder.

But then the doorbell went and she jumped up to let Howard and Carol in. Jack stood uncertainly, waiting for them to come through into the garden. Their two kids, whose names I could never remember, walked out behind them. There was a moment of quiet mutual appraisal, and then all three ran off towards the tree to play some game or other. They'd only ever met once before, on a trip we took to England, but obviously whatever they'd got up to then was still good for another day. As the evening began to darken, and the adults sat round the table and drank and ate, I could hear always in the background one of my favourite sounds of all, the sound of Jack laughing.

And smell Helena's barbecue sauce, wafting over from the grill; and feel Helena's leg, her thigh warm against my leg, her ankle hooked behind mine.

At ten I came out of the house, clutching more beers, and realized two things.

The first was that I was kind of drunk. Negotiating the step down from the kitchen was a little more difficult than it should have been, and the raucous figures around the trestle table looked less than clear. I shook my head, trying to get it back together: I didn't want to appear inebriated in front of my son. Not that he was on hand to watch—the kids were still tirelessly cavorting off in the darkness of the far end of the yard.

The second thing I noticed was less tangible. Something to do with atmosphere.

While I'd been in the kitchen, it had changed. People were still laughing, and laughing hard, but they'd moved, sitting in different positions around the table. I guess I'd been in the kitchen longer than I thought.

Becky and Jan were huddled at one end, and I perched myself on a chair nearby. But they were talking seriously about something, and didn't seem to want to involve me.

There was another burst of laughter from the other end. There was something harsh in the sound. Helena and Carol were leaned in tight together, their faces red and shiny. Howard was chortling with John and Julia. It was good to see them getting on, but I hadn't realized they were so chummy. Howard had only been with the firm for a year before upping stakes and going with Carol back to her own country. John and I had been friends for twenty years. Still, I guess it showed the evening was going well.

Then I saw something I couldn't understand. Helena's hand, reaching out and taking a cigarette from the packet lying on the table. I frowned vaguely, knowing something wasn't right, but she stuck the cigarette in her mouth and lit it with her lighter.

Then I remembered that she'd started a few months before, finally dragged into my habit. I felt guilty, wishing I'd been able to stop before she started. Too late now, I suppose.

I reached for the bottle of beer I'd perched on the end of the table, and missed. Well, not quite missed: I made enough contact to knock it off the table.

Janny rolled her eyes and started to lean down for it, but I beat her to it.

'It's okay, I'm not that drunk,' I said, slightly stiffly. This wasn't true, of course, because it took me longer than it should to find the bottle. In the end I had to completely lean over and look for where it had gone. This gave me a view of all the legs under the table, which was kind of neat, and I remained like that for a moment. Lots of shins, all standing together.

Some more together than others, I realized. Helena's foot was resting against John's.

I straightened up abruptly, cracking my head on the end of the table. Conversation stopped, and I found myself with seven pairs of eyes looking at me.

'Sorry,' I said, and went back into the kitchen to get another beer.

SAVE AS...

***

A couple beers later, really pretty drunk. Didn't want to sit back down at the table, felt like walking around. Besides, Janny and Becky were still in conference, Janny looking odd; Howard and Carol and Julia talking about something else. I didn't feel like butting in.

Headed off towards the tree, thinking I'd see what the kids were up to. Maybe they'd play with me for a while. Better make an effort to talk properly—didn't want Jack to see daddy zonked. Usually it's okay, as my voice stays pretty straight unless I'm completely loaded, and as I couldn't score any coke that afternoon, that wasn't the case.

Coke?

What the fuck was I talking about?

I ground to a halt, suddenly confused. I didn't do coke, never had. Well, once, a few years back: it had been fun, but not worth the money—and an obvious slippery slope. Too easy to take until it was all gone, and then just buy some more. Plus Helena would have gone ballistic—she didn't even like me *smoking*, for God's sake.

Then I remembered her taking a cigarette earlier, and felt cold. She hadn't started smoking. That was nonsense.

So why did I think she had?

I started moving again, not because I felt I'd solved anything, but because I heard a sound. It wasn't laughing. It was more like quiet tears.

At the far end of the yard I found Jack's camp, a little clearing which huddled up against the wisteria that clung to the fence. I pushed through the bushes, swearing quietly.

Jack was sitting in the middle, tears rolling down his moon-like face. His check shirt was covered in dirt, the leg of his pants torn. Howard's kids were standing around him, giggling and pointing. As I lumbered towards them the little girl hurled another clump of earth at Jack. It struck him in the face, just above the eye.

For a moment I was totally unable to move.

Then I lunged forward and grabbed her arm.

'Fuck off, you little bastards,' I hissed, yanking them away from my son. They stared up at me, faces full of some thought I couldn't read. Then the little boy pulled his arm free, and his sister did the same. They ran off laughing towards the house.

I turned again to Jack, who was staring at the fence.

'Come on, big guy,' I said, bending down to take him in my arms. 'What was that all about?'

His face slowly turned to mine, and my heart sank at what was always there to see. The glaze in the eyes, the slackness at one corner of his mouth.

'Dada,' he said. 'They dirt me.'

I went down onto my knees beside him, wrapping my arms around his thin shoulders. I held him tight, but as always sensed his eyes looking over my shoulder, gazing off into the middle distance at something no-one else could see.

Eventually I let go of him and rocked to my feet again, hand held down towards him. He took it and struggled to his feet. I led him out of the bushes and into the yard.

As we came close to the tree I saw Helena and John out of the darkness. I sensed some kind of rearrangement taking place as they saw us, but couldn't work out what it might have been.

'Oh shit, what's happened now?' Helena said, reading Jack's state instantly, and hurrying towards us. John hung back, in the deep shadows.

I couldn't answer. Partly just because I was drunk; I'd obviously over-compensated for my dealer's coke famine by drinking way more than usual. But mainly because there was something wrong with her face. Not her actual face, which was a beautiful as ever.

Her lipstick. It was smudged all round her lips.

'Christ, you're useless,' she snapped, and grabbed Jack's hand. I didn't watch as she hauled him back towards the house. Instead I stared into the darkness under the tree, where a faint glow showed John was lighting a cigarette.

'Having a good evening?' I asked.

'Oh yeah,' he said, laughing quietly. 'You guys throw such great parties.'

We walked back to the trestle table, neither of us saying anything.

I sat down next to the girls, glanced across at Becky. She looked a lot worse than the last time we'd seen her. The chemo obviously wasn't working.

'How are you feeling?' I asked.

SAVE AS...

She looked up, smiled tightly. 'Fine, just fine,' she said. She didn't want my sympathy, and never had since the afternoon I'd called round at her place, looking for some company.

Behind me I heard John getting up and going through into the kitchen. I'd never liked Julia, nor she me, and so it would be no comfort to look round and see her eyes following her husband into the house, where Helena would already have dispatched Jack up to bed with a slap on the behind, and would maybe be standing at the sink, washing something that didn't need washing.

Instead I watched Howard and Carol talking together. They at least looked happy.

I stood at the front door as the last set of tail lights turned into the road and faded away. Helena stood behind me. When I turned to take her hand she smiled meaninglessly, her face hard and distant, and walked away. I lumbered into my study to turn the computer off.

Instead I found myself waking it from sleep. I read an email from my sister, who seemed to be doing fine. She was redecorating her new house with her new boyfriend. I nodded to myself; it was good that things were finally going her way.

I turned at a sound behind me to find Helena standing there. She plonked a cup of coffee down on the desk beside me.

'There you go, Mister Man,' she said, and I smiled up at her. I didn't need the coffee, because I hadn't drunk much. Sitting close to Helena all evening was still all the intoxication I needed. But it would be nice anyway.

'Good evening?' she asked, running her fingers across the back of my neck.

'Good evening,' I said, looping my arm around her waist.

'Well don't stay down here too long,' she winked, 'Because we could make it even better.'

After she'd gone I applied myself to the screen, but before I could starting writing a reply to my little sis, I heard Helena's voice again. This time it was hard, and came as usual from outside the study.

'Put your fucking son to bed,' she said. 'I can't deal with him tonight.'

I turned, but she'd already gone. I sat with my head in my hands for a little while, then reached for the coffee. It wasn't there.

Then something on the screen caught my eye. Something I'd dismissed earlier.

'Read This!' it said.

As much to avoid going upstairs as anything, I clicked. A long text message burped up onto the screen, and I frowned. My kill file tests usually only ran a couple of lines. Blinking against the drunkenness slopping through my head I tried to focus on the first sentence.

I managed to read it, in the end. And then the next, and as I read all the way through I felt as if my chair was sinking, dropping lower and lower into the ground.

The message was from me, it was about Same Again, and finally I remembered.

Before I'd come home that afternoon I'd gone to their offices in the business district. It was the second time I'd visited, the first being when I signed up for the service, and had a preliminary backup done, a year before. When I'd got up that morning, woken by Jack's cheerful chatter and feeling the warmth of Helena's buttocks against mine under the sheets, I'd suddenly realized that if there were any day on which to make a backup of my life, today was surely that day.

I'd driven over to their offices, sat in the chair and they'd done their thing, archiving the current state of affairs into a data file. A file which, as their blurb promised, I could access at any time life had gone wrong and I needed to return to the saved version.

I heard a noise out in the hallway, the sound of a small person bumping into a piece of furniture. Jack. In a minute I should go out and help him, put him to bed. Maybe read to him a little, see if I could get a few more words into his head. If not, just hold him a while, as he slipped off into a sleep furnished with a vagueness I could never understand.

All it takes is one little sequence of DNA out of place, one infinitesimal chemical reaction going wrong. That's all the difference there is between the child he was, and could have been. Becky would understand that. One of her cells had misbehaved too, like a 1 or 0 out of place in some computer program.

Wet towels. Heavy rain. A leaking ceiling.

Suddenly, somehow, I remembered going to a dark office on Montague in the wet small hours of some future morning. The strange way the man standing outside with the towel had reacted (*would react*) when I said I needed to do a restore from the backup they held there. And I knew what had happened.

SAVE AS...

There'd been an accident. *Or there was going to be.* The same rain which would total the car which for the moment still sat out in the drive, was going to corrupt the data I'd spent so much money to save.

At the bottom of the mail message was a number.

I called it. Same Again's 24 hour switchboard was unobtainable. I listened to a recorded voice for a while, and then replaced the handset.

Maybe they'd gone out of business, in this differing reality. Backing up was, after all, illegal. Too easy for criminals to leap backwards before their mistakes, for politicians to run experiments. Wide scale, it would have caused chaos. So long as not many people knew, you could get away with it. The disturbance was undetectable.

But now I knew, and this disturbance was far too great.

I could feel, like a heavy weight, the aura of the woman lying in the bed above my head. Could predict the firmness with which her back would be turned towards me, the way John and I would dance around each other at work the next day, and the endless drudgery of the phone calls required to score enough coke to make it all go away for a while.

'Hi dad—you still up?'

Jack stood in the doorway. He'd taken three apples from the kitchen, and was attempting to juggle them. He couldn't quite do it, but I thought it wouldn't be too long now. Perhaps I would learn then too, and we could do that stuff where you swap balls with one another. That might be kind of cool.

'Yep,' I smiled, 'But not for much longer. How about you go up, get your teeth brushed, and then I'll read you a story?'

But he'd corrupted again by then, and the apples fell one by one, to bruise on the hardwood floor. His eyes stared, slightly out of kilter, at my dusty bookcase, his fingers struggling at a button on his shirt. I reached forward and wiped away the thin dribble of saliva that ran from the bad corner of his mouth.

'Come on, little guy,' I said, and hoisted him up.

As I carried him upstairs into the darkness, his head lolling against my shoulder, I wondered how much had changed, whether in nine months the crash would still come as we drove back from a happy evening in Gainesville.

And I wondered, if it did, whether I would do anything to avoid it. Or if I would steer the car even harder this time.

BEING **RIGHT**

It was Monday, the fourth day of their vacation, and the fourth solid day of rain.

This didn't unduly bother Dan—you didn't come to London, London in February, moreover, to work on your tan—and they'd packed accordingly. The city was moreover full of museums, galleries, stores: it had history up the wazoo, a ton of good restaurants and nearly as many Starbucks as at home. If you could bear to get a little damp in between stops, there was a good time to be had, whatever the precipitation situation. The forecast—which Dan knew *all* about, having been woken by it at five thirty that morning—said the weather was going to get better as the week went on. Which was hopeful.

Either way, it was something you couldn't do anything about. The weather was simply there. You had to just accept it, adjust your plans accordingly, move on. There was no point complaining. No point going on and on and *on*.

What you *could* affect, on the other hand, was jet lag.

If you were flying to Europe—which they had done many, *many* times since the kids left home—there was a simple procedure to follow. You'd be landing mid-morning, so it made sense to catch some sleep on the plane (however fractured and tossy-turny, even a little helps). Then, from the minute you arrived on foreign shores, you locked yourself mentally to the new slot, and stayed awake until the time you would normally at home. That way your body quickly got itself into a new kind of understanding, and you were so bushed by the time it came to turn in that you'd sleep regardless of the time zone change. Might be a couple of days where you felt draggy late afternoon, but otherwise you'd be okay.

This is what Dan had done. This is what he always did.

Marcia... She did it different.

Despite the fact they'd discussed it, she stayed awake the whole flight. Said she'd found it impossible to sleep, though Dan had managed to catch an hour or two—not much, but enough to make a difference, to con the body into believing it had been through some kind of night. Then when they'd gotten to the hotel just before lunch, she'd started yawning, muttering about a nap. Dan told her to keep going—but mid-afternoon still found her spark out on the bed. Dan left her there and went for a stroll around the surrounding blocks. Sure, he felt a little spacey and weird, but he kind of enjoyed the feeling, and the walk. It served as a first recon of the neighborhood, informing him where the cafés were, the nearest bookstore, all that. It reminded you also that you'd done a pretty strange thing, travelled a long way, and you weren't at home any more.

For Dan, this walk was the opening ceremony of the vacation. It said: Here I Am.

When he got back to the hotel, Marcia was in the shower. They went out, had another little walk, then dinner in the nearest restaurant. By ten o'clock Dan was utterly beat and ready for bed. Marcia was speeding, however, and wanted to talk up the issues around Proposition 7, the *cause du jour* back home in Oregon. Dan hadn't much cared about P7 when on his own turf (it was going to be defeated, which was a shame, but that's what people are like), and he sure as hell didn't care about it from five thousand miles away. What was the point of coming to another country if you were going to mire yourself in the same old crap?

When he eventually said this, yawning massively, Marcia led the discussion into a playful analysis of why he was apparently unable to enter into any kind of intellectual dialogue that wasn't about books, before deftly turning back to Proposition 7.

This lasted a further twenty-five minutes. When Dan finally said he was simply going to have to go to bed, she shook her head and stood up.

BEING RIGHT

First evening of the holiday ruined, her body language said. *Thank you again, my brutish husband. Thanks a lot.*

Dan slept like a baby that night.

Marcia, not so well.

They spent the next couple of days getting some tourism done, seeing iconic sights, ticking the big ones off the list. Dan was happy to do this, knowing they'd relax by the weekend, find their vacation feet, and be able to kick back and do their own thing. By Saturday he was locked on GMT, the lingering late-afternoon slump nothing that a triple-shot Americano couldn't shake off.

Marcia meanwhile was getting further and further out of sync. She was waking at six, five, four in the morning: sitting up in bed reading (and reading a novel set in America, naturally, or else one of the magazines she'd brought from home); alternatively, as on the Monday morning, turning the television on—quietly, of course, but you could still hear the crackle—and obsessing about the rain.

The real problem wasn't the jetlag, annoying though it was (and when it could have been so easily avoided). Dan could sympathize with jetlag. Not sleeping, it's no fun. You lie there on your back staring up at an unfamiliar ceiling and your brain goes round and round and round. He had sympathy with the sleeplessness. What drove him quietly nuts was the *mentioning* of it, the endless fricking...talk.

It was the same when Marcia had a cold.

If Dan got a cold, he took some tablets, waited for it to go away. He'd snuffle and wheeze a little, but you couldn't do anything about that. With Dan, a cold lasted four days, tops, soup to nuts, first sneeze to oh-it's-gone. With Marcia a cold was a two week miniseries, an HBO Big Season Event. The first signs would be noted, discussed, held up for scrutiny. The danger of an approaching malaise would be flagged, and the particular inconvenience of its timing loudly mourned. Nine times out of ten this phase would last a single evening—and then the symptoms would disappear, having never been anything more than two sneezes, or a mild headache. Sometimes the cold would arrive for real, however—and she would wander down the next morning wrapped in a blanket, face crumpled, nose red, hair crazy.

And then, for at least a week, the *mentioning of it*.

The constant updates—as if, twenty times a day, he'd said to her 'Now, darling, tell me *exactly* how every single little bit of your body feels, and don't stint on the detail. Really. I *have* to know.' The sinus report. The lower back state-of-play. The throat film-at-eleven—but first here's a message from our sponsor, Runny Noses R Us.

The cold would go away, eventually. After two days of noting its passing she'd be fine—would return, in fact, to the woman who claimed she never got colds, not ever. That's when Dan knew he was in trouble. Ten days of reduced conversation would mean she was full to the brim with observations of pith and moment, stuff that simply *had* to get out of her head before it popped. Any chat, no matter how relaxed, could get suddenly derailed into a discussion of the major or minor issues of the day/year/century, with Marcia being firm but fair, subtle but strident, as if performing to a sizable radio audience. His participation was tolerated once in a while, as a foil, a sentence thrown in as by an interviewer. Other than that, she'd just roll. Any suggestion that the length and depth of discussion was inappropriate to a dinner out at a local restaurant, to Sunday brunch, or to when he was trying to have a quiet bath, would be met with the masterfully oblique suggestion that he simply hadn't thought about the issues enough, and that anyway he'd had his say, and it was her turn now.

Followed by more discussion.

It was on one of these occasions, a romantic supper that had turned into a two-hour debate on their town's zoning regulations, that Dan first fantasized about the notion of some kind of independent adjudication: the idea that there might be some agency to which he could appeal, not with ill-will, but just so he could be proved *right*—just so that it could be established, once and for all, that she *did* hog discussions, that she did cheat in arguments (by deftly shifting the topic whenever she realized she was on shaky ground), and got mini-colds once a month.

He loved his wife, very much, and wouldn't want her any different. But just once in a while he wished there was some way of proving that *he was right*.

No-one was more surprised than him to find out that actually, there was.

***

BEING RIGHT

The bookstore was in a side street halfway down Charing Cross Road. When they'd last been to London, back in the mid-nineties, the whole area had been wall-to-wall books. Like everywhere else in the world it was now feeling the death-pinch of Amazon. The specialty shops were still in place, but the secondhand and antiquarian had closed or gone to seed, and there was a big hole left by the demise of a former Borders. Having left Marcia having a spa treatment back at the hotel for the morning, Dan was disappointed to find he'd done the street and still had an hour and a half to spare. He didn't want to go back early, kick his heels in the hotel. Marcia had been her most jetlagged yet that morning, and very down about the weather. He'd been unsympathetic on these two subjects, over which he considered himself powerless, and sharp words had been spoken.

On a whim, he started poking around the uncharted streets just behind the main road, and it was here he found Pandora's Books. A little wooden shop front, the name appropriately picked out in faded gold paint. The window was littered with an apparently random selection of ancient-looking volumes, none of which he'd heard of.

Perfect. Especially as it was beginning to drizzle. Again.

The smell made him smile as soon as he was inside. Old, forgotten paper, books foxed and creased and bumped. The scent of old shelves and venerable dust added their own welcome notes. It was the way these places *should* smell, the smell of peace and quiet and your own thoughts, the odor of not being in a hurry. The room wasn't that big—probably only twenty feet by fifteen—but the high shelves packed into it, along with the dim light, made it seem larger. In the back there were wooden staircases leading both up and down, neither marked 'Private', promising more of the same (and second-hand bookstores are all about promise). There was a little desk over on the right, piled high with books waiting categorization, but nobody behind it, or in sight.

Dan dithered, then propped his bag against the desk. Usually bookstores preferred it that way, to discourage shoplifters, and it would leave both hands free to browse.

He worked his way down from the top. They had a lot of books, that was for damned sure. Most of the stuff on the upper level was modern, and of no interest, though he did find a pulp paperback worth keeping in his hand. He thought he heard someone coming up the stairs while he turned this book over, debating the couple of pounds it would cost, but when he looked up no-one was there. By the time he got back to street level they'd evidently headed down to the basement.

He took his time around the shelves on the ground floor, as many were dedicated to local history. In the end he found one thing he thought was a definite, plus a couple of maybes. Depended on whether they shipped. The book he wanted was heavy—a Victorian facsimile of an older history of London—and he went over to prop it up against his bag. As he did so he thought he heard someone coming into the room from the back, but when he turned, a small loving-your-store smile on his face, there was no-one there. Evidently just a noise from upstairs. Booksellers creep in mysterious ways, their alphabetizing to perform.

It was in the basement that he found the book.

At first he thought there was nothing for him down there: the room was only half the size of the higher floors, and had none of their sense of order. Tomes of all ages and conditions were piled onto cases in danger of imminent collapse. There was a strong smell of damp too, doubtless caused or at least enhanced by grim-looking patches on the walls. The plaster had come away in many places, revealing seeping brickwork behind.

Dan poked around nonetheless, shoving aside piles of bashed-up book-length ephemera (do your own accounts, learn Spanish in twenty seconds, find your inner you and dream your inner dream), finding and quickly rejecting a few older tomes. It's a shame when the floor you look at last has the least of interest in it, but sometimes that's just the way it is. He was about to give up and go pay for what he'd already put aside, when a bookcase half-hidden right at the end caught his eye.

He decided to check it out. He was in no hurry, after all.

He'd thought from a distance these books were much older than the rest, but he soon saw they were not. Most were Everyman Editions, leather-bound and attractive, but commonplace and not worth the carrying. He had already turned away when something made him turn back and look again. He stood square onto the case and ran his eyes back and forth in a grid pattern. He'd evidently glimpsed something without really seeing it. He wasn't expecting much, but it would be mildly interesting to see what had caught his eye.

Eventually he found it, a book whose spine was much more scuffed than the rest.

He gently eased it out. It was called 'Hopes of a Lesser Demon, Part II', which was kind of odd, for a start. It was a small, chunky thing with battered boards and old leather covers; about an inch thick, six inches high, and four deep. The title on the spine seemed to have been handwritten in ink. When Dan turned to the front the frontispiece claimed the book had been published in Rome in 1641, but that couldn't be right. That meant it should have been in Latin, or Italian at the very least. It wasn't. It was in English, for the most part.

As he leafed through the book it also seemed clear that it could never actually have been published in this form at all. Chunks of it did look very old, the paper spotted and towelly, the text in languages he didn't understand and typefaces that were hard to read. Other parts had been printed far more recently; the paper fresh and glossy, the subjects contemporary. There were sections in French and German and something eastern European, plus something he guessed was Korean, from its similarity to the signs on a food market he walked past every day back home.

It was also far from clear what the book was *about*.

There was a sermon on chastity, and a few pages on deciduous trees. Part seemed to be a travel guide to Bavaria, with spotty black and white plates that must have been taken before the first world war. A polemic on some obscure Middle-Eastern sect was followed by a stretch of love poetry, which had mathematical equations in the footnotes, and preceded by two handwritten pages of what looked like the accounts of a sugar plantation in the West Indies in the eighteenth century. There was no sense to it whatsoever, and yet at the bottom of each page was a folio—a page number—and the ordering of these numerals was consistent from front to back, regardless of subject change or whether they were printed in decaying hand-plated gothic type or super-crisp computer-generated Gill Sans.

Dan flipped back to the front, and saw a price written there in pencil. Five pounds. Eight or nine bucks. Hmm. He already wanted the book, without really knowing why.

MICHAEL MARSHALL SMITH

He glanced through the pages a little further, looking for an excuse to turn his impulse into a no-brainer, and finding merely further pockets of unrelated non-information. A handful of reproductions of watercolors, none by artists he recognized, and few of them any good. A list of popular meadows in Armenia. A section on advanced electronic engineering, complete with circuit diagrams, then a Da Vinci-like ink sketch of a man holding an axe, followed by a long portion of what seemed to be an illustrated children's book, about a happy dog.

And then there were the 'invocations'.

The paper of this section was very, very old, and the text had been entered by hand. Portions had faded back almost to nothing, and even those that were strong weren't easy to read. The first page seemed to be a kind of index. Item one said: *'The Vision of Love's Arc invocation—for to glimpse what man or woman (or both) shall when come into your life, hopefully.'* Item eleven: *'The Sadness of Cattle invocation—the purpose being to make less gloomy your livestock in the night.'* Item twenty two: *'The Regeneration of Heat invocation - a most useful gesture for the revitalization of a time-cooled hot beverage.'*

A spell to warm up a cup of coffee? *What?*

That was silly. The whole index was dumb, in fact, the most stupid section of what was evidently a pretty stupid book. Dan had more-or-less changed his mind about buying it—five pounds was five pounds, after all, and the book was surprisingly heavy for its size—when he caught sight of the last entry in the index:

Item Thirty Eight: 'The Listening Angel—*an invocation for to prove whether you are right.*'

Frowning, Dan flicked to the indicated page and read just enough to establish that yes, this meant exactly what he thought it did.

He seemed then to hear a rushing noise, quite loud, like the tread of a hundred feet, or the beat of thousands of tiny wings. He closed the book and hurried up the stairs.

There was still no-one at the desk, though he saw an explanation for the sound he'd heard. It was raining properly outside now, raining hard. The store's dim lamps struggled against the lowering darkness.

Dan waited for a few moments, moving impatiently from foot to foot, then ventured to call out. There was no response. He waited a little longer, then strode to the back of the store and hiked up the stairs. There was no-one up there. No-one in the basement, either, when he went back down to look. He found himself back at street level, standing again in front of a desk which was still deserted.

Dan dug in his wallet and took out a five pound note. He put it on the desk and picked up his bag. He left the big Victorian book behind. It no longer seemed very interesting.

When he got back to the hotel he was soaked, and surprised to discover he was also late. Somehow it had become three o'clock. He was half-expecting to find Marcia waiting huffily in the lobby, but she wasn't. He took the elevator up to the room. It was empty. Baffled, he called the spa—and was relieved to find that a woman of his wife's description was currently fast asleep on one of the loungers around the pool.

Relieved and, of course, just a little irritated.

He left the book on the bed and wandered around the hotel room, drying his hair with a towel. He *could* go down and wake Marcia, remind her they were supposed to be...but what was the point? By the time she was dressed it would be too late to get to the Tate Gallery. And he would also, he realized, have to account for the fact he'd returned well after he'd said he would. It was not the first time, and 'looking at books' never seemed to be a good enough explanation.

He fired up the room's coffee machine and waited for it to do its thing. Meanwhile he sat in the chair at the desk, and watched the book on the bed. It wasn't moving, naturally, and there was no danger that it would.

And yet...it didn't feel as if he was merely looking at it. Of course you couldn't actually 'watch' something if it wasn't doing anything, though, right? And yet. And yet.

When coffee was made, he picked the book up. At first he couldn't find the Index of Invocations. After dipping into the book at random without success, he started at the beginning and rigorously leafed through from front to back. He saw a lot of odd things, but not the index. His heart, which had been beating rather faster than usual, gradually returned to normal. He flicked through the book again, more slowly, obscurely relieved. He had imagined it, that was all. Perhaps it had just been a kind of delayed jetlag fever: annoyance at the crossed words with his wife that morning, a fantasy born of the dust and damp of the shop...

But then he found them. The Invocations, sandwiched between two sections he *knew* he'd seen on the front-to-back pass. Whatever.

He scanned a few of the other entries:

'*Item Twenty Four: The Strengthening of Bark—a whisper for aiding the defenses of a tree or bush (of considerable size) that is under attack.*'

'*Item Ninety: The Hail of Destiny—a snap to force unto yourself the attentions of any passing taxi cab.*'

'*Item Six: The Flattening Stroke—for to redress a planet that has become mistakenly round. Use only once.*'

But they were just diversions. Quickly he made it down to Item Thirty Eight, then flicked through pages until he again found the one that entry referred to.

As he opened the page he heard the sound again, the beating of wings.

A glimpse out of the window confirmed that this was, for a second time, merely an increase in the volume of rain outside. Odd how it kept happening, though.

And how dark it had become.

The instructions on the page were short, and the ingredients it called for were not unduly hard to come by. Marcia still hadn't returned.

Dan didn't see how he had much choice but to give it a try.

Half an hour later he was standing on the roof of the hotel. This hadn't been easy to bring about, but the recipe stipulated that the invoker must be both outside (in the sense of "not within a structure") and at the highest place available within one hundred horizontal feet of his or her position when the book had been most recently opened. Once he'd worked out what this meant, Dan took the elevator to the highest floor of the hotel—the twelfth—but knew somehow this wouldn't be enough. Plus, if something was going to happen, he didn't want to be interrupted by another guest heading back to their room. A certain amount of poking around led him to a door around a corner, marked 'Stores'. There were indeed stores inside, and Dan helped himself to

BEING RIGHT

a bath towel, but at the back was another door. Opening this led to a dark interior staircase which led upwards.

At the top was a metal door. It was locked. Of course.

Dan kicked at it, impotently. He could hear the sound of rain beyond it. He was so close. He kicked again, the lock clicked, and the door swung open a foot.

The sound of rain was suddenly far louder, and Dan saw it was pelting down outside. Putting aside the question of why the door was now unlocked, he wrapped the towel around his head, left the book on the floor where it wouldn't get wet, and stepped outside.

A very large, flat area lay in front of him, the roof of the hotel. Various protuberances stuck up here and there, some disgorging steam or smoke, many with fans which lazily cycled round. Piles of forgotten wood and other detritus lay against the low wall which went right around the edges. The grey surface of the roof was hidden in places by sizable pools of water, which reflected a blackening sky which seemed to be getting lower and lower.

Dan walked right out into the center of the roof and stopped.

London was spread around him, albeit obscured by sheets of rain and gathering gloom. The towel was soon soaked, and he took it off. Evidently you just had to take this experience as it came. He had memorized the invocation. It wasn't hard. It was so straightforward, in fact, that it was ludicrous to believe it would achieve anything.

Nonetheless he unwrapped the hand towel he'd brought up from the room. Inside were three things. A small sample of his saliva, in one of the room's water glasses: a 'secretion' had been called for, and saliva was as far as he was prepared to go. A few strands of Marcia's hair, easily gleaned from her brush, wrapped in a piece of toilet tissue, and also put into the glass. Rather more trickily, a postcard to Marcia's sister. The recipe called for "a sample of both their words", and didn't explain it any more clearly than that. This defeated Dan until he noticed the postcard, written the previous evening in the bar and now lying on the desk awaiting a stamp. Most of it was in Marcia's hand, but he'd added a cheery sentence at the bottom. Would it do? Dan supposed he was about to find out. He rolled the postcard and put it into the glass too.

He straightened, and quickly threw his hand up into the air. He was a fool, he knew, and braced himself the immediate return of the glass, possibly onto his head.

It didn't come back down.

After a second he looked up, and saw that the glass had disappeared. The rain had started falling harder too, and now it really did sound like wings.

Parts of the sky slowly seemed to detach themselves from the rest, patches of darkness gathering as if a cloud was settling over the hotel, wisps of it catching on the buildings across the street, like the ghosts of future fires.

The sound of traffic seemed to get both louder and further away. Dan listened to it, and to the rain as it fell, until the two noises became one and entered his head, and disappeared, leaving it empty and still.

'Seventy-eight percent,' said a voice.

Dan turned. Something was now sitting on the low wall at the edge of the roof.

It was about twelve feet tall, its color the white of old, tarnished marble, and difficult to see. It seemed to sit hunched on the wall, huge wings hanging off its shoulders. It appeared a little uncomfortable, as if finding itself in the wrong place, somewhere either too hot or too cold.

'Are you the angel?' Dan said.

'Over the length of the marriage, you have spoken twenty-two percent of the time,' the figure said. Its face was turned away from him, hidden behind long wet hair. Its voice was cold, dry, and seemed to come to Dan both via his ears and up through his legs. 'If you limit the enquiry to periods of discussion that could be considered of academic or of purely hypothetical interest, then her contribution rises to eighty-six percent. This peaks, under the influence of alcohol, at ninety-four percent.'

'Then I am right,' Dan said. 'I knew it.'

The angel gave no indication it had heard. 'If considered in terms of total words uttered, rather than time spent speaking, the breakdown is about the same. The shortness and lack of fluidity of your sentences is somewhat counterbalanced by the speed of your attempts to pack them into the short intervals available.'

BEING RIGHT

'Now hold on,' Dan said. He started to walk forward, but a loud, heavy movement of the angel's wings warned him to stay where he was. Somewhere, far away, there was the rumble of thunder. 'What do you mean, lack of "fluidity"?'

'Caused merely by the lack of opportunity for you to get into your stride,' the angel said. 'Of course.'

Dan nodded, mollified. 'Thank you,' he said. 'Now. How do I…'

'Sometimes she even talks when you're not there,' the angel said. 'Quite often, in fact.'

'And you listen?'

'Of course. It's what I do.'

Dan frowned. 'What kind of things does she say?'

'She hopes your kids are safe.'

'Well, so do I.'

'Yes, But she says it out loud. And her words are heard.'

'Okay,' Dan said. He was cold. Unbelievably, it was starting to rain harder, the sky pressing closer down. His hair was plastered to his skull, water running down his face. 'What…else does she say?'

It seemed like the angel was turning to look at him, but when the movement was finished it was still looking another way. 'She says it makes her sad when the children call and you hand the phone straight to her, after merely grunting hello. She tries not to resent the fact you make little effort with her friends, and that—these are my figures, not hers—you are on average responsible for less than four percent of the conversation when they're around. She has issues with the fact that you seem to believe her having a massage once in a while is a big indulgence, when you spend three times as much every month on books you'll mostly never read, and often don't even open again. She feels hurt when you look at her as if wondering what she is harping on about, and why. She wishes that once in a while you would handle her in the way you do an interesting book—and says that you used to, once.'

Dan smiled tightly. 'Well, that's all very interesting. Thanks for your time. And your unbiased opinion.'

The angel rolled its shoulders, as if preparing to leave. 'She cares about things. Who do you think we're in favour of: those who care about things, or those who don't?'

Dan said nothing.

'And the colds,' the angel added. 'Who do you think they're worse for, her or you?'

'I've got to go,' Dan said. 'I assume you will let yourself out.'

He headed back toward the metal door, sloshing straight through the puddles. He didn't want this anymore. Sometimes the person you love is a pain in the ass. He wished he could have left it at that. The rain drummed on the roof like the turning of a million dusty pages. He felt suddenly tired, fifty years of coffee gone sour. With each step it became harder to remember what had just happened, or to believe it, or to remember why he'd wanted to know.

He was reaching for the handle on the door when the angel spoke again. It sounded different. Quieter, further away, as if only a memory of itself.

'When she cannot sleep she lies awake and hopes you still love her.'

Dan stopped dead in his tracks. 'Of course I do,' he said, stricken. 'She *must* know that, surely.'

The angel was fading now, the steady flap of its wings turning back to rain, the grey of its skin becoming cloud once more. As it stood, it turned into rising mist in front of his eyes, its words coming to him as cold wind, blown his way by the beating of those wings.

It said: 'For her, the sound of the two of you talking together is like the smell of books. Do you think she doesn't notice, when you believe you're being good about being bored? Sometimes that's precisely *why* she keeps talking, because she panics when she fears you might not find her interesting anymore.'

It said: 'This "peace and quiet" you believe you want so much: what is it for? What thoughts do you harbor, so valuable they are worth wishing quietness upon someone who loves you so much? Meanwhile she fears for all the ways that things can go wrong in the world, and become still, and lose strength and fall apart.'

It said: 'If she dies before you, which she might, will you then still wish you'd spent more time in silence? When you live in that endless quiet afterward, in those years of deadening cloud and solitude, what might you be prepared to promise, to give, to hear just one word more from her?'

Then the wind dropped and it was gone.

BEING RIGHT

Dan stood on the roof a full five minutes longer. When he stepped back through the metal door into the hotel, he found the book was gone. He hurried down the stairs, through the store cupboard, and ran to the elevator.

When he let himself back into the hotel room, he heard the sound of Marcia in the bath.

'Dan?' she said quickly. 'Is that you?'

'Yes,' he said.

'Where have you *been?*'

'Got caught out in the rain,' he said, carefully, not yet wanting to go in, not yet ready to see her face. 'I'm sorry. Had to hunker down and wait inside somewhere while it passed over. I called the room. You weren't here.'

'Fell asleep,' she said, sheepishly. There was silence for a moment. Then she said: 'I missed you.'

'I missed you too.' He took his jacket off and hung it up in the wardrobe to dry. 'You okay?'

'You know, I think I'm going down with a cold.'

Dan rolled his eyes, but called room service to bring up tea, lemon and honey, before going to help wash her hair. She told him about the spa in the hotel. He told her about his walk, leaving out Pandora's Books. The two of them sat companionably with their words in the warm bathroom, the world cold and wet outside. They decided to order food to their room. They watched TV, read a little, went to bed.

In the small hours of the night, while Marcia fitfully dozed, the listening angel came into the room and touched her brow, whispering to her to worry no more, for a while.

When Dan woke in the morning, Marcia was asleep next to him. It rained a little as they ate breakfast together, but after that the day was fine.

Actually, so much better than fine.

HELL HATH
ENLARGED HERSELF

I always assumed I was going to get old.

That there would come a time when merely getting dressed left me breathless, and I would count a day without a nap as a victory; when I would go into a barber's and some young thing would lift the remaining grey stragglers on my pate and look dubious if I asked her for anything more than a trim. I would have tried to be charming, and she might have thought to herself how game the old bird was, while cutting off rather less than I'd asked. I thought all that was going to come, some day, and in a perverse sort of way had even looked forward to it. A diminuendo, a slowing down, an ellipsis to some other place.

But now I know it will not happen, that I will remain unresolved, like a fugue which didn't work out. Or perhaps more like a voice in an unfinished symphony, because I won't be the only one.

I regret that. I'm going to miss having been old.

I left the facility at 6.30 yesterday evening, on the dot, as had been my practice. I took care to do everything as I always had, collating my notes, tidying my desk, and leaving upon it a list of things to do the next day. I hung my white coat on the back of my office door as usual, and said goodbye to Johnny on the gate with a wink. For six months we have been engaged in a game which involves making some joint statement on the weather every time I enter or leave the facility, without either of us making recourse to speech.

MICHAEL MARSHALL SMITH

Yesterday Johnny raised his eyebrows at the dark and heavy clouds, and rolled his eyes—a standard gambit. I turned one corner of my mouth down and shrugged with the opposite shoulder, a more adventurous riposte, in recognition of that fact this was the last time the game would ever be played.

For a moment I wanted to do more, to say something, reach out and shake his hand; but that would have been too obvious a goodbye. Perhaps no-one would have stopped me anyway, as it has become abundantly clear that I am as powerless as everyone else—but I didn't want to take the risk.

Then I found my car amongst the diminishing number which still park there, and left the compound for good.

The worst part, for me, is that I knew David Ely, and understand how it all started. I was sent to work at the facility because I am partly to blame for what has happened. The original work was done together, but I was the one who had always given creed to the paranormal. David had never paid much attention to such things, until they became an obsession. There may have been some chance remark of mine which made him open to the idea. Just having known me for so long may have been enough.

If so, then I'm sorry. There's not a great deal more I can say.

David and I met at the age of six, our fathers having taken up new positions at the same college—the University of Florida, in Gainesville. My father was in the Geography Faculty, David's in Sociology, but at that time—the late Eighties—the departments were drawing closer together and the two men became friends. Our families mingled closely, in countless back-yard barbecues and shared holidays on the coast, and David and I grew up more like brothers than friends. We read the same clever books and hacked the same stupid computers, and even ended up losing our virginity on the same evening. One spring when we were both sixteen I borrowed my mother's car and the two of us loaded it up with books and a laptop and headed off to Sarasota in search of sun and beer. We found both, in quantity, and also two young English girls on holiday. We spent a week in courting spirals of increasing tightness, playing pool and talking fizzy nonsense over cheap and exotic pizzas, and on the last night two couples walked up the beach in different directions.

HELL HATH ENLARGED HERSELF

Her name was Karen, and for a while I thought I was in love. I wrote a letter to her twice a week, and to this day she's probably received more mail from me than everyone else put together. Each morning I went running down to the mailbox, and ten years later the sight of an English postage stamp could still bring a faint rush of blood to my ears. But we were too far apart, and too young. Maybe she had to wait a day too long for a letter once, or perhaps it was me who without realizing it came back empty-handed from the mailbox one too many times. Either way the letters started to slacken in frequency after six months, and then, without either of us ever saying anything, they simply stopped altogether.

A little while later I was with David in a bar and, in between shots, he looked up at me.

'You ever hear from Karen anymore?' he asked.

I shook my head, only at that moment realizing that it had finally died. 'Not in a while.'

He nodded, and then took his shot, and missed, and as I lined up for the black I realized he'd probably been through a similar thing. For the first time in our lives we'd lost something. It didn't break our hearts. The original liaisons had only lasted a week, after all, and we were old enough to begin to realize that the world was full of girls, and that if we didn't hurry we'd hardly have got through any of them before it was time to get married.

But does anyone ever replace that first person? That first kiss, first fierce hug, hidden in sand dunes and darkness? Sometimes, I guess. I kept the letters from Karen for twenty years. Never read them, just kept them. Last week I threw them all away.

What I'm saying is this. I knew David for a long, long time, and I understood what we were trying to do. He was only trying to salve his pain, and I was trying to help him.

What happened wasn't our fault.

I spent the evening driving slowly along 75, letting the freeway take me down towards the Gulf coast of the panhandle. There were a few patches of rain but for the most part the clouds just scudded overhead, running to some other place. I didn't see many other cars. Either people have given up fleeing or all those capable of it have already fled.

I got off just after Jocca and headed down minor roads, trying to cut round Tampa and St Petersburg. I managed it, but it wasn't easy, and I wound up getting lost more than a few times. I would have brought a map but I'd thought I could remember the way. I couldn't. It had been too long.

We'd heard on the radio in the afternoon that things weren't going well around Tampa. It was the last thing we heard, just before the signal cut out. The six of us remaining in the facility sat around for a while afterward, as if we believed the radio would come back on again real soon now. When it didn't, we got up one by one and drifted back to work.

As I passed the city I could see it burning in the distance, and I was glad I had taken the back way, no matter how long it had taken. If you've seen what it's like when a large number of people go together, you'll understand what I mean.

Eventually I found 301 and headed down it towards 41, towards the old Coast Road.

Summer of 2005. For David and I it was time to make a decision. There was no question that we would go to college—both our families were book-bashers from way back. The money was already in place, some from our parents but most from vacation jobs we'd played at. The question was what we were going to study.

I'd thought long and hard but still couldn't come to a decision. I postponed for a year instead, and decided to take off round the world. My parents shrugged, said 'Okay, keep in touch, try not to get killed, and stop by your Aunt Kate's in Sydney.' They were that kind of people. I remember my sister bringing a friend of hers back to the house one time; the girl called herself Yax and her hair had been carefully dyed and sculpted to resemble an orange explosion. My mother just asked her where she had it done, and kept looking at it in a thoughtful way. I guess my dad must have talked her out of it.

David went for computers. Systems design. He got a place at Jacksonville's new center for Advanced Computing, which was a coup but no real surprise. David was always a hell of a bright guy. That was part of his problem.

HELL HATH ENLARGED HERSELF

It was strange saying goodbye to each other after so many years in each other's pockets, but I guess we knew it was going to happen sooner or later. The plan was that he'd come out and hook up with me for a couple of months during the year. It didn't happen, for the reason that pacts between old friends usually get forgotten.

Someone else entered the picture.

I did my grand tour. I saw Europe, started to head through the Middle East and then thought better of it and flew down to Australia instead. I stopped by and saw Aunt Kate, which earned me big brownie points back home and wasn't in any way arduous. She and her family were a lot of fun, and there was a long drunken evening when she seemed to be taking messages from beyond, which was kind of interesting. My mother's side of the family was always reputed to have a touch of the medium about them, and Aunt Kate certainly did. There was an even more entertaining evening when my cousin Jenny and I probably overstepped the bounds of conventional morality in the back seat of her jeep. After Australia I hacked up through the Far East for a while, until time and money ran out, and then went home.

I came back with a major tan, an empty wallet, and still without any real idea of what I was going to do with my life. With a couple months to go before I had to make a decision, I decided to go visit David. I hopped on a bus and made my way up to Jacksonville on a day that was warm and full of promise. Anything could happen, I believed, and everything was there for the taking. Adolescent naiveté perhaps, but I was basically an adolescent. How was I supposed to know otherwise? I'd led a pretty charmed life up till then, and didn't see any reason why that shouldn't continue. I sat in the bus and gazed out the window, watching the world go by and wishing it the very best. It was a good day, and I'm glad it was. Because though I didn't know it then, the new history of the world probably started at the end of it.

I arrived in Jacksonville late afternoon, and asked around for David. Eventually someone pointed me in the right direction, a house just off campus. I found the building and tramped up the stairs, wondering whether I shouldn't maybe have called ahead.

Eventually I found his door. I knocked, and after a few moments it was opened by some man I didn't recognize. It took me a couple of long seconds to work out it was David. He'd grown a beard. I decided not to hold it against him, yet, and we hugged like, well, like what we were. Two best friends, seeing each other after what suddenly seemed like far too long.

'*Major* bonding,' drawled a female voice. A head slipped into view from round the door, with wild brown hair and big green eyes.

That was the first time I saw Rebecca.

Four hours later we were in a bar somewhere. I'd met Rebecca properly, and realized she was special. In fact, it's probably a good thing they'd met six months before, and that she was so evidently in love with David. Had we met her at the same time she could have been the first thing we'd ever fallen out over. She was beautiful, in a strange and quirky way that always made me think of forests; and she was smart, in that particularly appealing fashion which meant she wasn't always trying to prove it, and was happy for other people to be right some of the time. She moved like a cat on a sleepy afternoon, but her eyes were always alive—even when they couldn't cooperate with each other sufficiently to allow her to accurately judge the distance to her glass. She was my best friend's girl, she was a good one, and I was very happy for him.

Rebecca was at the School of Medical Science. Nanotech was just going off big around then, and it looked like she was going to catch the wave and go with it. In fact, when the two of them talked about their work, it made me wish I hadn't taken the year off. Things were happening for them. They had a direction. All I had was goodwill towards the world and the belief that it loved me too. For the first time I had that terrible sensation that life is leaving you behind and you'll never catch up again; that if you don't match your speed to the train and jump on, you'll be forever left standing in the station.

At one am we were still going strong. David lurched in the general direction of the bar to get us more beer, navigating the treacherously level floor like a man using stilts for the first time.

'Why don't you come here?' Rebecca said, suddenly. I turned to her, and she shrugged. 'David misses you, I don't think you're too much of an asshole, and what else are you going to do?'

I looked down at the table for a moment, thinking it over. Immediately it sounded like a good idea. But on the other hand, what would I do? And could I handle being a third wheel, instead of half a bicycle? I asked the first question first.

'We've got plans,' Rebecca replied. 'Stuff we want to do. You could come in with us. I know David would want you to. He always says you're the cleverest guy he's ever met.'

I glanced at David, who was conversing affably with the barman. We'd decided that to save energy we should start buying drinks two at a time, and David appeared to be explaining this plan. As I watched, the barman laughed. David was like that. He could get on with absolutely anyone.

'And you're sure I'm not too much of an asshole?'

Deadpan: 'Nothing that I won't be able to kick out of you.'

And that's how I ended up applying for, and getting, a place on Jacksonville's nanotech program. When David got back to the table I wondered aloud whether I should come up to college, and his reaction was big enough to seal the decision there and then. It was him who suggested I go nanotech, and also him who explained their plan.

For years people had been trying to crack the nanotech nut. Building tiny biological 'machines', some of them little bigger than large molecules, designed to be introduced into the human body to perform some function or other: promoting the secretion of certain hormones; eroding calcium build-ups in arteries; destroying cells which looked like they were going cancerous. It had taken a long time before the first proper results started coming through—but in the last three years it had really been gathering pace. When David had met Rebecca, a couple of weeks into the first semester, they'd talked about their two subjects, and David immediately realized that sooner or later there'd be a second wave, and that they could be the first to achieve it.

Lots of independent little machines is one thing. But how about lots of little machines which worked *together*? All designed for particular functions, but coordinated by a neural relationship with each other, possessed of a power and intelligence that was greater than the sum of its parts. Imagine what *that* could do.

When I heard the idea I whistled. I tried to, anyway. My lips had gone all rubbery from too much beer and instead the sound came out as a sort of parping noise. But they understood what I meant. 'And no-one else is working on this?'

'Oh, of course,' David smirked, and I had to smile. We'd always both nurtured plans for world domination. 'But with the three of us together, no-one else stands a chance.'

And so it was decided, and ratified, and discussed, over just about all the beer the bar had left. At the end of the evening we crawled back to David and Rebecca's room on our hands and knees, and I passed out on the sofa. The next day, trembling under the weight of a hangover which passed all understanding, I found a place to stay in town and went to talk someone in the faculty of Medical Science. By the end of the week it was confirmed.

On the day I was officially enrolled in the next year's intake, the three of us went out to dinner. We went to a nice restaurant, and we ate and drank, and at the end of the meal we placed our hands on top of each other's in the center of the table. David's went down first, then Rebecca's, and then mine on top. With our other hands we raised our glasses.

'To us,' I said. It wasn't very original, I know, but it's what I meant. I bet all three of us wished there was a photographer present to immortalize the moment. We drank, and then the three of us clasped each other's hands until our knuckles were white.

Ten years later Rebecca was dead.

The coast road was deserted, as I'd expected. The one thing *nobody* is doing these days is heading off down to the beach to hang out and play volleyball. I passed a few vehicles abandoned by the side of the road, but took care not to drive too close. Often people will hide inside or behind one and then leap out at anyone who passes, regardless of whether that person is in a moving vehicle or not.

I kept my eyes on the sea for the most part, concentrating on what was the same rather than what was different. The ocean looked exactly as it always had, though I suppose usually there would have been ships to see, out on the horizon. There probably still are a few, floating aimlessly wherever the tide takes them, their decks echoing and empty. But I didn't see any.

When I reached Sarasota I slowed further, driving out onto Lido Key until I pulled to a halt in the center of St Armand's Circle. It's not a big place, but it has a certain class. Though the stores around the Circle were more than full enough of the usual kind of junk, the restaurants were good, and some of the old, small hotels were attractive, in a dated kind of way. Not as flashy as the deco strips on Old Miami Beach, but pleasant enough.

Last night the Circle was littered with burnt-out cars and the upscale pizzeria where we used to eat was still smoldering, embers glowing in the fading light.

We worked through our degrees and out into postgraduate years. At first I had a lot to catch up on. Sometimes Rebecca snuck me into classes, but most of the time I just pored over their notes and books, and we talked long into the night. Catching up wasn't so hard, but keeping up with both of them was a struggle. I never understood the nanotech side as well as Rebecca, or the computing as deeply as David, but that was probably an advantage. I stood between the two of them, and it was in my mind where the disciplines most equally met. Without me there it's probable none of it would have come to fruition. So maybe if you come right down to it, and it's anyone's fault, it's mine.

David's goal was designing a system which would take the input and imperatives of a number of small component parts and synthesize them into a greater whole—catering for the fact that the concerns of biological organisms are seldom clear-cut. Fuzzy logic wasn't difficult—God knows we were familiar with it, most noticeably in our ability to reason that we needed another beer when we couldn't even remember where the fridge was. More difficult was designing and implementing the means by which the different machines, or 'beckies', as we elected to call them, interfaced with each other.

Rebecca concentrated on the physical side of the problem, synthesizing beckies with intelligence coded into artificial DNA in a manner which enabled the 'brain' of each sub-model to link up with and transfer information to the others. And remember, when I say 'machines' I'm not talking about large metal objects which sit in the corner of the room making unattractive noises and drinking a lot of oil. I'm talking about strings of molecules hardwired together, invisible to the naked eye.

I helped them both with their specific areas, and did most of the development work in the middle, designing the overall system. It was me who came up with the first product to aim for, 'ImmunityWorks'.

The problem of diagnosing malfunction in the human body has always been the huge number of variables, many of which are difficult to monitor effectively from the outside. If someone sneezes, they could just have a cold. On the other hand, they could have flu, or the bubonic plague—or some dust up their nose. Unless you can test all the relevant parameters you're not going to know what the real problem is—or the best way of treating it. We were aiming for an integrated set of beckies which could examine all pertinent conditions, share their findings, and determine the best way of tackling the problem—everything happening at the molecular level, without human intervention of any kind. The system had to be robust enough to withstand interaction with the body's own immune system, and intelligent. We weren't intending to just tackle things which made you sneeze, either: we were never knowingly under-ambitious. Even for ImmunityWorks 1.0 we were aiming for a system which could cope with a wide range of viruses, bacteria and general senescence: a first aid kit to live in the body, anticipating problems and solving them before they got started. A guardian angel, which would co-exist with the human system and protect it from harm.

We were right at the edge of knowledge, and we knew it. The roots of disease in the human body still weren't properly understood, never mind the best ways to deal with them. An individual trying to do what we were doing would have needed about 300 years and a research grant bigger than God's. But we weren't just one person. We weren't even just three. Like the system we were trying to design, we were a perfect symbiosis, three minds whose joint product was incomparably greater than the sum of its parts.

Also, we worked like maniacs. After we'd received our doctorates we rented an old house together away from the campus, and turned the top floor into a private lab. Obviously there were arguments for putting it in the basement, historical 'mad scientist' precedents for example, but the top floor had a better view and as that's where we spent most of our time, that kind of thing was an issue. We got up in the mornings, did enough to maintain our positions at the university, and worked on our own project in secret.

HELL HATH ENLARGED HERSELF

David and Rebecca had each other. I had an intermittent string of short liaisons with fellow lecturers, students or waitresses, each of which felt I was being unfaithful to something, or to someone. It wasn't Rebecca I was thinking of. God knows she was beautiful enough, and lovely enough, to pine after, but I didn't. Lusting after Rebecca would have felt like one of our beckies deciding only to work with some, not all, of the others in its system. The whole thing would have imploded.

Unfaithful to us, I suppose is what I felt. To the three of us.

It took us four years to fully appreciate what we were getting into, and to establish just how much work was involved. The years after that were a slow, grinding process. David and I modeled an artificial body in software, creating an environment in which we could test virtual versions of the beckies Rebecca and I were busy trying to synthesize. Occasionally we'd enlist the assistance of someone from the medical faculty, when we needed more of an insight into a particular disease; but this was always done covertly, and without letting on what we were doing. This was our project, and we weren't going to share it with anyone.

By July of 2016 the software side of ImmunityWorks was in beta, and holding up pretty well. We'd created code equivalents of all of the major viruses and bacteria, and built creeping failures into the code of the virtual body itself—to represent the random processes of physical malfunction. An initial set of 137 different virtual beckies was doing a sterling job of keeping an eye out for problems, then charging in and sorting them out whenever they occurred.

The physical side was proceeding more slowly. Creating miniature biomachines is a difficult process, and when they didn't do what they were supposed to you couldn't exactly lift up the hood and poke around inside. The key problem, and the one which took the most time to solve, was that of imparting a sufficient degree of 'consciousness' to the system as a whole—the aptitude for the component parts to work together, exchanging information and determining the most profitable course of action in any given circumstance.

We probably built in a lot more intelligence than was necessary, in fact I know we did; but it was simpler than trying to hone down the necessary conditions right away. We could always streamline in ImmunityWorks 1.1, we felt, when the system had proved itself and we had patents nobody could crack. We also gave the beckies the ability to perform simple manipulations of the matter around them. It was an essential part of their role that they be able to take action on affected tissue once they'd determined what the problem was. Otherwise it would only have been a diagnostic tool, and we were aiming higher than that.

By October we were closing in, and were ready to run a test on a monkey which we'd infected with a copy of the Marburg strain of the Ebola virus. We'd pumped a whole lot of other shit into it as well, but it was the filovirus we were most interested in. If ImmunityWorks would handle that, we reckoned, we were really getting somewhere.

Yes *of course* it was a stupid thing to do. We had a monkey jacked full of one of the most communicable viruses known to mankind, *in our house*. The lab was heavily secured by then, but it was still an insane risk. In retrospect I realize we were so caught up in what we were doing, in our own joint *mind*, that normal considerations had ceased to register. We didn't even *need* to do the Ebola test. That's the tragic thing. It was unnecessary. It was pure arrogance, and also wildly illegal. We could have just tested ImmunityWorks on vanilla viruses or artificially-induced cancers. If it had worked we could have contacted the media and owned our own Caribbean islands within two years.

But no. We had to go the whole way.

The monkey sat in its cage, looking really very ill, with any number of sensors and electrodes taped and wired on and into its skull and body. Drips connected to bioanalysers gave a second-by-second readout of the muck that was floating around in the poor animal's bloodstream. About two hours before the animal was due to start throwing clots, David pulled the switch which would inject a solution of ImmunityWorks 0.9b7 into its body.

The time was 16:23, October 14th, 2016, and for the next 24 hours we watched.

At first the monkey continued to get worse. Arteries started clotting, and the heartbeat grew ragged and fitful. The artificial cancer which we'd induced in the animal's pancreas also appeared to be holding strong. We sat, and smoked, and drank coffee, our hearts sinking. Maybe, we began to think, we weren't so damned clever after all.

HELL HATH ENLARGED HERSELF

Then...*that moment*.

Even now, as I sit here in an abandoned hotel, listening for sounds of movement outside, I can remember the moment when the read-outs started to turn around.

The clots started to break up. The cancerous cells began to lose vitality. The breed of simian flu which we'd acquired illicitly from the University's labs went into remission.

The monkey started getting better.

And we felt like gods, and stayed that way even when the monkey suddenly died of shock a day later. We understood by then that there was a lot more work to do in buffering the stress effects the beckies had on the body. That wasn't important. It was just a detail. We had screeds of data from the experiment, and David's AI systems were already integrating it into the next version of the ImmunityWorks software. Rebecca and I made the tweaks to the beckies, stamping the revised software into the biomachines and refining the way they interfaced with the body's own immune system. We felt like the kings of the world.

We only really came down to earth the next day, when we realized that Rebecca had contracted Marburg.

Eventually the sight of the St Armand's dying heart palled, and I started the car up again. I drove a little further along the coast to the Lido Beach Inn, which stands just where the strip starts to diffuse into a line of small motels. I turned into the driveway and cruised slowly up to the entrance arch, peering into the lobby. There was nobody there, or if there was, they were crouching in darkness. I let the car roll down the slope until I was inside the motel court itself, then pulled into a space.

I climbed out, pulled my bag from the passenger seat, and locked the car up. I went to the trunk and took out the bag of groceries which I'd carefully culled from the stock back at the facility. I stood by the car for a moment, hearing nothing but the sound of waves over the wall at the end, and looked around. I saw no-one, and no signs of violence. I headed for the stairs to go up to the second floor, and towards room 211. I had an old copy of the key, 'accidentally' not returned many years ago, which was just as well. The hotel lobby was a pool of utter blackness in an evening which was already dark, and I had no intention of going anywhere near it.

For a moment, as I stood outside the door to the room, I thought I heard a girl's laughter, quiet and far away. I stood still, mouth slightly open to aid hearing, but heard nothing else.

Probably it was nothing no more than a memory.

Rebecca died two days later in an isolation chamber. She bled and crashed out in the small hours of the morning, as David and I watched through glass. My head hurt so much from crying that I thought it was going to split, and David's throat was so hoarse he could barely speak. David wanted to be in there with her, but I dissuaded him. To be frank, I punched him out until he was too groggy to fight any more. There was nothing he could do, and Rebecca didn't want him to die. She told me so through the intercom, and as that was her last comprehensible wish, I was determined that it would be so.

We knew enough about Marburg that we could almost feel her body cavities filling up with blood, smell the blackness as it coagulated in her. When she started bleeding from her eyes I turned away, but David watched every moment. We talked to her until there was nothing left to speak to, and then watched powerless as she drifted away, retreating into some upper and hidden hall while her body collapsed around her.

Of course we tried ImmunityWorks. Again, it nearly worked. Nearly, but not quite. When Rebecca's vital signs finally stopped, her body was as clean as a whistle. But it was still dead.

David and I stayed in the lab for three days, waiting. Neither of us contracted the disease.

Lucky old us.

We dressed in biohazard suits and sprayed the entire house with a solution of ImmunityWorks, top to bottom. Then we put the remains of Rebecca's body into a sealed casket, drove upstate, and buried it in a forest. She would have liked that. Her parents were dead, and she had no family to miss her, except us.

David left the day after the burial. We had barely spoken in the intervening period. I was sitting numbly in the kitchen that morning when he walked in with an overnight bag. He looked at me, nodded, and left. I didn't see him again for two years.

I stayed in the house, and once I'd determined that the lab was genuinely clean, I carried on. What else was there to do?

Working on the project by myself was like trying to play chess with two thirds of my mind burned out: the intuitive leaps which had been commonplace when the three of us were together simply didn't come, and had to be replaced by hours of painstaking, agonizingly slow experiment. On the other hand, I didn't kill anyone.

I worked. I ate. I drove most weekends to the forest where Rebecca lay, and became familiar with the paths and light beneath the trees which sheltered her.

I refined the beckies, eventually understanding the precise nature of the shock reaction which had killed our two subjects. I pumped more and more intelligence into the system, amping the ability of the component parts to interact with each other and make their own decisions. In a year I had the system to a point where it was faultless on common viruses, like common flu. Little did the world know, but while they were out there sniffing and coughing I had stuff sitting in ampoules which could have sorted them out for ever.

But that wasn't the point. ImmunityWorks had to work on everything. That had always been our goal, and if I was going to carry on, I was going to do it our way. I was doing it for us, or for the memory of how we'd been. The two best friends I'd ever had were gone, and if the only way I could hang onto some memory of them was through working on the project, that was what I would do.

Then one day…one of them reappeared.

I was in the lab, tinkering with the subset of the beckies designed to synthesize new materials out of damaged body cells. The newest strain of biomachines were capable of far, far more than the originals. Not only could they fight the organisms and processes which caused disease in the first place, but they could then directly repair essential cells and organs within the body, to ensure that it made a healthy recovery.

'Can you do anything about colds yet?' asked a voice, and I turned to see David, standing in the doorway to the lab. He'd lost about thiry pounds in weight, and looked exhausted beyond words. There were lines around his eyes that had nothing to do with laughter, and he looked older in other ways too. As I stared at him he coughed raggedly.

'Yes,' I said, struggling to keep my voice calm. David held out his arm and pulled up his sleeve. I found an ampoule of my most recent brew and spiked it with a hypo. 'Where did you pick it up?'

'England.'

'Is that where you've been?' I asked, as I slipped the needle into his arm and sent the beckies scurrying into his system.

'Some of the time.'

'Why?'

'Why not?' he shrugged, and rolled his sleeve back up.

I waited in the kitchen while he showered and changed, sipping a beer and feeling obscurely nervous. Eventually he reappeared, looking better but still tired. I suggested going out to a bar, and we did, carefully but unspokenly avoiding the ones we used to go to as a threesome. Neither of us had mentioned Rebecca yet, but she was there between us in everything we said, and didn't say. We walked down winter streets to a place I knew had only opened recently, and it was almost as if for the first time I felt I was grieving for her properly. While David had been away, it had been as if they'd just gone away somewhere together.

Now he was here, I could no longer deny that she was dead.

We didn't say much for a while, and all I learnt was that David had spent much of the last two years in Eastern Europe. I didn't push him, but let the conversation take its own course. It had always been David's way that he would get round to things in his own good time.

'I want to come back,' he said eventually.

'David, as far as I'm concerned you never went away.'

'That's not what I mean. I want to start the project up again, but different.'

'Different in what way?'

He told me. It took me a while to understand what he was talking about, and when I did I began to feel tired, and cold, and sad. David didn't want to refine ImmunityWorks. He had lost all interest in the body, except in the ways in which it supported the mind. He'd spent his time in Europe visiting people of a certain kind, trying to establish what made them different. Had I known, I could have recommended my Aunt Kate to him—not, I felt, that it would have made any difference.

I watched him covertly as he talked, as he became more and more animated, and all I could feel was a sense of dread, a realization that for the rest of his life my friend would be lost to me. He had come to believe that mediums, people who can communicate with the spirits of the dead, do not come about through some special spiritual power, but instead as a result of a difference in the physical make-up of their brain. He believed that it was some fundamental but minor idiosyncrasy in the wiring of their senses which enabled them to bridge a gap between this world and the next, to hear voices which had stopped speaking, or see faces which had faded away. He wanted to determine where this difference lay, pinpoint it and learn to replicate it. He wanted to develop a species of becky that anyone could take, which would rewire their soul and enable them to become a medium.

More specifically, he wanted to take it himself, and I understood why, and when I realized what he was hoping for I felt like crying for the first time in two years.

He wanted to be able to talk with Rebecca again, and I knew both that he was not insane and that there was nothing I could do, except help him.

Room 211 was as I remembered it. Nondescript. A decent-sized room in a low-range motel. I put my bags on one of the beds and checked out the bathroom. It was clean and the shower still gave a thin trickle of lukewarm water. I washed and changed into one of the two sets of casual clothes I had brought with me, and then I made a sandwich out of cold cuts and processed cheese, storing the remainder in the small fridge in the corner by the television. I turned the latter on and got snow across the board, though I heard the occasional half-word which suggested that someone was still trying somewhere.

I propped the door to the room open with a bible and dragged a chair out onto the walkway, and then I sat and ate my food and drank a beer looking down across the court. The pool was half full, and a deck chair floated in one end of it.

MICHAEL MARSHALL SMITH

***

Our approach was simple. Using some savings of mine we flew to Australia, where I talked Aunt Kate into letting us take minute tissue samples from her brain, using a battery of lymph-based beckies. We didn't tell her what the samples were for, simply that we were researching genetic traits. Jenny was now married to an accountant, it transpired, and they, Aunt Kate and David and I sat out that night on the porch and watched the sun turn red.

The next day we flew home and went straight on to Gainesville, where I had a much harder time persuading my mother to let us do the same thing. In the end she relented, and despite claiming that the beckies had 'tickled', admitted it hadn't hurt. She seemed fit, and well, as did my father when he returned from work. I saw them once again, briefly, about two months ago. I've tried calling them since, but the line is dead.

Back at Jacksonville David and I did the same thing with our own brains, and then the real work began. If, we reasoned, there genuinely was some kind of physiological basis to the phenomena we were searching for, then it ought to show up to varying degrees in my family line, and less so—or not at all—in David. We had no idea whether it would be down to some chemical balance, a difference in synaptic function, or a virtual 'sixth sense' which some sub-section of the brain was sensitive to—and so in the beginning we just used part of the samples to find out exactly what we'd got to work with. Of course we didn't have a wide enough sample to make any findings stand up to scrutiny: but we weren't ever going to tell anyone what we were doing, so that hardly mattered.

We drew the blinds and stayed inside, and worked 18 hours a day. David said little, and for much of the time seemed only half the person he used to be. I realized that until we succeeded in letting him talk with his love again, I would not see the friend I knew.

We both had our reasons for doing what we did.

It took a lot longer than we'd hoped, but we threw a lot of computing power at it and in the end began to see results. They were complex, and far from conclusive, but appeared to suggest that all three possibilities were partly true. My aunt showed a minute difference in synaptic function in certain areas of her brain, which I shared, but not the fractional chemical imbalances which were present in both my mother and me. On the other hand, there was evidence of a loose meta-structure of apparently unrelated areas of her brain which was only present in trace degrees in my mother, and not at all in me.

We took these results and correlated them against the findings from the samples of David's brain, and finally came to a tentative conclusion. The ability, if it truly was related to physiological morphology, seemed most directly related to an apparently insignificant variation in general synaptic function which appeared to create an almost intangible neural meta-structure within certain areas of the brain.

Not, perhaps, one of the most memorable slogans of scientific discovery, but that night David and I went out and got more drunk than we had in five years. We clasped hands on the table once more, and this time we believed that the hand that should have been between ours was nearly within reach. The next day we split into two overlapping teams, dividing our time and minds as always between the software and the beckies. The beckies needed redesigning to cope with the new environment, and the software required yet another quantum improvement to deal with the complexity of the tasks of synaptic manipulation. As we worked we joked that if the beckies got much more intelligent we'd have to give them the vote. It seemed funny back then.

September 12th, 2019 ought to have a significant place in the history of science, despite everything that happened afterwards. It was the day on which we tested MindWorks 1.0, a combination of computer and corporeal which was probably more subtle than anything else man has ever produced. David insisted on being the first subject, despite the fact that he had another cold, and in the early afternoon of that day I injected him with a tiny dose of the beckies. Then, in a flash of solidarity, I injected myself.

Together till the end, we said.

We sat around for five minutes, and then got on with some work. We knew that the effects, if there were any, wouldn't be immediate. To be honest, we weren't expecting much at all from the first batch. As everyone knows, anything with the version number '1' will have teething problems, and if it has a '.0' after it then it's going to crash and burn. We sat and tinkered with the plans for a 1.1 version, which was only different in that some of the algorithms were more elegant, but we couldn't seem to concentrate. Excitement, we assumed.

Then in the late afternoon David staggered, and dropped a flask of the solution he was working on. It was full of MindWorks, but that didn't matter—we had a whole vat of it in storage. I made David sit down and ran a series of tests on him. Physically he was okay, and protested that he felt fine. We shrugged and went back to work. I printed out ten copies of the code and becky specifications, and posted them to ten different places around the world. Of course the computers already laid automated and encrypted server backups all over the place, but if this worked it was going to be *ours*, and no-one else was taking credit for it. Such considerations were actually less important to us by then, because there was only one thing we wanted from the experiment—but old habits die hard. Ten minutes later I had a dizzy spell myself, but apart from that nothing seemed to be happening at all.

We only realized that we might have succeeded when I woke to hear David screaming in the night.

I ran into his room and found him crouched up against the wall, eyes wide, teeth chattering uncontrollably. He was staring at the opposite corner of the room. He didn't seem to be able to hear anything I said to him. As I stood there numbly, wondering what to do, I heard a voice from behind me—a voice I half-thought I recognized. I turned, but there was no-one there. Suddenly David looked at me, his eyes wide and terrified.

'Fuck,' he said. 'I think it's working.'

We spent the rest of the night in the kitchen, sitting round the table and drinking very strong coffee in very harsh light. David didn't seem to remember exactly what it was he'd seen, and I couldn't recapture the sound of the voice I'd heard, or what it might have said. Clearly we'd achieved *something*, but it wasn't clear what.

When nothing further happened by daybreak, we decided to get out of the house for a while. We were too keyed up to sit around any longer or try to work, but felt we should stay together. Something was happening, we knew: we could both feel it. We walked around campus for the morning, had lunch in the cafeteria, then spent the afternoon downtown. The streets seemed a little crowded, but nothing else weird happened.

HELL HATH ENLARGED HERSELF

In the evening we went out again. We'd been invited to a dinner party at the house of a couple on the medical staff, and thought we might as well attend. David and I were distracted at first, but once everyone had enough wine inside them we started to have a good time. The hosts got out their stock of pot, doubtless supplied by an accommodating member of the student body, and by midnight we were all a little high, comfortably sprawled around the living room.

And of course, eventually, David started talking about the work we'd been doing.

At first people just laughed, and that made me realize belatedly just how far outside the lanes of normal scientific endeavor we had moved. It also made me determined that we should be taken seriously, and so I started to back David up. It was stupid, and we should never have mentioned it. It was one of the people at that party who eventually gave our names to the police.

'So prove it,' this man said at one stage. 'Hey, is there a Ouija board in the house?'

The laughter which greeted this sally was enough to tip the balance. David rose unsteadily to his feet and went to stand in the center of the room. He sneezed twice, to general amusement, but then his head seemed to clear. Though he was swaying gently, the seriousness in his face was enough to quieten most people, although there was a certain amount of giggling. He looked gaunt, and tired, and everybody stopped talking, and the room went very quiet as they watched him.

'Hello?' he said, quietly. He didn't use a name, for obvious reasons, but I knew who he was asking for. 'Are you there?'

'And if so, did you bring any beer?' the hostess added, getting a big laugh. I shook my head, partly at how foolish we were seeming, partly because there seemed to be a faint glow in one corner of the room, as if some of the receptors in my eyes were firing strangely. I made a note to check the beckies when we got back, to make sure none of them could have had an unforeseen effect on the optic nerve.

I was about to say something, to help David out of an embarrassing position, when he turned to the hostess.

'Jackie, how many people did you invite tonight?'

'Eight,' she said. 'We always have eight. We've only got eight sets of table ware.'

David looked at me. 'How many people do you see?' he asked.

I looked round the room, counting.

'Eleven,' I said.

One of the guests laughed nervously. I counted them again. There were eleven people in the room. In addition to the eight of us who were slouched over the settees and floor, three people stood round the walls.

A tall man, with long and not especially clean brown hair. A woman in her forties, with blank eyes. A young girl, maybe eight years old.

Mouth hanging open, I slowly stood up. David and I looked from each of the extra figures to the other. They looked entirely real, as if they'd been there all along.

They stared back at us, silently.

'Come on guys,' the host said, nervously. 'Okay, I'll admit it—you had us fooled for a moment there. Now let's have another smoke.'

David ignored him, turning to the man with the long hair. 'What's your name?' he asked him.

There was a long pause, as if the man was having difficulty remembering. When he spoke, his voice sounded dry and cold. 'Nat,' he said. 'Nat Simon.'

'David,' I said. 'Be careful.'

David ignored me, and turned back to face the real guests. 'Does the name 'Nat Simon' mean anything to anyone?' he asked.

For a moment I thought it hadn't, and then we noticed the hostess. The smile had slipped from her face and her skin had gone white, and she was staring at David. With a sudden, ragged beat of my heart I knew we had succeeded.

'Who was he?' I asked. I wish I hadn't.

In a room that was now utterly silent she told us. Nat Simon had been a friend of one of her uncles. One summer, when she was nine years old, he had raped her just about every day of the two weeks she'd spent on vacation with her relatives. He was killed in a car accident when she was fourteen, and since then she'd thought she'd been free.

'Tell Jackie I've come back to see her,' Nat said proudly, 'And I'm all fired up and ready to go.' He had taken his penis out of his trousers and was stroking it towards erection.

HELL HATH ENLARGED HERSELF

'Go away,' I said. 'Fuck off back where you came from.'

Nat just smiled. 'Ain't ever been anywhere else,' he said. 'Like to stay as close to little Jackie as I can.'

David quickly asked the other two figures who they were. I tried to stop him, but the other guests encouraged him, at least until they heard the answers. Then the party ended abruptly. Voyeurism becomes a lot less amusing when it's you that people are staring at.

The blank-eyed woman was the first wife of the man who had joked about Ouija boards. After discovering his affair with one of his students, she had committed suicide in their living room. He'd falsely told everyone she'd suffered from depression to explain this, and that she drank in secret.

The little girl was the host's sister. She died in childhood, hit by a car while running across the road as part of a dare devised by her brother.

By the time David and I ran out of the house, two of the other guests had already started being able to see for themselves, and the number of people at the party had risen to fifteen.

After four beers my mind was a little fuzzy, and for a while I was almost able to forget. Then I heard a soft splashing sound from below, and looked to see a young boy climbing out of the stagnant water in the pool. He didn't look up. He just walked over the flagstones to the gate, and then padded out through the entrance to the motel. I could still hear the soft sound of his wet feet long after he'd disappeared into the darkness. The brother who'd held his head under a moment too long; the father who'd been too busy watching someone else's wife putting lotion on her thighs; or the mother who'd fallen asleep. I didn't know which of these it would be, but someone would be having a visitor tonight.

When we got back to the house after the party, and tried to get back into the lab, we found we couldn't open the door. The lock had fused. Something had attacked the metal of the tumblers, turning the mechanism into a solid lump of metal.

David and I stared at each other, by now feeling very sober, and then turned to look through the glass upper portion of the door. Everything inside looked the way it always had, but I now believe that even this early, before we really knew what was happening, everything had already been set in motion. The beckies work in strange and invisible ways.

David got the axe from the garage and we broke into the laboratory. We found the vat of MindWorks empty. A small hole had appeared in the bottom of the glass, and there was a faint trail where the contents had flowed across the floor, making small holes at several points. It had doubled back on itself, and in a couple of places it had also flowed against gravity. It ended in a larger hole which, it transpired, dripped through into a pipe.

A pipe which went out back into the municipal water system.

The first reports were on CNN at seven o'clock the next morning.

Eight murders in downtown Jacksonville, and three on the University campus. Reports of people suddenly going crazy, screaming at people who weren't there, running in terror from voices in their head and acting on impulses that they claimed weren't theirs. By lunchtime the problem wasn't just confined to people we might have come into contact with, or who David might have sneezed near the previous day: it had started to spread on its own.

I don't know why it happened. Maybe we made a mistake somewhere. Perhaps it was something as small and simple as a chiral isomer, some chemical the beckies created in a mirror image of the way it should be. That's what happened with Thalidomide, and that's what we created. A Thalidomide of the soul.

Or maybe there *was* no mistake. Perhaps that's just the way it is. Maybe the only spirits who stick around are the ones you don't want to see. The ones who can turn people into psychotics who riot, murder, or end their lives, through the hatred or guilt they bring with them. These things have always been here, all the time, staying close to the people who remember them. Only now they are no longer invisible. Or silent.

A day later there were reports in European cities, at first the ones where I'd sent my letters, then spreading rapidly across the entire land mass.

By the time my letters reached their recipients, the beckies I'd breathed over them had multiplied a thousandfold, breaking the paper down and reconstituting its molecules to create more of themselves. They were so very clever, our little children, and they shared the vaulting ambition of their creators. If they'd needed to, they could probably have formed themselves into new letters, and laid around until someone posted them all over the world. But they didn't, because coughing, or sneezing, or merely breathing is enough to spread the infection.

By the following week a state of emergency was in force in every country in the world.

A mob killed David before the police got to him. He never got to see Rebecca. I don't know why. She just didn't come. I was placed under house arrest, then taken to the facility to help with the feverish attempts to come up with a cure.

There is none, and there never will be. The beckies are too smart, too aggressive, and too powerful. They take any antidote, break it down, and use it to make more of themselves.

They don't need the vote. They're already in control.

The moon is out over the ocean, casting glints over the waves as they rustle back and forth with a sound like someone slowly running their finger across a piece of paper. A little while ago I heard a siren in the far distance. Apart from that, all is quiet.

I think it's unlikely I shall riot, or go on a killing spree. In the end, I will simply go.

The times when Karen comes to see me are bad. She didn't stop writing to me because she lost interest, it turns out. She stopped writing because she had been pregnant, and didn't want me involved, and died through some nightmare of childbirth without ever even telling her mother my name. I hadn't brought any contraception. I think we both figured life would let you get away with things like that. When David and I talked about Karen over that game of pool, she was already dead.

She will come again tonight, as she always does, and maybe tonight will be the night when I decide I cannot bear it any longer. Perhaps seeing her here, at the motel where David and I stayed that summer, will be enough to make me do what I have to do.

If it isn't her who gives me the strength, then someone else will, because I've started seeing other people now too. It's surprising how many—or maybe it isn't, when you consider that all of this is partly my fault. So many people have died, and will die, all of them with something to say to me. Every night there are more, as the world slowly winds down. There are three of them here now, standing in the court and looking up at me. Perhaps in the end I shall be the last person alive, surrounded by silent figures in ranks that reach out to the horizon.

Or maybe, as I hope, some night David and Rebecca will come for me, and I will go with them.

MORE
TOMORROW

I got a new job a couple of weeks ago. It's pretty much the same as my old job, but at a nicer company. What I do is troubleshoot computers and their software—and yes, I know that sounds dull. People tell me so all the time. Not in words, exactly, but in their glassy smiles and their awkward 'let's be nice to the geek' demeanor.

It's a strange phenomenon, the whole 'computer people are losers' mentality. All round the world, at desks in every office and every building, people are using computers. Day in, day out. Every now and then, these machines go wrong. They're bound to: they're complex systems, like a human body, or society. When someone gets hurt, you call in a doctor. When a riot breaks out, it's the police that—for once—you want to see on your doorstep. It's their job to sort it out. Similarly, if your word processor starts dumping files or your hard disk goes non-linear, it's someone like me you need. Someone who actually *understands* the magic box which sits on your desk, and can make it all lovely again.

But do we get any thanks, any kudos for being the emergency services of the late twentieth century?

Do we fuck.

I can understand this to a degree. There are enough hard-line nerds and social zero geeks around to make it seem like a losing way of life. But there are plenty of pretty basic earthlings doing all the other jobs too, and no-one expects them to turn up for work in a pinwheel hat and a T-shirt saying 'Programmers do it recursively'. For the record, I play reasonable blues guitar, I've been out with a girl and have worked undercover for the CIA. The last bit isn't true, of course, but you get the general idea.

Up until recently I worked for a computer company, which I'll admit *was* full of very perfunctory human beings. When people started passing around jokes which were written in C++, I decided it was time to move on. One of the advantages of knowing about computers is that unemployment isn't going to be a problem until the damn things start fixing themselves, and so I called a few contacts, posted a new CV up on my web site and within twenty-four hours had four opportunities to choose from. Most of them were other computer businesses, which I was kind of keen to avoid, and in the end I decided to have a crack at a company called the VCA. I put on my pinwheel hat, rubbed pizza on my shirt, and strolled along for an interview.

The VCA, it transpired, was a non-profit organization dedicated to promoting effective business communication. The suave but shifty chief executive who interviewed me seemed a little vague as to what this actually entailed, and in the end I let it go. The company was situated in tidy new offices right in the center of town, and seemed to be doing good trade at whatever it was they did. The reason they needed someone like me was they wanted to upgrade their system—computers, software and all. It was a month's contract work, at a very decent rate, and I said yes without a second thought.

Morehead, the guy in charge, took me for a gloating tour round the office. It looked the same as they always do, only emptier, because everyone was out at lunch. Then I settled down with their spreadsheet-basher to go find out what kind of system they could afford. His name was Cremmer, and he wasn't out at lunch because he was clearly one of those people who see working nine hour days as worthy of some form of admiration. Personally I view it as worthy of pity, at most. He seemed amiable enough, in a curly-haired, irritating sort of way, and within half an hour we'd thrashed out the necessary. I made some calls, arranged to come back in a few days, and spent the rest of the afternoon helping build a hospital in Rwanda. Well actually I spent it listening to loud music and catching up on my Internet newsgroups, but I could have done the other had I been so inclined.

MORE TOMORROW

The Internet is one of those things that more and more people have heard of without having any real idea of what it means. It's actually very simple. A while back a group of universities and government organizations experimented with a way of linking up all their computers so they could share resources, send little messages, and play *Star Trek* games with each other. There was also a military connection, and the servers linked in such a way that the system could take a hit somewhere and reroute information accordingly. After a time this network started to take on a momentum of its own, with everyone from Pentagon heavies to pinwheeling wireheads taking it upon themselves to find new ways of connecting things up and making more information available. Just about every major computer on the planet is now connected, and if you've got a modem and a phone line, you can get on there too. I can tell you can hardly wait.

What you find when you're there almost qualifies as a parallel universe. There are thousands of pieces of software, probably billions of text files by now. You can check the records of the New York Public Library, send a message to someone in Japan which will arrive within minutes, download a picture of the far side of Jupiter, and monitor how many cans of Dr Pepper there are in a soda machine in the computer science labs of American universities. A lot of this stuff is fairly chaotically organised, but there are a few systems which span the net as a whole. One of these is the World Wide Web, a hyper-text-based graphic system. Another is the newsgroups.

There are about 40,000 of these groups now, covering anything from computers to fine art, science fiction to tastelessness, the books of Stephen King to quirky sexual preferences. If it's not outright illegal, out there on the Infobahn people will be yakking about it 24 hours a day, every day of the year. Either that or posting images of it: there are paintings and animals, NASA archives and abstract art, and in the alt.binaries.pictures.tasteless group you can find anything from close-up shots of roadkill to people with acid burns on their face. Not very nice, but trust me, it's a minority interest. Now that I think of it, there is some illegal stuff (drugs, mainly)—there's a system by which you can send untraceable and anonymous messages, though I've never bothered to check it out.

Basically the newsgroups are the internet for traditionalists—or people who want the news as it breaks. They're little discussion centers that stick to their own specific topic, rather than wasting time with graphics and java applets which play weird tunes at you until you go insane. People read each other's messages and reply, or forward their own pronouncements or questions. Some groups are repositories of computer files, like software or pictures, others just have text messages. No-one, however sad, could hope to keep abreast of all of them, and nor would you want to. I personally don't give a toss about recent developments in Multilevel Marketing Businesses or the Nature of Chinchilla Farming in America Today, and have no interest in reading megabytes of losing burblings about them. So I, like most people, stick to a subset of the groups that carry stuff I'm interested in—Mac computers, guitar music, cats and the like.

So now you know.

The following Tuesday I got up bright and early and made my way to the VCA for my first morning's work. England was doing its best to be summery, which as always meant that it was humid without being hot, bright without being sunny, and every third commuter on the hellish tube journey was intermittently pebbledashing nearby passengers with hay-fever sneezes. I emerged moist and irritable from the station, more determined than ever to find a way of working that meant never having to leave my apartment. The walk from the station to the VCA was better, passing through an attractive square and a selection of interesting side streets with restaurants featuring unusual cuisines, and I was feeling chipper again by the time I got there.

My suppliers had done their work, and the main area of the VCA's open-plan office was piled high with exciting boxes. When I walked in just about all the staff were standing around the pile, coffee mugs in hand, regarding it with the wary enthusiasm of simple country folk confronted with a recently-landed UFO. There was a slightly toe-curling five minutes of introductions, embarrassing merely because I don't enjoy that kind of thing. Only one person, John, seemed to view me with the sniffy disdain of someone greeting an underling whose services are, unfortunately, in the ascendant. Everybody else seemed nice, some very much so.

Morehead eventually oiled out of his office and dispensed a few weak jokes which had the—possibly intentional—effect of scattering everyone back to their desks to get on with their work. I took off my jacket, rolled up my sleeves and got on with it.

I spent the morning cabling like a wild thing, placing the hardware of the network itself. As this involved a certain amount of disrupting everyone in turn by drilling, pulling up carpet and moving their desks, I was soon on apologetic grinning terms with most of them. I guess I could have done the wire-up over the weekend when nobody was there, but I like my weekends as they are. John gave me the invisibility routine that people once used on servants, but everyone else was fairly cool about it. One of the girls, Jeanette, actually engaged me in conversation while I worked nearby, and seemed genuinely interested in understanding what I was doing. When I broke it to her that it was actually pretty dull, she smiled.

The wiring took a little longer than I'd expected, and I stayed on after everybody else had gone. Everyone but Cremmer, that was, who remained, probably to make sure that I didn't run off with their plants, or database, or spoons. Either that or to get some brownie points with whoever it is he thought cared about people putting in long hours. The invoicing supremo was in expansive mood, and chatted endlessly about his adventures in computing, which were, to be honest, of slender interest to me. In the end he got bored of my monosyllabic grunts from beneath desks, and left me with some keys to the office instead.

The next day was pretty much the same, except I was setting up the computers themselves. This involved taking things out of boxes and installing interminable pieces of software on the server. This isn't quite such a sociable activity as disturbing people, and I spent most of the day in the affable but distant company of Sarah, their PR person. At the end of the day everyone gathered in the main room and then left together, apparently for a meal to celebrate someone's birthday. I thought I caught Jeanette casting a glance in my direction at one point, maybe embarrassed at the division between me and them. It didn't bother me, so I just got my head down and got on with swapping floppy disks in and out of the machines.

Well, it bothered me a *little*, to be honest. It wasn't their fault—there was no reason why they should make the effort to include someone they didn't know, who wasn't really a part of their group. People seldom do. You have to be thick-skinned about that kind of thing if you work freelance. There are tribes, everywhere you go. They owe their allegiance to shared time (if they're friends), or to an organization (if they're colleagues); but they're still tribes, just as much as if they'd tilled the same patch of desert for centuries. As a freelancer, especially in the cyber-areas, you tend to spend a lot of time wandering between them; occasionally being granted access to their watering hole, but never being one of the real people. Sometimes it can get on your nerves. That's all.

I finished up, locked the building carefully—I'm a complete anal-retentive about such things—and went home. I used my mobile to call for a pizza while I was en route, and it arrived two minutes after I got out of the shower. A perfect piece of timing, which sadly no-one was on hand to appreciate. My last experiment with living with someone did not end well, mainly because she was a touchy and irritable woman who needed her own space twenty-three and a half hours a day. Well it was more complicated than that, of course, but that was the main impression I took away with me. I mulled over those times as I sat and munched my 'Everything on it, and then a few more things as well' pizza, vague-eyed in front of white noise television, and ended up feeling rather grim.

Food event over, I made a jug of coffee and settled down in front of the Mac. I tweaked my invoicing database for a while, exciting young man that I am, and then wrote a letter to my sister in Australia. She doesn't have access to Internet email, unfortunately, otherwise she'd hear from me a lot more often. Write letter, print letter, put it in envelope, get stamps, get it to a post office. A chain of admin of that magnitude usually takes me about two weeks to get through, and it's a bit primitive, really, compared to 'Write letter, press button, there in seconds'.

I called my friend Nick, who's a freelance sub-editor on a trendy magazine, but he was chasing a deadline and not disposed to chat. I tried the television, but it was still outputting someone else's idea of entertainment. By nine o'clock I was very bored, and so I logged on to the net.

Probably because I was bored, and feeling a bit isolated, after I'd done my usual groups I found myself checking out alt.binaries.pictures.erotica. 'alt' means the group is an unofficial one; 'binaries' means it holds computer files rather than just messages; 'pictures' means those files are images. As for the last word, I'm prepared to be educational about this but you're going to have to work that one out for yourself.

The media has the impression that the minute you're in cyberspace countless pictures of this type come flooding at you down the phone, pouring like ravening hordes onto your hard disk and leaping out of the screen to take over your mind. This is not the case, and all of you worried about your little Timmy's soul can afford to relax a little. Even if you're only talking about the web, you need a computer, a modem, access to a phone line, and a credit card to pay for your Internet feed. With Usenet you need to find the right newsgroup, and download about three segments for each picture. You require several bits of software to piece them together, convert the result, and display it.

The naughty pictures don't come and get you, and if you see one, it ain't an accident. If your little Timmy has the kit, finance and inclination to go looking, then maybe it's you who needs the talking to. In fact, maybe you should be grounded.

The flipside of that, of course, is the implication that *I* have the inclination to go looking, which I guess I occasionally do. Not often—honest—but I do. I don't know how defensive to feel about that fact. Men of all shapes and sizes, ages and creeds, and states of marital or relationship bliss enjoy, every now and then, the sight of a woman with no clothes on. It's just as well we do, you know, otherwise there'd be no new little earthlings, would there? If you want to call that oppression or sexism or the commodification of the female body then go right ahead, but don't expect me to talk to you at dinner parties. I prefer to call it sexual attraction, but then I'm a sad fuck who spends half his life in front of a computer, so what the hell do I know?

Still, it's not something that people feel great about, and I'm not going to defend it too hard. I've talked about it for too long already now, and you're going to think I'm some Neanderthal with his tongue hanging to the ground who goes round looking up people's skirts. I'm not. Yes, there are rude pictures to be found on the net, and yes, I sometimes find them. What can I say? I'm a bloke.

Anyway, I scouted round for a while, but in the end didn't even download anything. From the descriptions of the files they seemed to be the same endless permutations of badly-lit crazy people, which is ultimately a bit tedious. Also, bullish talk notwithstanding, I don't feel great about looking at that kind of thing. I don't think it reflects well upon one, and you only have to read a few other people's slaverings to make you decide it is too sad to be a part of.

So in the end I played the guitar for a while and went to bed.

The next few days at the VCA passed pretty easily. I installed and configured, configured and installed. The birthday meal went pretty well, I gathered, and featured amongst other highlights the secretary Tanya literally sliding under the table through drunkenness. That was her story, at least. By the Monday of the following week everyone was calling me by name, and I was being included in the coffee-making rounds. England had called off its doomed attempt at summer, or at least imposed a time out, and had settled for a much more bearable cross between spring and autumn instead. All in all, things were going fairly well.

And as the week progressed, slightly better even than that. The reason for this was a person. Jeanette, to be precise.

I began, without even noticing at first, to find myself veering towards the computer nearest her when I needed to do some testing. I also found that I was slightly more likely to offer to go and make a round of coffees in the kitchen when she was already there, smoking one of her hourly cigarettes. Initially it was merely because she was the politest and most approachable of the staff, and it was a couple of days before I realized that I was looking out for her return from lunch, trying to be less dull when she was around, and noticing what she wore.

It was almost as if I was beginning to fancy her, for heaven's sake.

By the beginning of the next week I'd passed a kind of watershed, and went from undirected, subconscious behavior to facing the fact that I was actually attracted to her. I did this with a faint feeling of dread, coupled with occasional, mournful tinges of melancholy. It was like being back at school. It's awful, when you're grown-up, to be reminded of what it was like when a word from someone, a glance, even their mere presence, can be like the sun coming out from behind cloud. While it's nice, in a lyric, romantic novel sort of way, it also complicates things. Suddenly it matters if other people come into the kitchen when you're talking to her, and the way they interact with other people becomes more important. You start trying to engineer situations, trying to be near them, and it all just gets a bit weird.

Especially if the other person hasn't a clue what's going on in your head—and you've no intention of telling them.

I'm no good at that, the telling part. Ten years ago I carried a letter round with me for two weeks, trying to pluck up the courage to give it to someone. It was a girl who was part of the same crowd at college, who I knew well as a friend, and who'd just split up from someone else. The letter was a very carefully worded and tentative description of how I felt about her, ending with an invitation for a drink. Several times I was on the brink, I swear, but somehow in the end I didn't give it to her. I just didn't have what it took.

The computer stuff was going okay, if you're interested. By the middle of the week the system was pretty much in place, and people were happily sending pop-up messages to each other. Cremmer, in particular, thought it was just fab that he could boss people around from the comfort of his own den. Even John was bucked up by seeing how the new system was going to ease the progress of whatever dull task it was he performed, and all in all my stock at the VCA was rising high.

It was time, finally, to get down to the nitty-gritty of developing their new databases. I tend to enjoy that part more than the wireheading, because it's more of a challenge, gives scope for design and creativity, and I don't have to keep getting up from my chair. When I settled down to it on Thursday morning, I realized that it was going to have an additional benefit, too. Jeanette was the VCA's Events Organizer, and most of the databases they needed concerned various aspects of her job. In other words, it was her I genuinely had to talk to about them, and at some length.

We sat side by side at her desk, me keeping a respectful distance, and I asked her the kind of questions I had to ask. She answered them concisely and quickly, didn't pipe up with a lot of damn fool questions, and came up with some reasonable requests. It was rather a nice day outside, and sunlight that was for once not hazy and obstructive angled through the window to pick out the lighter hues amongst her chestnut hair, which was long, and wavy, and as far as I could see entirely beautiful. Her hands played carelessly with a biro as we talked, the fingers long and purposeful, the forearms a pleasing shade of skin color. I hate people who go sprinting out into parks at the first sign of summer, to spend their lunchtimes staked out with insectile brainlessness in the desperate quest for a tan. As far as I was concerned the fact that Jeanette clearly hadn't done so—in contrast to Tanya, who already looked like a hazelnut (and probably thought with the same fluency as one)—was just another thing to like her for.

It was a nice morning. Relaxed, and pleasant. Over the last week we'd started to speak more and more, and were ready for a period of actually having to converse with each other at length. I enjoyed it, but didn't get over-excited. Despite my losing status as a technodrone, I am wise in the ways of relationships. Just being able to get on with her, and have her look as if she didn't mind being with me—that was more than enough for the time being. I wasn't going to try for anything more. Or so I thought.

Then, at 12.30, I did something entirely unexpected. We were in the middle of an in-depth and speculative wrangle on the projected nature of their hotel-booking database, when I realized that we were approaching the time at which Jeanette generally took her lunch. Smoothly, and with a nonchalance which I found frankly impressive, I lofted the idea that we go grab a sandwich somewhere and continue the discussion outside. As the sentences slipped from my mouth I experienced an out-of-body sensation, as if watching myself from about three feet away, cowering behind a chair. 'Not bad,' I found myself thinking, incredulously. 'Clearly she'll say no, but that was a good, businesslike way of putting it.'

Bizarrely, instead of shrieking with horror or poking my eye out with a ruler, she said yes. We rose together, I grabbed my jacket, and we left the office, me trying not to smirk like a businessman recently ennobled for doing a lot of work for charity. We took the lift down to the lobby and stepped outside, and I chattered inanely to avoid coming to terms with the fact that I was now standing with her *outside* work, beyond our usual frame of reference.

She knew a snack bar round the corner, and within ten minutes we found ourselves at a table outside, ploughing through sandwiches. She even ate attractively, holding the food fluently and wolfing it down, as if she was a genuine human taking on sustenance rather than someone appearing in amateur dramatics. I audibly mulled over the database for a while, to give myself time to settle down, and before long we'd pretty much done the subject.

Luckily, as we each smoked a cigarette she pointed out with distaste a couple of blokes walking down the street, both of whom had taken their shirts off, and whose paunches were hanging over their jeans.

'Summer,' she said, with a sigh, and I was away. There are few people with a larger internal stock of complaints to make about summer than me, and I let myself rip.

Why, I asked her, did everyone think it was so nice? What were supposed to be the benefits? One of the worst things about summer, I maintained hotly, as she smiled and ordered a coffee, was the constant pressure to enjoy oneself in ways which are considerably less fun than death. Barbecues, for example. Now I don't mind barbecues, especially, except that *my* friends never have them. It's just not their kind of thing. If I end up at a barbecue it's because I've been dragged there by my partner, to stand round in someone else's scraggy back garden as the sky threatens rain, watching drunken blokes teasing a nasty barking dog and girls I don't know standing in hunched clumps gossiping about people I've never heard of, while I try to eat badly cooked food that I could have bought for £2.50 in MacDonald's *and* had somewhere to sit as well. That terrible weariness, a feeling of being washed out, exhausted and depressed, that comes from getting not quite drunk enough in the afternoon sun while standing up and either trying to make conversation with people I'll never see again, or putting up with them doing the same to me.

And going and sitting in parks. I hate it, as you may have gathered. Why? Because it's fucking *horrible*, that's why. Sitting on grass which is both papery and damp, surrounded by middle-class men with beards teaching their kids to unicycle, the air rent by the sound of some arsehole torturing a guitar to the delight of his hippy girlfriend. Drinking lukewarm soft drinks out of overpriced cans, and all the time being repetitively told how nice it all is, as if by some process of brainwashing you'll actually start to enjoy it.

Worst of all, the constant pressure to *go outside*. 'What are you doing inside on a day like this? You want to go outside, you do, get some fresh air.

MICHAEL MARSHALL SMITH

You want to go outside.' No. Wrong. I don't want to go outside. For a start, I like it *inside*. It's nice there. There are sofas, drinks, cigarettes, books. There is shade. Outside there's nothing but the sun, the mindless drudgery of suntan cultivation, and the perpetual sound of droning voices, yapping dogs and convention shouting at you to enjoy yourself. And always the constant refrain from everyone you meet, drumming on your mind like torrential rain on a tin roof: 'Isn't it a beautiful day?', 'Isn't it a beautiful day?', 'Isn't it a beautiful day?', 'Isn't it a beautiful day?'

No, say I. No, it fucking *isn't*.

There was all that, and some more, but I'm sure you get the drift. By halfway through Jeanette was laughing, partly at what I was saying, and partly—I'm sure—at the fact that I was getting quite so worked up about it. But she was fundamentally on my side, and chipped in some valuable observations about the horrors of sitting outside dull country pubs surrounded by red-faced career girls and loud-mouthed estate agents in shorts, deafened by the sound of open-topped cars being revved by people who clearly had no right to live. We banged on happily for quite a while, had another cup of coffee, and then were both surprised to realize that we'd gone into overtime on lunch. I paid, telling her she could get the next one, and although that sounds like a terrible line, it came out pretty much perfect and she didn't stab me or anything. We strode quickly back to the office, still chatting, and the rest of the afternoon passed in a hazy blur of contentment.

I could have chosen to leave the office at the same time as her, and walked to whichever station she used, but I elected not to. I judged that enough had happened for one day, and I didn't want to push my luck. Instead I went home alone, hung out by myself, and went to sleep with, I suspect, a small smile upon my face.

Next day I sprang out of bed with an enthusiasm which is utterly unlike me, and as I struggled to balance the recalcitrant taps of my shower I was already plotting my next moves. Part of my mind was sitting back with folded arms and watching me with indulgent amusement, but in general I just felt really quite happy and excited.

For most of the morning I quizzed Jeanette further on her database needs. She was lunching with a friend, I knew, so I wasn't expecting anything there. Instead I wandered vaguely round a couple of bookshops, wondering if there was any book I could legitimately buy for Jeanette. It would have to be something very specific, relevant to a conversation we'd had—and sufficiently inexpensive that it looked like a throwaway gift. In the end I came away empty-handed, which was just as well. Buying her a present was a ridiculous idea, out of proportion to the current situation. As I walked back to the office I told myself to be careful. I was in danger of getting carried away and disturbing the careful equilibrium of my life and mind.

Then, in the afternoon, something happened.

I was off the databases for a while, trying to work out why one of the servers was behaving like an arse. Tanya wandered up to ask Jeanette about something, and before she went reminded her that there'd been talk of everyone going out for a drink that evening. Jeanette hummed and ha-ed for a moment, and I bent further over the keyboard, giving them a chance to ignore me. Then, as from nowhere, Tanya said the magic words.

Why, she suggested, didn't I come too?

Careful to be nonchalant and cavalier, pausing as if sorting through my myriad of other social options, I said yes, why the hell not. Jeanette then said yes, she could probably make it, and for a moment I saw all the locks and chains around my life fall away, as if a cage had collapsed around me leaving only the open road.

For a moment it was like that, and then suddenly it wasn't. 'I'll have to check with Chris, though,' Jeanette added, and I realized she had a boyfriend.

I spent the rest of the afternoon alternating between trying to calm myself down and violently but silently cursing. I should have *known* that someone like her would already be taken—after all, they always are. Of course, it didn't mean it was a no-go area. People sometimes leave their partners. I know, I've done it myself. And people have left me. But suddenly it had changed, morphed from something that might—in my dreams, at least—have developed smoothly into a Nice Thing, becoming instead a miasma of potential grief which was unlikely to even start.

For about half an hour I was furious, with what… I don't know. With myself, for letting my feelings grow and complicate. With her, for having a boyfriend. With life, for always being that bit more disappointing than it absolutely has to be.

Then, because I'm an old hand at dealing with my inner conditions, I talked myself round. It didn't matter. Jeanette could simply become a pleasant aspect of a month-long contract, someone I could chat to. Then the job would end, I'd move on, and none of it would matter. I had to nail that conclusion down on myself pretty hard, but thought I could make it stick.

I decided that I might as well go out for the drink anyway. There was another party I could go to but it would involve trekking halfway across town. Nick was busy. I might as well be sociable, now that they'd made the offer.

So I went, and I wish I hadn't.

The evening was okay, in the way that they always are when people from the same office get together to drink and complain about their boss. Morehead wasn't there, thankfully, and Cremmer quickly got sufficiently drunk that he didn't qualify as a Morehead substitute. The evening was fine, for everyone else. It was only me who didn't have a good time.

Jeanette disappeared just before we left the office, and I found myself walking to the pub with everyone else. I sat drinking Budweiser and making conversation with John and Sarah, wondering where she was. She'd said she'd meet everyone there. So where was she?

At about half past eight the question was answered. She walked into the pub and I started to get up, a smile of greeting on my face. Then I realized she looked different somehow, and I noticed the man standing behind her.

The man was Chris Ayer. He was her boyfriend. He was also the nastiest man I've met in quite some time. That's going to sound like sour grapes, but it's not. He was perfectly presentable, in that he was good-looking and could talk to people, but everything else about him was wrong. There was something odd about the way he looked at people, both arrogant and closed off. His sense of his possession of Jeanette was complete. She sat at his side, hands in her lap, and said little throughout the evening. I couldn't get over how different she seemed to the funny and confident woman I'd had lunch with the day before, but nobody else seemed to notice it. After all, she joined in the office banter as usual, and smiled with her lips quite often. Nobody apart from me was looking for any more than that.

As the evening wore on I found myself feeling more and more uncomfortable. I exchanged a few words with Ayer, mainly concerning a new computer

MORE TOMORROW

he'd bought, but wasn't bothered when he turned to talk to someone else. The group from the office seemed to be closing in on itself, leaning over the table to shout jokes which they understood and I didn't. Ayer's harsh laugh cut across the smoke to me, and I felt impotently angry that someone like him should be able to sit with his arm around someone like Jeanette.

I drank another couple of beers and then abruptly decided that I simply wasn't having a good enough time. I stood up and took my leave, and was mildly touched when Tanya and Sarah tried to get me to stay. Jeanette didn't say anything, and when Ayer's eyes swept over me I saw that for him I didn't even exist. I backed out of the pub smiling, and then turned and stalked miserably down the road.

By Sunday evening I was fine. I met my ex-girlfriend-before-last for lunch on the Saturday, and we had a riotous time bitching and gossiping about mutual friends. In the evening I went to a restaurant that served food only from a particular four square mile region of Nepal, or so Nick claimed, such venues being his specialty. It tasted just like Indian to me, and I didn't see any sherpas, but the food was good. I spent Sunday doing my kind of thing, wandering round town and reading in cafes. I called my folks in the evening, and they were on good form, and then I watched a horror film before going to bed when I felt like it. The kind of weekend that only happily single people can have, in other words, and it suited me just fine.

Monday was okay too. I was regaled with various tales of drunkenness from Friday night, as if for the first time I had a right to know. I had all the information I needed from Jeanette for the time being, so I did most of my work at a different machine. We had a quick chat in the kitchen while I made some coffee, and it was more or less the same as it had been the week before—because she'd always *known* she had a boyfriend, of course. I caught myself sagging a couple of times on the afternoon, but bullied my mood into holding up. In a way it was kind of a relief, not to have to care.

The evening was warm and sunny, and I took my time walking home. Then I rustled myself up a chef's salad, which is my only claim to culinary skill. It has iceberg lettuce, black olives, grated cheese, julienned ham (that's 'sliced', to you and me), diced tomato and two types of home-made dressing:

which is more than enough ingredients to count as cooking in my book. When I was sufficiently gorged on roughage I sat in front of the computer and tooled around, and by the time it was dark outside found myself cruising round the net.

And, after a while, I found myself accessing alt.binaries.pictures.erotica. I was in a funny sort of mood, I guess. I scrolled through the list of files, not knowing what I was after. What I found was the usual stuff, like '-TH2xx.jpg-{m/f}-hot sex!'. Hot sex wasn't really what I was looking for, especially if it had an exclamation mark after it. Of all the people who access the group, I suspect it's less than about 5% who actually put pictures up there in the first place. It seems to be a matter of intense pride with them, and they compete with each other on the volume and 'quality' of their postings. Their tragically sad bickering is often more entertaining than the pictures themselves.

It's complete pot luck what is available at any given time, and no file stays on there for more than about two days. The servers which hold the information have only limited space, and files get rolled off the end pretty quickly in the high volume groups. I was about to give up when something suddenly caught my attention.

'j1.gif-{f}-"Young_woman, fully_clothed (part 1/3)".

Fuck *me*, I thought: that's a bit weird. The group caters for a fairly wide spectrum of human sexuality, and I'd seen titles which promised fat couples, skinny girls, interracial bonding and light S&M. What I'd never come across was something as perverted as a woman with all her clothes *on*. Intrigued, I did the necessary to download the picture's three segments onto my hard disk.

By the time I'd made a cup of coffee they were there, and I severed the net connection and stitched the three files together. Until they were converted they were just text files, which is one of the weird things about the newsgroups. Absolutely anything, from programs to articles to pictures, is up there as plain text. Without the appropriate decoders it looks like nonsense, which I guess is as good a metaphor as any for the net as a whole. Or indeed for life. Feel free to use that insight in your own conversations.

When the file was ready, I loaded up a graphics package and opened it. I was doing so with only half an eye, not really expecting anything very interesting. But when, after a few seconds of whirring, the image popped onto the screen, I dropped my cup of coffee and it teetered on the desk before falling to shatter on the floor.

It was Jeanette.

The image quality was not high, and looked as if it had been taken with some small automatic camera. But the girl in the picture was Jeanette, without a shadow of a doubt.

She was perched on the arm of an anonymous armchair, and with a lurch I realized it was probably taken in her flat. She was, as advertised, fully clothed, wearing a shortish skirt and a short-sleeved top which buttoned up at the front. She was looking in the general direction of the camera, and her expression was unreadable. She looked beautiful, as always, and somehow much, much more appealing than any of the buck-naked women who cavorted through the usual pictures to be found on the net.

After I'd got over my jaw-dropped surprise, I found I was feeling something else. Annoyance, possibly. I know I'm biased, but I didn't think it right that a picture of her was plastered up in cyberspace for everyone to gawk at, even if she was fully clothed. I realize that's hypocritical in the face of all the other women up there, but I can't help it. It was different.

Because I knew her.

I was also angry because I could only think of one way it could have got there. I'd mentioned a few net-related things in Jeanette's presence at work, and she'd showed no sign of recognition. It was a hell of a coincidence that I'd seen the picture at all, and I wasn't prepared to speculate about stray photos of her falling into unknown people's hands. There was only one person who was likely to have uploaded it. Her boyfriend.

The usual women (and men) in the pictures are getting paid for it. It's their job. Jeanette wasn't, and might not even know the picture was there.

I quickly logged back onto the net and found the original text files. I extricated the uploader information and pulled it onto the screen, and then swore.

Remember a while back I said it was possible to hide yourself when posting up to the net? Well, that's what he'd done. The email address of the person who'd uploaded the picture was listed as 'anon99989@penet.fi'. That meant that rather than posting it up in his real name, he'd routed the mail through an anonymity server in Finland called PENET. This server strips the journey information out of the posting and assigns a random address which is held on an encrypted database. I couldn't tell anything from it at all.

Feeling my lip curl with distaste, I quit out.

By the time I got to work the next day I knew there wasn't anything I could do about it. I could hardly pipe up with 'Hey! Saw your pic on the Internet porn board last night!' And after all, it was only a picture, the kind that people have plastic folders stuffed full of. The question was whether Jeanette knew Ayer had posted it up. If she did then, well, it just went to show that you didn't know much about people just because you worked with them. If she didn't, then I think she had a right both to know, and to be annoyed.

I dropped a few net-references into the conversations we had, but nothing came of them. I even mentioned the newsgroups, but got mild interest and nothing more. It was fairly clear she hadn't heard of them. In the end I sort of mentally shrugged. So her unpleasant boyfriend had posted up a picture. There was nothing I could do about it, except bury still further any feelings I might have entertained for her. She already had a life with someone else, and I had no business interfering.

In the evening I met up with Nick again, and we went and got quietly hammered in a small drinking club we frequented. I successfully fought off his ideas on going and getting some food, doubtless the cuisine of one particular village on the top of Kilimanjaro, and so by the end of the evening we were pretty far gone. I stumbled out of a cab, flolloped up the stairs and mainlined coffee for a while, in the hope of avoiding a hangover the next day.

And as I sat, weaving slightly, on the sofa, I conceived the idea of checking a certain newsgroup.

Once the notion had taken hold I couldn't seem to dislodge it. Most of my body and soul was engaged in remedial work, trying to save what brain cells they could from the onslaught of alcohol, and the idea was free to romp and run as it pleased. So I found myself slumped at my desk, listening to my hard disk doing its thing, and muttering quietly to myself. I don't know what I was saying. I think it was probably a verbal equivalent of that letter I never gave to someone, an explanation of how much better off Jeanette would be with me. I can get very maudlin when I'm drunk.

MORE TOMORROW

When the newsgroup appeared in front of me I blearily ran my eye over the list. The group had seen serious action in the last twenty four hours, and there were over 300 titles to contend with. I was beginning to lose heart and interest when I saw something about two thirds of the way down the list.

'j2.gif-{f}-"Young_woman"', one line said, and it was followed by 'j3.gif-{f}-"Young_woman"'.

These two titles started immediately to do what half a pint of coffee hadn't: sober me up. At a glance I could tell that there were two differences from the description of the first picture of Jeanette I'd seen. The numerals after the 'j' were different, implying they were not the same picture. Also, there were two words missing at the end of the title: the words 'fully clothed'.

I called the first few lines of the first file onto the screen, and saw that it too had come from anon99989@penet.fi. Then, reaching shakily for a cigarette, I downloaded the rest. When my connection was over I slowly stitched the text files together and then booted up the viewer.

It was Jeanette, again. Wincing slightly, hating myself for having access to photos of her under these circumstances when I had no right to know what they might show, I looked briefly at first one and then the other.

j2.gif looked as if it had been taken immediately after the first I'd seen. It showed Jeanette, still sitting on the arm of the chair. She was undoing the front of her top, and had got as far as the third button. Her head was down, and I couldn't see her face. Trembling slightly from a combination of emotions, I looked at j3.gif. Her top was now off, showing a flat stomach and a dark blue lacy bra. She was steadying herself on the chair with one arm, and her position looked uncomfortable. She was looking off to one side, away from the camera, and when I saw her face I thought I had the answer to at least one question. She didn't look very happy. She didn't look as if she was having fun.

She didn't look as if she wanted to be doing this at all.

I stood abruptly and paced around the room, unsure of what to do. If she hadn't been especially enthralled about having the photos taken in the first place, I couldn't believe that Jeanette condoned or even knew about their presence on the net. Quite apart from anything else, she wasn't that type of girl, if that type of girl indeed existed at all.

This constituted some very clear kind of invasion by her boyfriend, something that negated any rights he may have felt he had upon her. But what could I do about it?

I copied the two files onto a floppy, along with j1.gif, and threw them off my hard disk. It may seem like a small distinction, but I didn't want them on my main machine. It would have seemed like collusion.

I got up next morning with no more than a mild headache, and before I left for work decided to quickly log onto the net. There were no more pictures, but there was something that made me very angry indeed. Someone had posted up a message whose total text was the following:

'Re: j-pictures {f}: EXCELLENT! More pleeze!'.

In other words, the pictures had struck a chord with some nameless net-pervert, and they wanted to see some more.

I spent the whole morning trying to work out what to do. The only way I could think of broaching the subject would involve mentioning the alt.binaries.pictures.erotica group itself, which would be a bit of a nasty moment—I wasn't keen on revealing the fact that I was a nameless net pervert myself. I hardly got a chance to talk to her all morning anyway, because she was busy on the phone. She also seemed tired, and little disposed to chat on the two occasions we found ourselves in the kitchen together.

It felt as if parts of my mind were straining against each other, pulling in different directions. If she didn't know about it, it was wrong, and she should be put in the picture. If I did so, however, she'd never think the same of me again. There was a chance, of course, that the problem might go away: despite the net-loser's request, the expression on Jeanette's face in j3.gif made it seem unlikely there *were* any more pictures. And ultimately the whole situation probably wasn't any of my business, however much it felt like it was.

In the event, I missed the boat. About 4.30 I emerged from a long and vicious argument with the server software to discover that Jeanette had left for the day. 'A doctor's appointment'. In most of the places I've worked that phrase translates to 'A couple of hours off from work, *obviously* not spent at the doctors,' but that didn't seem to be the impression at the VCA. She'd probably just gone to the doctor's. Either way she was no longer in the office, and I was slightly ashamed to find myself relaxing now that I could no longer talk to her.

MORE TOMORROW

At 8.30 that evening, after my second salad of the week, I logged on and checked the group again. There was nothing there. I fretted and fidgeted around the apartment for a few hours, and then tried again at 11.00. This time I did find something.

Two things. j4.gif, and j5.gif, both from the anonymous address.

In the first picture Jeanette was standing. She was no longer wearing her skirt, and her long legs led up to underwear that matched the bra I'd already seen. She wasn't posing for the picture. Her hands were on her hips, and she looked angry. In j5 she was leaning back against the arm of the chair, and no longer wearing her bra. Her face was blank.

I stared at the second picture for a long time, mind completely split in two. If you ignored the expression on her face, she looked gorgeous. Her breasts were small but perfectly shaped, exactly in proportion to her long, slender body. It was, undeniably, an erotic picture. Except for her face, and the fact that she obviously didn't want to be photographed, and the fact that someone was doing it anyway. Not only that, but broadcasting it to the planet.

I decided enough was enough, that I had to do something.

After a while I came up with the best that I could. I loaded up my email software and sent a message to anon99989@penet.fi. The double-blind principle the server operated on meant that the recipient wouldn't know where it had come from, and that was fine by me.

The message was this: 'I know who you are'.

It wasn't much, but it was something at least. The idea that someone out there on the information superhighway could know his identity *might* be enough to stop him. It was only a stop-gap measure, anyway. I now knew I had to do something about the situation. It simply wasn't on.

And I had to do it soon. When I checked the next morning there were no more pictures, but two messages from people who'd downloaded them. 'Keep 'em cumming!' one wit from Japan had written. Some slob from Texas had posted in similar vein, but added a small request: 'Great work, but pick up the pace a little. I want to see more FLESH!'

All the way to work I geared myself up to talking to Jeanette, and I nearly punched the wall when I heard she was out at a venue meeting for the whole morning and half the afternoon. I got rid of the morning by concentrating hard on one of her databases, wanting to bring at least something positive into her life. I know it's not much, but all I know is computers, and that's the best that I could do.

At last three o'clock rolled round, and Jeanette reappeared in the office. She seemed tired and a little preoccupied, and sat straight down at her desk to work. I loitered in the main office area, willing people to fuck off out of it so hard my head started to ache. I couldn't get anywhere near the topic if there were other people around. It would be hard enough if we were alone.

Finally, bloody, *finally* she got up from her desk and went into the kitchen. I got up and followed her in. She smiled faintly and vaguely on seeing me, and, seeing that she had a bandage on her right forearm, I used that to start a conversation. A small mole, apparently, hence the visit to the doctor. I let her finish that topic, keeping half an eye out to make sure that no-one was approaching the kitchen.

'I bought a camera today,' I blurted, as cheerily as I could. It wasn't great, but I wanted to start slowly. She didn't respond for a moment, and then looked up, her face expressionless.

'Oh yes?' she said, eventually. 'What are you going to photograph?'

'Oh, you know, buildings, landscape. Black and white, that kind of thing.' She nodded distantly, and I ran out of things to say.

I ran out because in retrospect the topic didn't lead anywhere, but I stopped for another reason too. I stopped because as she turned to pick up the kettle, the look on her face knocked the wind out of me. The combination of unhappiness and loneliness, the sense of helplessness. It struck me again that despite the anger in her face in j4, in j5 she had not only taken her bra off but looked resigned and defeated. Suddenly I didn't care how it looked, didn't care what she thought of me.

'Jeanette,' I said, firmly, and she turned to look at me again. 'I saw a pict...'

'Hello boys and girls. Having a little tea party, are we?'

At the sound of Morehead's voice I wanted to turn round and smash his face in. Jeanette laughed prettily at her employer's sally, and moved out of the way to allow him access to the kettle. Morehead asked me some balls-achingly dull questions about the computer system, obviously keen to sound as if he had some faint idea of what it all meant. By the time I'd finished answering him Jeanette was back at her desk.

The next hour was one of the longest of my life. I'd gone over, crossed the line. I knew I was going to talk to her about what I'd seen. More than that, I'd realized that it didn't have to be as difficult as I'd assumed.

The first picture, j1.gif, simply showed a pretty girl sitting on a chair. It wasn't pornographic, and could have been posted up in any number of places on the net. All I had to do was say I'd seen *that* picture. It wouldn't implicate me, and she would know what her boyfriend was up to.

I lurked round the main office, ready to be after her the minute she looked like leaving, having decided that I'd walk with her to the tube and tell her then. So long as she didn't leave with anyone else, it would be perfect. In the meantime I watched her work, her eyes blank and isolated. At about quarter to five she got a phone call. She listened for a moment, said 'Yes, alright,' in a dull tone of voice, then put the phone down. There was nothing else to distract me from the constant cycling of draft gambits in my head.

At five she started tidying her desk, and I slipped out and got my jacket. I waited in the hallway until I could hear her coming, then went downstairs in the lift. I walked through the lobby as slowly as I could, and went and stood outside the building. My hands were sweating and I felt wired and frightened, but I knew I was going to go through with it. A moment later she came out.

'Hi,' I said, and she smiled warily, surprised to see me, I suppose. 'Look Jeanette, I need to talk to you about something.'

She stared at me, looked around, and then asked what.

'I've seen pictures of you.' In my nervousness I blew it, and used the plural rather than singular.

'Where?' she said, immediately. She knew what I was talking about. From the speed with which she latched on, I realized that whatever fun and games were going on between her and Ayer were at the forefront of her mind.

'The Newsgroups. It's...'

'I know what they are,' she said. 'What have you seen?'

'Five so far,' I said. 'Look, if there's anything I can do...'

'Like what?' she said, and laughed harshly, her eyes begin to blur. 'Like what?'

'Well, anything. Look, let's go talk about it. I could...'

'There's no use,' she said hurriedly, and started to pull away. I followed her, bewildered. How could she not want to do anything about it? I mean, alright, I may not have been much of a prospect, but surely *some* help was better than none.

'Jeanette...'

'Let's talk tomorrow,' she hissed, and suddenly I realized what was happening.

Her boyfriend had come to pick her up. She walked towards the curb where a white car was coming to a halt, and I rapidly about-faced and started striding the other way. It wasn't fear, or not purely. I also really didn't want to get her in trouble.

As I walked up the road I felt as if the back of my neck was burning, and at the last moment I glanced to the side. The white car was passing, and I could see Jeanette bolt upright in the passenger seat. Her boyfriend was looking out of the side window. At me.

Then he accelerated and the car sped away.

That night brought another two photographs. j6 had Jeanette naked, sitting in the chair with her legs slightly apart. Her face was stony. In j7 she was on all fours, photographed from behind. As I sat in my chair, filled with impotent fury, I noticed something in both pictures, and blew them up with the magnifier tool. In j6 one side of her face looked a little red, and when I looked carefully at j7 I could see that there was a trickle of blood running from a small cut on her right forearm.

And I realized, with help from memories of watching her hands and arms as she worked, that there had never been a mole on her arm.

She hadn't got the bandage because of the doctor.

She had it because of him.

I hardly slept that night. I stayed up till three, keeping an eye on the newsgroup. Its denizens were certainly becoming fans of the 'j' pictures, and I saw five requests for some more. As far as they knew all this involved was a bit more scanning originals from some magazine. They didn't realize that someone I knew was having them taken against her will.

MORE TOMORROW

I considered trying to do something within the group, like posting a message telling what I knew. While its frequenters are a bit tragic, they tend to have a reasonable moral stance about such things. It's not like the alt.binaries.pictures.tasteless group—where anything goes, the sicker the better. If the a.b.p.erotica crowd became convinced the pictures were being taken under coercion, there was a decent chance they might mailbomb Ayer off the net. It would be a big war to start, however, and one with potentially damaging consequences. The mailbombing would have to go through the anonymity server, and probably crash it. While I couldn't give a fuck about that, it would draw the attention of all manner of people. In any event, because of the anonymity, nothing would happen directly to Ayer apart from some inconvenience.

I decided to put the idea on hold, in case talking to Jeanette tomorrow made it unnecessary. Eventually I went to bed, where I thrashed and turned for hours. Sometime just before dawn I drifted off, and dreamt about a cat being caught in a lawnmower.

I was up at seven, there being no point in me staying in bed. I checked the group, but there were no new files. On an afterthought I checked my email, realizing that I'd been so out of it that I hadn't done so for days. There were about thirty messages for me, some from friends, the rest from a variety of virtual acquaintances around the world. I scanned through them quickly, seeing if any needed urgent attention, and then slap in the middle I noticed one from a particular address.

anon99989@penet.fi.

Heart thumping, I opened it. In the convention of such things, he'd quoted my message back at me, with a comment. The entire text of the mail read:

'> I know who you are.

>

Maybe. But I know where you live.'

When I got to work, at the dot of nine, I discovered Jeanette wasn't there. She'd left a message at eight thirty announcing she was taking the day off. Sarah was a bit sniffy about this, though she claimed to be great pals with Jeanette. I left her debating the morality of such cavalier leave-taking with

Tanya in the kitchen, as I walked slowly out to sit at Jeanette's desk to work. After five minutes' thought I went back to the kitchen and asked Sarah for Jeanette's number, claiming I had to ask her about the database. Sarah seemed only too pleased to provide the means of contacting a friend having a day off. I grabbed my jacket, muttered something about buying cigarettes, and left the office.

Round the corner I found a public phone box and called her number. As I listened to the phone ring I glanced at the prostitute cards which liberally covered the walls, but soon looked away. I didn't find their representation of the female form amusing any more. After six rings an answering machine cut in. A man's voice, Ayer's, announced that they were out. I rang again, with the same result, and then left the phone box and stood aimlessly on the pavement.

There was nothing I could do.

I went back to work. I worked. I ran home.

At six thirty I logged on for the first time, and the next two pictures were already there. I could tell immediately that something had changed. The wall behind her was a different color, for a start. The focus of the action seemed to have moved, to the bedroom, presumably, and the pictures were getting worse. j8 showed Jeanette spread-eagled on her back. Her legs were very wide open, and both her hands and feet were out of shot. j9 was much the same, except you could see that her hands were tied. You could also see her face, with its hopeless defiance and fear. As I erased the picture from my disk I felt my neck spasming.

Too late I realized that what I should have done was get Jeanette's address while I was at work. It would have been difficult, and viewed with suspicion, but I might have been able to do it. Now I couldn't. I didn't know the home numbers of anyone else from the VCA, and couldn't trace her address from her number. The operator wouldn't give it to me.

If I'd had the address I could have gone round. Maybe I would have found myself in the worst situation of my life, but it would have been something to try. The idea of her being in trouble somewhere in London, and me not knowing where, was almost too much to bear.

I decided that I had to do the one small thing I could.

MORE TOMORROW

I logged back onto the erotica group and prepared to start a flame war.

The classic knee-jerk reaction that people on the net use to express their displeasure is known as 'flaming'. Basically it involves bombarding the offender with massive mail messages until their virtual mail box collapses under the load. This draws the attention of the administrator of their site, and they get chucked off the net. What I had to do was post a message providing sufficient reason for the good citizens of Pornville to dump on anon99989@penet.fi.

So it might cause some trouble. I didn't fucking care.

I had a mail slip open and my hands poised over the keyboard before I noticed something which stopped me in my tracks.

There were two more files. Already. The slob from Texas was getting his wish: the pace was being picked up.

In j10 Jeanette was on her knees on a dirty mattress. Her hands appeared to be tied behind her, and her head was bowed. j11 showed her lying awkwardly on her side, as if she'd been pushed over. She was glaring at the camera, and when I magnified the left side of the image I could see a trickle of blood from her right nostril.

I leapt up from the keyboard, shouting.

I don't know what I was saying. It wasn't coherent. Jeanette's face stared up at me from the computer and I leant wildly across and hit the switch to turn the screen off. Just quitting out didn't seem enough. Then I realized the image was still there, even though I couldn't see it. The computer was still sending the information to the screen, and the minute I turned it back on, it would be there. So I hard-stopped the computer by just turning it off at the mains. Suddenly what had always been my domain felt like the outpost of someone very twisted and evil, and I wanted nothing to do with it.

Then, like a stone through glass, two ideas crashed into each other in my head.

Gospel Oak.

Police.

From somewhere came a faint half-memory, so tenuous that it might be illusory, of Jeanette mentioning Gospel Oak station. In other words, the rail station in Gospel Oak.

I knew where that was.

An operator wouldn't give me an address from a phone number. But the police would be able to get it. They had reverse directories.

I couldn't think of anything else.

I rang the police. I told them I had reason to believe that someone was in danger, and that she lived at the house with the phone number I had for Jeanette. They wanted to know who I was and all manner of other shit, but I rang off quickly, grabbed my coat and hit the street.

Gospel Oak is a small area, filling the gap between Highgate, Chalk Farm and Hampstead. I knew it well because Nick and I used to go play pool at a pub on Mansfield Road, which runs straight through it. I was familiar with the entrance and exit points of the area, and I got the cab to drop me off as near to the center as possible. Then I stood on the pavement, hopping from foot to foot and smoking, hoping against hope that this would work.

Ten minutes later a police car turned into Mansfield Road. I was very pleased to see them, and enormously relieved. I hadn't been very sure about the Gospel Oak part.

I shrank back against the nearest building until it had gone past, and then ran after it as inconspicuously as I could. It took a left into Estelle Road and I slowed at the corner to watch it pull up outside number 6. I slipped into the doorway of the corner shop and watched as two policemen took their own good time about untangling themselves from their car.

They walked up to the front of the house. One leant hard against the doorbell, while the other peered around the front of the house as if taking part in an officiousness competition. The door wasn't answered, which didn't surprise me. Ayer was hardly going to break off from torturing his girlfriend to take social calls. One of the policemen nodded to the other, who visibly sighed, and made his way round the back of the house.

'Oh come on, come *on*,' I hissed in the shadows. 'Break the fucking door down.'

About five minutes passed, and then the policeman reappeared. He shrugged flamboyantly at his colleague, and pressed the doorbell again.

A light suddenly appeared above the door, coming from the hallway behind it. My breath caught in my throat and I edged a little closer. I'm not sure what I was preparing to do. Dash over there and force my way in, past the policemen, to grab Ayer and smash his head against the wall? I really don't know.

The door opened, and I saw it wasn't Ayer or Jeanette. It was an elderly man with a crutch and grey hair that looked like it had seen action in a hurricane. He conversed irritably with the policemen for a moment and then shut the door in their faces. The two cops stared at each other for a moment, clearly considering busting the old bastard, but then turned and went back to their car. Still looking up at the house, the first policeman made a report into his radio, and I heard enough to understand why they then got into the car and drove away.

The old guy had told them that the young couple had gone away for the weekend. He'd seen them leave on Thursday evening. I was over 24 hours too late.

When the police car had turned the corner I found myself panting, not knowing what to do. The last two photographs, the one with the dirty mattress, hadn't been taken here at all. Jeanette was somewhere in the country, but I didn't know where, and there was no way of finding out. The pictures could have been posted from anywhere.

I walked quickly across the road towards the house. The policemen may not have felt they had probable cause, but I did, and I carefully made my way around the back of the house. This involved climbing over a gate and wending through the old guy's crowded little garden, and I came perilously close to knocking over a pile of flower pots. As luck would have it there was a kind of low wall which led to a complex exterior plumbing fixture, and I clambered on top of it. A slightly precarious upward step took me next to one of the second floor windows. It was dark, like all the others, but I kept my head bent just in case.

When I was closer to the window I saw it wasn't fastened at the bottom. They might have gone, and then returned. Ayer could have staged it so the old man saw them go, and then slipped back when he was out.

It was possible, but not likely. But on the other hand, the window was ajar.

Maybe they were just careless about such things. I slipped my fingers under the pane and pulled it open. Then I leant with my ear close to the open space and listened. There was no sound, and so I boosted myself up and quickly in.

I found myself in a bedroom. I didn't turn the light on, but there was enough coming from the moon and streetlights to pick out a couple of pieces of Jeanette's clothing, garments that I recognized, strewn over the floor. She wouldn't have left them like that, not if she'd had any choice. I walked carefully into the corridor, poking my head into the bathroom and kitchen, which were dead. Then I found myself in the living room.

The big chair stood in front of a wall I recognized, and at the far end a computer sat on a desk next to a picture scanner. Moving as quickly but quietly as possible, I frantically searched over the desk for anything that might tell me where Ayer had taken her. There was nothing there, and nothing in the rest of the room. I'd broken—well, *opened*—and entered for no purpose. There were no clues. No sign of where they'd gone. An empty box under the table confirmed what I'd already guessed: Ayer had a laptop as well. He could be posting the pictures onto the net from anywhere that had a phone socket.

Jeanette would be with him, and I needed to find her. I needed to find her *soon*.

I paced around the room, trying to pick up speed, trying to work out what I could possibly do. No-one at the VCA knew where they'd gone—they hadn't even known Jeanette wasn't going to be in. The old turd downstairs hadn't known. There was nothing in the flat that resembled a phone book or personal organizer, something that would have a friend or family member's number. I was prepared to do anything, call anyone, in the hope of finding where they'd gone. But there was nothing, unless...

I sat down at the desk, reached behind the computer and turned it on. Ayer had a fairly flash deck, together with a scanner and laser printer. He knew the Net. Chances were he was wirehead enough to keep his phone numbers somewhere on his computer.

As soon as the machine had booted up I went rifling through it, grimly enjoying the intrusion, the computer-rape. His files and programs were spread all over the disk, with no apparent system. Each time I finished looking through a folder, I erased it. It seemed the least I could do.

Then after about five minutes I found something, but not what I was looking for.

I found a folder named 'j'.

There were files called j12 to j16 inside, in addition to the others that I'd seen. Wherever Jeanette was, Ayer had come back here to scan the pictures. Presumably that meant they were still in London, for all the good that did me.

I'm not telling you what they were like, except that they showed Jeanette, and in some she was crying, and in j15 and j16 there was blood running from the corner of her mouth. A lot of blood. She was twisted and tied, face livid with bruises, and in j16 she was staring straight at the camera, face slack with terror.

Unthinkingly I slammed my fist down on the desk. There was a noise downstairs and I went absolutely motionless until I was sure the old man had lost interest. Then I turned the computer off, opened up the case and removed the hard disk. I climbed out the way I'd come and ran out down the street, flagged a taxi by jumping in front of it and headed for home.

I was going to the police, but I needed a computer, something to shove the hard disk into. I was going to show them what I'd found, and fuck the fact it was stolen. If they nicked me, so be it. But they had to do something about it. They had to try and find her. If he'd come back to do his scanning he had to be keeping her somewhere in London. They'd know where to look, or where to start. They'd know what to do.

They had to. They were the police. It was their job.

I ran up the stairs and into my flat, then dug in my spares cupboard for enough pieces to hack together a compatible computer. When I'd gathered them I went over to my desk to call the local police station, but then stopped and turned my computer on. I logged onto the net and kicked up my mail package, and sent a short, useless message.

'I'm coming after you,' I said.

It wasn't bravado. I didn't feel brave at all. I just felt furious, and wanted to do anything which might unsettle him, or make him stop. Anything to make him stop.

I logged quickly onto the newsgroups, to see when anon99989@penet.fi had most recently posted. A half hour ago, when I'd been in his apartment, j12-16 had been posted up. Two people had already responded: one hoping the blood was fake and asking if the group really wanted that kind of picture—the other asking for more. I viciously wished a violent death upon the second person, and was about to log off, having decided not to bother phoning but to just go straight to the cops, when I saw another text-only posting at the end of the list.

'Re: j-series' it said. It was from anon99989@penet.fi.

I opened it. 'End of series,' the message said. 'Hope you all enjoyed it. Next time, something tasteless.'

'And I hope,' I shouted at the screen, 'that you enjoy it when I ram your hard disk down your fucking throat.'

Then suddenly my blood ran cold.

'Next time, something tasteless.'

I hurriedly closed the group, and opened up alt.binaries.pictures.tasteless. As I scrolled past the titles for roadkills and people crapping I felt the first heavy, cold tear roll onto my cheek. My hand was shaking, my head full of some dark mist, and when I saw the last entry I knew suddenly and exactly what Jeanette had been looking at when j16 was taken.

'j17.gif,' it read. '{f} Pretty amputee'.

THE MOTEL
BUSINESS

I did not mean to get into the motel business. It came about when I was thirty-two because I got divorced and my ex-wife kept the house and after a while I realized I was hemorrhaging money on by-the-week rooms and so I put most of what I had left into a ramshackle property on a bluff above the ocean on the outskirts of Santa Cruz. It was small, old-fashioned, L-shaped, and had once been a fairly popular destination but become less successful after bigger and far nicer hotels were built in town and so it was eventually abandoned for several years. At the time I was semi-regularly drinking in the same bar as someone on the town council and he assured me that if I bought the place and vaguely implied I would be running it as a motel but in fact turned it into a private residence then nobody on the zoning commission would care. Soon after I completed the purchase he lost his seat on account of complicated financial wrong-doings and it turned out he was wrong about that—and other things, including the idea that his wife would continue to turn a blind eye to his relentless philandering—but by then I was in escrow and it was too late to back out and so I wound up owning a property in which stray dogs would not wish to abide and yet which had to be inhabited as a motel or not at all. I was unhappy about this but I was unhappy about pretty much everything in my life at that point so the situation didn't seem remarkable.

MICHAEL MARSHALL SMITH

I had a little money left after I'd taken ownership, cash I'd intended to spend on turning the place into a spacious and comfortable place for me to live. Instead it went on a few modifications and bringing the place up to code. I paid a contractor to fix the parts I knew would be futile or dangerous for me to attempt but did the rest of the work myself, including rewiring, learning as I went along. After a while I found I enjoyed the process, or at least that it was fairly successful in distracting me from the well-worn tracks of disillusion and impotent rage that my mind was prone to run around in the long, dark night that seemed to be mine to inhabit. My budget was small and so I made a virtue out of necessity, scouring yard sales and thrift stores and even using materials and furniture that people had left out on the street. I bought a bunch of old clock radios, and put one in each room. I found a cache of Bakelite bedside lamps. I tore up the carpets and rough-sanded the floors. Each room ended up a different color, based on what paint I could find cheaply that day. By the time I'd finished, to my surprise, the place was not only habitable but had something of a distinctive vibe. I guess now you'd call it shabby chic but then it was more just shabby so I pitched my prices accordingly.

I opened the following week. Business was slow at first. It's stayed that way. The motel is seldom more than a third full. That's okay. What with one thing and another I make enough to keep myself comfortable. It's sustainable. It doesn't attract attention. It's a life. It has been nearly thirty years now and during that time I've met a lot of people, come to know them a little, my path briefly entangling with theirs.

I'm going to tell you about one of them now.

She arrived in late afternoon as the light was fading. People often do. My motel is not a destination. Nobody books in advance. They turn into the lot either because they know they will not be able to afford the prices in town, or because they are not headed anywhere in particular and so my place is as good a place to stop as any.

She was driving a dark blue Camaro that looked like it had seen a lot of miles. That was my first clue. As a rule of thumb women don't drive Camaros.

I sat behind the desk—I spend most of each day there, reading, or staring out at the highway—and watched her get out. She stood for a moment as if becalmed. She looked to be in her late twenties and wore jeans and a denim shirt and had brown hair tied back and was only a few good weeks' sleep away from being very attractive.

Instead of coming to the office she wandered to the far side of the lot, from where you can look down over the ocean. I knew what she'd be seeing—grey sea disappearing into cold fog. That's the way it is for days at a stretch in the late Fall. She lit a cigarette and stood staring out, as if coming to a decision. Finally she dropped the butt to the ground and came walking in my direction.

When she was in front of the desk I could see it'd take more than sleep to fix things. The corners of her mouth were beginning to turn down, like someone who'd spent a few years forgetting—or never being reminded—how to smile.

'How many nights?'

'Two,' she said. 'Maybe more. Do I need to tell you now?'

I nodded toward the empty lot. 'Off season runs three hundred sixty-five days of the year.'

She laughed, briefly, in a way that changed her face. I looked up at her for a moment.

'What?'

'Deciding what room to put you in. They're all different. I choose the one I think people will enjoy.'

'Do you always get it right?'

'Never had any complaints.'

'So?'

I looked at her a moment longer. 'Number 9,' I said.

I watched as she moved in. In one hand, a small traveling bag. Under the other arm, a brown paper sack. Groceries, maybe. More likely something to drink and smoke.

She hung the Do Not Disturb tag on the knob, closed the door and drew the curtains, and that was the end of that.

Next morning the tag remained in place. I clean the rooms myself, so I let it be. At four o'clock—sitting once again behind the desk, reading a paperback novel a previous guest had left behind—I saw her door open. She was dressed the same as when she arrived and even from a distance you could tell she was badly hungover. She walked over to where she'd smoked a cigarette the day before and did it again.

I pulled my pack of Marlboros from under the counter and went outside. She saw me coming and registered my presence but didn't say anything.

'So is he going to come looking for it?'

'For what?'

'Your boyfriend,' I said. 'His car.'

'Husband. I doubt it. It's been three months.'

'Where'd you leave?'

'Richmond, Virginia.'

'Where you going?'

'Do I look like I know?'

I smiled. 'So what's the short-term?'

'Heading into town. Where's a good place?'

'For what?'

'Fun.'

'Define "fun".'

'Oh, I wish I knew.'

'Avoid Asti's. The Negative Space is okay. But I'd try the Blue Bar first, on Front Street. Relaxed place. The food isn't bad, either.'

'Good enough. I like my room, by the way,' she said. 'Guess you picked right.'

'I generally do.'

At a little after two a.m. I was woken by a noise outside. I raised my head from the pillow but I knew what it was. I've heard it before. It was the sound of a car running into the low metal fence around the parking lot, at low speed.

A pause. The sound of a car reversing, parking. Then the engine being turned off. Two doors opening, slamming. Low voices, a peal of laughter, footsteps on gravel, a room door shutting.

I went back to sleep.

The Do Not Disturb tag hung on Number 9 for the whole of the next day. When I saw her standing smoking and looking out at the sea at the end of the afternoon, she was alone and had something of a black eye. I let her be.

THE MOTEL BUSINESS

***

Next morning she came to the office. She looked tired and pale and pretty unhappy with herself.

'Going, or staying?'

'Staying,' she said. 'Though I won't be visiting the Blue Bar again.'

'Who was it?'

'Barman. I...forget his name.'

Never learned it, more likely. 'Rick. Tattoos on his knuckles?'

'That would be the guy. A little too vigorous maybe.'

'You want me to have someone talk to him?'

She looked at me. 'What?'

'Don't like to see a woman with a bruise on her face. Or anywhere else, come to that. There are people who could explain to him how not-cool it is.'

'You'd do that?'

'You're a guest in town. You're staying at my motel.'

She looked at me with an expression that was hard to name. 'I'm fine,' she said.

But on her way out the door she hesitated, and turned back. 'Thanks,' she said.

Next day a middle-aged salesman arrived on his way south to San Luis Obispo. I put him in Room 7. He left early the next morning.

Not much else happened, to be honest with you.

That evening I was sitting out on the stubby deck on the ocean side of the office, looking at the dim, fuzzy disk of the moon up above. The deck runs to the back, with a door giving access to the couple of rooms where I live. I heard someone coming and turned to see her standing diffidently at the little gate. She was holding a brown paper bag.

'Wondered if you drank on occasion.'

I lifted up the bottle of beer on the side table. 'Only when I'm awake. Not going into town?'

'Tonight I think I'd prefer to do it somewhere safe.'

'Sounds wise.'

'Am I safe?'

'Do you want to be?'

'Right now, yes I do.'

'Then this is the right place.'

She had a bottle of wine and once I'd opened it for her and got a glass from inside we sat in the two chairs and smoked and looked into the fog.

'So what's the deal?' I asked, eventually.

She didn't say anything for a while, then shrugged. 'Married at twenty-two. Walked out at twenty-nine. Driven a couple thousand miles since.'

'That's it?'

'I've had a while to boil it down. What about you? Is there a Mrs. Motel-keeper?'

'Long time ago. It didn't work out. That's how I wound up owning this place, in fact. I've spent some time with people since. But I'm not going down the wedding road again. For some, I think it's just not meant to be.'

She nodded. 'Maybe you're right.'

'Alone isn't so bad.'

She poured herself another drink. I'd meant to sound reassuring but I looked at her face in the light of the lamp on the wall and thought to myself that she didn't have much time to stop the lines at the corners of her mouth becoming permanent. That it might already be too late.

Next morning it was Friday and I had business in town. When I got back in the mid-afternoon the door to Room 9 was open.

I stood outside. She was sitting in the chair, smoking. The TV was on, some random re-run. Her head was pointed in that direction but I didn't think she was watching it. Her face was wholly without expression. Just wanted background noise. My motel is quiet. If the ocean's frisky, you'll hear waves. If not, nothing at all but for the sound of the occasional car on the highway, going somewhere other than here—which cannot help but, on some level, make you question whether here is the right place to be after all.

'Making chili,' I said. 'You'd be welcome.'

She shook her head. 'Need some fun tonight.' She realized what she'd said, made a face. 'No offense.'

'None taken.'

'What was that other bar you said? Not the Blue Bar?'
'The Negative Space.'
'Right. Thank you. And, you know, sorry.'
'Don't worry about it. Have fun. But not too much.'
She winked. It looked sad. It looked lonely.

At half past nine I was making a few adjustments to Room 8 when I heard a car coming into the lot. I left the room, locking the door behind me, in time to see her car bashing into the fence in pretty much the exact same place it had the other night. She reversed—I was glad to see she was alone in the car—made it into her own space, and got out.

'Keep screwing up that damned turn,' she said, as she got out. Her voice was slurred, her eyes unclear.

'It's a tough one,' I said, though it is not.

'Wait,' she said. She went around the passenger side and got a brown bag off the seat. 'Nearly forgot my fun.'

'Didn't find any downtown, huh.'

'I did not. Found that asshole Rick again, though.'

'Seriously?'

'Yep. He came in that other bar. Like I've got a homing device on my ass. But...' Her face changed, and when she spoke again her voice was quieter, and tired, and less drunk. 'He found some other dumb-ass, attached to a bigger pair of tits.'

'I have some chili left.'

'Tell the truth I'm more in the mood for wine.'

'I can tell. But get some food inside and it'll hurt less tomorrow. You can still get plenty drunk. Hell, I'll join you.'

She opened her mouth to say no but then said yes.

It was about two hours later. I'd given her a bowl of chili and she did finish it, because my chili is actually pretty good. Then she'd opened a bottle from her bag. That was gone now. She was halfway through another and had hit that stage of drunk where you hold steady for a while, getting deeper and colder rather than more incoherent.

'But in the end, you know what?'

'What?'

'All that stuff I just said, about his mother and his damn friends and his easy, know-nothing-and-proud-of-it take on everything... That's not even the problem.'

'So what is it?'

'*Was* it,' she said. 'I'm not going back.'

'Okay.'

'It was... Oh, it doesn't matter.'

'Sure it does.'

'It's...' She stopped. She poured herself another glass and this time instead of only filling it halfway, like you do when you're pretending, hey, this might be the last, she filled it right to the brim. Took a sip, and it was as though all the air slowly went out of her. 'It's me,' she said.

'What's you?'

'Sure, Steve's an asshole, or becoming one. And he cheats, or wants to. And his mom's a racist fuck. But every time you point a finger it points right back at you.'

'What do you mean?'

'I mean I didn't have to take his car and bail. I mean I could have tried talking to him, or tried harder, or longer. I loved him once and maybe I still do and it's not his fault that's not enough. It's not his fault that when we got married it looked like I was going to do something with my life and along the way I forgot what it was supposed to be. He goes to work every day and when he comes back I'm still there in Pjs and not in a sexy way but the way that says the person simply could not be bothered. The kitchen looks the same as when he left and there's breadcrumbs everywhere because toast is what I had for breakfast and for lunch and what I'd eat for dinner too except I know I should cook him something but the thought makes me feel so angry and bored that I get into an argument with him for no reason. During which he points out that the grocery store is literally ten minutes' walk away and some people might actually enjoy cooking for the person they love, an observation that incenses me even more and we wind up having a huge fight about nothing and everything, and it ends up with him walking out and me breaking something. And I stand there with the sound still ringing in my ears and the pieces all around and I know damned well it was my fault and I can remember being the person who wouldn't have done that and I can even picture that younger me standing there staring at the now-me saying "What the fuck *happened* to you?"—and it's like being an animal in a cage and you either whirl faster and faster in circles or you can stop and lie down and go to sleep. And that's what I did. Until three months ago, when I realized one morning that if I didn't get up and go, then I'd never get out of bed again. So I bailed. But you know what?'

'What?'

'I had this thing happen to me one time. There was this old woman in town, she used to clean for my mother once in a while. I'd known her since I was tiny. She was almost part of the family. And one day I drove her home and I was talking about boyfriends and how school wasn't working out and she listened patiently and when I stopped whining she said "You know, I'm not sure you're ever going to get what you want."'

'So she's a cranky old bitch.'

'Maybe, but there's more. Couple days later, we heard she died in her sleep that night. I'm likely the last person to ever talk to her. And so I carried that with me for years, thinking it was maybe like a prophecy or something.'

'It wasn't.'

'I know that now. But I know it because I eventually realized she had seen a bunch of stuff in her life and actually she was saying something different. She wasn't saying the world was stacked against me. She was warning me that I was stacked against *myself*. That I always managed to find the thing to be pissed or sad about, something or someone to blame. And she was right about that but I didn't get it until I was already up to my knees in the hole and sinking fast.'

'But now you know. So you can climb out.'

'No,' she said. 'I was *born* in the hole. Running doesn't change a thing. I have a god-given right to be mad about my life, right? Because I'm so special? *Bullshit.* Truth is I've done nothing in ten years but bitch about things I could change but never do. I can't even seem to give him kids because we've been fucking for years without protection and he keeps politely not saying anything about it to the point where I want to bash his brains in, but his mother got my number years ago—I hate her guts, but she isn't dumb—and makes no fucking bones about making it clear she thinks I'm just a drain on resources. A week before I blew town it was his birthday and she organized something for him because she knew I wouldn't get my shit together, and I did not, and she invited the girl he used to date before me. I mean, seriously, she actually did that. And the worst of it was I stood at the back of the room getting drunk and watched the two of them catching up on old times, and I thought "You know what, Stevie? You could do worse." Hell, you *have* done. You got me.'

'It was a dick move by his mom. You were self-protecting.'

'I really wasn't. I just didn't care.'

'That's not a good way to be.'

'Right. So, Mr. Motel-keeper...what do I do about it? How do I get from here to somewhere worth being? How do I stop feeling so sorry for myself and start giving a shit?'

I thought about it. Opened another bottle of beer. And in the end I shrugged and said 'Maybe you don't.'

She turned her head to look blearily at me. 'What?'

'Could be there's no way out. Maybe instead you got to say "Okay, this is me. So what do I do with that?"'

'How the fuck does that help?'

'Not saying it will. But pretending the world's going to change or that you're going to change is setting yourself up for bitter disappointment. Maybe you lower your expectations instead. Stop believing some prize or distraction or guy is going to come along to help you forget who you are. Accept that nothing's going to get better, deal with the world as it is.'

She was frowning and her eyes looked more focused now. 'I'm twenty-nine years old and you're telling me basically I'm *done*? Is that supposed to *help*?'

'I'm not your father.'

'No,' she said. 'You're not.' She stood up, unsteadily.

'Look,' I said. 'I apologize.'

'For what? You're right. Game over. So you play the same damn thing again or else turn off the machine.' She stomped half the way to the gate, realized she'd left the scant remains of her bottle of wine, came back for it. This gave me time to stand up. I accompanied her to the gate.

THE MOTEL BUSINESS

'I didn't mean to—' I said, but stopped talking, as a car turned into the lot. We watched it pull over and park next to hers. A guy got out of the driver's side.

'Huh,' she said. 'Would you look at that.'

'I'll tell him to leave.'

'Don't worry,' she said, and there was an awful change in her voice, a pathetic hopefulness. 'I'll see what he wants.'

She hurried across the lot toward Rick, who was standing there waiting, as if he knew she'd come.

I finished my beer on the deck with another cigarette and went to bed.

My head didn't feel great the next morning, but it often doesn't, so that didn't really affect my day one way or the other. I got up at seven and fixed myself some eggs and coffee and wrote down a list of jobs for the day.

I took a second coffee out for a walk around and as I left the office saw the door to Number 9 open. Rick came out.

And then another guy.

They both looked pretty pleased with themselves. Rick saw me there, and winked. They got in the car and drove away.

I went back into the office so if she came out she wouldn't realize what I'd seen.

I did not see her for the whole of the day.

I wasn't sure whether I would go out that evening. I had an open mind. When it got dark I sat on the deck with a beer and a smoke and waited to see what I would do.

She arrived at the gate a little after seven. She did not look good. She was pale and her hair was unwashed. Her eyes were evasive. She looked defeated. She looked terrible.

'Haven't seen you around today,' I said.

'Been in bed.' Her voice was quiet, almost a mumble.

'Sickening for something?'

She shook her head. 'Thinking.'

'How'd that go?'

'Can't face driving out tonight,' she said. 'Wondered if you had a couple beers I could borrow.'

'I'm sure I can find something.'

I went indoors. I did not have any beers but I found a bottle of vodka. When I came back out and offered it she took it gratefully. 'Have one with me?'

'I have to go out,' I said. 'Sorry.'

She nodded quickly. 'Sure, okay. Thanks.'

I went back indoors. She was still there, looking out toward the dark sea, when I came back out with my jacket on.

'What you said last night,' she said. Her voice was very quiet now. 'You really think that's the way it is?'

'I do,' I said. 'There's no big thing out there. Nothing to make it all okay. Doesn't matter how far you drive or how many bars you fall down in or how many different men you wake up next to thinking, Jesus—who the hell is this guy. There's just you. That's all there is in your life and all there's ever going to be. There is no magic. This is all she wrote.'

She nodded, more slowly this time.

When I drove out of the lot she was still standing there at my gate, looking out over the ocean.

I hoped it had been the right thing to say, that it might help push her in the right direction.

I had a solitary dinner down in Capitola, then drove slowly back up the coast, stopping at a couple bars.

I got home around midnight. There was no extra car in the lot. Just hers. I stayed up a while.

The Do Not Disturb tag wasn't hanging on her door next morning, but I left cleaning her room until last anyway. I didn't knock until nearly midday.

I left it a couple minutes, knocked again. I unlocked the door. The room was a mess.

She was in the bathtub. The water was cold and red. Her face was white and her eyes were open. The knife—one of the sharp ones from the kitchenette drawer—was lying on the floor. The cuts she'd made across her wrist were deep. She'd found a great deal of strength at the end.

I called the cops. They arrived and took pictures and the coroner came. He commiserated with me for having this happen in my place. He reassured me that what with her being from out of town, nobody needed to know what had happened. They took her away, one of the cops driving her car.

When they were gone I spent half an hour tidying up the mess, then an hour thoroughly cleaning up the bathroom. By the time I was done there would be no way of telling anything had happened there. It was ready for a new guest.

Then I went next door to Number 8. I took the tapes out of the cameras on tripods in front of the tiny holes in the wall opposite the main area of Room 9, and then from the two behind the false mirror in the bathroom. They are positioned so as to cover the entire matching space in the next room, including the bathtub.

I replaced the tapes with fresh ones from the box in the closet, double-checked the cameras facing Room 7 too. Then I left, putting the tapes that recorded what had happened in the night in a bag and taking it with me.

I would spent the afternoon making copies and then go out in the evening to pass the tapes to the three men in the area (and one woman) who will pay a great deal to watch that kind of material. I didn't need to pay Rick for his role—my calls to him, yielding advice as to which bars would yield a desperate woman in search of fun, had given him a couple of memorable nights, and he'd had no idea of the end to which I had directed him. But I'd buy him a drink or two. He'd played his part well. I'd likely use him again. I'd used him before.

After that I would come home and have a few beers on the deck and look up at the frail circle of the moon hanging in the fog over the ocean in a long dark night that has lasted my whole life and from which I do not expect ever to wake, and I would sit and smoke and drink until I was tired enough to sleep, and I would probably not think about anything at all.

DEAR **ALISON**

It is Friday the 25th of October, and beginning to turn cold. I'll put the heating on before I go.

I'm leaving in about half an hour. I've been building up to it all day, kept telling myself that I'd leave any minute now and spend the day waiting in the airport. But I think I always knew that I'd wait until this time, until the light was going. London is at its best in the autumn, and four o'clock in the afternoon is the autumn time. Four o'clock is when autumn is.

An eddy of leaves is turning hectically in the street outside my study window, flecks of green and brown lively against the tarmac. Earlier the sky was clear and blue, bright white clouds periodically changing the light which fell into the room; but now that light is fading, painting everything with a layer of grey dust. Smaller, drier leaves are falling on the other side of the street, collecting in a drift around the metal fence in front of Number 12.

I'll remember this sight. I remember most things. Everything goes in, and stays there, not tarnishing but bright like freshly-cut glass. An attic of experience to remind me what it is I've lost. The years will soften with their own dust, but dust is never hard to brush away.

I'll post the keys back through the door, so you'll know there is no need to look for me. And a spare set's always useful. I'm not sure what I'm going to do with this letter. I could print it out and put it somewhere, or take it with me and post it later. Or perhaps I should just leave it on the computer, hidden deep in a sub-folder, leaving it to chance whether it will ever be discovered. But if I do that then one of the children will find it first, and it's you I should be explaining this to, not Richard or Maddy; you to whom the primary apology is due.

I can't explain in person, because there wouldn't be any point. Either you wouldn't believe me, or you would: neither would change the facts or make them any better. In your heart of hearts, buried too firmly to ever reach conscious thought, you may already have begun to suspect. You've given no sign, but we've stopped communicating on those subtler levels and I can't really tell what you think any more. Telling you what you in some sense already know would just make you reject it, and me. And where would we go from there?

My desk is tidy. All of my outstanding work has been completed. All the bills are paid.

I'm going to walk. Not all the way—just our part. Down to Oxford Street.

I'll cross the road in front of our house, then turn down that alley you've always been scared of. (I can never remember what it's called; but I do remember an evening when you forgot your fear long enough for it to be rather interesting.) Then off down Kentish Town Road, past the Woolworth's and the Vulture's Perch pub, the mediocre sandwich bars and that shop the size of a football pitch which is filled only with spectacles. I remember ranting against the waste of space when you and I first met, and you finding it funny. I suppose the joke's grown old.

It's not an especially lovely area, and Falkland Road is hardly Bel Air. But we've lived here fifteen years, and we've always liked it, haven't we? At least until the last couple of years, when it all started to curdle; when I realized what was going to happen. Before that Kentish Town suited us well enough. We liked Cafe Renoir, where you could get a reasonable breakfast when the staff weren't feeling too cool to serve it to you. The Assembly House pub, with its wall-to-wall Victorian mirrors and a comprehensive selection of Irish folk on the jukebox. The corner store, where they always know what we want before we ask for it. All of that.

It was our place.

I couldn't talk to you about it when it started, because of how it happened. Even if it had come about some other way, I would probably have

DEAR ALISON

kept silent: by the time I realized what it meant there wasn't much I could do. I hope I'm right in thinking it's only the last two years which have been strained, that you were happy until then. I've covered my tracks as well as I could, kept it hidden.

So many little lies, all of them unsaid.

It was ten years ago, when we had only been in this house a few years and the children were still young and ours. I'm sure you remember John and Suzy's party—the one just after they'd moved into the new house? Or maybe not: it was just one of many, after all, and perhaps it is only my mind in which it retains a peculiar luminosity.

You'd just started working at Elders & Peterson, and weren't keen on going out. You wanted a weekend with a clear head, to tidy up the house, do some shopping, to hang out without a hangover. But we decided we ought to go, and I promised I wouldn't get too drunk, and you gave me that sweet, affectionate smile which said you believed I'd try but that you'd still move the aspirin to beside the bed. We engaged our dippy babysitter, spruced ourselves up and went out hand in hand, feeling for once as if we were in our twenties again. I think we even splashed out on a cab.

Nice house, in its way, though we both thought it was rather big for just the two of them. John was just getting successful around then, and the size of the property looked like a statement. We arrived early, having agreed we wouldn't stay too late, and stood talking in the kitchen with Suzy as she chopped vegetables for the dips. She was wearing the Whistles dress which you both owned, and you and I winked secretly to each other: after much deliberation you were wearing something different. The brown Jigsaw suit, with earrings from Monsoon that looked like little leaves. Do you still have those earrings somewhere? I suppose you must, though I haven't seen them in a while. I looked for them this morning, thinking that you wouldn't miss them and I might take them with me. But they're buried somewhere.

By ten the house was full and I was pretty drunk, talking hard and loud with John and Howard in the living room. I glanced around to check you were having a good enough time, and saw you leaning back against a table, a plastic cup of red wine hovering around your lips. You were listening to Jan rant on about something—her rubbish ex-boyfriend, probably. With your other hand you were fumbling in your bag for your cigarettes, wanting one pretty soon but trying not to let Jan see you weren't giving her familiar tale of woe your full attention. You are wonderful like that. Always doing the right thing, and in the right way. Always eager to be good, and not just so that people would admire you. Just because.

You finally found your packet, and offered it to Jan, and she took a cigarette and lit it without even pausing for breath, a particular skill of hers. As you raised your zippo to light your own you caught me looking at you. You gave a tiny wink, to let me know you'd seen me, and an infinitesimal roll of the eyes—but not enough to derail Jan. Your hand crept up to tuck your hair behind your ear—you'd just had it cut, and only I knew you weren't sure about the shorter style. In that moment I loved you so much, felt both lucky and charmed.

And then, just behind you, she walked into the room, and everything went wrong.

Remember Auntie's Kitchen, that West Indian cafe between Kentish Town and Camden? Whenever we passed it we'd peer inside at the cheerful checked tablecloths and say to each other that we must try it someday. We never did. We were always on the way somewhere else, usually to Camden Market to munch on noodles and browse at furniture we couldn't afford, and it never made sense to stop. I don't even know if it's still there. After we started going everywhere by car we stopped noticing things like that. I'll check tonight, on the way down into town, but either way it's too late. We should have done everything, while we had the chance. You never know how much things may change.

Then, over the crossroads and down past the site where the big Sainsbury's used to be. I remember the first time we shopped there together—Christ, must be twenty-five years ago—both of us discovering what the other liked to eat, giggling over the frozen goods, and getting home to discover that despite spending forty pounds we hadn't really bought a single proper meal. It's become a nest of bijou little shops now, of course, but we never really took to them: we'd liked the way things were when we started seeing each other, and there's a limit to how many little ceramic pots anyone can buy.

DEAR ALISON

By a coincidence I ate my first new meal just round the back of Sainsbury's, a week after the party. It was after midnight, and I knew you'd be wondering where I was, but I was desperate. Four days of the chills, of half-delirious hungers. Of feeling nauseous every time I looked at food, yet knowing I needed *something*. A young girl in her early twenties, staggering slightly, having reeled out of the Electric Ballroom still baked on ecstasy. I know that because I could taste it in her blood. She noticed me in the empty street, and giggled, and I suddenly knew what I needed. She didn't run away as I walked towards her.

I only took a little.

You and I went to Kentish Town library one morning, quite soon after we'd got the first flat together. You were interested in finding out a little more about the area, and found a couple of books by the Camden Historical Society. We discovered that no-one was very interested in Kentish Town, despite the fact it's actually older than Camden, and were grumpy about that, because we liked where we lived. But we learned some interesting snippets—like the fact that the area in front of Camden Town tube station, the part which juts out into the crossroads, had once housed a tiny jail and a stocks. Today the derelicts and drunks still collect there, as if there is something in that patch of ground which draws society's misfits and miscreants even now.

I'll cross that area on my way down, avoiding one of those tramps—who I think recognizes something in me, and may be one of us—and head off down Camden Road towards Mornington Crescent.

I don't understand why it happened.

You and I loved each other, we had the kids, and had just finished redecorating. We were happy. There was no reason for what I did. No *sense* to it. No excuse, unless there was something about her which simply drew me. But why me, and not somebody else?

She was tall and extremely slim. She had short blonde hair and nothing in her head except cheekbones. She came into the room alone, and John immediately signaled to her. Drunkenly he introduced her to Howard and me, telling us her name was Vanessa, and that she worked in publishing. I caught you glancing over, and then looking away again, unconcerned. John wurbled on at us for a while about some project or other, and then set off for more drinks, pulling Howard in his wake.

By then I was pretty drunk, but still able to function on the level of 'What do you do, blah, this is what I do, blah.' I talked with Vanessa for a while. She had very blue eyes, a little curl of hair in front of each ear, and the way her neck met her shoulders was pleasing. That was all I noticed. She wasn't really my type.

After ten minutes she darted to one side to greet someone else, a noisy drama of squeals and cheek-kisses. No great loss: I've never found publishing interesting. I revolved slowly about the vertical plane until I saw someone I knew, and then went and talked to them instead.

This person was an old friend I hadn't seen in some time—Roger, the one who got divorced last year—and the conversation took a while and involved several drinks. As I was returning from fetching one of these I noticed the Vanessa woman standing in the corner, holding a bottle of wine by the neck and listening patiently to someone complaining about babysitters. I suffered a brief moment of disquiet about ours—we suspected her of knowing where our stash of elderly dope was—and then made myself forget about it. When you're thirty all your friends can talk about are houses and marriage; a few years later babies and their sitters become the talk of the town. It's as if everyone collectively forgets that there's a real world out there, with interesting things in it, and becomes progressively more obsessed with what happens behind their own front doors.

I muttered something to this effect to Roger, glancing back across at the corner as I did so. The woman was swigging wine straight from the bottle, her body curved into a swan's neck of relaxed poise. I couldn't help wondering why she was here alone. Someone like that had to have a boyfriend.

Then I noticed that she was looking at me, the mouth of the bottle an inch from her wet lips. I smiled, uncertainly.

We never really spent much time in Mornington Crescent. Nothing to take us there, I suppose. Not even really a proper district as such, more a blur between Camden and the top of Tottenham Court Road. I remember once, when Maddy was small, telling her that the red two-story building we were

DEAR ALISON

driving past had once been a station like Kentish Town's, and that in fact there were many other disused stations, dotted over London. Mornington Crescent tube was shut and supposed to be being renovated, but I told Maddy I didn't believe them. She didn't believe *me* at first, but I showed her an old map, and after that she was always fascinated by the idea of abandoned stations. York Road, Down Street and South Kentish Town—which you can see when you pass it underground, if you know when to look. Places which had once meant something to the people who lived there, and which were now nothing but scar tissue in a city which had moved forward in time. Mornington Crescent opened again, in time, proving me wrong and providing both of us with a lesson in parental fallibility.

Then down towards the Euston Road, the part of the walk you never liked. It's a bit boring, I'll admit. Nothing but towering council blocks and busy roads, and by then you'd be complaining about your feet. But I'll walk it anyway. It's part of the trip, and by the time I come back it will all have changed. Maybe it'll be less boring. But it won't be the same.

One in the morning. The party was going strong—had, if anything, surged up to a new level. I saw that you were still okay, sitting cross-legged on the floor in the living room and happily arguing with Suzy about something.

By then I was very drunk, and on something like my seven billionth trip to the toilet. I reached down with my hand as I passed you, and you squeezed it for a moment. Then I flailed up two flights to the nearest unoccupied bathroom, cursing John for having so many stairs. The top floor of the house was darker than the rest, but I'd worn a channel in the new carpet by then and found my way easily enough.

Afterwards I washed my hands with expensive soap for a while, standing weaving in front of the mirror, giggling at my reflection and chuntering cheerfully at myself.

Back outside again and I seemed to have got more drunk. I tripped down the small flight of steps which led to the landing, and reached out to steady myself. Suddenly my mouth was filled with saliva and I had a horrible suspicion I was about to christen the house, but a minute of deep breathing and compulsive swallowing convinced me I'd survive to drink another drink.

I heard a rustling sound, and turned to peer through a nearby doorway. I recognized the room—it was one John had shown us earlier, destined to become his study. 'Where you'll sit becoming more and more successful,' I'd thought churlishly to myself. At that stage it didn't seem remotely likely that he would commit suicide six years later.

'Hello,' she said.

The woman called Vanessa was standing in the empty room, over by the window. Cold moonlight made her features look as if they'd been molded in glass, but whoever'd done it must have been pretty good. Without really knowing why, I stumbled into the room, pulling the door shut behind. As she walked towards me her dress rustled again, the sound like a shiver of leaves outside a window in the night.

We met in the middle. I don't remember her pulling her dress up, just the long white stretch of her thighs. I don't remember undoing my trousers, but someone must have. All I remember is saying 'But you must have a boyfriend,' and her just smiling at me.

It was insane. Someone could have come in at any moment.

But it happened.

Tottenham Court Road. Home of cut-price technology, and recipient of many an impulse buy on my part. When we walked down it towards Oxford Street you used to grab my arm and try to pull me past the stores, or throw yourself in front of the window displays to hide them from me. Then later I'd end up standing in Marks and Spenser's for hours, while you dithered over underwear. I moaned, and said it was unfair, but I didn't really mind.

Past the *Time Out* building, where Howard used to work, and then the walk will be over.

At the junction of Oxford Street and Tottenham Court Road I'll turn round and look back the way I've come, and say goodbye to it all. Sentimental, perhaps: but that walk means a lot to me. Then I'll go down into Oxford Street tube and sit on the Piccadilly Line to Heathrow.

I have a ticket, my passport and some dollars, but not many. I'm going to have to find a way of earning money sooner or later, so it may as well be sooner. I've left the rest for you. If you're stuck for a present for Maddy's birthday I've heard her mention the new Asylum Fields album a couple of times. Though probably she'll have bought it herself by then, I suppose. I keep forgetting how old they've got.

After those ten minutes in John's study I came back downstairs, suddenly shocked into sobriety. You were sitting exactly where I had left you, but it felt like everything else in the world had changed. I was terrified that you'd read something from my face, realize what I had done, but you just reached up and yanked me down to sit next to you. Everybody smiled, apparently glad to see me. Howard passed a joint.

These were my friends, and I felt like I didn't deserve them. Or you.

Especially not you.

We left an hour later. I sat a little apart from you in the cab, convinced you'd smell Vanessa on me, but I clutched your hand and you seemed happy enough. We got home and I had a shower while you clanked around in the kitchen making tea. Then we went to bed, and I held you tightly until you drifted off. I stared at the ceiling for an hour, chilled with self-loathing, and then surprised myself by falling asleep.

Within a few days I was calmer.

A drunken mistake: these things happen. I elected not to tell you about it—partly through self-serving cowardice, but more out of a genuine knowledge of how little it meant, and how much it would hurt you to know. The ratio between the two was too steep for me to say anything. After a fortnight it had sunk to the level of vague memory, the only lasting effect an increased realization of how much I wanted to be with you. That was the only time, in all our years together, that anything of that kind happened. I promise you.

It would all have been okay, a cautionary lesson learned, but then the first hunger pangs came and everything changed for me. To be honest, I feel lucky that we've had ten years, that I was able to hide it for that long. I developed the habit of occasional solitary walks in the evening, a cover that no-one seemed to question. I started going to the gym and eating healthily, and maybe that also helped to hide what was happening. At first you didn't notice, and then I think you were even a little proud that your husband was staying in such good shape.

But a couple of years ago that pride faded, around about the time the kids started looking at me curiously. Not often, and maybe not even consciously, but just as you started making unflattering remarks about your figure, how your body was not lasting compared to mine, I think at some level the children noticed something too. Maddy was always her daddy's girl. You said so yourself, many times. She isn't any more, and I don't think that's just because she's growing up and going out with that dickhead. She's uncomfortable with me. Richard's overly polite too, these days, and so are you. It's as if I've done something which none of us can remember, something small which nonetheless set me apart from you. As if we're all tiptoeing carefully around something we don't understand.

You'll work out some consensus between you. An affair. Depression. Something. I know you all care for me, and that it won't be easy, but it has to be this way. I'm not telling you where I'm going. It won't be one of the places we've been on holiday together, that's for sure. The memories would hurt too much.

After a while, a new identity. And then a new life, for what it's worth. New places, new things, new people: and none of them will be you.

I've never seen Vanessa since that night, incidentally. If anything, what I feel for her is hate. Not even for what she did to me, for that little bite disguised as passion. More just because, on that night ten years ago, I did something small and normal and stupid which would have hurt you had you known. The kind of mistake *anyone* can make, not just people like me.

I regret that more than anything: the last human mistake I made, on the last night I was still your husband and nothing else. That I was unfaithful to the only woman I've ever really loved, and with someone who didn't matter, and who only did it because she had to.

Because she was hungry.

I knew she must have had a boyfriend—I just didn't realize what kind of man he would be.

I can't send this letter, can I? Not now, and probably not even later. Perhaps it's been nothing more than an attempt to make myself feel better; a selfish confession for my own peace of mind. But I've been thinking of you while I've been writing it, so in that sense at least it is written to you. Maybe I'll

DEAR ALISON

find some way of keeping track of your lives, and send this when you're near the end. When it won't matter so much, and you may be asking yourself what exactly it was that happened.

But probably that's not fair either, and by then you won't want to know.

Perhaps if I'd told you earlier, when things were still good between us, we could have worked out a way of dealing with it. It's too late now.

It's nearly four o'clock.

I'll come back some day, when it's safe, when no-one who could recognize me is still alive. It will be a long wait, but I will come. That day's already planned.

I'll start at Oxford Street, and walk all the way back up, seeing what remains and what has changed. The distance at least will stay the same, and maybe I'll be able to pretend you're walking it with me, taking me home again. I could point out the differences, and we'd remember the way it was: and maybe, if I can recall it clearly enough, it will be like I never went away.

But I'll reach Falkland Road eventually, and stand outside looking up at this window; not knowing who lives here now, only that it isn't us. Perhaps if I shut my eyes I'll be able to hear your voice, imagine you sitting inside, conjure up the life that could have been.

I hope so. And I will always love you.

But it's time to go.

THE MAN WHO
DREW CATS

Tom was a very tall man, so tall he didn't even have a nickname for it. Ned Black, who was at least a head shorter, had been 'Tower Block' since the sixth grade, and Jack had a sign up over the door saying 'Mind Your Head, Ned'. But Tom was just Tom. It was like he was so tall it didn't bear mentioning even for a joke: be a bit like ragging someone for breathing.

Course there were other reasons too for not ragging Tom about his height or anything else. The guys you'll find perched on stools round Jack's bar watching the game and buying beers, they've known each other forever. Went to Miss Stadler's school together, gotten under each other's Mom's feet, double-dated right up to giving each other's best man's speech. Kingstown is a small place, you understand, and the old boys who come regular to Jack's mostly spent their childhoods in the same tree house. Course they'd since gone their separate ways after that, up to a point: Pete was an accountant now, had a small office down Union Street just off the Square and did pretty good, whereas Ned was still pumping gas and changing oil and after forty years he did that pretty good too. Comes a time when men have known each other so long they forget what they do for a living most the time, because it don't matter. When you talk there's a little bit of skimming stones down the quarry in second grade, a whisper of dolling up to go to that first dance, a tad of going to the housewarming when they moved twenty years back. There's all that, so much more than you can say, and none of it's important except for having happened. So we'll stop by and have a couple of beers and talk about the town and rag each other, and the pleasure's just in shooting the breeze and it don't really matter what's said, just the fact that we're all still there to say it.

But Tom, he was different.

We all remember the first time we saw him. It was a long hot summer like we haven't seen in the ten years since, and we were lolling under the fans at Jack's and complaining about the tourists. Kingstown does get its share in the summer, even though it's not near the sea and we don't have a MacDonald's and I'll be damned if I can figure out why folk'll go out of their way to see what's just a quiet little town near some mountains. It was as hot as Hell that afternoon and as much as a man could do to sit in his shirt sleeves and drink the coldest beer he could find. Jack's is the coldest for us, and always will be, I guess.

Then Tom walked in. His hair was already pretty white back then, and long, and his face was brown and tough with grey eyes like diamonds set in leather. He was dressed mainly in black with a long coat that made you hot just to look at it, but he looked comfortable, like he carried his very own weather around with him and he was just fine.

He got a beer, and sat down at a table and read the town *Bugle*, and that was that.

It was special because there wasn't anything special about it. Jack's Bar isn't exactly exclusive and we don't all turn round and stare at anyone new if they come in, but the place is like a monument to shared times. If a tourist couple comes in out of the heat and sits, nobody says anything—and maybe nobody even notices at the front of their mind—but it's like a little island of the alien in the water, and the currents just don't ebb and flow the way they usually do, if you get what I mean. Tom walked in and sat down and it was all right because it was like he was there just like we were, and could've been for thirty years. He sat and read his paper like part of the same river, and everyone just carried on downstream.

Pretty soon he goes up for another beer and a few of us got talking to him. We got his name and what he did—painting, he said—and after that it was just shooting the breeze. That quick. He came in that summer afternoon and fell into the conversation like he'd been there all his life, and sometimes

THE MAN WHO DREW CATS

it was hard to imagine he hadn't been. Nobody knew where he came from, or where he'd been, and there was something real quiet about him. A stillness, a man in a slightly different world. But he showed enough of himself to get along real well with us, and a bunch of old friends don't often let someone in like that.

Anyway, he stayed that whole summer. Rented himself a place just round the corner from the square, or so he said: I never saw it. I guess no-one did. He was a private man, private like a steel door with four bars and a couple of six-inch padlocks, and when he left the square at the end of the day for all we knew he could have vanished off the face of the earth as soon as he turned the corner. But he always came from that direction in the morning, with his easel on his back and paint box under his arm, and he always wore that black coat like it was a part of him. But he always looked cool, and the funny thing was when you stood near him you could swear you felt cooler yourself. I remember Pete saying over a beer that it wouldn't surprise him none if, assuming it ever rained again, Tom would walk round in his own column of dryness. He was just joking, of course, but Tom made you think things like that.

Jack's bar looks right out onto the square, the kind of square towns don't have much anymore: big and dusty with old roads out each corner, tall shops and houses on all the sides and some stone paving in the middle round a fountain that ain't worked in living memory. In the summer that old square is full of out-of-towners in pink toweling jumpsuits and nasty jackets standing round saying 'Wow' and taking pictures of our quaint old hall and our quaint old stores and even our quaint old selves if we stand still too long. Tom would sit out near the fountain and paint and those people would stand and watch for hours—but he didn't paint the houses or the square or the old Picture House. He painted animals, and painted them like you've never seen. Birds with huge blue speckled wings and cats with cutting green eyes; and whatever he painted it looked like it was just coiled up on the canvas ready to fly away. He didn't do them in their normal colors, they were all reds and purples and deep blues and greens—and yet they fair sparkled with life. It was a wonder to watch: he'd put up a fresh paper, sit looking at nothing in particular, then dip his brush into his paint and draw a line, maybe red, maybe blue. Then he'd add another, maybe the same color, maybe not.

MICHAEL MARSHALL SMITH

Stroke by stroke you could see the animal build up in front of your eyes and yet when it was finished you couldn't believe it hadn't always been there. When he'd finished he'd spray it with some stuff to fix the paints, and put a price on it, and you can believe me those paintings were sold before they hit the ground. Spreading businessmen from New Jersey or somesuch and their bored wives would come alive for maybe the first time in years, and walk away with one of those paintings and their arms round each other, like they'd found a bit of something they'd forgotten they'd lost.

Come about six o'clock Tom would finish up and walk across to Jack's, looking like a sailing ship amongst rowing boats, and saying yes he'd be back again tomorrow, and yes, he'd be happy to do a painting for them. He'd get a beer and sit with us and watch the game and there'd be no paint on his fingers or his clothes, not a spot. I figured he'd got so much control over that paint it went where it was told and nowhere else.

I asked him once how he could bear to let those paintings go. I know if I'd been able to make anything that good in my whole life I couldn't let it out of my sight, I'd want to keep it to look at sometimes. He thought for a moment and then he said he believed it depends how much of yourself you've put into it. If you've gone deep and pulled up what's inside and put it down, then you don't want to let it go: you want to keep it, so's you can check sometimes that it's still safely tied. Comes a time when a painting's so right and so good that it's private, and no-one'll understand it except the man who put it down. He's the only person who's going to know what he's talking about. But the everyday paintings, well they were mainly just because he liked to paint animals, and liked for people to have them. He could only put a piece of himself into something he was going to sell, but they paid for the beers and I guess it's like us fellows in Jack's Bar: if you like talking, you don't always have to be saying something important.

Why animals? Well if you'd seen him with them I guess you wouldn't have to ask. He loved them, is all, and they loved him right back. The cats were always his favorites. My old Pa used to say that cats weren't nothing but sleeping machines put on the earth to do some of the human's sleeping for them, and whenever Tom worked in the square there'd always be a couple curled up near his feet.

THE MAN WHO DREW CATS

And whenever he did a chalk drawing, he'd always do a cat.

Once in a while, you see, Tom seemed to get tired of painting on paper, and he'd get out some chalks and sit down on the baking flagstones and just do a drawing right there on the dusty rock. Now, I've told you about his paintings, but these drawings were something else again. It was like because they couldn't be bought but would be washed away, he was putting more of himself into it, doing more than just shooting the breeze. They were just chalk on dusty stone and they were still in these weird colors, but I tell you children wouldn't walk near them because they looked so real, and they weren't the only ones, either. People would stand a few feet back and stare and you could see the wonder in their eyes. If they could've been bought there were people who would have sold their houses. And it's a funny thing, but a couple of times when I walked over to open the store up in the mornings I saw a dead bird or two on top of those drawings, almost like they had landed on it and been so terrified to find themselves right on top of a cat they'd dropped dead of fright. But they must have been dumped there by some real cat, of course. I used to throw them in the bushes to tidy up and some of them were pretty broken up.

Old Tom was a godsend to a lot of mothers that summer, who found they could leave their little ones by him, do their shopping in peace and have a soda with their friends and come back to find the kids still sitting quietly watching Tom paint. He didn't mind them at all and would talk to them and make them laugh, and kids of that age laughing is one of the best sounds there is. It's the kind of sound that makes the trees grow. They're young and curious and the world spins round them and when they laugh they make it seem a brighter place, because it takes you back to the time when you knew no evil and everything was good, or if it wasn't, it would be over by tomorrow.

And here I guess I've finally come down to it, because there was one little boy who didn't laugh much, but sat quiet and watchful, and I guess he probably understands more of what happened that summer than any of us, though maybe not in words he could tell.

His name was Billy McNeill, and he was Jim Valentine's kid. Jim used to be a mechanic, worked with Ned up at the gas station and raced beat-up cars after hours. Which is why his kid is called McNeill now: one Sunday Jim took a corner too fast and the car rolled and the gas tank caught fire, and they never did find one of his hands. A year later his Mary married again. God alone knows why, her folks warned her, her friends warned her, but I guess love must just have been blind. Sam McNeill's work schedule was at best pretty empty, and mostly he just drank and hung out with friends who maybe weren't always this side of the law. I guess Mary had her own sad little miracle and got her sight back, because it wasn't long before Sam got free with his fists when the evenings got too long and he'd had a lot too many too drink. You didn't see Mary around much anymore. In these parts people tend to stare at black eyes on a woman, and a deaf man could hear the whisperings of 'We Told Her So'.

One morning Tom was sitting painting as usual, and little Billy was sitting watching him. Usually he just wandered off after a while but this morning Mary was at the Doctor's and she came over to collect him, walking quickly with her face lowered. But not low enough. I was watching from the store, it was kind of a slow day. Tom's face never showed much. He was a man for a quiet smile and a raised eyebrow, but he looked shocked that morning. Mary's eyes were puffed and purple and there was a cut on her cheek an inch long. I guess we'd sort of gotten used to seeing her like that and if the truth be known some of the wives thought she'd got remarried a bit on the fast side and I suppose we may all have been a bit cold towards her, Jim Valentine having been so well-liked and all.

Tom looked from the little boy who never laughed much, to his mom with her tired unhappy eyes and her beat-up face, and his own face went from shocked to stony and I can't describe it any other way but that I felt a cold chill cross my heart from right across the square.

But then he smiled, and ruffled Billy's hair, and Mary took Billy's hand and they walked off. They turned back once and Tom was still looking after them and he gave Billy a little wave and he waved back and mother and child smiled together.

That night in Jack's Tom put a quiet question about Mary and we told him the story. As he listened his face seemed to harden from within, his eyes growing flat and dead. We told him that old Lou Lachance, who lived next door to the McNeills', said that sometimes you could hear him shouting and her pleading till three in the morning, and on still nights the sound of Billy crying for even longer than that. Told him it was a shame, but what could you do? Folks keep themselves out of other people's faces round here, and I guess Sam and his drinking buddies didn't have much to fear from nearly-retireders like us anyhow. Told him it was a terrible thing, and none of us liked it, but these things happened and what could you do?

Tom listened and didn't say a word. Just sat there in his black coat and listened to us pass the buck. After a while the talk sort of petered out and we sat and watched the bubbles in our beers. I guess the bottom line was that none of us had really thought about it much except as another chapter of small-town gossip, and Jesus Christ did I feel ashamed about that by the time we'd finished telling it. Sitting there with Tom was no laughs at all. He had a real edge to him, and seemed more unknown than known that night. He stared at his laced fingers for a long time, and then he began, real slow, to talk.

He'd been married once, he said, a long time ago, and he'd lived in a place called Stephensburg with his wife Rachel. When he talked about her the air seemed to go softer, and we all sat quiet and supped our beers and remembered how it had been way back when we first loved our own wives. He talked of her smile and the look in her eyes and when we went home that night I guess there were a few women who were surprised at how tight they got hugged, and who went to sleep in their husband's arms feeling more loved and contented than they had in a long while.

He'd loved her and she him and for a few years they were the happiest people on earth. Then a third party had got involved. Tom didn't say his name, and he spoke real neutrally about him, but it was a gentleness like silk wrapped round a knife. Anyway his wife fell in love with him, or thought she had, or leastways she slept with him. In their bed, the bed they'd come to on their wedding night. As Tom spoke these words some of us looked up at him, startled, like we'd been slapped across the face.

Rachel did what so many do and live to regret till their dying day. She was so mixed up and getting so much pressure from the other guy that she decided to plough on with the one mistake and make it the biggest in the world.

She left Tom. He talked with her, pleaded even. It was almost impossible to imagine Tom doing that, but I guess the man we knew was a different guy from the one he was remembering. The pleading made no difference.

And so Tom had to carry on living in Stephensburg, walking the same tracks, seeing them around, wondering if she was as free and easy with this other guy, if the light in her eyes was shining on him now. And each time the man saw Tom he'd look straight at him and crease a little smile, a grin that said he knew about the pleading and he and his cronies had had a good laugh over the wedding bed — and yes, I'm going home with your wife tonight and I know just how she likes it, you want to compare notes?

And then he'd turn and kiss Rachel on the mouth, his eyes on Tom, smiling. And she let him do it.

It had kept stupid old women in stories for weeks, the way Tom kept losing weight and his temper and the will to live. He took three months of it and then left without even bothering to sell the house. Stephensburg was where he'd grown up and courted and loved, and now wherever he turned the good times had rotted and hung like fly-blown corpses in all the cherished places. He'd never been back.

It took an hour to tell, and then he stopped talking a while and lit another cigarette and Pete got us all some more beers. We were sitting sad and thoughtful, tired like we'd lived it ourselves. And I guess most of us had, some little bit of it. But had we ever loved anyone the way he'd loved her? I doubt it, not all of us put together.

Pete set the beers down and Ned asked Tom why he hadn't just beaten the living shit out of the guy. Now, no-one else would have actually asked that, but Ned's a good guy, and I guess we were all with him in feeling a piece of that oldest and most crushing hatred in the world, the hate of someone who's lost the person they love to another, and we knew what Ned was saying. I'm not saying it's a good thing and I know you're not supposed to feel like that these days but show me a man who says he doesn't and I'll show you a liar. Love is the only feeling worth a tin shit but you've got to know that it comes from both sides of a man's character and the deeper it runs the darker the pools it draws from.

THE MAN WHO DREW CATS

My guess was that Tom just hated the man too much to hit him. Comes a time when that isn't enough, when nothing is *ever* going to be enough, and so you can't do anything at all. And as he talked the pain just flowed out like a river that wasn't ever going to be stopped, a river that had cut a channel through every corner of his soul. I learnt something that night that you can go your whole life without realizing: that there are things that can be done that can mess someone up so badly, for so long, that they just cannot be allowed; that there are some kinds of pain that you cannot suffer to be brought into the world.

And then Tom was done telling and he raised a smile and said in the end he hadn't done anything to the man except paint him a picture, which I didn't understand, but Tom looked like he'd talked all he was going to. So we got some more beers and shot some quiet pool before going home.

But I guess we all knew what he'd been talking about.

Billy McNeill was just a child. He should have been dancing through a world like a big funfair full of sunlight and sounds, and instead he went home at night and saw his mom being beaten up by a man with shit for brains who struck out at a good woman because he was too stupid to deal with his life. Most kids go to sleep thinking about bikes and climbing apple trees and skimming stones, and there was Billy lying there hearing his mom get smashed in the stomach and then hit again as she threw up in the sink.

Tom didn't say any of that, but he did. And we knew he was right.

The summer kept up bright and hot, and we all had our businesses to attend to. Jack sold a lot of beer and I sold a lot of ice cream (Sorry ma'am, just the three flavors, and no, Bubblegum Pistachio ain't one of them) and Ned fixed a whole bunch of cracked radiators. Tom sat right out there in the square with a couple of cats by his feet and a crowd around him, magicking up animals in the sun.

And I do believe after that night that Mary maybe got a few more smiles as she did her shopping, and maybe a few more wives stopped to talk to her. She looked better too: Sam had a job by the sound of it and her face healed up pretty soon. You could often see her standing holding Billy's hand as they watched Tom paint for a while before they went home. I think she realized they had a friend in him. Sometimes Billy was there all afternoon, and he was happy there in the sun by Tom's feet and oftentimes he'd pick up a piece of chalk and sit scrawling on the pavement. Sometimes I'd see Tom lean over and say something to him and he'd look up and smile a simple child's smile that beamed in the sunlight.

The tourists kept coming and the sun kept shining and it was one of those summers that go on forever and stick in a child's mind, and tell you what summer should be like for the rest of your life. And I'm damn sure it sticks in Billy's mind, just like it does in all of ours.

Because one morning Mary didn't come into the store, which had gotten to being a regular sort of thing, and Billy wasn't out there in the square. After the way things had been the last few weeks that could only be bad news, and so I left the boy John in charge of the store and hurried over to have a word with Tom. I was kind of worried.

I was no more than halfway across to him when I saw Billy come running from the opposite corner of the square, going straight to Tom. He was crying fit to burst and leapt up at Tom and clung to him, his arms wrapped tight round his neck. Then his mother came across from the same direction, running as best she could. She got to Tom and they just looked at each other. Mary's a real pretty girl but you wouldn't have known it then. It looked like he'd actually broken her nose this time, and blood was streaming out of her lip.

She started sobbing, saying Sam had lost his job because he was back to drinking and what could she do—and then suddenly there was a roar and I was shoved aside and Sam was standing there, still wearing his slippers, weaving back and forth and radiating that aura of violence that keeps men like him safe. He started shouting at Mary to take the kid the fuck back home and she just flinched and cowered closer to Tom like she was huddling round a fire to keep out the cold. This just drove Sam even wilder and he staggered forward and told Tom to get the fuck out of it if he knew what was good for him, and grabbed Mary's arm and tried to yank her towards him, his face terrible with rage.

Then Tom stood up.

Now Tom was a *tall* man, but he wasn't a young man, and he was thin. Sam was thirty and built like the town hall. When he did get work it usually involved moving heavy things from one place to another, and his strength was supercharged by a whole pile of drunken nastiness.

But at that moment the crowd stepped back as one and I suddenly felt very afraid for Sam McNeill. Tom looked like you could take anything you cared to him and it would simply break, like he was a huge spike of granite wrapped in skin with two holes in the face where the rock showed through. And he was mad, not hot and blowing like Sam, but mad and *cold*.

There was a long pause. Then Sam weaved back a step and shouted:

'You just come on home, you hear? Gonna be trouble if you don't, Mary. *Real* trouble,' and then stormed off across the square the way he came, knocking his way through the tourist vultures soaking up the spicy local color.

Mary turned to Tom, so afraid that it hurt to see, and said she guessed she'd better be going. Tom looked at her for a moment and then spoke for the first time.

'Do you love him?'

Even if you wanted to, you ain't going to lie to eyes like that, for fear something inside you will break.

Real quiet she said: 'No.'

And began crying softly as she took Billy's hand and walked back across the square.

Tom packed up his stuff and walked over to Jack's. I went with him and had a beer but I had to get back to the shop and Tom was just sitting there like a trigger, completely silent and strung up tight as a drum. Somewhere down near the bottom of those still waters, something was stirring. Something I thought I didn't want to see.

About an hour later it was lunchtime and I'd just left the shop to have a break when suddenly something whacked into the back of my legs and nearly knocked me down. It was Billy. It was Billy and he had a bruise round his eye that was already closing it up.

I knew what the only thing to do was, and I did it.

I took his hand and led him across to the Bar, feeling a hard anger pushing against my throat. When he saw Tom, Billy ran to him again and Tom took him in his arms and looked over Billy's shoulder at me, and I felt my own anger collapse utterly, in the face of a fury I could never have generated.

I tried to find a word to describe it but they all just seemed like they were in the wrong language. All I can say is I wanted to be somewhere else and it felt real cold standing there facing that stranger in a black coat.

Then the moment passed and Tom was holding the kid close, ruffling his hair and talking to him in a low voice, murmuring the sounds I thought only mothers knew. He dried Billy's tears and checked his eye and then he got off his stool, smiled down at him and said:

'I think it's time we did some drawing, what d'you say?' and, taking the kid's hand, he picked up his chalk box and walked out into the square.

I don't know how many times I looked up and watched them that afternoon. They were sitting side by side on the stone, Billy's little hand wrapped round one of Tom's fingers, and Tom doing one of his chalk drawings. Every now and then Billy would reach across and add a little bit and Tom would smile and say something and Billy's gurgling laugh would float across the square. The store was real busy that afternoon and I was chained to that counter, but I could tell by the size of the crowd that a *lot* of Tom was going into that picture, and maybe a bit of Billy too.

It was about four o'clock before I could take a break. I walked across the crowded square in the mid-afternoon heat and shouldered my way through to where they sat with a couple of cold Cokes. And when I saw it my mouth just dropped open and took a vacation while I tried to take it in.

It was a cat alright, but not a normal cat. It was a life-size tiger.

I'd never seen Tom do anything near that big before, and as I stood there in the beating sun trying to get my mind round it, it almost seemed to stand in three dimensions, a nearly living thing. Its stomach was very lean and thin, its tail seemed to twitch with color, and as Tom worked on the eyes and jaws, his face set with a rigid concentration quite unlike his usual calm painting face, the snarling mask of the tiger came to life before my eyes. And I could see that he wasn't just putting a bit of himself in. This was a man at full stretch, giving all of himself and reaching down for more, pulling up bloody fistfuls and throwing them down. The tiger was all the rage I'd seen in his eyes, and more, and like his love for Rachel that rage simply seemed bigger than any other man could comprehend. He was pouring it out and sculpting it into the lean and ravenous creature coming to pulsating life in front of us on the pavement, and the weird purples and blues and reds just made it seem more vibrant and alive.

I watched him working furiously on it, the boy sometimes helping, adding a tiny bit here and there that strangely seemed to add to it, and thought I understood what he'd meant that evening a few weeks back. He said he'd done a painting for the man who'd given him so much pain. Then, as now, he must have found what I guess you'd call something fancy like 'catharsis' through his skill with chalks, had wrenched the pain up from within him and nailed it down onto something solid that he could walk away from. Now he was helping that little boy do the same, and the boy *did* look better, his bruised eye hardly showing with the wide smile on his face as he watched the big cat conjured up from nowhere in front of him.

The rest of us just stood and watched, like something out of an old story, the simple folk and the magical stranger. It always feels like you're giving a bit of yourself away when you praise someone else's creation, and it's often done grudgingly, but you could feel the awe that day like a warm wind. Comes a time when you realize something special is happening, something you're never going to see again, and there isn't anything you can do but watch.

Well, I had to go back to the store after a while. I hated to go but, well, John is a good boy, married now of course, but in those days his head was full of girls and it wasn't wise to leave him alone in a busy shop for too long.

And so the long hot day drew slowly to a close. I kept the store open till eight, when the light began to turn and the square emptied out with all the tourists going away to write postcards and see if we didn't have even just a *little* MacDonald's hidden away someplace. I suppose Mary had troubles enough at home, realized where the boy would be and figured he was safer there than anywhere else, and I guess she was right.

Tom and Billy finished drawing and then Tom sat and talked to him for some time. Then they got up and the kid walked slowly off to the corner of the square, looking back to wave at Tom a couple times. Tom stood and watched him go and when Billy had gone he stayed a while, head down, like a huge black statue in the gathering dark. He looked kind of creepy out there and I don't mind telling you I was glad when he finally moved and started walking over towards Jack's. I ran out to catch up with him and drew level just as we passed the drawing.

And then I had to stop. I couldn't look at that and move at the same time.

Finished, the drawing was like nothing on earth, and I suppose that's exactly what it was. I can't hope to describe it to you, although I've seen it in my dreams many times in the last ten years. You had to be there, on that heavy summer night, had to know what was going on. Otherwise it's going to sound like it was just a drawing.

That tiger was out and out terrifying.

It looked so mean and hungry, Christ I don't know what: it just looked like the darkest parts of mankind, the pain and the fury and the vengeful hate nailed down in front of you for you to see, and I just stood there and shivered in the humid evening air.

'We did him a picture.' Tom said, quietly.

'Yeah,' I said, and nodded. Like I said, I know what 'catharsis' means and I thought I understood what he was saying. But I really didn't want to look at it much longer. 'Let's go get a beer, hey?'

The storm in Tom hadn't passed, I could tell, and he still seemed to thrum with crackling emotions looking for something to earth them, but I thought the clouds might be breaking and I was glad.

And so we walked slowly over to Jack's and had a few beers and watched some pool being played. Tom seemed pretty tired, but still alert, and I relaxed a little. Come eleven most of the guys started getting on their way and I was surprised to see Tom get another beer. Pete, Ned and I stayed on, and Jack of course, though we knew our loving wives would have something to say about that when we eventually got home. It just didn't seem time to go. Outside it had gotten pretty dark, though the moon was keeping the square in a kind of twilight and the lights in the bar threw a pool of warmth out of the front window.

Then, about twelve o'clock, it happened, and I don't suppose any of us will ever see the same world we grew up in again. I've told this whole thing like it was just me who was there, but we all were, and we remember it together.

Because suddenly there was a wailing sound outside, a thin cutting cry, getting closer. Tom immediately snapped to his feet and stared out the window like he'd been waiting for it. As we looked out across the square we saw little Billy come running and we could see the blood on his face all the way from there. Some of us made to get up, but Tom snarled at us to stay there and so I guess we just stayed put, sitting back down like we'd been pushed.

He strode out the door and into the square and the boy saw him and ran to him and Tom folded him in his cloak and held him close and warm. But he didn't come back in. He just stood there, and he was waiting for something.

Now, there's a lot of crap talked about silences. I read novels when I've the time and you see things like 'Time stood still' and so on and you think: bullshit it did. So I'll just say I don't think anyone in the world breathed in that next minute. There was no wind, no movement. The stillness and silence were there like you could touch them, but more than that. They were like that's all there was and all there ever had been.

We felt the slow, red throb of violence from across the square, before we could even see the man. Then Sam came staggering into view waving a bottle like a flag and cursing his head off. At first he couldn't see Tom and the boy because they were the opposite side of the fountain, and he ground to a wavering halt, but then he started shouting, rough jags of sound that seemed to strike against the silence and die instead of breaking it, and he began charging across the square—and if ever there was a man with murder in his thoughts then it was Sam McNeill. He was like a man who'd given his soul the evening off.

I wanted to shout to Tom to get the hell out of the way, to come inside, but the words wouldn't come out of my throat and we all just waited, knuckles whitening as we clutched the bar and stared, our mouths open like we'd made a pact never to use them again. Tom stood watching Sam come towards him, getting closer, almost as far as the spot where Tom usually painted. It felt like we were looking out of the window at a picture of something that happened long ago in another place and time, and the closer Sam got the more I began to feel very afraid for him.

Then Sam stopped dead in his tracks, skidding forward like in some kid's cartoon, his shout dying off in his ragged throat. He was staring at the ground in front of him, his eyes wide and his mouth a stupid circle.

Then he began to scream.

It was a high shrill noise like a woman would make, and coming out of that bull of a man it sent fear racking down my spine. He started making thrashing movements like he was trying to move backwards, but he just stayed where he was.

His movements became unmistakable at about the same time his screams turned from terror to agony. He was trying to get his leg away from something.

Suddenly he seemed to fall forward on one knee, his other leg stuck out behind him, and he raised his head and shrieked at the dark skies and we saw his face then and I'm not going to forget that so long as I live. It was a face from before there were any words, the face behind our oldest fears and earliest nightmares, the face we're terrified of seeing on ourselves one night when we're alone in the dark and It finally comes out from under the bed to get us, like we always knew it would.

Then Sam fell forward, his leg buckled up—and still he thrashed and screamed and clawed at the ground with his hands, blood running from his broken fingernails as he twitched and struggled. Maybe the light was playing tricks, and my eyes were sparkling anyway on account of being too paralyzed with fear to even blink, but as he thrashed less and less it became harder and harder to see him at all, and as the breeze whipped up stronger his screams began to sound a lot like the wind. But still he writhed and moaned and then suddenly there was the most godawful crunching noise and then there was no movement or sound anymore.

Like they were on a string, our heads all turned together — and we saw Tom still standing there, his coat flapping in the wind. He had a hand on Billy's shoulder and as we looked we could see that Mary was there too now and he had one arm round her as she sobbed into his coat.

I don't know how long we just sat there staring but then we were ejected off our seats and out of the bar. Pete and Ned ran to Tom, but Jack and I went to where Sam had fallen, and we stared down, and I tell you the rest of my life now seems like a build up to and a climb down from that moment.

We were standing in front of a chalk drawing of a tiger. Even now my scalp seems to tighten when I think of it, and my chest feels like someone punched a hole in it and tipped a gallon of ice water inside. I'll just tell you the facts: Jack was there too, and he knows what we saw and what we didn't see.

What we didn't see was Sam McNeill. He just wasn't there. We saw a drawing of a tiger in purples and greens, a little bit scuffed, and there was a lot more red round the mouth of that tiger than there had been that afternoon and I'm sure that if either of us could have dreamed of reaching out and touching it, it would have been warm too.

And the hardest part to tell, is this. I'd seen that drawing in the afternoon, and Jack had too, and we knew that when it was done it was lean and thin.

I swear to God that tiger wasn't thin any more. What Jack and I were looking at was one fat tiger.

After a while I looked up and across at Tom. He was still with Mary and Billy, but they weren't crying anymore. Mary was hugging Billy so tight he squawked and Tom's face looked calm and alive and creased with a smile. And as we stood there, the skies opened for the first time in months and a cool rain hammered down. At my feet colors began to run and lines became less distinct. Jack and I stood and watched till there was just pools of meaningless colors and then we walked slowly over to the others, not even looking at the bottle lying on the ground, and we all stayed there a long time in the rain, facing each other, not saying a word.

Well, that was ten years ago, near enough. After a while Mary took Billy home and they turned to give us a little wave before they turned the corner. The cuts on Billy's face healed real quick, and he's a good looking boy now: he looks a lot like his dad and he's already fooling about in cars. Helps me in the store sometimes. His mom ain't aged a day and looks wonderful. She never married again, but she seems happy the way she is.

The rest of us just said a simple goodnight. Goodnight was all we could muster and maybe that's all there was to say. Then we walked off home in the directions of our wives. Tom gave me a small smile before he turned and walked off alone. I almost followed him, I wanted to say something, but the end I stayed where I was and watched him go. And that's how I'll always remember him best, because for a moment there was a spark in his eyes and I knew that some pain had been lifted deep down inside somewhere.

Then he walked and no-one has seen him since, and like I said it's been about ten years now. He wasn't there in the square the next morning, and he didn't come in for a beer. Like he'd never been, he just wasn't there. Except for the hole in our hearts: it's funny how much you can miss a quiet man.

We're all still here, of course, Jack, Ned, Pete and the boys, and all much the same, though even older and greyer. Pete lost his wife and Ned retired but things go on the same. The tourists come in the summer and we sit on the stools and drink our cold beers and shoot the breeze about ballgames and families and how the world's going to shit, and sometimes we'll draw close and talk about a night a long time ago, and about paintings and cats, and about the quietest man we ever knew, wondering where he is, and what he's doing.

And we've had a sixpack in the back of the fridge for ten years now, and the minute he walks through that door and pulls up a stool, that's his.

THIS **IS NOW**

'Okay,' Henry said. 'So now we're here.'

He was using his "So entertain me" voice and he was cold but trying not to show it. Pete and I were cold too. We were trying not to show it either. Being cold is not cool, and not manly. So you look at your condensing breath as if it's a total surprise to you, what with it being so balmy and all. Even when you've known each other for over thirty years, you do these things. Why? I don't know.

'Yep,' I agreed. It wasn't my job to entertain Henry.

Pete walked up to the thick wire fence. He tilted his head back until he was looking at the top, four feet above. A ten-foot wall of tautly crisscrossed wire. 'Who's going to test it?'

'Well, hey, you're closest.' Like the others, I was speaking quietly, though we were half a mile from the nearest road or house or person.

This side of the fence, anyhow.

'I did it last time.'

'Long while ago.'

'Still,' he said, stepping back. 'Your turn, Dave.'

I held up my hands. 'These are my tools, man.'

Henry sniggered. '*You're* a tool, that's for sure.'

Pete laughed too, and I had to smile, and for a moment it was like it *was* the last time. Hey presto—time travel on a budget. You don't need a machine, it turns out, you just need a friend to laugh like a teenager. Chronology shivers.

And so—quickly, before I could think about it—I flipped out my hand and touched the fence. My whole arm jolted, as if every bone in it had been tapped with a hammer. Tapped *hard*, and in different directions.

'Christ,' I hissed, spinning away, shaking my hand like I was trying to rid myself of it. 'Goddamn *Christ* that hurts.'

Henry nodded sagely. 'This stretch has current, then. Also, didn't we use a stick last time?'

'Always been the brains of the operation, right, Hank?'

Pete snickered again. I was annoyed, but the shock had pushed me over a line. It had brought it all back much more strongly.

I nodded up the line of the fence as it marched off into the trees. 'Further,' I said, and pointed at Henry. 'And you're testing the next section, bro.'

It was one of those things you do, one of those stupid, drunken things that afterwards seem impossible to understand. You ask yourself why, feeling confused and sad, like the ghost of a man killed through a careless step in front of a car. But then it's too late.

We could have *not* gone to The Junction, for a start, though it was a Thursday and the Thursday session is a winter tradition with us, a way of making January and February seem less like a living death. The two young guys could have given up the pool table, though, instead of bogarting it all night (by virtue of being better than us, and efficiently dismissing each of our challenges in turn): in which case we would have played a dozen slow frames and gone home around eleven, like usual—ready to get up the following morning feeling no more than a little fusty. This time of year it hardly matters if Henry yawns over the gas pump, or Pete zones out behind the counter in the Massaqua Mart, and I can sling a morning's worth of home fries and sausage patties in my sleep. We've been doing these things so long that we barely have to be present. Maybe that's the point. Maybe that's the real problem right there.

Anyway, by quarter after eight, proven pool-fools, we were sitting around the corner table. We always have, since back when it was Bill's Bar and beer tasted new and strange and metallic in our mouths. We were talking back and forth, laughing once in a while, none of us bothered about the pool but yes, a little bothered all the same. It wasn't some macho thing. I don't care about being beat by some guys who are passing through. I don't much care about being beat by anyone. Henry and Pete and I tend to win games about equally. If it weren't that way then probably we wouldn't play together. It's never been about winning.

It was more that I simply wished I was better at it. Had *assumed* I'd be better, one day, like I expected to wind up being something other than a short order cook. Don't get me wrong. If you eat one of my breakfasts you'll be set up right for the day and tomorrow you'll come back and likely order the same thing. I'm pretty good at what I do—it just wasn't what I had in mind when I was young. Not sure what I *did* have in mind—I used to think maybe I'd go over the mountains to Seattle, be in a band or something, but after that the thought got vague and lost direction—but it certainly wasn't being first in command at a hot griddle. None of our jobs are bad jobs, but they're the kind of jobs held by people in the background. People who are getting by. People who don't play pool very well, or else play it too well, because it's all they've got in life.

It also struck me, as I watched Pete banter with Nicole when she brought us round number four or five, that I was still smoking. I'd been assuming I would have given it up by now. Tried, once or twice. Didn't take. Would it ever happen? Probably not. Would it give me cancer sooner or later? Most likely. Better try again, then. At some point.

Henry watched Nicole's ass as it accompanied her back to the counter. 'Cute as hell,' he noted, approvingly, not for the first time.

Pete and I grunted, in the way we would of if he'd observed that the moon was smaller than the earth. Henry's observation was both true and something that had very little bearing on our lives. Nicole was twenty-three. We could give her twenty years each. That's not the kind of gift that cute girls covet.

So we sat and talked, and smoked, and didn't listen to the sound of balls being efficiently slotted into pockets by people who weren't us.

You walk for long enough in the woods at night, you'll start getting jittery. Forests have a way of making civilization seem less inevitable. In sunlight they may make you want to build yourself a cabin and get back to nature, get that whole Davy Crockett vibe going on. In the dark they remind you what a good thing chairs and hot meals and electric lights really are, and you thank God that you live now, instead of then.

Every once in a while we'd test the fence—using a stick. The current was on each time we tried. So we kept walking. We followed the line of the wire as it cut up the rise, then down into a shallow streambed, then up again steeply on the other side.

If you were seeing the fence for the first time you'd likely wonder at the straightness of it, the way the concrete posts had been planted at ten yard intervals deep into the rock. You might ask yourself if national forests normally went to these lengths to protect their boundaries, and you'd soon remember they didn't; that for the most part a cheerful little wooden sign by the side of the road was judged to be all that was needed.

If you kept on walking deeper, intrigued, sooner or later you'd see a notice attached to one of the posts. The notices are small, designed to convey authority rather than draw attention.

NO TRESPASSING, they say. MILITARY LAND.

That could strike you as a little strange, perhaps, because you might have believed that most of the marked-off military areas were down in the moonscapes of Nevada rather than up here in a quiet northeast corner of Washington State. But who knows what the military's up to, right? Apart from protecting us from foreign aggressors, of course, and The Ongoing Terrorist Threat, and if that means they need a few acres to themselves then that's actually kind of comforting. The army moves in mysterious ways, our freedoms to defend. Good for them, you'd think, and you'd likely turn and head back for town, having had enough of tramping through snow for the day. In the evening you'd come into Ruby's and eat hearty, some of my wings or a burger or the brisket—which, though I say so myself, isn't half bad. Next morning you'd drive back south and forget about it, and us.

I remember when the fences went up, though. Thirty years ago. 1985. Our parents knew what they were for. Hell, we were only eight and *we* knew.

There was a danger, and it was getting worse: the last decade had proved that. Four people had disappeared in the last year alone. One came back and was sick for a week, in an odd and dangerous kind of way, and then died. The others were never seen again. My aunt Jean was one of those. But there's danger to going in abandoned mine shafts, too, or talking to strangers, or juggling knives when you're drunk.

So...you just don't do it. You walk the town in pairs at night, and you observe the unspoken curfew. You kept an eye out for men who didn't blink, for slim women whose strides were too short—or so people said. There was never much passing trade in town. Massaqua isn't on the way to anywhere. Massaqua is a single guy who keeps his yard tidy and doesn't bother anyone. The tourist season up here is short and not exactly intense. There is no ski lodge or health spa and the motel frankly isn't great.

The fence seemed to keep the danger contained and out of town, and within a few years its existence was part of life. It wasn't like it was right there on our doorstep. No big-city reporter heard about it and came up looking to make a sensation—or, if they did, they didn't make it all the way here.

Life went on. Years passed.

Sometimes small signs work better than great big ones.

As we climbed deeper into the forest, Pete was in front. I was more or less beside him, and Henry lagged a few steps behind. It had been that way the last time, too, but then we hadn't had hip flasks to keep us fueled in our intentions. We hadn't needed to stop to catch our breath quite so often either.

'We just going to keep on walking?'

It was Henry asked the question, of course. Pete and I didn't even answer.

At quarter after ten we'd still been in the bar. The two guys remained at the pool table. When one leaned over to take a shot, the other stood judiciously sipping from a bottled beer. They weren't talking to each other, just slotting the balls down.

We were still drinking steadily, the conversation was often a two-way while one or other of us trekked back and forth to empty our bladder. By then we were resigned to just sitting around. We were a little too drunk to start playing pool, even if the table became free. We felt aimless. There was no news to catch up on. We already knew Pete was ten years married, that they had no children and it was likely going to stay that way. His wife is fine, and still pleasant to be with, though her collection of dolls is getting exponentially bigger. We knew Henry was married once too, had a little boy, and that though the kid and his mother now lived forty miles away relations between them remained cordial. Neither Pete nor I are much surprised that he has achieved this. Henry can be a royal pain in the ass at times, but he wouldn't still be our friend if that's all he was.

'Same again, boys? You're thirsty tonight.'

It was Pete's turn in the restroom, so it was Henry and I who looked up to see Nicole smiling down at us, thumb hovering over the repeat button on her pad. Deprived of Pete's easy manner (partly genetic, also honed over years of chatting to the public while totting and bagging groceries), our response was cluttered and vague.

Quick nods and smiles; I said thanks; and Henry got out a 'Hell, yes!' that sounded a little loud.

Nicole winked at me and went away again, as she has done many times over the last couple years. When she got to the bar I saw one of the pool-players looking at her, and felt a strange twist of something in my stomach. It wasn't because they were strangers, or because I suspected they might be something else, something that shouldn't be here. They were just younger guys, that's all. Of course they're going to look at her.

She's probably going to *want* them to.

I lit another cigarette and wondered why I still didn't really know how to deal with women. They've always seemed so different, somehow. So confident, so powerful, so present in themselves. Kind of scary, even. Most teenage boys feel that way, I guess, but I'd assumed age would help with this. That being older might make a difference. Apparently not. The opposite, if anything.

'Cute just doesn't cover it,' Henry said, again not for the first time. 'Going to have to come up with a whole new word. Supercute, how's that. Hyperhot. Ultra—'

How about just beautiful?

For a horrible moment I thought I'd said this out loud. I guess in a way I did, because what pronouncements ring louder than the ones you make only in your own head?

THIS IS NOW

Pete returned to the table at the same time as the new beers arrived, and with him around it was easier to come across like grown-ups. He came back looking thoughtful, too.

He waited until the three of us were alone again, and then reached across and took one of my Marlboros like he used to, back in the day, when he couldn't afford his own. He didn't seem to be aware he'd done it. He looked pretty drunk, in fact, and I realized I was too. Henry is generally at least a *little* drunk.

Pete lit the cigarette, took a long mouthful of beer, and then he said:

'You remember that time we went over the fence?'

The stick touched the wire, and nothing happened.

I did it again. Same result. We stopped walking. My legs ached and I was glad for the break.

Pete hesitated, then reached out and brushed the thick black wire with his hand. When we were kids he might have pretended it was charged, and jiggered back and forth, eyes rolling and tongue sticking out.

He didn't now. He just curled his fingers around it, gave it a light tug.

'Power's down,' he said, quietly.

Henry and I stepped up close. Even with Pete standing there grasping it, you still had to gird yourself to do the same.

Then all three of us were holding the fence, holding it with both hands, looking in.

That close up, the wire fuzzed out of focus and it was almost as if it wasn't there. You just saw the forest beyond. Moonlit trunks, snow. You heard the quietness. If you stood on the other side and looked out in our direction, the view would be exactly the same, I guess. With a fence that long, it could be difficult to tell which side was in, which was out.

This, too, was what had happened the previous time, when we were fifteen. We'd heard that sometimes a section of the fence went down for a brief period, and so we went looking. What with animals, snow fall, the random impacts of falling branches and a mountain wind that could blow hard and cold at most times of year, once in a while a cable stopped supplying the juice to one ten yard stretch. The power was never down for more than a day. There was a computer that kept track, and—somewhere, nobody knew where—a small station from which a couple of military engineers would quickly be dispatched to come to repair the outage.

But for now, a section was down.

We stood, a silent row of older men, and remembered what had happened back then.

Pete had gone up first. He shuffled along to one of the concrete posts so the wire wouldn't bag out, and started pulling himself up. As soon as his feet left the ground I didn't want to be left behind, so I went to the other post and went up just as quickly.

We reached the top at around the same time. Soon as we started down the other side—lowering ourselves at first, then just dropping—Henry started his own climb.

We all landed silently in the snow, with bent knees.

We were the other side, and we stood very still. Far as we knew, no-one had ever done this before.

To some people, this might have been enough.

Not to fifteen-year-old boys.

Moving very quietly, hearts beating hard—just from the exertion, none of us were scared, not *exactly*, not enough to admit it anyway—we moved away from the fence.

After about twenty yards I stopped and looked back.

'You chickening out?'

'No, Henry,' I said. His voice had been quiet and shaky. I took pains that mine sound firm. 'Memorizing. We want to be able to find that dead section again.'

He'd nodded. 'Good thinking, smart boy.'

Pete looked back with us. Stand of three trees close together there. Unusually big tree over on the right. Kind of a semi-clearing, on a crest. Shouldn't be hard to find again.

We glanced at each other, judged it logged in our heads, then turned and headed away, into a place no-one had been for nearly ten years.

The forest floor led away gently. There was enough moonlight to show the ground panning down towards a kind of high valley lined with thick trees.

THIS IS NOW

As we walked, bent over with unconscious caution, part of me was relishing how we'd remember this in the future, already leaping over the event into its retrospection. Not that we'd talk about it, outside the three of us. It was the kind of thing which might attract attention to the town, including maybe attention from this side of the fence.

There was one person I thought I might mention it to, though. Her name was Lauren and she was very cute, the kind of beautiful that doesn't have to open its mouth to call your name from across the street. I had talked to her a couple times, summoning bravery I hadn't known I possessed. It was she who had talked about Seattle, said she'd like to go hang out there some day. That sounded good to me, good and exciting and strange. What I didn't know, that long-ago night in the forest, was she would go on to do this, and I would not, and that she would leave without us ever having kissed.

I just assumed... I assumed a lot of stuff a lot back then.

After a couple of hundred yards we stopped, huddled together, and shared one of my cigarettes. Our hearts were beating heavily, even though we'd been coming downhill. The forest is hard work whatever direction it slopes. But it wasn't just that.

It felt a little colder here. There was also something about the light. It seemed to hold more shadows. You found your eyes flicking from side to side, checking things out, wanting to be reassured, but not being confident that you had been after all.

I bent down to put the cigarette out in the snow. It was extinguished in a hiss that seemed very loud.

We continued in the direction we'd been heading. We walked maybe another five, six hundred yards.

It was Henry who stopped.

Keyed up as we were, Pete and I halted immediately too. Henry was leaning forward, squinting.

'What?'

He pointed. Down at the bottom of the rocky valley was a shape. A big shape.

After a moment I could make out it was a building. Two wooden storeys high, and slanting.

You saw that kind of thing, sometimes. The sagging remnant of some pioneer's attempt to claim an area of this wilderness and pretend it could be a home.

Pete nudged me, and pointed in a slightly different direction. The remnants of another house further down. A little fancier, with a fallen-down porch.

And thirty yards further, another. Smaller, with a false front.

'Cool,' Henry said, and briefly I admired him.

We sidled onward, a lot more slowly and heading along the rise instead of down it. Ruined houses look very interesting during the day. At night they seem different, especially when lost high up in the forest. They sit at angles which do not seem quite right. Trees grow too close to them, pressing in. The lack of a road, long overgrown, can make the houses look like they were never built but instead made their own way to this forgotten place, in which you have now disturbed them.

I was beginning to wonder if maybe we'd done enough, come far enough, and I doubt I was the only one.

Then we saw the light.

After Pete asked his question in the bar, there was silence for a moment. Of course we remembered that night. It wasn't something you'd forget. It was a dumb question unless you were really asking something else, and we both knew Pete wasn't dumb.

Behind us, on the other side of the room, came the quiet, reproachful sound of pool balls hitting each other and then one of them going neatly down a pocket.

We could hear what each other was thinking. That it was a very cold evening, and there was thick snow on the ground — as there had been on that other night, when we were fifteen. That the rest of the town had pretty much gone to bed. That we could get in Henry's truck and be at the head of a hiking trail in twenty minutes, even driving drunkard slow.

I didn't hear anyone thinking a reason, though.

I didn't hear anyone think *why* we might do such a thing, or what might happen if we did.

By the time Pete had finished his cigarette, our glasses were empty. We put on our coats and left the bar and crunched across the lot to Henry's truck.

***

THIS IS NOW

Back *then*, on that long-ago night, suddenly my young heart hadn't seemed to be beating at all. When we saw the light in the second house, a faint and curdled glow in one of the downstairs windows, my whole body suddenly felt light and insubstantial.

One of us tried to speak. It came out like a dry click. I realized there was a light in the other house too, faint and golden.

Had I missed it before, or had it just come on?

I took a step backwards. The forest was silent but for the sound of my friends breathing.

'Oh, no,' Pete said. He started moving backwards, stumbling. Then I saw it too.

A figure, standing in front of the first house.

It was tall and slim, like a rake's shadow. It was a hundred yards away but still it seemed as though you could make out an oval shape on its shoulders, the color of milk diluted with water. It was looking in our direction.

Then another was standing near the other house.

No, two.

Henry moaned softly, and we three boys turned as one, and I have never, ever run like that before or since.

The first ten yards were fast but then the slope cut in and our feet started to slip, and after that we were down on hands half the time, scrabbling and pulling—every muscle working together in a headlong attempt to be somewhere else.

I heard a crash behind and flicked my head around to see Pete had gone down hard, banging his knee, falling on his side.

Henry kept on going but I made myself turn around to grab Pete's hand, not really helping but just pulling, trying to yank him back to his feet, or at least away.

Over his shoulder I glimpsed the valley below and I saw that the figures were down at the bottom of the rise, heading our way in jerky blurred-black movements, like half-seen spiders darting across an icy window pane.

Pete's face jerked up and I saw in it what I felt in myself, and it was not a cold fear but a hot one, a red-hot meltdown as if you were going to rattle and break apart.

Then he was on his feet again, moving past me, and I followed him towards the disappearing shape of Henry's back. It seemed *so* much further than we'd walked. It was uphill and the trees no longer formed a path, and even the wind seemed to be pushing us back.

We caught up with Henry, and passed him, streaking up the last hundred yards toward the fence. None of us turned around again. You didn't have to. You could feel them coming, *feel* them getting closer, like rocks thrown at your head, rocks only to be glimpsed at the last second, when there is time to flinch but not to turn.

I was sprinting straight at the fence when Henry called out. I was going too fast and didn't want to know what his problem was. I leapt up at the wire.

It was like a truck hit me from the side.

I crashed to the ground fizzing, arms sparking, with no idea which way was up. Then two pairs of hands were on me, pulling at my coat.

I thought the fingers would be long and pale and strong but then I realized it was my friends and they were pulling me away from the wrong section of the fence, dragging me to the side, to the right part, when they could have just left me where I fell and made their own escape.

The three of us jumped up at the wire at once, scrabbling like monkeys, stretching out for the top. I rolled over it wildly, grunting as I scored deep scratches down my back that would earn me a long, hard look from my mother when she happened to glimpse them a week later.

We landed heavily on the other side, still moving forward, having realized as one that we'd just given away the location of a portion of dead fence.

But now we *had* to look back, and what I saw—though my head was still vibrating from the electric shock I'd received, so I cannot swear to this—was at least three, maybe five, figures on the other side of the fence. Not right up against it, but a few yards back.

The wind whipped black hair up around their faces, and they looked like absences ill-lit.

Then they were gone.

We moved fast. We didn't know why they'd stopped, but we didn't hang around. We didn't stick too close to the fence either, in case they changed their minds.

THIS IS NOW

We half-walked, half-ran, and at first we were quiet but as we got further away and nothing came after us, we began to laugh and then to shout, punching the air, boys who had come triumphantly out the other side.

The forest felt like some huge football field, applauding its heroes with whispering leaves.

We got back to town a little after two in the morning. We walked down the middle of the deserted main street, slowly, untouchable, knowing the world had changed: that we were no longer the boys who had started the evening together, but men now, and that the stars were there to be touched.

That was then.

As older men, we stood together at the fence for a long time, recalling that night.

Parts of it are fuzzy now, of course, and it's reduced to snapshots: Pete's terrified face when he slipped, the first glimpse of light at the houses, Henry's shout as he tried to warn me, narrow faces the color of moonlight. The other guys most likely remembered other things, defined that night in different ways and were the center of their own recollections. As I looked now through the fence at the other forest I was thinking how long a decade had seemed back then, and how you could learn that it was actually no time at all.

Henry stepped away first.

I wasn't far behind. Pete stayed a moment longer, then took a couple of steps back. Nobody said anything. We looked at the fence a little longer, and then we turned and walked away.

Took us forty minutes to get back to the truck.

The next Thursday Henry couldn't make it, so it was just me and Pete at the pool table. Late in the evening, with many beers drunk, I mentioned the fence.

Not looking at me, chalking his cue, Pete said that if Henry hadn't stepped back when he did the week before, he'd have climbed it.

'And gone over?'

'Yeah,' he said.

This was bullshit, and I knew it. 'Really?'

There was a pause. 'No,' he said, eventually, and I wished I hadn't asked the second time. I could have left him with something, left *us* with it. Calling an ass cute isn't much, but it's better than just coming right out and admitting you'll never cup it in your hand.

The next week it was the three of us again, and our walk in the woods wasn't even mentioned. We've never brought it up since, and we can't talk about the first time any more either. We killed it.

I think about it sometimes, though. I know I could go out walking there myself some night, and there have been slow afternoons and dry, sleepless small hours when I think I might do it: when I tell myself such a thing isn't impossible now, that I am still who I once was. But I have learned a little since I was fifteen, and in the end I just go smoke another cigarette on the porch, or out back of the diner.

Because in my heart of hearts I know that was then, and this is now.

TO RECEIVE IS BETTER

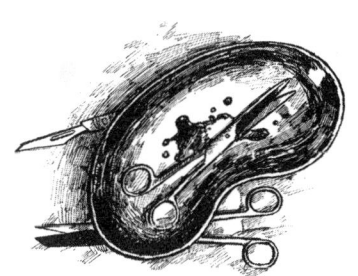

I'd like to be going by car, but of course I don't know how to drive and it would probably scare the shit out of me. A car would be much better, for lots of reasons. For a start, there's too many people out here. There's *so many* people. Wherever you turn there's more and more of them, looking tired, and rumpled, but whole.

That's the really strange thing. Everybody is whole.

A car would also be faster. Sooner or later they're going to track me down and I've got somewhere to go before they do. The public transport system sucks, incidentally. Long periods of being crowded into carriages that smell, interspersed with long waits for another line, and I don't have a lot of time. It's intimidating too. People stare. They look and look, and they don't know the danger they're in. Because in a minute one of them is going to look just one second too long and I'm going to pull his fucking face off, which will do neither of us any good.

So instead I turn and look out the window. There's nothing to see because we're in a tunnel, and I have to shut my eye to stop myself from screaming. The carriage is like another tunnel, a tunnel with windows, and I feel like I've been buried far too deep. I grew up in tunnels, ones that had no windows. The people who made them didn't bother to pretend there was something to look out on, something to look for. Because there wasn't. Nothing's coming up, nothing that isn't going to involve some fucker coming at you with a knife. So they don't pretend. I'll say that for them, at least: they don't taunt you with false hopes.

Manny did, in a way, which is why I feel complicated about him. He was the best thing that ever happened to us. But look at it another way, and maybe we'd have been better off without him. I'm being unreasonable. If it weren't for Manny, the whole thing would have been worse, thirty years of utter fucking pointlessness. I wouldn't have known this, of course, but I do now: and I'm glad it wasn't that way. Without Manny I wouldn't be where I am now.

Standing in a subway carriage, running out of time.

People are giving me a wide berth, which isn't surprising. Partly it'll be my face, and my leg. People don't like that kind of thing. But probably it's mainly me. I know the way I am, can feel the fury I radiate. It's not a nice way to be, I know, but my life has not been nice. Maybe you should try it, and see how calm you stay.

The other reason I feel weird towards Manny is I don't know why he did it. Why he helped us. Sue 2 says it doesn't matter, but I think it does. If it was just an experiment, a hobby, that makes a difference. I think I would have liked him less. But I don't think it was. I think it was simply humanity, whatever the fuck that is. I think if it was an experiment then what happened an hour ago would have panned out differently.

For a start, he probably wouldn't be dead.

If everything's gone okay, then Sue 2 will be nearly where she's going by now, much closer to her goal than I am to mine. (That's a habit I'm going to have to break. It's Sue now, just Sue. No numeral. And I'm just plain old Jack, or I will be if I get where I am going).

The first thing I can remember, the earliest glimpse of life, is the color blue. I understand now what I was seeing, but at the time I didn't know anything different, and I thought blue was the only color there was. A soft, hazy blue, a blue that had a soft hum in it and was always the same clammy temperature.

I have to get out of this subway very soon. I've taken an hour of it, and that's about as far as I can go. It's very noisy in here too, not a hum but a horrendous clattering. This is not the way I want to spend what may be the only time I have left. People keep surging around me and they've all got places to go. For the first time in my life, I'm surrounded by people who've actually got somewhere to go.

And the tunnel is the wrong color. Blue is the color of tunnels. I can't understand a tunnel unless it's blue. I spent the first four years of my life, as far as I can work out, in one of them. If it weren't for Manny, I'd be in one still. When he came to work at the Farm I could tell he was different straight away. I don't know how: I couldn't even think then, let alone speak. Maybe it was just he behaved differently when he was near us to the way the previous keeper had. I found out later that Manny's wife had died having a dead baby, so maybe that was it.

What he did was take some of us, and let us live outside the tunnels. At first it was just a few, and then about half of the entire stock of spares. Some of the others never took to the world outside the tunnels, such as it was. They'd just come out every now and then, moving hopelessly around, mouths opening and shutting, and they always looked kind of blue somehow, as if the tunnel light had seeped into their skin. There were a few who never came out of the tunnels at all, but that was mainly because they'd been used too much already. Three years old and no arms. Tell me that's fucking reasonable.

Manny let us have the run of the facility, and sometimes let us go outside. He had to be careful, because there was a road a little too close to one side of the farm. People would have noticed a group of naked people stumbling around in the grass, and of course we were naked, because *they didn't give us any fucking clothes*. Right to the end we didn't have any clothes, and for years I thought it was always raining on the outside, because that's the only time he'd let us out.

I'm wearing one of Manny's suits now, and Sue's got some blue jeans and a shirt. The pants itch like hell, but I feel like a prince. Princes used to live in castles and fight monsters and sometimes they'd marry princesses and live happy ever after. I know about princes because I've been told.

Manny told us stuff, taught us. He tried to, anyway. With most of us it was too late. With *me* it was too late, probably. I can't write, and I can't read. I know there's big gaps in my head. Every now and then I can follow something through, and the way that makes me feel makes me realize that most of the time it doesn't happen. Things fall between the tracks. I can talk quite well, though. I was one of Manny's favorites, and he used to talk to me a lot. I learnt from him. Part of what makes me so fucking angry is that I think I could have been clever. Manny said so. Sue says so. But it's too late now. It's far too fucking late.

I was ten when they first came for me. Manny got a phone call and suddenly he was in a panic. There were spares spread all over the facility and he had to run round, herding us all up. He got us into the tunnels just in time and we just sat there, wondering what was going on.

In a while Manny came to the tunnel I was in, and he had this other guy with him who was big and nasty. They walked down the tunnel, the big guy kicking people out of the way. Everyone knew enough not to say anything: Manny had told us about that. Some of the people who never came out of the tunnels were crawling and shambling around, banging off the walls like they do, and the big guy just shoved them out of the way. They fell over like lumps of meat and then kept moving, making noises with their mouths.

Eventually Manny got to where I was and pointed me out. His hand was shaking and his face looked strange, like he was trying not to cry. The big guy grabbed me by the arm and took me out of the tunnel. He dragged me down to the operating room, where there were two more guys in white clothes and they put me on the table in there and cut off two of my fingers.

That's why I can't write. I'm right-handed, and they cut off my fucking fingers.

Then they put a needle into my hand with see-through thread and sewed it up like they were in a hurry, and the big man took me back to the tunnel, opened the door and shoved me in. I didn't say anything. I didn't say anything the whole time.

Later Manny came and found me, and I shrank away from him, because I thought they were going to do something else. But he put his arms round me and I could tell the difference, and so I let him take me out into the main room. He put me in a chair and washed my hand which was all bloody, and then he sprayed it with some stuff that made it hurt a little less. Then he told me. He explained where I was, and why.

I was a spare, and I lived on a Farm. When people with money got pregnant, Manny said, doctors took a cell from the fetus and cloned another

TO RECEIVE IS BETTER

baby, so it had exactly the same cells as the baby that was going to be born. They grew the second baby until it could breathe, and then they sent it to a farm.

The spares live on the farm until something happens to the proper baby. If the proper baby damages a part of itself, then the doctors come to the farm and cut a bit off the spare and sew it onto the real baby, because it's easier that way because of cell rejection and stuff that I don't really understand. They sew the spare baby up again and push it back into the tunnels and the spare sits there until the real baby does something else to itself. And when it does, the doctors come back again.

Manny told me, and I told the others, and so we knew.

We were very, very lucky, and we knew it. There are farms dotted all over the place, and every one but ours was full of blue people that just crawled up and down the tunnels, like sheets of paper with nothing written on them. Manny said that some keepers made extra money by letting real people in at night. Sometimes the real people would just drink beer and laugh at the spares, or sometimes they would fuck them. Nobody knows, and nobody cares. There's no point teaching spares, no point giving them a life. All that's going to happen is they're going to get whittled down.

On the other hand, maybe they have it easier. Because once you know how things stand, it becomes very difficult to take it. You just sit around, and wait, like all the others, but you *know* what you're waiting for. And you know who's to blame.

Like my "brother" Jack, for example. Jamming two fingers in a door when he was ten was only the start of it. When he was eighteen he rolled his expensive car and smashed up the bones in his leg. That's another of the reasons I don't want to be on this fucking subway: people notice when something like that's missing. Just like they notice that the left side of my face is raw, where they took a graft off when some woman threw scalding water at him. He's got most of my stomach, too. Stupid fucker ate too much spicy food, drank too much wine. Don't know what those kind of things are like, of course: but they can't have been that nice. They can't have been nice enough. And then last year he went to some party, got drunk, got into a fight and lost his right eye. And so, of course, I lost mine.

It's a laugh being in a farm. It's a real riot. People stump around, dripping fluids, clapping hands with no fingers together and shitting into colostomy bags. I don't know what was worse: the ones who knew what was going on and felt hate like a cancer, or those who just ricocheted slowly round the tunnels like grubs. Sometimes the tunnel people would stay still for days, sometimes they would move around. There was no telling what they'd do, because there was no-one inside their heads. That's what Manny did for us, in fact, for Sue and Jenny and me: he put people inside our heads. Sometimes we used to sit around and talk about the real people, imagine what they were doing, what it would be like to be them instead of us. Manny said that wasn't good for us, but we did it anyway. Even spares should be allowed to dream.

It could have gone on like that forever, or until the real people started to get old and fall apart. The end comes quickly then, I'm told. There's a limit to what you can cut off. Or at least there's supposed to be: but when you've seen blind spares with no arms and legs wriggling in dark corners, you wonder.

But then this afternoon the phone went, and we all dutifully stood up and limped into the tunnel. I went with Sue 2, and we sat next to each other. Manny used to say we loved each other, but how the fuck do I know. I feel happier when she's around, that's all I understand. She doesn't have any teeth and her left arm's gone and they've taken both of her ovaries, but I like her. She makes me laugh.

Eventually Manny came in with the usual kind of heavy guy and I saw that this time Manny looked worse than ever. He took a long time walking around, until the guy with him started shouting, and then in the end he found Jenny 2, and pointed at her.

Jenny 2 was one of Manny's favorites. Her and Sue and me, we were the ones he could talk to. The man took Jenny out and Manny watched him go. When the door was shut he sat down and started to cry.

The real Jenny was in a hotel fire. All her skin was gone.

Jenny 2 wasn't going to be coming back.

We sat with Manny, and waited, and then suddenly he stood up. He grabbed Sue by the hand and told me to follow and he took us to his quarters and gave me the clothes I'm wearing now. He gave us some money, and told us where to go. I think somehow he knew what was going to happen. Either that, or he just couldn't take it anymore.

We'd hardly got our clothes on when all hell broke loose. We hid when the men came to find Manny, and we heard what happened.

Jenny 2 had said something.

They don't use drugs or anesthetic, except when the shock of the operation will actually kill the spare. Obviously. Why bother? Jenny 2 was in a terminal operation, so she was left awake. When the guy stood over her, smiling as he was about to take the first slice out of her face, she couldn't help herself, and I don't blame her.

'Please,' she said. 'Please don't.'

Three words. It isn't much. It isn't so fucking much. But it was enough. She shouldn't have been able to say anything at all.

Manny got in the way as they tried to open the tunnels and so they shot him and went in anyway. We ran then, so I don't know what they did. I shouldn't think they killed them, because most had lots of parts left. Cut out bits of their brain, probably, to make sure they were all tunnel people and stayed that way.

We ran, and we walked and we finally made the city. I said goodbye to Sue at the subway, because she was going home on foot. I've got further to go, and they'll be looking for us, so we had to split up. We knew it made sense, and I don't know about love, but I'd lose both of my hands to have her with me now.

Time's running out, but I don't care. Manny got addresses for us, so we know where to go. Sue thinks we'll be able to take their places. I don't, but I couldn't tell her. We would give ourselves away too soon, because we just don't know enough. We wouldn't have a chance.

It was always just a dream, really, something to talk about.

But one thing I am going to do. I'm going to meet him. I'm going to find Jack's house, and walk up to his door, and I'm going to look at him face to face.

And before they come and get me, I'm *going to take a few things back.*

THEY ALSO
SERVE

The years had shown that 5:35pm was the most likely time for Mr. Torrence to have a shower, and so the cubicle turned itself on to save him the trouble. The vertical LED strips by the sink unit flickered into life, the towel rail began to warm, and water issued at a predetermined rate from the four nozzles placed equidistantly around the shower area. After a moment the water's temperature was exactly equal to the average of all those to which it had previously been adjusted, and there it stayed. Preparations complete, the cubicle waited for the man to arrive, with the brute patience of no-patience: the patience of a machine.

In a very small room just off the bridge area, David Torrence put down his bitflip wrench and looked at his watch. The watch was analog, as had several times been the fashion, and told him it was time to knock off for the evening. Torrence knew the shower cubicle would be warm and ready, as it always was; after thirty years he was no longer sure whether it took its schedule from him, or vice versa, but supposed it didn't matter.

He poked the straggling mess of fiber optics and boards back into its nest in the wall. On a ship that did nothing but revolve slowly around its axis, day in and day out, a routine service of the optical matrices could wait. The truth was that the only wear and tear the damned things suffered was through his testing of them.

As he stood, Torrence winced comfortably at the sound of his joints creaking. An unwelcome reminder of advancing years, but somehow satisfying nonetheless. Another day's work completed, another day fought and won.

After replacing the access panel and dusting off his hands, he turned to his android, who had been sitting in the corner all afternoon, companionably watching him work.

'I'm done, Cat,' he said. 'That job will have to drift into fifteen minutes of tomorrow.'

'We'll survive, Dave.'

Torrence smiled. Cat was the only machine on board the ship who called him by his first name. When he'd come on board, three decades ago, all the machines had been factory-set to call him by his surname, prefixed by 'Mr.', and Cat was the only one it had occurred to him to tell to call him Dave instead. All the rest were still calling him Mr. Torrence, because he hadn't told them not to. They were like that. They were all…very much like that.

Cat raised himself a few inches off the ground and quickly hoovered up a few stray pieces of plastic. This done, he followed the man out of the service room.

'Any preferences on dinner?'

'Whatever,' Torrence said absently, drifting off down the corridor towards the living quarters.

Then he stopped. 'No, wait. Chicken. Something with chicken in it.'

Cat took the short cut through the ventilation ducts to the kitchen area. There was no chicken on board, and never had been, but manipulation of Gastronomic ProtoMatter would provide an excellent facsimile. It was not an exact science, and fifteen years ago Dave had chipped a tooth on a coq au vin that for some reason had come out made of bronze, but the element of chance was one of the reasons the machine liked cooking.

Cat was a VariTronique C7i—a compact rectangle only eighteen inches long, four inches across and eight inches high. He was nonetheless fully equipped to provide full technical, social and—if necessary—military backup for his human. By a quirk of a randomization process popular in neurocircuitry at the time of their creation, the C7s had come out as amiable,

THEY ALSO SERVE

capable and somewhat unaccountable, good companions as well as excellent workers. It was this, coupled with a tendency to follow curved paths and to rest in apparently random positions on top of, or underneath, things, or sometimes just in the middle of the floor, that had earned the C7s the generic nickname 'cats'.

They were also the qualities that had made the C7s particularly suitable for posting to Sentry Stations. Positioned in deep space in the run-up to The War, when it had finally become obvious that interstellar conflict was not only inevitable but likely to go on for some time, the Sentry Stations were small, totally independent modules whose sole function was to relay video, radar and electromagnetic information on what was happening in their locality. Because the maintenance of such a craft only justified one human crew member, and because that person would be stranded in deep space well beyond the shipping lanes for however long the war lasted, cats were felt to be the ideal companions.

Once the Station was in position there was no contact from Home, as any transmissions could just as easily be eavesdropped on by enemy craft. There was merely the routine servicing and maintenance of a ship that relayed blind information, one that cycled and recycled the closed system of the raw materials on board. Sentry Officers, chosen for their perceived ability to withstand such conditions of service, needed dependable backup, technical support, and someone to talk to.

Cats fitted the bill perfectly. The series' motto was 'To serve, and to protect'. Cat had always felt that it would ring better the other way around, but apparently it had already been used.

A small red light above the cooking area flashed briefly, a signal from the shower cubicle that Dave had finished washing. There was plenty of time, Cat knew. Dave liked to dress for dinner, and to have a drink in the recreation area before eating. It had taken four years for the recreation area and the human to reach a modus operandi on that one. At first the room insisted on trying to pre-guess what drink Dave would want, and have it ready, even though it seemed the human really did prefer to do that for himself. After a period of covert struggle in which the man had deliberately switched drinks at unpredictable intervals, and the recreation area had countered with a complex series of increasingly inaccurate predictive algorithms, a compromise had been reached.

Now the room simply had a glass and a bowl of ice ready, though Cat knew that it was secretly keeping an internal tally of how often its guesses would've been correct.

Torrence considered the question for a moment, and then decided to have a simple scotch on the rocks. The basic material in each of the bottles was the same, albeit with carefully applied flavorings. Like everything else he ingested, it had passed through him more than once already, though he tried not to think too hard about that.

There'd been a time, very many years ago, when he'd had to lay off any variant of alcohol, on Cat's advice. Back before he'd got fully used to his life and his role, when the evenings had begun to seem too long, the tomorrows too similar to all the yesterdays.

He couldn't remember much about that period, and was glad about that. As a pleasure, drink was a fine one: as a problem it was the worst. It crept up on you, befriending you: knowing the routes to the hearts of the lonely, making them believe they'd invited it in. You could have a good time with the stuff, but that didn't mean it was your friend. Torrence now only shook hands with it twice a day.

Swirling the ice in his glass, he wandered over to the observation window, appreciating the smells of cooking that Cat was piping in from the kitchen area. The view outside the window remained unedifying. The relative positions of the points of light slowly changed, but ultimately a star was a star was a star. Thirty years of looking out at Christmas lights, with no tree in sight. Thirty years without ever seeing a single other human being. Thirty years simply passing, one by one, like a drop of cold water running down a very long sheet of glass.

He just hoped that at least *one* interesting or useful piece of information had been relayed by the ship's automatic sensors in all that time.

He had never regretted the job, was proud of it and fulfilled by it. When he'd taken the tests and applied to be a Sentry Officer he'd been twenty eight and directionless, needing something to believe in, something to achieve, and the War had provided it. If, hundreds of millions of miles away, there were people looking out their windows onto a view that was more interesting, onto fields or streets, they were doing so because of the people like him. Men and women who'd been prepared to give up those things in order to help keep them safe. He'd never expected the conflict to go on this long—nobody had—but he intended to do his duty for as long as it took.

He could remember what Home was like, of course, but it had become increasingly stylized in recollection, and the early years on the ship itself were blurred and indistinct. With little to mark one day from the next, the past was simply what one remembered. It was an odd kind of life. But when they finally came to collect him, when it was all over, he'd be able to look at them down thirty or more years of service and know he'd done his part.

'Nearly ready, Dave,' came Cat's voice over the intercom. 'I'll just—shit, hang on.' After a hectic pause Cat resumed: 'Sorry, sauce got a bit out of control there. Be about five minutes.'

'Fine,' Torrence said.

They hadn't known how good a decision it was to send cats up with the Sentries. He couldn't have lasted this long without his, and he was willing to bet the other sentries dotted about the cosmos would agree. About twenty years ago the machine had sustained some internal damage, and had to turn itself off for a week while its auto-repair modules grew replacement chips. Torrence couldn't remember how he'd whiled that time away, and didn't want ever to have to relearn. He secretly hoped that he'd be allowed to keep Cat when he was eventually fetched back to Earth. He thought he might need him. For the same reasons, perhaps, that mankind had always sought the company of certain animals. Because they brought out the best in us, and protected us from our worst.

The blue light in the middle of the recreation room's circular table flashed, signaling Cat was on his way with the meal. Torrence seated himself, and within moments Cat scythed out of the ventilation duct, steaming plate clutched in a field.

'Chicken à la King,' he announced, 'with rice and some other stuff that's very nearly broccoli.'

'A la King...' mused Torrence, '...have I had that before?'

'One hundred fifty-eight times,' Cat said, settling himself not quite underneath the occasional table near the entertainment system's plasma screen. 'But not in the last two years.'

As he ate the 'chicken', which was excellent, and the 'a bit like mango' ice cream that followed, Torrence was surprised to find himself thinking further about his life. Introspection was something he rarely had time for. He was very busy keeping up with a largely self-imposed schedule of servicing and checking, and in the evening the ship's immense store of film and book material helped him while away the hours without too much thought.

But as his sixtieth birthday approached, he found himself thinking about the past more and more. Sixty was pensionable age back Home. Sixty was people opening doors for you, giving up their seat. He wished he at least knew how the War was going, could trace who was doing what, have some feeling of direct involvement. Would he be a hero when he got home, or merely an old man with nothing to do?

If. *If* he got Home. As the years went by he was beginning to realize he might have to confront the idea he might never get Home at all.

That he might die alone out here, still holding the fort.

'It can't last for ever, Dave,' Cat said, quietly.

Dave stared at the machine, surprised into a smile.

Later, when Torrence had finished filing the day's report, Cat reappeared from wherever he went when he wasn't around, bearing a glass of brandy—or something that tasted like it. Perching to one side of the console, he clicked briskly for a while in a way Torrence had come to assume signified contentment, and asked what movie the man wanted to watch. Wandering over to the window as Cat and the recreation room silently liaised over the entertainment, Torrence reflected that, all in all, things could be a whole lot worse.

'Um, Dave,' Cat said suddenly, 'You might want to come look at this.'

Torrence turned. 'What's...'

He stopped, breath escaping him in a small grunt, and stared at the console.

A large screen, subdivided into many sections, constantly-updated information on the performance of the essential functions of the ship. Torrence gave it a glance several times an hour whenever he was in the rec room to make sure everything was in order.

In the bottom right-hand corner lay an area that had remained unused in all the time he had been on the ship. The area was labelled 'Communication', and a word lit in red was now flashing in it.

The word was Incoming.

It was impossible to get the ship to even *register* attempted contact unless the sender knew a sequence of codes. That one flashing word could only mean one thing.

The War was over.

Cat hovered by his side and watched the blinking lights with him, and not for the first time Torrence wished he could know what the machine was thinking.

It was Cat who broke the silence. 'Aren't you going to answer it?'

Shaking his head, and grinning like an idiot, Torrence tapped in the code which permitted contact, a code he'd practiced so many, many times in his head over the years.

The word Incoming continued to flash for a moment, and then was replaced by Contact Established.

'Hello? Is that David Torrence? Hello? Am I through?'

With some difficulty, Torrence replied. 'This is Sentry Officer David Torrence. I can hear you clearly.'

He had to struggle to find the words, feeling tongue-tied and inarticulate. He'd spent hours every day talking to Cat, to the recreation room or shower, but this was different. 'It's...it's good to hear your voice. Who am I speaking to?'

'Field Lieutenant Jack Pols, Retrieval Forces. Good to hear you too, Dave. I've come a very long way to pick you up. My friend? You're going home.'

Home. That word again.

Torrence felt the ship, his ship, round him like an embrace. It would have taken the approaching ship several years to make the journey from Home System, and would take the same to return. By the time he set foot on Home Planet, the War would have been over for the better part of a decade.

'Where are you now?'

'Still a few hours away, uh, currently at co-ords 348.22/56.68. I figured you might not have your eye on the Comms channel every minute of the day, so I flashed ahead of time. I anticipate arrival circa 22:50.'

'I'll wait up', said Torrence. 'So…it's over.'

'Yep—two years back. They finally caved.'

'*Two* years? It only took you two years to get here?'

'Ships have come on a little while you've been out here, Dave. One of the reasons we won. You want to make sure the defenses are turned off before I get there?'

'Your ship's beacon coding will do it.'

'Yeah, I know, but that's an old ship you've got there. Kind of a downer to come all this way to get fried by accident only an hour away, wouldn't you say?'

Laughing, Torrence started to key in the codes. Cat floated up from behind him and placed a freshened drink on the console.

Pols's voice crackled over the speakers. 'Dave, I got something flashing at me here. Back with you in a moment.'

The Established sign was replaced by a Hold.

Coding finished, and the ship's automatic defenses disarmed, Torrence turned to Cat, and saw that the machine was holding a glass of its own. There was nothing in it, but Torrence knew what he meant, and felt absurdly touched.

'You made it, Dave,' Cat said, raising his glass.

'*We* did.' Torrence clinked the rim of his glass against Cat's, and drank.

For half an hour Torrence pummeled Pols with questions, how the War had finished, what life was like back in Home System now. Eventually he ground to a halt, nowhere near empty of questions but already full of answers, swamped with the new and barely expected.

'I can still hardly believe it.'

'Believe it, Dave. All round the outer fringes the same thing's happening. There's one hundred forty Sentry Stations, and right now someone's on the way to every single one.'

Torrence shook his head. It was strange to think of so many other men and women, coming to the end of the same journey. Between them, several thousand years of watching and waiting were over.

Suddenly a siren crashed over the speakers, half-deafening him.

THEY ALSO SERVE

Startled, he ran his eyes over the screen, trying to work out what the issue was. As far as he could see, *most* of the panel was flashing. Beneath the noise he heard Pols's voice asking if there was a problem.

He put the microphone on mute, scanning the screen more methodically. Cat, oddly silent, drifted over to the observation window.

Most of the flashing, Dave realized, was in subsidiary areas of the screen, signifying readiness of response. Thin red tracks of light linked these areas to a central zone, in which the main message was contained.

Warning, it said, in red. Approaching Craft Fails Hull Coding Test.

Torrence stepped back from the console. Tiny micro-beacons the size of pinheads were spread randomly through the ship's hull, each broadcasting part of a coding matrix. This matrix, through a process of cumulative self-reference, produced a code both greater and different to the sum of its parts, and was further mutated by interaction with the hull coding of any Home ship it approached. If the result was acceptable, contact was allowed. If it wasn't, the security system went bananas.

If he hadn't already disarmed the ship's auto-defense mechanisms, Pols's ship would by now be dispersed over most of the surrounding parsec, in pieces scarcely bigger than molecular size.

'Weird' he muttered. He switched the alarm off and turned to face Cat, who was still floating facing the window. 'What's *that* about?'

'Well,' said Cat, 'The Station doesn't accept Pol's ship's coding matrix.'

'Yes, but what does *that* mean?'

'As he said, this is an old ship, and his is very recent. But it seems unlikely they'd change the system. It'd be backwards-compatible, at least. So…it's down to a glitch in the security system on the Station.'

'How likely is that?'

'It's possible. The Securicore module is the only mode of the distributed system I can't access. It's too heavily encrypted. Even if I could, I can't test anything. Essential functions are controlled by organic neurocircuitry. It may have lost its grip. I don't know.'

Torrence noticed that the Incoming light was flashing in the Communication panel. Pols, doubtless wondering what was going on. 'You don't sound very convinced.'

Cat paused. 'Well, how convinced are you, Dave?'

He *wanted* to assume that was the problem—Pols had known the right communication codes, after all—and it made sense. Thirty years of War just made that assumption difficult to run with. He tapped in the Contact code.

Pols's voice came back on immediately. 'Problem there, Dave?'

'Just as well I turned off the defense system, Pols. The Station doesn't like your ship's hull coding very much.'

Pols sounded utterly unconcerned. 'Right. It's happened before. That's why I warned you. And make it Jack, yeah?'

Torrence paused for a moment, chewing his lip.

Right from the start Pols had called him Dave. He realized belatedly that this had rankled, despite the good news he brought: Torrence was an officer, still on active war duty. Perhaps Pols was merely being friendly, and after two years' journey to collect someone, maybe you felt you'd earned the right to use their Christian name. Perhaps they did things differently now.

Or maybe he had just become too used to everyone except Cat calling him Mr. Torrence.

'Why does it happen?'

'You think I *understand* those boxes? All I know is they've found that senior active ships can get a bit picky. I heard of two examples right before I left. Luckily they both got worked out before the nukes went off, but who wants to take the risk? Show me a perfect machine and I'll show you figures on the annual turnover of the repair business. Nothing lasts forever.'

'I guess that's true.'

Torrence leaned on the console, head hanging, eyes closed. He felt dumb, and pedantic, and he wanted so much to simply believe. But although what the man said made sense, Torrence had done things by the book too long to be able to immediately accept a discrepancy.

'I know it looks odd,' said Cat, quietly, so not as to be picked up by the microphone, 'but he did know the codings.'

Torrence nodded. 'But why,' he said, loud enough to be overheard, 'haven't we heard anything about this? If the War has been over for two years, why didn't Home broadcast the news?'

'Because it *was* two years ago,' Pols said. 'Say they beam you information that the War's over. Then you've got two years to wait, knowing you're no longer serving a purpose, but just waiting for the ship to arrive. That's a *long fucking Sunday afternoon*, man. Isn't it better for me to just arrive, so then it's over and you're going home both at the same time?'

That did make sense. Two years of sitting watching the console with your bags already packed would drive anyone nuts. You'd know you had to wait, of course, but if everything was over except for that waiting, how easy would it be to get through it?

Torrence opened his eyes and started to turn, but then stopped. Silently he motioned to Cat, and the machine floated up to look at the console.

A different message was now flashing.

Warning. Approaching Craft fails Backup Hull Test. View Vessel with Code Red Suspicion.

'Backup?' asked Torrence. He knew he should remember what that entailed. He didn't.

'The Station's run the backup test,' Cat said. 'It's actually a subset of the initial tests, and so is less stringent.'

'Easier to pass, you mean. Recreation Room?' called Torrence, wondering absently, and for the first time, if this wasn't the equivalent of it calling him "Mr. Torrence", and if he should just be calling it 'Rec' or 'Reccy' or something, 'Get me a juice, would you?'

'I'll fetch it,' Cat volunteered quickly.

'I'm sorry Pols,' Torrence said, 'but I'm... going to have to think about this.'

'Dave, relax. That's cool. You want to do this by the book, I get that, and with the coding kicking off I don't blame you. They figured at Home that this could be a tricky moment psychologically, even if the alarms didn't go off. That's why they sent me to get you.'

'Why should you make any difference?'

There was a pause. When Pols spoke again, he did so slowly and carefully. 'Well, because you know me.'

'What are you talking about?'

For the first time, Pols sounded irritated. 'Who better to pick you up than the only person you saw in all the time you were on the Station? Come on, Dave. So the alarm's gone off, but, Christ, it's *Jack Pols*, okay?'

'I spoke to you for the first time twenty minutes ago.'

'Oh Jesus.' Concern was now present in the man's tone, which made it worse. 'February 20th, 2043. Okay, it's over twenty years ago, but Jesus, how many visitors have you *had*?'

Struggling to keep his voice level, Torrence stared straight at the speaker. His chest felt cold and empty.

'It is forbidden to visit or even approach Sentry Stations during war time, because of the risk of signaling their position to the enemy. I have never met or spoken to you before this evening, Pols. I do not know what you are talking about. I have had no visitors while I have been on this Station. I do not know who you are.'

'I *know* it's forbidden to approach Stations: I knew it then, too. I was caught on the fringes of the Fifth Battle. My cruiser was deeply fucked, and I needed somewhere to dock, and someone to help me fix it. I knew there was a Station in the area, so I took the risk.'

'Cat?' Torrence broke in, 'does this ring any bells with you?'

'No.'

'Odd. I though your memory was quite good.'

'Christ, Torrence, is this some kind of test? Do I have to remember a secret song or something?'

'I'd be likely to remember a visitor, Pols. Not only would you have been the only person I'd seen in the last thirty years, your visit would have been highly irregular, whether your craft was damaged or not.'

'I *know*, and that's why you agreed not to enter it in the logs.'

'What?' said Torrence suspiciously.

'You should have written it up, right? You didn't.'

'I didn't write it up because it didn't happen.'

'I can confirm Officer Torrence's statements,' Cat said. 'Neither you nor anyone else has ever visited this Station.'

'You weren't around, machine.'

'Where was I? Back Home on leave?'

'You'd banged into a post or something and turned yourself off for a few days, to self-repair. Christ. Come on, guys, this isn't funny.'

Torrence didn't hear Pols' next few sentences. He'd felt bad when Pols had first claimed to know him, as if the ground had shaken under his feet.

THEY ALSO SERVE

This was worse. The ground wasn't merely shaking: a huge crack seemed to be opening in front of him. He still believed he hadn't met Pols. It wasn't something you could just forget.

But Cat *had* been out of action for a week.

Back in the days when Torrence hadn't been dealing with things too well. A time he couldn't remember very clearly at all.

He knew Cat was looking at him, but when the machine spoke, it was to Pols. 'Don't you think it likely that I would still know something about it?' it said. 'That Officer Torrence might have thought it worth mentioning when I reactivated?'

'Ordinarily, yes. But ordinarily I wouldn't have expected a Sentry Officer to have been shitfaced.'

Cat saw Dave flinch.

'One of the reasons I was so happy to find a Station in the area,' Pols continued, 'was that I knew that a Sentry Officer was going to have to be handy with mechanics. And he was. Of course I had to keep telling him which of the several images of things he was seeing was the one he was supposed to be repairing.'

'It's not true.' Torrence said, shaking his head. 'This just isn't true.'

'It's okay, man. I never told anyone, and I never will. It's not on your record. Hell, drunk or not, you saved my ship, right? And I remember getting pretty wasted myself on the last evening I was with you. It was a good night, man, one of the best I had in the whole damned War. That's why I'm here today. Retrieval is a volunteer service, Dave.'

'So,' Cat said, 'Officer Torrence was so much under the influence that not only did he neglect to mention single-handedly repairing a damaged cruiser, but also what was by all accounts the social event of the War?'

'He didn't *neglect* it, he said he straight-up wasn't going to tell you. Seemed pretty psyched about the idea actually. I think you were pissing him off.'

'That's bullshit,' Torrence said, loudly. 'Cat is the...'

He broke off, first becoming aware of what he was about to say, and then realizing it was true. 'Cat is the best friend I've ever had.'

'Woh, dude, talk about the Lost Weekend. You weren't going to tell your machine because it'd only rag you out. Said it was trying to take over. You knew the machine would go bananas at the breach of security, that it'd think you'd lost your grip.'

Torrence felt his eyes pricking, and saw that his knuckles were white. He'd never said that. This had still never happened. But it was the kind of thing that *could* have happened, the sort of thing he might have said at one time.

But he hadn't. Had he?

Pols kept pushing. 'You told me that only the week before the machine had told you to knock off drinking, for Christ's sake!'

Torrence shoved himself away from the console and stumbled into the center of the room.

Cat, showing marginally less confidence now, continued the defense. 'Such a decision to not divulge information, even if it were to take place, would not work. The recreation room, the bridge, the shower cubicle, the docking module; they would have remembered you, and they would have told me. They haven't.'

'They were turned off too, machine. He locked out everything except the maintenance functions. He just wanted a week where he could drink, and crash out, without having the shower coming on, without having the recreation room give him a hard time, without having fucking *machines* wish him good morning just because they were programmed to. Look. You want proof? I've got it. When I was on the ship, I left something behind.'

Torrence turned. His eyes were huge and dark.

'What?' Cat asked.

'A book. A paper book. It was a novel by Ray Bradbury—*The October Country*. I was big into the classics back then.'

'Even if that were true, it would have been cleared away many years ago.'

'But not *thrown* away, right? It's a closed system. Somewhere on the Station is that book. Find it.'

'This is a very large craft. To have the Station do a full self-inventory will take a couple of hours.'

'So don't let me on board until you find it. I'll dock with the Station, but stay in my ship. Tell the rec room to get looking.'

'The recreation room is already engaged on another function,' said Cat distantly. 'Dave, what do you think?'

THEY ALSO SERVE

There was a long silence before Torrence answered. When he did, his voice was barely audible. It wasn't that he had a vague memory of the event, or thought it might have happened. He simply couldn't be sure. He couldn't remember that it definitely hadn't happened, and so in his heart of hearts he knew it could.

'I think we'd better check.'

Cat patched into the console and spoke directly to the bridge, instructing it to perform an exhaustive inventory of every object on the Station.

'In the meantime,' Cat added, speaking to Pols, 'I think Officer Torrence and I should discuss this. Contact will be re-established later. Goodbye.'

He snapped the channel off.

One look at Dave was enough to show that the man, strong for so many years, was near the end of his tether. Thirty years was too long to leave a man in a ship, without contact, without support, without continuing proof of his importance. Far too long.

It was Torrence who broke the silence.

'I don't remember any of this. I know you think it must be true, but I can't, I don't...'

'Dave,' Cat said gently, 'I don't believe it at all.'

Torrence turned, a look of childish surprise on his face. 'Then why did you agree to an inventory?'

'The same reason Pols suggested one. To buy time. I needed to talk to you. All the while we were talking, Pols' ship was getting closer.'

'But the inventory will take ages. By the time it's finished, his ship will be docked.'

'If we wait that long.'

Torrence stared at the machine, struggling to keep up. He felt old and confused. 'But we've *got* to wait.'

'Tell me, Dave — how do you see the situation? Doesn't it go something like this? Relief has arrived from Home. The War is over, and he has come to collect you. His ship fails the hull coding test, even the reduced version, after he has conveniently suggested you turn the auto-defenses off. Even though all you want to do is let him on, you rightly become concerned.'

'But then he proves that he's alright.'

'Does he, Dave?'

'Well.' Torrence stopped, upset. 'I can't remember. I'm old, Cat. I never realized. I'm old now.'

'Yes. And you can't be expected to remember everything. Pols knows that. Think of all the other Sentry Officers. Think of someone, like you, by himself on a Station. Think of him spending five years, ten years, doing the same things, and never talking to anyone else. Then double and triple that. Isn't it *likely* that some of them started to drink too much after a while? How many Sentry Officers do you think have stayed absolutely straight for thirty years?'

Torrence considered. 'Not many, I guess. So what?'

'So you could probably safely assume a period when an Officer's memories aren't what they could be. When he may have been bitter. When the advice and company of machines got on his nerves. When he might even have turned them off for a period.'

'He knew the communication codes. He knew that you had to repair yourself that time.'

'I doubt there are many Cats who haven't, at one time or another. We take knocks. As for the codes...we don't actually know how the War's going, do we?'

Torrence paused, trying to re-order things in his mind. Once Pols had told him what he wanted to hear, a switch flipped in his head: War Over, Good Guys in Charge.

But the only evidence of that... was Pols's word.

And if the War *wasn't* over, and if Home Planet was in trouble, communications protocols could be breached, passwords stolen.

But not hull codings. They, like the Sentry Officers, had to be taken the hard way.

He'd been all too ready to take responsibility, to admit weakness. But he'd stuck it out for thirty years, so why the hell should he take Pols's word for it now?

'Okay,' he said finally, his voice steadier. 'But if Pols *isn't* who he says he is, then he's taking a hell of a risk on a bluff like this self-inventory.'

THEY ALSO SERVE

'Would you let him on otherwise? However calm he stayed, whatever chapter and verse he could produce on hull coding errors, would you have let him on? However long he talked of Home, and of the welcome you'd receive, whatever he came up with, *would you let him on?*'

Torrence didn't have to look far into himself to know the answer. 'No.' he said. 'I wouldn't, would I?'

'You would not. They weren't screwing around when they selected Sentry Officers. There'll be some who've had a long battle with the bottle, and there will be many who will not be fit for much when they get back Home. But not a single one of you will risk blowing it. Not thirty years of solitary service. Not a life's work. And so if things start getting complicated, if there's a glitch in the plan, what will someone like Pols have to do?'

'Make me believe that I've lost it. That I was so out of it one time that I don't even remember turning the whole ship off so I could get drunk in peace.'

'His ship's getting closer, Dave. You have to make a decision. After his cruiser is docked you can't destroy it. Once he's docked, whoever he may be, he's as good as in. The airlock is tough, but if that's what he's come for then he'll get through eventually.'

'But until the inventory is done, I don't *know*. You know what I was like back then, Cat. He could be telling the truth. He could be here to take us Home.'

'Either he's telling the truth, or he's from The Others. I can't tell you what to do. You're the commanding officer. It's your call.'

Cat floated over to the console. 'The cruiser is a hour and twenty minutes away. In thirty minutes he'll be too close for us to safely use General Displacement on him. It'll be down to a shoot-out. At the very least the Station will be badly damaged. At worst it will be taken. The decision has to be quick, sir.'

Torrence walked to the window. For five minutes he stood there, running back over every sentence of the conversation with Pols, checking off what actually amounted to anything. In all the time he'd been on the ship, all he'd had to do was maintain. Keep things running. Perhaps some Officers had been forced to make these kinds of decisions every year, every few months. Some of the Stations were probably in ruins, or taken, through the wrong calls being made.

It was very late in the day to have to make a decision like this. Very, very late.

He just wanted to go Home.

Most of all, he racked his brains for some hint of memory, the ringing of however distant a bell. And in the end he forgot all of it and went on gut feeling.

Abruptly he strode over to the console and opened the communication channel. 'Pols?'

Pols laughed. 'Hey! All coming back to you now?'

'There's nothing I'd like more than to believe you. But I have to do what I think is right. It's my job. If you're who you say you are, then I'm very sorry.'

He tapped a seven figure number into the console. The dimmed auto-defense panel came alight.

Pols' voice was no longer light-hearted. 'Shit, Dave...'

Two more codes.

'Dave! Don't fucking... Jesus!'

Torrence paused, then tapped in the final digit.

He didn't turn to face the window. He didn't have to.

The entire room lit up, as the Station's defense system caused the position of Pols's craft to become the exact center of a displacement reaction that rotated every molecule within half a cubic mile randomly about its axis.

What had been a ship, or a man, was instantly mere chemicals. Same atoms, different bonds, like water and the Sun. Just to make sure, the ship also placed a nuclear warhead in the middle of the cloud of chemicals, and blew them still further apart.

Overkill, the cocktail of war.

When the glow had faded, Torrence turned to look. Nothing was visible but the occasional sparkle of a spinning speck of debris.

The next hour and a half seemed longer to Torrence than the previous thirty years. He sat on the couch, not speaking, watching the stars. He was either a hero, or an idiot. In some ways it was difficult to know which was worse.

Eventually Cat floated over to the console, alerted on an internal channel that the bridge had completed its inventory.

Torrence stood, walked over. He felt as if he was floating. 'Okay. What?'

THEY ALSO SERVE

The bridge's voice came clearly over the speakers. 'I have performed a complete inventory, as requested, and compared every object on this ship with what was here before we left Home Planet.'

'And?' Torrence's voice was hoarse.

'I understand you were looking for a book. The number and titles of the books on board is exactly equal to the number and titles of the books we started with. There has been no increase in quantity of any other object at all. Nothing has come in. Nothing at all.'

Throat tight, eyes pricking, the man turned to his Cat.

'I was right,' he said.

Torrence went to bed at midnight, tired and happy. With Cat's aid he'd reworked his maintenance schedule so as to keep everything in top condition on a shorter cycle, with particular stress on the defense systems. When there was a War on, you had to be vigilant.

And he'd been that, alright. Faced with the most difficult choice a man could make, he'd done okay. He'd got it *right*. He was still the man he'd always been. They'd been right to trust him with his mission. When Home System eventually won, as he knew they would, then up there with the Fleet Commanders, up there with the Star Generals, in his own small way, up there too would be Sentry Officer David Torrence. In the meantime the mission continued, and Torrence was confident in his ability to keep on fighting.

Through his success he'd found a renewed spirit and pride, which never left him.

When he was sure Torrence was asleep, Cat floated over to the bed and settled himself near the man's feet. After a moment, very quietly, he began to emit a brisk clicking sound.

He too was content with the day's work. He'd known for over a year that The War was over, and that Home System had lost. The ship had been alerted to this effect fourteen months ago, over an internal band. Cat had known since then that the Sentry Officers would never be collected, that they were never going home. It had taken all that time to come up with the plan, to perfect the script for the Recreation Room to perform, faking incoming communication signals and simulating the lines of a Field Lieutenant who had never existed.

But it had worked, and he was glad. For Cat was a good cat, and took his job very seriously.

To serve, and to protect.

THE SCARIEST THING IN THE WORLD

I got the cab to pull up a hundred yards short and paid the guy in cash, adding a generous tip despite having been told multiple times that people didn't do that here in Finland. A few euros here or there make little difference to me, but might to the driver. I worked as a waiter for a couple years, back in the day. What goes around comes around.

"Halloween party?"

"No," I said. "Well, sure, tonight's the night, I guess. But this is part of the Festival of the Fantastique."

"Ah, yes. I heard of this."

Hard not to. European cities tend to care a lot more openly about the arts, and the center of Helsinki was presently festooned with banners for this celebration of the Gothic and weird, in prose, film and art—with big posters at most of the bus stops, and on the trams too. The venue for Greg's event was an imposing neoclassical stone frontage that looked like a museum or embassy or church, strikingly uplit on either side of a large central doorway. I'd asked to be dropped down the street to have a private moment for a cigarette, and also see how the land lay. The line snaked a hundred feet down the cold, dark street.

"Big crowd, huh?"

"Looks that way," I said.

MICHAEL MARSHALL SMITH

I climbed out, wrapping my coat around as a chill wind came whipping down the road, and used half of my grasp of the Finnish language in one sentence. "*Kiitos*."

After the cab pulled away I blinked, stretched my mouth and eyes wide, and lit my cigarette. I was, I noticed, pretty drunk. That's unusual for me now, especially at a festival, though in the early days it was near-mandatory. We'd arrive in a chaotic flock, get our work hung or installations set up as quickly as possible, and immediately head *en masse* for the nearest dive-bar to talk arty bullshit and get flamboyantly wasted into the small hours. Repeat for however many nights the event lasted, ending with a wretched train ride home.

But I don't go to festivals by train any more. Or doze my hungover way home in the back of some guy's truck, buffeted by unsold prints and paintings. I fly. Actually, I am flown. If I find myself in a bar it's an invite-only party and I arrive escorted by the organizer and their assistant, the PR, sometimes a gallery owner, probably several other people whose identity I never learn. I am deferentially handed a glass of obligatory champagne and sip it while chatting with whoever's allowed through the cordon. I'll have a glass of wine during dinner, two at most, before switching to espressos and water. Being drunk in public is fine for *enfants terribles*. Not for me. Instead I'll retire to my hotel room, catch up on e-mail, stand a while looking out the window at whatever city it happens to be. And go to bed.

Tonight the party hadn't been at a public venue, but—as sometimes happens—the home of a notable collector of my work.

And that's where the trouble started.

I dropped the cigarette butt in the trash and headed across the street.

Something of a *frisson* ran through the line as I walked toward the entrance. Half the crowd was in Halloween costume, thankfully all horror-related instead of the ballerinas and baseball players and other random crap you'll see at home. I considered democratically joining the end of the line, but only for about a second. That simply doesn't work. People leave their positions to come say "hi," and the whole system goes to shit and it's hassle the organizers don't need when they're trying to get an event started in a timely manner.

THE SCARIEST THING IN THE WORLD

The Festival secretary was at the front of the line, standing with the people checking tickets. Her eyes widened as I approached: not three hours previously I'd told her I wasn't coming to this event.

"Mr. Williams," she said. She'd gotten into the spirit of the night in a low-key way, up-spraying her hair like the Bride of Frankenstein, completing the effect with curved brows and bee-sting lipstick. "What a pleasure to see you here."

"Figured I'd come support an old friend."

"Aha," she said. "And did you announce you might be attending, on the social media?"

"I may have mentioned it."

She smiled, and looked at the people snaking away down the sidewalk. "So that explains this."

"No, no," I said. "It's been a while since he had a show. I'm sure there's a lot of interest in what Greg's come up with."

She winked, as if we both knew that wasn't true. "Still no costume for you?"

"I am what I am. That's scary enough." I held up my hands like claws and made a deliberately lame growling sound.

She laughed, but then her face turned a little more serious. "I should warn you," she said. "Your friend...he's in a strange mood, I think."

"Probably nervous. It's a big crowd."

She nodded, as if reassured. "I'm sure that's all it is."

The ticket-collectors stood aside to let me pass, and the people at the front of the line nodded and grinned at me. That's the weirdest thing, the aspect I still haven't gotten used to after all these years. I mean, sure—I'm recognizable, somewhat, in certain *milieux*. The TV show did that, along with being laughably characterized as "the Anthony Bourdain of art," and simple self-marketing tricks like always wearing a charcoal suit.

But why does that mean I get to jump the line? I don't get it.

For a moment I considered stopping, briefly joining the front of the line as a gesture of solidarity with the masses. But then realized I was being a bit drunk and that in reality I needed both a piss and some more to drink and I didn't want to wait for either, and so I swanned in as God intended.

A short, dark corridor led to a large, circular room with a domed ceiling. This was crowded with a couple of hundred people, chattering and milling about and waiting for the event to start. I wrongly assumed the gents would be at the far side of the room, and found myself heading down some stone stairs into a sepulchral space beneath the building, like a crypt made of corridors. There were big bundles of straw and rolls of cotton wool piled up against the walls throughout, and large barriers of corrugated cardboard, painted black. Sound baffles, presumably. But nowhere to piss.

I went back upstairs and found the john, and as I came out a festival underling spotted me and hectically drew me to one side. She was shy, her English rather more heavily accented than most of the Finns I'd encountered so far, and so it took me a moment to understand where she was taking me.

But then, there he was.

Rather more overweight than his picture in the festival program suggested, significantly more balding, standing by himself in a cordoned-off area and holding a bottle of champagne bullishly by the neck.

"Danny *boy*," he said. "As I live and breathe."

"Greg," I said. "Looking good."

"That's horseshit and you know it. You of course look exactly how you do on the TV. I guess that's what a shit-ton of money will do for you."

That, and going to the gym, and watching what I eat, I thought, *and making the effort to do all the other tiresome things required not to look like crap at our age.* Didn't say it. "You going to give me some of that drink?"

"Oh yeah." He peered around, eventually spotted the clearly-visible array of glasses on the table behind him, and slopped a random amount of champagne more-or-less into one of them. "There were a couple of the festival people here, but I said something borderline rude to that organizer woman and they all kind of drifted off."

"Rude about what?"

"*You*, to be honest."

I laughed. "What did you say?"

"Just I didn't think you were all you were cracked up to be. 'Course at that point I had no idea you'd actually be turning up. Look at 'em..." He gestured out at the crowds milling around the room, more than a few of

THE SCARIEST THING IN THE WORLD

whom were sneaking glances over at us. "...Isn't that fucking weird? Them wanting to *look* at you like that? Or are you used to it?"

"Doesn't bother me," I said, giving a little wave to a couple of people who seemed familiar. They looked delighted, and waved back.

"Having been recognized by their lord, the peasants rejoiced."

"Piss off, Greg."

"Why are you even here?"

"Dude," I said. "It's been a long time. But back in the day... I'd say we were friends, wouldn't you?"

"Sure," he said, reluctantly. "But I didn't mean that. I meant at this festival. It's all horror stuff. They can call it "Gothic" or "fantastique" or whatever they like, but that's basically what it is, right? Horror movies, horror books, horror art. The genre slum. You haven't done anything like than in fucking *decades*."

"My 'Dark Side' series two years ago—"

"Oh fuck off. Putting in more shadows and ladling on the burnt umber does not make you a master of the macabre."

"I'm flattered you've been keeping up with my work."

"Can't fucking avoid it. Any idea what *I've* been doing?"

"To be honest, no. Not since."

I left it there. He looked away, then back. It was the first time in the entire exchange we'd had direct eye contact. He looked drunk, also tired and hurt. "Installations."

"Well, yeah, I know that. Which is what the thing tonight is, right? That's great. I always said that was your best medium in the early days."

"Are you taking the piss? These still *are* the early days for me, Danny. I am literally back where I fucking started."

"Careers can be like that."

"Not yours."

"Look, what do you want me to say? I've been lucky."

"Plus you sold out."

"That's unfair."

"Is it? The annoying thing, the thing that really *pisses me off*, is you were *good*. You painted stuff that unnerved the crap out of people. But then you figured out there was no money in it, and so you jumped into the abstractosphere."

MICHAEL MARSHALL SMITH

"We all make choices."

"Meaning?"

I shook my head. He knew I was referring to his defining moment. The point where—resentful at not receiving the recognition that in all honesty he probably deserved—he spiraled off into using a genuinely remarkable level of technical skill to start forging art, instead of creating it. Of course faking is an act of creation, of a kind, not least in the level of attention to detail required to convincingly replicate the techniques of others, especially the old masters. But it's a road to nowhere good, especially if you have an ego as big as Greg's.

They say many serial killers get to the point where they actually want to be caught, either to be put out of their misery or—more likely—finally get the attention they've always craved. It's the same with forgers. Almost none of them are in it for the money. They want to get one over on the gallery owners and collectors and other so-called experts who turn some artists into rock stars and consign others to obscurity. For a while it's enough for you alone to know you're doing this. Not for long, though. Consciously or otherwise, eventually you'll leave a clue. Greg tried to pull the same trick twice (painting a semi-obvious forgery on top of a much better one, thus getting the latter accepted as real) and was caught. And vilified.

"Fuck you," Greg said. He said it very clearly. Several people outside the cordon heard him, and quickly looked away.

"Thanks. I was the sole person from the old days who stood up for you. Literally the only one."

"And *that's* why fuck you. It was that which pushed me over the fucking edge. How do you think it felt, charity from somebody who gets his assistants to do all the work?"

"Yeah, I've heard that rumor," I said, knocking back the glass of wine. "It isn't true. Everything with my name on it is mine. I work long hours. And I work hard."

"With your eyes closed?"

I was saved from having to answer this by the approach of the Festival Secretary. She'd been hovering the background for a few minutes. "I'm sorry to…interrupt," she said. "I just wanted to remind you it's due to start in twenty minutes."

THE SCARIEST THING IN THE WORLD

"I know," Greg said. "I can tell the fucking time."

"Thank you," I told her. She backed away.

"That's why there's a crowd here tonight, isn't it?" Greg said to me, angrily. "You fucking tweeted it. Didn't you? You couldn't even let me have *that*."

"Fuck's sake. I'm going outside for a cigarette."

"You still smoke? I'm genuinely amazed."

"We all have a dark side, Greg. I just hide mine. Whereas you get yours out like your cock, and wave it around."

"At least I'm honest."

"Maybe. But the problem is then everybody's already seen your dick and you've got nothing left to shock them with."

There was still a line at the door, though shorter. It was getting close to show time. I walked quickly past with my head down and went far enough up the street that I could stand in a doorway without being seen. Not that I give a damn about people knowing I smoke. I'm fifty-two. My parents are dead and my wife is now an ex-wife, so there's not really anybody's judgement that I have to take seriously.

Except my own, of course. I stood huddled in shadow and sucked down the first cigarette quickly, decided to have another, on the grounds I had no idea how long this event was going to take: the description merely said it was something everybody experienced together, rather than wandered through in their own time.

Seeing Greg had affected me in ways I hadn't anticipated, too. Most of my reason for being here was genuinely to show support. But sure, I'll admit a portion of it was to present myself to him. To the guy who'd always had so much more flair in the old days, always attracted the lion's share of attention, who had no qualms about elbowing "friends" aside in order to get to the reviewer, gallery owner—or girl. The alpha creator, the hare, who'd burned out and let the beta male tortoise overtake him on the long haul.

Being in the same physical space for the first time in probably twenty years, however, had caused that to fall away. Instead it reminded me of the days when you hung out with people because of a spark, not because of their status, and you created things not because they'd be good investments, but because they touched people. Because what you did was real.

As I was lighting the second cigarette I realized someone was approaching. My heart sank. The glass of champagne I'd thrown back had topped me back up to pretty-drunk level, and I didn't want to undergo a stilted conversation with a fan.

"Can I bum one of those?"

It was Greg. I held out the pack. He took one and accepted a light. Stood for a moment, looking along the dark street. Shook his head. "Sorry I was such a cunt."

"I enjoyed it. Reminded me of the old days."

He laughed. "You win that one."

"Well, I'm a winner, to the bone."

This had been a catch-phrase of Greg's, thirty years ago. He remembered. "Yeah yeah, fuck you. Look, seriously though. And this is important. Why are you actually here?"

"What difference does it make?"

"I wasn't kidding earlier. During that whole dumpster fire four years back, after I was dumb enough to try to sell a fake to a celebrity and wound up being the poster boy for pricks everywhere, it was you coming to my defense that pushed me over the edge. I spent the next three years raging drunk."

I started to speak but he rode over me. "I know, I know. I'm sure you did it with the best intentions, because you've always been a good boy, but that's what happened. My shit is closer to being back together now. And so I just want to know how much charity is involved here."

"Not at all," I said. "If you want to know, it's this. Punching a hole. Remember that?"

He did, and the act of recollection made him look much younger for a moment. "Of course. What I used to say we were going to do. Or *should* do. Not just put rectangular shit on people's walls, but make things that changed the world. Things that would be remembered forever."

"Right. Did you bring the champagne out with you?"

"The Finns are open-minded, but not *that* open-minded," he said. "However." He pulled a small flask out of his coat. I unscrewed it and took a long pull of what turned out to be vodka. "But I don't get what you're saying."

THE SCARIEST THING IN THE WORLD

"I was at a dinner this evening," I said. The vodka felt good and warm inside me. It did what ill-advised drinks always do, which is make you want to have a dozen more. "At the home of the biggest collector of my work in Finland. Whole of Europe, in fact. Roasted boar. Appetizers with seven different types of smoked fish. Champagne that was older than the pert little things who were serving it."

"I went to McDonald's."

"Whatever, Greg. Just listen. The Festival committee was there. A couple of super-fans. The freakin' mayor. And this collector and her husband, of course. And before the food is served we were all led—with enormous ceremony—to a separate wing they've had built to showcase their art. One room of which, the *main* room, the reason the wing was *built*, is specifically for me. I hadn't realized how much of my stuff she had. It was like seeing my entire life nailed to the walls. And there, at the end of this gallery, is a huge space dedicated to a single painting from my 'Dark Side' series. It's very big. I used nearly a bucket of burnt umber on that one alone. Spot-lit, in full glory, probably the best thing I've ever done. And the hostess stands there and regales everybody with how, in the nine months since the wing was built, she's made sure every guest comes and sees this work of mine, and how they all tell her how marvelous it is. And she raised her glass to me, and then to the painting, and the assembled company spontaneously broke into applause."

Greg was looking down at the sidewalk now. I knew how he'd be feeling, and also that we were running out of time. "So what's your point?" he muttered.

"It'd been hung sideways," I said.

As we walked back to the building I saw the festival organizer waiting in the doorway. She looked relieved to see us.

"Everybody is downstairs," she said. "Waiting. It's amazing. There's over three hundred people."

"Cool," Greg said. "Let them get settled. Five minutes. You not going down?"

She shook her head apologetically. "I don't like the dark."

I followed Greg into the big antechamber, which was now empty. "So what is this thing of yours tonight anyway?"

"Borderline plagiarism," Greg said, looking slightly embarrassed. "Which is why you were in my mind, and probably why I dissed you to that woman earlier, if I'm honest. Actually, I'm pretty sure we talked it into shape together, some long drunken night of yesteryear. But the initial idea was yours."

"Idea for what?"

"'The Scariest Thing in the World.'"

For a second I had no idea what he was talking about. Then I remembered. "*Christ*," I said.

He rolled his eyes. "I know, right? The years go by."

I nodded, though he'd misunderstood. I hadn't meant how long it was since we'd talked about a "psychological horror" installation—though yes, it had to be a quarter of a century. I'd meant how dumb and sad it was to go ahead and actually do it.

It had seemed grown-up and cool back then, before we were real adults. Get people down into a confined space. Turn off the lights, deaden the sound, close the door so that nobody can find their way out, and make them stay there for half an hour.

The idea being to demonstrate that it wasn't horror, or the fantastical, that was truly frightening. That those are merely entertainments, distractions, safe spaces, crèches for our anxieties—and the real and oldest horror, the scariest thing in the world, is being alone in the dark.

Very big, right? Very *deep*.

Back then. Now it felt woefully simplistic and juvenile, cool and edgy only before you'd had to deal with grown-up stuff like the lingering death of parents or marriages exploding into bloody shards: before you'd learned that the deepest pit is not the dark, but our own fears and doubts, regrets and wrong paths and mistakes: before you'd found yourself looking around in panic and not understanding where you are or how you got there, or in which direction—if any—a meaningful future lies. All Hallow's Eve is supposed to be when the walls of reality come down, and the dark spirits walk abroad and knock on doors.

But the truth is, they're already inside.

The idea we'd once nurtured was adolescent and naïve, and I knew that when people left the venue tonight, Greg's career would be over forever, killed with quiet laughter.

THE SCARIEST THING IN THE WORLD

The scandal would have been a better way to go.

"Well, good luck," I said, however. "And the funny thing is, I remember the idea being yours anyhow."

He looked at me with an expression I'd never seen on his face before. Or anybody's, probably. Only someone pretty close to the very end of their tether lets emotions like that out of the back of their mind, and far enough to show in the eyes.

Bitter gratitude, mangled with utter desperation.

"Your stuff's okay," he said, quietly. "You know that. And I know you didn't actually sell out."

"You don't think?"

"No. You just choked."

He said this with offhand authority, and for a moment I was back to being the twenty-three-year-old I was when I first met Greg. He was a couple of years older than me. Far more self-assured. Better-connected, part of the scene. Already making waves. Confident he was going to carve his mark on the world.

"Of all of us," he said, "you were the one who could have punched a hole. I knew it then. Which is why I was kind of an asshole to you at times." He shrugged. "Ah well. That ship sailed, I guess. Too late for any of us now."

"Life goes on."

"For better or worse." He smiled, genuinely. And gestured with his head. "Show time."

I followed him to the big door in the corner of the room, and started down the stairs after him into the lower area. Basement, crypt, whatever it was. All the lights down there had been turned off. There was a distant rustle of all the people wandering around the corridors, in the pitch-dark, waiting for this thing to start, not yet knowing what it was, but the sound was soft, deadened. Dead.

Before we were even at the bottom of the stairs I realized Greg wasn't as dumb as I'd thought.

This felt like going somewhere unsafe.

This was a place where, like everybody else, I'd be forced to look inside. To think about a world in which I'd stuck with what I'd been doing, and turned out to be the same kind of genuinely interesting footnote to history Greg was, and possibly even remained his friend. Or where I'd parlayed the TV show into one on a bigger network, maybe even taken up one of several offers to direct a movie, instead of listening to the quiet inner voices that told me no, I'd screw it up. Where I'd had the courage to turn down endless commissions and instead spend sufficient time on the woman I loved, giving her enough attention to still have her, instead of losing her to a broken heart.

But I didn't. I choked each time. I got to the edge but couldn't make myself jump over. Couldn't take the risk of stretching my soul until it broke, and instead failed my way upwards into something that only looked like success from the outside.

The scariest thing in the world is the widening gap between who you are, and who you *wanted* to be, and the truth was that Greg wasn't the only faker here tonight.

That was a fact worth learning. But I didn't have to spend half an hour having it hammered home. "I've got to take a piss," I said. "I'll be right back."

"Sure," Greg said, face blank. "Close the door on the way out. And keep having a great life." He walked away into the darkness, dismissing me. He knew I wasn't intending to come back.

I hesitated. Maybe it would actually be good for me to confront myself, to stumble those interior corridors for a while, trying to find a way out. But I didn't want to.

I turned and headed back up the stairs.

The festival organizer was standing outside on the street. She looked around quickly when I came out of the building, caught in the act of having a cigarette break.

"Your secret's safe with me," I said.

Surprised, and side-lit by the uplighter by the door, she actually did look kind of like Elsa Lanchester, or close enough. She smiled gratefully. "You're not staying?"

"It's been a long day. And I don't want there to be any distractions after the show. It's going to be a big success, and I want to make sure Greg gets all the credit. He's going to get what he always wanted."

THE SCARIEST THING IN THE WORLD

"And what was that?"

"To be remembered."

"I suppose it's what we all want, yes?"

I just smiled and walked away.

After a few minutes I found a cab and got in and sat in the back, not listening as a chatty driver took me to the Hilton through dark, wet streets: back to another hotel in yet another city, back to my great life.

I was glad that I had not stayed for the show, that instead of following the path of least resistance I had made a decision and done something. I was glad that I, for once, had not choked. And I felt fine about the fact that, before securely closing the heavy door to the basement full of people come to see the installation, I'd held my lighter down to the nearest bundle of straw, waited until it caught alight, and then watched as the flames started to spread.

THE SEVENTEENTH
KIND

Hi. I'm James Richard.

No, not 'Richards', but 'Richard'. Dumb name, I think you'll agree. No, it's okay. Really. I've had many years to savor it, to laboriously spell it out over the phone and yet find parcels arriving at my door marked for Richard James anyhow. I didn't even make it up. It's not a stage name. My parents gave it to me when I was born, bless them—along with a straight nose, wavy brown hair and virtually no talent at all.

'Why,' I asked my father one time, back when I was young in years and full of hope, 'Why in the name of sweet Jesus did you call me James Richard?'

He stared down at me, confused, and I belatedly realized he was in the same predicament. His name was David. David Richard. Maybe when he was young his peers also snarled, "Hey, shithead—why have you got two first names?" For a moment I felt a strange and poignant affinity with my dad, as if we were holding hands down the years, two small boys a generation apart who'd shouldered a similar burden. Then I kicked him in the shin.

Anyway. This isn't about my name. This is about what I do, and what I do is I'm a presenter on a shopping channel. No, go ahead. Laugh all you like. Just the stupidest job in the whole damned universe, right? Well, you know what, *screw you*. If I hear one more person say a chimp could do my job, then I'm going to take some innovative and durable kitchen implement—retailing in stores for $19.99 but available for this hour only at the low-low price of $11.99 plus postage and packing—and shove it up their ass. This is a skill. It really is.

And it saved my life.

I wound up in home shopping via a circuitous route. Everyone does. Nobody wakes up one morning thinking "Hey, I want to be on live cable selling people shit they don't need." Or perhaps they do, in which case they genuinely *are* stupid. Maybe they think it counts as television, and is therefore glamorous. It's not. The point of being on the tube is first, to earn big bucks; second, to be recognized in the street. Anyone who tells you different is a moron. What—they instead want the unsociable hours, the danger of being sacked at any moment, the ever-present threat of exposure and embarrassment, not to mention the joy of standing under hot lights while hairy-backed yahoos point cameras at you and swop impenetrable menial jokes behind your back? The money in cable really isn't that great, and the people you actually *want* to recognize you are pretty young things of the opposite sex. Or of the same sex, whatever. You work a shopping channel, then these are not the people who are going to be recognizing you. They're going to be...well, I'll come to that.

I was an actor originally. I was profoundly average, and there's only so many times you can emote your heart out to scraggly-bearded directors to then be told you're insufficiently tall or Turkish-looking or female or frankly even any *good*. So I switched to stand-up as a kind of holding pattern. Easier to get gigs, but the money stinks like fish and I couldn't write my own jokes so I was going nowhere fast. Finally there was a spell on a local radio news station for which cattle made up the main demographic. That was *really* grim. It was while I was there, reading out the weather and listening to the neurons in my brain popping one by one, that I saw a trade ad for a presenter on a cable channel. I combed the straw out of my hair, jumped on a plane and went and did my thing. I dug deep, gave it everything I had. I was desperate.

I got the gig.

Now. If you don't do any home shopping then I'm going to have to explain the deal to you. (If you do, then just skip-read or have a sandwich or something. I'll be back in a minute). How it works is this. The channels

THE SEVENTEENTH KIND

basically have a pile of goods which they want to sell. Pots and pans. Jewelry. Gardening implements. Technical gizmos for the home. Limited Edition Star Trek™ bathmats. The buy-me inducements they offer are severalfold. First, the goods are cheap. No store overheads, plus the advantages of buying in bulk. Two, you just pick up the phone and give a credit card number (hell, just your *name*, if you're a returning customer) and the thing will be with you in a couple days—without you even having to get up off your couch. I assume when it drops through your mailbox you have to get up and go fetch it, or maybe these people have someone who does that for them too.

The third inducement is people like me. The presenters. Your friend on the screen.

As the audience, this is what you see. A live picture of the object in question, with a panel at one side telling you the cost and the product code and just how beguilingly cheap it is compared to regular in-store prices. You listen to a voice-over, with cutaways to the presenter's face and upper body as he or she tells you how much the thing costs (in case you can't read), how many are left to buy ('Only three quarters of stock left now—this one's moving *incredibly* quickly everybody, so hurry hurry, pick up your phone and make that call, operators are standing by...') and also explains to the hard-of-thinking why they should want the damn thing in the first place. If it's a ring, for example, my job would be to remind you that you could put it on your finger and wear it for cosmetic purposes, in order to enhance your attractiveness and/or perceived status. You think I'm kidding. I'm really not.

Sounds easy, but wait. Sometimes you may have to fill twenty minutes with this crap. *You* try talking for *half* that time, non-stop—with no help, no cues and moreover with people pointing cameras at you and some fool chattering in your ear—explaining why someone would want to buy an enormous cookie jar shaped like a chicken, and you'll begin to see it's not as easy as it sounds. Most of the presenters cheat. They'll repeat themselves endlessly, rehearsing the remaining stock levels time and again just to give themselves something to say. I never did that. I never dried. I also never said anything like "Today's special value today is really special," as one of my colleagues once did; nor "In the sixteenth century was the Renaissance, and garnet was a stone", another of my personal favorites.

MICHAEL MARSHALL SMITH

I didn't do these things because when I found myself in this weird job it was like I'd come home. I knew it was worthless, but on the other hand I thought: Hey—perhaps this is something I could be *good* at. Maybe this was a corner of an ill-regarded field which I could make forever James Richard. Most of the stuff the channel pushed was skull-crushingly dull, but that didn't mean you couldn't talk about it. Okay, so it might be a hideous hexagonal pendant in faux gold with a miniscule pseudo-emerald in the middle: but you could point out how *delightfully* hexagonal it was, and how neatly the 'emeraldite' sat in its exact center. You could measure it with the special Home Mall ruler, just in case someone in the audience didn't understand perspective and was worried that the pendant was as big as a house. You could tell them how *many* different occasions they'd find to wear it, and list them, and generally evoke just how unspeakably lovely their lives would become—all because of this twenty dollar piece of costume jewelry.

The whole time you're working you have the director talking at you, relaying sales information through a plug in your ear. But I only mentioned availability twice, three times in each hour. At most. Just enough to keep people on their toes, to convince them they ought to get working that phone. And you can believe this—when I was doing the selling, the units started shifting. That sounds arrogant, I guess. Well, maybe; and so what? For all the times some shithead casting agent dumped on me; for all the times I died on a small stage because the jokes I wrote weren't funny; for all the times I was shown I couldn't do a job well enough to be proud of myself—now I had Home Mall to demonstrate I could do *something*.

So what if no-one respected it? I could *do it*.

That's what counts.

Which is why, after a couple of months, I found myself doing a lot of the Specials.

Every evening there'd be a product the station had some particular deal on. They'd wheel on the manufacturer or some other front person with the promise of shifting extra units, and stick him or her on the screen to demonstrate the product. These slots lasted a whole hour, and of course needed a professional to guide the civilian through the live television experience. To keep things running smoothly. And increasingly that professional was me.

THE SEVENTEENTH KIND

Talking about something for ten minutes is one thing. An hour is a *whole* different kettle of ballgames. The big factor you have in your favor is that you aren't just a talking torso any more. You're there, live on camera, standing next to some guy demonstrating a Blu-ray player or salad shooter or car wrench. You can use everything about yourself, not just your voice. Employ your body to suggest things, use hand movements, shrug; if you weren't too proud you could even pout winsomely. God knows I've pouted on occasion, winsomely and otherwise.

All that helped, but the Specials were still tough, and I enjoyed the challenge. As the months went on I might resort to a little cocaine on occasion to keep myself humming along; but my main juice was pure adrenaline. That and a genuine drive to dance the jig of semi-relevance, to keep the balls in the air when they didn't deserve to be up there in the first place—to *just keep talking.*

To communicate with the viewer at home.

Once the products were shifting nicely, you see, we'd start taking calls from people who were buying the merchandise. Initially this was the part of the job that most freaked me out. I mean, who the hell *were* these people? What were they doing, calling a shopping channel at 1.30 a.m. on a Wednesday night to tell us why they'd bought some neo-bosnium trinket? And why? Didn't they have beds to go to? Didn't they have *lives?* Ninety-five percent of the callers were middle-aged women, too, which I found especially hard to get my head around. I could have understood guys in their twenties, maybe, too stoned to change the channel, or thinking they were being ironic. I even suggested to Rod that we should have a Stoner Hour, where we sold big bags of candy and potato chips along with small glittering baubles which might appeal to the chemically-enhanced mind. People would call up in droves, go to bed later and forget all about it, and then be completely bemused when boxes of munchies arrived a couple days later. We could probably get away with not sending out the product at all, which would be a big fat profit all round. (The idea wasn't taken up, which I think reveals commercial timidity).

I quickly realized that taking the calls was a crucial part of the selling process, however, and made it my specialty. Because nobody called in to say that something they'd bought was a piece of shit—they rang in to say it was fabulous. They wanted to say something nice, which meant that everyone else listening got a ringing product endorsement from *someone who was just like them*. I would imagine these callers, dumpy and dough-faced, sitting in darkened rooms around the country, their faces lit by the flicker of the selling screen. Just occasionally I believed that once they'd finished talking to us they abruptly switched off, like abandoned robots, their heads tilting forwards onto their chests, hands folded in their laps—and that they would remain that way until the following night, when they got a chance to talk about their obsessions again. Sometimes this impression was stronger, and I felt I could imagine them all at once, all sitting in their rooms, bathed in the twinkling eeriness of television light, eyes focused on the screen, their loneliness and need pouring back through the cables towards me.

God Bless Cocaine.

The job settled into a rhythm. I'd do a couple of sessions late afternoon or early evening, standard stuff—then at the beginning of the late shift, somewhere between 10 p.m. and 1 a.m., I'd do a Special. The late shift is when the real action starts, when the heavy hitters of couch potato-purchasing settle down with their buckets of soda and sacks of potato chips and get into their stride. The products varied wildly but that was part of the fun. The manufacturers were also mixed, from a monosyllabic sauté pan dude who said maybe three words all hour, to a woman I worked with selling a home organ, who was damned nearly as good as me. *Christ* did that woman know a lot about organs. I thought she'd never shut up.

Then...okay: here we go.

The night in question I was doing a Special for a cleaning product called Supa Shine. Some guy from Texas had spent ten years working on polishes and finally come up with a real humdinger. The stuff had been on the channel once before but this was the first time it had got its own segment. When I heard what the Special was that evening I thought even *I* was going to have some trouble. Metal polish: it's useful, it may even be essential to some people. But say what you like, it's really just not very exciting.

An hour before we were due to go on air I dropped by the green room to meet the guy. Rusty, his name was. He was about fifty, grey-haired, bearded

THE SEVENTEENTH KIND

and kind of heavy round the gut, but affable enough in a good-old-boy kind of way—and wow, did he like his job. I'm not kidding. Polishing was this guy's *life*. He'd got into town early that morning and straightaway gone trawling junk stores and antiqueries picking up old bits of silver and copper to use on the show. He showed me how to use the product. The polish was a silvery paste which came in a very small tin. You put a subliminal amount on a rag, wiped it over your metal in a desultory way and then rubbed it off.

And it worked. It worked to a freakish degree. I was genuinely impressed. He took an old coin, so dirty and corroded it looked more like a disk of wood, and after about ten seconds it looked better than the day it popped out of the mint. I relaxed. Okay, so polish was dull. But this stuff worked, by Jesus. Selling something that works is never too hard.

I hung out for a while, took a couple of minutes in the john to tip my chemical balance in the direction of enthusiasm, then got the five minute call. I murmured encouraging things to Rusty—who'd begun to tremble slightly—and strode out under the lights. I don't know why I did that, because we weren't on air. They always cut in with you already in position. But I always stride on anyway. Call it professional pride.

Then the floor manager counts you down, the light on Camera One goes red, and you're on. It's showtime. Suddenly it's not just you and some perspiring Southerner—it's you and the rest of the world. Well, the world that's up and watching a shopping channel at 12:02 a.m., anyway.

I started the hour with a searching but light-hearted meditation on the amount of old metal ware in people's houses, and went on to muse how folks would get a lot more fun out of antique stores and yard sales if it weren't for the prospect of having to *clean* their prizes when they got them home. I didn't mention the other metal in people's houses—the silverware, furniture, the facias of ovens and TVs. Not yet. Throw out all your ideas in the first minute on a Special, and by twenty after the hour you're going to be treading water until you drown.

I segued direct from this into Rusty doing his thing. He was okay, even pretty good. There was something so down-home about him that you couldn't help but watch. 'Christ,' you were soon thinking, 'this guy's fucking *obsessed*. If he gets off this much on polishing, there's *got* to be something in it. Let me have a try.'

He took a pair of old candlesticks, equally tarnished. Talking slowly, he described the process of using his wonder-polish, demonstrating as he went. I didn't do much more than provide an echo every now and then—'Okay, so you put it on a *cloth*, right?'—because I knew as the hour progressed he'd run out of steam. A minute later one of the candlesticks was looking brighter than the day it was made. I'd kind of preferred it with the tarnish, to be honest: for me taking an antique and making it look new was like sprucing up Stonehenge with fiberglass. But I knew that the audience would feel differently, and Rod the director was already chattering happily in my earpiece. The calls had started right away, and Supa Shine was out of the starting blocks.

For the next fifteen minutes Rusty tirelessly polished and buffed. I tried it myself, of course, affably pouring the full weight of my personality into restoring the shine to a variety of pieces of old trash—while being careful to make it clear that James Richard, like the viewer at home, had no pre-existing expertise in the field. We did gold, we did silver, we did copper, we did chrome. They all worked spectacularly. We actually had to start being careful about the way we held the pieces because the glitter was throwing the cameras off.

Twenty-five minutes in I took over from Rusty, helping him out of a circuitous ramble he'd trapped himself into. The calls were really flooding in by now; Supa Shine was shifting big time.

It was time to start talking to people.

Our first call was typical. Lori from Black Falls rang to say that she'd bought Supa Shine when it'd been on before and it had changed her life. She described in detail how she's polished everything in her street and how happy that had made her. She'd called this evening to buy stocks for her sisters, daughters and friends. She was so patently sincere that I let her run on for quite some while, knowing she was doing our job for us. Rusty nodded benignly, dislodging a small droplet of sweat from his hairline, which rolled slowly onto his forehead. I covertly signaled the director to switch to a close up product shot, and Mandy the makeup girl darted on to powder us both.

THE SEVENTEENTH KIND

No more than six seconds, then back to a medium shot of the two of us, and all the while I kept the banter going with the caller until she'd said all she had to say.

Lori finally stopped yakking and went off to polish her dog's head and we took a call from Ann in Raenord. Ann had called because she was concerned that Supa Shine might harm her gold-plated jewelry. Rusty whipped a piece of plated stuff off the pile and polished it there and then. It came up beautifully, and Ann was mollified. She thanked us for talking to her and was transferred to the purchase operators.

It was a natural point to take five, and so I signaled to Rod and talked us into a short break…giving just a hint of some of the exciting polishing action still to come.

As soon as the ident was on the screen I winked at Rusty, and disappeared behind the set and into the green room. None of the production staff batted an eyelid. I'd left a line chopped and ready on the one table which wasn't covered with various crap from previous specials, and so it was the matter of a moment to get the marching dust into my bloodstream.

I strode back into the studio—taking care to grab a glass of water for cover—and stood next to Rusty. 'Going great,' I enthused. 'Just had a word with the guys—you're selling by the *shit*load.'

Rusty smiled shyly, and I noticed that another droplet of sweat was forming. Mandy swabbed, Rod counted us back in and we were on air less than three minutes after I'd left.

The next five minutes were fine. Rusty told us how it would only take two cans of Supa Shine to clean an entire 747, and it didn't seem hard to believe. I must admit that by this time I was kind of wondering what was in the stuff: the pile of metal in front of us was gleaming so much it was starting to hurt my eyes. I got Rusty to tell his story about working in his mother's garage for ten years coming up with the formula, then decided it was time to take another call.

And that's…where the evening went a little *weird*.

'Hi,' I said, smiling direct to Camera One. 'So, who do we have come to talk with us now?'

The normal response to this is the caller's name and location, uttered promptly and clearly. They've been briefed by an operator and most of them blurt the information out super-fast, as if eager to prove they can follow instructions properly and will make a great addition to the show.

This time, however, there was a silence.

Which is fine, it happens—sometimes people get overawed once they realize they're really on air. The tactic then is to ask them a *very simple question* to start them off.

'Have you already experienced Supa Shine's cleaning miracles, caller?' I asked. 'Or do you have a question for our friend Rusty here before you try it?'

Usually that'll do it. The silence continued, however, and I began to let my right hand wander up towards my neck—in preparation for the agreed code for cutting a caller off.

But then the caller spoke. 'He's not Rusty.'

The voice was deep and ragged and wet and rough. My heart sank. Every now and then one of the directors, Rod in particular, would let a weird one slip through. The stated intention was 'keeping it real', but as Rod wouldn't know real if it slapped him upside the head I believed it was more likely to be about fucking up the presenter for the delight of the assembled spear carriers. Kind of irresponsible when the product was shifting so well, but that's assholes for you.

'Well, not *literally*, of course,' I pouted (winsomely). 'But you know what? It wouldn't surprise me one bit to find that Supa Shine wasn't only great with stains and tarnish—but could handle a little spot of rust as well. In fact, I was just going to ask...'

'His *name* isn't Rusty,' the voice said. It sounded like the guy had the world's worst ever cold. Or flu. Or maybe the plague.

'Well, no, it's kind of a nickname, isn't it?' I chuckled. 'No-one gets called Rusty right off the bat, do they? Just like some of my friends call me Jim. And so caller, while we're talking, what's *your* name?'

There was no reply.

Screw this, I thought. I very obviously scratched my Adam's apple. In other words, *get this loser off the air*. Meanwhile I turned to Rusty, who was

THE SEVENTEENTH KIND

starting to look nervous. That's often the way with the guests. When things start well they can get lulled into forgetting they're on live television—but it's a perilous relaxation. The smallest upset can unsettle them for good.

'So how *about* that, Rusty?' I asked, holding his eyes to lock him back into where he was, and what he was doing. 'Obviously Supa Shine isn't going to be able to cope if something's totally *covered* in rust, kind of falling apart, but how about a little spot or two?'

Rusty opened his mouth to speak, but then a very bizarre noise came over the studio monitor. It sounded like a loud, liquid cough, mixed up with the sound of a handful of nails being dropped on a metal surface.

'Whoa! I apologize for that, viewers,' I laughed. 'Little technical glitch here in the studio, don't know if you heard it at home—just goes to show that we really are *live* tonight in your living room, live and *alive*, bringing you the very best in bargains 24/7. So...'

Then the noise happened again.

I laughed once more, throwing my hands up in the air for good measure—as if helpless with mirth at the hilarious events which tumbled through life: not just *my* life, you understand, but the lives of the viewers at home too.

Then something else came over the speakers. The deep, broken voice said: 'That's my name.'

'What?' I said, momentarily thrown.

'That's my name,' the voice repeated. Then the strange liquid noise rumbled through the speakers again. 'That's it.'

'That...noise is your name?'

'Yes.'

'Well make sure you spell it out when you talk to our purchase operators...' I said, with a wink directly into camera—to the normal man and woman on the couch, 'because I'm not sure they'll have come across that one before. Eastern European, is it?'

'No.'

'Well okay then. I know that we have many, *many* other viewers out there who really want to share their experiences with Rusty's Supa Shine polish with us, so maybe if...'

'It's not his.'

By now I was finally beginning to get pissed off. The entire exchange had probably only actually taken forty seconds, but that's a *long* time on live television. Rusty was looking extremely wary again now, and a whole army of perspiration drops were massed at the hair line, ready to roll down his face. That could *not* happen, not on my watch. Nobody wants to buy something from a guy who's sweating like a pig.

I made the cut sign again, even more clearly.

'Jim, there's something odd going on.'

This voice didn't come out over the speakers, but only into my earpiece. It was Rod.

I turned to Rusty and cheerfully suggested he show us his polish working magic on the second candlestick, which was a weak gambit, but I needed a few seconds' cover.

As I watched him get to this, I raised my eyebrows quickly, just about the only way I could communicate to the box that I needed to hear more.

Rod spoke again, and what he said was strange. 'We can't get this joker off the air.'

I risked a glance off. Normally you never do this. You look direct to the camera, at the object, or at your civilian co-host. Anywhere else looks weird to the viewer at home, reminding them you're in a studio. But I swept my eyes quickly over the window to the director's booth—their lair was sealed from the studio so chatter and techspeak didn't leak onto live microphones—and saw Rod standing and looking directly at me, his hands held up in professional mime-quality 'I have no fucking clue what is going on' pose.

Behind him a couple of techs were moving quickly about the room fiddling with wires. By this time I had done many, many hours of live television. I'd never seen something like that before. I realized there and then that I was entering new and uncharted territory.

'He has stolen it,' said the speaker voice, loudly.

'Stolen what?' I said.

'His so-called polish. It is not his. It belongs to us.'

I was still trying conjure a response to this when I heard Rod's voice in my ear once more. He wasn't speaking directly to me this time, but what he said was so weird I decided that from then on I was just going to ignore everything except what was happening in front of me. Rod's voice was on the edge of cracking.

'What the fuck do you mean?' he was shouting, to someone, 'Time is slowing *down*?'

I assumed he was bawling out some technician and it was some geek wires-and-sockets thing. Whatever. Their problem, not mine. If they couldn't get this idiot off the air I'd just have to plough on regardless. The show must go on, always. This was precisely what I got paid the big bucks for, Well, the bucks, anyway.

I smiled at Camera Two, the one currently showing a red light. 'Well, *thank* you caller, it's been great to hear your own special perspective on this. But right now I want to ask Rusty here something.'

I turned to my co-host, the first time I'd looked directly at him for maybe a minute or two. I should have checked back before. He'd got stressed, nervous, a big old dose of stage fright. The line of sweat droplets I'd seen forming earlier had decided to all go over the top at once, and fresh ranks were following in their wake—taking with them what appeared to be a thick layer of make-up. Every guest gets some pancake, to smooth out blotches and variations and make everyone look nice under the lights. This make-up was a lot thicker than that, though. And, I noticed, looked kind of like...latex.

I stared at Rusty.

Rusty looked back at me.

I noticed then that his eyes were perhaps suspiciously blue, too, as if they were contacts. And that where the make-up was running or melting or whatever it was doing, the skin underneath seemed to be both rough and warty and also an unusual color.

'Rusty,' I said, suspiciously, 'Are you...green?'

He turned away suddenly, tilting his head toward the speaker hanging above us, out of shot. He barked something angrily at it and now his voice didn't sound like it had before. It didn't sound like he was from the South. It sounded like a large bucket of nuts and bolts dropped down an old drain pipe. Then he made another sound, even louder. The force of the utterance caused a whole strip of skin to fall off one side of his face, revealing something that looked like a piece of steak that had been lying in a parking lot for a couple weeks.

'Okay,' I said, into the silence. 'So I'm guessing maybe you're not from East Texas after all?'

The voice from the speaker spoke once again. 'No, he is not,' it said. 'And his polish belongs to us. In reality it is a foodstuff. And we are running perilously low. It must be returned to us.'

'Okay, wait,' I said. 'Back up. Who's "us"? Who am I talking to?'

All around me, cameramen and production assistants and random techs were frozen like statues. No-one was doing anything anymore. They were staring up at the speaker from which the voice was coming, and all looked like they'd never move again, like their minds so wanted to be somewhere else that their bodies had been left to their own devices for a while.

But I'm different. Used to the challenges of going live.

And a goddamned professional, too.

'We are from a planet you do not have a name for,' the voice said. 'In our tongue it is called…' And he made a sound I'm not even going to try to describe. You wouldn't want to hear it outside your house late at night, that's for sure. 'The being you call "Rusty" is one of us. We are allowed to leave the ship every now and then on a strict rotation basis. But he has outstayed his leave. And he is selling what belongs to us alone.'

'Wait there a second,' I said, holding my hand up. 'Ship? What kind of ship?'

'A scout ship.'

'From where? Okay, right, the unpronounceable place.' I turned to the being that I had previously been introduced to as Rusty. 'But what are you *doing* here?'

'We have been experiencing technical difficulties,' Rusty/it muttered, his voice now halfway between Southern drawl and hacking flu-cough. 'Because the captain is a complete…'

And then suddenly he/it vanished.

The thing that had been Rusty was gone, leaving only a small pile of clothes, two vivid blue contact lenses and a head and beard wig, lying on the floor.

And over the speaker came the sound of something very bad and physical and permanent happening.

Suddenly there *was* movement amongst the assembled people in the studio. Some running, a little shrieking, a lot of men and women crying out. But it didn't amount to much. I heard someone in back shouting that all the doors had mysteriously become locked. I glanced over at the window to the control booth once more and saw everyone in there was still standing still, watching me through the glass. I think Rod was still shouting things in my ear, too, but I wasn't listening. He was never any help.

'If you're some kind of scout ship,' I said, talking directly to the disembodied voice again, 'how come you can't just phone home? Contact the mothership or whatever, tell them you've got issues and to send help?'

There was a pause, then something that sounded a little like a human cough.

'We're not supposed to be here,' the voice said.

'Why?'

'Long story,' the voice said.

'You got lost?'

'No,' the voice said, irritably, as if I'd opened a huge great can of worms. 'We were going to invade. But there was some last-minute discussion onboard over the ethics of the thing. Your world is protected, theoretically, and there was some…heated discussion. A small amount of equipment damage ensued. The remote control for the radial neo-transponder matrix got stepped on, and without it the ship doesn't work.'

'So you're *stuck?*'

'Yes.'

'For how long?'

There was something like a sigh, a sound that reverberated through the studio like a gust of wind wandering alone through the Grand Canyon, in the dead of night.

'Eleven point five thousand of your years.'

'Jesus,' I said. 'That's quite a layover.'

'Yes. To be honest, the time's beginning to drag.'

'I'm not surprised. Holy cow. Where are you, exactly?'

'In a mountain.'

'In a…'

'I don't want to talk about it.'

'And you're completely alone here?'

'There's a crew down in Key West. But not our kind. They're spindly. And assholes, actually. And they won't help.'

'Have you tried changing the batteries?'

There was a pause. 'Excuse me?'

'Well,' I said, 'this radial neo-transponder matrix widget or whatever sounds like the kind of thing that's going to need some juice, right? Couldn't it just be the batteries went flat? Have you checked?'

There was a long, long pause. I mean—really, *really* long. Another cough. Then a further pause. Finally: 'I don't believe our technicians have explicitly evaluated that possibility, no.'

'You think maybe they...should?'

'Even if your suggestion had merit, the batteries of our kind are completely different from yours. Actually...do you say different "from" or different "to"?'

'Whichever,' I said. 'You're the boss.'

'They are both different from and different to your batteries. They are transquantum piso-structures one mile square in five dimensions. And not available here.'

'Have you tried a universal remote?'

'Universal remote?'

'Sure,' I said. 'In fact...wait here.'

I ran out of the studio, back into the green room, and searched through the various piles of crap spread all over it. Spare jackets and ties, bits and pieces left from other random segments, free samples from previous Special hours. After a minute—thank god—I found what I was looking for, and which I *thought* I'd remembered seeing a couple nights before.

Then I strode back out into the studio, already talking direct to camera as I hit the floor.

'Do *you* suffer from "remote proliferation"?' I asked. 'Is *your* den deluged under a pile of remotes, your sitting room swamped with switches and kitchen ka-flumped with kontrols, each one designed to work with only one piece of equipment? Do you have one for the television, one for the satellite, one for DVD, CD...maybe even one for the cat? You do, right? So do I. Or I *did*, that is, until I discovered the Relco Universal OmniRemote.'

I triumphantly held up the remote I'd found. It caught one of the big lights overhead, and glittered like a chalice.

THE SEVENTEENTH KIND

'Truly, my friends, this is a leap forward in both technology and tidiness, a breakthrough in convenience and style. I'll tell you right now—and regular viewers know I don't say this often—I've even got one of these babies myself at home. I'd have two, but...'—and here I paused for a trademark winsome smile to camera: I was back in the zone—'...you'll only *need* one, right?'

'We don't have a den,' said the voice over the speaker. 'This is a spaceship.'

'I get that,' I said, 'My point is you could maybe use one of these things. Reprogram it to work a radial neo-transponder monkey, or whatever it is you said.'

'Hmm,' said the voice. 'Hold on a minute.'

There was a brief humming sound, followed by utter silence. Then the voice came back.

'Put it in the middle of the floor.'

'What?'

'The device of which you speak. Put it in the middle of the floor with a minimum of two Trajelian Nippits of clear space all around it. That's approximately a 'yard', in your currency.'

I walked out from behind the counter and placed the remote carefully in the middle of the floor. Then I stepped back, shooing the cameramen and production flunkies away, so there was a lot of space around it.

'You got it,' I said. 'Now what?'

There was a sudden rushing sound, followed by a brief whirr. Both sounded as if they came from inside my own head. Then a simple and very loud *ping*.

And the remote on the floor had disappeared.

And everything was silent.

There was not a sound in the studio. Everyone stood, waiting. It was as if the world outside had disappeared.

Then, from over the speaker, came a noise that sounded like distant and somewhat relieved cheering.

Everyone in the studio looked at each other.

'Well, who knew,' said the rough, liquid voice, coming back. 'So the monkey-people finally came up with something useful. Point to you.'

'You're welcome,' I said. 'So now you're free to go?'

'Our engines are coming up to speed as we speak. We are going to need that tin of 'polish' on the counter there, though. Leave no man behind. Or evidence, I mean.'

I picked up the tin of Supa Shine and went around to put it in the cleared space in the floor. Wind/whirr/ping—and it was gone.

'Remain right where you are,' the voice said.

I stayed put, frozen in the middle of the floor.

'You have been helpful, people of Earth. We are grateful. Now...we're going to have to destroy you all.'

'What?'

'You know too much.'

'We know shit,' I protested. 'Really. Zip. Nada. Especially me.'

'Sorry,' the voice said. 'Health and safety.'

People began to break down in earnest then. They knew this was the end. They understood suddenly that this was irrevocable, that no argument, however cogent, well-argued or frankly even *right*, would ever make a difference once the twin godhead of health and safety had been invoked.

'Well, look, Christ,' I spluttered anyway, knowing I had to keep talking until the very end. 'That seems kind of harsh, you know? We fixed your, you know, that thing that was broken. We helped you out, right?'

'No,' the voice said. '*You did.* Say goodbye.'

I looked around the studio, at the people all terrified and flinching, the tear-running faces and trembling shoulders. I glanced at Max and Clive and Jeff, the camera and lights crew, not looking so tough now. At Mandy from make-up, and Trix and Pinky the PA girls, and finally through the window at Rod and his open-mouthed producers and other familiars: at these people, my colleagues and acquaintances, the people I had worked with, these fellow-toilers at the sharp end of retail.

These humans. Every single one of them remains burned into my mind. They're the last I ever saw.

'Goodby...' was all I got out.

Then my mind went white, and there was the sound of wind, and then a whir, and then a ping.

***

THE SEVENTEENTH KIND

The viewers at home never saw me vanish, or what happened to Rusty. They never even heard the strange voice over the speakers—all they saw was a whacky few seconds where James Richard seemed to be going seriously off message...before the Home Mall signal went fuzzy for a couple minutes. Then the channel abruptly left the air forever, as the studio, warehouse and surrounding city block was vaporized—by what was later explained, I gather, as an unexpected meteorite. I guess the CIA or NSA or some other bunch of spooks covered the whole thing up somehow. Clearly *someone* back at home knows where Earth stands in the bigger picture—since I've been away I discovered there's even a secret website at www...oh, I guess I shouldn't say. But that's how I know the official US government classification for what happened to me: a close encounter of the seventeenth kind, one involving 'a commercial transaction conducted over some form of mass telecommunication (including but not limited to television, radio or particle net sub-rotation) and involving individual items valued at one hundred dollars or less'. It's kind of rare. In fact I think I may have been the first. To survive, anyhow.

So—there's the scoop on how I came to be here, like you asked.

Edit as you see fit, of course—I know it's kind of long for a press release. I'm sure my new agent will want other cuts too: the stuff about my name won't mean a lot to a guy called fLKccHL±±sgd0273-fx2, I guess.

Anyhoo. Got to go, bro. The bright lights call. I'm five minutes away from a two-hour pan-galactic Special for a consignment of mesquite-roasted Alpha Centaurian pengulnuts and their associated serving dishes and cookware. Yum yum. The buying public awaits eagerly, always, and James Richard is their friend, adviser and honest guide through the retail jungle...

...whatever damned planet they're from.

WHAT YOU MAKE IT

Finding a child was easy. It always was. You waited outside one of the convenience stores that lined the approach, or just trawled a strip mall at the nearby intersections for half an hour. There were always kids hanging around at night, pan-handling change for a burger or twenty minutes on a coin-op video game in one of the arcades. Or sometimes simply hanging there with nothing in particular in mind. You have to have seen something of the world to know what's worth looking for. These kids, the just-hanging kids, had seen nothing—and were often willing to be shown pretty much whatever you had in mind.

The only question was which one to pick.

Too old, either sex, and it looked weird at the Gate. Too young, and people tend to wonder where the kid's mother is at. And of course sometimes it depended, and you had to find one that looked right for the night.

Early teens was usually best. Acquiescent, not too scuffed up.

It only took Ricky ten minutes. She was sitting by herself on one of the benches outside Subway, looking at her feet or nothing in particular, alone in a yellow glow. Ricky cruised by the sandwich store twice in the twilight, noted that though there were two groups of kids nearby, one a little along the sidewalk and another loitering outside Publix, the girl didn't seem to have any link to either. She was all by herself. Mistake.

He parked the car, let the motor tick down to silence, and watched her a while. The nearest group of kids walked right by her, in and out of her pool of light, without a word being exchanged. She didn't even look up. She wasn't expecting friends.

Ricky grabbed his cigarettes off the dash, locked the car, and walked over.

She glanced at him as he approached, but without much curiosity. Something told him this wasn't indifference but a genuine ignorance of the kind of situations the world could provide. That meant she was even more likely to be what he needed, and it was good luck for her that it was Ricky's eye she'd caught, instead of some kind of fucking pervert.

'Waiting for someone?' he asked, stopping when he was a couple of yards away.

She looked up, then away. Didn't even shake her head.

He sat casually on the next bench along. 'Right. I know. Just a good place to sit.'

Ricky took out a cigarette and lit it, unhurried. She looked maybe twelve years old, pretty face. Blue eyes, fair hair in a ponytail. White T-shirt, blue jeans. Both recently clean. He noticed her eyes follow his discarded match as it skittered across the way and went out. Despite appearances, he had her attention.

'You hungry?'

She blinked, and her head turned a little toward him. Something changed. It always did. It's an elemental question. Even if you've just eaten enough to kill a man, you think about it. *Am I hungry? Have I had enough? Will I be okay?* And if you're really hungry, the question comes at you like you've been goosed, like someone's guessed your worst secret, how close you are to being cancelled out. Ricky knew how it worked. He'd been hungry in his time. Often, and very. You answer the hungry question quietly, so the vultures don't hear.

'Kinda,' she admitted, eventually.

He nodded, looking across the parking lot. Partly to check how many couples were hefting grocery bags to their breeder wagons; mainly to let the conversation settle.

'I could buy you something,' he said, casually. 'What's the matter? Your mom didn't feed you tonight?'

'Don't have a mom,' she said.

WHAT YOU MAKE IT

'What about your old man? Where's he at?'

The girl shrugged. Didn't matter whether she didn't know, or didn't want to know. Ricky knew now that she was his.

Ten minutes later, as he watched her wolf down her sandwich and fries, Ricky asked the question.

'How'd you like to visit Wonder World tonight?'

It was after eight by the time they got to the entrance. The line was pretty short. Ricky had known it would be: there was a parade every night at eight thirty, down 1st Street, and anyone with park-visiting in mind made sure they were already inside by then. Even the girl, whose name was Nicola, knew about the parade. Ricky told her this week it was at nine fifteen because it was a special parade. She looked at him dubiously, but seemed hopeful.

As he turned into one of the lanes and pulled up to the gate Ricky felt a faint flicker of anxiety. This was the part where it could all go wrong. It hadn't yet, because the kids had always wanted what they thought they were getting, but it could. It could go wrong tonight. It could go wrong any time. He wound down the window.

The gateman's head immediately bobbed out to grin at him. 'Hi there! I'm Marty the Gateman! How you doing?'

Marty the Gateman was in his fifties, dressed in an exaggerated version of the uniform of a cop from the 1940s. His face was pink with good cheer and makeup. Or alcohol. The gatemen in all the other lanes looked the same, and said exactly the same things.

Ricky grinned right back. 'I'm good. You?'

'Me? I'm great!' the man said, and laughed uproariously. When he did this, he leant back from the waist, placed a splayed hand on either side of his ribcage, and rubbed them up and down with each chortle, like a cartoon.

Nicola giggled.

Ricky let one hand drop to where the gun rested between the seat and the door, waited for the man to stop. Fucking loser. He imagined the guy going home after his shift, removing his stupid fucking costume, whacking off in front of the Internet. He had to do something like that, surely. Rick knew *he* would have done, that's for sure.

Eventually the man stopped laughing, wiped his eyes. 'Sheesh! So! Two happy travelers bound for the Wonder World! You just here for rides and fun and all the magic you can find?'

'No,' Nicola said, leaning over Ricky so she could smile up at the guy through the window. 'We're visiting Grandma too!'

Ricky relaxed. The girl was going to behave. Better still, she'd gotten into the part. They did, sometimes. Kids loved make-believe.

Marty winked. 'Lucky grandma! She know you're coming?'

'It's a surprise,' Nicola said, confidingly. 'She lives in Homeland 3.'

'Okeydokey!' the gateman yelped joyously, pulling a deck of tickets out of one of the oversize pockets on his uniform. 'So, Mr. Dad—how long you going to be spending with us?'

'An hour, maybe two,' Rick smiled. 'Depends on how strong Grandma's feeling.'

'Why don't we say three? Can always get you a rebate when you come out if she's too tired.'

'Sure, Marty. That'd be great.'

'All-righty!' Tongue sticking out of the corner of his mouth, Marty the Gateman tapped some buttons on the control unit on the side of his booth. As he tapped, the buttons got a little larger, and started moving around, so he had to keep his hand darting back and forth to keep up. Two twinkling animatronic eyes appeared at the top of the control unit, and one of them winked at Nicola. Within a few seconds, the buttons, brightly colored in primary hues, were a few inches long and bending every which way, evading Marty's fingers. Still the man poked at them, huffing and puffing.

'Hey!' he said, and Nicola laughed, when a couple of the buttons got even longer and started poking him back. When this gag was done, the gate man held a ticket out towards the machine, a slit opened in the unit in the shape of a cheerful mouth, and the ticket was popped inside, chewed for a moment, and then spat out, authorized. The eye winked at Nicola again, and suddenly the control unit returned to normal and Marty was waggling the ticket right under Ricky's nose.

Any other time or place, Marty would have lost his hand. But Ricky gave him the money, and the gate opened. The gateman waved at Nicola through the back window.

WHAT YOU MAKE IT

As the car started to pull forward, all of the faces in the gate structure—each a classic character from a Wonder World cartoon, every one hand-tweaked by liars into joyous perfection—swiveled their eyes towards the car and started to sing.

China Duck was there, Loopy Hound and Careful Cat, Bud and Slap the Happy Rats and Goren the fucking Gecko and countless others, every face already hard-wired into your mind, no matter how hard you'd always ignored them.

'The magic is what you make it,' they sang, a sonic tower of saccharine harmonies. 'Make it, make it... The magic is what you...'

Ricky wound up the windows.

Lit a cigarette and stepped on the gas.

The kid was quiet as they headed towards Homeland 3. She had plenty to look at, and she drank it in as though—even in darkness—it was the greatest thing she had ever seen. Maybe it was. Ricky had seen it all before.

Monorail tracks arced gracefully in all directions, linking park to park. Mostly quiet for the evening, but occasionally a streamlined shape would swoosh past the road or over their heads. Taking happy families out for the evening, or back: out to ridiculous themed restaurants, or back to dumb-looking resort hotels where over-excited kids would make so much noise you'd want to throttle them, and parents would reconcile themselves to another night without screwing and send out for overpriced room service booze instead. Probably even this would be delivered by a fucking chipmunk.

In fact, Ricky had never stayed in one of the hotels. Never even been in one: the security was too good. But he felt he knew exactly how it would be. A great big stupid con, like everything else in Wonder World. Set up fifty years ago and now so vast and sprawling it put some real cities in the shade. Rides and enclosures and parks and theatres and 'experiences' and crap, all based around a bunch of cartoons and some asshole's idea of the perfect world. There was a fake big game reservation. A bunch of fake lakes, where fish and dolphins and shit swam about, like anyone cared. A fake downtown strip the size of a regular town, where people who were too scared to walk to the corner store in their own stupid bergs could wander around and buy up all the crap they wanted. Some sort of stupid futuristic park, where it was supposed to be like what it would be in a hundred years: as if we were all going to be shopping from home and wearing pastel nylon and using video phones—while standing in tight little nuclear family groups and talking to Gramps on Mars.

Ricky knew what it was really going to be like in a hundred years, and it wasn't going to be cutesy characters posing for photographs and making the little kids laugh. It wasn't going to be restaurants where the family could get good food and great service for ten bucks a head; it wasn't going to be endless fucking stores full of t-shirts and candy in painted tins, and being able to leave your door unlocked at night and no litter anywhere.

It was going to be guns and stealing things. It was going to be dog eat dog, like always, and he wasn't talking the kind of dog which had some fuck-ass pimply kid inside, earning chump change for pot. It was going to be taking what you wanted, and fucking up anyone who got in your way. It had been that way since the dawn of time, and only fools pretended otherwise. *That's* what kids needed to learn, not bullshit with talking bunnies.

Wonder World pained Ricky personally, which is one of the reasons why he did what he did for a living. He hated the bright colors, the cheer, the stupid kiddie nonsense, the lies about how the world was, the conspiracy to believe there was magic somewhere in the world. He hated it all. *It was a crock of utter shit.*

The kid was good while he drove, even though weird and miraculous buildings kept appearing in the darkness, each promising fun and games. She didn't ask to stop at every single one, like most of them did. She kept quiet until the car swung around in the front of the massive portal into the heart of Wonder World, the original Beautiful Realm park. The gate was like a massive googie castle, every ludicrous 50s drive-in and coffee shop-erama mashed joyously together into an eight-story extravagance that would have taken the Jetsons' breath away. Whirling spotlights sent beams of light chopping merrily through the night, and characters capered around the entrance, beckoning people inside.

The girl had wound her window back down by then, and could hear in the distance the sound of drums and music, the singing and dancing inside. 'The parade,' she said.

WHAT YOU MAKE IT

He shrugged. 'Fuckers did it early. Or maybe it's just starting.'

She was calm, reasonable. 'You said we'd see the parade.'

'We will. It goes on for, like, an hour. We'll just do this thing, then we'll go catch the end. It's better that way. Most of the people have gone home, you get closer to all the characters.'

'Really?' She was looking at him closely, her mouth wanting to smile, but wary of being let down. Just then one of the lights cut through into the car, showing her in every detail. Pretty little face, red lips that had never been kissed. Big eyes, wanting him to tell her good news, wanting to see nice things. And tiny new breasts outlined in a T-shirt that was one size too small.

She was perfect, all the more so because she wouldn't even understand what he was thinking.

Ricky decided this one was going to play the game a little longer than most of the others, that she going to learn the facts of life. The facts that had to do with taking whatever he wanted to put inside her. A training session. Save some guy time and effort later on, except Ricky knew there wasn't going to be a later. Usually he lay the kid over the back seat on the way out, put a blanket over them like they were sleeping, winked at some guy at the gate and laughed with him about how the child had too much excitement for one day.

Tonight he'd find a way of getting this one out alive. He'd work it out.

'Really,' he said. 'Trust me.'

She smiled.

Ten minutes later he was scanning street names as he cruised down Homeland 3's main drag. Every now and then they'd pass a toon character who'd stop and wave at Nicola. Ranging from three foot dancing toadstools to six foot ducks, they were freaking Ricky out. You didn't normally see characters roaming this late: they were there to magic the place up through the day, the most popular visiting hours. Ricky was having trouble sorting through the names of the streets, which were also the names of fucking characters. Loopy Drive IV, Careful Crescent VI, how the fuck were you supposed to keep track?

Nicola wasn't helping, having decided to tell him her life story. She was thinking of shortening her name, and spelling it Nicci, because she thought it was classy. She liked cats, like Careful Cat, but dogs were sometimes cute too. She didn't know where Daddy was because she'd never known. She said she didn't have a mommy because real mommies didn't do what hers did, and so two days ago she'd run away and she wasn't going back this time.

Jesus, only two days, Ricky was thinking. You're lucky you ran into me so quick. Going to save you six months of turning into your mommy and then a short lifetime waiting for the hammer to fall. You're a lucky girl, little Nicola. Lucky, lucky, lucky.

Part of him was also shaking, because of what he knew he was going to do later. He didn't normally. He just disposed of them. Take a drive down to the 'glades, dump the body, no-one's going to know or give a shit. He didn't like doing anything else, it made him feel like a pervert, though he wasn't, he was a professional. Every now and then was okay though, even if the prospect was clouding his mind, making it hard to make out the street names. Some guys bought themselves new guns, went on a coke bender, hired a couple of whores. Everyone needs a treat. Incentive scheme. Keeps your wheels turning.

Ricky gripped the wheel tightly, tuned out the noise of the kid's nattering, got himself straight.

Eventually he got himself in the right direction. Found his way down the grid of streets, each lined with houses, some streets like the 1940s, some the 1950s or 1960s. Or like those times would have been if they hadn't been shit, anyhow. Like those decades were if you looked back at them now and forgot everything what was wrong with them. The streets were quiet, because mostly the people in the houses were too old to be out walking this late.

Homeland 3, along with the four other near-identical districts which spread in a fan around the Beautiful Realm, was one of the newest parts of the Wonder World.

Five years ago, the suits who ran the parks realized they had another goldmine on their hands: managed communities of old farts. Cutesy little neighborhoods in the sun where the oldsters could come waste their final years, safe from the world outside and bad afternoons where they could be walking home from the store and suddenly find three guys with knives standing on the corner. Not only safe, but coddled, living somewhere their

WHAT YOU MAKE IT

grandkids could be guaranteed to come see them. You want to go visit Granny in Roanoke? I don't think so. But Wonder World?—that's a very easy sell.

They built the houses, any size, any style, so everyone from trailer trash to leather-faced zillionaires had somewhere to hang their trusses: houses that looked like whatever you wanted—from a space podule to a mud hut on the planet Zog. All this and stores and banks and shit, all built to look like what they sold. That's what made it so difficult to find your way around. It was like wandering around a toy store on acid.

It got so popular that even the smaller houses started getting expensive, and a year ago Ricky had an idea. You've got house after house of old people. With money. People who can't defend themselves too well. With things worth stealing. So you get yourself into one of the Homelands—with a cute kid, who's going to question you?—and you help yourself to some stuff, using the kid's voice to get the door open. You're in and out before anyone knows there's a few old people who've just gone to meet their maker: the kid's the only living witness, and not for long. All you got to do is make sure you never get recognized at the gate, and with millions of people going in and out every week, that's never going to happen.

And the kicker—Wonder World covered the burglaries up.

Of course they did. Very bad for business, because they showed the magic retreat was a crock of shit. Plus—and here Ricky witnessed something which made perfect sense to him, something which placed the whole world in context as he understood it—the families often didn't make too much fuss. Why? Same reason that, after a couple months, Ricky had a new idea and moved onto a different line of business, made himself a true professional.

A lot of times the families weren't even sad to see the old folks go, because they wanted the old people's money.

Which is why Ricky didn't bother to steal any more. Ricky took contracts instead, and made it look natural. Safer, more secret, more lucrative—for the time being. Sooner or later the suits would catch on and increase security, and Ricky would work the change-up…and instead start blackmailing the families he'd already done jobs for. The kind of people who'd pay to have gramps whacked had to be living in a Wonder World of their own, if they didn't realize it would come back to haunt them some day.

MICHAEL MARSHALL SMITH

Ricky finally found Gecko Super Terrace III, drove a little way along. Pulled over to the curb, looked up at a house and checked the address. Grunted with satisfaction. He was in the right place.

Margaret Harris, eighty-four years old, was worth maybe eight hundred and fifty thousand dollars, all told, including the Homeland house. Not such a hell of a lot, but her son and daughter-in-law could get the bigger boat, without working all those unsociable hours and missing cocktail hour. Upgrade the car, too, make that down payment on the beach house even. Maybe they'd throw their children a bone too. A games station. A better bike. A last visit to Wonder World. As John Harris, Margaret's son, had put it while slurping a large scotch to blur his conscience: they were merely realizing an asset a little early. That's all.

Margaret Harris had herself a kind of tiny storybook Tudor cottage, dark beams and whitewash, exaggerated leans in the walls and gingerbread thatch. There was a light on in a downstairs room behind a curtain. The grass in the yard was all the same perfect fucking length. Maybe it was animatronic grass. Maybe it sang a happy wake-up call in the morning, a million blades in unison.

Nicola looked at the house. 'Is this where she lives?'

'That's right. You remember what I want you to do?'

She looked away. 'I had a grandma,' she said. 'I saw her twice. She gave me a ring, but Mommy took it and sold it. She died when I was six. Mommy got so drunk that night she wet herself.'

Ricky nearly hit her then, but stopped himself in time. It was like that with the ones like her. Part of wanting to fuck them was finding them too fucking irritating to bear. He forced himself to speak calmly.

'This isn't your grandma, okay? Do you remember, Nicola? What I want you to do?'

'Of course,' the girl said. She opened the door and got out.

Swearing quietly, Ricky got out, slipped the gun into his pocket, and followed her up the path to the Harris house.

Nicola rang the doorbell a second time, and Ricky heard someone moving inside the house. He stepped back into shadow. Nicola stood in front of the door, waiting.

WHAT YOU MAKE IT

'Who is it?' The voice was old but functional, cracked but not quavery. The kind of voice that says I'm pretty ancient but not ready to drop dead just yet, thank you.

'Hi, Grandma!' Nicola piped, leaning to peer through the diamond of swirled glass in the door. She waved her hand. 'I've come to see you!'

'Theresa?' The oldster's voice was uncertain, but Ricky caught the sound of locks being tentatively drawn. This was the second key moment. This was the one where the kid had to be good enough so that the old woman didn't press the Worry Button positioned beside the door of every Homeland house. The button that would alert Wonder World's version of security to the fact that something was sharp and spikey in the dream tonight.

The final slide bolt, and the door opened a crack. 'Theresa?'

Margaret Harris was small, barely over five feet tall. She was grandma-shaped and had white hair done up in a curly style. Her face was plump and lined and she was wearing one of those dresses old bitches wear, flowers on a dark background. You opened a dictionary and looked up 'Grandma', she was pretty much what you'd see.

'You're not Theresa,' she said.

'Oh no,' Nicola laughed. 'I'm Theresa's friend. Theresa said if we were passing we should call in and say hi.'

Ricky stepped into the light, an apologetic smile on his face. 'Hey there, Mrs. Harris. Hope this is okay—Theresa's telling Nicola here about you all the time. John said you probably wouldn't mind. Meant to call ahead, but you know how it is.'

'You're a friend of John's?'

'Work right across the hall at First Virtual.'

Mrs. Harris hesitated, but then smiled back, her face crinkling in a pattern which started from the eyes. 'Well I guess it's okay then. Come on in.'

The hallway looked like a painted background from an old Wonder World cartoon: higgledy stairs, everything neat, colors washed and clean. When the door was shut again behind them, Ricky knew the job was done.

'You can't be too careful these days,' the old woman said, predictably, leading Nicola through to the kitchen.

Right, thought Ricky, following at a distance: *and you haven't been nearly careful enough.*

He hung back for a moment, scoping the place, listening with half an ear to Nicola chatting with the old bag in the kitchen. Jeez, the kid could spin a story: what's happening at school, party she went to with Theresa last week, Theresa borrowing her shoes. Listening to her, you'd think she really *did* know the woman's granddaughter. More make believe, he realized: some better life she wished she had.

Ricky debated disabling the Worry Button, decided it wasn't necessary. Difficult to do, anyhow—and smashing it would leave a clue. This one was too easy to make it worth the risk.

The kitchen was small, cozy, tricked up to look like the kind of place where there would always be something baking in the oven, instead of ready-made shit from the microwave. Pots, pastry cutters, a rolling pin. Probably Wonder World sent someone into everyone's house every day, made sure the props looked right.

Grandma Harris turned as Ricky entered, and handed a cup of coffee up to him. She smiled, twinkle-eyed, relaxed—the kid had put her at ease.

Ricky made a mental note that the cup and saucer would need wiping when he was done. Nicola had a glass of Dr. Pepper—that would need washing too. He sipped the coffee—might as well—and deflected a couple of questions about working with the great John Harris. Pathetic, really, the way the old woman was eager for any snippet of news about her son, wanted telling how much people liked him. Ricky wanted to lash out and shove his cup right down the old fart's throat. It would be a whole lot quicker, and put her out of the misery she didn't even know she was in. But he knew how it had to look, and death by ingestion of china tea set wouldn't play.

Meantime Nicola and Grandma sat at the table, yakking nineteen to the dozen. Nicola had a lot of grandma-talking to do, even if she had to make do with someone else's. Ricky let his eyes glaze, mulling what he was going to do to the kid later. He enjoyed doing that, getting the comparison, just as he liked looking at girls in the street and imagining them on the job, their hands or mouth busy, face wet with sweat. They'd never know, but they'd been his.

WHAT YOU MAKE IT

Ricky rode that line, that fine line, between the life they lived and the life that could come and find them in the night.

'Isn't that right, Daddy?'

'Huh?' Ricky looked at the girl dully, having missed the question. 'What's that?'

'Nicola was saying how you and John were planning a joint vacation for the families later in the year,' Mrs. Harris said. 'That's wonderful news. Do you think you might be able to make it up here? We'd have such fun.'

'Sure,' Ricky said, abruptly deciding this had gone on long enough and was getting out of hand. 'No question. Hey, Mrs. Harris—meant to ask you something.'

'Of course.' Grandma was beside herself at the prospect of another visit later in the year. She'd have agreed to anything. 'What is it?'

'John told me about some pictures, old photos, you've got at the top of the stairs? Kind of an interest of mine. He said you might let me take a peek at them.'

'I'd be *delighted* to show you,' the old woman said. 'Come, let's go up.' Nicola jumped to her feet, but Ricky flashed a glare at her.

Grandma raised an eyebrow. 'Wouldn't you like to come too, dear?'

Nicola avoided Ricky's eye. 'Could I have another Dr. Pepper first, please?'

'Help yourself, then follow us up. Now come on—Rick, isn't it?—let's go take a look.'

Ricky sent another 'Stay here' look at the kid, and followed Grandma out. Made interested grunts every now and then as the old woman talked and led him across the hall to the stairs. A couple of sellable-looking objects caught Ricky's eye on the way, and he planned on picking them up later, before he left. Little bonus.

Up the stairs behind her. Feeling no fear, no excitement. Just watching for the moment. Mrs. Harris took the steps slowly, hitching one leg up after the other. Her voice might be strong but her body was saying goodbye. She wouldn't be losing much.

They got to the landing and Ricky saw there were indeed a whole bunch of really fucking dull-looking black and whites in frames on the wall. John Harris had the whole thing planned out, gave Ricky this way of getting her up to the scaffold. Ricky debated telling the old woman about this, letting her see what lay beyond her wonder world, that the son she'd raised had sat in his study one night drinking scotch and working out how she would die.

But by then Margaret Harris was standing right by Rick, and he knew the time was right and he wanted to get it over with. The real bonus was waiting for him in the kitchen, drinking Dr. Pepper. He didn't need any cheap thrills first.

This picture was her mother, that one her grandpapa. Gone-away people, stiff in fading monotone.

Ricky leaned toward her, ostensively to get a closer look at a bunch of people grouped in front of a raggedy farm building—but actually to get himself at the right angle.

For a moment then he was distracted, by a scent. It seemed to come from the old woman's clothes, a combination of things: milk and cinnamon, rich coffee and apples cooking on the stove. Leaves barely on the trees in autumn, and the smell of sun on grass in summer. These things weren't a part of his life, but for a moment he had them in his mind—like they were part of some story he'd read long ago, as a child, and dismissed.

Then he pushed her down the stairs.

Palm flat against her shoulder, feeling the bones inside the old, thin flesh. He straightened his arm firmly, which was enough—and wouldn't leave a bruise that some forensic smartass might be able to talk up into evidence.

The old woman teetered, without making a sound, and then her center of gravity was all wrong and she tumbled over sideways, over the edge and down the stairs.

Thump, crash, thud, splat.

Like a loose bag of old, grey sticks.

Ricky walked briskly down the stairs, reached the bottom bare seconds after she did. Held back from kicking her head, which would have been risky and was clearly unnecessary. Huge dent in the skull already, eyes turned upwards and out of sight. Arm twisted a strange way, one leg bent back on itself. The usual anti-climax.

Job done.

WHAT YOU MAKE IT

He stepped over the body and into the kitchen, stopping Nicola already on her way out. She ran into him, crashed against his body. He grabbed her shoulders, warm through the thin T-shirt.

'What happened? I heard a crash.'

Usually he killed the kid at this point, before they got hysterical and made too much noise or ran out of the house. Ricky pushed Nicola gently back into the kitchen, felt his temperature rising. He needed her alive to do things with, but he couldn't do them here. 'Nothing. Just an accident. Mrs. Harris fell down the stairs.'

'Grandma?'

'She's not your grandma, sweetie. You know that.'

'We've got to get help...'

Ricky smiled down at her. 'We will. That's exactly what we'll do. We'll get in the car, go find one of the security wagons. They'll help her out. She'll get fixed up and we'll catch the end of the parade.'

The girl was near tears now. 'I want to stay here with her.'

He pretended to think about it, then shook his head. 'Can't do. Security gets here while I'm away, finds you with an old lady at the bottom of the stairs, what are they going to think? They're going to think *you* pushed her.'

'They won't. She was my grandma. Why would I hurt her?'

Ricky glared at her, good humor fast disappearing. 'She wasn't your fucking grandma. Just some old woman.'

Nicola pushed hard against him, momentarily rocking him back on his heels. 'She was *too*. She knew about me. She knew things. She said not to worry about my mom any more. She said she loved me.'

Ricky lashed out with his hand, shoved the kid hard. She flew back, ricocheted off the table and knocked the coffee pot flying. It struck the wall, spraying brown gunk everywhere, as Nicola crashed to the floor.

Ricky cursed himself. Not clever. It was just going to make it more difficult to get her out of the house, plus now there were signs of a struggle.

He took a deep breath, stepped towards her. Maybe he was going to have to simply kill her after all.

'Nicola? Are you okay, dear?'

Ricky froze. Turned slowly round.

Grandma stood in the doorway. One eye fluttered slowly, the one below the huge dent which pulled most of the side of her face out of kilter. The arm was still bent way out of place. Her body was completely fucked up, but somehow she'd managed to drag herself to the door, and to her feet.

Nicola struggled into a sitting position against the wall behind Ricky. 'Grandma—are you alright?'

Of course she's not fucking alright, Ricky thought. *No way.*

Grandma leant against the door frame, as if tired. 'I'm fine, dear. Just had a little fall, isn't that right, Rick?' Her working eye fixed on him.

Ricky felt the hairs on the back of his neck rise, like a thousand tiny erections.

Then her other eye stopped flickering. Closed for a moment, re-opened—and he had two strong eyes looking at him. Tough old bitch.

Ricky reached for the table, grabbed the rolling pin lying there. This job was getting badly fucked up, but he was going to finish it now.

'Close your eyes, dear,' Grandma said. She wasn't talking to him, but the kid. 'Would you do that, for Grandma? Just close your eyes for a while.'

'Close them tight?' Nicola asked, voice small.

'Yes, close them extra tight,' Grandma said, trying to smile. 'I'll tell you when you can open them again.'

Ricky saw the girl shut her eyes and cover her ears. He shook his head and turned back to the old woman, rolling pin held with loose ease.

He took a measured stride toward her, not hurrying. Ricky had been in bad situations all his life, been beaten up and half-killed on a hundred occasions, starting with the times that happened in his own bedroom, a room that had no posters on the walls or books on the shelves or little figures of cartoon animals. Ricky's old man hadn't believed in make-believe; was proud of being cynical—'That's what I am, boy, I'm nobody's fool'—and working the angles and telling God's honest truth however fucking dull it might be. His lessons had been painful, but Ricky knew he'd been right.

Ricky wasn't afraid of an old woman, no matter how tough she was. He grinned at her, looking forward to seeing what extra damage the pin was going to do to her face.

WHAT YOU MAKE IT

She looked back, head tilted up, grey hair awry and skin papery, and then her head popped back out.

One minute her skull was caved in, the next it was back where it should be, like someone pumped exactly the right amount of air back into a punctured balloon. It made a sound like cellophane.

Ricky gawped, arm aloft.

Grandma swallowed, blinked, then did something with her fucked-up arm. Swung it around from behind—and as it came it seemed to become more solid, finding the correct planes to rotate in once more. She bent it experimentally, found it worked, and used it to pat her hair more or less back into place.

'You're a very bad boy, Ricky,' she said softly, too quietly for Nicola to hear. 'And bad boys never get to see Santa Claus. Hear what I'm saying, motherfucker?'

Before Ricky could even process this, Margaret Harris hurled herself at him.

He tried to turn, to bring the rolling pin down, but only managed to twist halfway at the waist. She smacked into him sideways and the two of them spun off the corner of the table to crash into the wall. Ricky felt his nose bend and melt, and realized now there was going to be blood to clean up, as well as everything else.

He tried to push the old woman away, but she looped a fist straight into his face. It cracked hard against his cheekbone, far too hard.

The rolling pin went spinning across the floor.

Ricky kicked and scrambled, lashing out with his feet, hands and elbows in a flurry of compact violence. Each time he thought he was going to be able to dislodge her, she seemed to gain a notch in strength.

They rolled back and forth under the table, smashing a chair to firewood, and out the other side. Ricky heard Nicola squeal, and part of his mind was able to hope the neighbors hadn't heard. Then he found himself with two gnarled hands tight around his throat, and almost wished they *had* heard, and were sending help. For *him*.

He finally managed to pull his knee up under the old bitch, and gradually forced his hands in between hers. When they were in position he steadied himself, got his breath—and threw everything he had, chopping his hands in opposite directions, and kicking out hard.

The old woman flew a yard and hit the stove like an egg.

Ricky was on his feet immediately, hands on his knees and coughing. When he swallowed, something clicked alarmingly in his throat. Nicola was still squeaking, eyes shut, but he heard it as from a great distance. He could taste his own blood, see it spattered on the wall and floor—in amongst the coffee and a few lumps of grey hair that he managed to yank out of the robot.

A fucking animatronic.

He'd been set up.

John Harris had changed his mind, or more likely been a plant from minute one and there'd never been a real Grandma Harris. Fuckers. Wonder World weren't working with the cops. They were settling things their own way.

And so would Ricky.

The job was over, and it didn't matter how much mess he left. He was getting out, and then he was going to find Mr. John Harris. The fee for this fucked-up job had just accelerated to include every single thing the asshole owned, including his wife. And daughter.

Grandma Harris was slumped on the floor, back against the cooker. Her throat was arced up like a twisted branch, a perfect target, but then jerked back into position as Ricky pulled out his gun.

No matter. The face would do just as well.

He held the gun in a straight-arm grip, sighted down the barrel.

'Don't even think about it,' the rolling pin said.

Ricky turned very slowly. 'Excuse me?'

The rolling pin had grown legs, and was standing with little hands on where its hips would be. Two stern eyes glared out of the wooden cylinder of its body. It looked like a strange, wide crab.

Ricky stared at it. Knew suddenly that it wasn't a machine, but an actual rolling pin with eyes and arms.

He fired at it. The pin flipped out of the way, then switched direction and flick-flacked towards him, like a crazy little wooden gymnast.

Ricky backed hurriedly away, fired another shot. It missed, and the rolling pin flicked itself into the air like a muscular missile. Ricky wrenched his head out of the way just in time, and the pin embedded itself in the wall behind him.

'Careful,' said the wall, slowly opening its eyes.

WHAT YOU MAKE IT

Over at the stove, Grandma Harris was pulling herself upright. Ricky blinked at her. She smiled, a sweet old lady smile that wasn't for him.

Ricky decided he didn't have to mop up this mess after all. He'd go straight to talk with John Harris instead. He fired a couple of rounds into the wall, between its huge eyes. It made a grumpy sound, but didn't seem much inconvenienced. A huge mouth opened sleepily, as if yawning, as if it was only just getting up to speed.

The pin meanwhile pushed itself out with a dry popping sound, and turned its beady eyes on Ricky.

'Shit on this,' Ricky muttered, as it scuttled towards him.

He swung a kick at the rolling pin, sent it howling across the room. Fired straight at Margaret Harris, but didn't wait to see if it hit.

He turned on his heel, bounded down the hallway and yanked at the front door. It wouldn't open, and when Ricky tried to pull his hand away, he saw the handle had turned into a brown wooden hand and was gripping his like he was a prime business opportunity and they were testing each other's strength. Ricky braced his foot against the wall and tugged, for the first time hearing the sound of the beams whispering above. He glanced up and saw some of them were wriggling in place, limbering up, getting ready for action. He didn't want to see their action.

The door handle wasn't letting go, and so he placed the muzzle of the gun against it and let it have one.

It took the tip of one of Ricky's fingers with it, but it let go. Ricky reared back, kicked the door with all his strength. It splintered and he barreled through it, tripped and fell full length on the lawn.

Face to face with the grass, he saw he'd been right, and there *was* a tiny face on every blade. He heard a noise like a million little voices tuning up, and knew its song wasn't likely to be one he wanted to hear.

He scrambled to his feet and careened down the path towards the car, bloody hand reaching for the keys. Before he got half-way there, two trash cans came running from next door. They made it to the car before him, and started levering one side off up the ground.

Meanwhile the rolling pin shot out of the house from behind him, narrowly missed his head, and went through the windscreen of the car like a torpedo. Barely had the spray of glass hit the ground before the pin emerged the other side, turned in mid-air and looped back to punch through a door panel. It kept going, faster and faster, looping and punching, until the car began to look like a battered atom being mugged by a psycho electron.

Ricky began to realize just how badly his hand hurt, and that the car wasn't going to be a viable transportation option. He diverted his course in mid stride, heading toward the road instead, for a straight line to run in. He cleared the sidewalk, barely keeping his balance, and leant into the turn. Ricky could run. He'd had practice, down many dark streets and darker nights, always running away from something, instead of toward. The way was clear in front of him.

Then a vehicle appeared at the corner, and he realized what the grass had been singing.

It hadn't been a song. It was a siren.

Wonder World's designers hadn't stinted themselves on the cop wagon. It was black, half as big as a house, all retro fins and intimidating wheel arches spiked with chrome. The windows in the sides were blacker still, and the doors in the back might as well have had 'Abandon hope all ye who enter here' scrawled across them.

Ricky skidded to a halt, whirled around. An identical vehicle had arrived on the other side of the remains of his car. Behind it a bunch of mushrooms and toadstools were moving into position.

The doors of the first wagon opened, and a figure got out each side. Both seven foot tall, with long tails and claws that glinted. Bud and Slap, though rats, had been friendly rats in the countless cartoons they'd appeared in over the last thirty years. They were almost as popular as Loopy and Careful and China Duck, and even Ricky recognized them. Cute, well-meaning villains, they always ended up joining the right side in the end.

But this Bud and Slap weren't like that.

These toons were just for Ricky. As he held his ground, knowing there was nowhere to run, they walked toward him with heavy tread. They were stuffed into parodies of uniforms, torn at the seams and stained with bad things. Bud had a lazy, damaged eye, and was holding a big wooden truncheon in an unreassuring way. Slap had a sore on his upper lip, and kept running his long blue tongue over it, to collect the juice. Both had huge guns stuffed down the front of the pants of their uniforms. At least…that's what Ricky hoped they were. From five yards away he could smell the rats' odor, the gust of sweat and stickiness and decay, and for a moment he caught an echo of all the screams and death rattles they'd heard.

'Hey, Ricky,' said Slap. His voice was low and oily, full of unpleasant good humor. 'Got business with you. Lots of different kinds of business, matter of fact. You can get in the wagon, or we can start it right here. What d'you say?'

Behind him, Bud giggled, and started to undo his pants.

Nicola stood at the window with Grandma, and watched the parade in the road. It wasn't the real parade, like the one in the Beautiful Realm where they had fireworks and Careful Cat and Loopy, but Grandma said they were going to see that tomorrow instead. This was a little parade, with just Bud and Slap, and Percival Pin and Terrance and Terry the Trash Cans: sometimes they put on little parades of their own, Grandma said, just because they enjoyed it so.

They laughed as they watched the characters play. Nicola had thought the man she'd come with had been a bad man, but he couldn't have been as bad as all that. Bud and Slap the Happy Rats were each holding one of his hands, and they were dancing with him, leading him to their wagon. They looked as if they liked him a lot. The man's mouth opened and shut very wide as he danced, and Nicola thought he was probably laughing. She would be, in his position. They all looked like they were having such fun.

Finally the wagon doors were shut with the man inside, and Bud and Slap bowed at Grandma's window before getting back into their police car. The trashcans went somersaulting back to next door's yard, and the rolling pin came hand-springing up the path, leaving a trail of little firework stars in its wake.

Nicola clapped her hands and Grandma laughed, and put her arm around the little girl.

Now it was time for supper and pie, and tomorrow would be a new and different day. They turned from the window and went to start cooking, in a kitchen where the tables and chairs had already tidied everything up, as if nothing bad had ever happened, or ever could.

***

MICHAEL MARSHALL SMITH

Meanwhile, well outside Wonder World, over on a splintered porch outside a small house the other side of the beltway, Marty the gateman sat in his chair enjoying his bedtime cigarette. His back ached a little from standing up all day, but didn't bother him too badly. It was a small price to pay for seeing all the faces as they went into the parks, and when they came out again. The kids went in bright-eyed and hopeful, the parents tired and watchful. You could see them thinking how much it was all going to cost, and wondering whether it would be worth it. When you saw them come out, hours or days later, you could see they knew that it had been. For a little while the grown-ups had realized cynicism was an emotional short-cut which meant they missed everything worth seeing along the way, and the children had proof of what they'd already believed: the world was cool.

The gateman's job was very important, Marty knew. You said the first hello to the visitors, and you bid them goodbye. You welcomed them and helped them acclimatize; and you sent them on their way afterward, letting them see in your eyes the truth of what they believed—they were leaving a little lighter inside.

Marty's house was small and looked like all the others nearby, and he lived in it alone. As he sat in the warmth of the evening, looking up at the stars, he didn't mind that very much. His wife now lived with someone who was better at earning money, and who came home after a day's work in a far worse mood. Marty missed her, but he'd survive. The house he lived in could have been fancier, but he'd painted it last summer and he liked his yard.

He had the last couple of puffs of his cigarette, and stubbed it out carefully in the ashtray he kept by the chair. He yawned, sipped the last of his iced tea, and decided that was that. It was early yet, but a good time for sleep.

It always is, when you're looking forward to the next day.

As he lay in his bed later, gently settling into the warm train which would take him into tomorrow, he dimly wondered what he'd do with the rest of his life. Work for as long as he could, he supposed, and then stop. Sit out on the porch, live out his days bathed in the memory of all the faces he'd seen, lit for a moment by magic.

Smile at passersby. Drink iced tea in the twilight.

That sounded okay. Better than okay.

It sounded good.

NOT **WAVING**

Sometimes when we're in a car, driving along country roads in autumn, I see poppies splashed in amongst the grasses and it makes me want to cut my throat and let the blood spill out of the window to make more poppies, many more, until the roadside is a blaze of red.

Instead I just watch the road. In a while the poppies will be behind us, as they always are.

On the morning of October 10th I was in a state of high excitement. I was at home, and I was supposed to be working. What I was actually doing, however, was sitting thrumming at my desk, leaping to my feet whenever I heard the sound of traffic outside the window. I was also peeking at the two large cardboard boxes sitting in the middle of the floor. These contained, respectively, a new computer and a new monitor. After a year of denying my inbuilt technophile need to own the brightest and best in silicon-based goodies, I'd finally succumbed and upgraded my computer. Credit card in hand, I'd picked up the phone and ordered myself a piece of science fiction, in the shape of a machine which not only went like a train but also had built-in telecommunications and speech recognition. The future was finally here, and sitting on my living room floor.

However.

While I had £3000 worth of Macintosh and monitor, what I didn't have was the £15 cable which connected the two together. The manufacturer, it transpired, felt that constituted an optional extra—despite the fact that without it the two system components were little more than bulky white ornaments of a particularly tantalizing and frustrating kind. The cable had to be ordered separately, and there weren't any in the country at the moment.

They were all in Belgium.

I was only told this a week after I ordered the system, and I endeavored to make my feelings on the matter clear to my supplier during the further week in which they playfully promised to deliver the system first on one day, then another, all such promises evaporating like the morning dew. The two boxes had finally made it to my door the day before, and, by a bizarre coincidence, the cable had today crawled tired and overwrought into the supplier's warehouse. My contact at Calldriven Direct knew just how firmly one of those cables had my name on it, and had phoned to grudgingly admit they were available. I'd immediately called the courier firm which I occasionally used to send design roughs to clients. Calldriven had offered to put it in the post, but I somehow sensed that they wouldn't quite get around to it *today*, and I'd waited long enough. The bike firm I used specializes in riders who look as if they've been chucked out of the Hell's Angels for being unruly. A large man in leathers turning up in Calldriven's offices, with instructions not to leave without my cable, was just the sort of incentive I felt they needed—and so I was waiting, drinking endless cups of coffee, for such a person to arrive at the flat brandishing said component above his head in triumph.

When the buzzer finally went I nearly fell off my chair. Without bothering to check who it was I left the flat and pounded down the house stairs to the front door, swinging it open with, I suspect, a look of something like lust upon my face. I get a lot of pleasure out of technology. It's a bit sad, I realize that—God knows Nancy has told me so often enough—but hell, it's my life. Each to their own.

An expanse of black leather was standing outside, topped with a shining black helmet. The biker was a lot slighter than their usual type, but quite tall. Tall enough to have done the job, evidently.

'Bloody marvelous,' I said. 'Is that a cable?'

'Sure is,' the biker said, indistinctly. A hand raised the visor on the helmet, and I saw with some surprise that there was a woman inside. 'They didn't seem too keen to let it go.'

NOT WAVING

'I'll bet'. I laughed and took the package from her. Sure enough, it said 'AV adapter cable' on the outside. 'You've made my day,' I said, a little hysterically, 'and I'm more than tempted to kiss you.'

'That seems rather forward,' the girl said, reaching up to her helmet. 'Cup of coffee would be nice, though. I've been driving since five this morning and my tongue feels like it's made of brick.'

Taken aback, I hesitated for a moment. I'd never had a motorcycle courier in for coffee before. I'm not sure *anyone* has. Also, it would mean a delay before I could ravage through the boxes and start connecting things up. But it was still only eleven in the morning, and another fifteen minutes wouldn't harm. I was also a little pleased at the thought of such an unusual encounter.

'You would be,' I said, with a kind of mock-Arthurian courtliness which doubtless sounds horrific but was what the moment required, 'most welcome.'

'Thank you, kind sir,' the courier said, and pulled her helmet off. A great deal of dark brown hair spilled out around her face, and as she swung her head the sun shot threads of chestnut through it. Her face was strong, with a wide mouth and vivid green eyes.

Bloody hell, I thought, the cable for a moment forgotten in my hand.

Then I stood to one side to let her in.

Her name was Alice, and she stood looking at the books on the shelves as I made a couple of cups of coffee.

'Your girlfriend's in Personnel,' she said.

'How did you guess?' I said, handing her a cup.

She indicated the raft of books on Human Resource Development, Managing for Success and Stating the Bleeding Obvious in Five Minutes a Day, which take up half our shelves.

'You don't look the type. Is this it?' She pointed her mug at the two boxes on the floor.

I nodded, slightly sheepishly. 'Well,' she said, 'Aren't you going to open them?'

I glanced up at her, surprised. Her face was turned towards me, a small smile in the corners of her mouth. Her skin was the pale tawny color which goes with rich hair, I noticed, and flawless. I shrugged, slightly embarrassed.

'I guess so,' I said, noncommittally. 'I've got some work I ought to do first.'

'Rubbish,' she said firmly. 'Let's have a look.'

And so I bent down and pulled open the boxes, while she settled down on the sofa to watch. What was odd was that I didn't mind doing it. Normally when I'm doing something that's to do with me and the things I enjoy, I want to do it alone. Other people seldom understand the things which give you the most pleasure, and I'd rather not have them around to undermine the occasion. But Alice seemed genuinely interested, and ten minutes later I had the system sitting on the desk. In the meantime I'd babbled about voice recognition and video input, the eight gigabyte hard disk and ultra-zippy CD-ROM. She'd listened, and even asked questions, questions that followed from what I was saying rather than simply set me up to drivel on some more. It wasn't that she knew a vast amount about computers. She just understood what was exciting about them.

When the screen threw up the standard message saying all was well we looked at each other. 'You're not going to get much work done today, are you?' she said.

'Probably not,' I agreed, and she laughed.

Just then a protracted squawking noise erupted from the sofa, and I jumped. The courier rolled her eyes and reached over to pick up her unit. A voice of stunning brutality informed her that she had to pick something up from the other side of town, urgently, like five minutes ago, and why wasn't she there already, darlin'?

'Grr,' she said, like a little tiger, and reached for her helmet. 'Duty calls.'

'But I haven't told you about the telecommunications stuff yet,' I said, joking.

'Some other time,' she winked.

I saw her out, and we stood for a moment on the doorstep. I was wondering what to say. I didn't know her, would never see her again, but wanted to thank her for sharing something with me. Then I noticed one of the local cats ambling past the bottom of the steps. I love cats, but Nancy doesn't, so we don't have one. Just one of the little compromises you make, I guess. I recognized this particular furball, and had long since given up hope of appealing to it. I made the sound universally employed for gaining cats' attention, as usual with no result. It merely glanced wearily up at me and cruised on by.

Then Alice sat down on her heels and made the same noise.

NOT WAVING

The cat stopped in its tracks and looked at her. She made the noise again and the cat turned, glanced down the street for no discernible reason, and then confidently made its way up the steps to weave in and out of her legs.

'That is truly amazing,' I said. 'He is not a friendly cat.'

She took the cat in her arms and stood up. 'Oh, I don't know,' she said. The cat sat up against her chest, looking around with the air of a monarch inspecting his kingdom and finding all was well. I reached out to rub its nose and felt the warm vibration of a purr.

The two of us made a fuss of him for a few moments, and then Alice put him down. She replaced her helmet, climbed on her bike, and, with a wave, set off.

Back in the flat I tidied away the boxes, anal retentive that I am, before settling down to immerse myself in the new machine. On impulse I called Nancy, to let her know the system had finally arrived. I got one of her assistants, Trish, instead. She didn't put me on hold, merely cupped the mouthpiece, and I heard Nancy say 'Tell him I'll call him back,' in the background. I said goodbye to Trish with fairly good grace, trying not to mind.

Voice recognition software hadn't been included, it turned out, nor anything to put in the CD-ROM drive. The telecommunications functions wouldn't work without an expensive add-on, which Calldriven didn't expect for four to six weeks. Apart from that, it was great.

Nancy cooked that evening. We tended to take it in turns, though she was much better at it than me. Nancy is good at most things. She's accomplished.

There's a lot of in-fighting in the selfless world of Personnel Development, it would appear, and Nancy was in feisty form that evening, having tastily outmaneuvered some colleague. I drank a glass of red wine and leaned against the counter while she whirled ingredients around. She told me about her day, and I listened and laughed. I didn't tell her much about mine, only that it had gone okay. Her threshold for hearing about the world of freelance graphic design is pretty low. She'd listen with relatively good grace if I really had to get something out of my system, but didn't understand it and didn't seem to want to. No reason why she should, of course. I didn't mention the new computer sitting on my desk, and neither did she.

Dinner was very good. It was chicken, but she'd done something intriguing to it with spices. I ate as much as I could, but there was a little left. I tried to get her to finish it, but she wouldn't. I reassured her that she hadn't eaten too much, in the way that sometimes seemed to help, but her mood dipped and she didn't have any dessert. I steered her towards the sofa and took the stuff out to wash up and make some coffee.

While I was standing at the sink, scrubbing the plates and thinking vaguely about the mountain of things I had to do the next day, I noticed a dark brown cat sitting on a wall across the street. I hadn't seen this one before. It was crouched watching a twittering bird, with that catty concentration that combines complete attention with the sense that they might at any moment break off and wash their foot instead.

The bird eventually fluttered chaotically off and the cat tracked its progress for a moment before sitting upright, as if drawing a line under that particular diversion.

Then the cat's head turned, and it looked straight at me.

It was a good twenty yards away, but I could see its eyes very clearly. It kept looking, and after a while I laughed, slightly taken aback. I even turned away for a moment, but when I looked back it was still there, still looking.

Then the kettle boiled and I turned to tip water into a couple of mugs of Nescafé. When I glanced through the window on the way out of the kitchen, the cat was gone.

Nancy wasn't in the lounge when I got there, so I settled on the sofa and lit a cigarette. After about five minutes the toilet flushed upstairs, and I sighed.

A couple of days came and went, as they do, with the usual flurry of deadlines and committee redesigns. I went to a social evening at Nancy's office and spent a few hours being patronized by her power-dressed colleagues, while she sparkled in the center. I messed up a print job and had to cover the cost of doing it again. Good things happened too, I guess, but all too often it's the others that stick in your mind.

One afternoon the buzzer went and I wandered absentmindedly downstairs to get the door. As I opened it there was a flick of brown hair, and I saw that it was Alice.

NOT WAVING

'Hello there,' I said, strangely pleased.

'Hello yourself,' she smiled. 'Got a parcel for you.' I took it and looked at the label. Color proofs from the repro house. Yawn. She must have been looking at my face, because she laughed. 'Nothing very exciting?'

'Hardly.' After I'd signed the delivery note, I looked up at her. She was still smiling, I think, though it was difficult to tell. Her face looked as though it always was.

'Well,' she said, 'I can either go straight to Peckham to pick up something else really dull, or you can tell me about the telecommunications features.'

I stepped back to let her in.

'*Bastards*,' she said indignantly, when I told her about the things that hadn't been shipped with the machine. I told her about the telecoms stuff anyway, as we sat on the sofa and drank coffee, but not for very long. Mainly we just chatted, and when she got to the end of the road on her bike she turned and waved before disappearing around the corner.

That night Nancy went to Sainsbury's on the way home from work. I caught her eye as she unpacked the biscuits and brownies, potato chips and pastries, but she just stared back at me, and I looked away. She was having a hard time at work. Deflecting my gaze to the window, I noticed the dark cat was sitting on the wall opposite. It wasn't doing much, simply peering vaguely this way and that, watching things I couldn't see. It seemed to look up at the window for a moment, but then leapt down off the wall and wandered away down the street.

I cooked dinner and Nancy didn't eat much, but she stayed in the kitchen when I went into the living room to finish off a job. When I made our cups of tea to drink in bed I noticed that the bin had been emptied, and the rubbish bag stood, neatly tied, to one side. I nudged it with my foot and it rustled, full of empty packets.

Upstairs the bathroom door was pulled shut, and the key turned in the lock.

I saw Alice a few more times during the following weeks. A couple of major design jobs were reaching crisis point at the same time, and there was a semi-constant flurry of bikes coming and going from the house. On three or four of those occasions it was Alice who I saw when I opened the door.

Apart from once, when she had to turn straight around on pain of death, she always came in for a coffee. We'd chat about this and that, and when the voice recognition software finally arrived I showed her how it worked. I had a rip-off copy, from a friend who'd sourced it from the States. You had to do an impersonation of an American accent to get the machine to understand anything you said, and my attempts to do so made Alice laugh a lot. Which is curious, because it made Nancy merely sniff and ask me whether I'd put the new computer on the insurance.

Nancy was preoccupied, those couple of weeks. Her so-called boss was dumping more and more responsibility onto her, while stalwartly refusing to give her more credit or money. Nancy's world was very real to her, and she relentlessly kept me up to date on it: the doings of her boss were more familiar to me by then than the activities of most of my friends. She did manage to get her company car upgraded, however, which was a nice thing. She screeched up to the house one evening in something small and red and sporty, and hollered up to the window. I scampered down and she took us hurtling around North London, driving with her customary verve and confidence. On impulse we stopped at an Italian restaurant we sometimes went to, and they miraculously had a table. Over coffee we took each other's hands and said we loved one another, which we hadn't done for a while.

When we parked outside the house I saw the dark cat sitting under a tree on the other side of the street. I pointed it out to Nancy but she just shrugged. She went in first and as I turned to close the door I saw the cat was still sitting there, a dark shape in the half-light. I wondered who it belonged to, and wished that it was ours.

A couple of days later I was walking down the street in the late afternoon when I noticed a motorbike parked outside Sad Café. I seemed to have become sensitized to bikes over the previous few weeks: probably because I'd used so many couriers. 'Sad' wasn't the café's real name, but what Nancy and I used to call it, back in the times when we would stagger hungover down the road on Sunday mornings on a quest for a cooked breakfast. The first time we'd slumped over one of its Formica tables we'd been slowly surrounded by middle-aged men in zip-up jackets and beige bobble hats, a party of mentally-challenged teenagers with broken glasses, and old women on the verge of death. The pathos attack we'd suffered had nearly finished us off, and it had been dubbed the Sad Café ever since. We hadn't been there in a while: Nancy usually had work in the evenings in those days, even at weekends, and fried breakfasts appeared to be off the map again.

The bike resting outside made me glance through the window, and with a shock of recognition I saw Alice in there, sitting at a table nursing a mug of something or other. I nearly walked on, but then thought what the hell, and poked my head inside. Alice looked startled to see me out of my usual context, but then smiled, and I sat down and ordered a cup of tea.

She'd finished for the day, and was killing time before heading home. I was at a loose end myself; Nancy was out for the evening, entertaining clients. It was odd seeing Alice outside the flat, and this was also the first time we'd met outside working hours. Possibly it was this which made the next thing coalesce in front of us.

Before we knew how the idea had arisen, we were wheeling her bike down the road to prop it up outside the Bengal Lancer, the area's bravest stab in the direction of a decent restaurant. I loitered awkwardly to one side while she took off her leathers and packed them into the bike's carrier. She was wearing jeans and a green sweatshirt underneath, a green that matched her eyes. Then she ran her hands through her hair, said 'Close enough,' and strode towards the door. Momentarily reminded of Nancy's standard hour-and-a-half preparation for going out, I followed her into the restaurant.

We took our time, and had four courses, and by the end were absolutely stuffed. We talked of things beyond computers and design, but I can't remember what they were. We had a couple of bottles of wine, a gallon of coffee, and smoked most of two packets of cigarettes.

When we were done I stood outside again, far more relaxed by now, as she climbed back into her work clothes. She waved as she rode off, and I watched her go. Then I turned and walked for home.

It was a nice meal. It was also the big mistake.

The next time I rang for a bike to send a package, I asked for Alice by name. After that, it seemed the natural thing to do. And Alice seemed to end up doing almost all of the deliveries to me, more than you could put down to chance.

If we hadn't gone for that meal, perhaps it wouldn't have happened. Nothing was said, and no glances exchanged: I didn't note the date in my diary.

But we'd started falling in love.

The following night Nancy and I had a row, the first full-blown one in a while. We rarely argued. Nancy was a good manager.

This one was short, and also very odd. It was late and I was sitting in the lounge, trying to summon up the energy to turn on the television. I didn't have much hope for what I would find on it, but was too tired to read. I'd been listening to a CD which had run its course, and was staring at the stereo, half-mesmerized by the green and red LEDs. Nancy was working at the table in the kitchen, which was dark apart from the lamp which shed yellow light over her papers.

Suddenly she marched into the living room, already at maximum temper, and shouted incoherently at me.

Shocked, I half-stood, trying to work out what she was saying. In retrospect I was probably half asleep, and her anger seemed to fill the room with its harsh intensity.

She was shouting at me for getting a cat. There was no point me denying it, because she'd seen it. She'd seen the cat under the table in the kitchen, it was in there still, and I was to go and throw it out. I knew how much she disliked cats, and anyway, how could I do it without asking her, and the whole thing was a classic example of what a selfish and hateful man I was.

It took me a while to get to the bottom of this and start denying it. I was too baffled to get angry. In the end I went with her into the kitchen, and looked under the table. She was very insistent. By then I was a little spooked, to be honest. After that we looked in the hallway, the bedroom and the bathroom. Then we looked in the kitchen again, and in the living room.

There was, of course, no cat. Anywhere.

I sat Nancy on the sofa. She was still shaking, though her anger was gone. I tried to talk to her, to work out what exactly was wrong. Her reaction was disproportionate, misdirected: I'm not sure even she knew what it was about. The cat, of course, could have been nothing more than a discarded shoe seen in near-darkness, maybe even her own foot moving. After leaving my parents' house, where there had always been a cat, I'd often startled myself by thinking I saw them in similar ways. Nancy's family had never had one, but the same principle still held. Maybe.

She didn't seem convinced, but did calm a little. She was so timid, and quiet, and as always I found it difficult to reconcile her as she was then with her fire-eating Corporate Woman routine, the way she spent so much of the time. I turned the fire on and we sat in front of it and talked, and even discussed her eating. Nobody else knew about that part of her life. I didn't understand it, not really. I sensed that it was something to do with feelings of lack of control, of trying to shape herself and her world, but couldn't get much closer than that. There appeared to be nothing I could do except listen, but I hoped that was better than nothing.

We went to bed a little later, and made careful, gentle love. As she relaxed towards sleep, huddled in my arms, I caught myself for the first time feeling for her something that was a little like pity.

Alice and I had dinner again about a week later. This time it was less of an accident, and took place further from home. I had a late meeting in town, and by coincidence Alice would be in the area at around about the same time. I told Nancy I might end up having dinner with my client, but she didn't seem to hear. She was preoccupied, some new power struggle at work edging towards climax.

Though it was several weeks since the previous occasion, it didn't feel at all strange seeing Alice in the evening, not least because we'd talked to each other often in the meantime. She'd started having two cups of coffee, rather than one, each time she dropped something off, and had once phoned me for advice on computers.

While it didn't feel odd, I was aware of what I was doing. Meeting another woman for dinner, basically, and enjoying it. Enormously. When I talked to Alice, my feelings and what I did seemed more important, as if they were a part of someone worth talking to. Part of me felt that was more important than a little economy with the truth. To be honest, I tried not to think too hard about it.

When I got home Nancy was sitting in the living room, reading. 'How was your meeting?' she asked.

'Fine,' I replied. 'Fine.'

'Good,' she said, and went back to scanning her magazine. I could have tried to make conversation, but knew it would have come out tinny and forced. In the end I went to bed and lay tightly curled on my side, wide awake.

I was drifting off to sleep when I heard a low voice in the silence, speaking next to my ear.

'Go away,' it said. 'Go away.'

I opened my eyes, expecting…I don't know what. Nancy's face, I suppose, hanging over mine. There was no-one there. I was relaxing, prepared to believe it had been a fragment of a dream, when I heard her voice again, saying the same words in the same low tone.

I climbed carefully out of bed and crept towards the kitchen. Through it I could see into the living room, where Nancy was standing in front of the main window in the darkness. She was looking down at something in the street.

'Go away,' she said again, softly.

I turned quietly around and went back to bed.

A couple of weeks passed quickly. Time seemed to, that autumn. I was very immersed, what with one thing and another. Each day held something that fixed my attention, and pulled me through it. I'd look up, and a week would have gone by, with me barely having noticed.

Speaking to Alice was now a regular part of most days. We talked about things that Nancy and I never touched upon, things Nancy simply didn't understand or care about. Alice read, for example. Nancy read too, in the sense that she studied memos, and reports, and genned up on the current corporate claptrap being imported from the States. She didn't read books, however, or even paragraphs. She read sentences, to asset-strip from them what she needed to do her job, find out what was on television, or hold her own on current affairs. Every piece of text was a bullet point, a step towards some bottom line.

Alice read for its own sake. She wrote, too, hence her growing interest in computers. I mentioned once that I'd written a few articles, years back, before I settled on being a barely competent graphic designer instead. She said she'd written some stories, and after regular nagging from me, diffidently gave up copies. They were vignettes about life in London and about being a motorcycle courier, a profession with its own heroes and lore. I don't know anything about fiction from a professional point of view, so I can't say how innovative or clever the pieces were or whether the TLS would have described them as 'A new synthesis of narrative dialectics'. But they held my attention, and I read them more than once, and that's good enough for me. I told her so, and she seemed pleased.

We saw each other a couple of times a week. She delivered things to me, or picked them up, and sometimes I chanced by Sad Café when she was sipping a cup of tea. It all felt very low key, very friendly—though in retrospect it was a long simmer, a relationship reducing towards an ever more intense flavor.

Nancy and I got on with each other, in an occasional, space-sharing sort of way. She had her friends, and I had mine. Sometimes we saw them together, and performed as a social pair. We looked good together, like a series of stills from a lifestyle magazine. Life, if that's what it was, went on. Her eating vacillated between not good and pretty bad, and I carried on being bleakly accepting of the fact that there didn't seem much I could do to help. So much of our lives seemed geared up to perpetuating her idea of how two young people should live together, that I somehow didn't feel that I could call her bluff and point out what was lurking beneath the stones in our existence. I also didn't mention the night I'd seen her in the lounge. There didn't seem any way of tabling it for discussion.

Apart from having Alice to chat to, the other good news was the new cat in the neighborhood. When I glanced out of the living room window it would usually be there, ambling smoothly past or hunkered down on the pavement, watching movement in the air. It had a habit of sitting in the middle of the road, daring traffic to give it any trouble, as if it knew what the road was for but was having no truck with it. The twitch of her tail seemed to say that she knew this had once been a meadow, and that as far as she was concerned, it still was.

One morning I was walking back from the corner shop, clutching some cigarettes and milk, and came upon her, perched on a wall. If you like cats there's something rather depressing about having them run away from you, so I approached cautiously. I wanted to get to at least within a yard of this one before it went shooting off into hyperspace. To my delight, it didn't move away at all. When I got up next to her she stood up, and I thought that was it, but it turned out to be just a recognition that I was there. She was happy to be stroked, and to have the fur on her head runkled, and responded with a purr so deep it was almost below the threshold of hearing. Now that I was closer I could see the chestnut gleams in the dark brown of her fur. She was a very beautiful cat.

After a couple of minutes of this I moved away, thinking I ought to get on, but the cat immediately jumped off the wall and wove in figure eights about my feet, pressing up against my calves. I find it difficult enough to walk away from a cat at the best of times. When they're being ultra-friendly it's impossible. So I bent down and tickled, and talked fond nonsense.

I finally got to my door and looked back to see her, still sitting on the pavement. She was peering around as if wondering what to do next, after all that excitement. I had to fight down the impulse to wave.

I closed the door behind me, feeling for a moment very lonely, and then went back upstairs to work.

Then one Friday night Alice and I met again, and things changed.

Nancy was out at yet another works get-together, in the center of town. Her company seemed to enjoy controlling the social lives of its staff, like some evangelical church intent on infiltrating every activity of its congregation. Nancy mentioned the event in a way that made it clear that my attendance was far from mandatory, and I was happy to take the hint. I do my best at these things, but doubt I look as if I'm having the time of my life.

I didn't have anything else planned, so I just flopped about the house for a while, reading and watching television. It was easier to relax when Nancy wasn't there, when we weren't busy being a Couple. I couldn't settle, though. I kept thinking how pleasant it would be *not* to feel that way, that it would be nice to want your girlfriend to be home so you could laze about together. It didn't work that way with Nancy, not any more. Getting her to consider a half-hour lie-in on one particular Saturday was a major project in itself. I probably hadn't tried very hard in a while, either. She got up, I got up. I'd been developed as a human resource.

My reading grew fitful and in the end I grabbed my coat and went for a walk along streets which were dark and cold. A few couples and solitary figures floated up and down the roads, in mid-evening transit between pubs and Indian restaurants and homes and buses. On the way elsewhere. The apparent formlessness of the activity around me, the Brownian motion of its random wandering, made me feel quietly content. Though I'd no idea where it was, I could picture the room in which Nancy and her colleagues stood, robotically passing catch-phrases and info-nuggets up and down the office hierarchy. I would much rather be here than there.

But then I felt the whole of London spread out around me, and my contentment faded. Nancy at least had somewhere to *go*. All I had was miles of roads in winter light, black houses leaning in towards each other. I could walk, and I could run, and in the end come to the edge of the city. Then there would be nothing I could do except turn around, and come back. I couldn't feel anything beyond the gates, couldn't believe anything was out there. This wasn't some yearning for the countryside, or far climes: I like London, and the great outdoors irritates me. It was more a sense that a place which should hold endless possibilities had been tamed by something, bleached out by my lack of imagination and courage, by the limits of my life.

I headed down the road towards Camden, so wrapped up in heroic melancholy that I nearly got myself run over at the junction with Prince of Wales Road. Rather shaken, I stumbled back onto the curb, dazed by a passing flash of yellow light and a blurred obscenity. Fuck that, I thought, and crossed at a different place, sending me down a different road, towards a different evening.

Camden was busy as hell, and I skirted the purposeful crowds and ended up in a backroad instead. It was there that I saw Alice.

I felt my heart lurch, and I stopped in my tracks. She was walking along the road, dressed in a long skirt and dark blouse, hands in pockets. She appeared to be alone, and wandering the street much as I was, in a world of her own.

It was too welcome a coincidence not to take advantage of, and, careful not to surprise her, I crossed the road and met her on the other side.

We spent the next three hours in a noisy, smoky pub. The only seats were very close together, crowded round one corner of a table in the center of the room. We drank a lot, but the alcohol seemed to work in an unusual way. I didn't get drunk, merely felt warmer and more relaxed. The reeling crowds of locals gave us ample ammunition to talk about, until we were going fast enough not to need any help at all. We just drank, and talked, and talked and drank, and the bell for last orders came as a complete surprise.

When we walked out of the pub the alcohol suddenly kicked in, and we stumbled in unison on an unexpected step, to fall together laughing and shh-ing each other. Without even discussing it we knew neither of us felt like going home yet, and we ended up walking down the steps to stroll by the canal instead. We walked slowly past the backs of houses and speculated what might be going on beyond the curtains; we looked up at the sky and pointed out stars; we listened to the quiet splashes of occasional ducks coming in to land on the still waters. After about fifteen minutes we found a bench, and sat down for a cigarette.

When she'd put her lighter back in her pocket Alice's hand fell near mine. I was very conscious of it being there, of the smallness of the distance mine would have to travel, and I smoked left-handed so as not to move it. I wasn't forgetting myself. I still knew Nancy existed, was aware of how my life was set up. But I didn't move my hand.

Then, like a chess game of perfect simplicity and naturalness, the conversation took us there. I said that work seemed to be slackening off, after the busy period of the last couple of months.

Alice said that she hoped it didn't drop off too much.

I smiled. 'So I can continue to afford expensive computers that don't do quite what I expect?'

'No,' she said. 'So that I can keep coming to see you.'

I turned and stared at her. She looked nervous but defiant, and her hand moved the inch that put it on top of mine.

'You might as well know,' she said, 'if you don't already. There are three important things in my life. My bike, my stories, and you.'

People don't change their lives; evenings do. There are nights that have their own momentum, their own purpose and agenda. They come from nowhere and take people with them. That's why you can never understand, the next day, quite how you came to do what you did—because it wasn't you. It was the evening. The universe itself comes and takes you by the hand and leads you through a revolving door after which things are never the same.

My life stopped that evening, and started up again, and everything was a different color.

We sat on the bench for another two hours, wrapped up close to each other. We admitted when we'd first thought about each other, and laughed quietly about the distance we'd kept. Alice admitted it hadn't been pure coincidence that had brought her to Camden that evening, but a faint hope that we might just bump into each other. She was embarrassed to admit it, but I thought it was pure magic. After weeks of denying what I felt, of simply not realizing, now that I had hold of her hand I couldn't let go. It felt extraordinary to be that close to her, to be able to feel the texture of her skin on mine and her nails against my palm.

People change when you get that close to them, become much more real. If you're already in love with them then they expand to fill the world.

In the end we got on to Nancy. We were bound to, sooner or later. Alice asked how I felt about her, and I tried to explain, tried to understand it myself. In the end we let the topic lapse.

'It's not going to be easy,' I said, squeezing her hand. I was thinking glumly to myself that it might not happen at all. Knowing the way Nancy would react, it looked like a very high mountain to climb. Alice glanced at me, nodded, and then turned back towards the canal.

A cat was sitting there, peering out over the water.

First moving myself even closer to Alice, so that strands of her hair tickled against my face, I made a noise at the cat. It turned to look at us, and then ambled over towards the bench. 'I like a friendly cat,' I said, reaching out to stroke its head.

Alice smiled, and made a noise of her own. I was puzzled that she wasn't looking at the cat while she made it, but then saw that another was making its way out of the shadows. This one was smaller and more lithe, and walked right up to the bench. I was still a little befuddled with drink, and when Alice turned to look in a different direction it took me a moment to catch up.

A third cat was coming down the canal walk in our direction, followed by another.

When a fifth emerged from the bushes behind our bench, I turned and stared at Alice. She was already looking at me, the smile on her lips like the first one of hers I'd seen. She laughed at the expression on my face, and made her noise again. The cats around us sat to attention, and two more appeared from the other direction, almost trotting in their haste to join the collection. We were now so outnumbered that I felt rather beset.

When the next one appeared I had to ask. 'Alice, what's going on?'

She leaned her head against my shoulder.

'A long time ago,' she said, as if making up a story for a child, 'None of this was here. There was no canal, no streets and houses, and all around was trees, and grass.' One of the cats around the bench briefly licked its paw, and I saw another couple padding out of the darkness towards us. 'The big people have changed all of that. They've cut down the trees, and buried the earth, and they've even leveled the ground. There used to be a hill here, a hill that was steep on one side but gentle on the other. They've taken all that away, and made it look like this. It's not that it's so bad. It's just different. The cats still remember the way it was ten thousand years ago.'

It was a nice idea, but it couldn't be true, and it didn't explain all the cats around us. There were now about twenty, and somehow that was too many. Not for my taste, but for common sense. Where the hell were they all coming from?

'But they didn't have cats in those days,' I said, nervously. 'Not like this, anyway. This kind of cat is modern, surely. An import, or crossbreed or something.'

She shook her head. 'That's what they say,' she said, 'and that's what people think. They've always been here. It's just that people haven't always known.'

'Alice, what are you talking about?' I was beginning to get genuinely spooked by the softly milling cats. They were still coming, in ones and twos, and now surrounded us for yards around. The canal was dark apart from soft glints of moonlight off the water, and the lines of the banks and walkway seemed somehow stark, sketched out, as if modeled on a computer screen. They'd been rendered well, and looked convincing, but something wasn't quite right about the way they sat together, as if some angle was one degree out.

NOT WAVING

'Five thousand years ago cats used to come to this hill, because it was their meeting place. They would come, and discuss their business, and then they would go away. This was their place, and it still is. But they don't mind us.'

'Why?'

'Because I love you,' she said, and kissed me for the first time.

It was ten minutes before I looked up again. Only two cats were left. I pulled my arm tighter around Alice and thought how simply and unutterably happy I was.

'Was that all true?'

'It's true that I love you,' she said, and smiled. 'The rest was just a story.' She pushed her nose up against mine and nuzzled, and our heads melted into one.

At two o'clock I realized I was going to have to go home. We got up and walked slowly back to the road. I waited shivering with her for a mini-cab, and endured the driver's histrionic sighing as we we took our time saying goodbye. I stood on the corner and waved until the cab was out of sight, and then walked back home.

It wasn't until I turned into our road and saw that the house lights were still on that I understood just how real the evening had been. As I walked up the steps the door opened. Nancy stood there in a dressing gown, looking angry and frightened.

'Where the hell have you *been?*' she said. I straightened my shoulders and girded myself to lie.

I apologized. I told her I'd been out drinking with a male friend, lying calmly and with convincing determination. I didn't even feel bad about it, except in a self-serving, academic sort of way.

Some switch had finally been thrown in my mind, and as we lay beneath the duvet afterwards I realized that I wasn't in bed with my girlfriend any more. There was just someone in my bed. When Nancy rolled towards me, her body open in a way that suggested that she might not be thinking of going to sleep, I felt my chest tighten with something like dread. I found a way of suggesting that I might be a bit drunk for anything other than unconsciousness, and she curled up beside me and went to sleep instead. I lay awake for an hour, feeling as if I was lying on a slab of marble in a room open to the sky.

Breakfast the next morning was a festival of leaden politeness. The kitchen seemed very bright, and noise rebounded harshly off the walls. Nancy was in a good mood, but there was nothing I could do except force tight smiles and talk much louder than usual, waiting for her to go to work.

The next ten days were both dismal and the best of my life.

Alice and I managed to see each other every couple of days, occasionally for an evening but more often just for a cup of coffee. We didn't do any more than talk, and hold hands. Our kisses were brief, a sketching out of the way things could be. Bad starts will always undermine a relationship, for fear it could happen again. So we were restrained and honest with each other, and it was wonderful, but it was also difficult.

Being home was no fun at all. Nancy hadn't changed, but I had, and so I didn't know her any more. She was a stranger who was all the worse for reminding me of someone I had once loved, and of someone I had once been. The things that were the closest to the old ways were the things which made me most irritable, and I found myself avoiding anything that might promote them. Any signs of intimacy, or real friendship, in other words—the only things which make a relationship worthwhile.

Something had to be done, and it had to be done by me. The problem was gearing myself up to it. Nancy and I had been living together for four years. Most of our friends assumed we'd be engaged before long; I'd already heard a few jokes. We knew each other very well, and that does count for something. As I moved warily around Nancy during those weeks, trying not to seem too close, I was also conscious of how much we had shared together, of how affectionate a part of me still felt towards her. She was a friend, and I cared about her. I didn't want her to be hurt. I wasn't just her boyfriend. I knew some of the reasons her eating was as bad as it was, things no-one else would ever know. I'd talked it through with her, and knew how to live with it, knew how to not make her feel any worse. She needed support, and I was the only person there to give it. Ripping that away when she was already having such a bad time would be very difficult to forgive.

And so things went on, for a little while. I saw Alice when I could, but always at the end I would have to go, and we would part, and each time it felt more and more arbitrary and I found it harder to remember why I should have to leave. I grew terrified of saying her name in my sleep, or of letting something slip, and felt as if I was living my life on stage in front of a predatory audience waiting for a mistake. I'd go out for walks in the evening and return as slowly up the road as possible, stopping to talk to the cat, stroking her for as long as she liked and walking up and down the pavement with her, doing anything to avoid going back into the house.

I spent most of the second week looking forward to the Saturday. At the beginning of the week Nancy announced she would be going on a team-building day at the weekend. She explained to me what was involved, the chasm of corporate vacuity into which she and her colleagues were cheerfully leaping. She was talking to me a lot more at the time, wanting to share her life. I tried to take in what the day's programme would be, but I couldn't really listen. All I could think about was that I was due to be driving up to Cambridge that day, to drop work off at a client's. I'd assumed that I'd be going alone.

With Nancy firmly occupied somewhere else, another possibility sprang to mind.

When I saw Alice for coffee that afternoon I asked if she'd like to come. The warmth of her reply helped me through the remaining evenings of the week, and we talked about it every day on the phone. The plan was that I'd ring home early evening, when Nancy was back from her day, and say that I'd run into someone up there and wouldn't be back until late. It was a bending of our unspoken 'doing things by the book' rule, but it was unavoidable. Alice and I needed a whole afternoon and evening together, if I was ever going to be able to psych myself up to doing what had to be done.

By mid-evening on Friday I was at fever pitch. I was pacing round the house not settling at anything, so much in my own little world that it took me a while to notice that something was up with Nancy too.

She was sitting in the living room going over some papers, but kept glancing angrily out of the window as if expecting to see someone. When I rather irritably asked her about this, she denied she was doing it, but then ten minutes later I saw her do it again. I retreated to the kitchen and did something dull to a shelf that I'd been putting off for months. When Nancy stalked in to make some more coffee she saw what I was doing, and seemed genuinely touched that I'd finally got around to it. My smile of self-deprecating good nature felt as if it was stretched across the lips of a corpse.

Then she was back out in the lounge again, glaring nervously out of the window, as if fearing immanent invasion from a Martian army. It reminded me of the night I'd seen her standing by the window, and it was a little scary. She was looking very flaky that evening, and I'd run out of pity. I simply found it irritating, and hated myself for that.

Eventually, finally, at long last, it was time for bed. Nancy went ahead and I volunteered to close windows and tidy ashtrays. It's funny how you can seem most solicitous and endearing when you don't want to be there at all.

What I actually wanted was a few moments to wrap a novel I was going to give to Alice as a gift. When I heard the bathroom door shut, I leapt for the filing cabinet and took out the book. I grabbed tape and paper from a drawer and started wrapping. As I folded I glanced out of the window and saw the cat sitting outside in the road, and smiled to myself. With Alice I'd be able to have a cat of my own, could work with furry company and doze with a warm bundle on my lap. The bathroom door opened again and I paused, ready for instant action. When Nancy's feet had padded safely into the bedroom I continued wrapping. When it was done I slipped the present in a drawer, and took out the card I was going to give with it, already composing in my head the message for the inside.

'Mark?'

I nearly died when I heard Nancy's voice. She was striding through the kitchen towards me, and the card was still lying on my desk. I quickly yanked a sheaf of papers towards me and covered it, but only just in time. I turned to look at her, my heart beating horribly, trying to haul an expression of bland normality across my face.

'What's this?' she demanded, holding her hand up in front of me. It was dark in the room, and I couldn't see at first. Then I saw. It was a hair. A dark brown hair.

'It looks like a hair,' I said, carefully, shuffling papers on the desk.

'I know what it fucking is,' she snapped. 'It was in the bed. I wonder how it got there.'

Jesus Christ, I thought. *She knows.*

NOT WAVING

I stared at her with my mouth clamped shut, and wavered on the edge of telling the truth, of getting it over with. I'd thought it would happen some other, calmer, way, but you never know. Perhaps this was the pause into which I had to drop the information that I was in love with someone else.

Then, belatedly, I realized Alice had never been in the bedroom. Even since the night of the canal, she'd only ever been in the living room and the downstairs hall. Maybe the kitchen, but certainly not the bedroom.

I blinked at Nancy, confused.

'It's that bloody cat,' she shouted, instantly livid in the way that always disarmed and frightened me. 'It's been on our fucking bed.'

'What cat?'

'The cat who's always fucking outside. Your little *friend*,' she sneered violently, face almost unrecognizable. 'You've had it in here.'

'I haven't. What are you *talking* about?'

'Don't you deny, don't you...'

Unable to finish, Nancy simply threw herself at me and smacked me across the face.

Shocked, I stumbled backwards and she whacked me across the chin, and then pummeled her fists against my chest as I struggled to grab hold of her hands. She was trying to say something but it keep breaking up into furious sobs. In the end, before I could catch her hands, she took a step backwards and stood very still.

She stared at me for a moment, and then turned and walked out of the room.

I spent the night on the sofa, and was awake for hours after the last long, moaning sound had floated out to me from the bedroom. I felt I couldn't go to comfort her. It may sound like selfish evasion, but the only way I could make her feel better was by lying, so in the end I stayed away.

I had plenty of time to finish writing the card to Alice, but found it difficult to remember exactly what I'd been going to say. In the end I struggled into a shallow, cramped sleep, and Nancy was already gone by the time I woke up.

I felt tired and hollow as I drove to meet Alice in the center of town. I still didn't actually know where she lived, or even her phone number. She hadn't volunteered the information, and I could always contact her via the courier firm. I was content with that until I could enter her life without any skulking around.

I remember very clearly the way she looked, standing on the pavement and watching out for my car. She was wearing a long black woolen skirt and a thick sweater of various dark browns. Her hair was backlit by morning light and when she smiled as I pulled over towards her I had a moment of plunging doubt. I don't have any right to be with her, I thought. I already had someone, and Alice was far and away too wonderful. But she put her arms round me, and kissed my nose, and the feeling went away.

I have never driven as slowly on a motorway as that morning with Alice. I'd put some tapes in the car, music I knew we both liked, but they never made it out of the glove compartment. They simply weren't necessary. I sat in the slow lane and pootled along at sixty miles an hour, and we talked, or sat in silence, sometimes glancing across at each other and grinning.

The road cuts through several hills, and when we reached the first cutting we both gasped at once. The embankment was a blaze of poppies, nodding in a gathering wind, and when we'd left them behind I turned to Alice and for the first time said I loved her. She stared at me for a long time, and in the end I had to glance away at the road. When I looked back she was looking straight ahead and smiling, her eyes shining with held-back tears.

My meeting took a little under fifteen minutes—a personal record. I think my client was rather taken aback, but I didn't care. Alice and I spent the rest of the day walking around the shops, picking up books and looking at them, stopping for two cups of tea. As we came laughing out of a record store she slung her arm around my back, and very conscious of what I was doing, I put mine around her shoulders. Though she was tall it felt comfortable, and there it stayed. We fitted.

By about five I was getting tense, and we pulled into another café to have more tea, and so I could make my phone call. I left Alice sitting at the table waiting to order and went to the other side of the restaurant to use the booth. As I listened to the phone ringing at the other end I willed myself to be calm, and turned my back on the room to concentrate on what I was saying.

'Hello?'

NOT WAVING

When Nancy answered I barely recognized her. Her voice was like that of a querulously frightened old woman who'd not been expecting a call. I nearly put the phone down, but she realized who it was and immediately started crying.

It took me about twenty minutes to calm her even a little. She'd left the team-building at lunchtime, claiming illness. Then she'd gone to Sainsbury's. She had eaten two Sara Lee chocolate cakes, a fudge roll, a box of cereal and four packets of biscuits. She'd gone to the bathroom, vomited, and then started again. I think she'd been sick again at least once, but I couldn't really make sense of part of what she said. It was so mixed up with abject apologies to me that the sentences became confused, and I couldn't tell whether at one moment she was talking about the night before or about the half-eaten packet of jelly she still had in her hand.

Feeling a little frightened, and completely unaware of anything outside the cubicle I was standing in, I did what I could to focus her until what she was saying made a little more sense. I gave up trying to say that no apology was needed for the previous night, and in the end just told her everything was alright. She promised to stop eating for a while and to watch television instead. I said I'd be back as soon as I could.

I loved her. There was nothing else I could do.

When the last of my change was running out I told her to take care until I got back, and slowly replaced the handset. I stared at the wood paneling in front of me and gradually became aware of the noise from the restaurant on the other side of the glass door behind me. Eventually I turned, and looked out.

Alice was sitting at the table, watching the passing throng. She looked beautiful, and strong, and about two hundred thousand miles away.

We drove back to London in silence. Most of the talking was done in the restaurant. It didn't take very long. I said I couldn't leave Nancy in her current state, and Alice nodded once, and put her cigarettes in her bag.

She said that she'd sort of known, perhaps even before we'd got to Cambridge. I got angry then, and said she couldn't have, because I hadn't known myself. She got angry back when I said we'd still be friends, and she was right, I suppose. It was a stupid thing to say.

Awkwardly I asked if she'd be alright, and she said yes, in the sense that she'd survive. I tried to explain that was the difference, that Nancy might not. She shrugged and said that was the other difference: Nancy would never have to find out. The more we talked the more my head felt it was going to explode, as if eyes would burst with the pain and run in bloody lines down my cold cheeks. In the end she grew business-like and paid the bill, and we walked slowly back to the car in silence.

Neither of us could bring ourselves to small talk on the journey, and for the most part the only sound was that of the wheels upon the road. It was dark by then, and the rain began before we'd been on the motorway for very long. When we passed through the first cut in the hillside, I felt the poppies all around us, heads battered down by the falling water. Alice turned to me.

'I *did* know,' she said.

'How?' I asked, trying not to cry, trying to watch what the cars around me were doing.

'When you said you loved me, you sounded so unhappy.'

I dropped her in town, on the corner where I'd picked her up. She said a few things to help me, to make me feel less bad about what I'd done.

Then she walked off around the corner, and I never saw her again.

When I'd parked outside the house I sat for a moment, trying to pull myself together. Nancy would need to see me looking whole and at her disposal. I got out, looking half-heartedly for the cat. It wasn't there.

Nancy opened the door with a shy smile, and I followed her into the kitchen. As I hugged her, and told her everything was alright, I gazed blankly over her shoulder at the room. The kitchen was immaculate, no sign left of the afternoon's festivities. The rubbish had been taken out, and something was bubbling on the stove. She'd cooked me dinner.

She didn't eat, but sat at the table with me. The chicken was okay, but not up to her usual standard. There was a lot of meat but it was tough, and for once there was a little too much spice. It tasted odd, to be honest. She noticed a look on my face and said she'd gone to a different butcher. We talked a little about her afternoon, but she was feeling much better. She seemed more interested in discussing the way her office reorganization was shaping up.

NOT WAVING

Afterwards she went through into the lounge and turned the television on, and I set about making coffee and washing up, moving woodenly around the kitchen as if on abandoned rails. As Nancy's favourite televisual inanity boomed out from the living room I looked around for a bin bag to shovel the remains of my dinner into, but she'd evidently used them all. Sighing with a complete lack of feeling, I opened the back door and went out to put my scraps directly into the bin. There were two sacks already there, both tied with Nancy's distinctive knot. I undid the nearest and opened it up. Then, just before I pushed the bones off my plate, something in the bag caught my eye.

A patch of darkness amidst the garish wrappers of high-calorie comfort foods. An oddly-shaped piece of thick fabric, perhaps. I pulled the edge of the bag back a little further to look, and the light from the kitchen window above fell across the contents of the bag.

The darkness changed to a rich chestnut brown matted with red, and I saw it wasn't fabric at all.

We moved six months later, after we got engaged. I was glad to move. The flat never felt like home again. Sometimes I go back and stand in that street, remembering the weeks in which I stared out of the window, pointlessly watching the road. I called the courier firm after a couple of days. I was expecting a stonewall, and knew it was unlikely they'd give an address. But they denied she'd ever worked there at all.

After a couple of years Nancy and I had our first child, and she'll be eight this November. She has a sister now. Some evenings I'll leave them with their mother, and go out for a walk. I'll walk with heavy calm through black streets beneath featureless houses, and sometimes go down to the canal. I sit on the bench and close my eyes, and sometimes I think I can see it. Sometimes I think I can feel the way it was when a hill was there, and meetings were held in secret.

In the end I always stand up slowly, and walk the streets back to the house. The hill has gone and things have changed, and it's not like that anymore. No matter how long I sit and wait, the cats will never come.

LATER

I remember standing in the bedroom before we went out, fiddling with my tie and fretting mildly about the time. As yet we had plenty, but that was nothing to be complacent about. The minutes had a way of disappearing when Rachel was getting ready, early starts culminating in a breathless search for a taxi. We were going to a party, so it didn't really matter what time we left, but I tend to be a little dull about time. I used to, anyway.

When I had the tie as close to a tidy knot as I was able I turned from the mirror, and opened my mouth to call out to Rachel. But then I caught sight of what was on the bed, and closed it again. For a moment I just stood and looked, and then walked over towards it.

It wasn't anything very spectacular, just a dress made of sheeny white material. A few years ago, when we started going out, Rachel used to make a lot of her clothes. Not because she had to, but because she enjoyed it. She used to haul me endlessly round dress-making shops, browsing patterns and asking my opinion on a million different fabrics, while I half-heartedly protested and moaned.

On impulse I leant down and felt the material, and found I could remember touching it for the first time in the shop on Mill Road, could recall surfacing up through contented boredom to say that yes, I liked this one. On that recommendation she'd bought it, and made this dress, and as a reward for traipsing around after her she'd bought me dinner too. We were poorer then, so the meal was cheap, but there was lots and it was good.

The strange thing was, I didn't even really mind the dress shops. You know how sometimes, when you're just walking around, living your life, you'll see someone on the street and fall hopelessly in love with them? How something in the way they look, the way they are, makes you stop dead in your tracks and stare: and how for that instant you're convinced that if you could just meet them, you'd be able to love them forever? Wild schemes and unlikely chance meetings pass through your head, and yet as they stand on the other side of the street or the room, talking to someone else, they haven't the faintest idea of what's going through your mind. Something has clicked, though only inside you. You know you'll never speak to them, that they'll never know what you're feeling, and that they'll never want to. But something about them forces you to keep looking, until you wish they'd leave so you could be free.

The first time I saw Rachel was like that, and now she was in my bath. I didn't call out to hurry her along. I decided it didn't really matter.

A few minutes later a protracted squawking noise announced the letting out of the bath water, and Rachel wafted into the bedroom swaddled in thick towels and glowing high spirits. Suddenly I lost all interest in going to the party, punctually or otherwise. She marched up to me, set her head at a silly angle to kiss me on the lips and jerked my tie vigorously in about three different directions. When I looked in the mirror I saw that somehow, as always, she'd turned it into a perfect knot.

Half an hour later we left the flat, still in plenty of time. If anything, I'd held her up.

'Later,' she'd said, smiling in the way that showed she meant it. 'Later, and for a long time, my man.'

I turned from locking the door to see her standing on the pavement outside the house, looking perfect in her white dress, looking happy. As I walked smiling down the steps towards her she skipped backwards into the road, laughing for no reason, laughing because she was with me.

'Come on,' she said, holding out her hand like a dancer, and a yellow van came round the corner and smashed into her.

She span backwards as if tugged on a rope, rebounded off a parked car and toppled into the road. As I stood frozen on the bottom step she half sat

LATER

up and looked at me, an expression of wordless surprise on her face, and then she fell back again.

By the time I reached her, blood was already pulsing up into the white of her dress and welling out of her mouth. It ran out over her makeup and I saw she'd been right: she hadn't quite blended the colors above her eyes. I'd told her it didn't matter.

She tried to move her head again and there was a sticky sound as it almost left the tarmac and then slumped back. Her hair fell back from around her face, but not as it usually did. There was a faint flicker in her eyelids, and then she died.

I knelt there in the road beside her, holding her hand. I heard every word the small crowd said, but I don't know what they were muttering about. All I could think was that there wasn't going to be a later, not to kiss her some more, not for anything.

Later was gone.

When I got home from the hospital I phoned her mother. I did it as soon as I got back, though I didn't want to. I didn't want to tell anyone, didn't want to make it official. It was a bad phone call, very, very bad. Then I sat in the flat, looking at the drawers Rachel had left open, at the towels on the floor, at the party invitation on the dressing table, feeling my stomach crawl.

I was back at the flat, as if we'd come back home from the party. I should have been making coffee while Rachel had yet another bath, coffee we'd drink on the sofa in front of the fire. But the fire was off and the bath was empty. So what was I supposed to do?

I sat for an hour, feeling as if somehow I'd slipped too far forward in time and left Rachel behind, as if I could turn and see her desperately running to try to catch me up. When it felt as if my throat was going to burst I called my parents and they came and took me home. My mother gently made me change my clothes, but she didn't wash them. Not until I was asleep, anyway. When I came down and saw them clean I hated her, but I knew she was right and the hate went away. There wouldn't have been much point in just keeping them in a drawer.

The funeral was short. I guess they all are, really, but there's no point in them being any longer. Nothing more would be said. I was a little better by then, and not crying so much, though I did before we went to the church because I couldn't get my tie to sit right.

Rachel was buried near her grandparents, which she would have liked. Her parents gave me her dress afterwards, because I'd asked for it. It had been thoroughly cleaned and large patches had lost their sheen and died, looking as much unlike Rachel's dress as the cloth had on the roll in the shop where she'd bought it. I'd almost have preferred the bloodstains still to have been there: at least that way I could have believed that the cloth still sparkled beneath them. But they were right in their way, as my mother was. Some people seem to have pragmatic, accepting souls, an ability with death.

I don't, I'm afraid. I don't understand it at all.

Afterwards I stood at the graveside for a while, but not for long because I knew my parents were waiting at the car. As I stood by the mound of earth that lay on top of her I tried to concentrate, to send some final thought to her, some final love, but the world kept pressing in on me through the sound of cars on the road and some bird that was cawing up in a tree. I couldn't shut it out. I couldn't believe that I was noticing how cold it was; I couldn't believe that somewhere lives were being led and televisions being watched, that the inside of my parents' car would smell the same as it always had. I wanted to feel something, wanted to sense her presence, but I couldn't. All I could feel was the world round me, the same old world. But it wasn't a world that had been there a week ago, and I couldn't understand how it could look so much the same.

It was the same because nothing had changed, I supposed, and I turned and walked to the car.

The wake was worse than the funeral, much worse, and I stood with a tuna sandwich feeling something very cold building up inside. Rachel's oldest friend Lisa held court with her old school friends, swiftly running the range of emotions from stoic resilience to trembling incoherence.

'I've just realized,' she sobbed to me, 'Rachel's not going to be at my wedding.'

'She's not going to be at mine either,' I said numbly, and immediately hated myself for it.

I went and stood by the window, out of harm's way. I couldn't react properly. I knew why everyone was standing here, that in some ways it was like a wedding. Instead of gathering together to bear witness to a bond, they were here to prove she was dead. In the weeks to come they'd know they'd stood together in a room, and eaten crisps, and would be able to accept she was gone. I couldn't.

I said goodbye to Rachel's parents before I left. We looked at each other oddly, and shook hands, as if we were strangers again. Then I went back to the flat and changed into some old clothes. My 'Someday' clothes, Rachel used to call them, as in 'some day you must throw those away'. Then I made a cup of tea and stared out of the window for a while. I knew damn well what I was going to do, and it was a relief to give in to it.

That night I went back to the cemetery and dug her up.

It was hard work, and it took a lot longer than I expected, but in another way it was surprisingly easy. I mean yes, it was creepy, and yes, I felt like a lunatic, but after the shovel had gone in once, the second time seemed less strange. It was like waking up in the mornings after the accident. The first time I clutched at myself and couldn't understand, but after that I knew what to expect. There were no cracks of thunder, there was no web of lightning and I actually felt very calm. There was just me and, beneath the earth, my friend. I simply wanted to find her.

When I did I laid her down by the side of the grave and then filled it back up again, being careful to make it look how it had. Then I carried her to the car in my arms and brought her home.

The flat seemed very quiet as I sat her on the sofa, and the cushion rustled and creaked as it took her weight again. When she was settled I knelt and looked up at her face. It looked much the same as it always had, though the color of the skin was different, didn't have the glow she always had. That's where life is, you know, not in the heart but in the little things, like the way hair falls around someone's neck. Her nose looked the same and her forehead was smooth. It was the same face.

I knew the dress she was wearing was hiding a lot of things I would rather not see, but I took it off anyway. It was her going-away dress, bought by her family specially for the occasion, and it didn't mean anything to me or to her. I knew what the damage would be and what it meant. As it turned out the patchers and menders had done a good job, not glossing because it wouldn't be seen. It wasn't so bad.

When she was sitting up again in her white dress I walked over and turned the light down, and I cried a little then, because she looked so much the same. She could have fallen asleep, warmed by the fire and dozy with wine, as if we'd just come back from the party.

I went and had a bath. We both used to when we came back in from an evening, to feel clean and fresh for when we slipped between the sheets. It wouldn't be like that this evening, of course, but I had dirt all over me, and I wanted to feel normal. For one night at least I just wanted things to be as they had.

I sat in the bath for a while, knowing she was in the living room, and slowly washed myself clean. I really wasn't thinking much. It felt nice to know that I wouldn't be alone when I walked back in there. That was better than nothing, was part of what had made her alive. I dropped my Someday clothes in the bin and put on the ones from the evening of the accident. They didn't mean as much as her dress, but at least they were from before.

When I returned to the living room her head had lolled slightly, but it would have done if she'd fallen asleep. I made us both a cup of coffee. The only time she ever took sugar was in last cup of the day, so I put one in.

Then I sat down next to her on the sofa and I was glad that the cushions had her dent in them, that as always they drew me slightly towards her, didn't leave me perched there by myself.

The first time I saw Rachel was at a party. I saw her across the room and simply stared at her, but we didn't speak. We didn't meet properly for a month or two, and first kissed a few weeks after that. As I sat there on the sofa next to her body I reached out tentatively and took her hand, as I had done on that first night. It was cooler than it should have been, but not too bad because of the fire, and I held it, feeling the lines on her palm, lines I knew better than my own.

I let myself feel calm and I held her hand in the half light, not looking at her, as also on that first night, when I'd been too happy to push my luck. She's letting you hold her hand, I'd thought, don't expect to be able to look at her too. Holding her hand is more than enough: don't look, you'll break the spell.

LATER

My face creased, not knowing whether to smile or cry, but it felt alright. It really did.

I sat there for a long time, watching the flames, still not thinking, just holding her hand and letting the minutes run. The longer I sat, the more normal it felt, and finally I turned slowly to look at her. She looked tired and asleep, so deeply asleep, but still there with me and still mine.

When her eyelid first moved I thought it was a trick of the light, a flicker cast by the fire.

But then it stirred again, and for the smallest of moments I thought I was going to die. The other eyelid moved and my fear simply disappeared, and that made the difference, I think. She had a long way to come, and if I'd felt frightened, or rejected her, I think that would have finished it then. I didn't question it.

A few minutes later both her eyes were open, and it wasn't long before she was able to slowly turn her head.

I still go to work, and put in the occasional appearance at social events, but my tie never looks quite as it did. She can't move her fingers precisely enough to help me with that any more. She can't come with me, and nobody can come here, but that doesn't matter. We always spent a lot of time by ourselves. We wanted to.

I have to do a lot of things for her, but I can live with that. Lots of people have accidents, bad ones: if Rachel had survived she could have been disabled, or brain-damaged, so that her movements were as they are now, so slow and clumsy. I wish she could talk, but there's no air in her lungs, so I'm learning to read her lips. Her mouth moves slowly, but I know she's trying to speak, and I want to hear what she's saying.

But she gets round the flat, and she holds my hand, and she smiles as best she can. If she'd just been injured I would have loved her still.

It's not so very different.

WALKING **WOUNDED**

When after two days the discomfort in his side had not lessened, merely mutated, Richard began finally to get mildly concerned. It didn't hurt as often as it had at first, and he could make a wider range of movements without triggering epic discomfort; but when the pain did come it was somehow deeper, as if settled into the bone.

Christine's solution to the problem was straightforward in its logic, and strident in delivery. He should go to Casualty, or at the very least to the doctor's surgery not far down the street from their new flat in Kingsley Road.

Richard's view, though unspoken, was just as definite: *bollocks to that*.

There were more than enough dull post-move tasks to be endured without traipsing up to the Royal Free and sitting amongst stoic old women and bleeding youths in a purgatory of peeling linoleum. As they were now condemned to living on a different branch of the Northern line to Hampstead, it would require a dogleg trip down to Camden and back out again—together with a potentially limitless spell on a waiting room bench—and burn up a whole afternoon. Even less appealing was the prospect of going down the road and explaining in front of an audience of whey-faced locals that he had been living somewhere else, now lived just across the road, and wished to both register with the surgery and have the doctor's doubtless apathetic opinion on a rather unspecific pain in Richard's side. And that he was very sorry for being middle-class and would they please not beat him up.

MICHAEL MARSHALL SMITH

He couldn't be bothered, in other words, and instead decided to dedicate Monday to taking a variety of objects out of cardboard boxes and trying to work out where they could be least unattractively placed. Christine had returned to work, at least, which meant she couldn't see his winces or hear the swearing which greeted every new object for which there simply wasn't room.

The weekend had been hell, and not just because Richard hadn't wanted to move in the first place. He *had* wanted to, to some extent; or at least he'd believed they *should* do. It had come to him one night while lying in bed in the flat in Belsize Park, listening to the even cadence of Chris' breathing and wondering at what point in the last couple of months they had stopped falling asleep together. At first they'd drifted off simultaneously, facing each other, four hands clasped into a declaration, determined not to leave each other even for the hours they spent in another realm. Richard half-remembered a poem by someone long dead—Herrick, possibly?—the gist of which had been that though we all inhabit the same place during the day, at night each one of us is hurled into a several world. Well it hadn't been that way with them, not at first. Yet after nine months there he was, lying awake, happy to be in the same bed as Chris but wondering where she was.

Eventually he'd got up and wandered through into the sitting room. In the half-light it looked the same as it always had. You couldn't see which pictures had been taken down, which objects had been removed from shelves and hidden in boxes at the bottom of cupboards. You couldn't tell that for three years he had lived there with someone else.

But Richard knew that he had, and so did Christine.

As he gazed out over the garden in which Susan's attempts as horticulture still struggled for life in the face of indifference, Richard finally realized that they should move. Understood, suddenly and with cold guilt, that Chris probably didn't like living here. It was a lovely flat, with huge rooms and high ceilings. It was on Belsize Avenue, which meant not only was it within three minutes' walk of Haverstock Hill, with its cafés, stores and tube station, but Belsize 'village' was just around the corner. A small enclave of shops specifically designed to cater to the needs of the local well-heeled, the village was so comprehensively stocked with pâtés, wine, videos and magazines that you hardly ever actually needed to go up to Hampstead, itself only a pleasant ten minutes' stroll away. The view from the front of the flat itself was onto the Avenue, wide and spaced with ancient trees. The back was onto a garden neatly bordered by an old brick wall, and although only a few plants grew with any real enthusiasm, the overall effect was pleasing.

But the view through Christine's eyes was probably different.

She perhaps saw the local pubs and restaurants in which Richard and Susan had spent years of happy evenings. She maybe felt the tightness with which her predecessor had held Richard's hand as they walked down to the village, past the gnarled mulberry tree which was the sole survivor of the garden of a country house which had originally stood there.

She certainly wondered which particular patches of carpet within the flat had provided arenas for cheerful, drunken sex. This had come out one night after they'd come back drunk and irritable from an unsuccessful dinner party at one of Chris' friends. Richard had been bored enough by the evening to respond angrily to the question, and the matter had been dropped.

Standing there in the middle of the night, staring around a room stripped of its familiarity by darkness, he remembered the conversation, the nearest thing they'd yet had to a full-blown row. For a moment he saw the flat as she did, and almost believed he could hear the rustling of gifts from another woman, condemned to storage but stirring in their boxes, remembering the places where they had once stood.

The next morning, over cappuccinos on Haverstock Hill, he'd suggested they move.

At the eagerness of her response he felt a band loosen in his chest that he hadn't even realized was there, and the rest of the day was wonderful.

Not so the move. Three years' worth of flotsam, fifty boxes full of stuff. Possessions and belongings that he'd believed to be individual objects metamorphosed into a mass of generic crap to be manhandled and sorted through. The flat they'd finally found to move into was tiny. Well, not *tiny*: the living room and kitchen were big enough, and there was a roof terrace. But a good deal smaller than Belsize Avenue, and nearly twenty boxes of Richard's stuff had to go into storage. Books which he seldom looked at, but would have preferred to have around; DVDs which he didn't want to watch next week, but might in a couple of months; old clothes which he never wore but had too much sentimental value to be thrown away.

And, of course, the Susan collection. Objects in boxes, rounded up and buried deeper by putting in further boxes, then sent off to be hidden in some warehouse in Kings Cross.

At a cost of fifteen pounds a week this was going to make living in the new flat even more expensive than the old one—despite the fact it was in Kentish Town and you couldn't buy a decent chicken liver and hazelnut pâté for love or money.

On Friday night the two of them huddled together baffled and exhausted in the huge living room in Belsize Avenue, surrounded by mountains of cardboard. They drank cups of coffee and tried to watch television, but the flat had already taken its leave of them. When they went to bed it was if they were lying on a cold hillside in some country where their visa had expired.

The next morning two affable Australians arrived with a van the size of Denmark, and Richard watched, vicariously exhausted, as they trotted up and down the stairs, taking his life away. Chris bristled with female know-how in the kitchen, periodically sweeping past him with a damp cloth in her hand, humming to herself. As the final pieces of furniture were dragged away Richard tried to say goodbye to the flat, but the walls stared back at him with vacant indifference, and offered nothing more than dust in corners which had previously been hidden. Dust, some particles of which were probably Susan's skin—and his and Chris's, of course. He left to the sound of a hoover, and followed the van to their new home.

Where, it transpired, his main bookcase could not be taken up the stairs.

The two Australians, by now rather bedraggled and hot, struggled gamely in the dying light but eventually had to confess themselves beaten. Richard, rather depressed, allowed them to put the bookcase back in the van, to be taken off with the other storage items. Much later he held out a tenner tip to each of them, watched the van squeeze off down the narrow road, and then turned and walked into his new home.

Chris was still at Belsize Avenue, putting finishing touches to the cleaning and negotiating with the old twonk who owned the place. While he

WALKING WOUNDED

waited for her to arrive, Richard moved a few boxes around, not wanting to do anything significant before Chris was there to share it with him, but too tired to simply sit still. The lower hallway was almost completely impassable, and he resolved to carry a couple of boxes up to the living room.

It was while he was struggling up the stairs with one of them that he hurt himself.

He was about halfway up, panting under a box which seemed to weigh more than the house itself, when he slipped on a cushion lying on the stairs. Muscles which he hadn't used since his athletic glory days at school kicked into action, and he managed to avoid falling, but collided heavily with the wall instead. The corner of the box he was carrying crunched solidly into his ribs.

For a moment the pain was truly startling, and a small voice in his head said 'Well, that's done it'.

He let the box slide to the floor, and stood panting for a while, fingers tentatively feeling for what he was sure must be at least one broken rib. He half expected it to be protruding from his body. He couldn't find anything which yielded more than usual, however, and after a recuperative cigarette he carefully pushed the box the remainder of the journey up the stairs.

Half an hour later Chris arrived, cheerfully grumpy about their previous landlord's attempts to whittle money off their deposit, and set to work on the kitchen.

They fell asleep together that night, three of their hands together; one of Richard's unconsciously guarding his side.

The next morning it hurt like hell, but as a fully-fledged male human, Richard knew exactly how to deal with the situation: he ignored it. After four days of looking at the cardboard boxes cheerfully emblazoned with the logo of the removal firm, he had begun to hate the sight of them, and concentrated first on unpacking everything so he could be rid of them.

In the morning he worked in the living room, unpacking to the sound of Chris whistling in the kitchen and bathroom. He discovered that two of the boxes shouldn't even have been there at all, but were supposed to have been taken with the others and put in storage. One was full of manuals for software he either never used, or knew back to front; the other was a box of Susan Objects.

As he opened it, Richard realized why it had hurt quite so much when making contact with his ribs. It contained, amongst other things, a heavy and angular bronze which she had made and presented to him. He was lucky it hadn't impaled him to the wall.

As it wasn't worth calling the removal men out to collect the boxes, they both ended up in his microscopic study, squatting on top of the filing cabinet. More precious space taken up by stuff which shouldn't even be there; either in the flat, or in his life.

The rest of the weekend disappeared in a blur of tidal movement and pizza. Objects migrated from room to room, in smaller and slower circles, before finally finding their resting places. Chris efficiently unpacked all the clothes and put them in the fitted wardrobes, cooing over the increase in hanging space. Richard tried to organize his books into his *decreased* shelving space, eventually having to lay many on their side and pile them up vertically. He tried to tell himself this looked funky and less anal-retentive, but couldn't get the idea to take. He set his desk and computer up.

By Monday most of it was done, and Richard spent the morning trying to make his study habitable by clearing the few remaining boxes. At eleven Chris called from work, cheerful and full of vim, and he was glad to sense that the move had made her happy. As they were chatting he realized that he must at some point have scraped his left hand, because there were a series of shallow scratches, like paper cuts, over the palm and underside of the fingers.

They hardly seemed significant against the pain in his side, and aside from washing his hands when the conversation was over, he ignored them.

In the afternoon he took a break and walked down to the local corner store for cigarettes. It was only his second visit, but he knew he'd already seen all it had to offer. The equivalent store in Belsize Village had stocked American magazines, fresh-baked bread and three different types of hand-fashioned pesto. Next door had been the delicatessen with home-made duck's liver and port pâté. 'Raj's EZShop' sold precisely none of these things, having elected instead to focus rather single-mindedly on the instant noodle and cheap toilet-paper end of the market.

WALKING WOUNDED

When he left the shop Richard went and peered dispiritedly at the grubby menu hanging in the window of the restaurant opposite. Eritrean food, whatever the hell that was. One of the dishes was described as 'three pieces of cooked meat', which seemed both strangely specific and discomfortingly vague.

Huddling into his jacket against the cold, he turned and walked for home, feeling—he imagined—rather like a deposed Russian aristocrat, allowed against all odds to remain alive after the revolution, but condemned to lack everything which he had once held dear. The sight of a small white dog scuttling by only seemed to underline his isolation.

When Chris returned at six she couldn't understand his quietness, and he didn't have the heart to try to explain it to her.

'What's that?'

The answer, Richard saw, appeared to be "a scratch". About four inches long, it ran across his chest, directly over his heart. He hadn't noticed it before, but it seemed to have healed and thus must have been there for a day or two.

'Another souvenir from the move,' he guessed. It was after midnight and they were lying in bed, having just abandoned an attempt to make love. It wasn't any lack of enthusiasm—far from it—simply that the pain in Richard's ribs was too bracing to ignore. He was fine so long as he kept his chest facing directly forwards. Any twisting and it felt as if someone was stoving in his rib cage with a well-aimed boot. 'And no, I'm not going to the doctor about it.'

Chris smiled, started to tickle him, and then realized she shouldn't. Instead she sighed theatrically, and kissed him on the nose before turning to lie on her side.

'You'd better get well soon,' she said, 'Or I'm going to have to buy a do-it-yourself book.'

'You'll go blind,' he said, turning off the bedside light, and she giggled quietly in the dark. He rolled gingerly so that he was snuggled into her back, and lightly stroked her shoulder, waiting for sleep.

After a moment he noticed a wetness under his hand, and stopped, pulling it out from under the duvet. In the threadbare moonlight he confirmed what he'd already suspected. Earlier in the evening he'd noticed that the little cuts on his hand seemed to be exuding tiny amounts of blood. It was still happening. Constantly being reopened when he lugged boxes around, presumably.

'S'nice,' Chris murmured sleepily. 'Don't stop.'

Richard slid his hand back under the duvet and moved it gently against her shoulder again, using the back of his fingers, and cupping his palm away from her.

The bathroom was tiny, but very adequately equipped with mirrors. Richard couldn't help noticing the change as soon as he took off his dressing gown the next morning.

There was still no sign of bruising over his ribs, which worried him. Something which hurt that much ought to have an external manifestation, he believed, unless it indicated internal damage. The pain was a little different this morning, less like a kicking, more as if two of the ribs were moving tightly against each other. A kind of cartilaginous twisting.

There were also a number of new scratches.

Mostly short, they were primarily congregated over his stomach and chest. It looked as though a cat with its claws out had run over him in the night. As they didn't have a cat, this seemed unlikely, and Richard frowned as he regarded himself in the mirror.

Also odd was the mark on his chest.

Perhaps it was merely seeing it in proper light, but this morning it looked like more than just a scratch. By spreading his fingers out on either side, he found he could pull the edges of the cut slightly apart, and that it was a millimeter or so deep. When he allowed it to close again it did so with a faint liquidity, the sides tacky with lymph. It wasn't healing properly. In fact—and Richard held up his left hand to confirm this—it was doing the same as the cuts on his palm. They too seemed as fresh as the day before—maybe even a little fresher.

Glad that Chris had left the house before he'd made it out of bed, Richard quickly showered, patting himself dry around the cuts, and covered them with clothes.

By lunchtime the flat was finally in order, and Richard had to admit that parts of it looked pretty good. The kitchen was the sole room which was

WALKING WOUNDED

bigger than he'd been used to in the previous flat, and in slanting light in the late morning, it was actually very attractive. The table was a little larger than would have been ideal, but at least you could get at the fridge without performing contortions.

The living room upstairs also looked pretty bijou, if you ignored the way half his books were crammed sideways into the bookcases. Chris had already established a nest on the larger of the two sofas; her book, ashtray and an empty coffee mug placed within easy reach. Richard perched on the other sofa for a while, eyes vaguely running over his books, and realizing he ought to make an effort to colonize a corner of the room for his own, too.

Human, All Too Human.

The title brought Richard out of his reverie. A second-hand volume of Nietzsche, bought for him as a joke by Susan. It shouldn't have been on the shelf, but in one of the storage boxes. Chris didn't know it had been a present from Susan, but then it hadn't been Chris who'd insisted he take the other stuff down. It had simply seemed to be the right thing to do, and Richard had methodically worked around the old flat hiding things, the day before Chris moved in. Hiding them from whom, he hadn't been sure. It had been six months by then since he and Susan had split up, and she wasn't even seeing the man she'd left him for any more. To have the old mementos still out didn't cause him any pain, and he'd thought he'd put them away purely out of consideration for Chris.

But as he looked over the bookcase he realized how much the book of Nietzsche stood out in their new flat. It smelled of Susan. Some tiny part of her, a speck of skin or smear of oil, must surely still be on it somewhere. If he could sense that, surely Chris could too.

He walked across the room, took the book from the shelf, and walked downstairs to put it in the box on top of his filing cabinet in the study. On the way he diverted into the bathroom. As he absently opened his fly, he noticed an unexpected sensation at his fingertips.

He brushed them around inside his trousers again, trying to work out what he'd felt. Then he slowly removed them, and held his hand up.

His fingers were spotted with blood.

Richard stared coldly at them for a while, and then calmly undid the button of his trousers. Carefully he lowered them, and then pushed down his boxer shorts.

More cuts.

A long red line ran from the middle of his right thigh around to within a couple of inches of his testicles. A similar one lay across the very bottom of his stomach. A much shorter but deeper slit lay across the base of his penis, and it was from this that the majority of the blood was flowing. It wasn't a bad cut, and hardly put one in mind of the *Texas Chainsaw Massacre*, but Richard would have much preferred it not to have been there.

Looking up at the mirror above the toilet, he reached up and undid the buttons on his shirt. The scratches on his stomach now looked more like cuts, and a small thin line of blood rolled down from the cut on his chest.

Like many people—men especially—Richard wasn't fond of doctors. It wasn't the sepulchral gloom of waiting rooms, or the grim pleasure their receptionists took in patronizing you. It was the boredom and the sense of potential catastrophe, combined with a knowledge that there probably wasn't a great deal they could do in any event. If you had something really bad, they sent you to a hospital. If it was trivial, it would go away of its own accord.

It was partly for these reasons that Richard simply did his shirt and trousers back up again, after patting at some of the cuts with pieces of toilet tissue.

It was partly also because he was afraid.

He didn't know where the scratches were coming from, but the fact that far from healing, they seemed to be getting worse, was worrying. With his vague semi-understanding of such things, he wondered if it meant his blood had stopped clotting, and if so, what that meant in turn. He didn't think you could suddenly develop hemophilia. It didn't seem very likely. But what then? Perhaps he was tired, run-down after the move, and that was making a difference.

In the end he resolved to simply go on ignoring it a little longer, like that mole which keeps growing but which you don't wish to believe might be malignant.

He spent the afternoon sitting carefully at his desk, trying to work and resisting the urge to peek at parts of his body. It was almost certainly his imagination, he believed, which made it feel as if a warm, plump drop of blood had sweated from the cut on his chest and rolled slowly down beneath his shirt; and the dampness he felt around his crotch was the result of his having turned the heating up high.

Absolutely.

He took care to shower well before Chris was due back. The cuts were still there, and had been joined by another on his upper arm.

When he was dry he took some surgical dressing and micropore tape from the bathroom cabinet and covered the ones which were bleeding most. He then chose his darkest shirt from the wardrobe and sat in the kitchen, waiting for Chris to come home. He would have gone upstairs, but didn't really feel comfortable up there by himself yet. Although most of the objects in the room were his, Chris had arranged them, and the room seemed a little forlorn without her to fill in their underlying structure.

That evening they went out to a pub in Soho, a birthday drink for one of Chris' mates. Chris had several different groups of friends, Richard had discovered. He had also discovered that the ones she regarded as her closest were the ones he found hardest to like. It wasn't because of anything intrinsically unpleasant, more an insufferable air of having known each other since before the dawn of time, like some heroic group, the Knights of the Pine Table. Unless you could remember the hilarious occasion when they all went down to the Dangling Cock in Mulchester and good old 'Kipper' Philips sang 'Bohemian Rhapsody' straight through while lying on the bar with a pint on his head before going on to amusingly prang his father's car on the steps of the village church, you were clearly no more than one of life's spear carriers—even after you'd been going out with one of them for nearly a year. In their terms, God was a bit of a Johnny-come-lately, and the Devil, even had he turned up to dinner with a small hostess gift and a bottle of very good wine, would have been treated with the cloying indulgence reserved for friends' younger siblings.

Luckily that evening they were seeing a different and more recent group, some of whom were certified human beings. Richard stood at the bar affably enough, slowly downing a series of Kronenbourgs while Chris alternately went to talk to people or brought them to talk to him. One of the latter, a doctor whom Richard believed to be called Kate, peered hard at him as soon as she hove into view.

'What's that?' she asked, bluntly.

Richard was about to tell her that what he was holding was called a "pint", that it consisted of the liquid alcoholic byproducts of the soaking, boiling and fermenting of certain natural vegetative species, and that he had every intention—regardless of any objections she or anyone else might have—of drinking it, when he realized she was looking at his left hand. Too late, he tried to slip it into his pocket, but she reached out and snatched it up.

'Been in a fight, have you?' she asked. Behind her Chris turned from the man she was talking to, and looked over Kate's shoulder at Richard's hand.

'No,' he said. 'Just a bizarre flat relocation accident.'

'Hmm,' Kate said, her mouth pursed into a moue of consideration. 'Looks like someone's come at you with a knife, if you ask me.'

Chris looked at Richard, eyes wide, and he groaned inwardly.

'Well, things between Chris and I haven't been so good lately...' he tried, and got a laugh from both of them. Kate wasn't to be deflected, however.

'I'm serious,' she said, holding up her own hand to demonstrate. 'Someone tries to kill you with a knife, what do you do? You hold your hands up. And so what happens is often the blade will nick the defending hands a couple of times before the knife gets through. See it all the time in Casualty. Little cuts, just like those.'

Richard pretended to examine the cuts on his hand, and shrugged.

'Maybe Kate could look at your ribs,' Chris said.

'I'm sure there's nothing she'd like better,' he said. 'After a hard day at the coal face there's probably nothing she'd like more than to look at another piece of fossilized wood.'

'What's wrong with your ribs?' Kate asked, squinting at him closely.

'Nothing,' he said. 'Just banged them.'

'Does this hurt?' she asked, and suddenly cuffed him around the back of the head.

'No,' he said, laughing.

WALKING WOUNDED

'Then you're probably alright,' she winked, and disappeared to get a drink. Chris frowned for a moment, caught between irritation at not having got to the bottom of Richard's rib problem, and happiness at seeing him get on well with one of her friends.

Just then a fresh influx of people arrived at the door, and Richard was saved from having to watch her choose which emotion to go with.

Mid-evening he went to the gents and shut himself into one of the cubicles. He changed the dressings on his penis and chest, and noted that some of the cuts on his stomach were now slick with blood. He didn't have enough micropore to dress them, and would have to hope that they stayed manageable until he got home. The cuts on his hands didn't seem to be getting any deeper.

Obviously they were just nicks. Almost, as Kate had said, as if someone had come at him with a knife.

They got home well after midnight. Chris was more drunk than Richard, but he didn't mind. She was one of those rare people who got cuter when she was plastered, instead of maudlin or argumentative.

Chris staggered straight into the bathroom, to do whatever the hell it was she spent all that time in there doing. Richard made his way into the study to check the answer phone, gently banging into walls whose positions he still hadn't internalized yet.

One message.

Sitting heavily down on his chair, Richard pressed play. Without noticing he was doing it, he reached forward and turned down the volume so only he would hear what was on the tape. This was a habit born of the first weeks of his relationship with Chris, when Susan was still calling regularly. Her messages, though generally short and uncontroversial, were not things he wanted Chris to hear. Again, a programme of protection, now no longer needed.

Feeling self-righteous, and burping gently, Richard turned the volume back up.

He almost jumped out of his skin when he realized the message actually *was* from Susan, and hurriedly turned the volume back down.

She said hello, in the diffident way she had, and went on to observe that they hadn't seen each other that year. There was no reproach, simply a statement of fact. She asked him to call her soon, to arrange a drink.

The message had just finished when Chris lurched out of the bathroom smelling of toothpaste and moisturizer. "ny messages?'

'Just a wrong number,' he said.

She shook her head slightly, apparently to clear it, rather than in negation. 'Coming to bed then?' she asked, slyly. Waggling her eyebrows, she performed a slow grind with her pelvis, managing both not to fall over and not to look silly, which was a hell of a trick. Richard made his "Sex Life in Ancient Rome" face, inspired by a book he'd read many years before.

'Hell yes,' he said. 'Be there in a minute.'

But he stayed in the study for twenty minutes, long enough to ensure that Chris would have fallen asleep. Wearing pajamas for the first time in years, he slipped quietly in beside her and waited for the morning.

The bedroom seemed very small as he lay there, and whereas in Belsize Park the moonlight had sliced in, casting attractive shadows on the wall, in Kingsley Road the only visitors in the night were the curdled orange of a streetlight outside and the sound of a siren in the distance.

As soon as Chris had dragged herself groaning out of the house the next morning, Richard got up and went through to the bathroom. He knew before he took his nightclothes off what he was going to find. He could feel parts of the pajama top sticking to areas on his chest and stomach, and his crotch felt warm and wet.

The marks on his stomach now looked like proper cuts, and the gash on his chest had opened still further. His penis was covered in dark blood, and the gashes around it were nasty. He looked as if he had collided with a threshing machine. His ribs still hurt a great deal, though the pain seemed to be constricting, concentrating around a specific point rather than applying to the whole of his side.

He stood there for ten minutes, staring at himself in the mirror. So much damage. As he watched, he saw a faint line slowly draw itself down three inches of his forearm; a thin raised scab. He knew that by the end of the day it would have reverted into a cut.

WALKING WOUNDED

Mid-morning he called Susan at her office. As always he was surprised by how official she sounded when he spoke to her there. She had always been languid of voice, in complete contrast to her physical and emotional vivacity—but when you talked to her at work she sounded like a headmistress.

Her tone mellowed when she realized who it was. She tried to pin him down to a date for a drink, but he skirted the issue. They'd seen each other twice since she'd left him for John Simmons; once while he'd been living with Chris. Chris had been relaxed about the meetings, but Richard hadn't. On both occasions he and Susan had spent a good deal of time talking about Simmons: the first time focusing on why Susan had left Richard for him, the second on how unhappy she was about the fact that Simmons had in turn left her without even saying goodbye.

Either she hadn't realized how much the conversations would hurt Richard, or she hadn't even thought about it. Most likely she had just taken comfort from talking to him in the way she always had.

'You're avoiding it, aren't you,' Susan said, eventually.

'What?'

'Naming a day. Why?'

'I'm not,' he protested, feebly. 'I'm just, busy, you know. I don't want to say a date and then have to cancel.'

'I really want to see you,' she said. 'I miss you.'

Don't say that, thought Richard miserably. *Please don't say that.*

'And there's something else,' she added. 'It was a year ago today when...'

'When what?' Richard asked, confused. They'd split up eighteen months ago.

'The last time I saw John,' she said, and finally Richard understood.

That afternoon he took a walk to kill time, trolling up and down the surrounding streets, trying to find something to like. He discovered another corner store, but it didn't stock Parma ham either. Little dusty bags of fuses hung behind the counter, and the plastic strips of the cold cabinet were completely opaque. A little further afield he found a local video store, but he'd seen every thriller they had, most more than once. The storekeeper seemed to stare at him as he left, as if wondering what he was doing there.

After a while he simply walked, not looking for anything. Slab-faced women stomped by, screaming at children already getting into method for their five minutes of fame on *CrimeWatch*. Pipe-cleaner men stalked the streets in brown trousers and zip-up jackets, heads fizzing with racing results. The pavements seemed unnaturally grey, as if waiting for a second coat of reality, and hard green leaves spiraled down to join brown ashes already fallen.

And yet as he started to head back towards Kingsley Road, he noticed a small dog standing on a corner, different to the one he'd seen before. White with a black head and lolling tongue, the dog stood still and looked at him, big brown eyes rolling with good humor. It didn't bark, merely panted, ready to play some game he didn't know.

Richard stared at the dog, suddenly sensing that some other life was possible here, that he was occluding something from himself.

The dog skittered on the spot slightly, keeping his eyes on Richard, and then abruptly sat down. Ready to wait. Ready to still be there.

Richard looked at him a moment longer, and then set off for the tube station. On the way he called and left a message at the house phone on Kingsley Road, telling Chris he'd gone out, and might be back late.

At eleven he left The George pub and walked down Belsize Avenue. He didn't know how important the precise time was, and he couldn't actually remember it, but eleven felt about right. Earlier in the evening he had walked past the old flat, establishing that the 'For Let' sign was still outside. Probably the landlord had jacked the rent up so high he couldn't find any takers.

During the hours he had spent in the pub he had checked the cuts only twice. After that he'd ignored them, his only concession being to roll the sleeve of his shirt down to hide what was now a deep gash on his forearm. When he looked at himself in the mirror of the gents his face seemed pale; whether from the lighting or blood loss he didn't know. As he could now push his fingers deep enough into the slash on his chest to feel his sternum, he suspected it was probably the latter. When he used the toilet he did so with his eyes closed. He didn't want to know what it looked like down there: the sensation of his fingers on ragged and sliced flesh was more than enough. The pain in his side had continued to condense, and was now restricted to a circle about four inches in diameter.

It was time to go.

He slowed as he approached the flat, trying to time it so that he drew outside when there was no-one else in sight. As he waited, he marveled at how different the sounds were to those in Kentish Town. There was no shouting, no roar of maniac traffic or young bloods looking for damage. All you could hear was distant laughter, the sound of people having dinner, braving the cold and sitting outside Café Pasta or the Pizza Express. This area was different, and it wasn't his home any more. As he realized that, it was with relief.

It was time to say goodbye.

When the street was empty he walked along the side of the building to the wall. Only about six feet tall, it held a gate through to the garden. Both sets of keys had been yielded, but Richard knew from experience that he could climb over. More than once he or Susan had forgotten their keys on the way out to get drunk, and he'd had to let them back in this way.

He jumped up, arms extended, and grabbed the top of the wall. His side tore at him, but he ignored the pain and scrabbled up. He slid over the top without pausing and dropped silently onto the other side, leaving a few slithers of blood behind.

The window to the kitchen was there in the wall, dark and cold. Chris had left a dishcloth neatly folded over the tap in the sink. Other than that the room looked as if it had been molded in an alien's mind. Richard turned away and walked out into the garden.

He limped towards the middle, trying to recall how it had gone. In some ways it felt as if he could remember everything; in others it was as though it had never actually happened to him, but was a second-hand tale told by someone else.

A phone call to an office number he'd copied from Susan's filofax before she left.

An agreement to meet for a drink, on a night Richard knew that Susan would be out of town.

Two men, meeting to sort things out in a gentlemanly fashion.

The stalks of Susan's abandoned plants nodded suddenly in a faint breeze, and an eddy of leaves chased each other slowly around the walls. Richard glanced towards the living room window. Inside it was empty, a couple of pieces of furniture stark against walls painted with dark triangular shadows. It was too dark to see, and he was too far away, but he knew the dust was gone. Even that little part of the past had been sucked up and buried away.

He felt a strange sensation on his forearm, and looked down in time to see the gash there disappearing, from bottom to top, from finish to start. It went quickly, as quickly as it had been made.

He turned to look at the verdant patch of grass, expecting to see it move, but it was still. Then he felt a warm sensation in his crotch, and knew it too would soon be whole. He had hacked at him there long after he knew Simmons was dead; hacked symbolically and pointlessly until the penis which had rootled and snuffled into Susan had been reduced to a scrap of offal.

The leaves moved again, faster, and the garden grew darker, as if a huge cloud had moved into position overhead. It was now difficult to see as far as the end wall of the garden, and when he heard the distant sounds from there Richard realized the ground was not going to open up. No, first the wound in his chest, the fatal wound, would disappear. Then the cuts on his stomach, and the nicks on his hands from where Simmons had resisted, trying to be angry but so scared he had pissed his designer jeans.

Finally the pain in his side would go; the first pain, the pain caused by Richard's initial vicious kick after he had pushed his drunken rival over. A spasm of hate, flashes of violence, wipe pans of memory.

Then they would be back to that moment, or a few seconds before. Something would come towards him, out of the dry, rasping shadows, and they would talk again. How it would go Richard didn't know, but he knew he could win, that he could walk away back to Chris and never come back here again. It was time. Time to go.

Time to move on.

THE GIST

'I'm not doing it,' I said.

Portnoy gazed coolly back at me. 'Oh? Why?'

'Where do I begin? Ah, I know—let's start with the fact you haven't paid me for the last job...'

'That situation could be remedied.'

'...or the one before that.'

The man behind the desk in front of me sighed. This made his sleek, moisturized cheeks vibrate in a way that couldn't help but put you in mind of a successful pig, exhaling contentedly in its sty, confident that the fate that stalked its kind was not going to befall him tonight, or indeed ever. A pig with friends in high places, a pig with pull. Pork with an exit strategy. The impression was so strong you could almost smell the straw the pig lay in—along with a faint whiff of shit.

'Ditto.'

'Great,' I said, briskly. 'We'll attend to the financial backlog first, shall we? Then I'll get onto the other reason.'

'You sadden me, John,' Portnoy said, as he reached down to the side and opened the top drawer of his desk. This meant, as the desk was double-sided, that the corresponding drawer-front on my side disappeared. From his end he withdrew a cheque book that was covered in dust. Literally. 'Anyone would think you do this only for the money.'

'Anyone would be absolutely right.'

'I don't believe you.' He tilted his head forward and allowed his spectacles to slide down his nose, the better to inspect the means of payment now laid in front of him. After a long pause he flipped it open, and peered bemusedly at the contents.

'Forgotten how to use it?'

He looked at me over the rims of his glasses, as if disappointed. 'Surely you can do better, my boy.'

'Perplexed by the instructions printed thereon?' I elaborated, 'Which must presumably be in Latin, at least, or Indo-European? Perhaps even facsimiles of petroglyphs representing routes to local lunching spots, with crosses indicating wine bars and the nearest cab rank?'

'Better. What manner of total were you expecting? For the two alleged late payments?'

'Seven hundred and fifty quid. Because it's three. *The Diary of Anna Kourilovicz*, remember?'

'Good lord.' Portnoy shook his head, evidently wondering what had overcome him to promise such outlandish sums. I said nothing, however. I'd come this far in a settlement negotiation before to find Portnoy suddenly derailed by a phone call, an ill-advised comment on my part, or some movement of the spheres only he could sense. If that happened then the whole process would have to start again, at a later date, and so I wasn't going to let it go pear-shaped this time. I needed the money, badly.

He took a pen from his tweed jacket—a pen which had, I entertained no doubt, cost him far more than the sum currently causing him such pain—and wrote in the book, concluding with his ponderous signature. He tore out the cheque with an oddly decisive movement and waved it in the air to dry the ink, before finally laying it on the desk.

I grabbed it and stuffed it in my wallet with a thick wash of relief. The rent was paid. Say what you like about Portnoy—and people did say many things, on the quiet—but his cheques never bounced.

'You're a gent.'

He grunted, and sat looking at me while reigniting the fat and noxious cigar which had been idling in a saucer at his elbow. I watched, and waited,

THE GIST

casting half an eye over a page of Shakespeare's *A Midsummer Night's Dream*, purporting to be from the original folio edition, that Portnoy had framed on the wall behind his desk. Those who knew Portnoy only slightly suspected the page of being fake, there to impress the naïve. People who knew him a little better, as I did, were prone to believe it was genuine—and that he'd started the rumor of it being fake just to mess with people's heads. Along with many other aspects of Portnoy's life and business, it was unlikely the real truth would ever be known.

As always, his basement office was murky, lit only by a small, old lamp on the corner of the desk, and thin slats of light striking down from a high, pavement-level window on the far wall, enlivened by turning motes of dust. The effect was so subdued that you couldn't see what lined all four walls, or stood in haphazard-seeming piles over most of the floor, to almost shoulder height. You could smell them, though, even through the permanent fug of cigar smoke.

Books. Thousands of them.

'Well?' he said, eventually.

'Well what?'

'We're square. So what was the other reason?'

'Simple.' I picked up the object that had been the initial focus of our conversation. 'It's a fake. Or nonsense. Or both.'

'I don't believe so. The gentleman I obtained it from has an immaculate record in providing me with titbits.'

Titbits. An interesting word for volumes that routinely fetched Portnoy upwards of ten, twenty or even a hundred thousand pounds. 'He's let you down this time. What's the provenance?'

For a moment the dealer looked shifty. This intrigued me. Despite being roguishly disheveled, and somewhere in that indefinable age (amongst the portly and ruddy-faced) between mid-forties and mid-sixties, there was a word I always applied to Portnoy in my head. *Sleek*.

But now, for a period of time perhaps equal to that required for a hummingbird to flap its wings (once), he didn't look sleek.

'You needn't concern yourself with that,' he muttered. 'I already have. I'm satisfied.'

'Well, that's okay then,' I said, standing. I had a mind to celebrate payday with a visit to the pub, starting immediately. 'You don't need me to—'

'A thousand,' Portnoy said.

I sat back down. I realized immediately how very like him this was—not merely doubling my usual fee, but going straight for the financial jugular. He had the measure of me, and knew it. So did I.

'Maurice,' I said.

He winced. Apparently I always said it wrong, making it sound either too much or not enough like "Morris", I'd never been clear which.

'I honestly think it's a fake, or a joke.'

'It's neither.'

'In which case I'm still not the man for the job.'

'You are.'

I laughed. This was ridiculous. 'How can I translate something out of a tongue I've never seen before? Which I don't even think is a real language?'

'I'm confident you'll uncover the gist.'

'Look...'

'For twelve hundred pounds.'

Twelve hundred meant not just next month's rent, but a replacement laptop (second hand, naturally, and scuffed after its most recent descent from the back of a lorry), of which I was in dire need. It meant a small gift for Cass (assuming I could track her down), in which case she might consent to being my sort-of girlfriend again, or at least going through the motions once or twice.

It meant a *very long* evening in the pub.

Portnoy reached into his jacket and pulled out his wallet. From this he drew a wad of notes, and slowly sorted the wheat from the chaff. I read them from where I sat. Six hundred quid. He coughed, a long, wet-sounding eruption bedded deep in his lungs.

'Half now, half when you come back,' he said, when he'd finished.

My head was spinning. Portnoy *never* paid except on completion—and this was nearly as much as the sum I'd just levered out of him, much of which had been owed for nearly two months.

'Just do what you can, my boy,' he said. 'Hmm?'

I picked up the book and the cash and left before he could change his mind.

THE GIST

***

In a break from my usual practice, I'd bothered to pop home to stow Portnoy's book there before going to the pub. It was, therefore, lying safely on the table when I jack-knifed to a sitting position on the sofa, at three o'clock the following afternoon.

A quick fumble through my wallet confirmed what I'd suspected immediately upon waking. The bulk of the six hundred quid was gone. Three hundred on an under-the-counter laptop, to be fair—but where was the rest? Some of it in my stomach, a portion of it up my nose, plus I seemed to have a new and much groovier mobile phone that I didn't remember acquiring via the usual high street channels—but that couldn't account for all of it, surely?

I was exceeding glad I'd brought the book home first, or it would have become Schrödinger's Tome, equally likely to be at any random point in London—or at least the subset of those points which lay within easy lurching distance of The Southampton Arms.

Christ.

Being me is not a fate everyone would enjoy. There are risks, and frequent disappointments. I'm not all that keen on the arrangement myself, to be honest.

I braced myself by drinking a huge amount of coffee and going through the process of transferring my files from the old laptop, feeling like a military policeman supervising the last desperate airlift from Saigon. The screen flashed at regular intervals, staying blank for up to five seconds at a time. The hard disk was far too audible, and smelled alarming, like a digital grave.

When everything was safely transferred to the new one I shut the old machine with relief, and lobbed it into the corner of the room which holds things broken, empty, or otherwise held in disdain. Like the other three corners of the room, in fact. My flat is a craphole, or so I've been told. I don't see it myself. It's a single-room studio with a tiny bathroom off the far end, and a laughable kitchenette which I've never used. The place is certainly untidy, but that's not my fault. I've tried tidying it and within hours it's untidy again, far more quickly than can be accounted for by any normal means. Evidently that's simply its natural state, and there's nothing I can do about it.

MICHAEL MARSHALL SMITH

Three walls are lined with bookshelves which sag under the weight of dictionaries, grammars, other reference and theoretical texts. Actually, the fourth wall is too, now. This has a pair of windows in it, but I don't like a lot of sunlight because it makes it harder to read a computer screen (not to mention it's bad for old books, and manuscripts, and hangovers), and so the blinds are permanently down and the piles of extra dictionaries, grammars, reference and theoretical texts have gradually grown to block most of their span.

I have a couch/bed thing, a big table, and a useful collection of pub ashtrays and pint glasses. What else do you need? I don't think it's a craphole.

Eventually I left off tinkering with the new laptop (whose own hard drive had a disconcertingly choppy whine, but at least the screen worked properly) and pulled Portnoy's book toward me.

It was time to start earning the rest of the money.

What I do for Portnoy, as you may have gathered, is translate. I can read nine languages fluently, another eight or ten given a bit of warning, and pick my way through fragments of quite a few more. It's just something I can do, and doesn't betoken any great intelligence in other spheres, more's the pity.

The annoying thing is that I can't actually *speak* any of them. Give me a tattered document in Medieval High German or Welsh or even Basque—which is as near a Stone Age remnant as you'll find, and really hard—and I'll be able to tell you what it says. The gist, at the very least. Put me in a café in Paris, however, and while I can understand perfectly what people are saying, I can't seem to say much in reply. It's like there's a barrier in my head, a glass wall that the words get trapped behind. I have the vocabulary, I know the grammar so well it's as if I don't know it—which is exactly how it should be—but the words just won't come out of my head and dance on my tongue. I went to Calais for a boozy weekend with Cass once, and she did far better than I with the waiters just by bellowing English nouns.

The upside, almost as if it's there to compensate, is that I'm unusually good at the written or printed word—which is why Maurice Portnoy pays me (when he remembers).

The core of the antiquarian book trade naturally lies in providing clients with books they're actually looking for. Through an immense and spidery

THE GIST

network of contacts, Portnoy keeps his eye out for works on customers' wish lists, or those he knows he can find a home for: first editions, modern and ancient; short-run autobiography or privately produced ephemera; seminal illustrated volumes of botany, alchemy or alarmingly frank (and to modern tastes, downright illegal) pornography—whatever these men have set their fetid collectors' hearts on (and the majority of them are men, members of our obsessive and fetish-friendly sex). In this regard Portnoy is much the same as other dealers, and plies an unexceptional trade.

His real business, however, is in the books that people don't know about. The books that got lost.

I got talking to this bloke once in the pub, a novelist. He told me he'd just discovered there was a Romanian edition of one of his novels. An acquaintance happened to be on holiday in the region, recognized the writer's name on the spine of a battered paperback on a second-hand stall in the market of a small town. Otherwise, the author would never have known about it. Granted, that's just a translation, but bear in mind this was only a couple of years ago, too. Think back over the hundreds of years we've been printing books—and the centuries before that, when they were copied by hand. How are you going to know that a book once existed, long after anyone involved with it is dead? If there's a copy somewhere, yes, or a reference to it in another book. Otherwise...they've vanished. People didn't keep records like they do now. You printed a book, sold it, and when it was gone, it was gone. Often books were printed privately, in runs of a hundred, twenty, even just five, and proudly so—it's said that Goethe's old man viewed his son's willingness to appeal to a more 'mass' market with permanent disdain.

It's different now, of course. Our entire culture has turned obsessive-compulsive, recording everything and storing it on servers across the world, the better to information-swamp us into a state of baffled ignorance. But a book hand-copied by unknown scriveners in the twelfth century? It's history. Vanished into the undertow, as if it had never existed.

Until...someone finds one.

That's what Portnoy's 'titbits' are. Lost books. Not in the sense that no-one can find a copy, but because no-one knew there was a copy out there to be found.

MICHAEL MARSHALL SMITH

Some are merely volumes by unknown authors, or previously-unknown titles by established names. Others turn up in more mysterious states, missing covers or whole chunks and without any indication of who wrote it, or when. Portnoy can fill in the 'when'—expertise in bookbinding techniques, the evolution of paper stock and modes of printing or handwritten script will generally give you a date within twenty-five years either way. You have to be on the lookout for fakes, of course (when someone's tried to make a manuscript look older than it is) or occasions when a genuinely eldritch tome has been rebound at a much later date, an old book now lurking between younger covers. Portnoy has an eagle eye for this kind of thing, too.

Most collectors are searching for the known, of course. Being known—and merely rare—is precisely what makes something conventionally collectable. That's why Gutenberg Bibles, the first 'mass' printing of that venerable fantasy tale, fetch the head-spinning sums they command. Only about fifty copies survive from the original paper edition of one hundred and eighty, and examples of the much smaller vellum edition are even more scarce. Most are in museums, and they're genuine works of art over and above their state of precedence. But what if an unknown rival had done a small trial printing the year before—of which only one copy remained, lost and forgotten in some hidden attic? And what about copies of other, more unknown books, collections of words now vanished from public awareness—like dinosaurs who left no discovered bones or fossilized tracks to mark their passing?

There are people out there who want this stuff, and want it *very much indeed*.

So Portnoy receives these books, often battered and torn and water-damaged, and makes a judgement on their age. If they're in English, he passes them by people he knows who can make guesses at authorship. These people can further refine the date, too, from clues in the use of language. There's the issue of semantic drift, for example, where words start out meaning one thing and over time morph into something different. 'Henchman' is a mildly interesting English example. In the fourteenth century it was a positive term, literally meaning a 'horse attendant'—the squire who walked beside high-ranking men and kept an eye on their boss's steed. It continued to mean this for a few centuries, and appears thus in *A Midsummer Night's Dream*, as a matter of fact, where Oberon says 'I do but beg a little changeling boy/To be

THE GIST

my henchman'. By the eighteenth century it had sidestepped to designate the chief sidekick of Scottish Highland chiefs, and then by nineteenth century America the word had strayed yet further, to mean a 'political supporter'—a fairly short step from its current meaning of 'a criminal associate', ha ha. Working out the precise sense in which these shape-shifting words are being used can help nail a text to quite a specific time frame.

Sometimes they're not in English, however, and that's where I come in.

If it's in one of my fluent languages, I can do it right there in the basement beneath Portnoy's deceptively bland shop in Cecil Court, one of London's few remaining book alleys. I don't like to do it that way, because it makes Portnoy feel he can pay me even less, but he's too wily to fall for any nonsense about me needing reference books, when the thing's obviously in a seventeenth century strand of one of the regional variations that eventually became subsumed into modern-day French.

Whenever I can, however, I take them home, and get to the bottom of them there. Most of the time, the results are mundane. A previously-unknown pamphlet on the history of a one-horse town in Umbria in the 1760s remains dull, however few people knew it existed. There are collectors who revel in the purity of simply owning a book no-one else knows exists, but that's a precarious thrill. Portnoy knows about it now, of course, as do I…and as soon as anyone else comes across a reference to it somewhere, the bubble bursts. So there's naturally a higher attraction to books that aren't just unknown, but possess fascination in their own right. That's when the price truly leaps up into the sky.

The *Diary of Anna Kourilovicz* was a case in point—a bound manuscript in a version of Russian used in the mid-1800s. Ms. Kourilovicz had very bad handwriting. She also had an extremely colorful life—or imagination, I was never sure which—that she set down in detail, and that involved varied, frequent and eyebrow-raising couplings with men, women and pets of note in St. Petersburg society of the time. There is a lot of cash swilling around the former Soviet Union these days, and the kinky stuff always goes for the highest prices. I don't know how much Portnoy made when he sold *The Diary*, but for several weeks his sleekness went up a very significant notch. The next time I was in his office he even gave me a cigar, which I tried to enjoy, though it tasted like someone had set fire to a wet dog. It didn't stop him paying me late, of course, but then he hadn't offered me twelve hundred quid to do it, either.

Which made me think whatever I now held in my hands must be something he was hoping would turn out to be very interesting indeed.

At first glance, the book had one obvious thing going for it—it was attractive. It had been laid out in a style somewhere between Arts & Crafts and Roycroft (tight and detailed typography, with woodcut-style design ornaments), and was actually a curious blend of the two, putting its publication—even to my graphically untrained eye—somewhere between 1890 to the early 1900s, and most likely in America, England, Germany or Austria.

So far, so good.

The problem was that it was nonsense.

There was text—rather a lot of it, in fact—but it wasn't in any language I'd ever seen.

There used to be a lot more languages than there are now, of course. The Languedoc region of France was so named to distinguish its inhabitants as those who said 'oc' to mean 'yes', rather than 'oui', as used elsewhere—and when Italy began to standardize its tongue late in the nineteenth century, only three percent of the population were speaking the dialect which has now come to be known as 'Italian'. The lost varieties are generally at least recognizable, however. What was in front of me didn't look like any breed of English, French, Italian, German, Spanish, Scandinavian or Slavic language that I'd ever seen, and the lack of Cyrillic characters help rule out a slew of others.

The obvious answer was that it was a code. If so, then Portnoy was out of luck. One of the many things I have no talent for is puzzles. I hate them, actually. I suspected he had reason to believe this wasn't a cipher, however, as in that case he'd have given it to someone who possessed those skills. In fact, he'd possibly already done so—ending up with me as a last resort.

So what made him think it was worth twelve hundred notes to work out what it was? It had to be the provenance—where the book had come from. One of his shadowy procurers must have told him the context of its discovery was very good indeed. After three hours of flicking through the book, however, it still looked like bollocks to me.

I photocopied a few random pages on the little printer/scanner/copier thing I have, and took them with me to the pub.

At some point in the evening I lost track of them, a little before I lost track of myself.

When I woke in the middle of the following night, it took me a few moments to work out where I was. I'll be honest and admit this is not an unknown phenomenon. What is unusual is for the location not to be my own dwelling, however. Once in a while I've regained consciousness in someone else's house—that of a random woman, generally, in whose rumpled waking face I see mirrored my own weary disappointment at our mutual fate—but usually it's my own gaff that I wake to find myself face-down on the carpet of. Not this time.

I sat up, and saw I was in a park.

Not a large one—only about eighty yards square—but with quite a lot of trees, the rest of the space given over to instruments designed to beguile the energies of children of pre-school age. A roundabout, and a pair of swings. A couple of slides, one in the manner of a pirate ship. Something in the shape of a horse, on which I could have rocked hectically back and forth, had I been much smaller and determined to make myself sick.

Inspection of a metal waste bin a few yards away suggested I was in something called Dalmeny Park. This was promising, as I was pretty sure there was a Dalmeny Road not too far away from where I lived. The park in general looked very vaguely familiar, in fact, though it was hard to understand why. It was surrounded by houses and gardens except at the gate, which was accessed down an alley between a couple of unremarkable dwellings. It would be hard to even know of its existence, unless you were already inside, and I could imagine no circumstances in which I would have been in the park before.

Less positive was the fact that when I got to the gate, I found it was locked.

This was not some small and easy-to-vault-over affair, either, but ten feet high, evidently designed to stop the place being used as an alfresco drugs den and/or informal homeless shelter. A sign on the gate alleged the place shut at dusk. As I hadn't left the pub until well after closing time—the Southampton operates a generous lock-in policy—it didn't seem likely that I'd entered the park this way.

I turned around and saw that much of the perimeter of the park gave onto people's back gardens, the walls to which varied from five to eight feet in height. So it was more likely I'd come in via that route.

But... How had I got into someone's garden, and then over the back of their wall and into here? And why, more to the point? What on earth had possessed me?

And *how was I going to get out?*

I lurched around the edge of the park, pushing behind the tall shrubs which lined most of it. I was relieved to find that in the far corner was another gate, which—though it didn't give onto public space—at least looked like it might lead by the side of a mansion block, beyond which the road presumably lay.

This gate was only about eight feet high. I stared up at it, feeling drunk, bilious and far from confident.

'What the hell are you doing?'

At first I couldn't work out where the voice was coming from. Then I saw that someone was approaching the gate from the other side, occluded behind a hellishly bright torch beam.

'I don't know,' I said.

'What do you mean you don't know? What are you *doing* in there?'

It was a man's voice, and had an odd rhythm to it.

'I don't know that either,' I said.

'You're drunk.'

'Yes,' I agreed quickly, eager to be helpful. 'I think that's a large part of the problem.'

He lowered his torch enough to allow me to glimpse a man in late middle age, wearing a dressing gown.

'I'm really sorry,' I said.

He unlocked the gate, giving me a comprehensive ticking off in the process, rehearsing a number of things he should be doing—calling the police, the council, my mother—but I found it hard to make out the individual words, or to form a more comprehensive apology.

THE GIST

Instead I thanked him and hurried up the path past the side of the block. It occurred to me as I made it to the road that I'd only solved part one of the problem, as I still didn't actually know where I was. But I didn't want to push my luck.

It took forty minutes of wandering the streets to find my road, which—had I not been travelling in shambling circles for most of it—was actually only about half a mile from the park. I let myself into the house and climbed up the stairs on hands and knees, as if undertaking the final desperate assault on a very high and idiosyncratically carpeted mountainside.

Only when I was safely inside my flat did I realize I could still hear the rhythm of the voice of the man with the torch, beating inside my head.

When I woke again late the next morning, my location was more explicable. I was exactly where I had been when I'd fallen back to sleep. Face-down on my own sofa. I was sufficiently relieved by this that I didn't even much mind when rolling over sent me over the edge, to land with a crash on the floor.

I drank a lot of water while sitting at the table. I still didn't understand what had happened. Sure, I'd drunk a lot of beer. But I've done that before (the previous night, for example, and the one before that). How I'd got from drunk-in-the-Southampton-Arms to being unconscious-inside-Dalmeny Park remained a mystery. As I'd scurried away under the torch-wielding man's scrutiny, I'd had time to note that the side of the building didn't look even remotely familiar. I suspected this meant it hadn't been the way I'd gained access to the park. Climbing over even that lower gate would have been a major undertaking, one which you'd have thought should have stuck in my beer-addled brain.

So how had I got in there? Via someone's garden?

In which case, had I also gone via someone's house?

It suddenly seemed horribly possible that I'd met someone in the pub, gone back to their house with them, and then—for one reason or another—left by a rear exit, making it as far as the park before crashing out.

Not ideal, obviously. Not the outline of a classy evening, a soirée of distinction and restraint. Oh bloody hell. Why did I have to be me? Wasn't it someone else's turn yet? Wasn't there anyone else who fancied taking on the job for a while, so I could have a rest?

In the end I decided to simply forget about it. I find that's the best approach to events in your past which you'd prefer not to bring into your present or future. Just pretend they didn't happen. In the meantime, distract yourself.

To aid this I reached once more for Portnoy's tome. I dimly remembered having spent a fairly diligent hour or so in the pub the previous evening, trying to make sense of the photocopied pages I'd taken with me—even swapping words back to front, in the hope it was some simple code which Portnoy's other sages might have missed through lack of familiarity with foreign or obsolete languages.

Nothing had come out of it, and at first glance the text looked no more explicable this morning than it had the day before. After a few minutes of flipping back and forth through the pages, however, something was tugging at my brain, trying to bring itself to my attention. It wasn't until I tried saying some of the words out loud that I understood what it was.

The words remained nonsensical, but there was a rhythm to them.

I never paid much attention in class during the parts where they explained iambic pentameters and all that jazz (nor during quite a lot of the other bits, to be honest) so I couldn't put an actual name to the rhythm, but as I turned to other pages at random and read out further chunks, I became convinced I'd finally spotted something. The ratio of long and short words, the way in which the blocks of text were organised and contained by commas and full stops, seemed to have a kind of pattern.

It wasn't universal—it's not like the whole thing went ti-tum-ti-tum ti-tum-ti-tum—but each section did seem to have a kind of aural organizing principle, when you said the words aloud. By chance I happened to come across one of the passages I'd photocopied the night before, and as I read through it, I realized something else.

It was this rhythm I'd heard in the voice of the man with the torch, who'd let me out of the park I'd found myself in. It hadn't been in his words, but in my mind—put there through reading and re-reading this section while pouring beer into my head.

Which was kind of weird.

THE GIST

***

Portnoy took a long puff on his cigar and looked at me.

'Yes?' he said. 'And?'

'Well, that's it,' I said.

My head was splitting, and it was becoming clear that the hope that this insight would do—and be worth the other six hundred quid—had been overly optimistic. 'I still can't make anything of the actual words—and I've tried everything I know. But these rhythms can't be unintentional. It must be what the thing is about.'

'A book of rhythms.'

'Yeah.'

Portnoy just looked at me some more.

'I mean, that must be pretty unusual, right? Very rare?' I could sense this wasn't at all what Portnoy had been hoping for, but ploughed on regardless. 'Maybe it's a manual of poetic meter, or something.'

'Oh, that's wonderful news,' he snorted. 'Those go for simply enormous sums, as I'm sure you can imagine.'

He thought for a while in silence, staring down at the surface of his desk, gently biting his lip.

'No,' he said eventually. 'I'm not convinced. You're not there yet. You need to keep on trying.'

'Christ,' I said, 'Look, it's something. And I honestly don't think there's anything else there to be found. I spent all yesterday evening in the pub with this bloody thing, trying everything I could—'

'You took this book to the pub?' Portnoy said, sharply.

'No,' I said, hurriedly. 'Obviously not. I photocopied some pages, and—'

'Which pub?'

'Um, the Southampton Arms,' I said. 'On Junction Road. You won't know—'

'Of course I know it,' he snapped. 'I had the misfortune to grow up in that very area.'

'Oh,' I said, surprised.

'Don't ever do that again,' he said. 'Do you have any idea what would happen to the value of this book, if it got out that it existed?'

'Trust me, I don't think there are any antiquarian book dealers working undercover in my local boozer.'

'Your fellow sops probably don't imagine that amongst their number is someone who can sight-read medieval Dutch,' he bellowed, semi-reasonably. 'And yet there you are, getting merrily shit-faced and falling off stools.'

'Sorry,' I said, chastened. 'I just didn't think that...well, sorry. Sorry.'

For the second time in three days, Portnoy wasn't looking sleek. In fact, he was looking the closest I've ever seen to angry. And a little scary, too.

'Where are the photocopies now?'

'Um,' I said.

Even to someone well-acquainted with the practice of drinking in the afternoon, pubs look different during the day. Natural light is friendly to neither their interiors nor denizens, and since the Nazi health bastards stopped us smoking inside, they smell bad too. Stale alcohol, a waft of disinfectant from the toilets, whatever vile gunk they use to clean out the pumps—all overlaid with the background tang of dust in ancient carpets. Now this olfactory assault is no longer hidden below the welcoming fug of cigarette smoke, walking into a pub of a late morning can make you wonder why on earth you spent the whole of the previous evening there. Luckily, a quick pint can usually remind you.

I got half of one down me before asking what I'd come to ask.

'Ron?' I said, addressing the slab-faced landlord. It would be romantic to imagine he'd once been a boxer, a plucky local hopeful gone spectacularly to seed—and Ron wasn't averse to that rumor being spread around—but it's more likely he merely spent his youth and post-youth engaged in the kind of villainous pursuits that come hand in hand with outbursts of spirited violence. Even in his sixties he remains an extremely handy-looking geezer, and I definitely wouldn't want to wind up on the wrong end of either of his ham-sized fists.

'John,' he replied, in his courtly fashion.

'Your rubbish. What happens to it?'

Ron cast a droll eye around the bar, but the only other person sitting at it was already too drunk to provide much of an audience.

THE GIST

'We throw it away,' Ron said. 'Is that...wrong?'

'But, I meant, at what time? First thing, or...?'

'Nah. We like to save it. The bloke comes round to collect, and we say "No, you're alright mate, we'll keep it until next week."'

'And what time does he come round?'

Ron abruptly dropped the show, realizing I was going to be dogged about it. 'It's still out the back. Why? You lost something?'

'Few bits of paper I had with me last night. Forgot them when I left.'

'Not surprised,' he said. 'You was bladdered, mate. Muttering to yourself like a twat, you were. Almost thought about not serving you the last four or five pints.'

'Muttering?'

'Yeah. Same thing, over and over. Couldn't make it out. Sounded like a sodding poem, or something.'

That sounded weird, but I didn't want to risk being diverted from what I was driving at. I opened my mouth to ask the next question, but had to pause while I underwent a long coughing fit. Ron watched the process with some satisfaction.

'Sounds nasty,' he said, when I'd finished.

'Yeah,' I said. 'It feels it.' The cough was harsh and glassy—a legacy, no doubt, of having spent a portion of a cold night crashed out on damp grass in a park. 'Look, Ron—has your rubbish been taken, or not? I need those pages, is what it is.'

He jerked his head toward the side door. 'Help yourself.'

I swallowed the rest of my pint, indicated I'd like another, and spent twenty minutes in the alley that ran down the side of the pub, sifting through bin bags. Cass used to call bin bags—especially when stacked in a black pile by the side of a building—'house poo'. I always liked that, and trust me, the bin bags of pubs deserve the term more than most. I wouldn't have been rummaging through them at all, had Portnoy's response to the pages being lost not been as strong as it was. He really was not happy about it at all, which made me all the more intrigued as to what the hell the story was behind this book.

I found the photocopies, eventually, in about the eighth bag. I remembered bringing approximately six pages with me, and that's how many I managed to dredge up. I'm not sure what most of them were covered in, but I hope to Christ it wasn't on the pub menu—or, at least, that no-one had eaten it. Especially me.

I wiped the pages off as best I could, and in doing so saw that the second sheet contained the passage that had taken me to Portnoy's that morning. The liquid in the gloop smeared over it had done something strange to the laser print, making it look as though it was standing off the page a little. I still thought I could determine some kind of consistent rhythm in the collections of letters, and it still meant nothing.

In the end I folded the pages in half, and half again, and stuffed them in my pocket. I had a well-earned cigarette and then went back in the pub, where—after washing my hands in the gents—I took my place back at the bar. I didn't know what to do next. I wanted (needed) the rest of the cash Portnoy had promised. I had no idea what else to try, however, and the combination of a hangover and whatever bug I'd picked up wasn't making my head a place of clarity. Neither was the new beer entering my system, most likely, though it was at least making me feel slightly better. I decided I'd have one more pint then go back to the flat and...dunno. Try looking through the book some more.

'You're doing it again.'

I raised my head to see both Ron and the nearly-comatose other bloke at the bar looking at me.

'Doing what?'

'The muttering.'

I frowned. 'Really?'

Ron turned to the bloke. 'Was he muttering?'

'You was...muttering,' the man said, laboriously.

I realized that yes, I had been, and was again, that my lips were soundlessly shaping the same phrase over and over. It was as if, suddenly and after all this time, I could vocalize a foreign language after all. It just wasn't one that I knew.

I got off the stool without ordering another beer, and walked quickly home.

Portnoy wasn't in when I called, and he cleaved to the incredibly annoying habit of not having an answer phone. He'd been extremely insistent that I let

THE GIST

him know immediately about the fate of the pages, however, so I remained where I was and waited to call him again.

In the meantime I sat at my table, putting the book in front of me. After a moment I opened it, somewhat more cautiously than on previous occasions.

It was just a book. Of course.

But things get under your skin.

I remembered the first time I'd met Cass, for example. It was in a pub, obviously. She'd been there with a couple of mates, as had I, and somehow over the course of many drinks the two groups wound up mingling. At the end of the evening, two new—and very temporary—couples disappeared off into the night. Cass and I were not one of them, though we did talk for hours and swap phone numbers.

The next morning I woke with her in my head.

I was alone in what serves for my bed, but bang in the center of a head seared with hangover, was this petite, red-haired girl. Not saying anything. Just there. She remained in vision for the whole of the day—sometimes right in front of me, sometimes glimpsed out of the corner of my internal eye. When I woke up the next morning and found that she was again my first waking thought, I bit the bullet and called her.

I'm not sure we ever quite 'went out with each other', as such, though we did spend quite a lot of time together in pubs for a while, and took that one day-trip to France; and on days when I feel scratchy and crap, and put at least some of this down to the vague sensation of missing someone, I suspect it's her that I miss.

Portnoy's book, or its contents, had started to feel the same way. Not as if I wanted to snog it, obviously. As if it had climbed into my head. This could just be for self-evident reasons: having pissed away the first half of the money, I needed the other six hundred even more urgently, and he clearly wasn't going to give it up without due cause—which meant me getting to the bottom of this sodding tome. The cold, flu or whatever I had was getting worse too, making my head muddy and unclear. My cough had by now reached epic proportions. I was trying to unleash it as seldom as possible, on the grounds that it stirred reserves of phlegm so deep it felt like it was endangering the foundations of the house.

I called Portnoy's office again. He still wasn't there. Then, maybe because she was in my head from remembering her from being in my head, I called Cass's mobile.

'You've got a bloody nerve,' she said, before I'd even had time to say hello.

'Have I?'

'You don't remember?' she said.

Two hours later I was back in the Southampton, sitting fretfully at a table and waiting for her. In the meantime I'd managed to get hold of Portnoy and reassure him about the missing pages. He sounded less scary afterwards, and listened to me wheeze and cough with something like paternal concern.

'If I might make an observation,' he said, 'you're bottling it up, my boy. Let it all go. Release it. Will you try doing that, John?'

I said I would. I then spent a few minutes trying to position my lack of further ideas about his book as being an analysis worth six hundred quid. He heard me out with good grace, appeared to even think about it for a nano-second, but then said he was confident I would have made more progress soon—and that he'd look forward to an update in his office on Monday... which was days and days away, so at least I didn't have to sort it out right now.

On the way to the pub I took his advice, however, and (when no-one else was around) treated myself to a good old cough, a third-hangover-in-a-row and let-yourself-go-red-in-the-face and double-up-and-really-go-for-it job.

It felt like something important was coming loose inside, but then—bam: it was over, and I felt fine. Well, better, anyway. Head still fuzzy, but chest suddenly back to normal.

I'd been in the pub half an hour, and was on my second pint, when I noticed someone was standing in front of my table. I glanced up to find Cass looking down at me. You have to be sitting down for her to do that—she's pretty tiny. I've always liked skinny, petite girls. There's such a weird contrast between the amount of space they appear to take up, and their actual weight, both physical and psychic. It's as if they extend beyond the range of their bodies. Because they look so small, it's surprising, too, how much mass they actually contain. Someone so light on the planet still weighs in at over a hundred pounds, which is a lot to have in your arms, or on top of you—and the

THE GIST

difference between the sight of them and their unexpected physical heft has a great attraction, not least because of the surprise and shock of them actually being there, voluntarily that close to you. This density also means that once encountered, the attraction continues, as a matter of their gravitational pull.

This, I knew even as I was thinking it, was not the kind of thought that usually ran through my mind. It sounded rather grown-up and brainy, in fact. I wondered about telling Cass some of it, but then saw she was frowning at me pretty severely.

'What?' I said.

'Was all that supposed to mean something?'

'Christ—was I talking out loud?'

'You was saying something, but God knows what. Are you calling me fat?'

As she sat down I saw she'd already got herself a drink, which made me feel a bit rubbish, because I knew she'd have done this on the assumption I might not have the cash to buy one for her, and that I might actually be intending to let her buy all mine.

I realized suddenly that I was thirty-four and really not making a very good job of it. 'Thanks for coming.'

'Haven't got long,' she said, business-like. 'Me and Lisa is going clubbing.'

'On a Wednesday?'

'It's Friday, you nutter.'

'Really?' That explained why the pub was so full. It also meant that I had less time than I'd thought to come up with something sensible about Portnoy's book. Christ.

Cass sipped her bucket of Chardonnay and looked at me pretty seriously. 'You alright, babe?'

'I think so,' I said. 'Got flu, or something. Head's a bit ropey, that's all.'

'Still hungover, I should think.'

'Look—what actually happened the other night?'

'You was in here,' she said, briskly, as if reading back dictation. Do people still do dictation these days, sit there writing down the gist and rhythm of what people say? No idea. 'You'd had a few already. You called me, said come over and have a beer. I wasn't doing nothing, so I said okay. Got here about an hour later, which time you was three sheets and scribbling all over some bits of paper you had with you—but we had a laugh and I'm thinking, okay, he's pissed as a fart but I do like him, so, you know. We stayed for the lock-in, gave it some welly, an' all. Then you said you'd walk me home.'

'That doesn't sound so bad,' I said, relieved. I mean, by my standards, that's like a week working for a charity in Botswana.

'But you didn't, see.'

'Oh.'

'We got halfway there, and you suddenly said you wanted to show me something. I said "Yeah, right, and I bet I know what it is, an' all," but you said no, it wasn't that, and be honest I was so pissed by then I thought sod it, why not, even if it is a shag he's after. So you start leading me down these side roads and it didn't look like you knew where you were going, but then there's this alleyway and at the end there's a kiddie's park or something. Locked up. And you said you used to play there when you was little, and why don't we climb the fence and go have a look around.'

'Okay,' I said, feeling cold. Maybe Cass remembered that I'd grown up out in Essex, and had never even been to London before I was eighteen. Maybe she didn't.

'Nearly killed yourself getting over that fence. Nearly killed me, an' all. But we get inside, and it's cold enough that I'm feeling even more pissed, and I'm thinking "Well, this is one to tell the grandchildren anyway" though not if we actually *do* shag, leave that bit out, obviously, but then...'

She stopped talking. Her face went hard.

'What?'

'You went funny.'

'Funny how?'

'You'd been doing this muttering thing half the way there, saying something over and over really quietly. But now you're standing in the middle of the park, and you don't even look like yourself. You was...you was being really *odd*.'

'What do you mean?'

'Dunno. You just didn't look like yourself. And you was saying things, but it didn't sound like you.'

'Then what happened?'

THE GIST

'I sat on a bench, had a ciggy. Thought "let him get on with it". Then just as I've put out me fag, suddenly you make this weird sound, and fall down.'

'What, just keeled over?'

'Flat on your back. I laughed my head off until I realized you was out cold.'

'So what did you do?'

'I pissed off home, didn't I. Checked you was breathing and everything, but you know, bloody hell, babe, it was sodding freezing and I'd had enough.'

I didn't know what to say. I sat looking at her.

She rolled her eyes. 'You know you're doing it again, don't you.'

'Doing what?'

'Saying things, under your breath.'

'Yeah, of course,' I lied. 'It's, uh, I'm memorizing something. For work.'

'You're barmy, you are.'

She drained the rest of her glass in a swallow, and stood up. 'Got to go. If I don't get to Lisa's before she opens the second bottle then we won't be going nowhere, and I really fancy a boogie tonight.'

She gave me a quick peck on the cheek and then she was off, cutting through the crowds at the bar like a fish through reeds it had known all its life.

I honestly didn't mean to have another pint. I was just sitting there, looking at all the people, trying to gather the strength to leave, and to find some distraction from the fact I was a bit freaked out by what Cass had just told me. Ron caught my eye from behind the bar, and I gave him a quick upwards nod, just meaning 'hello'—one of those things you can say without saying, a physical utterance—but he mistranslated my intentions and starting pulling me another Stella instead.

And so it went.

I don't know how many hours later it is, but I'm standing outside somewhere and it's very cold. My hands hurt and I look down and I see I've cut the back of one. How?

Climbing the fence, presumably.

Because I'm back there again. In the park.

I turn around and recognize the things in it. The big slide, the small one. The pirate ship. The swings and the little wooden house.

But when it comes to this last item, I'm not recognizing it in the right way.

It's drizzling a bit and so I walk over to the wooden house. It's small and battered, about four feet by three feet, open at both ends and with a roof over it, painted yellow some time ago. I go in the front end and perch on the tiny bench inside, and I know I've been there before; that though all the rest of the children's stuff in the park is fairly recent, this house has been here a long time, as long as the park itself.

I get out a cigarette, and try to sort through my memories of the other night, the one Cass told me about. She didn't say anything about me sitting in a little house, and she would have mentioned it, if I had. I didn't sit in there after I woke up, either—I just tried to find a way out.

So why do I think I've been in there before?

I put my head in my hands. I don't feel right. My mind is full of beer and I can't think straight. Having my eyes shut isn't helping either, and so I raise my head and open them again, and as I do I'm suddenly overcome by a memory, so sharp and vivid that for a split second it's more real than anything else.

In the memory I'm sitting exactly where I am now, on this bench in this little wooden house. I'm not here because I'm drunk and sheltering from the rain, however. I'm here because it's a wooden house and I always sit in here for a while when we come to the park.

I do not feel cramped. There's plenty of room.

And then I turn toward the little door at the front, and...

Suddenly I jerk up, banging my head on the roof, and lunge outside.

But he isn't there.

I know who I'm expecting to...no, not 'expecting' to see, because I know now that what I've just experienced was a memory, and not happening in real time. I know who I was remembering looking up to see, on some unimportant Saturday morning a long time ago.

I look around, still convinced he's going to be here somewhere, maybe over at the bench, or looking vaguely at the houses, or slipping behind a tree.

It's my dad.

This is our park, the one we come to together.

THE GIST

And when I find I can't see him, and the memory suddenly starts to fade, I feel miserable, because it has been so long since I've seen my father's face, so many years since he died, and I miss him.

Then it's gone, whatever long-ago morning I'm remembering, and I'm just a very pissed man standing in the middle of a park, in the rain and the dark, and feeling alone and pretty scared.

I lurch over to the main gate and very slowly, very laboriously and very carefully, clamber back out—on only three or four occasions coming close to tumbling off and smashing my skull to smithereens.

I trudge up the alley and find a street I think I recognize. I walk along it, and keep going, and by the time I get back to the house in which I live, I've remembered both that my dad isn't actually dead, and that the bastard never took me to a park in his life.

Saturday and Sunday blurred into one. I spent some of it in the pub, some in the park, some of it walking the streets, but most of it in my flat. Whenever I was at home, I found myself reading from the book.

Not 'reading' from it in a literal sense, I suppose, but letting it sit in front of my eyes. The conscious extraction of meaning from a procession of words is not, after all, the only way of interacting with a text, or with anything else in the world. By now I had become sufficiently familiar with the book's contents that I'd realized there was more than one rhythm to the words, that in the beginning they fell into one loose pattern—the one I thought I'd heard in the voice of the man who'd let me out of the park—but that by the end it had changed. No matter how much time I spent looking at the middle sections, however, I couldn't put my finger on where the transition occurred. I found that I was intrigued rather than bothered by this. I cannot, after all, recall the point where I became the person who lives in this flat and exists how I do, after being the person who was so far in advance of the other students at university that the lecturers just let me do my own thing, convinced I would amount to a great deal. I cannot recall when the four-year marriage I abandoned, toward the end of my twenties, started to be something I no longer wished to be involved in—nor at what point I stopped bothering to send birthday and Christmas cards to the daughter that I'd gained from it. I cannot remember when I became exhausted instead of merely tired.

MICHAEL MARSHALL SMITH

Things rarely stop and start at easily identifiable points, after all. If they did, then it would be much easier to know when to hold up your hand and say 'Wait, hang on, *hang on*, stop—I'm not sure I like where this is going.' Life tends to shade from one state to the next, to evolve or devolve, to grow and develop or fade and fall apart. Books and sentences and words hide this, with their quantized approach to reality, their pretense that meanings and events and emotions stop and start—that you can be in one state and then another that is different and that the whole of life is not one long, continual flux. Whole languages collude too, especially the European ones, setting object against subject and giving precedence to the latter over the former: only rare exceptions like certain Amerind dialects structuring themselves to say 'a forest, a clearing, and me in it,' instead of the individual-as-god delivery of 'I am in a clearing in a forest.'

I think of these things as I sit. I find other things changing, too, aspects of the world becoming different. In the local corner store, for example, I discover myself chatting fluently to the strikingly beautiful Polish girl behind the counter, in her own language. I find myself walking away with her phone number, too, which is not the kind of thing that usually happens in my life.

I begin to feel hopeful that change is still possible, and that it is happening to me.

I arrived at Portnoy's shop at mid-day on Monday, as requested. I'd made no further progress, but had stopped worrying about it. He wanted to meet, so we'd meet. I'd tell him I didn't know what the book was supposed to be about, and he wouldn't give me the remaining six hundred pounds, and that would be that. Life would go on.

When I got to Cecil Court I saw through the window that Portnoy was with a customer, so I lurked outside with a cigarette. Though the cough hadn't come back, the smoke felt weird in my lungs, and so mostly I just held it in my mouth instead. Portnoy's book was in a carrier bag in my hand. There had been times over the weekend where I'd found it difficult to imagine handing it back to him, so much a part of my life had it become. At some point in the night that had changed. I was tired of it now, tired of its music and transitions, tired of not knowing what it was about. Ignorance isn't always bliss.

THE GIST

Sometimes it's just a huge pain in the arse, especially when it's about to cost you six hundred quid.

The customer eventually left, clutching something in a neat brown paper bag. An early Wodehouse first, most likely, one of Portnoy's minor stocks in trade. I entered the shop to the sound of him coughing.

'Sounds like you've got what I had.'

He nodded. 'Could be, my boy, could be.'

Clear grey light was coming through the shop window, and it struck me how seldom I'd seen him lit by anything other than his subterranean lair's murky glow. Today his skin looked very pale, and waxy.

I held the carrier bag up toward him and started to speak, but he shook his head.

'Downstairs,' he said, and reached over to flip the sign on the door to CLOSED.

I followed him down the narrow and abruptly-turning staircase that led to the basement office. The gloom down there seemed even more sepulchral than normal, so much so that I was halfway across the floor before I spotted that something was different; even then it was the smell that gave it away first, or the lack of it.

I stopped, looked around. 'What happened to all the books?'

'Moved them on,' he said.

'What, *all* of them?' The room was entirely empty. Aside from the desk and its two chairs, everything was gone. Even the framed page of *The Dream* on the wall. All that remained was dust.

'Some were sold, others put in storage.'

He sat at his side of the desk, and I sat at the other.

'Are you shutting up shop?'

'Good lord, no,' he said, lighting one of his cigars. 'Well, in a way, I suppose. I'm moving on.'

'Moving on? Why?' I felt panicky.

'The cost of living where I do has simply become too high, especially as the fabric is falling apart. The lease is up.'

'But you don't actually *live* here, do you? In this building?'

He smiled. 'I meant it figuratively.'

I had no idea what he was talking about, and didn't really care. I put the bag with the book in it on the desk. He looked at it, then back up at me. 'What's that?'

'The book,' I said. 'I'm giving it back. I can't do what you asked.'

'And what did I ask you to do?'

'Translate it. Tell you what the book was about.'

'No. All I asked for was the gist.'

'How could I give you that without translating it?'

He smiled again, kindly. 'A good question. But you have. Can't you feel it?'

I was distracted by the smell of his cigar. It smelled good. It made me wonder, in fact, why I smoked cigarettes.

He noticed me looking at the object in his hand, and held it out to me. 'Want to try?'

I took it, put it in between my lips. Drew some of the smoke into my mouth, and let it lie there a while.

'Nice,' I said, putting the cigar back in the ashtray.

'I have to be elsewhere in an hour,' Portnoy said, 'So I suggest we get down to business right away.'

'Business?' My head felt fuzzy, as if I'd drunk far too much coffee. The cigar smoke, perhaps. But I allowed myself to hope that—as he appeared to be claiming that I had done what he asked—he might actually be intending to pay me the other six hundred pounds. 'What business?'

He reached into his jacket pocket, and took out a small set of keys and a piece of paper with an address written on it. He put them on the table.

'There are six months left on this building,' he said, indicating two of the keys. 'I'm afraid that will be more than sufficient, given your condition.'

'What are you talking about?'

'The address on that piece of paper is where you live. A *pied a terre* in Fitzroy Square. Not overly large, but extremely comfortable. I have left a substantial sum of money in a suitcase under the bed.'

I stared at the young man opposite me. 'Portnoy, what the hell are you talking about?'

'I'm not a bad person,' he said. 'I'd like you to be at ease in the time that's left. The money should see to that. I've left a note in the drawer of the bedside

THE GIST

table, too, should you decide to, ah, self-medicate. The phone number on the note is that of an extremely reliable and discrete gentleman who can supply morphine at short notice.'

'Morphine?'

'The pain can be very bad,' he said, apologetically. 'It's only going to get worse, I'm afraid.'

Only then did I realize that, instead of having my back to the room, the wall was behind me. That I was sitting on the opposite side of the desk to normal.

And then that the man I was facing was not Portnoy.

It was me.

I tried to say something about this, but was derailed by a cough. It went on for a long time, and hurt a very great deal. When I finally pulled my hand away from my mouth, I stared at it. It was Portnoy's hand.

'What have you done to me?'

'Not so much,' the other man said. 'Think of it as somatic drift, if you need a term. It's never a book's cover that matters, after all, but what's inside. The gist. You found him in the end.'

'"Him"? Don't you mean "it"?'

'No,' he said, standing. 'Good luck. And remember that gentleman I mentioned.' He picked up the bag from the desk, and replaced it with something in a frame. 'A leaving present.'

I reached out for it, feeling tired and old and unwell. I tilted it toward me, and saw it was what had always hung on the wall behind him, that single page from the first folio of *A Midsummer Night's Dream*. Seeing it close up for the first time, I noticed that three words had been lightly underlined, in pencil.

Thou art translated.

'I don't understand.'

'From the Latin "translatus",' Portnoy said, 'serving as a past participle of "transferre"—to bring over.'

He picked up the cigar from the ashtray, and stuck it in his mouth.

Around it he said 'Goodbye, dear boy,' and left.

In a month the deterioration has already become marked. From notes left in Portnoy's flat I learned that my new body has lung cancer, of a belligerently terminal variety. Nothing that can be done about it—except, I suppose, what he did. I wouldn't know how to even embark upon such a course, even if I still had the book, which I do not. It is with him, wherever he is, in whichever quarter of the world he is starting upon his new life. Or a new chapter of it, at least.

I wonder how many times he has done it before, how many younger men, like me, have allowed his meaning to be substituted between their covers. A great many, I suspect.

My days are comfortable, in any event. I sit in the large leather chair in his sitting room and look through the books he left behind, or out of the window at the trees in the square. If the pain gets very bad, I avail myself of the substance I now obtain from the gentleman Portnoy recommended. It beats knocking back pints of Stella, that's for sure.

On afternoons when I don't feel too dreadful I go for walks, watching the leaves turn, feeling the weight of the city around me, appreciating these things while I still have time.

Last week I even took the tube a few stops north, early one evening, and sat at a table in the corner of the Southampton for a while. Yes, naturally I was hoping that Cass might come in, and wondrously, she did. Her eyes skated over me, not recognizing the portly, grey-skinned covers in which I now find myself bound. She enjoyed a few raucous glasses of wine with some guy I didn't recognize, but finally took herself off into the night alone.

I wish her well, wherever she is.

After she left I walked slowly around to Dalmeny Park, and down the alleyway, and looked through the closed gates. There's no way I could climb them now, and it's not really my place, after all. My body knows it, however. It remembers being there as a child, with its father, and so I let it stand there for a while, before wheezing my way back up the road and waiting until a cab came to take me back to my nest.

Where I continue to die.

The odd thing is I don't even mind too much. Some stories, some people, deserve their length and span. They merit a novel-length treatment, have things to tell and other lives to illuminate. The real Portnoy—whoever or whatever he was—is one of those, and I'm sure he's already making far better

THE GIST

use of my body than I ever did. There are others, people like the man I was, who should aspire only to being a novella, or perhaps not even that.

Short stories have their place in the world, after all. The tale remains afterwards, beyond death, and perhaps one day someone will read mine and understand what I amounted to.

A few events and mistakes, several hangovers and a kiss, and then a final line.

AUTHOR OF
THE DEATH

Finally I decided I'd had enough and I wasn't going to put up with it anymore and it was high time something was done the hell about it. My father was a vague character at best but there's one way in which I evidently do take after him. Once he'd decided to do something, apparently, that was it. That thing was going to happen, and it was going to happen *now*. As soon as I realized I was clinically fed up with the situation, compelling verbs were required—and there was only one immediate course of action I could think of.

I grabbed my coat and looked for my gun, but I couldn't find it. Sometimes it's here, sometimes it's not, and probably it wasn't such a great idea to take it anyhow. I had a mission, a simple goal. I didn't need a weapon.

I needed focus.

I knew tracking down a writer wasn't going to be an easy task. They're everywhere but yet nowhere, too—a state of affairs I'm sure reminds some of them of one conception of deity. (Is it called 'Pantheism'? I can't remember. I probably shouldn't know anyway.) I have only ever been in New York, except for a couple of short chapters in a small town nearby called Westerford. It was never clear to me how I even got to Westerford, however—as I was just cut there and back on chapter breaks—so that idea was a non-starter and to be absolutely honest I suspect he just made the place up anyhow.

Bottom line was that I was stuck with looking for him in the city. If I'd believed he knew the place very well then this would have been a very daunting prospect—NYC is a hell of a big patch of ground even if you stick to the island and don't start on the other boroughs. I had reason to suspect that his knowledge was limited to Manhattan, however, and far from comprehensive even there.

I made a list of locations, the places I knew well, and got out into the streets.

Six hours later my feet hurt and I was getting irritable. I'd looked everywhere. Everywhere I could remember having been, or where scenes with other characters had taken place, or that I'd heard described by other people—finally washing up at the Campbell Apartment in Grand Central Station, a bar surprisingly few people know about. I'd been there once for a meeting about a job that got derailed. The meeting had always felt to me like filler, but I'd liked the venue. Dark, subterranean-feeling, dirty light filtered through a big stained glass window. It looked and felt exactly as described, and so I thought it likely the guy had actually been there, rather than merely having read about it. He wasn't there now, though.

I had a drink anyway and left and started to walk wearily back down 5th Avenue, cigarette in hand. It was mid-afternoon and starting to get colder. I'd had plenty of time to consider whether what I was doing was a good idea (and if it even made any kind of ontological sense), but something I evidently inherited from my mother (much better fleshed out as a character than my father, featuring in two long, bucolic memory sequences and a series of late-climax flashbacks) is that once I've embarked on a project, it does tend to get done.

So I walked, and then I walked some more. Instead of cutting over to 3rd and down into the East Village—which is where I live, for better or worse—I went the other way, switching back and forth between 6th, 7th and 8th, down through Chelsea, back over to Union Square, then over and down into Meatpacking, though only briefly, because I didn't seem to know it very well.

No sign of him, anywhere. I didn't know what I was expecting, if I was hoping I'd just run into him on a street corner or something, but it didn't happen.

He evidently didn't know what was going to happen next, how to get me on to the next series of events.

The short paragraphs were a giveaway.

AUTHOR OF THE DEATH

He was treading water.
It was a hiatus.
So I made my own choice.

I was down on the fringes of Soho when I spotted another Starbucks. I'd already been in about ten. He is forever dropping a Starbucks into the run of play—situating events there, revisiting recollections, or having people pick up a take-out to engineer a beat of 'real life' texture. Each was well-described, as though he'd actually been there, and so I'd taken the trouble to seek them out. This one was new to me, however.

The interior was big enough to have three separate seating areas, and looked comfortable and welcoming. It smelled like they always do. There was the harsh cough of steam being pumped through yet another portion of espresso. Quiet chatter. Anodyne music. People reading Lethem and Frantzen or Derrida and Barthes.

Weird thing was, it felt familiar.

Not familiar to *me*, but still...familiar. I know that sounds strange. I knew I didn't know the place personally, but it felt like I *could* have done. I decided I might as well have yet another Americano, and was wandering over toward the line when I realized some guy was looking at me.

I turned and looked back at him. He was in an armchair by a table close to the window. Late twenties, with sharply defined and well-described facial features. Something about him said he was no stranger to criminal behavior, but that's not what struck me most about him.

He looked how I felt. He looked weary.

He looked stuck.

I took a pace in his direction. 'Do I know you?'

'Don't see how.'

'That's what I thought. So why are you staring at me?'

'You look familiar,' he said. 'Like... I dunno.'

'Can't be. I've never been in here before.'

'You sure?'

'Yes. I've done stuff in the Starbucks on the corner of 42nd and 6th, the one on 6th between 46th and Times Square, and another at an unspecified street address up near Columbus Circle. Also I've stuck my head in a bunch more today, uptown, and on the way down here, just in case. But I've never been in this particular one. I'm sure.'

He shook his head, sat back in his chair, ready to disengage. 'Sorry to have bothered you.'

I was struck by a crazy thought.

'Who's your writer?'

'Michael Marshall Smith,' he said, diffidently, fully expecting the name not to mean anything to me.

I stared at him. 'No way.'

'What?' he said. He sat forward again in his chair, looking wary. 'You're... you're one of his too?'

'Well, yes, and no. Actually I'm in a Michael Marshall novel—different name, different genre, but the same guy.'

'Holy shit.' He looked at me, dumbfounded. 'That's outside the *box*. I never met someone else before. I mean, the people in this place, obviously, but not someone from a whole other *story*.'

'Me neither,' I said. I pulled a chair over to the table. 'You mind?'

'Go ahead,' he said, and I sat.

We looked at each other for a full minute. It felt very weird. I've met other characters before, of course—but only ones from my own story, like the guy said. They had their place and were all situated in relation to the star at the center of their firmament: which would be me.

This guy wasn't like that. He was totally other. I had no idea what he was about.

'How come you're here?' he asked eventually. 'I mean, suddenly, like this. You've never been in this place before. But now here you are.'

'I got tired of waiting,' I said. 'Bored of being in that scummy apartment in the East Village. He barely even knows the area. Spent half a morning walking around it, like, five years ago. That's all. There's a couple of streets that are pretty convincing and he nailed a few local shops—including a deli and a liquor store, thank God—but after that it's basically atmosphere and a few well-chosen adjectives.'

'How long do you have?'

'About a hundred and fifteen thousand words.'

He stared at me. 'You're in a *novel?*'

'I'm the protagonist, dude.'

'Shit.'

I shrugged. He sat back in his chair, caught between envy and resentment. 'Jesus, then you don't know you're born. I'm only in a short story, and even by the standards of the form, it's pretty fucking brief. Three thousand words. Whole thing takes place right here in this Starbucks. I don't even get to go *out the door.* I don't know shit about the city. I can see it, through the window, but that's all I get.'

'Hell,' I said. 'That's tough.'

'Tough is right. And look at what I'm wearing.'

I'd already noticed his clothes were nondescript. Jeans. A shirt in some indeterminate color. Shoes that I couldn't even see. 'Pretty vague.'

'Exactly,' he said. 'I don't have a coat because I don't do anything but be in here and so he didn't bother to describe one, not even a thin jacket hanging over the back of my chair, for Christ's sake.'

'That's understandable,' I said. 'He can't be bogging down with extraneous details, not at your kind of word length. Plus if he did mention a coat, people might assume it was going to become relevant at some point and get pissed off when it wasn't. Any good editor would pick him up on it, blue line it out.'

'Yeah, maybe so. But it gets *cold* in here, come the middle of the night.'

I thought about that, and about the idea of being trapped in one location forever, pinned to one small location for eternity. It made me feel cold too.

'I'm going to find the guy,' I said. 'Tell him I'm grateful for being—though some pretty harsh things happen to me, especially in back story—but I'd like some broader horizons now.'

'*Find* him? How the hell do you hope to do that?'

I shrugged. Again. I shrug a lot. 'By searching the city—the parts of it he knows, at least. That's what I'm doing now. It's how I ran into you. Which is something that's never happened to me before, and that makes me think that I'm achieving *something*, at least.'

'But what are the odds of banging into him?'

'Not good. I know that. But weren't there any coincidences in your story?'

'Like what?'

'I don't know. Things that were kind of convenient, that helped drive the plot forward without too much hard work?'

He thought about it. 'Not really.'

'There were in mine. Small things, he didn't take the piss with it, but—'

'"Take the piss"? What's that supposed to mean?'

'See, that's interesting. We don't say that here, do we? It's a British expression, I think. I'm supposed to be American born and bred, yet once in a while I'll say something that's a little bit off.'

'Maybe the guy *is* British, but sets his stuff here in the US. Blame the copyeditor for not picking up on it.'

'Could be. But my point is that while he didn't fall back on any whopper coincidences, he was happy to ease the way every now and then with a combination of circumstances that was just a little convenient.'

'I guess in a novel you have to, maybe. My thing, it happens in real time, so he didn't need to resort to that kind of kludge.'

'Right. But given I'm driving *this* story, I'm hoping that my rules apply. And so it's possible, if I keep walking, there's a small coincidence out there waiting to happen. Like meeting you.'

I waited for him to think about this. It was strange, but also exciting, to be dealing with someone new, *completely* new, who wasn't subservient to my protagonist status. It felt as though doors might be opening. I didn't know where they'd lead, but I was starting to think I could find them. If I *believed* enough. Maybe I could make it back to Westerford after all, that leafy town upstate where I'd been for those brief chapters. I could start a new life, do new things. Perhaps I could even get to the beach down in Florida featured in a small flashback. That would be great, but actually *anywhere* would do. Somewhere new. A place I could stretch my wings and find some other way to be.

The guy was frowning at me. 'Are you okay?'

'What do you mean?'

'You stopped talking. Just sat there looking intense.'

'Sorry. I had a stretch of interior monologue. Slightly lyrical. Takes a while to get through.'

AUTHOR OF THE DEATH

'I guess you first-person guys get a lot of that. Me, I'm in third. I just *do* stuff, pretty much.'

'So let's *do* stuff,' I said. 'Let's get out of this generic coffee house and go looking for him.'

'I can't.'

'Why?'

He looked sheepish. 'I don't think I can leave here. I've never been through that door. My whole life, I've been in here. I think that's it for me.'

'Have you ever tried? Gone up to the door and pulled on the handle and seen what happens?'

He looked down at his feet. 'Well, no. I'm just supposed to do what I do, right?'

'Not necessarily,' I said. 'I've spent longer with the guy than you, remember. I think he kind of likes it when one of us does something off our own bat. There was a minor character in my book, he dies in the end, but he sometimes got the chance to go do his own thing, and the writer would work around it. Maybe you're the same way.'

'I don't want to die in the end.'

'No, of course. Not saying that's going to happen. Just...if you're like me, if you're the narrator, the audience *knows* you're going to live—unless the guy's prepared to do something tricksy or flip into unreliable narrator at the end. So there's a set arc for me, and I kind of have to stick to it, because I manifest the story and vice versa and he can't screw with that. But with the more minor characters, like you—no offense—he can let them roam free a little more, see where they end up.'

'"Unreliable narrator"? What the hell is that?'

'It's a literary term. Not sure how I know it, given that I used to be a cop, but...'

The guy looked nervous. 'You're a *cop?*'

'No. *Ex*-cop. That way he could shorthand me as a tough guy with certain skill sets and a troubled past without having to do much actual research, or getting stuck with writing a police procedural.'

'That's a relief. My character's not a very nice guy, I don't think. There's a pervading sense of guilt throughout, though it's never clear what for.'

'Doesn't matter. I'm not going to arrest you, even if I still could. Come on. Let's go.'

I stood, and waited for him to follow suit.

'I just don't think I can, dude,' he muttered, looking wretched. 'I look out that window and all I see is two-dimensional.'

We turned and looked together. The light outside was beginning to fade. 'Barely even that,' he said. 'It's just two sentences, to me. "It was cold and grey and flat outside." And "A couple of leaves zigzagged slowly down from the tree along the sidewalk, falling brown and gold and dead." That's it.'

'Look,' I said, pointing. Two leaves were doing just what he'd said, and it *did* look cold out there, and the light was grey and flat.

'Every day,' he said. 'Every day they do that.'

'So evidently what happens out there *is* your domain, at least to a degree. You could—'

He shook his head. 'I can't do it. I'm sorry.'

I felt bad for him, and realized how lucky I was. 'I'll come back,' I said. 'I have to keep looking, but I will come back.'

'Really?'

'Sure. I know where you live, right? And you're in this new story now, too. That's something, at least. You branched out. You're recurring.'

'Yeah, I guess. Though I'm still stuck in the same place.'

'I'll come back tomorrow.'

'Okay,' he said, shyly. 'That...that would be cool.'

We shook hands. 'The name's John.'

'Oh,' he said. 'So's mine.'

I laughed. 'Guess we were never supposed to wind up on the same pages. Never mind. We'll cope. I'm going to find the guy, and when I do, we'll talk.'

'Good luck,' he smiled.

I felt jealous. I'd never been allowed to do that. I have to *say* things, or *ask* them. Shout them, once in a while. I can't 'smile' them. There's tougher editing on the novels than with the short stories, I guess, or a more restrictive house style. Though...right now I was *in* a short, wasn't I?

'Thanks,' I smiled, and took off my coat. 'Here.'

'Don't you need it?'

AUTHOR OF THE DEATH

'I've got an apartment. There are closets. I've never looked inside, but there must be something. Worst case, I can put on a sweater or another shirt.'

'Thanks, man.'

When I got to the door I heard him wish me luck again.

I turned back and winked. 'Thanks. And keep the faith, my friend.'

When I stepped out onto the sidewalk, however, everything changed. I knew right away that a decision had been made. It's happened to me before. I stroll aimlessly through a chapter, with lots of thinking and not much doing, and then suddenly there's a blank line break and the next event arrives.

I noticed a man on the other side of the street. He was wandering along, aimlessly, smoking a cigarette. He glanced across at the Starbucks I'd just left and I could see him wondering if he could face yet another coffee. There wasn't so much traffic, but what there was, was moving fast enough that he'd have to go back to the corner to cross. It was enough to make him decide it wasn't worth it.

I'd never seen the man before, but I knew who he was. I knew I'd found him.

I thought it again, for emphasis.

I knew.

He looked a little like me and also a little like the guy I'd just left in the Starbucks, the other John. A bit shorter, and a little older, with a touch of grey in the temples. Less distinctive overall. He looked tired, too. Jet-lagged, was my guess. Come over from London for a meeting with his publisher and some research, doggedly using his first day in the city to walk the streets. Not for him, I knew, the hours of reading or scanning the Internet or using Google Streetview™. He liked to do his research with his feet, wanted to get to know the city through the miles he moved through it.

Suddenly I realized what this could mean.

The writer *could* merely be reminding himself of these streets for the sake of it, because that's what he always did and it was better than lurking in his hotel room. Or it could merely wind up as background in another short story.

But...it *could* also be that there was a sequel in the works. A sequel to *my book*.

He could be *considering* doing it, at least. He didn't normally. He usually came up with a new bunch of characters for each novel, which was why we ended up in such fixed and limited worlds, without a future. But maybe he was clueing in to the fact that many readers don't *want* to sit through the wheel being reinvented each time, but would prefer to settle back into a recurring set of characters like a comfortable old chair.

The more I thought about it, the more plausible it seemed. I'd always felt that there were elements in my story that hadn't been tied up as satisfyingly as they could have. I'd been left on a cautiously upbeat note, but there was a lot more to be said.

Maybe he was going to do it.

Maybe there was going to be *more*.

I felt myself smiling. Meanwhile the writer ground to a halt, looking up and down the street. I saw his eyes lighting on this and that—store fronts, fire escapes, passers by—absorbing everything without noticing, passing it down to the part of his mind that stored these snippets of local color for later use.

I turned away, not wanting him to see my face. When I'd left the apartment that morning, a meeting had been exactly what I wanted. Now I didn't. I didn't want to run the risk of derailing him. I wanted whatever was going through his head to run its course, just in case there was a chance that I was right.

I heard a noise behind me.

I turned to see the guy from the Starbucks, the other John. He was standing in the doorway of the coffee shop, and the sound he'd made was a grunt of disbelief.

He'd done it. He'd tried the door, and opened it.

He stepped cautiously out onto the sidewalk. 'Holy crap, John,' he said, seeing me. 'Look!'

'You *did* it, man.'

The joy I felt was partly for him, but mainly for myself. He'd come out because of me, after all. I'd met him and I'd *changed* things. If that much was possible, then maybe everything else was too. Perhaps the writer was considering a sequel precisely *because* I'd started to prove myself capable of independent movement, worthy of further development.

Maybe I was even going to be a series.

The other John was staring around in wonder. He took a couple of steps up the sidewalk. He turned and looked back the other way. Another pair of leaves came zigzagging gently down from the tree, falling brown and golden.

He reached out and grabbed one, crumpling it in his hands. 'I did that,' he shouted. 'I *did* that!'

'Way to go,' I said.

He waved his hands in the air triumphantly, still shouting. He was making a lot of noise now. Enough that it reached across the street, evidently...

...because at that moment, the writer looked up.

He saw John, of course. John was the guy making all the noise, dancing around on the sidewalk, brandishing a crushed leaf in his hand.

The writer frowned, cigarette halfway to his mouth, as though something about John struck him, but he wasn't sure what. It could be that he was merely wondering if he could use the guy in something, not realizing that he already had.

But then his eyes skated past John, and landed on me. And he froze.

He knew who I was.

He was bound to, I guess. I'd recognized *him* immediately, after all, and he'd spent nearly a year with me inside his head, every day, every working hour. Could be that he'd already been thinking about me, too, moments before, if he genuinely was considering pulling me out of the backlist for another turn in the light, as I hoped.

He kept on looking at me. He blinked.

'Hey,' I said. 'You're Michael, right?'

He started to back away up the street.

I was confused—this was the last thing I'd expected—but then I realized. He was scared. I'd assumed he'd understand how things work, but maybe not. I guess these guys just put down the words and chase their deadlines, not realizing what comes to life between the sentences that come out of their heads in torrents or fits and starts.

He thought he was losing his mind.

'No, it's okay,' I said, hurrying up my side of the street, trying to catch up with him. There were too many people and so I darted across the road instead.

'Go away,' he said, between clenched teeth, hurrying backwards as I got closer. His eyes were wide. 'Go *away*.'

'It's *okay*,' I said, trying to sound soothing. 'I got no problem with you. Not anymore. I... I think I know why you're here. And that's cool. It's *great*, in fact. I don't want to freak you out. I just wanted to say "hi," and, you know, wish you good luck.'

'You are *not* real,' he hissed, and kept backing away—but he realized he was right up against a crossroads, and had to stop. 'I am *very* tired, that's all.'

'Absolutely,' I said. 'That's all it is. And I just happen to look a little like a guy you wrote. Look, we'll go our separate ways. It's the way it should be. But let's at least shake hands, okay? No hard feelings. And, you know, obviously I love your work.'

I raised my right hand. His eyes got wider still.

I realized my hand felt cold and heavy, and when I glanced down at it I remembered that actually, I *had* found my gun before I left the apartment. It seemed like he was prepared to go down the unreliable narrator route after all. I tried to throw it away, to prove I was harmless, but it wouldn't leave my hand.

'Michael,' I said, trying to sound reassuring. 'It's okay. You know me—I'm not a killer. I'm basically a good person. More sinned against than sinning, like all your protagonists. Just ignore the gun, okay?'

But he'd started to back away again, so scared now that he'd forgotten where he was standing, and he stepped back into the road and lost his balance and a cab came around the corner and smacked straight into him.

I haven't been back to the Starbucks in Soho. I said I would, and I will, but I haven't yet. I don't know what to say to John. I don't know how to explain what happened. I don't want to have to describe how it felt to look down at the writer's head on the street, with all the blood leaking out of it, or to watch his eyes as they went from clear to glassy to frosted. I don't want to admit to the fact that I was the author of that event.

I also don't want to see John yet because afterwards I tracked down one of the writer's story collections. I found it in the discount section in a Borders. Borders may be history in the real world—more's the pity—but my novel was set back in 2006, so for me they're still around. I found the short story John's in, and I read it. It's pretty good, but it's kind of spooky and heads toward a dark, bad conclusion. I don't want to have to explain to John that he dies in the end after all, or why that may be better than being me.

Because...I do not.

I do not die. I walk these streets and these pages forever, and there will never be a sequel now.

I should have just stuck to my arc, to my own story, been satisfied with what I had. Now I'm trapped in this dead end.

Down at the bottom of this chunk of words.

It doesn't even end properly.

It just stops.

THE DARK
LAND

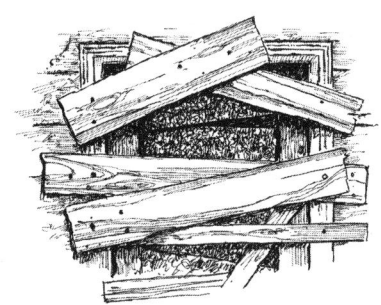

I t started with the bed.

After three years at college I'd come back home, returning to the bedroom I'd grown up in. It was going to be a while before I could afford to move out for good, and so in the intervening month I'd redecorated the room: covering the very 1970s orange with a more soothing shade, and badgering my mother into getting some new curtains that didn't look like they had been designed on drugs by someone who liked the color brown a great deal. I'd also moved most of the furniture around, trying to breathe new life into a space I'd known since I was ten. It hadn't worked. It still felt as if I should be doing French verbs or preparing conkers, musing on what kissing a girl might be like. I knew it was largely an excuse for not doing anything more constructive—like filling out the pile of job applications which sat on the desk—but that afternoon I decided to move the bed away from its traditional place by the wall and try it in another couple of positions. It was hard work. One of the legs was rather fragile and the bed had to be virtually lifted off the floor rather than dragged around—which is why I hadn't tried moving it before, I now remembered. After half an hour I was hot and irritated and developing a stoop. I had also become convinced that the original position had been not only the optimal but in fact the *only* place the bed could go.

It was as I struggled to shove it back up against the wall that I began to feel a bit strange. Light-headed, nauseous. Out of breath, I assumed. When the bed was finally back in place I lay back on it for a moment, feeling rather ill—and I suppose I just fell asleep.

I woke up about half an hour later, half-remembering a dream in which I had been doing nothing more than lying on my bed and remembering that my parents had said that they were going to extend the wood paneling in the downstairs hallway. For a moment I was disorientated, confused by being in the same place in reality as I had been in the dream, and then I drifted off again.

Sometime later I woke up again. I found it very difficult to fight my way up out of sleep, but eventually managed to haul myself sluggishly upright. After a while I lurched to my feet and across to the sink to get a glass of water. Drinking it made the inside of my mouth a little less dry, but no more appealing. I decided that a cup of tea would be a good idea, and headed out of the bedroom to go downstairs.

As I reached the top of the staircase I remembered the dream about the paneling, and wondered where a strange notion like that could have come from. I'd worked hard for my psychology paper at college, and was confident that Freud hadn't felt that wood paneling was even worth a mention. I trudged downstairs, still feeling odd, my thoughts dislocated and fragmented.

When I reached the halfway landing I ground to a halt, and stared around me, astonished. They *had* extended the paneling.

When you enter my parents' house you come into a two story hallway, with a staircase that climbs up three walls to the second floor. The paneling used to only go about eight feet up the wall of the front hall, but now it soared right up to the ceiling. And they'd done it in exactly the same wood as the original. There wasn't a join to be seen. How had they managed that? Come to that, *when* had they managed it? It hadn't been like this that morning, but both my parents were at work and would be for hours and…well, it was just impossible. I reached out and touched the wood, bewildered at how even the grain matched, and that the new wood looked just as aged as the original, which had been there fifty years.

Then:

Wait a minute, I thought. That isn't right. There hadn't used to be *any* paneling in the hall. Just simple white walls. The stairs themselves had been paneled in wood, but the walls were plain white plaster. How could I have forgotten that? What had made me think that the front hall had been paneled, and believe it so unquestioningly? I remembered that I'd recently noticed, sensitized to these things by having repainted my room, that the white in the hall was a little grubby, especially round the light switches.

So what was all this paneling doing here? Where had it come from? And why had I been so sure that at least some of it had always been there?

Something wasn't right.

I walked into the kitchen, casting bewildered glances back into the hall. I absentlymindedly registered a soft clinking sound outside, and automatically headed to the back door—too puzzled about the paneling to realize that it was late in the day for a milk delivery.

Both the front and back doors of the house open onto the driveway, the back door from a little corridor full of muddy shoes and rusting tools which connects the kitchen to the garage. I threaded my way through the gardening implements and wrenched the stiff door open. It was late afternoon by then, but the light outside seemed very intense, the colors rich as they are before a storm.

I looked down and saw the milk bottle holder, with four bottles of milk in it. They weren't normal milk bottles, however, but large American-style quart containers somehow jammed into slots meant to take pints. Someone had taken the silver tops off.

A movement at the periphery of my vision caught my attention, and I glanced up towards the top of the driveway. There, about thirty yards away, were two children. One was fat and sitting on a bike, the other slim and standing.

I was seized with sudden irritation, and started quickly up the drive towards them—convinced that the clinking sound I'd heard was them stealing the tops off the milk.

I had covered scarcely five yards when someone who'd been at my school appeared from behind me, and walked quickly past me up the drive, staring straight ahead. I couldn't remember his name, had barely known him. He'd been two or three years older than me, and I'd completely forgotten he'd existed, but as I stared after him now I remembered he'd been one of the more amiable seniors. I could recall being proud of having some small kind of communication with one of the big boys, how it had made me feel a bit older myself, more a man of the world. And I remembered the way he used to greet my yelling his nickname, with a half-smile and a coolly raised eyebrow.

All this came back with the instantaneous impact of memory, but something was wrong. The man didn't seem to register that I was there. I felt disturbed, not by the genuinely strange fact that he was in the driveway—or that he was wearing school athletic gear—but merely because he didn't smile and tilt his head back the way he used to. It was so bizarre that I wondered briefly if I was dreaming, but if you can ask yourself the question you always know the answer. I wasn't.

My attention was distracted by a reflection in the glass of the window in the back hallway. A man seemed to be standing behind me. He wore glasses, had a chubby face and basin-cut blond hair, and was carrying a bicycle. I whirled round to face where he should have been, but he wasn't there.

Then I remembered the kids at the top of the driveway, and turned to shout at them again, needing something to take my bewilderment out on. Almost immediately a tall slim man in a dark suit came walking down the drive: briskly, as if slightly late. Maybe it was a trick of the light in the gathering dusk, but I couldn't seem to fix on his face. My eyes just seemed to slide off it, as if it were slippery, or made of ice.

'Stop shouting at them,' he snapped. He strode past me, towards the back door. I stared at him open-mouthed. 'They're not doing anything wrong,' he said. 'Leave them alone.'

The kids took themselves off, one on the bike, the other walking alongside, and I turned to the suited man. For some reason I felt anxious to placate him, and yet at the same time I was outraged at his invasion of our property.

'I'm sorry,' I said, 'It's just, well, I'm a bit confused. I thought I saw someone I knew in the drive. Did you see him? Wavy brown hair, athletics kit?'

For some reason I thought that the man would say that he had, and that that would make me feel better. All I got was a curt 'No' as he entered the back hallway.

Then another voice spoke. 'Well then. Shall we go into your old house?'

Someone else was standing in the back hall. The man with the blond hair and glasses. And he really was carrying a bicycle. He wasn't talking to me, but to the man in the suit.

THE DARK LAND

'What?' I said, and hurried after them, catching a glimpse of the suited man's face. 'But it's *you*...' I stopped again, baffled, as I realized that the man in the suit was the same man who had been in athletics gear.

The two men marched straight into the kitchen. I followed, impotently enraged. *Was* this his old house? Even so, wasn't it customary to ask the current occupants' permission if you wanted to visit?

The suited man was peering round the kitchen, which looked very messy. He poked at some fried rice I'd left cooling in a pan on the stove. At least, I *seemed* to have left it there, though I wasn't sure when I would have done so. I don't just cook up rice in the afternoon for the pure hell of it. I still felt the urge to placate the man, however, and hoped he would eat some of the rice.

He merely grimaced with distaste and joined his colleague at the window, looking out onto the drive, hands on hips. 'Dear God,' he muttered. The other man grunted in agreement.

I noticed that I'd picked up the milk from outside the back door, and appeared to have spilt some of it on the floor. I tried to clean it up with a piece of kitchen roll which seemed very dirty and yellowed as if with age. I was trying to buy time. I felt very strongly that there must be some sense to the situation somewhere, some logic I was missing. Even if the man had lived here once, he had no right to just march in here with his friend, but as I continued trying to swab up the milk before he noticed it—*why?*—I realized that there was something far more wrong than a mere breach of protocol at stake.

The suited man looked about thirty-five, much older than he should have been if he was indeed the guy I'd been to school with. Yet that would still leave him far too young to ever have lived here. Between our family and the previous occupants, I knew who'd lived in the house for the last forty years. So how could it be his old house? It didn't make sense.

And was it actually *him*? The boy from my school? Apart from being too old, it looked like him, but was it actually *him*?

I did the best I could with the milk and then straightened up, staggering slightly. My perception seemed to have become both heightened and jumbled, as if I was very drunk. Everything pulsed with an unusual intensity and exaggerated emotional charge, yet there also seemed to be gaps in what I was perceiving, as if I was receiving an edited version of what was going on.

Things began to flick from one state to another—with the bits in between, the becoming, missing like a series of jump cuts. I felt hot and dizzy and the kitchen looked small and indescribably messy, the orange of the walls—the same color my bedroom had once been painted—seeming to push in at me beneath a low and unsteady ceiling. I wondered if I was seeing the kitchen as *they* saw it, and then immediately wondered what I meant by that.

Meanwhile they stood at the window, occasionally turning to stare balefully at me, radiating distaste and impatience. They were evidently waiting for something. But what?

Noticing that I still had the piece of kitchen roll in my hand, I stepped over all the rubbish on the floor—*what the hell had been going on in this kitchen?*—to put it in the overflowing bin. I squeezed my temples with my fingers, struggling to stand upright against the weight of the air, and squared up to the men.

'L-look', I stuttered, leaning on the fridge for support, 'what exactly is going on?'

I immediately wished I'd kept quiet. The suited man slowly turned his head. It kept turning and turning, until it was looking directly at me — while his body stayed facing the other way. Like an owl, though he wasn't blinking. I could feel my stomach trying to crawl away and fought the need to gag. I sensed he'd done it deliberately, done it because he knew it would make me want to throw up, and I thought he might well be right.

'Why don't you just *shut up?*' he said. Then he twisted his head slowly back round until he was looking out onto the drive once more.

I decided not to ask any more questions.

Meanwhile, the mess in the kitchen seemed to be getting worse. Every time I looked there were more dirty pans and bits of rubbish and old food on the floor. My head felt thicker and heavier, as if everything was slipping away from me. I slumped against the fridge and clung to it, almost pulling it away from the wall. I began to cry too, my tears cutting channels in the thick grime on the fridge door. I dimly remembered that my parents had bought a brand new one only a few weeks before, but they must have changed it again. This one looked like something out of the 1950s. Very retro. Or original. To be honest it was hard to tell, because it was swimming back and forth and there was a lot of white in my eyes. Both the men were both watching me now, as if mildly interested to see when I'd fall.

Suddenly there was a terrible jangling impact in my head. I flapped hysterically at my ears, as if to stop someone hammering pencils into them. Then the pain happened again, and I recognized first that it was a sound rather than a blow, and then that it was the doorbell.

Someone was at the front door.

The two men glanced at each other, and the blond one nodded wearily. The suited man turned to me.

'Do you know what that is?' he asked.

'It's the front door,' I said quickly, still trying to please him.

'So you'd better answer it, hadn't you?'

'Yes.'

'Answer the *door*.'

'Should I answer it?' I queried, stupidly. I couldn't seem to remember what words meant anymore.

'*Yes*,' he shouted, and picked up a mug—my mug, the mug I'd came downstairs, I remembered, to put tea in—and hurled it straight at me. It smashed into the fridge door by my face. I struggled to pull myself upright, head aching and ears ringing, aware of a soft crump as a fragment of the mug broke under my foot.

The doorbell jangled again, the harshness of the noise making me realize how muted all other sounds had become. I fell towards the kitchen door, sliding across the front of the fridge, my feet tangling in the boxes and cartons that now covered the filthy floor. I could feel the orange of the walls seeping in through my ears and mouth, and kept missing whole seconds of time—as if I was blacking out and coming to like a stroboscope.

As I lurched across to the kitchen door and grabbed the handle to hold myself up, I heard the blond man say, 'He may not go through. If he does, we wait.'

It didn't mean anything to me. None of it did.

I made my way towards the front door, ploughing clumsily through drifts of rubbish in the hallway. The chime of the doorbell had pushed the air hard, and I could see it lapping towards me in waves. Ducking to avoid the sound, I slipped on the mat and almost fell into the living room. As I crouched there on my hands and knees I saw it was getting dark in there, really dark, and I could hear the plants talking. I couldn't catch the words, but they were definitely conversing, beneath the night sounds and a soft rustling which sounded a hundred yards away. The living room must have grown.

I picked myself up and turned to the front door. The bell clanged again, and this time the sound caught me full in the face, stinging bitterly. It should have been about four paces across the hall from the living room door to the front door, but I thought it was only going to take one and then it took twenty, past all the paneling and over the huge folds in the mat. It was not an easy journey.

Then I had my hand on the doorknob and then the door was open and I stepped out of the house.

'Oh hello, Michael,' said a voice. 'I thought someone must be in, because all the lights were on.'

'Wuh?' I said, blinking in the fading sunlight.

The woman in front of me smiled. 'I hope I didn't disturb you?'

'No, that's fine.' Suddenly I recognized her. It was Mrs. Steinberg, the woman who brings us our cat food in bulk. 'Fine. Sorry.' I glanced covertly behind me into the hallway, which was solid and unpannelled and four paces wide and led to the living room—which was light and airy and the size it had always been.

'I've brought your delivery' the woman said, and then frowned. 'Are you alright?'

'I'm fine,' I replied, turning to grin broadly at her. My mind felt like a runaway lift, soaring back upwards to reality. 'I just nodded off for a moment, in the kitchen. I still feel a bit, you know.'

Mrs. Steinberg smiled. 'Of course. Give me a hand?'

I followed her to the top of the drive and heaved a box of cat food out of her van, watching the house. There was nothing to see. I thanked her and carried the box back down the drive as she drove off. I walked back into the house and shut the front door behind me.

I felt absolutely fine.

I walked into the kitchen. As I'd expected, the men had disappeared. I looked slowly around a kitchen which looked exactly as it had since before I was too young to remember. Everything was normal.

THE DARK LAND

I must have fallen asleep while making tea, and then struggled over to the front door to open it while still half asleep. I could remember asking myself if I was having a dream, and deciding that I wasn't—but that just showed how wrong you could be. It had been unusually vivid, and it was odd how I'd been suddenly awake and alright again as soon as I stepped out of the front door. But it had been a dream. Here I was in the kitchen again, and everything was normal. Clean and tidy, spick and span, with all the rubbish in the bin and the pans in the right places and the milk in the fridge and a smashed mug on the floor.

That was less good. It was my mug, and it lay smashed at the bottom of the fridge.

How had that happened?

Maybe I'd fallen asleep holding it. Not terribly likely, but possible. Or perhaps I'd knocked it over on waking, and incorporated the sound into my dream. This was slightly more credible, but where exactly was I supposed to have fallen asleep? Just leaning against the counter—or actually stretched out on it, using the kettle as a pillow?

Then I noticed the fridge door. There was a little dent in it, with a couple of flecks of paint missing. At about head height. That wasn't good either.

I cleared up the mug and switched the kettle on. While it was boiling I wandered into the hall and the living room. Everything was fine, tidy, normal. Super. I went back into the kitchen. The same. Great.

Apart from a little dent in the fridge door at about head height.

I made my cup of tea in a different, non-broken mug, and drank it looking out of the kitchen window at the drive. I felt unsettled and nervous, and unsure of what to do with either of those emotions. Even if it *had* been a dream, it was a very odd one, particularly the way it had fought so hard against melting away. Maybe I was more tired than I realized. Or ill. Food poisoning could make your head go very strange, as I'd learned after a couple of college friends' attempts at cooking anything more complex than toast. But I felt fine. Physically, at least.

I carried the box of cat food into the pantry, unpacked it, and stacked the cans in the corner. Then I switched the kettle on again. Suddenly my heart seemed to stop.

Before I had time to understand why, the cause repeated itself. A soft chinking noise outside the back door.

I moved quickly to the window and looked out. There was no-one in the drive. I craned my neck, trying to see around to the back door, but could only see the large pile of firewood that lay to one side of it.

Then I heard the noise again. I walked slowly into the back hallway and listened, slowly clenching my fists. I could hear nothing except the sound of blood pumping in my ears. I grabbed the knob and swung the door open.

Stillness outside. A rectangle of late afternoon light, a patch of driveway, and a dark hedge waving quietly. I stepped out into the drive, and stood and listened again.

After a moment I heard a faint crunching noise. It sounded like pebbles softly rubbing against each other. Then I heard it again. I looked more closely at the drive, peering at the actual stones, and noticed that a small patch about ten yards in front of me appeared to be moving slightly. Wriggling, almost.

They stopped, and then the sound came again — and another patch stirred briefly, about a yard closer than the first. As if registering the weight of invisible feet.

I was so engrossed that I didn't notice the whistling straight away. When I did, I looked up. The blond man was back. He was standing at the top of the driveway, carrying a bicycle with the wheels slowly spinning in the dusk. He whistled the top line of a perfect harmony, the lower line just the sound of the wind. As I stared at him, backing slowly towards the house, the crunching noise got louder and louder.

Then the suited man was standing with his nose almost touching mine.

'Hello again,' he said.

The blond man started down the driveway. 'Greetings indeed,' he laughed. 'Come on, in we go.'

Abruptly I realized that the very last thing I should do was let them back into the house.

I leapt back through the door into the hallway. The suited man, caught by surprise, started forward but I was quick and whipped the door shut in his face and locked it. That felt good, but then he started banging on the door very hard, grotesquely hard, and I saw that the kitchen was getting messy again, and the fridge was old, and I could barely see out of the window because it was so grimy. A slight flicker in my mind made me think that maybe I'd missed the smallest fraction of a second, and I realized that it really hadn't been a dream. I was back in the bad place. As I backed into the kitchen I tripped and fell, sprawling amongst cartons and bacon rind and dirt and what appeared to be puke on the floor. The banging on the back door got louder, and louder, and louder. He was going to break it, I knew. He was going to break the door down. I'd let them back and they had to come in through the back door. I'd come in through the wrong door…

Suddenly understanding what I must do, I scrambled to my feet and kicked my way through the rubbish. The fridge door swung open to block my path. The inside was dark and dirty and there was something rotted inside, but I slammed it out of the way, biting hard on my lip to keep my head clear.

I had to get to the front door.

I had to open it, step out, and then step back in again. The front door was the *right door*. And I had to do it soon, before the back door broke and let them in. I could already hear a splintering quality to the sound of the blows. And the back door was about two inches thick.

The hallway was worse than I expected. I skidded to a halt, at first unable to even *see* the front door. I thought that I must be looking in the wrong direction, but I wasn't, because I finally spotted it over to the left, where it was supposed to be. But the angles were all wrong, and to see it I had to look behind me and to the right, although when I saw it I could see that in reality it was still over to the left. And it looked so close—could it really be less than a yard away?—but when I held my hand out to it I groped into nothing, the fingers still in front of the door when it should have been past it.

I stared wildly around, disorientated and unsure even of which way to go. Suddenly the banging behind me got markedly louder, probably as the blond man joined in, and this helped to marginally restore my sense of direction. I found the front door again, concentrated hard on its apparent position, and started to walk towards it.

I immediately fell over, because the floor was much lower than I expected. It actually seemed be tilted in some way, although it looked flat and level, because although one of my legs reached it easily enough the other dangled in space. I pulled myself up onto my knees and found I was looking at a sort of sloped wall between the wall and the ceiling, a wall which bent back from the wall and yet out from the ceiling. The door was still over on the left, although to see it I now had to look straight ahead and up.

Then I noticed another sound beneath the eternal banging, and whirled to face the direction it was coming from. I found that I was looking through the living room door, and that it gave into sheer darkness, a darkness which was seeping out into the hallway like smoke, clinging to the angles in the air like the inside of a dark prism. I heard the noise again. It was a deep rumbling growl, far, far away in there, almost obscured by the night noises and the sound of vegetation moving in the wind. The sound didn't seem to be getting any closer, but I knew that was because the living room now extended out far beyond the house, into hundreds and hundreds of miles of dense jungle. As I listened carefully I could hear the gurgling of some dark river far off to the right, the sound of water mixing with the warm rustling of the breeze in the darkness. It sounded very peaceful and for a moment I was still, transfixed.

Then the sound of another splintering crack wrenched me away, and I turned my back on the living room and flailed towards where the front door must be. The hall table loomed above me and I thought I could walk upright beneath it—but tripped over it and fell again, headlong onto the cool floorboards. The mat had moved, no, was *moving*, sliding slowly up the stairs like a draught, and as I rolled over and looked at the ceiling I saw the floor coming towards me, the walls shortening in little jerks.

As I lay there panting, a clear cool waft of air stroked my cheek. At first I thought that it must have come from the living room, although it had been warm in there, but then I remembered that I was lying on the floor. The breeze had to be a draft coming under the front door. I must nearly be there. I looked all around me but all I could see was paneling and floor and what was behind me. I closed my eyes and tried to grope for it, but it was even worse inside my head so I opened them again. Then I caught a glimpse of the door, far away, obscured from view round a corner but just visible once you knew where to look.

THE DARK LAND

On impulse I reached my hand out in not quite the opposite direction and felt it fall upon warm grainy wood.

The door. I'd found it.

I pulled myself along the floor towards it, and tried to stand up. I got no more than a few inches before I fell back down again. I tried once more, with the same result, feeling as if I was trying to do something entirely against nature. Again, and this time I reached a semi-crouching position, muscles straining. I started to slump almost immediately — but as I did so I threw myself forwards. I found myself curled up, my feet a couple of feet from the floor, lying on the door. Electing to not even *try* to come to terms with this, I groped by my side and found the doorknob. I tried to twist it but the sweat on my hand made them spin uselessly on the shiny metal. I wiped it on my shirt and tried again, and this time I got some purchase and heard the catch withdraw as the knob turned. Exultantly I tugged at it, as with a tremendous crash the back door finally gave way.

The door wouldn't budge. Panicking, I tried again. Nothing. By peering down the crack I could see that no lock or bolt was impeding it, so why wouldn't it bloody move?

There were footsteps in the back hall.

Suddenly I realized that I was lying on the door, and trying to pull it towards me against my own weight.

The footsteps reached the kitchen.

I rolled over off the door onto the wall beside it and reached for the handle, but I'd slid too far. As the footsteps came closer I scrambled back across the slippery wall, grabbed and twisted the doorknob with all my strength. It opened just as they entered the hall and I rolled out through it, fell and landed awkwardly and painfully on something hard and bristly and for a few moments had no clear idea of where or who I was, and just lay there fighting for breath.

After some time I sat up slowly. I was sitting outside the house on the doormat, my back to the front door. At the top of the drive a young couple were staring at me curiously. I stood up and smiled, trying to suggest that I often sat on the doormat and that they ought to try it as it was actually a lot of fun—hoping that they hadn't seen me fall there from about two-thirds of the way up the door. They smiled back and carried on walking, mollified or maybe even hurrying off home to try it for themselves.

I turned hesitantly back towards the door, and looked in.

It had worked. It was all okay again.

The mat was on the floor, right angles looked like 90°, and the ceiling was back where it was supposed to be. I stepped back a pace and looked down the driveway at the back door. It had been utterly smashed, and now looked like little more than an extension of the firewood pile.

I stepped back into the house through the front door, the right door, and shut it behind me. I walked carefully and quietly into the living room, and then the kitchen. Everything was fine, everything was normal. It was just a nice normal house.

If you came in through the right door.

The wrong door was in about a thousand pieces. I thought about that for some time, with another cup of tea and what felt like my first cigarette in months. I saw with frank disbelief that less than half an hour had elapsed since I'd first come downstairs. The back door. The *wrong* door. It was coming in through there that took me to wherever it was that the house became. Coming in through the *front* door brought me back to where I normally lived. So presumably I was safe, so long as I didn't leave the house and come back in through the back door. They couldn't get me. Presumably.

But I didn't like having that door in pieces. Being safe was only half of the issue. I wasn't going to feel *secure* until that portal was well and truly closed.

I walked into the back hall and looked nervously out through the wreckage onto the drive. Everything was fine. There was nothing I needed protecting from. But I still didn't like it. Did it have to be me who came through the door, or what if a falling leaf or maybe even just a soft breeze came inside? Would that be enough?

Could I take the risk?

As I stood there indecisively, I noticed once more the pile of firewood propped up against the outside wall of the back hall. I probably still wouldn't have put two and two together had not a very large proportion of the pile been thick old floorboards—a donation from a neighbor. I looked at the tool shelf on the inside wall and saw a hammer and a big box of good long nails. Then I looked at the wood again.

I could nail the damn thing shut.

I flicked my cigarette butt out onto the drive and rolled up my sleeves. The hammer was big and heavy, which was just as well because when I nailed the planks across the door frame I'd be hammering into solid brickwork. I was going to have to board right the way up, but that was alright as there were loads of planks, and if I reinforced it enough it should be well-nigh impregnable.

Feeling much better, I set to work. I may even have hummed. Kneeling just inside the door, I reached out and began pulling the floorboards in, taking care to select the thickest and least weathered. I judged that I'd need about fifteen to make the doorway really secure, although that was largely guesswork as I'd never tried to turn the back hall into a fortress before. Pulling them in was heavy work. I had to stretch out to reach them, and I began to get hot and tired, and anxious to begin the nailing. Outside it was getting darker as the evening began, and the air was very cool and still.

As the pile in the back hall increased in size it became more difficult, and I had to lean further and further out to reach the next plank. This made me nervous. I was still inside, and my feet were still on the ground in the back hall. I wasn't 'coming back in'. I was just leaning out and then, well, *sort of* coming back in but not really, because my feet never left the back hall. But it made me nervous nonetheless, and I began to work quicker and quicker, perspiration running down my face as, clinging to the doorframe with my left hand, I stretched out to bring the last few boards in. Eleven, twelve. Just a couple more. Now the last one I could possibly reach: that would have to be enough. Hooking my left foot behind the frame and gripping it hard with my left hand, I stretched out towards the plank, waving fingers little more than an inch from the end. Just a little further... I let my hooking foot slide slightly, allowed my fingers to slip round half an inch, and tried to extend my back as far as it would go. My fingers just scraping the end, I tried a last yearning lunge.

And then suddenly a stray thought struck me.

Here I was, pulled out as if on some invisible rack. Why hadn't I just gone out of the front door, picked up piles of wood, and brought them back into the house through the front door? It would have been easier, it would have been quicker, and it wouldn't have involved all this monkeying around at the wrong door. Not that it mattered now, because as it happened even if I didn't get this last plank I'd probably have plenty, but I wouldn't have been so hot and tired. It was also worrying that in my haste I'd been putting myself in needless danger. I'd better slow down, calm down, take a rest.

It was an unimportant, contemplative thought, but one that distracted me for a fraction of a second too long. As I finally got the tips of my fingers round the plank I realized with horror that the hand on the doorframe was slipping. Desperately I tried to scrabble back, but my hands were too sweaty and the doorframe itself was slippery now. I felt the tendons in my hand stretch as I tried to defy my center of gravity and think my weight backwards, and then suddenly my forehead walloped onto the ground and I was lying flat on my face.

I was up in a second, and I swear to God that both feet never left the hall floor at once. I leapt back into the hallway, grabbing that last bloody piece of wood without even noticing it.

I crouched in the doorframe, panting hysterically. Everything looked normal outside. The driveway was quiet, the pebbles were still and there was none of the faint deadening of sound that I associated with the other place. I was furious with myself for having taken the risk, for not having thought to bring them in through the front door—and especially for falling, which had been painful quite apart from anything else.

But I hadn't fallen out, not really. I hadn't come back in, as such. The drive was fine, the kitchen was fine. Everything was okay.

Soothed by the sounds of early evening traffic in the distance, my heart gradually slowed to only about twice its normal rate. I forced myself to take a break, and had a cigarette perched on the pile of planks. During the fall my right foot had caught the tool shelf, and there were nails all over the place, both inside and outside the door. But there were plenty left and the ones outside could stay there. I wasn't going to make the same damn fool mistake twice.

Gathering up the hammer and a fistful of nails, I laid a plank across the door and started work. Getting the nails through the wood and into the masonry was even harder than I'd expected, but within a couple of minutes it was in place, and felt reassuringly solid. I heaved another plank into position and set about securing it. This was actually going to work.

After half an hour I was into the swing of it and the wood now reached almost halfway up the doorframe. My arms were aching and head ringing from the hammering, which was very loud in the confined space of the back hall. I had a break leaning on the completed section, staring blankly out onto the drive. I was jolted back from reverie by the realization that a piece of dust or something must have landed in my eye, distorting my vision. I blinked to remove it, but it didn't disappear. It didn't hurt, just made a small patch of the drive up near the road look a bit ruffled. I rubbed and shut both eyes individually, and discovered with mounting unease that the distortion was present in both.

I stood upright. Something was definitely going on at the top of the drive.

The patch still looked crumpled, as if seen through a heat haze, and whichever way I turned my head the patch stayed in the same place. It was flickering very slightly now too, like a bad quality film print, although the flecks weren't white, they were dark. I rubbed my eyes hard again, but once I'd stopped seeing stars I saw that the effect was still there. I peered at it, trying to discern something that I could interpret. The flecks seemed to organize into broken and shifting vertical lines as I watched, as if something was hidden behind a curtain of rain, rain so colored as to make up a picture of that patch of the drive. This impression gradually strengthened until it was like looking at one of those plastic strip doors, where you walk through the hanging strips. It was as if there was one of those at the top of the drive, a patch of driveway pictured on it in living three dimensions. With something moving just the other side.

Then suddenly the balance shifted, like one of those drawings made up of black and white dots where if you stare at it long enough you can see a Dalmatian. I dropped to my knees behind the partially completed barrier.

They were back.

Standing at the top of the drive, their images both underlying and superimposed on it as if woven together, were the two men.

They were standing in a frozen and unnatural position, like a freeze-frame. Their faces looked pallid and washed out, the colors uneven and the image flickering and dancing in front of my eyes. And still they stood, not there, and yet in some sense there.

As I stared, transfixed, I noticed that the suited man's foot appeared to be moving. It was hard to focus on, and happening incomprehensibly slowly, but it was moving, gradually leaving the ground. Over the course of a minute it was raised and then lowered back down a couple of feet in front of its original position, leaving the man's body leaning slightly forward.

I realized what I was seeing. In extraordinary and flickering slow motion, somehow projected onto the drive like an old home movie, the suited man was beginning to walk down towards the house. The image wasn't flickering so much anymore, the colors were getting stronger, and I could no longer see the driveway through them. Somehow they were coming back through. I thought I'd got away with it, but I hadn't.

I'd fallen out. Not very far by anyone's standards, but far enough. Far enough to have come back in through the wrong door. And now they were tearing their way back into the world, or hauling me back towards theirs. And very slowly they were getting closer.

Fighting to stay calm, I grabbed a plank, put it into position above the others and nailed it into place. Then another, and another, not pausing for breath or thought. Through the narrowing gap I could see them getting closer. They didn't look two-dimensional any longer, and they were moving more quickly too. As I leaned towards the kitchen for a plank I saw that there was a single dusty carton on the floor. It had started.

I smacked another plank into place and hammered it down. The men were real again, and they were also much nearer to the house, though still moving at a weirdly graceful tenth of normal speed. Hammering wildly, ignoring increasingly frequent whacks on the fingers, I cast occasional wild glances aside into the kitchen. The fridge was beginning to look strange, the stark 1990s geometry softening, regressing, and the rubbish was gathering. I never saw any of it arrive, but each time I looked there was another piece of cardboard, a few more scraps, one more layer of grime. It had only just started, and was still happening very slowly, maybe because I'd barely fallen out. But it was happening. The house was going over.

THE DARK LAND

I kept on hammering. I knew that what I had to do at some point was run to the front door, go out and come back in again, come in through the right door. But that could wait, would *have* to wait. It was coming on very slowly this time, and I still felt completely clear-headed. What I had to do first was seal off the back door, and soon. The two men, always at the vanguard of the change, were well and truly here, and getting closer all the time. I had to make sure that the back door was secure against anything those two could do to it, for long enough for me to get to the front door and jump out. I had no idea what the front hall would be like by the time I got there, and if I left the back door unfinished and got lost trying to get to the front door, I'd be in real trouble.

I slammed planks into place as fast as I could. Outside they got steadily closer and closer, and inside another carton appeared in the kitchen. As I jammed the last horizontal board into place the suited man and the blond man were only a couple of yards away, now moving at full pace. I'd barely nailed it in before the first blow crashed into it, bending it and making me leap back with shock. I hurriedly picked up more wood and slapped planks over the barrier in vertical slats and crosses, nailing them in hard, reinforcing and making sure that the barrier was securely fastened to the wall on all sides, furiously hammering and building.

After a while I couldn't feel the ache in my back or see the blood on my hands: all I could hear was the beating of the hammer, and all I could see was the heads of the nails as I piled more and more wood onto the barrier. I had wood to spare—I hadn't even needed that last bloody plank—and by the time I finished it was four pieces thick in some places, with the reinforcing strips spread several feet either side of the frame. I used the last three pieces as bracing struts, forcing them horizontally across the hallway, one end of each lodged in niches in the barrier, the other jammed tight against the opposite wall.

Finally it was finished, and I stood back and looked at it. It looked pretty damn solid. 'Let's see you get through *that*,' I shouted, half sitting and half collapsing to the ground.

After a moment I noticed how quiet it was. At some point they must have stopped banging against the door. I'd been making far too much noise to notice, and my head was still ringing. I put my ear against the barrier and listened. Silence.

I lit a cigarette and let tiredness and a blessed feeling of safeness wash over me. The sound of the match striking was slightly muted, but that could've been the ringing in my ears, and the kitchen looked pretty grubby but no more than that. I felt fine. I wondered what the two outside were up to, and whether there was any chance that they might have given up and be waiting for the change to take its course—not realizing that I understood about the right door and the wrong door. For a few minutes I actually savored the sensation of being balanced between two worlds, secure in the knowledge that in a moment I would just walk out that front door and the house would come back and none of it would matter at all.

Eventually I stood up, wincing in pain. I was really going to ache tomorrow. I stepped into the kitchen, narrowly avoiding a large black spider that scuttled out of one of the cartons. The floor was getting very messy, strewn with scraps of dried-up meat covered with the corpses of dead maggots, interspersed with small piles of stuff I really didn't want to look at too closely. I threaded my way past the now bizarrely misshapen fridge, and into the hall.

The hallway was still clear of debris, and as far as I could see, utterly normal. As I crossed towards the front door, anxious now to get the whole thing over with—and wondering how I was going to explain the state of the back door to my parents—I noticed a faint tapping sound in the far distance. After a moment it stopped, and then restarted from a slightly different direction. Odd, but scarcely a primary concern. Right now my priority was getting out of that front door before the hall got any stranger. Feeling like an actor about to bound onto the stage, I reached out to the doorknob, twisted it and pulled it towards me.

At first I couldn't take it in. I couldn't work out why instead of the driveway all I could see was brown. Brown flatness.

As I adjusted my focal length, pulling it in for something much closer than the drive I'd been expecting, I understood. The view looked rather familiar. I'd seen something like it very recently.

It was a barrier. An impregnable wooden barrier nailed across the door into the walls from the outside. Now I knew what they'd been doing as I finished nailing them out.

THE DARK LAND

They'd been *nailing me in*.

I tried everything I could think of. My fists, my shoulder, a chair. The planks were there to stay.

I couldn't get out. I couldn't come back in through the right door, and for the moment they couldn't get in through the wrong door. A sort of stalemate. But a very poor sort for me, because they were much the stronger and getting more so all the time, and because the house was still going over and now I couldn't stop it.

I strode into the kitchen, rubbing my bruised shoulder and thinking furiously. There had to be something I could do, and I had to do it fast. The change was speeding up. Although the hall still looked normal the kitchen was now filthy, and the fifties fridge was fully back. In a retro kind of way it was quite attractive. But it was wrong.

In the background I could still hear the faint tapping noise. Maybe they were trying to get in through the roof.

I had to get out, had to find a way. I tried lateral thinking. You leave a house by a door. How else? No other way. You always leave by a door. But was there any other way you *could* leave, if you were in, say, a desperate emergency? The doors... The windows. What about the windows? If there was a right door and a wrong door, maybe there were right and wrong windows too, and perhaps the right ones looked out onto the real world. Maybe, just maybe, you could smash one and then climb out and then back in again. Perhaps that would work.

I had no idea whether it would or not. I wasn't kidding myself that I understood anything, and God alone knew where I might land if I chose the wrong window. Perhaps I'd go out the wrong one and then be chased round the house by the two maniacs outside, as I tried to find a right window to break back in through. That would be a barrel of laughs. That would be Fun City. But what choice did I have? I ran into the living room, heading for the big picture window. *Through the square window today, children.*

I don't know how I could have missed making the connection. Possibly because the taps were so quiet. I stood in the living room, my mouth open. This time they were one jump ahead. They'd boarded up the fucking windows.

I ran back into the hall, through into the dining room, then upstairs to the bedrooms. Every single window was boarded up. I knew where they'd got the nails from, because I'd spilt more than enough when I fell, but how...? Then I realized how they'd nailed them in without a hammer, why the tapping had been so quiet. With sudden unpleasant clarity I could imagine the suited man clubbing the nails in with his fists, smashing them in with his forehead and grinning while he did it.

Oh, Jesus.

I walked downstairs again, slowly now. Every single window was boarded up, even the ones that were too small to climb through. As I stood once more in the kitchen, amidst the growing piles of shit, the pounding on the back door started. There was no way I could get out of the house, and I couldn't stop what was happening. This time it was going over all the way, and taking me with it. And meanwhile they were going to smash their way in to come along for the ride. To get me.

I listened, watching the rubbish, as the pounding got louder and louder.

It's still getting louder, and I can tell from the sound that some of the planks are beginning to give way. The house stopped balancing long ago, and the change is coming on more quickly. The kitchen looks like a bomb site and there are an awful lot of spiders in there now. Eventually I left them to it and came through the hall into here, only making one or two wrong turnings. Into the living room. And that's where I am now, just sitting and waiting. There's nothing I can do about the change, nothing. I can't get out. I can't stop them getting in.

But there is one thing I can do. I'm going to stay here, in the living room. I can see small shadows now, gathering in corners and darting out from under the chairs, and it's quite dark down by the end wall. The wall itself seems less important, less substantial, no longer a barrier. I think I can hear the sound of running water somewhere far away, and smell the faintest hint of dark and lush vegetation.

I won't let them get me. I'll wait, in the gathering darkness, listening to the coming of the night sounds and feeling a soft breeze on my face as I sense the room opening out as the walls shade away, as I sit here quietly in the dark warm air. And then I'll get up and start walking out into the dark land, into the jungle and amidst the trees that stand all around behind the darkness,

THE DARK LAND

smelling the greenness that surrounds me and hearing the gentle river off somewhere to the right. And I'll feel happy walking away into the night, and maybe far away I'll meet whatever makes the growling sounds I begin to hear in the distance, and we'll sit together by running water and be at peace in the darkness.

DIFFERENT **NOW**

She was out of the door before Chris had time to grasp what was going on. What had started as a run of the mill argument had suddenly escalated out of control, bored misery giving way to alarm. Then the flat seemed very empty, and she was gone.

Until moments before it had just been the usual depressing bickering, the holding up of past hurts for inspection, and he'd been wondering how much longer he was going to defend his corner. There had been a time when he'd been prepared to stay up all night, had felt bound to hang on in there until the swapping of grievances could be steered towards a new compromise. A time when he could not have contemplated sleeping next to her unless they did so as friends.

But *so many nights*.

For a few months or weeks things would be alright, and then the familiar slow spiral towards confrontation would start. She would shout, and he would mutter: both completely in the right, and both utterly in the wrong. These days he didn't have the energy to argue until dawn when he knew any truce was only temporary; or the stomach to put up with melodrama when what they needed was discussion. When the point of diminishing returns had clearly been reached he usually went to bed, to be joined an hour later by Jo, vicious and sniffling. The next day would be very unpleasant, the day after less so. Sooner or later both would apologize so they could start living their lie for a little longer, go on inhabiting the same fragile world.

Chris grabbed his keys and ran for the door. He tripped over the pile of newspapers left in the middle of the floor by leave-it-where-it-drops Jo, and almost fell, but his beat of irritation was perfunctory. This was very bad. He'd looked at her and for the first time seen that he didn't know her any more, as if he was in the room with a stranger. Suddenly it hadn't been just another row, a chance for both to be flamboyantly hurt; the cord which had always somehow remained between them had lain there, exposed, waiting for the axe.

Fumbling to lock the door, Chris dropped his keys and swore. He didn't like the note of slight hysteria in his voice. It wasn't like him. However loud the shouting, he always stayed distant enough to watch, even when he was center stage. Stuffing the keys in his jeans, he leapt down the steps to the hall four at a time.

The outside door was open, swaying slightly from the strong wind outside. Rain spattered the familiar black plastic bags habitually left in the hall by the tenants of the downstairs flat, who he suspected were also responsible for the grey camper van which had sat outside on four flat tires since before he'd moved in.

He shouted at their door with all his strength, throat rasping: 'Oh what a surprise: someone's left some fucking rubbish in the hall again!'

Frightened by his fury he bolted out of the door and ran to the end of the short path, wildly looking up and down the street. All he could see was waving branches and wet moonlit patches. He'd hoped that she would grind to a halt just outside the house, but clearly she'd got further. Swearing desperately, he trotted back and pulled the door shut before heading out onto the pavement.

She couldn't have had much more than two minutes' start, which made it very likely that she'd gone right. Though it was theoretically possible she could have covered the two hundred yards or so to the end of the road on the left side, it seemed unlikely.

Chris jogged to the nearer corner and stood at the insignificant crossroads, straining his ears for the sound of footsteps. All he heard was the sound of distant traffic on the Seven Sisters Road; the featureless cramped streets of terraced houses facing him were silent apart from the sound of rain

DIFFERENT NOW

on swaying leaves. He called her name and heard nothing more than the thin sound of his own voice. Head down and shoulders hunched against the wind-whipped rain, he trotted out of Cornwall Road, across the small junction and into the road that was the start of the most direct route to the station.

After a couple of minutes he stopped, panting slightly. There was still no sign of Jo, and there were now a couple of choices as to which way she might have gone. Assuming she would have been walking towards the station to head for home, she should have taken the left fork—but she had only walked the route a couple of times, and always with him. Chances were that she wouldn't have had any clear idea of the way, and the alternative road was slightly wider than the one which led to the station. Chris had a sneaking suspicion that faced with the choice she might have assumed that was the best way to go. Not that there was any real way of telling: he didn't know if she had headed for the station at all.

Shivering, simultaneously wishing he'd thought to bring a coat and realizing that going back for one would lose him any chance of catching up, Chris headed for the wider road, walking quickly.

It was impossible to see very far down the road, as it curved quite sharply round to the left, presenting a blank face of wall broken by occasional squares of light. From his level all Chris could see was patches of ceiling and snatches of curtain. It seemed easy to believe there was no-one in any of the rooms, that they were empty and always had been. In one ground-floor room a black and white television flickered by itself, somehow making the sight even less hospitable than the windows that were dark and reflective black. Disturbed, Chris turned his attention back to the pavement. Somewhere, a long way off, a car horn sounded.

Suddenly he saw a movement some way ahead, and hurried forwards. It was difficult to see clearly in the steadily falling rain, and hard to see what might be there against the pocks and puddles in the pavement. A shape moved out from behind a car, but it was only a small dog, white and shivering. Wiping rain from his face, Chris trotted up to the next junction.

The streets all looked the same. All bent slightly, all had pavements torn apart and uneven through years of patching, and all looked orange and shiny black with water, the patterns of light changing as branches of grey leaves slashed in front of the streetlights. There was still no sign of Jo, no sign of anyone. Chris picked a road at random and headed down it.

He was far from sure what would happen when he found her. Nothing like this had ever happened before. If she'd headed for home, which would involve a tube to a mainline station and then an hour on a train, that was bad. If she'd not even been thinking as clearly as that, but had just set off, that was even worse, given her paranoia about walking any streets late at night. Either way it seemed possible that things might finally have broken down, and he understood suddenly that he didn't want them to. However bad things might be between them, she was the only person who really knew him. And more than that, he loved her.

Another turning, another road. Chris felt increasingly desperate, sensed an already bad situation getting away from him, and he was now far from sure where he was. Not having a car meant that he didn't know the area very well, his movements restricted to walking to the station and the nearest shops. He thought that the station was probably still over to the left, but when he started to choose left turns the roads bent and doglegged, bringing him back or taking him in the wrong direction, through rows and rows of three storey brick punctuated by sheets of dark glass.

Finally he stopped and rested, hands on his knees and chest aching.

After a few moments the pain felt at once less urgent but more deep-seated, a feeling he remembered from horrific cross-country runs at school. Then, too, the rain had sheeted down, as if settled in for ever. Chris raised his head, squinting into the lines of water.

Someone was standing at the top of the street.

Chris straightened, and took a pace forward. About fifty yards away, motionless and grey behind the rain stood a woman of Jo's size and shape. It had to be Jo. Feeling a lurch of compassion, Chris walked quickly towards her, and then started to trot.

As he neared her he slowed to a walk. She was facing away from him, shoulders slumped, heedless of the rain which coursed down her soaking hair and clothes. She made no movement as he approached and Chris felt tears welling up; Jo hated the rain, and there are always things about someone which, however trivial, make them more them than anyone else.

DIFFERENT NOW

He stood at her side for a moment, and then gently touched her shoulder. For a moment there was no response, and then she looked up slowly, timidly.

It wasn't Jo.

Chris took a step backwards, confused. The woman continued to look at him as rain streamed down her face, not staring, just including him in her gaze.

'I'm sorry, I thought...' Chris stopped, unable to finish the obvious sentence, transfixed by her face. It wasn't Jo, but it so nearly was. The face was so similar, so *equal* to Jo's face, and yet something was different. He took a few more steps backwards, shrugging to show his harmlessness, and started to turn away.

As he did so the woman turned too, and he caught a glimpse of her face in three-quarter view. The woman began slowly to step through the puddles, heading up a road he'd already tried. Chris stared after her, and knew what it was about her face.

It was the face of someone he didn't know. The face of someone you catch sight of across a room, the face of a stranger you don't understand yet, a face before you've seen it thousands of times, loved and kissed each inch of it, seen its every smile and frown. It was the face that Jo would always have had, if he'd not plucked up his courage on a night four years ago, and walked across the room to timidly make her acquaintance.

Had he not met her and loved her, had she not become his world, she would always have had that face. The woman's face was Jo's in a world where they'd never met.

Chris started up the road after her, just as she turned the corner. Anxious to keep sight of her, he slipped on a patch of lurid moss glistening blackly on the pavement. Narrowly avoiding a sprawling fall, he awkwardly maintained his balance, twisting his knee. Slowing to a fast lurch he painfully rounded the corner in time to see the flap of a coat disappearing from sight. He rubbed his knee for a moment and then set off in pursuit.

He hadn't tried this particular road, and didn't recognize it or the turning. Wiping water from his face, he trotted into the sheets of rain, feeling the silence behind the hissing patter of drops. He slipped again navigating the turn at speed but kept his balance. At the end he stopped, chest heaving again. She had disappeared.

There was no obvious way she could have gone. The other three roads stretched straight for many yards before curving, and it should have been possible to see her whichever way she'd taken. Chris glanced about wildly, peering into the rain. Then he noticed something. The road opposite was Cornwall Road.

Bewildered, he took a few steps forward, into the middle of the road. He turned and looked the way he'd come. The road was unfamiliar, curving a wholly different way to the road he walked down to the station. The road that cut across was different too: it was narrower and had more trees. The whole junction was different, and yet...

He walked slowly into Cornwall Road. There, about ten yards up on the left, was the familiar white gateway, the entrance to Number 7. Light fell weakly down from the upper window. Proceeding forwards like a nervous gunfighter, casting frequent glances behind, Chris tried to marry the two views in his mind. But they wouldn't gel, couldn't.

Cornwall Road now joined with different roads, and the grey camper van was gone.

He pushed open the dark green gate and stepped up to the door. Through misted glass he saw that the hallway was clear. He turned and looked at the entryphone. The label by the topmost buzzer said 'Price', which was not his name. He wondered briefly where Jo was now, but already the name seemed unfamiliar, ordinary, like that of someone he'd met once at a party, some years ago. His key did not turn the lock, was made for a different door.

Chris took a last look at the house and then turned and faced the rain, pausing for a moment before stepping out into it. He had no idea where he lived, who he loved, where he should go.

Things were different now.

THE THINGS HE SAID

My father said something to me one time. Matter of fact he said a lot of things to me, over the years, and many of them weren't what you'd call helpful, or polite—or loving, come to that. But in the last couple months I've found myself thinking back over some of them, and often find they held a grain of truth. I consider what he said in the new light of things, and move on, and then they're done. This one thing, though, has kept coming back to me. It's not very original, but I can't help that. He was not an original man.

What he said was, you had to take care of yourself, first and foremost and always, because there wasn't no-one else in the world who was going to do it for you. Look after Number One, was how he put it.

About this he was absolutely right. Of that I have no doubt.

I start every day to a schedule. Live the whole day by it, actually. I don't know if it makes much difference in the wider scheme of things, but having a set of tasks certainly helps the day kick off more positively. It gets you over that hump.

I wake around 6:00 am, or a little earlier. So far that has meant the dawn has either been here, or coming. As the weeks go by it will mean a period of darkness after waking, a time spent waiting in the cabin. It will not make a great deal of difference apart from that.

I wash with the can of water I set aside the night before, and eat whatever I put next to it. The washing is not strictly necessary but, again, I have always found it a good way to greet the day. You wash after a period of work, after all, and what else is a night of sleep, if not work, or a journey at least?

You wash, and the day starts, a period of life marked off from what has gone before. In the meantime I have another can of water heating over a fire. The chimney is blocked up and the doors and windows are sealed overnight against the cold, so the fire must of necessity be small. That's fine—all I need is to make enough water for a cup of coffee.

I take this with me when I open the cabin and step outside, which will generally be at about 6:20 am. I live within an area that is in the shade of mountains, and largely forested. Though the cabin itself is obscured by trees, from my door I have a good view down over the ten or so acres between it and the next thicker stretch of woods. I tend to sit there on the stoop a couple minutes, sipping my coffee, looking around. You can't always see what you're looking for, though, which is why I do what I do next.

I leave the door open behind me and walk a distance which is about three hundred yards in length—I measured it with strides when I set it up—made of four unequal sides. This contains the cabin and my shed, and a few trees, and is bounded by wires. I call them wires, but really they're lengths of fishing line, connected between a series of trees. The fact that I'm there checking them, on schedule, means they're very likely to be in place, but I check them anyway. First, to make sure none of them need refixing because of wind—but also that there's no sign something came close without actually tripping them.

I walk them all slowly, looking carefully at where they're attached to the trees, and checking the ground on the other side for signs anything got that far, and then stopped—either by accident or because they saw the wires. This is a good, slow, task for that time in the morning, wakes you up nice and easy. I once met a woman who'd been in therapy—hired a vacation cottage over near Elum for half a summer, a long time ago this was—and it seemed like the big thing she'd learned was to ignore everything she thought in the first hour of the day. That's when the negative stuff will try to bring you down, she said, and she was right about that, if not much else. You come back from the night with your head and soul empty, and bad things try to

THE THINGS HE SAID

fill you up. There's a lot to get exercised about, if you let it. But if you've got a task, something to fill your head and move your limbs, by the time you've finished it the day has begun and you're on to the next thing. You're over that hump, like I said.

When that job's finished I go back to the cabin and have the second cup of coffee, which I keep kind-of warm by laying my breakfast plate over the top of the mug while I'm outside. I'll have put the fire out before checking the wires, so there's no more hot water for the time being. I used to have one of those vacuum flasks, and that was great, but it got broken. I'm on the lookout for a replacement. No luck yet. The colder it gets, the more that's going to become a real priority.

I'll drink this second cup planning what I'm going to do that day. I could do this the night before, but usually I don't. It's what I do between 7:30 and 8:00 am. It's in the schedule.

Most days, the next thing is going into the woods. I used to have a vegetable patch behind the cabin, but the soil here isn't that great and it was always kind of hit-and-miss. After the thing, it would also be too much of a clue that someone is living here.

There's plenty to find out in the woods, if you know what to look for. Wild versions of the vegetables in stores, other plants that don't actually taste so good but give you some of the green stuff you need. Sometimes you'll even see something you can kill to eat—a rabbit or a deer, that kind of thing—but not often. With time I assume I may start to see more, but for now stocks are low. With winter coming on, it's going to get a little harder for all this stuff. Maybe a *lot* harder.

We'll see. No point in worrying about it now. Worry don't get nothing but worry, as my father also used to say.

Maybe a couple hours spent out in the woods, then I carry back what I've found and store it in the shed. I'll check on the things already waiting, see what stage they're at when it comes to eating. The hanging process is important. While I'm there I'll also check the walls and roof are still sound, and that the canvas I've layered around the inside is still watertight. As close to airtight as possible, too.

MICHAEL MARSHALL SMITH

I don't know if there are bears in these parts any more—I've lived here forty years, man and boy, and I haven't seen one in a long time, nor wolves either—but you may as well be sure. One of them catches a scent of food, and they're bound to come have a look-see, blundering through the wires and screwing up all that stuff. Fixing it would throw the schedule right out. I'm joking, mainly, but you know, it really would be kind of a pain, and my stock of fishing wire is not inexhaustible.

It's important to live within your means, within what you know you can replace. A long game way of life, as my father used to say. I had someone living here with me for a while, and it was kind of nice, but she found it hard to understand the importance of this, of playing that long game. Her name was Ramona, and she came from over Noqualmi way. The arrangement didn't last long. Less than ten days, in fact. Even so, I did miss her a little after she walked out the door. But things are simpler again now she's gone.

Time'll be about 10:30 am by then, maybe coming up for 11:00, and I'm ready for a third cup of coffee. So I go back to the cabin, shut and seal up all the doors and windows again, and light the fire. Do the same as when I get up, make two cups, cover one to keep it semi-warm for later. I'll check around the inside of the cabin while the water's heating, making sure everything's in good shape. It's a simple house. No electricity—lines don't come out this far—and no running water.

I got a septic tank under the house I put in ten years back, and I get drinking and washing water from the well. There's not much to go wrong and it doesn't need checking every day. But if something's on the schedule then it gets done, and if it gets done, then you know it's done, and it's not something you have to worry about.

I go back outside, leaving the door open behind me again, and check the exterior of the house. That does need an eye kept on it. The worse the weather gets, the more there'll be a little of this or that needs doing. That's okay. I've got tools, and I know how to use them. I was a handyman before the thing, and I am, therefore, kind of handy. I'm glad about that now. Probably a lot of people thought being computer programmers or bankers or TV stars was a better deal, the real cool beans. It's likely by now they may have changed their minds.

THE THINGS HE SAID

I'll check the shingles on the roof, make sure the joints between the logs are still tight. I do not mess with any of the grasses or bushes that lie in the area within the wires, or outside either. I like them the way they are.

Now, it's about midday. I'll fill half an hour with my sculpturing, then. There's a patch of ground about a hundred yards the other side of the wires on the east side of the house, where I'm arranging rocks. There's a central area where they're piled up higher, and around that they're just strewn to look natural. You might think this is a weird thing to do for someone who won't have a vegetable patch in case someone sees it, but I'm very careful with the rocks. Spent a long time studying how the natural formations look around here. Spent even longer walking back from distant points with just the right kind of rocks. I was born right on this hillside. I know the area better'n probably anyone. The way I'm working it, the central area is going to look like just another outcrop, and the stuff around, like it just fell off and has been laying there for years.

It passes the time, anyway.

I eat my meal around 1:00 p.m. Kind of late, but otherwise the afternoon can feel a little long. I eat what I left over from supper the night before. Saves a fire. Although leaving the door open when I'm around the property disperses most of the smoke, letting it out slowly, a portion is always going to linger in the cabin, I guess. If it's been a still day, then when I wake up the next morning my chest can feel kind of clotted. Better than having it all shoot up the chimney, but it's still not a perfect system. It could be improved. I'm thinking about it, in my spare time, which occurs between 1:30 and 2:00 p.m.

The afternoons are where the schedule becomes a tad more freeform. It depends on my needs. At first, after the thing, I would walk out to stock up on whatever I could find in the local towns. There's two within reasonable foot distance—Elum, which is about six miles away, and Noqualmi, a little further in the other direction. But they were both real small towns, and there's really nothing left in them now. Stores, houses, they're all empty and stripped even if not actually burned down. This left me in a bit of a spot for a while, but then, when I was walking back through the woods from Noqualmi empty-handed one afternoon, I spied a little gully I didn't think

I knew. Walked up it, and realized there might be other sources I hadn't yet found. Felt dumb for not thinking of it before, in fact.

So that's what I do some afternoons. This area was never home to that many vacation cabins or cottages, on account of the skiing never really took off and the winter here is really just kind of cold, instead of picturesque cold—but there are a few. I've found nine, so far. First half-dozen were ones where I'd done some handiwork at some point—like for the therapy woman—so they were easier to find. Others I've come upon while out wandering. They've kept me going on tinned vegetables, extra blankets. I even had a little gas stove for a while, which was great. Got right around the whole smoke problem, and I had hot coffee all day long. Ran out of gas after a while, of course. Finding some more is a way up my wish list, I'll tell you, just below a new vacuum flask.

Problem is, those places were never year-round dwellings, and the owners didn't leave much stuff on site, and I haven't even found a new one in a couple weeks. But I live in hope. I'm searching in a semi-organised grid pattern. Could be more rigorous about it, but something tells me it's a good idea to leave open the possibility you might have missed a place earlier, that when you're finished you're not actually *finished*—that's it and it's all done, and so what now?

Living in hope takes work, and thinking ahead. A schedule does no harm, either, of course.

Those lessons you learn at a parent's knee—or bent over it—have a way of coming back, even if you thought you weren't listening.

What I'm concentrating on most of all right now, though, is building my stocks of food. The winter is upon us, there is no doubt, and the sky and the trees and the way the wind's coming down off the mountain says it's going to land hard and bed itself down for the duration. This area is going to be very isolated. It was that way before the thing, and sure as hell no-one's going to be going out of their way to head out here now.

There's not a whole lot you can do to increase the chance of finding stuff. At first I would go to the towns, and had some success there. It made sense that they'd come to sniff around the houses and bins. Towns were a draw, however small. But that doesn't seem to happen so much now. Stocks have got depleted in general and—like I say—it's cold and getting colder and that's not the time of year when you think hey, I'll head into the mountains.

So what I mainly do now is head out back into the woods. From the back of the cabin there's three roads you can get to in an hour or so's walking, in various directions. One used to be the main route down to Oregon, past Yakima and such. Wasn't ever like it was a constant stream of traffic, but that was where I got lucky the last two times, and so you tend to get superstitious, and head back to the same place until you realize it's just not working any more.

The first time was just a single, middle-aged guy, staggering down the middle of the road. I don't even know where he'd come from, or where he thought he was going. This was not a man who knew how to forage or find stuff, and he was thin and half-delirious. Cheered right up when he met me. The last time was better. A young guy and girl, in a car. They hadn't been an item before the thing, but they were now. He believed so, anyway. He was pretty on the button, or thought he was.

They had guns and a trunk full of cans and clothes, back seat packed with plastic containers of gasoline. I stopped them by standing in the middle of the road. He was wary as hell and kept his hand on his gun the whole time, but the girl was worn out and lonely and some folks have just not yet got out of the habit of wanting to see people, to mix with other humans once in a while.

I told them Noqualmi still had some houses worth holing up in, and that there'd been no trouble there in a while on account of it had been empty in months, and so the tide had drifted on. I know he thought I was going to ask to come in the car with them, but after I'd talked with them a while I just stepped back and wished them luck. I watched them drive on up the road, then walked off in a different direction.

Middle of that evening—in a marked diversion from the usual schedule, but I judged it worth it—I went down through the woods and came into Noqualmi via a back way. Didn't take too long to find their car, parked up behind one of the houses. They weren't ever going to last that long, I'm afraid. They had a candle burning, for heaven's sake. You could see it from out in the back yard, and that is the one thing that you really *can't* do. Three nights out of five I could have got there and been too late already. I got lucky, I guess. I waited until they put the light out, and then a little longer.

MICHAEL MARSHALL SMITH

The guy looked like he'd have just enough wits about him to trick the doors, so I went in by one of the windows. They were asleep. Worse things could have happened to them, to be honest, much worse. There should have been one of them keeping watch. He should have known that. He could have done better by her, I think.

Getting them back to the cabin took most of the next day, one trip for each. I left the car right where it was. I don't need a car, and they're too conspicuous. He was kind of skinny, but she has a little bulk. Right now they're the reason why the winter isn't worrying me quite as much as it probably should. Them, plus a few others I've been lucky enough to come across—and yes, I do thank my luck. Sure, there's method in what I've done, and most people wouldn't have enjoyed the success rate I've had.

But in the end, like my father used to say, any time you're out looking for deer, it's luck that's driving the day. A string of chances and decisions that are out of your hands, that will put you in the right place at the right time, and brings what you're looking for rambling your way.

If I don't go out hunting in the afternoon, then either I'll nap a while or go do a little more sculpting. It only occurred to me to start that project a few weeks ago, and I'd like to get some more done before it starts to snow.

At first, after the thing, it looked like everything just fell apart at once, that the change was done and dusted. Then it started to become clear it didn't work that way, that there were waves. So, if you'd started to assume maybe something wasn't going to happen, that wasn't necessarily correct. Further precautions seemed like a good idea.

Either way, by 5:00 p.m. the light's starting to go and it's time to close up the day. I'll go out to the shed and cut a portion of something down for dinner, grab something of a plant or vegetable nature to go with it, or—every fourth day—open a small can of corn. Got a whole lot of corn still, which figures, because I don't really like it that much.

I'll cook the meat over the day's third fire, straight away, before it gets dark, next to a final can of water—I really need to find myself another of those vacuum flasks, because not having warm coffee in the evening is what gets me closest to feeling down—and have that whole process finished as quick as I can.

THE THINGS HE SAID

I've gotten used to the regime as a whole, but that portion of the day is where you can still find your heart beating, just a little. I grew up used to the idea that the dark wasn't anything to fear, that nothing was going to come and do anything bad to you—from outside your house, anyway. Night meant quietness outside and nothing but forest sounds which—if you understood what was causing them—were no real cause for alarm.

It's not that way now, after the thing, and so that point in the schedule where you seal up the property and trust that your preparations, and the wires, are going to do their job, is where it all comes home. You recall the reality of the situation.

Otherwise, apart from a few things like the nature of the food I eat, it's really not so different to the way life was before. I understand the food thing might seem like a big deal, but really it isn't. Waste not, want not—and yes, he said that too. Plenty other animals do it, and now isn't the time for beggars to be choosers. That's what we're become, bottom line—animals, doing what's required to get by, and there isn't any shame in that at all. It's all we ever were, if we'd stopped to think about it. We believed we had the whole deal nailed down pretty good, were shooting up in some pre-ordained arc to the sky. Then someone, somewhere, fucked up. I never heard an explanation that made much sense. People talked a lot about a variety of things, but then people always talked a lot, didn't they? Either way, you go past Noqualmi cemetery now, or the one in Elum, and the ground there looks like Swiss cheese. A lot of empty holes, though there are some sites yet to burst out, later waves in waiting.

Few of them didn't get far past the gates, of course. I took down a handful myself, in the early days. I remember the first one I saw up here, too, a couple weeks after the thing. It came by itself, blundering slowly up the rise. It was night-time, of course, so I heard it coming rather than seeing anything. First I thought it was someone real, was even dumb enough to go outside, shine a light, try to see who it was. I soon realized my error, I can tell you that. It was warmer then, and the smell coming off up the hill was what gave it away. I went back indoors, got the gun. Only thing I use it for now, as shells are at a premium. Everything else, I use a knife.

Afterwards I had a good look, though I didn't touch it. Poked it with a stick, turned it over. It really did smell awful bad, and they're not something you're going to consider eating—even if there wasn't a possibility you could catch something off the flesh. I don't know if there's some disease *to* be caught, if that's how it even works, but it's a risk I'm not taking now or likely ever. I wrapped the body up in a sheet and dragged it a long, long way from the property. Do the same with any others that make it up here from time to time. Dump them in different directions, too, just in case. I don't know what level of intelligence is at work, but they're going to have to try harder at it if they ever hope to get to me—especially since I put in the wires.

I have never seen any of them abroad during the day, but that doesn't mean they aren't, or won't be in the future. So wherever I go, I'm very careful. I don't let smoke come out of my chimney, instead dispersing it out the doors and window—and only during the day. The wires go through to trips with bells inside the cabin. Not loud bells—no sense in broadcasting to one of them that they just shambled through something significant. The biggest danger is the shed, naturally—hence trying to make it air-tight. Unlike just about everything else, however, that problem's going to get easier as it gets colder. There's going to come a point where I'll be chipping dinner off with a chisel, but at least the danger of smell leaking out the cracks will drop right down to nothing.

Once everything's secured for the night, I eat my meal in the last of the daylight, with the last hot cup of coffee of the day. I set aside a little food for the morning. I do not stay up late.

The windows are all covered with blackout material, naturally, but I still don't like to take the risk. So I sit there in the dark for a spell, thinking things over. I get some of my best ideas under those conditions, in fact—there's something about the lack of distraction that makes it like a waking dream, lets you think laterally. My latest notion is a sign. I'm considering putting one up, somewhere along one of the roads, that just says THIS WAY, and points. I'm thinking if someone came along and saw a sign like that, they'd hope maybe there was a little group of people along there, some folks getting organised, safety in numbers and all that, and so they'd go along to see what's what.

And find me, waiting for them, a little way into the woods.

I'll not catch all of them—the smart guy in the car would have driven straight by, for example, though his girl might have had something to say on

THE THINGS HE SAID

the subject—but a few would find my web. I have to think the idea through properly—don't know for sure that the others can't read, for example, though at night they wouldn't be able to see the sign anyway, if I carve it the right way—but I have hopes for it as a plan. We'll see.

It's hard not to listen out, when you've climbed in bed, but I've been doing that all my life. Listening for the wind, or for bears snuffling around, back when you saw them up here. Listening for the sound of footsteps coming slowly toward the door of the room I used to sleep in when I was a kid. I know the wires will warn me, though, and you can bet I've got my response to such a thing rigorously worked out.

I generally do not have much trouble getting off to sleep, and that's on account of the schedule as much as anything. It keeps me active, so the body's ready for some rest come the end of day. It also gives me a structure, stops me getting het up about the general situation.

Sure, it is not ideal. But, you know, it's not that different on the day-to-day. I don't miss the television because I never had one. Listening to the radio these days would only freak you out. Don't hanker after company because there was never much of that after my father died. Might have been nice if the Ramona thing had worked out, but she didn't understand the importance of the schedule, of thinking things through, of sticking to a set of rules that have been proven to work.

She was kind of husky and lasted a good long time, though, so it's not like there wasn't advantages to the way things panned out. I caught her halfway down the hill, making a big noise about what she found in the shed. She was not an athletic person. Wasn't any real possibility she was going to get away, or that she would have lasted long out there without me to guide her. What happened was for the best, except I broke the vacuum flask on the back of her head, which I have since come to regret.

Otherwise I'm at peace with what occurred. The real important thing is when you wake up, you know what's what—that you've got something to do, a task to get you over the hump of remembering, yet again, what the world's come to. I'm lucky that way.

The sculpting's the one area I'd like to get ahead of. The central part is pretty much done—it's coming up for three feet high, and I believe it would be hard to get up through that. But sometimes, when I'm lying in the dark waiting for sleep to come, I wonder if I shouldn't extend that higher portion; just in case there's a degree of tunneling possible, sideways and then up. I want to be sure there's enough weight, and that it's spread widely enough over the grave.

I owe my father a lot, when I think over it. In his way, through the things he said, he taught me a great deal of what it turned out I needed to know. I am grateful to him for that, I guess.

But I still don't want to see him again.

THE WINDOW
OF ERICH ZANN

She arrived, like so many, on a Greyhound bus.

Also as with many, she had little clue where to go, no idea how to find a home. Until the moment when she first glimpsed the iconic Golden Gate Bridge looming in the sun-warmed fog, it hadn't properly occurred to her that this was going to be an issue. Sure, she'd need somewhere to sleep, and wash, but the city would provide, right? Everything she needed was waiting there for her, for *them*—manifest destiny reinvented for the first generation to realize they were a generation, a harbor from which to set off for parts unknown.

Not every person on the bus was on that journey. Some were leading regular lives. Coming back from visiting family. Going to the city to look for work. But history tends to forget that majority who are merely keeping on keeping on, and one in five believed they were going on to something bigger and better, traveling inexorably toward some higher place—ignoring the fact that in reality many of them were also moving *away*. Leaving behind old places, old people, old lives, casting them off like old clothes, skins that chaffed and constrained. Most who arrived in San Francisco that year were barely old enough to have given old lives a chance, but all knew they were ready for something new. Something different.

That this was their time.

And so Marion clamped down on the tension in her guts, telling herself it was unworthy of this great adventure, that worrying about where she was going to sleep was precisely the style of petty bourgeois bullshit she'd left Illinois to escape. Nonetheless, she was relieved when the girl next to her—a petite and serious-looking girl from South Dakota, wearing what Marion guessed was her grandfather's waistcoat (over otherwise very straight clothes) in an attempt to look fashionably old-timey, a single layer of hippie on top of a hometown girl—turned nervously to her.

Her name was Katie, and she'd climbed onto the bus late the previous evening, in Montana. It had been pretty full, with many seats taken up with people crashed out full-length, and the girl had stood in the aisle, looking apprehensive.

Marion moved along her seat and smiled up at her. "There's room next to me."

Katie sat gratefully. The two girls had talked a little since, though Marion spent much of the night looking at the darkness out the window. Katie had slept, or read.

"Do you have somewhere to stay tonight?"

"No," Marion admitted. She had enough money for maybe three nights in a cheap hotel, five if it was *really* cheap. After that she'd be putting herself in the hands of fate.

"So what are you going to do?"

Marion shrugged, glad of the chance to appear unfazed, cool, and finding that—for a moment at least—it made her feel that way too. "I don't know. Ask around, I guess?"

"Can we do it together? Look for a place?"

"Sure," Marion said, and smiled. She was aware this would make it harder, but she could tell that Katie needed reassurance, and a temporary friend.

"Don't worry about a thing," a voice said from behind.

Marion and Katie turned cautiously. A girl with a huge frizz of red hair was leaning toward them, elbows on the back of their seat. "My cousin," she said. "Been here a month, got a place. He says there's space for me. If we scrunch up small, there's space for three, right? I'm Cindy, by the way."

"Are you sure?"

The girl grinned, broad and crooked, the grin of a girl who was sure about pretty much everything. "My mom's annoying as hell, but I don't think she'd lie to me about my actual *name*."

Marion laughed. "About the house, she means."

"That too. Done deal. And it's right in Haight. You've heard of Haight, yes?"

Of course they had. Haight-Ashbury, the well-spring of everything that was going on in the city—of the whole world—and the epicenter of cool. Marion nodded, her stomach relaxing. See? The world was on her side.

She was inevitable.

Forty minutes later the three girls got off the bus together, brave new spirits arriving in the promised land.

Five weeks later Marion moved out of the house. It was a Sunday, and she left in the late morning and tried to find Katie and Cindy before she went. Though she was tired and hungover, she was dogged, and eventually located Cindy under some guy in one of the bedrooms. Both were passed out, as were the six other people spread around the room. Thirty seconds of poking in the side from Marion resulted in the redhead eventually opening her eyes, one more slowly than the other.

"I'm leaving," Marion said. "Catch you soon, okay?"

Cindy looked at her without apparent recognition, blinked, and then passed out again.

Katie was nowhere to be found. The girl had steered clear of anything stronger than pot since the disaster at the end of the first week, so Marion thought she was most likely fine, and at her waitressing job. Katie's shit was pretty much together.

On the way out Marion passed the kitchen. She preferred to pass this room whenever possible, on the grounds that it was safer than actually going in. The place was a health hazard, as she knew to both her cost and benefit.

Everybody was super-enthusiastic about experimenting with new ways of cooking—on very limited budgets, people who until recently had relied upon their moms to fill their plates, and who therefore had only vague and idealistic ideas of how you turned raw ingredients into something edible— but much less good about clearing up the mess afterward. That'd be too square, too obsessed with appearances, too much the way their appallingly unhip parents did things. And so the sink was piled precariously high with dirty plates, and the cold, murky water a minefield of silverware; while the counters, floor and parts of the walls were encrusted with multiple layers of grime and spilled remnants of food.

Marion estimated that she'd lost seven pounds in weight since arriving in Frisco. Katie was holding steady, because she got one square meal a day where she worked and could actually cook a little, too. Marion had long-ago clocked the fact that Katie's timid request that they find a berth together on that first day had been not a sign of weakness but indicative of a quiet, focused ability to judge the best way of achieving what she needed. Meanwhile, a diet of sex and drugs seemed to be suiting Cindy just fine.

There was a guy in the kitchen. At first Marion didn't realize who it was, because everybody looked pretty similar. Denim. Layers of shirts and waistcoats. Long hair. When he turned toward the door, she saw it was Dylan.

"Hey," he said. His voice was a croak, his eyes bloodshot. He peered at her face for a long moment, then at her backpack. "You, you've, like, got your bag."

"Right. I'm leaving."

"Cool. I mean, why?"

Dylan was Cindy's cousin. The guy who'd opened the door when they arrived, already majestically high, and said sure, come join the fun, step right in and pull up a joint. Which was basically how it had gone on—a tidal, day-after-day party, under the influence of one thing or another, or more often several things at the same time.

On that first night, and for the next week or so, it had seemed utterly exotic and far out and exactly what they'd come to the city for. Everybody was talking nonstop about the Revolution, and what they could do to help set the old ways on fire. Planning meetings for anti-war protests. Impromptu jam sessions, where an inability to play an instrument was no barrier. Long—freakin' endless—discussions about how to get the message of what was happening from here out into the world at large.

It was only as the second week wore on and the effects of consecutive hangovers began to take their toll, that Marion began to get a clearer fix on her situation.

The house—though a tall, narrow, and dilapidated Victorian of approximately the same style—was not in the Haight district after all, but fifteen minutes' uphill walk away in a neighborhood that was far less happening and much more scary, especially at night. Each room looked like some other entire house had been upended into it: an ever-evolving chaos of guitars, art materials, half-finished canvasses—some of which had been used multiple times, shadows of earlier terrible paintings dimly visible under the current image—stained mattresses, dirty clothes, fliers and posters, discarded take-out food containers, and a screen-printing contraption that a number of very stoned people had tried to fix several times and so was destined to never work again.

And people.

God, yes, people.

When Marion and Katie arrived, there were already at least four sleeping to a room. Every day, though people came and went, that average had increased. Generally, newcomers knew at least one person in the house, or had met someone before. It had been getting up in the small hours to take a pee—and don't even try to imagine what the bathroom was like—to find a complete stranger passed out in there, his penis hanging flaccidly out of his pants, that made up Marion's mind to leave. This was not the scene she'd come to be a part of. There was somewhere better, and she was the girl to find it.

"You know there's some half-naked dude in the john?"

"I just talked to him. He's okay."

"So who is he?"

"I have literally no idea."

He beamed. Marion liked Dylan, she really did. Though apparently incapable of turning down any intoxicant that was passed in front of him, he seemed solid in the core. Or relatively so. Some of the others...not so much. A few, not even a little bit. There were people who'd brought darkness with them, or an emptiness so deep and profound it was somehow even worse. Marion needed to spend longer in the city before unconditional acceptance of others was going to play for her, and preferably do it somewhere that didn't smell of burned lentils and armpits. She knew there were houses where the cool/chaos balance was better. She needed to find one of those.

Dylan took a gulp of coffee, and winced. "So where are you going?"

"Met a guy in City Lights yesterday. He said he knew somewhere I could stay. Less crowded."

Dylan raised an eyebrow. "Hot guy?"

She laughed. "No. Old."

"They're the worst."

"Not this one. Or, I don't think. He seems cool. If it's a problem I'll bail."

"Cindy will be bummed you've gone."

Marion wasn't too sure about that. The primary message she'd been getting from the other girl in the last couple weeks was that she felt Marion wasn't letting her hair down hard or fast or often enough, and that she was bordering on being officially uncool. "Tell her I'll see her soon."

"But you're coming Tuesday afternoon, right?"

The event half the house had been preparing for. "Of course. And look, also tell Katie I'll drop by in the next couple days, okay? Tell her especially."

"You got it."

Marion was pretty sure he'd have forgotten by the time she left the house, but she thanked him and walked out the door into the sunshine on a mission.

He'd said he'd meet her in the bookstore at five-thirty, but at nearly seven o'clock she was still in the poetry room upstairs, waiting. Wondering, too, if she'd made a mistake. It wasn't unrecoverable: if the guy failed to turn up, she could simply hike back to the house and say it didn't work out and people would shrug and pass a joint and that would be that.

But she didn't want to. It would feel dumb.

It would be a big fail.

So she stayed there, as the day faded outside, watching people cooing over the books, explaining poems to each other, necking, hanging out. After a while the lights began to look strange to her, a souvenir of the disaster in the first week. After three days in the house she'd gone with Katie and Cindy to a big happening in the park—somewhat reluctantly, because though she totally wanted to go, her stomach had been feeling weird since breakfast. It was crowded and sunny and loud and fun, and The Dead played a set, and there had been buckets of Kool-Aid and friendly people encouraging newcomers to quench their thirst, and maybe some of the drinkers had known what they were getting into, but certainly not all.

Sure as hell not Marion and Katie, and that's why Marion had reason to be thankful for the unsanitary conditions of the kitchen of the house. It turned out her stomach gripes were the harbinger of a violent food poisoning episode that suddenly had her vomiting into the bushes—purging her body of a large portion of the LSD before it had time to kick in.

Katie had not been so lucky. She'd spent the next eight hours on a roller coaster of alternating laugh-out-loud euphoria and catastrophic paranoia, including a long episode where she'd been convinced that the wide grass of the park was in fact a part of the bay. She'd infected Marion with this vision, and the two of them spent a period of unknown duration clinging to each other, trembling, convinced they were on an invisible raft slowly spiraling around a cove, while everybody else danced and sang and ran in circles.

Eventually Marion (who'd only been suffering about 20% of the effects, but was still intermittently barfing), managed to get the two of them back to the house, where someone far more experienced managed to plane them back toward normality with a regimen of herb teas, chocolate, and pot.

Marion and Katie decided the next morning that the doors of their perception were quite wide enough already, thank you, and had steered the hell clear of LSD ever since. There were times when Marion still felt affected, though that had to be an illusion, surely. It'd been a month now. But certain types of light still looked strange, as if the glow existed between her and the object causing it, rather than in the lamp or bulb itself. And once in a while she heard…

She could hear it now, in fact.

Music.

A faint single line of notes, which—though she assumed it was something she'd heard in the park that afternoon, and had become locked in her head—was unlike anything she'd heard before. Different to what she'd normally think of as music, in fact—though a lot of local musicians liked to explore those kind of sounds, to show how liberated they were from outdated conceptions of melodic yadda yadda yadda.

This was a little louder than she'd heard it before—so much so that she turned in her seat to look out of the window, expecting to see some guy with a flute (she thought that's probably what it was, though she wasn't sure, maybe a piccolo or something) busking on the sidewalk.

Fog had begun to roll in. The Broadway/Columbus crossroads was pretty crowded—this borderland between Chinatown and North Beach had become a Mecca for both real hippies and buses of tourists come to gawp at them—but there was nobody obviously playing.

After a moment, however, she spotted something (or someone) else, and got up and hurried down, out of the store.

The man was standing on the corner.

Short, half-bald, rather stooped and overweight. His nose was large, the skin of his face liberally sprinkled with moles, some disconcertingly large. Though his clothes looked as though they had once been well-tailored, they were now somewhat shabby. Not at all a hot guy, bottom line.

"Hey," Marion said, diffidently, as she approached. "I thought you weren't coming."

"Aha," he said. His voice was soft, with the trace of an accent. "There you are."

"You said to meet inside. At five-thirty."

"I'm sorry," he said. "It was hard today. I couldn't finish in time."

"Finish what?"

He shook his head. "It's done. Come. Follow me."

Twenty minutes later he suddenly stopped walking. Marion had been getting more and more confused—they were heading away from the places where people actually lived, the kind of people she knew anyhow—but for an older guy he walked fast, a relentless beetling motion that covered the ground quickly. She asked at one point if they could take a streetcar instead, but he just shook his head again.

"Why are we here?"

They were standing in front of a tall, weathered building in the Financial District, on a narrow side street at the corner of California and Battery. The structures here were tall, constructed of stone or sometimes brick, making the alleyway feel like a canyon. There was a sense of heavy permanence to the area, despite the excavations they'd passed farther up Market, part of the process of installing the new BART/Muni system. Everything in sight seemed to be either a bank or business, apart from a battered neon sign on the opposite corner for something called YUGGOTH, wreathed in the fog coming in more and more thickly from the bay.

The old man didn't answer. Instead he stood looking at her, head cocked to the side, his sharp blue eyes narrowed, as he'd been doing when Marion first noticed him in City Lights on the previous afternoon. "Do you see me?" he'd asked then.

She'd frowned. "Well, yeah."

He nodded, and somehow from there they'd got to how she came to be in the city, and where she was living, and its insufficiency. He'd made the offer of somewhere to stay, and her initial reaction had been to laugh—she'd been hit on at least three times a day since she'd been there, though you weren't supposed to see it that way because everybody (or the guys, mainly) were framing rampant promiscuity as "generosity of spirit," something they were all supposed to have.

Cindy had discovered enormous generosity within herself, very quickly. The very first night, in fact. Katie was having no truck with the whole concept—you can take the girl out of the prairie, but extracting the prairie from the girl is a whole other thing. Marion was adopting a wait-and-see policy and trying to be open about it, but she was damned sure this elderly, foreign-looking guy wasn't going to break the dam.

She realized he wasn't looking salacious, however, or hopeful or even desperate. More thoughtful, even a little sad. Sometimes you'd see that in older guys—an awareness of how undignified and gross their lingering drives were making them appear—but it didn't seem to be that either. If anything he looked paternal, and not in a weird way.

So she'd agreed.

The building they were now standing in front of looked even more ancient than the others around it. Battered, stained, stoic. As the old man got out keys, Marion noticed the name PENTIMENTO chiseled into the stone above the door.

"Italian?" she asked.

"I believe so."

He opened the door and they stepped into a cramped vestibule. The old man flicked a switch and a pale, dusty bulb illuminated the space. Scuffed-up floorboards, stone walls. In the corner, rusted ironwork in front of a tiny elevator.

"Doesn't work, I'm afraid," he said, indicating the narrow steps which led from the other side.

Six flights later, she was glad to see they'd reached the top of the building. There had been no windows on the ascent—just another old bulb on each landing. Then finally this upper space, with a single wooden door.

"This is it," the old man said, as he unlocked it. "Now, don't get your hopes up. It was the caretaker's place."

The other side lay a room, perhaps ten feet wide and twenty long. It was bare, with dusty gray floorboards and peeling wallpaper that looked old. They were up in the roof, and so the ceiling bore sharply inward on one side, revealing beams. A single bed had been pushed into the corner. A small table. One chair. A small area on the right-hand side evidently designed to serve as a kitchenette, with a hotplate. There was a narrow doorway open next to it. Beyond was a tiny room with a toilet and a shower-stall, both of which looked like they had not been used in twenty years. Overall, it felt like a cabin below-decks on an old wooden ship.

In truth, it would have been a pretty depressing place, were it not for one thing. Marion walked straight toward it. "Wow," she said. "That's cool."

The old man stayed where he was, back by the door to the stairs. "I suppose so. There are two conditions. The first is that you bring nobody else up here. *Ever*. This cannot become another flophouse filled with free spirits and freeloaders."

"Works for me," Marion said. "That's exactly the scene I'm bailing from."

"The second is that on Tuesday evenings I need this space myself. Not for long—a couple of hours. Between eight and ten. I require you to be elsewhere during that time."

"Sure thing."

"That's all."

"And you really don't want me to pay anything?"

THE WINDOW OF ERICH ZANN

He shook his head, handed her a pair of keys, and turned away. She said thank you to his back, and he raised a hand in return as he started down the stairs.

As the sound of his footsteps receded, Marion closed the door and took stock. Sure it was dusty and smelled weird, and the ceiling made it feel kind of cramped, and in general it was a long way from nice, but listen…

It was silent.

Nobody talking. Nobody playing the guitar badly. Nobody snoring. Nobody…just *nobody*.

She smiled, then wandered back down to the room's biggest and most redeeming feature. A window. *The* window, in fact.

It was the only one, but it was large. Circular, with different colored panes divided by spokes that came out from the center: the panes broken up into further sections by a tracery of leading. What they called a "rose window," in a church. She dimly remembered from childhood—there'd been such a feature in the chapel back home—that they were usually placed at the western aspect, and wondered if this was the case here. Maybe.

She stood for a while and looked out, across the rooftops, at the city lights that stretched toward Nob Hill and beyond. Without realizing she was doing it, after a few minutes she slipped the pack off her back and set it gently on the floor, continuing to stare through the multicolored glass as night fell.

She followed the people as they marched, and after a while they were all singing and shouting, and if you've never been part of a crowd like that, a swell of humanity all driven by the same cause and dreaming the same dream, then you simply don't know how it feels. You can't know what it's like to become a part of something that blurs every individual into one, all their single candles turning a bright and shining afternoon into a sea of infinite light—a light that each one of them believes will be enough to illuminate the universe in ways it has never been before.

They strode along the streets together, chanting the same slogans, waving at the straights and squares mired on the sidewalks, as they frowned confusedly at the free spirits in their midst—and as they progressed toward Haight, more and more people started to join them at the back, and from the sides, impulsively throwing off the shackles of their lives and swelling this tide of humanity into a fleet of souls too powerful to resist.

People sang, and played instruments, weaving together one enormous song. Guitars, flutes, drums. And after a while Marion realized she could hear something else, too—a high, keening melody played on a single violin.

The thing she'd been hearing for days now, and that spoke to her, sang in a way that was dark but direct and true. It took all this noise and joy and condensed it to a single note.

She turned her head back and forth, tried to see where it was coming from, but there was no sign. By then the crowd around her was so loud that it sounded as if the tune was coming from between her own ears, and so she forgot about it and rhythmically punched the air with her fist like all the others.

And they marched on.

That evening she ate sitting at the little table. The meal consisted of two vegetable egg rolls from a place she'd found five minutes' walk away, all she convinced herself she could afford. It wasn't impossible to find casual work in the city. She'd washed dishes. Waited tables. A few nights of bar work before they found out she'd lied about her age and was only eighteen. What was tougher was keeping your position. Hardly anyone was offering stable employment, because they knew there were countless other girls and boys out there desperate to earn a little cash, and they didn't trust hippies to be reliable. Most people got hired by the day, or even the hour. The only person Marion knew with an actual job was Katie.

After eating she read for a while, a water-damaged copy of *The Naked Ape* that an older guy named Karl, the manager in City Lights, had let her take on permanent loan.

At ten o'clock she went to bed.

Haight-Ashbury. Ground zero. Heaving with humanity. Placards. Chanting. Protest songs. Men and women on soapboxes, all shouting different things, but they were all the same thing at heart, and so it spiraled up into an extraordinary new music, a choral symphony of those who would upend the universe.

For the next forty minutes, Marion was happier than she had been in her entire life. Happier than on the sporadic days as a young child when her mother remembered she was around, and spent some actual time with her. Happier than when a little older, and her bedroom door for once did not open in the middle of the night. Happier even than when she went to sit alone in her grandmother's yard, away from everyone. Away from her uncle especially. Happy as only a person can be when their mind, every molecule of their bodies, their very soul is in tune with the world around them.

Happy, happy, happy.

She saw Cindy walking by, swigging from a plastic cup, her arm around some guy, grinning and pumping her fist. She ran over when she saw Marion and planted a big kiss on her lips before dancing back away into the crowds. Marion spotted Dylan too, and some of the others from the house, and for a moment felt a keen stab of loneliness, but convinced herself it didn't matter because, look: here they all were together again—that all of them would always be together, preserved in moments like this, when they stood together and changed the world, fierce insects frozen in the warm amber of history.

They all sang together, and somewhere in the background or deep inside, that simple un-melody played.

When Marion woke, at first she wondered if she'd heard a noise. She lay in the narrow bed, listening, before realizing it was more likely the *lack* of noise that was unusual. For weeks she'd been living under the kind of conditions they use to soften up political prisoners prior to interrogation. There was no noise here. There were no people.

Once she'd realized that was the difference, she turned on her side and tried to get back to sleep. Soon it felt as if the silence was pounding in her eardrums, however—so loud it was almost like tinnitus, a single note, varying in pitch. It compelled you to listen, to unsuccessfully predict where it was going next, like the strangest kind of experimental music. She'd heard more than her share of that over recent weeks (Dylan was an enthusiastic, though unschooled, bass player), and learned something.

If you could actually play—and a few people in the house could—then your hands and ears wouldn't let you leave the path. However much a real musician tried to be random and free, previously-learned patterns ensnared them. Muscle memory pulled you back to the norm, to the established shipping lanes of melody. You had to be wholly ignorant of the process to play something truly new, and even then a vestige of recognizable rhythm would eventually emerge as utter incompetents bashed clumsily on out-of-tune guitars with only four strings. Humanity, the things we learn without even realizing, intervenes and regathers. To truly throw the past aside and become new requires both strength and a willingness to throw yourself into the void.

This sound, the sound her ears or brain made without intervention...it sounded like that. After a while it had woken her sufficiently that she sat up. It was only then that she understood what had really roused her.

She got out of bed and walked to the window.

It was light out there. Not like during the day, of course—she checked her watch and found it was a little before 3:00 a.m.—but starkly moonlit, bright enough to flood a multitude of colors into the room. Below that shining level, the buildings all around were wreathed and enveloped in fog.

In the moonlight, everything looked psychedelic.

Marion pulled the chair over to where she could sit and look out. Though she'd spent a while gazing out of the window earlier, she must have been looking at a slightly different angle. Fog, like snow, will make a place look unfamiliar. Presumably that's what was making the angles between the buildings look altered. And presumably it was the fog that was turning the few lights a curdled yellow, almost as if they were running on gas, instead of electricity.

She moved the chair right up close to the window, noticing something. Sounds, from outside. This wasn't the single note thing, but the kind of noise people made. Distant shouting. Not in anger, but workmanlike shouts, the kind you heard when men were engaged in some kind of task.

Then a screeching cry, like a seagull.

Perfectly possible, of course—the building was only a ten-minute walk along Market from the Bay, and the moldering piers and warehouses there—but combined with the shouts, it reminded her of something. She couldn't work out what it might be.

Now she was close to the window, she could see some of the individual panes in the design were mottled, making the views through them crooked, twisted. They also somehow magnified the effect of the fog, causing it to seem to move more quickly, sinuously, as if with intent. As she panned her gaze slowly down one of the nearest buildings, she noticed tendrils of it feeling their way around some bricked-up windows and then move on, as if seeking some easier mode of entry. Silly, of course, just a night-time thought, but nonetheless she was glad the fog didn't reach up as high as her own window.

She kept bending her head, slowly, looking farther and farther down, then suddenly stopped.

For just a moment the fog had parted, giving her a glimpse right down to street level. But it hadn't been a street she'd seen, or even a sidewalk.

It was water.

She knew from the time before, that first happening in the park, not to drink anything that anybody passed her, however much it looked and smelled innocent, and if they told her it was fruit juice.

But she was hungry, as well as thirsty—and there were cookies and brownies being passed around. And once she'd had a few of those her guard started to slip, and probably she did have a drink, or two, and then there was some guy with tabs and blotters, and Marion was standing with Cindy at that point, and when Marion shook her head and said no, she didn't want any of that scene, no thank you and no way, Cindy rolled her eyes and made fun about how her time in the city wasn't changing Marion at all, she was still the same uptight small-town girl she'd always been, nothing was ever going to help her evolve—and she'd never dance like the rest of them.

The other people with them thought Cindy was joking, just playing around. But Marion looked at her and saw twinkling lights around the girl's eyes, probably only the sun glinting off glitter and make-up but still so bright and sharp, and in their lights she saw every girl in school and high school who'd looked at her the same way, those exact same girls, the girls who've always been there, and realized Cindy was no different even if she floated like an angel with layers of velvet and denim and second-hand silk, even if her skin was clear and shone like milk, even if she walked though this place like a fairy queen. The uniforms change, the times change, but deep inside everybody stays the same.

Marion looked Cindy straight in the eye and took the tab.

And she danced.

"And then I woke up," Marion said. She shrugged and laughed. "Weird, huh?"

"Woke up where?"

"In bed, in the attic. I hadn't gotten up at all. I'd fallen asleep, and just dreamed that I did."

"I had a dream like that once," Katie said. "Where I dreamed I was where I actually was. It was freaky."

They were at a table outside the café next door to City Lights, making a pair of coffees last as long as they could. After a morning trying unsuccessfully to find work, Marion had wound up at the bookstore by default. She'd spent a couple hours reading—the staff were cool about people doing that, and the manager (Karl) positively encouraged it—and then looked up to see Katie standing over her. Katie had played it all "Oh, what a coincidence," but she knew Marion often spent chunks of the afternoon in the store, and the longer they'd sat outside together, the less Marion believed their meeting had been an accident.

"You okay?" she asked eventually, after a pause in the conversation had stretched to a full minute.

Katie took a moment before replying, looking down into her coffee cup. When she looked up, Marion realized how tired the other girl looked. Tired, but resolute.

"I'm fine," she said. "But I'm done."

"Done how?"

"I'm out of here. The city. This whole scene."

Marion felt her stomach turn over. "For real? Why?"

"Because it's bullshit," Katie said. "I mean, not all of it. I get that. There's stuff going down. This is…it's a thing. No doubt. People are going to look back and say wow, far out. But right now, for *most* of us, that's not in reach. It's the other side of the windowpane. We can see it, but we can't touch it. There're people who are making a real difference, doing real things, having a real good time. I'm not. Any of those things. And I'm done pretending otherwise."

"So what are you going to do?"

"Go home."

"Doesn't that feel like…"

"Failing? Giving up? Nope." The girl's eyes were hard, thoughtful. "There's a 1% getting things done here. The rest of us are only adding weight. Having 'fun'—except a lot of the time it's really not fun—and hanging around. This city right now is like a hundred thousand people jumping in the air at once, and it's great while they're still up, but gravity is strong and at some point the love-bubble's going to burst and they're going to fall back to earth—hard. 'Failing' would be sticking it out until that happens, and finding yourself stranded here afterward. I'm just getting a head start on the inevitable."

"When are you going?"

"Today. I called my dad last night and told him. He sounded happy, and said cool, and he'd be waiting to give me a hug. He trusted me to make my own decision six weeks ago, and he trusts me again now. Including when I said I might bring a friend back with me."

"A friend? Who?"

"You. If you wanted. You never really talk about what you left back at home. If it wasn't good, and you wanted to leave here, there's a place for you in South Dakota."

Marion looked at her, blinking rapidly. "But why?"

"When I climbed on the bus that got me here, in the middle of the night, everybody else looked away. You smiled right up at me and said, 'There's room next to me.' You're a nice person, and my friend, and always will be."

"Thank you," Marion managed to say, quietly.

"But that's a 'no?'"

Marion realized again how sharp the other girl was, and for a long moment teetered toward a different future. One where she said yes, and traveled with this girl back to the prairies, and they let the world unfold after that. She'd never been to that part of the country, but she imagined herself standing wholesomely in a waving field under a huge sky, smiling, looking into the distance. Maybe wearing a check shirt. The vision was so strong that she almost thought she could smell the wheat around her, but then she realized the smell was fog instead—the fog that was starting to creep up the street toward where they sat. A fog that smelled of the sea and old things, and said she was staying here because it was where she belonged. The fog that was here even when it wasn't. A fog that sounded of something.

"I don't think I'm done here yet," Marion said.

MICHAEL MARSHALL SMITH

Katie pulled a pen out of her bag and scribbled something on a napkin. She gave it to Marion. "My address back home," she said. "And take care of yourself, okay?"

Marion smiled brightly.

Katie got up and looked down at her before walking off down the street, quickly swallowed up by the sea mist.

It was too early to head back to the place where she now slept. There was nothing else she particularly wanted to do. So Marion wound up back in City Lights, in the basement, scrunched up in a tatty chair in the corner, trying to read some Kerouac. The light wasn't good, and the bulbs in the lamps dotted around the space also seemed to be flickering intermittently. The pages blurred in front of her.

"Now, what's going on here?"

Marion looked up to see Karl, the manager, crouched in front of her. He was heavy-set, paunchy, with chaotic gray hair that wisped up from his temples to make him look like a kindly owl.

"What do you mean?" she asked.

He reached his hand toward her, slowly, giving her plenty of time to understand his intention, and gently ran his thumb over her left cheek, and then the right. She realized both were wet, and she'd been crying, and that's why the light had seemed strange. And because it was the first time in a long while that someone had done something like that, she wound up telling him about her dream too, and that her friend was blowing town, and she wondered whether she maybe should too.

Karl listened and said the right things, and left the right pauses, and let her make up her own mind, and eventually got her laughing about some of the store's more notoriously weird patrons, and by the end of that she felt okay again.

He walked with her up the stairs and told her to go home and get some sleep, and to eat more, she was looking thin.

"Here's a thing, though," he said, before she left.

"What?"

"Your dream. The place where you're living now. You know that area used to be under water, right?"

THE WINDOW OF ERICH ZANN

"Huh?"

"Yeah. I mean, forever ago. But half of the Financial District used to be part of the bay. There was a thing about it a few years back. They found some stuff during an excavation or something. You should look it up."

She stepped out into the evening. It felt cold, and the streetlights looked strange.

Three hours later she was cross-legged on her bed, surrounded by paper. She'd stopped off at the main library on the way back to the building, expecting it to only take a few minutes. Instead she lost an hour of time—and six bucks she absolutely couldn't afford—duplicating several old maps, along with sections from a couple of books.

She was holding two of these now, trying to compare them. The picture in her left hand was an old photo. A daguerreotype taken by a man called William Shaw in 1852, showing a wide panorama of the San Francisco Bay, taken from Rincon Point. The far left of the picture held a few shacks and low buildings, and gave a sense of the area stretching behind. Much more interesting was the way in which, as it panned across this part of the Bay—a shallow portion called the Yerba Buena Cove—the view became at first dotted and then positively cluttered with sailing ships. Some looked ready to roll, as if they could head straight out for pastures new. Others less so, and a few were in advanced states of disrepair. On the far right of the picture, the two closest to the camera had lost their masts and significant chunks of their sides, looking like sad, bedraggled ghosts.

One of the books had informed her that over sixty thousand people arrived in the city in the 1850s, come to try their luck in the Gold Rush. They came on ships like these, and abandoned them in the Bay. Not completely—some had caretakers, men who lived in the gradually declining hulks, much as she now sat alone in this room—but the truth was, almost none of these ships ever sailed the open seas again.

In her other hand she was holding a reproduction of a section of an old map published by a San Francisco company called Britton & Rey, some years later. It showed approximately the same area as the daguerreotype, though looking rather different. Yerba Buena Cove, which had once stretched from

Rincon Point to Clark's Point, had disappeared. It remained indicated as a dotted line on the map, but where once had been water now lay streets, some of the main ones—like Market, California, and Sacramento—clearly following what had used to be the line of the old wharfs into the cove.

From reading a history from 1922, pages of which she'd also copied, Marion knew how one view had turned into the other. As the city grew and grew (bolstered by men returning empty-handed from the gold fields), the pressure for land increased, especially that which had coveted Bay access. By scuppering the old ships still languishing there, speculators had been able to make sanctioned land-grabs of small portions of the cove. The section of land under your sunken ship became yours by right. Some had even towed ships into position before dropping them. They then got busy with dumping sand and debris into water which in parts had only ever been a few feet deep, and before long the entire cove had disappeared into prime real estate that eventually became the Financial District.

Marion looked more closely at the map and confirmed that half of Battery Street had once been in the cove, and all of California south of Montgomery. This included the point where Battery and California intersected.

Where she was sitting, right now. Or, at least, where the foot of this building met the ground six stories below.

And more than that. She reached across to the last bundle of photocopies, and pulled out the portion reproducing a newspaper article from 1963. She found the sketch map and bent over it. As she did so, she noticed a couple of spots of moisture on it. She looked up, and watched as another drop of water gathered and fell from the wooden roof a couple of feet above her head.

It wasn't raining. The fog, perhaps, condensing in sufficient quantities to drip. She kept watching for a moment, but it didn't happen again.

So she went back to her documents.

It was the sound of shouting that woke her this time. Again, not angry shouting. The distant bellows of men working, attracting the attention of others, calling instructions.

She knew now what the sound reminded her of. The noise you hear at a busy harbor, the hubbub of sailors and the men who work the docks.

Loading, unloading. Moving cargo to and fro. She got quickly out of bed and went to the window.

The moon was bright once again, but it looked different to the night before. Then it had been almost full. Tonight it was only a sharp sliver. That didn't make much sense, but she immediately forgot about it.

All the other buildings had disappeared.

Though fog billowed below, she could see through it right down to a shallow cove. A few large shapes lurked within it, prows and sterns, and here and there a mast tilted like the charred remnant of a forest fire.

Marion pinched herself. It hurt, as she'd known it would. She grabbed her coat and ran over to the door.

She clattered down the steps as fast as she could, and was breathless by the time she got to the bottom. She yanked the big door open and stuck her head out.

It wasn't there. What she'd seen from above.

Instead she was looking out onto a grimy backstreet, murky in the shadows of the same old buildings. It looked just the same as it had when she'd returned home from the library. All she could hear was the sound of distant traffic.

On the other side of the street, a middle-aged man shambled by, broken by drugs or alcohol. He shouted something incoherent at her.

She closed the door and walked slowly back up the stairs. She went back to the window and stood looking out, even though all she could see now were the buildings everybody else saw. She couldn't hear the far-away shouting any more.

But she could hear something else. Again. Something so faint it could almost have been her imagination. A melody. It sounded as though someone must be standing somewhere nearby, perhaps even on one of the rooftops, playing this composition to himself, or perhaps up toward the stars above.

Then it was later.

Back at the house. The one where she'd lived for over a month. Even more crowded now. Even dirtier than it had been. It smelled like damp wood and seawater, like rot and decay.

Even louder, too. Different music in every room. Two groups of people who couldn't play, but played nonetheless. And people who danced nonetheless, too, arms flailing, bodies contorting, faces smeared with movement and incoherence.

Marion staggered around for a while, looking for Katie. Her vision was foggy at the edges, and sometimes at the center too. She got lost in one room for ages, and couldn't find her way out even after she remembered that Katie wouldn't be there or anywhere else in the house. Katie was gone.

It was getting later.

It was getting darker too.

Then she was in the downstairs hallway and somebody gave her another drink. She was very happy again for ten minutes, laughing and laughing, and made it into the living room. But she fell over there and lay on the floor for a while, as people walked and danced around and over her.

She couldn't get up because she couldn't work out which way that was. It seemed like she was lying there on her back for about a thousand years, and then she saw blurry shapes and realized it was Dylan and Cindy, kneeling on either side and leaning over her. She smiled and tried to say hi, but couldn't.

And then the ceiling was coming down to get her, and she was afraid. The ceiling was covered in mold, dripping with salty water, creaking as in a high wind.

"She's having a bad trip," Dylan said, indistinctly.

"There are no bad trips," she heard Cindy say, as the girl pulled at Marion's belt buckle. "Only bad people. We have to help them see the light."

She overslept. When she hauled herself out of bed at 9:30, she felt exhausted. Her calves hurt, as if she'd walked a tremendous distance, though she knew it was probably just because she'd waited for so long in the dead of night, looking out of the window, seeing if it would change. It did not.

She stood under the near-cold of the weak shower for a long time. It smelled weird, rusty, salty. It didn't help much. Her clothes smelled that way too, when she climbed back into them, and she realized it had been a week or more since she'd taken her scant set of outfits to a laundromat. She needed to find one soon.

Late-morning she walked to the café where Katie worked. The owner confirmed that the girl quit the day before. Marion hadn't doubted her friend's resolve. But she'd had to check, and the city now felt very big. Katie was gone.

After that she walked over to City Lights for want of anything better to do. Karl wasn't there when she arrived, so she sat in a window seat, watching all the people outside walking back and forth, feeling her eyelids start to droop. She wondered how many of them had real places to go, real things to do, and how many were just ballast, ships rocking gently up and down on a shallow tide, with no onward voyage charted. It seemed busier out there than normal, a lot of people headed in a particular direction, so maybe so.

She woke at the sound of her own name. It wasn't someone talking directly to her, however.

"Her name's Marion." She recognized Karl's voice, even though he was keeping it low. "She's good people."

Marion opened her eyes. She couldn't see him, and realized he was the other side of the half-wall, near the register.

"Has she ever actually bought a book?"

Marion recognized this voice too. Carol, the older woman who acted as manager when Karl wasn't in.

"Yes," Karl said. "*The Naked Ape*. I...sold it to her. Several weeks ago."

"What an excellent memory you have. She's rather young, though, isn't she?"

"Fuck off, Carol."

"Teenagers don't care about the likes of us, Karl. They're off on their own journey. Isn't that what they like to say? It's true. We're just the lands they leave behind."

"If you say so."

"Well, it's up to you. But even in these enlightened days, free love comes with strings attached. Baggage. And to be honest, she smells."

"She does not."

"Not always, I'll admit. But she does today."

There was a little more of the conversation, but Marion didn't listen. She pulled herself upright on the window seat, feeling dizzy. Hunger. She'd forgotten to eat anything this morning. Last night, too, though then it had been more of a choice, after she'd spent her money on the photocopying. She was about to stand when Karl came through.

"Oh, hi," he said, as though he'd no idea she was in the store. A lie, but a small one, and forgivable. Kind.

"Don't worry," she said. "I'm leaving."

"You don't have to."

She shook her head, though she wasn't sure what she meant. "I only came by to say thanks."

"For what?"

"Yesterday. Cheering me up. And telling me stuff. I looked into it."

"Interesting, huh?"

"You know they're still there?"

"What are?"

"The boats," she said. "They sunk them, then filled in over the top. Easier than taking them away or breaking them up. The ships are still down there, and sometimes contractors find the remains when they're redigging foundations or fixing pipes. The BART goes right through one. There's a map showing where some of the others are."

"I'd love to see that," he said. "After you'd gone, I found out something else that might interest you. You told me there was a name on the building you're staying in. I thought I'd look it up, see if I could find anything about it."

Marion nodded. Whatever she might think of Carol, one thing was true: Karl was being very thoughtful about Marion. Attentive. "I wondered if it was Italian," she said.

"It is, but it's not a name. Or at least, I couldn't find anybody called *Pentimento* in city history. And you think they'd have had to make at least some mark, to have a building in their name. Wait here a moment."

He darted off toward one of the stacks. Marion stood, feeling woozy. She saw Carol behind the register, making a not-very-fairly subtle job of watching her. Marion held out her hands, fingers wide, to show she wasn't trying to steal anything. Carol looked away. Slowly.

"Here," Karl said, having returned, holding a battered old paperback. "It's an art history term."

Marion looked at the page he was holding open. The word was there, with an explanation: *Pentimento (noun)—A trace of an earlier painting, beneath the top layer of paint on a canvas.* She shrugged.

THE WINDOW OF ERICH ZANN

"Yeah, I know," Karl said. "Can't see why you'd name a building for that. So maybe there *was* someone by that name, and I simply couldn't find them. I did find out a bit more about the building, though. It was owned by some guy called Erich Zann. There wasn't much about him. He seems to have been a musician or something, came over from Europe sometime in the early 1920s. Couldn't find out anything about him since then, I'm afraid, or who owns the building now."

Marion wasn't really listening. She could tell that, at the periphery of her vision, Carol was still keeping an eye on her. "She's right about one thing," she said.

"Who is?" Karl asked, confused.

"The register bitch. Carol. I do smell funny."

"You really don't."

"You can't smell it? You can't smell the sea?"

"No," he said. But Marion thought he was lying.

She left him standing there awkwardly and walked out of the store, flipping the bird at Carol in passing.

Outside, she joined the crowds now concertedly heading in a particular direction, and finally remembered that today was Tuesday, which meant today was *the day*—the occasion of the big protest in Haight that Dylan and Cindy and the others at the house had been planning for weeks. Marion thought that she might as well see if, for a few hours at least, she could float up and join the people who were doing something real. Whatever that meant.

And that is how she wound up back at the house, where it all happened, and she learned that the new ways are just the same as the old ones, and that we live in the shadows of the very dark and very old things that came even before that.

A period of time that Marion would never be able to get back to, even in her most lucid moments. Impossible to tell how long it lasted. An hour, two, three. Split-second snapshots were all she brought with her out of it, and they were more than enough. They were far too much.

Dylan was so high she suspected he barely knew what he was doing. But he still did it.

And so did the other men. She recognized a few of them. The rest were strangers. Either new in the house since she'd left, or part of the protest. Random guys. And a couple of girls, rubbing themselves in her face.

In every snapshot, the people doing these things to her were laughing or smiling. Most because they were deliciously high and assumed this was all part of some generous and giddy game, Marion giving up what she had, because that's how it worked in this big, new happy world they were making. A wet ritual to the new gods, a way of disappearing inside one another, of them all becoming one.

Others had faces that looked like they were smiling, but in the cracks between their teeth and the dark holes in their eyes you could see the old blackness that pools up there between the stars above our heads, and in their grunts you could hear the animals that wrapped themselves in these human disguises. So many hands, so many fingers, so many other things. Going into her, time and again. Like tentacles.

Marion said no. She said no *a hundred times. All she heard in response was the distant noise of men shouting, of miserable cargo being loaded.*

And most of all, the sound of Cindy laughing.

And then somehow, some time later, in the dark and alone, she was back outside the building. Outside *Pentimento*. With no memory of how she got out of the house, or away from the people there. No memory of her journey.

She was dressed, more or less. Her face stung from where she'd been hit. Her lips were bruised. She was battered all over, bleeding in places. Every means of entry to her body hurt.

She saw two men in dark suits walking quickly up the street toward her. Cops? Maybe. She should tell them what had just happened. But she didn't want to. She couldn't.

She opened the door and fell in.

Got to her knees and slammed the door shut.

Crawled up the staircase. Maybe there was a loud knocking sound from below. She didn't care and didn't stop crawling. It was a long way and took a long time, but what she could hear from up there kept her going.

The door was ajar on the top floor, and yes, the music was coming from the other side.

She pulled herself to her feet, and lurched in.

THE WINDOW OF ERICH ZANN

The old man stood at the other end of the room, in front of the window, with a violin under his chin. The last unearthly note of his music still hung in the air, like smoke, like fog.

"Oh, child," he said, when he saw her.

"They hurt me," she murmured. There was no reason for him to care, but she had nobody else to tell.

"They will. People always will."

"But why?"

"Because there is no 'us.' There is no 'together.' We are just sheep milling around the same pen. We are all food. Mouthfuls of sustenance for things we cannot see."

"Why?"

"Because they are hungry."

"No—why are *you* here?"

"Every Tuesday," he said. "I told you. Every Tuesday night I must be here, and do this. Some other days and nights I do it somewhere else. There is a schedule. Recently it has been hard, even more of a struggle. That's why I let you stay. I thought perhaps you seeing might help, that another set of eyes through the window would keep what's out there at bay, and our world in place. This layer of it, at least. But you saw through it, didn't you? You saw to the other side."

"I don't know what you mean."

"I think you do. And it's too late to change it now."

He walked over to the table and put his viol in the case lying upon it. "I'm sorry for your pain," he said. "But that is food for them too, and perhaps you have bought us a little time. For that, I thank you."

And with that, he left the room.

An unknowable period of time later, Marion realized that the view had changed outside. She had spent the intervening minutes or hours standing in front of the window, but mired deep inside her head, feeling as though she was running after a musical note, chasing it, trying to catch it—the otherworldly note that the old man had left with her in the attic.

Then she was aware of herself again, and seeing past the fractured reflections of herself in the colored glass to what lay beyond.

It was different now.

No buildings, only the dark ships and the fog. The shouts of men as they loaded cargo, and as she stared down at the cove she finally glimpsed what they were shoving aboard the rotting hulks—the lines of pale men and women, naked and filthy and tied together with chains.

Not slaves. *Food.*

For the things that live in the star-oceans above.

She turned and limped to the door, and descended the flights of stairs, step by painful step, gripping the handrail to stop herself stumbling and falling, half the fingernails on each hand ripped off in her attempts to pull people off her in the house near Haight that afternoon. The walls of the stairwell seemed to pulse as she passed, as if breathing, the ever-moving intestine of some vast and terrible creature as it digested her, as it digested all of them.

But she kept going down. At the bottom, she tugged the street door open and stepped outside. This time the modern city had not reappeared and the men in the suits were gone.

It was how it should be.

Her feet, which were bare—and had been for her staggering return from the house up near Haight—stood upon wood, not paving stones. The splintered planks of a narrow old wharf. She turned left, knowing what she would see.

She knew, because the sketch map in the article she had upstairs showed the positions of the fossil ships that had never made it back out of Yerba Buena Cove—and so she had known that the remains of one had been buried beneath the foundations of this very building. A ship from Europe.

And there it was. Double-masted, but with no sails. The sides damaged and sliding. A ship called the *Pentimento.*

A gust of wind came rolling down the wharf, turning the fog into a roiling cloud. She heard a slamming sound behind her. The door to the building closing.

She turned, but the building wasn't there any more, just the sound. It didn't matter. She hadn't brought the key down. There was no turning back now, and that was the way it was.

She staggered instead along the wharf toward the ship, smelling its rotting interior more clearly with every step. A gangplank reached out to a dark, gaping opening in its side.

THE WINDOW OF ERICH ZANN

This was her ship. This was how she could sail away. It was no coincidence that it had lain all these years beneath the building she'd found herself in, to which the city had steered her. It had been waiting for her all this time.

She stepped out onto the gangway, leaving another bloody footstep on the wharf.

Took another step, and then another.

The rotted wood snapped beneath her, and she plunged down into the water.

Marion could swim, but she chose not to. The water was not deep, but she remembered her grandmother telling her once—long, long ago—that you can lose your life in just two inches of water, if you're facing down.

She turned face-down, and listened to the faint melody born on the fog, or from it, as she slowly drowned.

There is one place you can make your own. A place they can't stop you being. It is a land in flux, somewhere you find not with a ship but with your feet, a realm that is yours alone. Unique, defensible through constant movement, created through twists and turns and exhausted footstep after footstep.

If you walk far and long enough you'll find it, and whatever else people do to you, they can't stop you being there. You can be there forever, in your kingdom of one.

Marion did not die that day, though others did that Summer of Love—before, during and after the counterculture bubble burst and all those pretty birds lost the wind beneath their wings, and they came crashing to earth, a city full of offerings to dark forces they'd never understood.

In every era there must be a great sacrifice. There must be blood.

Some perished in random accidents. Many—like Dylan, seven weeks later—through overdoses. Others survived against the odds, in some cases for a long time. Cindy lived to the age of seventy, leaving a fifty-year trail of broken lives and casual destruction in her wake, as she unwittingly served the Elder Gods that live beyond the last layer that sane humans can see or understand. She never understood this, or cared, and died a peaceful death that she did not deserve.

Marion did not die in those years either, though for much of the time that followed she had no idea who she was.

Others knew her as the crazy lady on the street corner, or the woman in rags standing screaming at the Bay, demanding that the ships come and take her.

MICHAEL MARSHALL SMITH

Then, when she was a little older, coming up on thirty, as the huddle of filth that spent the day in bushes at the side of the park, talking and whispering to herself.

But every evening she walked, round and round those streets, following a route that made sense only to her, as she was the sole person who knew that her path took her over every single one of the deeply-buried hulks of the ships underground, the vessels that had refused her passage, instead trapping her in the city as a final sacrifice, one whose soul bled for them. Year after year after year.

One scream at a time.

Until one weekend, mid-afternoon, when Marion was nearly forty years old, crouched in a doorway right by the *Pentimento* building, gnawing on a three-day-old pizza crust.

A family of tourists slowed to look as they passed. Twin girls in their early teens winced at the acrid smell coming from the woman on the ground. Their father shook his head, and tried to keep them moving, wishing they hadn't taken this shortcut—sympathetic, but knowing there was nothing that could be done. That every city holds creatures like these, and they belong there, as part of their fabric.

His wife stopped dead in her tracks, however. Despite the thick layers of grime, she could see who lay below.

"*Marion?*" she said.

Marion looked blearily up at her, seeing the handsome, confident woman Katie had become. The girl who'd seen through it all, back then, and survived to come out the other side, not just in one piece, but twice the size.

It broke Marion's heart, the distance, and she tried to turn away.

But Katie was firm, and reached down to take Marion's hand, to pull her to her feet. To yank her back up out of a shallow, turgid Bay that nobody else could see.

"Come with us," she said.

Marion's voice had soured and broken long ago, and was now little more than a rasp. "Where...?"

"To South Dakota," Katie said. "You should have done it then, but you can still do it now."

"But how can I get there?"

"There's room next to me. And it's time to go home."

EVERYTHING YOU NEED

Sheila supposed their marriage had been old-fashioned right from the start. They met in 1961 and married in 1963, a year which now sounded—and felt, sometimes, though not always—an awfully long time ago; but even back in those dim and distant days the world had been changing. Women had begun to quietly reassess and realign their roles in the home and the workplace. 'Quietly' was how women had most often done things in those days. It worked, too. Nobody likes being shouted at. Sometimes a soft voice gets heard more clearly.

She and John had been perfectly well aware of the changes in society, and had paid due attention. On the other hand...their way worked. He was cheerfully useless in the kitchen. Sheila was a decent cook and a whizz at keeping the place clean and tidy. He pitched in with both from time to time but it was a chore for him and a pleasure for her, so what was the point of reversing roles for the sake of it? Likewise with the children, and the washing and ironing. Yes, you could insist these household tasks be shared evenly—just as he could have insisted that, once the children were old enough, she go out and get a job—but neither felt the need for that any more than Sheila fancied going without a bra.

Doing what the new people tell you, for the sake of it, is surely no more sensible than doing what the *old* people had said, for the sake of *that*. The traditional division of labor worked for them, and once both had realized this they let it be, with some relief.

Not that she'd been the little wife indoors—far from it. She drove, of course (though he kept track of the car's service records, and when it needed an MOT). She was the one who dealt face-to-face with plumbers or electricians when something in the house needed fixing (though it was John who filed the maintenance contracts, and could lay his hand on them when required). He knew where the bank statements were, the mortgage agreement, receipts for major household expenses like furniture and white goods; he knew who the car was insured with, who held their medical insurance, what it covered and what it did not, and how much they were paying each month for any number of other things and services, and to whom, and which were on direct debit, and how on earth that worked.

She fretted from time to time that it was ridiculous she didn't know any of these details but simply handed it all over to him. Usually this concern stayed within her own head but sometimes she would articulate it. He'd shrug and say it was all boring stuff and he had a system and there was no point both of them wasting time and energy over it when there were more interesting discussions to be had, and cups of tea to make and drink, and long walks down country lanes to enjoy together.

Whenever some household matter required clarification or resolving, he'd quickly and easily find whatever document was needed. Afterwards he'd put it back in its designated drop file and push the drawer shut. If she happened to be nearby, he'd smile at her.

'Remember,' he'd say. 'Everything you need—it's in here.'

'Here' was the three-drawer filing cabinet that stood in the middle of the wall of the small upstairs room John used as an occasional office. In the days after he died, this was the room Sheila found most difficult to traverse. It had nothing to do with her. It had been his, just as the kitchen had been hers. She felt like a tourist in his office, with neither local currency nor any understanding of the language. When they'd gone on holidays to France as a family it was her schoolgirl French that got them fed and into hotel rooms: John limited his input to standing in the background looking affable.

In the office, however, she couldn't even say her own name.

EVERYTHING YOU NEED

She found it particularly hard when confronted with some aspect of the process of death that required documentary evidence. 'John dealt with all that,' she'd say, feeling old and small and stupid. Fiona didn't actually roll her eyes, but you could tell she wanted to. Fiona had been climbing the corporate ladder—with a good deal of success—since the age of eighteen. She had a spreadsheet for everything and backed them up to the cloud, whatever that was. She didn't understand that a way of being had existed between her parents, a tacit agreement, or that her mother's lack of engagement with ten thousand pieces of household management over the decades demonstrated neither lack of will, nor intelligence, nor a failure of fealty to the sisterhood—but had just been the way things worked.

John would have known what the cloud was. He wouldn't have used it—he believed in bits of paper, documents you could touch and hold (and wave imperiously at someone, if required)—but he would have at least brought it within his ken.

Sheila was slowly starting to realize that, when it came to the administration of the life she'd lived and now had to keep on living, her ken was entirely empty.

Each time this happened Fiona would dart up to the little office and open the filing cabinet and quickly track down whatever document was needed.

'Say what you like,' she'd say, returning in triumph. 'Dad's systems worked. It's all in there.'

'Everything I need,' her mother said, quietly.

'What?'

'Nothing,' she said, and put the kettle on again.

The funeral came and went, a somber train arriving out of darkness to pause in a station for a couple hours before pulling smoothly back out into the fog, never to return. Sometime during the following night a team of invisible workers came and removed all the track, abandoning Sheila on a platform from which there was no evident way forward, or back.

Friends came to visit. So did Fiona, every day. Sometimes with her husband, occasionally with her children. Neither of these seemed to know how to deal with a grandma who was now no longer always smiling as she bustled around a kitchen filled with steam; and Mark—who Sheila privately thought was okay, though no John—stood around looking as if he could hear the unanswered emails mounting up on his phone.

After the second week their visits tailed off, but Fiona kept popping in. She was a good daughter. She had a little of both parents in her, of course, and was unconsciously compensating for her father's absence.

Sheila didn't miss her husband's efficiency, however. She missed *him*.

She missed the man.

After ten days Fiona brought up the idea of going to Brighton. 'You always liked it there, Mum,' she said. 'I'll come with you. I could do with a break and It'll do you good to get out of this house. We could have tea at The Grand.'

She must have seen how horrified the idea made her mother. 'I know it'll be weird, without Dad,' she added, quickly. 'But you have to start making new memories. He wouldn't have wanted you to just stop living.'

But Sheila didn't want new memories. The idea of them made her furiously sad. What possible use could they be, if she couldn't share them with John? What would she do with such memories? What would they be *for*?

Fiona dropped the subject, but three days later mentioned it again, in passing, careful to move the conversation on quickly afterwards. Her mother knew she was being 'managed' now, that the tactic had become to drip-feed her until the idea became lodged, and came to seem reasonable, less of a denial of how the world had once stood. John had tried something similar with Sheila a few times, back in the early days. She had firmly put him right over it. He'd never tried it again. Fiona had yet to learn, evidently, that people aren't as dim as you think they are, and that taking over her father's role wasn't as simple as downloading a backup of him from the 'cloud'.

After Fiona had left, Sheila went and sat in her chair in the living room. She had never realized how loudly the clock ticked.

The next morning a man called from the mobile phone company. He had an Indian accent but said his name was Bob. He said he had great news about their phone contract.

EVERYTHING YOU NEED

'My husband deals with all that,' Sheila said, before she had time to realize what she was saying.

Bob cheerfully asked if he could talk to her husband, then. Sheila said that would not be possible, and put the phone down.

When Fiona popped in later she could tell something was wrong, but her mother wouldn't tell her what it was. She stayed a little longer than usual, as if hoping that would wear her mother down. It did not. Sheila felt sad, yes; today she felt wretched. That did not mean she had reverted to being a child. Dimly she sensed it was important her daughter understand this, too—that the road to role reversal between the generations was much more of a one-way street than it ever had been between the sexes.

Just before she went, Fiona mentioned that she'd heard a new bistro had opened down on the sea front in Brighton. Locally-sourced food, all organic.

'Hmm,' her mother said. She had not felt hungry for several days.

That night there didn't seemed to be anything on television. Sheila had adopted a temporary policy of not watching the programmes she and John used to enjoy together. Not for ever, just for now. Settling down in front of *University Challenge* or that chef they both liked, Rick Stein, was simply not a tolerable prospect.

Unfortunately all of the other television seemed to have been made with someone different to Sheila in mind. She watched almost all of what was evidently supposed to be a comedy without feeling moved to smile. This wasn't because she was grieving. It was because it wasn't funny. When something wasn't funny and you were watching it with someone, you could enjoy not finding it funny together. By yourself, it simply wasn't funny.

Although everyone in the audience seemed to be laughing.

For a moment Sheila felt very afraid, wondering if the show was funny after all, but she was unable to see it. She'd always known what funny was. She and John used to make each other laugh all the time. Even in bed. But what if that hadn't been her? She used to say things that would make John laugh, but what if it was his laughter that made them funny, rather than what she said? What if—without realizing it—she'd left all of that to him, too?

***

Half an hour later she found herself upstairs, outside the little office. The door was open and the filing cabinet was visible. It was a murky green color, with beige drawers. John bought it from a catalogue and for years afterwards they got a laugh out of an occasional update arriving at their door, addressed to 'The Office Furniture Buyer'. John would open up the kitchen waste bin, bend down and call, 'More post for you, Cyril...' and drop the catalogue in.

Their mobile phone contract would be in the cabinet somewhere. Sheila knew she didn't have to look for it. She understood that any news "Bob" might have had for her would have been nothing more than a covert means of getting her to upgrade, thereby committing herself to a longer contract with the same provider. A history of leaving things to someone else didn't make her a complete dimwit.

It seemed important, however. It felt symbolic of something or other. It was a useful test case, too. If Bob or one of his familiars called back, she could hear him out—armed with the relevant documentation—and simply say "No, thank you,", if she so chose. There was nothing to lose.

She walked into the office and up to the cabinet. She put her hand on it. The metal felt cool to the touch. It was strange. Despite the fact that John would have had far more contact with other objects in the room—the desk, the chair, his biros in the little pot—the cabinet felt like the essence of the space.

She opened the top drawer. It was easier than she'd thought it would be. Not just that she was able to reach out and do it, but also because it slid out faster and more smoothly than she'd anticipated.

Ka-thunk, it went. It was a capable sound.

The smell of old papers wafted out. Each drop file had a neat plastic tag at the top, arranged so as to progress from left to right, all visible at once. Every one held a tiny rectangle of paper in John's extremely legible capitals, saying things like CAR, KITCHEN and MEDICAL. Big nouns, concrete and abstract. The building blocks, tangible or otherwise, of a life lived.

Sheila ran her hand over the top of the files, causing some to open a little. Lots of pieces of paper lay within. Letters, receipts, contracts. Even though many of them presumably related to things she was still using, she had never seen anything that looked so dead. Deader even than John. He at least still lived—to some degree—in her mind.

EVERYTHING YOU NEED

These things…they were just dead.

She closed the drawer, not having been able to spot a tag that appeared to relate to mobile phones, and feeling neither inclined nor strong enough to work through the contents of all the drop files one by one.

She opened the second drawer. This didn't come so easily. Perhaps the mechanism had rusted, or a piece of paper inside had got caught. She pulled harder, and it eventually withdrew.

It wasn't just a mechanical problem, however. She was crying now. Crying hard enough that all of the energy in her body seemed focused on yanking muscles tightly in the wrong directions, stretching the tendons in her throat. There was little power left for anything else.

She dragged her sleeve across her eyes and forced herself to read the tags in this drawer.

GAS & ELECTRICITY. BROADBAND. TAX. She couldn't imagine why she would ever, ever want to open drop files labeled thus. There were more, but still not the one she was looking for.

She pushed the drawer. It suddenly slammed shut, far more easily than it had opened. The noise scared and unnerved her.

She reached down and took hold of the handle on the lowest drawer. She pulled, but nothing happened. She tugged, with all her might, but it would not open.

It wasn't locked—it gave a little—but there was evidently something jammed in it, stopping the drawer from sliding out more than about half an inch. A few more half-hearted yanks at it changed nothing. She stopped.

She'd tried. Evidently the drawer was broken.

She left the room and went back downstairs. Later she went to bed, and lay there, sleepless, for several hours. What if he'd been wrong?

What if everything she needed *wasn't* in there?

What then?

Fiona's visit next day was a fly-by, mid-morning, on her way to some meeting or other. She seemed distracted at first, as if these daily visits to her mother—never part of their routine before John's death—were beginning to feel a little like…not a chore, exactly, but an errand secondary to the main order of business.

Sheila caught herself thinking this, and felt depressed and sad. Not at the thought, but at herself for entertaining it. That wasn't how Fiona would be feeling, and Sheila knew it. Fiona was busy. Her life went on, as all lives must. The dead die in order to remind us how non-dead are those who remain; we have children to provide us with role models to remind us the way we think now is not the only way to think. Fiona was not "distracted", merely a woman leading her own life, one that currently involved the death of her father and dealing with a grieving mother, but which also still held commitments to the living, and to the future.

Sheila understood this. But still, when Fiona dropped a mention of how The Grand in Brighton was doing out-of-season deals, it was all she could do to turn away and remain silent, rather than saying something she would have regretted.

Mid-afternoon Bob rang again. Actually he said his name was Kevin this time but he appeared to be fundamentally the same man. He also wanted to talk to her about her mobile phone contract. Sheila did not say that John dealt with those things. She told him instead that she was unable to find their phone contract. The man assured her that this was not a problem, not in the slightest, and that the great offers he wished to make available to her were not dependent upon it.

Sheila listened for a few moments but then gently put the phone down. Of course it mattered whether she could find the contract. Otherwise why would they have such things?

She spent the rest of the afternoon in her chair in the sitting room, in silence. She was waiting for something.

What, she didn't know.

Later, she stood in front of the window onto the garden, watching twilight darken and fade. When it was properly dark, she went upstairs.

This time she looked through the top cabinet properly, searching each drop file. Although she found many, many pieces of paper—John had evidently maintained a policy of retaining absolutely everything, even for appliances that she knew for a fact had gone to the great dump in the sky many years previously—there was nothing in there about their mobile phones.

EVERYTHING YOU NEED

She closed the drawer. She realized it was now after nine in the evening. She realized too that she hadn't eaten anything for dinner. Or lunch. She couldn't remember the last time she'd drunk anything, either.

Had she made tea again after Fiona left, late morning? She wasn't sure. She didn't think so. She felt dry, and tired, but knew that she had to do this, and do it tonight.

The second drawer was as hard to pull out as it had been the night before. She still couldn't work out why, and tonight at least she wasn't crying. It simply didn't slide properly. She searched through all of the files, going straight to BROADBAND to begin with, as it had occurred to her that whoever was supplying them/her with that service might be in the market to sell mobile phones too, and John might have taken advantage of some special deal or other (he had always read direct mail diligently, rather than throwing it away, in case they were offering something worth having. Sheila had never understood how he was able to tell if something was worth having or not).

Their Internet supplier apparently did not also provide their mobile phones. Neither did anyone else in any of the second drawer's drop files. By the time she was only halfway through it, Sheila's back was aching. She pulled John's old chair over from the desk, but it didn't help much. For the last few files she was leaning her elbows on the sides of the drawer. Her stomach had stopped growling some while ago, as if it had lost faith. Her mouth felt arid. When she blinked she could hear the lids scrape across her eyeballs, or it seemed like she could. She felt a little light-headed as she sat upright. It didn't matter. She could have a snack afterward if she felt like it. The clock on the desk said it was now well after eleven, in fact coming up for midnight. The house was silent and cold around her.

That made no difference. She was finishing this tonight. She had to find the thing, and if everything she needed was in here, then here was where it had to be.

She closed the second drawer.

Ten minutes later she was crying. She didn't know whether the tears were of grief or frustration or both and it didn't matter. What mattered was that she couldn't open the bottom drawer. As with the night before, it would slide back about a centimeter but then come no further. She'd gone down on hands and knees in front of it, holding the handle with both hands, and pulled with all her might. She'd got one of the pens from the desk and poked it through the gap at the top, running it right along the edge, in the hope of dislodging anything that might be obstructing it within. She had done that one way, then the other, then back—faster and faster, until a combination of despair and fury broke the pen into three pieces.

She'd broken a pen that John had used to write things and sign things, but achieved nothing else.

She tugged at the handle some more. She hit the drawer with her fists. Her tears were constant now, and she felt dizzy and her head was aching. The room seemed to sway around her as she pushed herself back up to her feet.

'You said it would be in here,' she shouted, catching herself unawares. She'd had no idea she was going to say anything, much less shout it. 'YOU SAID THIS HAD EVERYTHING I NEED.'

She kicked the drawer, hard, and then again, heedless of the pain in her toes. She relished it, in fact, bitterly triumphant at being able to make herself feel *something*, breaking out of the endless grey fog. She felt even dizzier now but didn't care—she felt as if she'd finally understood what people feel in the moment before they end it all, a kind of frantic glee, a rich dedication to self-harm and self-destruction and to the realization that none of it mattered and you could just keep escalating the pain until it exploded into silence.

She pulled her foot back, screaming incoherently now, and kicked the drawer with all her force.

There was a soft *thunk*.

Sheila stopped. The sound hadn't been loud, but it cut through the haze all the same.

Something had happened inside the drawer. Something had been dislodged or freed.

She staggered back toward the cabinet and leaned down, panting. She grasped the handle. She pulled. It slid open smoothly.

John was inside.

He was bent and folded and turned over on himself, like a blanket stuffed into a too-small drawer. He had been so very thin at the end. His head seemed to lie on top of the rest of him, top toward the front, face pointing upwards. His eyes were open.

They swiveled to look at her. 'Hello, dear,' he said.

Sheila fell to her knees, reaching for him. She tried to pull him out but he was far too tightly jammed into the drawer. There was no way of ever getting him free.

She gave up trying, and though her eyes were so tear-blurred so she could barely see, she saw him start to smile in the same old way, as she leaned over to bring her lips toward his mouth.

She woke the following morning in her bed. When she remembered what had happened she got up, wrapped her robe around her, and went through to the office. The bottom drawer was shut. She knelt down in front of it and pulled, gently, not expecting it to open.

But it did. It was empty inside but for ten hanging files. Each had a plastic tag at the top, but no label yet.

She flicked slowly through them.

In the last she found a single index card. She took it out and found something written in John's handwriting. Not as she remembered it from their first letters to each other, or on so many birthday and Christmas cards, but as it had become in the final six months, in the last days. Weaker, but defiantly neat, and still characteristically his.

'For your filing,' the note said. 'Put everything you need in here. Love, J.'

Fiona arrived at midday, this time bearing lunch from Marks & Spensers. She looked tired. Sheila helped her unwrap the sandwiches in silence, and then the two of them stood side by side for a few moments, looking out at the street outside.

'I don't want to go to The Grand for tea, not this time,' Sheila said. 'Let's try the Metropole instead.'

Fiona turned to her and smiled, properly, for the first time since her father died.

Bob from the mobile phone company rang again, in the afternoon. This time he was called Justin. He still had a great new offer to discuss.

Sheila told him to bugger off.

WHAT HAPPENS WHEN YOU WAKE UP IN THE NIGHT

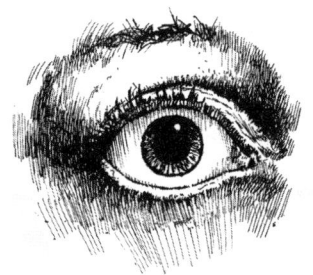

The first thing I was unhappy about was the dark. I do not like the dark very much. It is not the worst thing in the world but it is also not the best thing in the world, either. When I was very smaller I used to wake up sometimes in the middle of the night and be scared when I woke up, because it was so dark. I went to bed with my light on, the light that turns round and round, on the drawers by the side of my bed. It has animals on it and it turns around and it makes shapes and patterns on the ceiling and it is pretty and my mummy's friend Jeanette gave it to me. It is not too bright but it is bright enough and you can see what is what.

But then it started that when I woke up in the middle of the night, the light would not be on any more and it would be completely dark instead and it would make me sad. I didn't understand this but one night when I'd woken up and cried a lot my mummy told me that she came in every night and turned off the light after I was asleep, so it didn't wake me up. But I said that wasn't any good, because if I *did* wake up in the night and the light wasn't on, then I might be scared, and cry. She said it seemed that I was waking every night, and she and Daddy had worked out that it might be the light that woke me, and after I was awake I'd get up and go into their room and see what was up with them, which meant she got no sleep any night ever and it was driving her completely nuts.

So we made a deal, and the deal said I could have the light on all night *but* I promised that I would not go into their room in the night unless it was *really* important, and it is a good deal and so I'm allowed to have my light on again now, which is why the first thing I noticed when I woke up was that it was dark.

Mummy had broken the deal. I was cross about this but I was also very sleepy and so I wasn't completely sure if I was going to shout about it or not.

Then I noticed it was cold.

Before I go to bed, Mummy puts a heater on in my room while I am having my bath, and also I have two blankets on top of my duvet, and so I am a warm little bunny and it is fine. Sometimes if I wake in the middle of the night it feels a bit cold but if I snuggle down again it's okay.

But this felt really cold. My light was not on and I was cold.

I put my hand out to put my light on, which was the first thing to do. There is a switch on a white wire that comes from the light and I can turn it on myself—I can even find it in the dark when there is no light.

I tried to do that but I could not find the wire with my hand.

So I sat up and tried again, but still I could not find it, and I wondered if Mummy had moved it, and I thought I might go and ask her. But I could not see the door. It had been so long since I had been in my room in the night without my light being on that I had forgotten how dark it gets. It's *really* dark. I knew it would be hard to find the door if I could not see it, so I did it a clever way.

I used my imagination.

I sat still for a moment and remembered what my bedroom is like. It is like a rectangle and has some drawers by the top of my bed where my head goes. My light is on the drawers, usually. My room also has a table where my coloring books go and some small toys, and two more sets of drawers, and windows down the other end. They have curtains so the street lights do not keep me awake, and because in summer it gets bright too early in the morning and so I wake everybody up when they should still be asleep because they have work to do and they need some sleep. And there is a big chair but it is always covered in toys and it is not important.

I turned to the side so my legs hung off the bed and down onto the floor. In my imagination I could see that if I stood up and walked straight in front of me, I would nearly be at my door, but that I would have to go a little way...left, too.

WHAT HAPPENS WHEN YOU WAKE UP IN THE NIGHT

So I stood up and did this walking.

It was strange doing it in the dark. I stepped on something soft with one of my feet, I think it was a toy that had fallen off the chair. Then I touched one of the other drawers with my hand, and I knew I was close to the door, so I turned left and walked that way a bit.

I reached out with my hands then and tried to find my dressing gown. I was trying to find it because I was cold, but also because it hangs off the back of my bedroom door on a little hook and so when I found the dressing gown I would know I had got to the right place to open the door.

But I could not find the dressing gown. Sometimes my mummy takes things downstairs and washes them in the washing machine in the kitchen and then dries them in another machine that makes them hot, so maybe that was where it was. I was quite awake now and very cold so I decided not to keep trying to find the gown and just go wake Mummy and Daddy and say to them that I was awake.

But I couldn't find my doorknob. I knew I must be where the door is, because it is in the corner where the two walls of my room come together. I reached out with my hands and could feel the two sides of the corner, but I could not find the doorknob, even though I moved my hands all over where it should be. When I was smaller the doorknob came off once, and Mummy was very scared because she thought if it happened again I would be trapped in my bedroom and I wouldn't be able to get out, so she shouted at Daddy until he fixed it with a different screw. But it had never come off again, so I did not know where it could be now. I wondered if I had got off my bed in the wrong way because it was dark and I had got it mixed up in my imagination, and maybe I should go back to my bed and start again.

Then a voice said: 'Maddy, what are you *doing*?'

I was so surprised I made a scared sound, and jumped.

I trod on something, and the same voice said 'Ow!' I heard someone moving and sitting up. Even though it was in the dark I knew it was my mummy.

'Mummy?' I said. 'Where are you?'

'Maddy, I've *told* you about coming into our room.'

'I'm not.'

'It's just not *fair*. Mummy has to go to work and Daddy has to go to work and you have to go to school and we *all* need our sleep. We made a *deal*, remember?'

'But *you* broke the deal. You took away my light.'

'I haven't touched your light.'

'You did!'

'Maddy, don't lie. We've talked about lying.'

'You took my light!'

'I haven't taken your light and I didn't turn it off.'

'But it's not turned on.'

She made a sighing sound. 'Maybe the bulb went.'

'Went to where?'

'I mean, got broken.'

'No, my whole *light* is not there.'

'Maddy...'

'It's not! I put my hand out and I couldn't find it!'

My mummy made a sound like she was very cross or very tired, I don't know which. Sometimes they sound the same. She didn't say anything for a little minute.

'Look,' she said then, and she did not sound very cross now, just sleepy and as if she loved me but wished I was still asleep. 'It's the middle of the night and everyone should be in bed. Their *own* bed.'

'I'm sorry, Mummy.'

'That's okay.' I heard her standing up. 'Come on. Let's go back to your room.'

'What do you mean?' I said.

'Back to your room. Now. I'll tuck you in, and then we can all go back to sleep.'

'I *am* in my room.'

'Maddy—don't start.'

'I *am* in my room!'

'Maddy, this is just silly. Why would you... Why is it so dark in here?'

'Because my light is off. I told you.'

'Maddy, your light is in *your* room. Don't—'

She stopped talking suddenly. I heard her fingers moving against something, the wall, maybe. 'What the hell?'

WHAT HAPPENS WHEN YOU WAKE UP IN THE NIGHT

Her voice sounded different.

'"Hell" is a naughty word,' I told her.

'Shush.'

I heard her fingers swishing over the wall again. She had been asleep on the floor, right next to the wall. I heard her feet moving on the carpet and then there was a banging sound and she said a naughty word again, but she did not sound angry but like she did not understand something. It was like a question mark sound.

'For the love of *Christ*.'

This was not my mummy talking.

'Dan?'

'Who the hell else? Any chance you'll just take her back to bed? Or I can do it. I don't care. But let's *one* of us do it. It's the middle of the fucking night.'

'Dan!'

'Fucking is a *very* naughty—'

'Yes, yes, I'm terribly sorry,' my daddy said. He sounded as if he was only half not in a dream. 'But we have *talked* about you coming into our room in the middle of the night, Maddy. Talked about it endlessly. And—'

'Dan,' my mummy said, starting to talk when he was still talking, which is not good and can be rude. 'Where *are* you?'

'I'm right *here*,' he said. 'For god's *sake*. I'm... Did you put up new curtains or something?'

'No,' Mummy said.

'It's not normally this dark in here, is it?'

'My light has gone,' I said. 'That's why it is so dark.'

'Your light is in *your* room,' Daddy said.

I could hear him sitting up. I could hear his hands, too. They were not right next to Mummy, but at the other end of my room. I could hear them moving around on the carpet.

'Am I on the floor?' he asked. 'What the hell am I doing *on the floor?*'

I heard him stand up. I did not tell him 'hell' is a naughty word. I did not think that he would like it.

I heard him move around some more, his hands knocking into things.

'Maddy,' Mummy said, 'where do you think you are?'

'I'm in my *room*,' I said.

'Dan?' she said, to Daddy. My daddy's other name is 'Dan.' It is like 'Dad' but has a nuh-sound at the end instead of a duh-sound. '*Is* this Maddy's room?'

I heard him moving around again, as if he was checking things with his hands.

'What are we doing in here?' he said, sounding as if he was not certain. 'Is this her room?'

'Yes, it's *my room*,' I said.

I was beginning to think Daddy or Mummy could not hear properly, because I kept saying things over and over but they did not listen.

I told them again. 'I woke up, and my light was off, and this is my room.'

'Have you tried the switch by the door?' Daddy asked Mummy.

I heard Mummy move to the door, and her fingers swishing on the wall, swishing and patting. 'It's not there.'

'What do you mean it's not there?'

'What do you *think* I mean?'

'For Christ's sake.'

I heard Daddy walking carefully across the room to where Mummy was. Mummy said: 'Satisfied?'

'How *can* it not be there? Maddy—can you turn the light by your bed on, please?' Daddy sounded cross now.

'She says it isn't there.'

'What do you mean, not there?'

'It's not *there*,' I said. 'I already told Mummy, like, fourteen times. I was coming into your room to tell you, and then Mummy woke up and she was on the floor.'

'Are the street lamps out?'

This was Mummy asking. I heard Daddy go away from the door and go back to the other end of the room, where he had woken up from. He knocked into the table as he was moving and made a cross sound but kept on moving again.

'Dan? Is that why it's so dark? Is it a power cut?'

'I don't know,' he said. 'I...can't find the curtains.'

'Can't find the gap, you mean?'

'No. Can't find the *curtains*. They're not here.'

WHAT HAPPENS WHEN YOU WAKE UP IN THE NIGHT

'You're sure you're in the right—'

'Of course I'm in the right place. They're not here. I can't feel them. It's just wall.'

'It is just wall where my door is too,' I said. I was happy that Daddy had found the same thing as me, because if he had found it too then I could not be wrong.

I heard Mummy check the wall near us with her hands. She was breathing a little quickly. 'She's right. It's just wall,' she said, so we all knew the same thing now. 'It's just wall, everywhere.'

But Mummy's voice sounded quiet and a bit scared and so it did not make me so happy when she said it.

'Okay, this is ridiculous,' Daddy said. 'Stay where you are. Don't move.'

I could hear what he was doing. He was going along the sides of the room, with his fingers on the walls. He went around the drawers near the window, then past where my calendar hangs, where I put what day it is in the mornings, then along my bed.

'She's right,' he said. 'The lamp isn't here.'

'I'm really cold,' Mummy said.

Daddy went past me and into the corner where Mummy had been sleeping, where I had trod on her when I was trying to find the door.

But he couldn't find the door either.

He said the door had gone, and the windows, and all the walls felt like they were made of stone. Mummy tried to find the curtains, but she couldn't.

They tried to find the door and the window for a long time but they still couldn't find them and then my mummy started crying.

Daddy said crying would not help, which he says to me sometimes, and he kept on looking in the dark for some more time, trying to find the door.

But in the end he stopped, and he came and sat down with us. I don't know how long ago that was. It's hard to remember in the dark. But I think it was quite long ago.

Sometimes we sleep, but later we wake up and everything is still the same. I do not get hungry but it is always dark and it is always very cold.

Mummy and Daddy had ideas and used their imaginations. Mummy thought there was a fire, and it burned all our house down and us in it. Daddy says we *think* we are in my room because I woke up first, but he says really we are in a small place made of stone, near a church somewhere. I don't know but we have been here a very long time now and still it is not morning yet.

It is quiet and I do not like it. Mummy and Daddy do not talk much anymore, and this is why, if you wake up in the night, you should never ever get up out of bed.

FAILURE

It is always difficult to discern the boundaries of existence. Children valiantly insist upon putting black lines around the shapes and people they draw, in an attempt to divide and master the continuum of being, but real life does not come with such clear separation. It's hard to tell where your existence stops and the external world begins, and equally tough to determine within that what counts as work, and what is merely "life": or, perhaps, what is merely work, and what has been the thing that, when you look back from the final precipice, will constitute the life you have just lived.

Many people never even stop to consider these questions. Jonathan did, however. He monitored his progress, paying increasing attention as he entered his late fifties and became ever more aware of his advancing position on life's journey. Often the process of scrutiny was reassuring. He felt broadly content, for example, with his performance as Operations Director of a growing chain of copy shops, and had reason to believe they were content with him too. His thirty-year marriage to Elaine was similarly successful. They'd weathered storms large and small with patience and good humor, and there was no-one in the world with whom he'd rather spend time. They always found something to talk about. They told each other they loved one another, often, and with patent sincerity.

Even as solid a relationship would ultimately be terminated by death, however, and Jonathan would one day retire. The things you do by your own hand pass and fade away. The most important and lasting marks, therefore, are the ones you leave behind, the deeper scratches you make on the world—and it was here that Jonathan had begun to lose confidence in what he'd achieved.

Here, and specifically in the shape of his son.

He told Elaine he was going for a drive. This had long been his habit in the evenings, and she wished him well without bothering to look up from the copy of *Sunset Magazine* she was reading on the sofa. He picked up the keys to her 4Runner—the area's default domestic vehicle, and less noticeable than his own Boxter (itself a rare indulgence in a life that was otherwise remarkably unshowy)—and walked out into the evening. It had been unusually hot all day, without the welcome breeze that normally freshens Northern California afternoons, and the air retained warmth even in twilight.

As he opened the car door he raised a hand in greeting to his neighbor, who stood peaceably watering her front yard. Everyone in the neighborhood employed teams of very competent Mexicans to perform such tasks—in most cases aided by automated sprinkler systems—and so this could only be a self-imposed diversion, an excuse for being out of doors on a pleasant night. And why not? She waved back as he drove away.

He passed a car parked fifty yards away down the street, in the shadow of trees. Beyond noticing it was another 4Runner, he did not give it any thought.

He found it hard to recall when he'd first started to feel concern that things were not going as they should. Ryan had been a mercurial toddler and a fractious boy, sure, prone to pout and to sweeping things to the floor while possessed with inarticulate fury, but Jonathan suspected you could say the same of many children unless you were determined to maintain a pretense of perfection in front of other parents.

There were other times when the child was as sweet and helpful as you could wish for. The two poles balanced, for the most part, more or less.

Nonetheless Jonathan gradually became aware of how many times he'd picked up some treat or trinket while away on business, telling himself he'd give it to his son to reward a notable piece of good behavior, only to discover

FAILURE

the object in a drawer six months later, no obvious occasion for such celebration having presented itself in the meantime.

Ryan grew more even-tempered as he entered his teens. His schoolwork was uniformly better than adequate, keeping him in the second tier of students year after year. He was a good-looking boy, decent at sport, charming when it suited him. This combination meant that, after he entered high school, his father and mother became accustomed to meeting and welcoming girls with whom their son had became involved.

And it was at this point, perhaps, that Jonathan had started to observe more closely, though he hadn't been consciously aware of it at the time.

There were four girlfriends worthy of the name during the teenage years. All had been attractive, polite and evidently enamored of their son. Then, a few months later, the liaison would prove to have been discontinued. Ryan never volunteered anything beyond saying it hadn't worked out, and hadn't seemed to suffer any particular emotional turmoil or distress. There would simply be a period where he did not have a girlfriend, after which a new one would materialize.

The pattern did not have long enough to assert itself as notable, however, before Ryan finished school and left town to attend law school on the other side of the country.

Jonathan drove in an aimless fashion for an hour, tracing shapes around a town he had known for most of his life. When it finally got the other side of nine o'clock he looped back and headed for the Jury Room.

Santa Cruz's most barefaced example of a hardcore drinkers' bar, the Jury Room lurks at the northern end of town, close to the highway, a ramshackle sign above the door proclaiming it has been proudly manufacturing and servicing hangovers since 1976. It's open from six in the morning until two on the other side of midnight, after which the staff presumably crash out on the floor for four hours before starting again. Jonathan had never been inside.

He drove into the lot and to its darkest corner. He turned off the engine and settled to wait.

Ryan emerged from university with a good degree. He'd always been skilled at arguing, presenting the facts of a situation—or selected subsets of them—to his advantage. He'd evidently developed the ability to perform this task on the behalf of clients. His mother was delighted when he elected to return to Santa Cruz, and Jonathan had been pleased too, while privately wondering if it betrayed a lack of ambition. Ryan quickly got himself taken on by a small local firm, however, and used this as a stepping stone to a larger and more prestigious outfit over the hill in Los Gatos. His success was not conspicuous, but solid and sustained. The kind of success, in fact, that his father had always counselled him to seek.

After six years, he got married. Jonathan liked Maria the first time they met, an informal bar-snacks meal upstairs at the Crow's Nest restaurant, by the beach. She was very pretty, of course, but he could see at once that she possessed a good deal more character than the previous girls his son had been aligned with. She was smart, and excellent company, and Ryan's parents were delighted when the engagement was announced.

For several years all went well. Ryan achieved further promotions, taking him within a step of junior partner. He and Maria moved into a large house in Scott's Valley, halfway between his work and Santa Cruz. The two couples met for dinner once a month (Maria's family lived on the opposite coast, and were not involved in these events). Elaine increasingly allowed herself to speculate—with pleasure, and only to her husband—how long it would be before they became grandparents.

Then one night Maria was absent from a dinner. Ryan brought her heartfelt apologies, explaining that an excess of Dungeness crab the night before (they were in season, and Maria an ardent fan) had turned bad on her. Jonathan and Elaine e-mailed their condolences. At the next gathering, Maria was amusing at her own expense.

Four months later it happened again.

Crab was no longer in season. This time it was a revised deadline for a report relating to the environmental agency for which she worked. A shame, but Ryan's parents agreed that her commitment to her job was admirable, and sufficiently within character that it raised no flag.

Two months after that, it was the flu.

By chance, Jonathan's schedule took him through Scott's Valley the following afternoon. He stopped by his son's house with a vial of the foul-tasting herbal concoction Elaine swore by when plagued by viral demons (and which genuinely seemed to lop a few days off the recovery period). At first there was no answer, but Maria's car was in the driveway and so he persisted.

When she eventually opened the door she stood well back, and the extra make-up had been well-applied. The bruising was obvious nonetheless.

By the end of the year, the marriage was over. Aided in the closing stages by Elaine (who remained ignorant of what he'd seen that afternoon, and the previous instances which had prevented her attendance at other meals), Jonathan did what he could. The relationship could not be saved, however, and privately he admired his daughter-in-law for her decisiveness in determining that there was a point after which it was no longer worth trying.

She finally left town one Thursday morning. She stopped by Jonathan's office, told him what she was doing, and explained that Ryan did not yet know she wouldn't be there when he got home from work.

Jonathan hugged her tightly and implored her to keep in touch. He watched her drive away toward the highway south, his hands bunched down by his sides. He then drove to his son's place of work, hauled him from his office and into a discrete corner of the parking lot. Within ten minutes he had secured a promise that Ryan would never behave in this way again. So far as Jonathan knew, he had not.

Not in that precise way, anyhow.

After forty minutes Jonathan saw his son coming up the street. He watched him head into the Jury Room. He knew Ryan couldn't have walked the ten miles from Scott's Valley, and so he must have parked discreetly nearby. That was something, at least.

Jonathan put his head in his hands. He thought about going home, or calling his wife, but not seriously, and not for long. The love between a boy and his mother is a wonderful thing, of that there is no doubt.

The responsibility for a son and his life, however, lies with the father.

Of course it does.

**

A year and a half after the break-up of his marriage, Ryan made partner in his law firm. That night there was a celebratory dinner with Jonathan and Elaine, three at a table that would have felt better with four. The regular dinners they'd enjoyed during their son's marriage had never resumed. Instead there had been occasional brief encounters with Ryan and a succession of partners, most of whom appeared rather bemused by the experience. Few of these women lasted long. None was on hand to help celebrate his partnership.

Eventually the tickling in the back of his mind grew too acute to ignore, and Jonathan tracked down his son's most recent girlfriend (the only thing he remembered her saying was that she worked in administration for the Santa Clara mall, but that had been enough).

Six weeks after the end of her affair with Ryan, a limp was still discernible. She declined to discuss their relationship.

By now wearily, and with a growing, leaden anger that felt horribly impotent, the next week Jonathan found and spoke to one of his son's high school girlfriends, making it look like an accidental encounter. Jessica Friedkin had gained three children and sixty pounds in the intervening years. She remained as cheerful as he recalled, however, until the subject of her break-up with Ryan came up (or, in fact, had been laboriously brought into the conversation by Jonathan). At this point she became evasive. Jonathan persevered gently.

"He was my first," she admitted, eventually. "He was…I don't know. Well, I didn't know *then*. I had no comparison. But…he was kinda…*rough*. I'm sure he was just finding his way, though, right? None of us knew anything about that whole kit and kaboodle back then."

Jonathan nodded and smiled, and stayed long enough to steer the conversation back to more positive matters. Then he paid for coffee and left.

On the way back to the house he took a detour and parked close to the vast expanse of meadow and redwood forest that bordered the upper west side of town, stretching unbroken up into the Santa Cruz mountains. He walked out into it, not knowing what to feel or what to do. Along the path he came across the sturdy sign showing a map of the area. He had walked past it many times before. Occasionally, as now, there was a handmade addition stuck on one side, warning of recent mountain lion sightings.

FAILURE

Wild animals, in the neighborhood. Creatures that could not be trusted to treat humans kindly—who did not even comprehend the rules by which others felt honor-bound to live; and who in the dead of night lifted their heads to listen to the silent call of the wilderness.

Jonathan looked at the sign for a while and then walked back to his car.

He didn't know how much to blame himself for not having connected his son to the intermittent spate of local rapes. Area women enticed from cafés and bars, then brutalized in cars or alleys: all resistant to the idea of discussing their assailant, a man whose methods of operation seemed different every time. Local police—and the *Santa Cruz Sentinel*—took this to indicate that a number of men were attacking women within the same period.

Jonathan was less sure. He came to fear—though he tried to push the idea away—this merely meant that one man was being crafty about his deeds, and that he'd been able to firmly impress upon his victims the dangers of trying to identify him to the authorities.

Why did Jonathan care? Because one long evening after his wife had gone to bed, it finally occurred to him to wonder whether he might know who that man might be.

There was no reason to think it was his son. Not really. Ryan evidently nursed a tendency toward excessive physical dominance with women, but there were plenty of marriages and partnerships that worked this way, and (though the idea was abhorrent to Jonathan) he could see how, within the strange shorthands and hidden language of relationships, such a situation might continue without a couple splitting up. Maria had clearly tolerated it for a number of years, and Jonathan would always ask himself whether his visit to her the day after the alleged flu might have provoked her departure; whether, had he been engaged in business on some other side of town, things might have gone differently.

Having your weakness and pain witnessed makes it real. Jonathan had done that for Maria, for better or worse. And she had left.

He'd only received one e-mail from her afterward. He knew enough about technical matters to notice it had been sent via a means that stripped all geographical information from the chain of servers that had delivered it to his computer. Either Maria had not been sure whether to trust her erstwhile father-in-law, or had simply been very cautious indeed. He didn't blame her. In the conversation they'd had the afternoon with the opened door and facial bruising, she'd eventually—in a whisper, her head hung low with shame—revealed some of what it was like to share a sex life with Jonathan's son.

This was despite the fact that Ryan had *loved* Maria. Of that Jonathan had no doubt. The nagging question was what he might be prepared to do—what dire avenues he might feel drawn to explore—with girls casually picked up in clubs and bars.

Somebody was doing this to women in town. Once the idea had entered Jonathan's head that it might be his son it proved tough to dislodge, however hard it might be to reconcile with his internal collection of images of Ryan as a little boy, looking up at him with amusement, or love.

It was also difficult to dislodge the notion that, should someone not step in, the results could get worse.

Thirty-five minutes later Jonathan sat upright when he saw a woman striding along the street toward the Jury Room. It was hard to tell much in a darkness slashed by harsh streetlights, but she looked young and had a tight body in a short dress, and also—despite the strut in her walk—betrayed clear signs of drunkenness. About twenty feet from the door she lost her balance for a moment, teetering on very high heels. Jonathan's window was open. He heard her swear under her breath. She regained control. He watched as she went inside, poise more-or-less re-established.

The die was cast, he knew.

Three weeks previously, Jonathan had spent the evening in a similar way. That time the bar had been The Grinder, in Watsonville, a twenty-minute drive from Santa Cruz. It, like the Jury Room, had featured in news reports as a place where a victim had been picked up. This evidently hadn't been enough to stop women coming there.

Or Ryan, either.

Jonathan had recognized his son's car in the lot as soon as he arrived. He parked and went over to check. Then he returned to his own vehicle and sat in darkness for two hours.

FAILURE

At a quarter of eleven a couple emerged from the bar, spilling loud music and light for a moment before the door slammed behind them. The man had his arm around the woman's waist, and was leading her firmly. The woman was very drunk.

The man was Ryan.

Brazen, calculated, or dumb? It was hard to be sure. This didn't prove that Jonathan's son was the attacker, of course. He could simply have been at The Grinder hoping to score cheap and easy sex, coincidentally visiting a venue the local attacker had also frequented. Nonetheless Jonathan was glad he'd taken the opportunity to drive an expensive four-inch vegetable paring knife—borrowed from Elaine's kitchen, purchased at some expense from Williams-Sonoma in Los Gatos—into three of the tires of his son's car.

Ryan's fury at seeing the damage had been enough to convince his companion that he wasn't the right guy to be going home with. She tottered back to the bar and disappeared inside. Ryan watched her go, hands on his hips, then got out his phone to call AAA.

Jonathan started his car and drove quietly away.

It wasn't proof.

But it was.

Brazen, calculated, dumb.

Or innocent?

That was the question that had plagued Jonathan over the last three weeks. Had Ryan gone to the Grinder because he was too arrogant to believe he might be caught, because he was crafty enough to think the cops would assume no-one would be dumb enough to return to the scene of a previous crime, or because he was too dumb to even consider the question?

Ryan wasn't dumb. He never had been. So he was brazen or calculating.

Or...innocent, of course.

Still there remained that possibility, and that's why Jonathan had come out again tonight, to wait in the dark outside the Jury Room. He'd waited there the previous night too, and the night before, and the night before that—in vain. But tonight Ryan had finally come, and an hour and a half later he emerged back into the night, lurching slightly, the hardbody girl in the short skirt by his side. Jonathan didn't think Ryan's stumbling was genuine, but tonight he'd left the tires on his son's car alone.

To be sure.

He watched, his breathing shallow, as Ryan led the girl across the lot and let her into his car. He waited as his son drove out onto the street, and then followed.

He thought it would only be a little while before he saw his son indicate and turn onto a side road, somewhere close by. That's what had happened in the previous attacks, according to the victims' accounts. His heart sank—and his stomach turned cold—as he realized this wasn't going to happen. Before long he understood that Ryan was heading onto Highway 17 instead, taking the most direct route back to Scott's Valley. Where he had a house.

Innocence remained possible. But if not, then neither brazen, calculating nor dumb would describe Ryan's actions any more. If his son *was* the attacker, and had now decided to take a woman back to where he lived—with the far higher risks for identification that entailed—then it was likely he'd done so in order to give himself the time and freedom in which to do *very* bad things.

If that's what he had in mind, Ryan was now out of control. And, as his father's position on his tail demonstrated, incapable of adequately covering his tracks.

Jonathan stopped following when Ryan's car turned off the highway. He was horribly confident of the destination now. He parked a mile from his son's house, around the back of a *tacquería* long-ago closed for the night. He walked at a steady pace up the long incline that led into the upscale neighborhood where his son lived.

His palms were damp. The front of his mind felt empty, the back heavy and dark.

He drew to a halt at the end of the driveway. This was long, snaking through a front yard that had once been striking in its design and planting. Maria's work. It was still presentable—this neighborhood had its share of hard-working Mexican gardeners, too—but had lost focus, and looked dead in the moonlight. Ryan's house was hidden from the street by a stand of

FAILURE

cypress trees, but Jonathan could hear the faint sounds of music. There was a party going on, evidently. A party for two.

He took a deep breath and started up the driveway, knowing this was an event he had to break up, before a little boy grown big started to snarl and shout, before he swept his arm across the table. Before something got broken.

On the other side of the trees he saw a light in the kitchen. The music was coming from there, too.

When he got to the window, however, he could see the room was empty. A bottle of wine stood on the counter, half-empty. Ryan's jacket had been thrown over a chair. Nearby on the floor lay a pair of black high-heeled shoes.

Jonathan moved silently to the french doors. He let himself in. The music was very loud. Grotesquely so. He hadn't done much preparation for this moment. All he saw ahead was telling the girl to get out of here, then trying to have a conversation with his son.

Assuming he wasn't too late.

He felt panicky, wondering whether he should have driven right up to the street instead of parking down the way. Surely half-an-hour wouldn't have been enough for things to have gotten out of hand, even if that's what Ryan had intended all along?

And assuming his son wasn't innocent after all?

In a break between songs Jonathan heard the sound of voices, deeper in the house. A woman's voice.

That was a relief, but he had to stop wasting time.

He hurried into the corridor on the other side of the kitchen and toward the door which led to the large living space at the heart of the house. He heard the woman's voice again, raised this time.

He started to run, bursting into the living room. The main lights were off, the area illuminated only by dim lamps. He stopped, staring at the figure tied to the chair in the center of the space, head slumped forward. At the pool of blood on the floor in front of it.

"Who the fuck are you?"

Jonathan whirled to see the woman standing right behind him. Her eyes were hard but she looked amused. It was the girl his son had picked up from the Jury Room, and she was holding a long, sharp knife.

Seen closer, he half-recognized her. "What...are you doing?" he asked.

"Oh," she said, stepping closer. "It's Daddy. Huh."

The figure tied to the chair raised his head. "Dad?" he said. His voice was hoarse. "Is that you?"

Jonathan saw that his son's face was badly cut. One eye appeared punctured. When he took a step closer it became more evident that the liquid on the hardwood floor around him was not just blood, but urine too.

He turned back to the girl. "Let him go."

"Sooooooo not going to happen," she said, flipping the knife so it spun a languid 360 degrees in the air. The handle smacked back into her palm, loudly establishing her level of acquaintanceship with the weapon. "This isn't good, Jonathan. This is...*not okay*."

"I can make him stop."

"Doubt it. That's not the point anyway, as you well know. The *point* is that he's crap at it. The cops in this town are dumb as a sack of rocks, but if *you* managed to put it together, sooner rather than later they will too. Then what?"

"He gets arrested. And it stops."

"No. Then the police and the media start nosing around your family. Are you sure all *your* bodies are buried deep enough, Jonathan? That none of the girls you've met on your evening drives are ever going to be found? And are you sure Ryan won't remember some evening when he was super-small and supposed to be asleep, a night you and Elaine held a party for our special friends, and little boy Ryan maybe peeked out his window and saw bad funky stuff happening out there at the dark back-end of the garden? From what I hear Elaine was *quite* the party girl once, though she always left the wet work to you. Personally, that's my favourite part."

"He won't talk. He never saw anything. I made sure of it."

"No? So how come he's out there hurting people? And how come he's so fucking *bad* at it?"

The girl picked a bag off the nearest chair and put the knife inside. She didn't put the bag back down, however, or pull her hand back out. "You know

FAILURE

the deal," she said. "Either the kids don't know anything about what we do, or else you train them up so they're *better* than you at it. Generation upon generation. This *has not happened* here, Jonathan. Your boy is the worst of both worlds—and whose fault is that?"

"Mine," he said, numbly.

"Dad?" Ryan said, his voice slurred. "What are you talking about?"

"Let him go," Jonathan asked, again. What was the girl's name—Miranda? Cassandra? Something like that. He now recalled seeing her, briefly, at a very private party at someone else's house, down in Los Angeles, seven or eight or ten years ago. She'd been very young then, not much more than a child, but laughed and clapped with ferocious glee when blood started to spill: the kid of someone who'd done a much better job of passing their secret world on, of pulling their child into the fold. "I'll make it right."

"Too late," she said.

"You're nobody. You don't get to make that call."

"Screw you, and anyway I'm not making it. This is from the top. The Upright Man himself. You failed. End of story."

"Not just me," he said, grimly. "You think no-one will remember you being with him in that bar tonight? If he dies, someone who looks like you will be suspect number one. The assholes in the Jury Room may be drunk out of their minds, but they'll remember you—and *they'll* talk to the cops."

"It won't get that far. Not with the neat father-ends-his-errant-son's-miserable-life-and-then-takes-his-own scenario we're going to be giving them."

She brought her hand out of her bag, and held out a gun to him.

"Seriously? You expect me to do that?"

"I know you will. And not just because you understand the consequences if you don't. You'll do it because you're one of us, and you know the rules."

Jonathan took the gun. He looked at Ryan, still peering blearily at him with his terribly damaged little boy's face. They hadn't wanted him to kill. He and Elaine had done everything they could to keep him away from the life, in fact, going against everything the group was supposed to stand for. They had loved Ryan, very much, even when he was bad and ill-tempered. Even when he'd been hard to love. Jonathan had tried to be a good father. He'd tried to bring his son up to be happy and healthy, even at the risk of putting himself in danger by failing to mistreat the boy in the ways prescribed.

In vain, it turned out, because somehow Ryan had found his own path to the same destination.

"Elaine's already dead, isn't she?"

The woman gestured toward a side-table. On it, Jonathan now realized, lay a copy of the current issue of *Sunset Magazine*. He doubted this was a periodical that Ryan read, and he knew where he'd very recently seen it, and in whose hands, and he remembered the 4Runner he'd seen parked just down the road from the house when he came out.

"You bitch. Why?"

"We tie up the loose ends. Have to. You know that."

Jonathan took the gun and walked over to Ryan. He put his hand on his son's head, gently. "I loved you," he said.

"Dad?"

Jonathan shot the boy through the temple. Then he raised the gun to his own head, and closed his eyes. "And I loved you most of all, my dear," he whispered, quietly, to Elaine. "I'll fight through all the ghosts we made, until I am by your side."

He pulled the trigger a second time.

When she was convinced that neither of the men were going to move ever again, the girl—whose name, the one she used most often at least, was indeed Cassandra—left the house, and walked away down the driveway.

She took the copy of *Sunset Magazine* with her.

She hadn't read that issue yet.

CHARMS

Once she reached the high street Carol's walk slowed. She took a few deep breaths and shrugged her shoulders to dislodge some of the tenseness, making slow fists of her hands and releasing them quickly, as if trying to flick off insects. The street was crowded in the sunshine, and she threaded her way down the wide pavement, wondering where to go. She had no reason to be in town, and before her parents had started arguing had been looking forward to a desultory afternoon at their house.

Then something had happened.

Nothing unusual; the same old thing. Whatever it was.

She always missed it, somehow, the actual moment when things turned sour. Most of the time being at home was like wading in a stream of warm flowing water, comforting and secure. She knew the history of everything in every room, and the spaces were secure, dependable. So too her parents: Mother would potter about in the kitchen, asking her how she was, what she was doing; Father would read the paper and listen to her answers while Mother pounced in with another question.

Then the warmth would be gone, as if Carol had carelessly stepped into a deep cavity filled with icy water. Suddenly the air was taut with the unspoken, and objects seemed to stand isolated with an unpleasant starkness, cut adrift from each other, as what her parents said to each other started to take on cutting subtexts. Until she'd left home Carol had subconsciously blamed her father, probably because it was always him who ended up storming out of the room. Distance had helped her see that her mother was at least as much to blame.

She'd left the house fifteen minutes after stepping into the cold. By that time Mother was furiously cooking unnecessary brownies, and Father was in his study. As she walked down the drive Carol winced at the music coming loudly from the window. The arguments always ended in the same way—with her mother burying herself in trivia, and her father in his study, sitting bolt upright in his chair and listening to his old 45's. Early Beatles, Stones. Other bands whose names fate hadn't blessed with memorability. Carol had never been able to hear those songs with pleasure, and always flinched when they came on at parties now. They were irretrievably associated with suddenly finding herself in a wasteland, lost between two warring factions whose feelings and grievances she had never understood.

Everyone in the high street seemed to have somewhere to go, urgent tasks to perform. A glance at their faces showed they weren't even seeing their surroundings, just running breathlessly on rails. Carol felt strangely dislocated, in a town that was no longer hers, wandering aimlessly among projectile people as they ricocheted from car to shop to shop to car. At last a task occurred to her, and she crossed the street and headed for Tony's Records. It was her mother's birthday in a couple of weeks, and she might not get a chance for a leisurely shop again before then. She could probably find something in the record store her mother would like, though she'd have to be diplomatic about giving it to her.

Her mother had a CD player, and classical tastes. Her father had his 45's. And never, it appeared, did the twain meet. She'd always been a little perplexed by that, as it had been her father who had encouraged her to have piano lessons when she was young. Every now and then she caught a glimpse of something irrational between her parents, something made so rigid and obscure by time that even they probably didn't understand it any more. The still water between them ran very deep, and the smallest coin created huge ripples. She'd give her mother the CD on the quiet.

Saturday afternoon in Loughton was a time for the big guns of shopping, the DIY mercenaries and the Sainsburys SWAT teams. The record shop was almost deserted, and as she headed for the classical CDs she cast a glance at the only other customer. He was in his late forties, and she was a little surprised to notice herself finding him rather attractive. Older men weren't her thing at all, but there was something about him that kept the eye.

The classical section of Tony's was laughably small, market forces evidently having declared proper music played by actual musicians to be a cultural dead end. The single rack of CDs hung like an appendix on the end of the Soul section, and in five years it probably wouldn't be there at all. But by then Tony's would probably have folded anyway, and you'd have to go twenty miles to buy music from a hyperstore the size of Denmark.

For just a moment, Carol suddenly felt terribly old.

She spent five minutes flicking irritably through the CDs, trying to find something that wasn't either music from a TV advert or Nigel bloody Kennedy playing the Four sodding Seasons. She was about to give up when a hand reached from beside her and plucked a double CD case from the 'B' section.

'What about this?'

Startled, Carol turned to see the other customer standing beside her. Now that she could see his face properly she couldn't imagine how she could have thought him middle-aged. He was no more than early thirties, and had a smile that was younger still.

'Are you buying for yourself,' he asked, 'or someone else?' His grin was infectious, and Carol found herself returning it.

'For my mother.'

He nodded, and looked at her for a moment. 'I think these, then.'

He handed her the CD, and she turned it over to read the cover. It showed a relatively youthful Paul Tortelier, sternly poised behind a cello.

'Bach Solo Cello Suites,' she said, looking up at him. 'I don't think I know them. Are they nice?'

He frowned at her. 'They're not "nice", no. To the best of my knowledge they have not helped sell a single brand of car, bank or nationalized industry.'

She laughed. 'Good. They sound perfect.'

'Would you like an ice cream?'

Carol double-took at the question, but the offer was evidently serious. She shrugged. 'Why not?'

As she waited for the teenaged assistant behind the counter to remember that she had a role to play in helping customers make purchases, Carol glanced at the man. He was waiting near the door, and raised his eyebrows at her. She smiled at him, then turned back. For some reason she felt quite excited. From the minute he'd first spoken to her she'd known that he wasn't trying to pick her up. She'd fielded more than enough charming lechers and drink-buying madmen to be able to tell immediately. He had talked to her because he wanted to, nothing more. And when he'd spoken, he'd spoken to her, to Carol, not just to a pretty girl who might be worth a try.

It was so unusual it was a bit weird. But nice.

On the first warm day, suburban England goes into Summer mode as if a giant switch has been thrown. Men walk around with no shirts on while still wearing trousers, every moron with a white car cruises the high street pumping out anonymous dance music, and sure enough, there was an ice cream van only ten yards down the street. The man's courteousness in ordering their ice creams so blew the frazzled kiosk attendant's mind that he even got a smile from her. Then he led Carol to the bench that sat beneath the one tree in the high street.

As she sat and lapped her cone, Carol felt curiously cool and calm, and she turned to look at the man. 'So why that CD?'

'What brought you out to this mayhem this afternoon?'

'I asked first,' Carol said. As she did so she felt a faint brush of embarrassment, then realized she didn't really feel embarrassed at all. It was like being with someone back in the days when things were simple, when you didn't have jealous ex-boyfriends on your back, and weren't talking to someone with a closet full of hang-ups and probably a wife somewhere in the background; when the game had been fun, instead of just a tortuous and repetitive way of ending up with a record collection you didn't even recognize any more.

'And I shall answer,' he smiled. 'Eventually.'

'Well, I came out,' Carol paused, then decided to go on anyway. 'I came out because my parents were having a row.'

'Over what?'

'Over nothing. Over everything. I don't know.'

CHARMS

He nodded, and she noticed that his eyes were very green, with a ring of brown round the irises. They reminded her of leaves, some fallen, some still on the trees, down by a stream in the autumn.

'I've never known. They're both...they're both so *nice*. I mean, individually, they're the two nicest people I know. They must have loved each other once, otherwise they wouldn't have married each other, but somewhere down the line...'

She trailed off. Somewhere down the line two people who had loved each other very much had simply drifted off course.

'Maybe something happened, maybe nothing,' the man said.

Carol looked up at him, startled but grateful to realize that he'd picked up the train of her thoughts. Then she looked down at her lap again.

Something had simply gone wrong somewhere, and now her father sat in his study listening to old records that had lost their magic, and her mother grew old in the living room. She found her eyes filling with tears. Although she'd thought about her parents many times, she'd never had the realization before. This was all they had, it wasn't working, and they were just waiting for everything to be over.

Maybe something, maybe nothing. That's all it had taken.

It wasn't fair, wasn't right that people who had loved each other should end up bound together by their feelings for two people who weren't there anymore, and she suddenly felt very miserable.

The man turned from looking out across the road, and smiled gently at her. 'Shall I tell you what I like about that CD?'

She nodded. She was happy to listen to him talk about anything.

'Bach is very different to any other composer,' he said. 'When you listen to Vivaldi, or Handel, you can tell that the music was composed for an audience. It's like a blockbuster film: it's good, but it's good because it's *supposed* to be good. It's been designed that way. When you listen to Bach, it's different. You're not being performed to. You're being allowed to overhear.'

An open-topped white Golf cruised by, spilling trance jungle garage at a volume that would have had Led Zeppelin shaking their heads in grim disapproval.

The man smiled. 'Ten years from now, no-one will be listening to that crap any more, thank God. It's moment music, no more. But it's the same with the better stuff too. All the old 45's stashed in people's rooms, they're like a butterfly collection. They look as if they're still alive, as if they could fly away, but they've been dead for decades. Old feelings and memories pinned to pieces of vinyl. In a hundred years no-one will have associations for those songs any more, and most of them will be dead. But in five hundred years, a thousand years, when people sit in houses on planets we don't even know exist yet, they'll still listen to Bach, and they'll still hear the same things. It's like listening to a charm. It doesn't fade.'

His smile broadened, ridiculing the flamboyance of what he was saying. She smiled back, properly this time. He nodded approvingly.

'Better. And there's something else about that record, too.' He reached across and took the CD from her. 'Look. Recorded in 1961. When you listen to it, remember that.'

Slightly puzzled, she smiled again. 'I will. But you still haven't answered my question. And I'm intrigued now, I want to go listen to this and it's not even for me.'

'Well, maybe you should.'

'But,' Carol fought hard, but then said it as simply as she could. 'It's nice being with you.' *Great*, she thought. *You sound, what—about fourteen years old?*

'That's alright,' the man said. 'I'll come with you, if I may.'

Carol leapt at the chance. Apart from anything else, her turning up with a guest might diffuse the atmosphere back at the house. Her parents always liked meeting people she knew.

'Of course, I mean, yes. I'll say I bumped into a friend by accident.'

Which wouldn't, she thought as they headed for his car, feel as if she was straying very far from the truth.

Carol knew nothing about cars, but there was something undeniably classic about his, a diffident and unassuming open-topped sports car in darkest green. It looked like something from another era that had lasted very well, like the deepest pockets of Epping Forest where the trees had never been pollarded, and still looked like trees.

There was a comprehensive-looking CD player built into the front console, but she couldn't see any CDs anywhere, and she didn't want to break the wrapping on the Cello Suites. It was still going to be a present for her mother, though not for her birthday, and it would only take a few minutes to get home.

When they pulled up in the drive all was quiet, and Carol knew from experience that her father would now be out in the garden, pottering quietly, thinking his own thoughts.

Her mother looked a little quiet when she opened the door, but brightened considerably on seeing Carol had a guest.

'Hi, Ma,' Carol said, 'I ran into a friend in town, thought I'd bring him home to meet you.'

'How nice,' her mother said warmly, reached out her hand.

Realizing too late she didn't know the man's name, Carol scrabbled and came up with one that would have to do.

'So, er...Mother—*Mark*, Mark—Mother.'

The man accepted this without batting an eyelid, and took her mother's hand. 'How do you do. I've heard a lot about you.'

'Oh, I hope not,' her mother laughed.

'Are you bored with people saying how alike you and Carol look?' he asked as she led them into the sitting room. Carol blinked: how did he know her name? Had she told him, and forgotten? She must have.

'No, not at all,' her mother giggled, and Carol stared at her curiously. She didn't think she'd ever heard her mother giggle before. Certainly not like that.

Carol felt the house relax about them as Mother set about making tea, chatting with the man. She'd never been like this with any of the boyfriends she'd brought home. Polite, yes, friendly in a reserved and parental way, but not like this. 'Vivacious' was something she hadn't realized her mother had in her armory.

'And that,' said the man, nodding out at the garden, 'is presumably your husband, Mrs. Peters?'

Carol steeled herself. It was generally a few hours after an argument before either of them would acknowledge the other's existence.

'Yes,' said her mother, 'that's John. And call me Gillian.'

'Okay,' he said, 'Is that your name?'

Giggling again, her mother punched him lightly on the shoulder and turned to hand Carol her tea. 'Your friend is a twit, Carol,' she said.

'Perhaps I should go introduce myself to your father,' the man said. His eyes drifted over the small package Carol held in her lap, and she realized that he was giving her a chance to present it to her mother undisturbed.

'Do you want me to...'

'No, I'll be fine.'

They watched him go, and then mother and daughter turned to each other.

'Well,' her mother said after a pause, 'if you're not going out with him yet you want to bloody well get a move on.'

They looked at each other soberly for a moment and then started laughing. When they tailed off, still hiccupping every now and then, Carol felt an enormous wave of relief. Not only had the tension in the house disappeared as it had never existed, but her mother looked so relaxed, so vital.

'I bought you a present,' she said.

Her mother hadn't heard the Suites either, and they decided to give the first one a quick listen. Carol settled back in her chair as her mother set up the CD, realizing that was something that she liked about her mother that she'd never noticed before. Most people past a certain age seemed to make a decision to refuse to come to terms with new technology. To give up, and become old. But not her mother: as she wielded the CD remote she looked just like Carol's flatmate Suz. Or like a capable older sister, the kind who goes off travelling round the world for six months, and doesn't come back with dysentery.

There was a faint hiss before the music started, and Carol remembered what the man had said. 'Recorded in 1961,' she observed to her mother, who nodded.

Then there was the sound of the cello.

It had something of the austere beauty of an equation, an irreducible expression, but it touched you very deeply: it was like seeing truth with your ears. It *was* like a charm, she realized, like looking at the inside of a perfect crystal and observing an expression of natural forces which you could appreciate but not understand. That was why you could often tell what was coming next when you listen to Bach. Not because it was predictable, but because it was *right*. When clouds darkened, it was going to rain: when they broke, the sun would shine. Some things happened after something else. That was all there was to it.

All her favourite songs, the albums in her flat and the battered singles archived in her old bedroom upstairs, they captured moments. This music captured time itself.

As they listened, she focused on every note as it passed, listening to sounds recorded in 1961: before the Beatles, before the Stones, before the Sixties themselves got into their stride. On the day those notes were recorded the world was a completely different place, yet however you listened to it, in those grooves, in that tape, in those digits, was 1961. Outside the room Tortelier was playing in was another room, where men with Brylcreamed hair ran an old-fashioned recording desk which was state-of-the-art to them. Behind them was a window, and outside the birds were singing. And somewhere out there would be a newspaper seller, and he'd be hawking papers with the date 1961 on them, maybe a Thursday. Perhaps if you listened hard enough you could hear him, and the moment had never really died.

As the Prelude finished, reducing itself to a broken chord which hung on the air, Carol turned and looked at her mother.

She was crying gently, and pressed the Stop button on the handset. Then she looked up at her daughter, and Carol saw that her mother had heard the same things.

In a different house, on a different planet, it would always be there to be heard.

Her mother wiped her eyes and smiled with genuine warmth. 'They've been out there a long time.'

They walked into the kitchen, to look out of the window into the back garden. The man was standing talking to her father, and though you couldn't hear what they were saying, her father's laugh drifted through the window to them. Carol glanced at her mother, and held her breath when she saw the expression on her face.

There was a faint smile on her lips, and small tears still in her eyes. It was the face of someone who was looking at a photo of a friend who'd died long ago, and finding that the mourning was not over yet.

When she spoke, her voice was fractured, and hesitant. 'It's funny. Standing out there, he looks just like he used to look.'

As they watched, the two men laughed again, and her father ran his hand carelessly back through his hair. Carol heard the intake of her mother's breath.

'He always...' Her mother reached her own hand up, and ran it gently through her own hair, at the side. 'I loved him for that.'

The two men burst into a fresh gale of laughter, her father almost doubling up. They looked like two young friends out there, planning some old-fashioned devilry, and it would be very easy to love either one of them. Tears ran down her mother's face.

'Mum—what happened?'

Her mother looked at her, her face clouded. 'Nothing,' she said, shaking her head with puzzled misery. 'Nothing that I can remember.'

The two men looked back towards the house, and then headed towards the back door, still talking.

'They're coming back,' her mother said, wiping her face with a tea towel. 'Is the tea still warm?'

As Carol poured two cups, the back door opened and her father came in, followed by the man. Her father made it halfway across the kitchen, and then stopped, faltering, rubbing his hands nervously on his hips. He looked about sixteen.

Carol watched her mother. She was looking at her husband, eyes bright and wide, also nervous. They seemed awkward, unsure of themselves, as if meeting for the first time, or after a long time apart.

Then her father ran his hand unconsciously through his hair, and Carol noticed his grace as he smiled tentatively, a lopsided grin that could break anyone's heart. Her mother handed him a cup of tea, not taking her eyes off his, head tilted to one side.

'Never mind tea,' said the man from behind her father. 'It's a lovely day. Let's drive.'

He led Carol out to his car, and she stood to one side to let her parents climb into the back seat, which they did with an agility Carol doubted she could have mustered. They settled back, and as Carol noticed her father's

CHARMS

hand brush her mother's, and saw her grab hold of it, her father drawled in a surprisingly good American accent.

'So what are we waiting for?'

The man pulled the car quickly out into the road and turned away from town, out to where the houses shaded away to fields. 'In the glove compartment,' he said quietly.

Carol opened it, found the CD, and slotted it in the machine. The sound of the cello whipped up into the wind as they flashed towards the country, but she believed that if you strained your ears hard enough, you could hear those sounds, you could hear that year: you could slip through that channel and step out into the fresh sunlight of that day. As the fields spread out beside them and the car shot out into the afternoon, her mother whooped deliriously, and Carol turned round to see them, faces bright and hair dancing in the wind, clasping each other tight and waving at the trees, the wheat, the birds.

THE BURNING WOODS

1

I'd been there a couple weeks before he mentioned the island, which I guess would make it the third or fourth time we'd talked. For the first few days he left me alone. I checked into the resort (a designation accurate only in the old-fashioned sense, of a collection of old, mossy cabins somewhere mountainous and remote) late one cold, dark afternoon, smelling of wood smoke and with one small suitcase and a demeanor that said company and conversation were nowhere on my list of priorities. It's possible Ralph had encountered people like me before. It's equally likely he was glad of anybody's money out of season and didn't give a damn.

He led me to the cabin furthest from his own, which stood in the middle of the compound and also served as the office. Mine had a sitting area with kitchenette, bedroom, basic bathroom, and a narrow deck along the front. It smelled damp but he showed me where the wood lay in a neat pile around the side and lit a starter fire in the grate while he explained what there was to explain. He told me the nearest store was a mile back down the road but I knew this already, having bought beer and cigarettes half an hour before. I'd kept the brim of my cap low while I gathered my goods and paid. Ralph further informed me that the nearest bar was three miles in the other direction and they served food from midday until eight most days but it wasn't great. Nearest actual town was another twenty miles beyond that.

Then he left me to it, wandering back in the direction of his cabin. A couple minutes later I heard his door shut.

I put my bag in the closet, not sufficiently confident of the duration of my stay to make it worth the five minutes of unpacking. I opened a beer instead and took it onto the deck where I sat in one of the battered chairs and smoked.

The cabin was sparsely surrounded by trees on all sides and backed up against where the forest started in earnest. About fifty yards below, at the bottom of a gentle slope, was the shore of the lake.

I could see four other cabins from where I sat, not including Ralph's. I'd seen nine hooks on the wall behind his desk so presumably there were additional ones not in line of sight. A thin hook of smoke spiraled out of the office chimney but from none of the others, and it was already cold and would get a lot colder when the light faded. That suggested Ralph had been telling the truth when he said I had the place to myself. I'd no reason to disbelieve him but I don't trust most things until I've established them for myself.

It was very quiet.

Twilight came seeping toward me from between the trees and off the surface of the frigid lake. He'd told me its name but it was a long adaptation of some Native American original and I forgot it immediately. It was very large, surrounded by thousands of acres of forest and dotted with small islands. It was right there in front of me.

I didn't need to know its name.

Over the next few days I settled in. I walked back down to the ramshackle general store and gathered further supplies from its few shelves. It dealt mainly in tinned goods and alcohol, basic provisions for small groups of men on their way into the woods for annual rebonding exercises. As these trips usually involve the attempted destruction of wildlife, the store also sold ammunition. I did not buy any. I did however allow the clerk to see my face this time. He was entirely uncurious.

I came back with a couple bags of things that could be turned into basic meals and when I'd put them on the shelf in the kitchen area decided I may as well unpack my suitcase too. I had just finished when I heard a knock on the cabin door.

I opened it to find Ralph standing diffidently on the porch. Tall, angular, a face of big planes, deep creases in his forehead, sharp in the lamp light. Late fifties. 'Just checking everything's working out for you.'

I'd seen him a couple times during the week, from afar, when setting off or returning from my excursions in the woods. These were not taken out of a desire to experience nature, which I can take or leave, but to maintain a basic level of fitness. I would walk for an hour, run for thirty minutes, repeat, until it was time to head back to the cabin. I set off at a different angle each day. I did not try to find a path because there aren't any. I had seen a lot of trees.

I had also stood on the shore of the lake, looking at the small islands in the distance. If you wanted, you could presumably drag a boat or kayak to the water and spend a day navigating between them. In summer, people likely did just that.

'Fine,' I told him. 'Need more wood soon, though.'

He pointed into the trees. 'Main pile is over there. You got enough for tonight?'

'Yes.'

'I'll bring some by in the morning.'

'I can do it, now I know where it's at.'

'It's what I'm here for. Anything else?'

I shook my head. He walked away. I stood a few minutes longer looking up at the sky. It was grey and frosted. Snow was coming.

It didn't fall that night, however, so I walked down to the store the next morning and this time bought some ammunition. Not much. Just enough.

2

A few evenings later the first snows came, enough to put a couple inches on the ground and the roof of the cabin. I sat on my deck and watched it slowly fall. After a while I saw Ralph trudging from cabin to cabin in the half-light, making sure they were mothballed against the heavier falls to come. As he passed he looked up at me.

'Shipshape?'

'As it's gonna be.' He stood looking around into a gloom flecked with falling white. 'We're closed now,' he said. 'For the winter.'

'But I'm good?'

'From what I seen, you being here is no more trouble than you not being here.'

I had a six-pack on the deck next to the chair. I lifted one out, held it up. He thought a moment, came up and sat in the other chair.

We each drank one, in silence, and he left.

Next morning I made a few trips to the wood pile, making sure I had plenty for the days ahead. I took another walk to the store in the late afternoon, laying in supplies in advance of the first inevitable heavy snow fall. On my way back, on a whim, I kept going past the turn-off to the cabins.

The bar up the road was a featureless oblong with a door and a sign. The parking lot was empty. Inside was a deserted pool table of considerable age, a non-functioning juke box and three people drinking in silence. I stood at the counter for ten minutes. Nobody appeared, and none of the patrons offered an explanation. I left.

The night I dreamed of a house. I was inside and it was long and low and it was humid and dark and I was running. I passed a wall covered in a spray of blood. As I turned the corner I realized I had a gun in my hand, its muzzle pressed into my own temple. I ran faster.

When I woke, the world was white.

I went out into the woods but only for half a day. Impossible to run in the snow, hard to even walk any distance. The edge of the lake was turning opaque, icing up. I stepped a couple of feet out onto it, heard it cracking.

That evening I sat on the deck again. It was so quiet that I heard the click of Ralph's cabin door opening. I turned my head and watched, curious as to why he'd come out. He didn't seem clear on the subject either. He lurched a few yards and then came to a standstill, visible at the edge of the glow from the lamp above his door. Stood, as if listening for something. Then glanced in the direction of my cabin.

THE BURNING WOODS

I lifted the hand in which I was holding a bottle of beer. He seemed to take this as an invitation. Perhaps it was.

He stayed longer this time, and we talked a little. I learned he'd inherited the place from his father and spent the last thirty years running it. That it got busy in the summer, people come to fish and kayak around the lake, grilling up a storm in the evenings. That the reason I hadn't been able to get served at the bar was the proprietor was a drinker and spent a portion of every off-season day passed out on a pile of sacking in the back. Regulars knew to serve themselves and leave payment on the bar, even adding a tip, because the owner was basically a decent guy and if the place shut down there'd be nowhere to go to escape their lives for a while, and being trapped in your home with your beloved family for weeks at a time can be a heavy burden for all concerned.

I learned also that Ralph read a lot, armfuls of secondhand paperbacks from a thrift store twenty miles up the road in Renton, where he drove once a month for supplies. That his wife died ten years ago of cancer. No children.

I learned all this while we drank three beers, in no special hurry. He didn't learn anything about me.

3

More days passed. It snowed, twice heavily. Walking in the woods became an exercise in frustration. I did it anyway, though I stuck mainly to the shore of the lake. The ice gradually spread further over the water. I stood for a time one afternoon looking down through its frosting at the pebbles and rocks beneath, before squatting and using my knuckles to break the thin coating of ice. I picked up a stone and turned it over in my cold fingers. An anonymous piece of rock, rounded by millions of years of history, none of which mattered or would ever be known. Countless small events over a span twenty times longer than the tenancy of humankind on the earth. Now lying there, on the edge of a frigid lake in the back of nowhere, its past and future amounting to nothing because it was on the way nowhere. No path, no trajectory, nothing to wait for except the waiting itself. I would in all probability be the only person to ever pay it attention. To weigh it, examine it. To whom it would be real. There were countless others like it around this lake—cold, muddy pebbles of no importance—and unless they happened to scrape the underside of your boat, you'd never know or care.

I considered keeping the pebble, raising it above its peers, making it something, instead of just a thing, but I had no need for it and dropped it back onto the ice a yard from where I'd found it, another random step along its stoic progress through time.

I walked away feeling as if it was watching me go but knowing I hadn't even been a blink in its life. I wondered if God felt the same about me.

Or if he thought about any of us, at all.

That night I had to call Ralph over to the cabin because the stove wasn't functioning properly. Normally I like to fix things myself but propane is something I fundamentally distrust.

He fiddled around until he had it working again. When he reopened his bag to put his tools back I saw a six-pack in there. He didn't hurry to close the bag. He'd drunk my beer. I knew he'd feel this should be returned in kind, if not tonight then soon. It might as well be now.

'I could help lessen the load you got there.'

'Hoped that might be the case,' he said.

It was too cold to sit out on the deck. I had a fire going. We sat in chairs on opposite sides.

'Snow getting in the way of your hiking, huh.'

'I'll be out again tomorrow, though.'

'Looking for something?'

'Like what?'

'I don't know,' he said. 'Just until the last few days you've been out there eight hours at a stretch. That's a lot of walking. Wondered if you were looking for something.'

'Nothing in particular,' I said.

'Find much?'

'Trees.'

He nodded, took a sip. 'Used to walk a lot too, back in the day. When my wife was alive. Felt like I needed time to myself then. Now she's gone and it's all I've got.'

THE BURNING WOODS

'A person needs space.'

'I guess. Though now I think maybe I could have survived with less of it. And I never found anything either.'

'Except trees.'

He smiled. 'Plenty of those. I did use to go looking for something, though, sometimes.'

'What?'

'The burning woods.'

'The what?'

He shook his head ruefully. 'My dad told me about them one time. Like a bedtime story. He said there was part of the forest that was on fire, always had been.'

'How would that work?'

He shrugged. 'Special trees, he said—that grew and then burned up and grew again from the ashes. He said you could get there and back in a day, if you went in the right direction and it was the right time for you to find it. I fell asleep while he was telling me, and maybe that's why it stuck. Got into my mind by the back route. I used to go looking, anyway, and maybe I even half-believed in them. Started again when I took to walking later in life. Didn't believe then, of course. Though maybe I wanted to.'

'Like how older kids go along with the idea of Santa,' I said. 'Because it'd be nicer if it was true. And there are times when you need something to look for. Whether it's real or not.'

'True, both. But I didn't find it.'

'Sometimes that's better.'

'Maybe. And could be the whole thing was just his way of getting me out of the house for the day, too. Dads are cunning with that crap. Mine was, anyway.'

We drank and looked at the fire. I thought about my own father, but found it difficult to bring anything to mind.

'Pretty sure I saw the island once, though,' he said.

'The island?'

I could see him wondering whether he should have mentioned this, whatever it was. I didn't press. But I opened a couple more beers. He sat looking into the flames. I waited. Eventually he spoke again.

'That one, it was Granddad told me. I don't know if he even told my dad. Dad never mentioned it.'

'Your grandfather owned this place before?'

'He built it. He was the most antisocial human being I ever met. People were just not his thing. Yet he built this camp around their homestead—that fell apart years ago, but it used to be where my cabin is now—and so he wound up spending most of the year having to deal with people. A lot of them, pretty dumb people.'

'No other way to earn a living, maybe.'

'No, he could of. He was uncanny good at trapping. Had lines going out into the woods in all directions. Could catch anything, skin it after, make it look like it never died.'

'Enough to support a family?'

Ralph shrugged. 'Maybe not. But I asked him about the resort one time, why he built it. He told me that when you lived in a place like this, it was a good idea to have people around. I pushed him on it, a few weeks later, one night when the place was full and everybody was partying loud. How could he like having all these people up in his face, when he was such a solitary soul that even the company of his own family seemed to try his patience a lot of the time? He said "Didn't say I liked it. Said it was a good idea".'

'What'd he mean by that?'

'I have no idea. He'd already answered two questions in a row. I didn't push my luck. You knew my grandfather, you wouldn't either. He was okay some of the time but others it'd be like he was hanging around for something he knew was never going to come, and had gotten tired of the process.'

I stayed quiet, assuming Ralph would get back to the island he'd mentioned. We'd finished his six-pack and started on one of mine, though, and his mind had begun to go in slow circles.

'I talked with my dad about the burning woods one other time, which is what made me wonder if maybe it wasn't just a story. Though he was dying of cancer then and cruising high on pain drugs, so maybe it didn't mean anything. There's a lot of waiting when someone's leaving that way. You can run out of things to say. One afternoon I told him I'd gone looking for the burning woods when I was a kid. I was twenty-five by then. Guess I was trying

THE BURNING WOODS

to signal that the guy he was handing over to wasn't a child any more. That I understood it had been a joke, and I was older now. Man enough to take his place. My dad nodded, and I figured that was that, maybe he'd got my point, maybe not, and probably he was going to sleep now. But then he said "I think I nearly found them".'

'Huh.'

'Well, right. So I told him—I thought you were just kidding. He shook his head. His father told him about them, and just like me—he knew I'd gone out looking, day after day, I don't know how he knew, but he knew—he'd tried to find them. One afternoon it was cold, bitter cold, but the sky was frosting over. He knew snow would be coming soon so he walked harder and faster than usual, and instead of stopping and turning around at midday—my granddad had told him it was a half day hike, like he'd told me—he kept going. Meanwhile the sky's getting heavier and darker and lower. It's coming on for three o'clock and he knows he's got himself in a pickle and it's time to turn round now because he's got the same hike back plus his legs are a lot tireder than they were. But then...he saw something.'

'What?'

'A glow. Up ahead, through the trees. You've spent time in these woods now. You know what you're going to see.'

'Silvers, dark green, greys, black.'

'Right. Ain't nothing that glows. A kind of yellow with some orange in it, he said. Way up ahead. So now he doesn't know what to do. He really wants to go on. His father never found the burning woods. So he wants to. He wants to be the one. But it's late already. And finally it starts to snow. For a while it's just a light fall, like how it started here last week. But then it comes on stronger and stronger. He's got his work cut out getting home already. With this kind of snow? He's grown up in these woods and he knows he's putting himself in danger with every minute he dicks around.'

'So what did he do?'

'He turned back. And good call, say I. Otherwise I wouldn't be here right now. And still he barely made it. There was a record fall that year and a lot of it came down that first day and night. He didn't get home until two in the morning, half-dead, probably three-*quarters* dead by the time his mother finished bawling him out for scaring her to death. My grandmother was a small woman but I wouldn't have bet against her in a bar fight.'

'Did your dad try to get back there?'

'Of course. Wasn't able to for a few days, though, until he'd got his strength back. And guess what?'

'He couldn't remember where he's seen the glow.'

'Not a clue. He'd tried to mark it on the way back but gave up and focused on staying alive and anything he'd left was buried with snow for weeks, and gone by the time it thawed. He never saw the glow again.'

'So maybe it's true after all.'

'Or maybe not. He died a couple hours after he told me that story. Could be he was confused and it wasn't a memory of anything that happened, and instead he was talking about some other kind of light. A light he could see in the distance that afternoon, as he lay dying.'

I waited to see if Ralph would say anything more about the island but he just finished his beer and left.

4

Next afternoon I found myself standing on the edge of the lake again. This time I did not look down at the pebbles but at the water itself. It was grey/blue. The nearest of the islands was a couple hundred feet away. It was small, home to six trees, tall and straight and meaningless in the context of the hundreds of thousands in the forest.

There's something about an island, though. The fact that it's set apart from the land, and from the water, even from other islands—no matter how similar they may be, or how close—confers a singularity upon it. Every island is different to every other island, because it is an island.

And John Donne was wrong. Not every man is a piece of the continent, or a part of the main. Some men are just islands. We know that. It's why we're drawn to islands in the first place. To the idea of being an island on an island.

Never having to listen to any bell tolling but your own, and you never hear that one until it's too late to do anything but sing along.

THE BURNING WOODS

***

Ralph didn't seem surprised when I said I was thinking about going out on the lake. He'd evidently been expecting it.

'The islands are there,' he said. 'Limit to how long a man's going to be able to resist setting foot on one.'

He asked if I'd used a kayak before and I said yes. He took me to the shed where they were stored for the winter and handed me a life jacket. We both knew I wasn't going to wear it. He asked if I wanted help moving the craft to where I could get it in the water and I said no.

'Beer, later?'

'Sure,' I said.

I dragged the kayak down across the snow using the rope loop at the front provided for the purpose. I had to keep dragging it for a while, as the lake had iced up twenty yards from the shore, and was barely deep enough to navigate for another twenty after that.

The gloves I had were not thick and my hands were very cold before I even got in the kayak. My weight pushed it down onto pebbles and I was reminded of the one I'd looked at a few days ago. I had to shove at the lake bottom for several minutes with the paddle before the kayak started to move more freely.

But then suddenly it was floating, carrying me out into the silence. The sky was low and white. The water was silver-grey. Except for when my paddle touched the water everything was utterly without sound, the quietest place I had ever been.

There were no birds.

I'd been on the lake for an hour before I decided to head toward an island. It took that long for me to get over the initial rush of moving freely, after days of trudging through snow and weeks tramping through forest undergrowth. I felt as though I could paddle forever, but knew this was an illusion. I'd already done enough that I was going to feel it in my arms and shoulders the next day. And it's as well to remember—when you do anything in life—that you're not just going outward. You have to conserve the energy to get back to where you started. And you've got to remember where it was.

MICHAEL MARSHALL SMITH

The nearest island was a hundred yards away. It was thirty yards long, twenty across, dropping steeply into the lake without a shore. I paddled round until I found an accessible tree root and tied up to it. Knowing there was a good chance I was about to wind up in the freezing water, I steadied the kayak as best I could and grabbed the root. I wondered whether I should go find an easier island instead, but that would have felt like a defeat.

So I pulled hard and pushed up with my legs. The kayak tried to fly out backward, but the knot held.

I kept pulling, reaching out and grabbing another root with my other hand and jamming one foot into the mud. I didn't fall. My gloved hands weren't secure on the slippery roots, however, so I went straight to scrabbling up the slope, keeping my movements steady and even so I didn't slip.

One end of the island held a few trees, the same green-black pines that filled the forest around the lake. The other was just mossy rock. I walked around it. As a quantity of space it felt constrained—because it was surrounded by water—but not oppressively so. It was about the same area that most of us live out the bulk of our lives in, after all: the size of a house with a small yard. The amount of space we're used to. The size of the average human cage.

It wasn't clear what I'd achieved, but returning to the kayak was going to be even harder than getting out of it, so I hung around a while, smoking and looking out across the lake. I stood on the side I'd come from, then went and stood on the other. The difference still felt clear, and I wondered how far from your starting point you had to go before that ceased to be the case, before you'd truly left the place you were before. The point where you became committed. There's probably no kind of math that will work that out. It depends how much you're leaving behind, and what kind of person you are, and what—if anything—you hope to find in the other direction. How far you're prepared to keep walking without looking back.

I managed to get back in the kayak without incident. I paddled back to the resort and spent the afternoon in front of the fire, looking into the flames. Ralph came over in the evening and we drank a few beers but didn't talk much.

I thought I would sleep well, but I did not. Smoke from the dying fire seemed to permeate the cabin, lying over me like a shroud. In the middle of the night I was woken by something like the sound of a gunshot, very close by, almost as though it was in the room. It must have been a branch outside breaking under the weight of snow.

But the echo seemed to go on for a long time.

5

When I got up next morning the sky was low and heavy. My arms and shoulders felt tight. On the back of these facts it made sense to walk in the woods instead of going out on the water again. Or to simply stay indoors.

Ralph was standing by his cabin smoking as I dragged the kayak down toward the shore. He'd told me his wife didn't like the smell and so smoking had always been something he did outdoors. Even after ten years of living alone it seemed this was still true. The dead get their way more than the living, it seems.

He glanced up at the sky. I didn't say anything.

I took it easy at first. One of the advantages of having no destination is that slow will get you there as quick as fast.

I was soon out past the island I'd visited the day before. As soon as you've been so far, it becomes near, and you can't help but wonder what's past it. I kept going.

The next few islands were small, including one barely a couple of yards across and home to a single tree. It was the most solitary thing I'd ever seen, and I wondered what John Donne would have had to say about it.

There was a patch of open water after that, but I didn't feel done. As I paddled out into it the first flakes started to come down. It was quite something to be moving near-silently across the water, while snow dropped all around.

The fall was light. I figured it would stay that way for a while.

It started to come down in earnest when I was on another island. I'd been there only a few minutes and had already decided to leave—the sole reason I'd visited was it had a conveniently gentle slope on one side, and a few feet of rocky shoreline, making it an easier proposition than the one I'd been on the day before. But there was nothing to see. Just a piece of rock, without even the distinction of being the first I'd stood upon. I ate half the sandwich I'd brought with me and decided I was done being there.

As I walked back to the kayak the snow increased in volume, suddenly, all at once, as if someone had turned a knob. Nothing like a blizzard—six on the dial at most, not all the way up to ten—but pretty hard all the same.

I got in the kayak and pushed back, knowing now was the time to head home. It was beautiful, though. Within a couple of minutes I couldn't see the island I'd just left—it, or anything else. A shifting curtain of falling white, appearing as if by magic out of a steel-grey sky, now hung so low it felt like I could reach up and touch it.

I let my reversing strokes carry me around in a half circle and then started forward again. Slow, measured back and forths, until I hit a rhythm that felt eternal, forging out into the white, squinting to stop it going in my eyes.

I had no idea what direction I was going, and it didn't matter. There was no destination. My mind blanked out but my muscles kept moving, as if grateful to have stillness in which to do their work for once. It is a blessed relief when you stop trying to think, when you commit to a course and keep going. It was certainly the closest I had felt to peace in a long time, and after a while I stopped having any sense of where I was or what I was doing.

6

I don't know how long it was before I came back into myself.

The process was sudden. I had been somewhere else, deep in my head, and then I was back in reality—warm under my coat, but very cold at the extremities, unable to feel my fingers, my ears hurting, aware that the snow falling around me was even thicker than before. The front of the kayak had over an inch lying on it.

I stopped paddling, let the craft keep moving under its own momentum. Looked around.

I couldn't see a damned thing.

THE BURNING WOODS

The day before, the whole time I'd been out on the lake, either the shore or an island had been in view, however distantly and however small. Now there was nothing to be seen in any direction, and of course that was partly due to snow reducing visibility to thirty feet but for all I knew I'd got myself out into a portion of the lake where there weren't any islands. And so nothing to navigate by.

As soon as I'd had this thought, I realized it was dumb. For an unknown period (I don't wear a watch, but some internal clock said at least half an hour, maybe longer) I'd been driving myself out into nothingness. In a straight line, theoretically, but I'm not a good enough kayaker that it would have been absolutely straight, and so there was actually no telling where I was now, and any fixed point I found would tell me nothing other than that I was…here.

The snow was now up to around eight on the dial with no sign of slackening, and I accepted the fact that I'd got myself into something of a situation.

When you're young there's an unspoken assumption that everything can be put right, pulled back on track. You feel this partly because most of your missteps are in truth pretty small, within the parameters of common human error, and you have other people—usually your parents—with the experience and compassion to reach out, lift you up, and put you back on the rails.

Then you get older, and experience shows there are actions for which there is no undo button. With most of these you just reconcile yourself to taking the hit, sometimes a big one, and steer cautiously forward into an altered future.

But there are some dark days and nights where you realize you've gone ahead and rowed yourself right off the edge of the world. Where you do something that feels as natural and right as continuing to paddle, but find you've gone the wrong way and there's no road back, that you were burning the path behind you with every step you took—and are now in freefall.

I didn't think I was in trouble that serious. Yet. I was cold but continuing to row would keep my core temperature elevated. The kayak was made of very thick plastic and had evidently been bashed around plenty in the past without springing a leak. I had a little food left. It could be worse.

I basically had two options. Stay where I was, hoping the snow dropped and visibility increased. There was no reason to believe this would happen any time soon, and I was mindful of tales Ralph had told about years where it had dropped steadily for two days straight. The alternative was to head back to base, as best I could.

I let the kayak cruise to a halt while I considered the question, but really I'd decided as soon as the choice was articulated in my mind. I made sure the paddle was secure across my lap and got out the rest of the sandwich. I ate every scrap and then used the wrapping as a half-assed shovel to get some snow up to my mouth. I'd sweated a lot already and dehydration would do more harm than hunger, ironic though that would be, given where I was. The chances were the lake water was drinkable, but I'd put myself sufficiently at risk.

Then I took the paddle and cautiously turned round a hundred and eighty degrees, or as near as I could judge it.

The view looked exactly the same in that direction. The snow was still coming down relentlessly. I felt a twist of panic in the pit of my stomach, and waited it out. Setting off fast would be a dumb idea. The feeling faded.

I dipped the right tip of the paddle into the water and pulled it back, then did the same on the other side.

It seemed to take longer than it should for the kayak to come up to speed, as if the water was thickening, freezing up. That made no sense, though. Or at least I hoped it didn't. More likely it was my tired, cold arms protesting against being put back to work. I was going to be hurting in bed tonight.

Assuming I made it back there.

Within a few minutes I started to warm, the kayak moving smoothly in what I hoped was the right direction. Slow and steady should get me to the general area of where I'd been.

Wherever that was.

I told the doubting parts of my mind to shut up, and settled to sustained work. But a few minutes later I stopped again, staring into the snow ahead.

At first I wondered if it was merely an especially thick patch of snow fall. Wind was starting to pick up, making the snow chaotically variable in both strength and direction.

The kayak kept moving forward, however, and soon it was clear that it was something else.

THE BURNING WOODS

An island.

Visibility was too bad to get a sense of how big it was, but the curve of the craggy rock face ahead and the size of the trees on top suggested it was notably larger than any previous ones I'd seen.

On my current course I was going to run right into it. And that wasn't good. It meant I couldn't have turned the kayak around accurately, because I would have had to have come right *through* this island to get to where I'd been when I stopped. Evidently I hadn't judged the hundred and eighty degree turn perfectly. But logic said that I must have at least come *past* this island, sufficiently to the side that I hadn't been able to see it in the snow. So what I had to do now was angle to the left and head in that direction.

Maybe this was even good news. Without the island to demonstrate my turning error, I could have continued paddling in a direction that must be at least twenty degrees wrong.

I made the maneuver and started off.

I watched the side of the island as I paddled alongside, realizing another option would be to hole up on it instead. I didn't know how long it was going to take for the snow to slacken, however, and while there might be shelter up among the trees, it would remain a very cold way of spending a number of hours, more likely the night. It must be getting toward mid-afternoon, which meant only an hour or two of light remained, at best. If trying to paddle back to the resort in a snowstorm was dumb, it'd be dumb squared to attempt it in the dark. Better stick with the lesser of two dumbs, not least as the island was continuing to present a steep, rocky aspect straight up from the water to a height of maybe fifty feet. Nowhere to moor the kayak, and no way to get up to the top.

After a few minutes the island started to curve away. I realized it would soon stop providing an indication of the direction I should take, and tried to figure a way of ensuring I maintained a consistent bearing after I left it behind. I couldn't, and decided to hope instead that so long as I failed to zone out, I'd be able to keep paddling in a straight line without a marker.

I found myself reluctant to leave the island behind, however, and allowed my course to bend to the right, keeping a consistent distance from it while it was still there.

Then I found myself braking.

***

I was thirty yards away, the falling snow between it and me turning most of it into nothing more than blocky masses in shades of grey. But I realized that the island looked different on top—and then I understood why.

There was a house on it.

A long structure, multi-level, predominantly of grey wood. This was no mere cabin, either, some rudimentary structure thrown up a hundred years ago. It had the look of something that had weathered both time and storms but whoever put it there did so either with the help of an architect or natural talent. It was the kind of thing Frank Lloyd Wright might have come up with on a limited budget and if challenged to build only with what was available on the island, which made sense. Getting materials out here would have been time-consuming and expensive. As I stared up at it, letting my momentum carry me along the remaining stretch, I saw chunks of rock had also been incorporated into the structure. At the end there was a deck sticking ten feet out over the water.

There was someone standing on it.

The deck was sixty feet above my head and the snow made it look like something glimpsed in old black and white footage, fractured with jittering vertical lines. A woman was standing there. She had dark hair, curly, not long. I couldn't make out what she was wearing. She was up against the railing, arms folded, looking out into the snow.

'Hey.'

She didn't hear, or at least gave no indication of having heard. I tried again, louder, with the same result, although by then I was almost directly in front of her.

She stood, arms tightly crossed, staring out into the falling white, as though either not seeing what lay in front or looking so intently for one thing in particular that anything else—like me—simply failed to register.

I stopped paddling. The house and the woman proved there had to be some way onto the island. There was shelter up there. There would be warmth and maybe food.

I shouted again, but still she did not hear. I turned and paddled back to where I was a few yards from its rocky face. I pulled around the end and set off up the other side, knowing there must be a landing somewhere.

THE BURNING WOODS

***

Except there wasn't.

I kept close, because the snow was now falling so heavily it seemed continuous. It was three inches deep on the front of the kayak, and I had to stay within ten feet of the island to even be able to see it.

I paddled right the way around, down the long side, past the other end, and then, baffled, back along the side I'd already paddled past. There was no beach, no dock. Just the same wall of slippery, jagged rock all around the island.

And when I got back to where the deck stuck out over the lake, there was no-one on it any more.

I couldn't land. I couldn't stay where I was.

I turned the kayak and set off into the white.

7

I have no idea how long I was out there. Hours. Long enough to go through alternating stages of dogged effort and mounting panic. Long enough for exhaustion to set in. I stopped being able to feel my hands, much less my fingers. My toes and feet were also lost to me, and patches of my face. For long periods I kept my eyes shut against the constant jabs of snowflakes flying into them. My ears sung with sharp, deep pain.

The water felt like frozen treacle. I fought it in one direction for a long time, then in desperation altered my course more or less at random and fought in another direction instead. After a while this came to seem like the stupidest decision on a long day of stupid decisions, and I tried to right myself back to my original course, but naturally I could not—especially as what little light there had been had started to fade. The falling snow stopped seeming dimly lit from within and began to turn grey instead: at first faintly, then darker and darker by shades—until I was paddling in pitch darkness, nothing but the cold sting of flake after flake against my face to tell me it was still coming down.

All I could hear was the jagged rhythm of my strokes, each a self-contained little noise, like a sound effect on repeat. I considered turning and heading back to the island, trying to shout up at the house once again, but by then I had absolutely no idea of what direction it would be in. For all I knew I was back there already, only yards away, paddling round and round it in the swaddling, deadening blackness, gripped in its gravitational field and unable to escape.

My body told me to give up and die, but the mind would not. Then my mind told me the same, but found the body had reevaluated and now would not listen. The cold settled deeper until my ears ached so badly that for a while I thought I could hear singing, the absent-minded song of a child brushing her hair after a shower, wrapped in a towel too big for her, happy in a home she assumed would be eternal, warmed by adults she thought would be there forever.

I kept going, stroke after stroke, my eyes sparkling against the cold and the undifferentiated darkness, until I realized there was something in the distance, that instead of retinal flashes I was perceiving something real, something that lay ahead.

The island. It had to be.

Suddenly I knew that I'd been right, that I'd somehow managed to do nothing more than go round and around it, sometimes close, sometimes far, held within its orbit by my soul yearning for somewhere to be, somewhere safe to go. Yearning for landfall of some kind. Any kind.

I headed for the light, knowing that the woman had come back out onto the deck, perhaps hearing the sound of my paddling. I headed for the light, knowing that she would shout down this time, explaining that I'd missed an easy way onto the island, telling me where to go and how to climb out of the kayak and onto the land where I could rest. I paddled with what remained of my strength, my face a frozen mask, grunting with exertion, knowing that it was her, guiding me home.

But then I saw it wasn't.

It was Ralph, standing on the edge of the shore at the resort, holding up a lantern.

8

I came back to consciousness to find myself in one of the chairs in my cabin. The fire was burning. There was a thick blanket over me. The entire surface of my skin was tingling. There was a soft glow around everything.

I blinked, slowly. Turned my head, which felt like it was splitting in two. Ralph was in the other chair. He had a beer in his hand. There was another on the table between us, already open, next to a couple of empties.

'Be dumbass to drink that,' he said. 'But it was a dumbass idea to go out today in the first place.'

It was a while before I felt able to bring my arm from under the blanket. The bottle felt like it weighed twenty pounds. It nearly slipped from my hand on the way to my mouth. I drank half of it slowly, before trying to speak.

'Cigarettes.'

Ralph nodded toward the arm of my chair. I hadn't even noticed they were there. I eventually got one lit with fingers that felt swollen and dead. 'How'd I get here?'

'Carried you from the shore. Well, dragged. You got the kayak to within a couple yards and then tried to get out. I got to you just before you fell over.'

'Thanks. And for coming to look for me.'

He didn't respond. It felt strange being in the cabin, like a dream. Now it was over, part of me was acknowledging I hadn't been at all sure I was going to make it back. That I'd been very scared. To be somewhere warm, where it wasn't relentlessly snowing, and where I knew where I actually was... The little things you take for granted can seem magical when you get them back. But consequently fragile, and undependable.

'Is it still coming down out there?'

'Yeah.'

'Christ.'

'It's the big one. Why'd you stay on the lake so long?'

'I got lost. Got out too far, didn't have anything to take my bearings by. Couldn't see a damned thing.'

'You're lucky you made it back.'

'I guess.'

'Someone vanishing on the lake—it doesn't look good.'

'Has it happened before?'

He looked preoccupied, like he had something else on his mind. 'Of course.'

'How often?'

'Couple times. While back.'

'Together?'

'Separate.' He said this as though it had been a dumb question.

'What happened?'

'Same as you. Went out when they shouldn't of.'

'Did anybody miss them?'

He shook his head.

'You think anybody would have missed me?'

He looked me straight in the eye. 'I'm assuming not.'

Fuzzy-headed though I was, it was obvious Ralph's manner was different tonight. Perhaps out of concern for me, or out of time spent worrying. Perhaps not. 'Are we okay?'

'Do you want another beer?'

'Sure.'

We drank in silence for a while.

'So what happened? Out there?'

I'd gone into a daze. My skin wasn't hurting so much, settling into the dull sparkle you get after a bad dose of pins and needles. The pain in my ears was receding, too, though it still sounded a little as though someone was singing, a very long distance away.

'Snow started coming hard, and I lost visibility. Tried to turn around and thought I'd judged it, but obviously not.'

'How did you know, if you didn't know where you were?'

'I saw something I hadn't before.'

He looked into the fire, as if to avoid my eye. 'What did you think you saw?'

'An island.'

'Lots of those out there.'

'Not like this. It was bigger. And it had a house on it.'

He shook his head. 'No inhabited islands on that lake.'

'This one was.'

'Maybe back in the day.'

'No. There was a deck. I saw someone on it.'

'Who did you think you saw?'

'A woman. Late thirties, early forties. Mid-length hair, curly. I didn't see her clearly.'

'You didn't see anything at all.'

'Excuse me?'

'Nobody lives out there. There's no island with a house on it. You didn't see it. You just thought you did.'

'Are you serious?'

'You were cold, exhausted, lost. In a snowstorm. The eyes will play tricks. The mind, too. That's all.'

'Bullshit.'

'It's the truth.'

'I don't get it. I don't understand why you're even saying this.'

'Because it's true.'

'You can't have any idea of what I saw.'

'Yeah, I do. And you didn't see it.'

We finished our drinks in silence, and then Ralph stood.

'You're welcome to stay to the end of the week,' he said. 'After that, I think we're done.'

9

I woke up next morning in the same place, in the chair. The world outside the window was white. The fire had died to a few embers and the end of my nose was cold. I tried to pull the blanket up over my face, but every part of my body ached. Arms, shoulders and back worst of all, and my stomach, but there wasn't a bit of me that didn't feel badly used, strained, leaden. I stayed where I was until I felt strong enough, then gingerly levered up out of the chair. I laboriously put a few pieces of wood on the fire and made a cup of coffee and took it with me into the cabin's tiny shower and ran warm water over my body until it felt more like it belonged to me.

I spent the rest of the morning in the chair, drinking cup after cup of warm water, waiting to feel better.

***

By the afternoon I had moved to the bench near the window. It was still snowing, though not as heavily.

Yesterday felt as if it had happened a year ago. The hours I'd spent lost and flailing, though intensely real at the time, now seemed insubstantial. The few parts where something specific and different happened began to swell, like islands of substance in a cloud of white.

Foremost amongst these, of course, was the house. And the deck, and the person on it. If I closed my eyes I could see her clearly, or as much as I'd been able to see her at the time. The description I'd given Ralph wasn't great but it was enough. Couldn't be too many full-time residents in this area. The woman must have to visit the store, perhaps even the bar up the road. Ralph had been here all his life. There was a good chance he knew who she was. So how come he'd denied not only this, but that she'd been there at all?

Come to think of it, hadn't he been laying the way for denial before I even mentioned her—asking what I'd *thought* I'd seen out on the lake, rather than what I *saw*? My memories of the conversation were not sharp, but that sounded right.

I didn't know how seriously to take his suggestion that I be on my way. I hadn't done anything wrong, except unnerve him by nearly coming to grief out on the lake. Sure, the place was closed for the season and had been for a couple weeks. He'd be within his rights. But up until last night he'd seemed content for me to be there.

As I sat mulling this over I saw movement down toward the lake. The door to Ralph's cabin opened and he came out. He was dressed in a coat, on his way somewhere.

He glanced toward my cabin, as if wondering whether he should come check on me. But then he stomped off into the snow in the direction of where he parked his truck.

A couple minutes later I heard the engine start, and the sound of him driving away.

I wound up back in the other chair in front of the fire, where I dozed for a while. When I woke up I felt better. Well enough that I took a coffee and cigarette out onto the deck. The snow was light, sparkles drifting through muted light.

THE BURNING WOODS

The question of Ralph's change in manner had evidently been picking at me while I slept, because it was front and center in my head now I was back up on my feet. And it suddenly occurred to me that it might have nothing to do with me being out on the lake at all.

I went back indoors. I didn't know how long I'd been passed out in the chair after he got me back in the cabin, but I'd bet it was a half hour or more. There'd been two empty bottles on the table.

I walked to the kitchenette and opened the cupboard. My meagre groceries were there, cans and a couple boxes and jars. But there used to be a small paper bag stashed behind them.

It was gone.

10

I stewed on it for a while. There didn't seem to be much else I could do right away.

Maybe there was even a rule about it, though it seemed unlikely. In hunting season there had to be a bunch of guys who'd come up here to go hunting, and came prepared. I doubt Ralph made them store their bullets in his shed or a safe.

Either way, he could have talked to me about it instead of doing what he'd done, and he shouldn't have been looking in the first place. Poking around a guy's stuff when he's unconscious, and taking his ammunition, is not okay.

After a while the snow started to grow heavy again.

And I got tired of waiting.

I hadn't heard his truck coming back but that didn't mean he hadn't returned. Snow will play tricks with sound. If he wasn't home then I'd slip the note I'd written under his door. I'd kept it short and polite, only saying I'd like my ammunition back. As I tramped from my cabin to his my fingers and toes start to complain, immediately. They'd had a narrow escape the day before and didn't want me fucking with their welfare again.

Ralph's truck wasn't there. I trudged up to his door and was about to bend down to shove the note under it when a thought struck me. I reached for the door handle and gave it a twist. Sure enough, it was unlocked.

MICHAEL MARSHALL SMITH

There was a different way of handling this, and the fact it came so swiftly to mind showed me how pissed I was at what he'd done. Instead of leaving the note, I could go in there. Take a look around. I wouldn't ransack the place or open cupboards or drawers, but if he'd set it down on a counter when he got back last night, then I would pick it up and leave. To get angry about my doing this would involve him opening the box of what he'd done in the first place.

I knew the moral math on this was shaky—and there were arguments that he owned the place and could set whatever rules he wanted and he was only in my cabin last night because he'd helped me out of a tight spot—but I knew I was going to do it anyway, so I might as well get on with it.

The cabin was warmer than outside but not by much—he hadn't lit a fire yet, and the smell of smoke from yesterday was thin and weak. The floor plan was similar to my own cabin, though a little larger, with a real kitchen and a small second bedroom. I guess people who live alone decide either it doesn't matter how the place looks, or go the other way. He'd gone the other way. It was very tidy, everywhere, which made scanning around for a small paper bag very easy.

I found it in the kitchen, on the counter.

I headed back out through the sitting room, feeling a dull, childish triumph at getting back something that belonged to me. I remembered when I must have been about eleven, and another boy at the school had taken one of my marbles, to which I had been attached. I eventually got it back, and had felt much the same as I did now. This recollection diminished my achievement, making it even smaller than I'd already understood it to be.

Was this all there was? Did forty years of life take you nowhere but a return to "that's mine, give it back"? So I had my bullets. Big deal. I didn't even have a gun.

I was a couple of steps from the door when something caught my eye. It was on the mantel, above a fireplace from which yesterday's ashes had already been tidily removed.

I stared at it, understanding that Ralph's change in manner was nothing to do with the bag of shells after all.

THE BURNING WOODS

11

The knock came a little before eight. I already knew he was back. I'd been watching out of my window late afternoon, thinking things through, and saw his truck return. He went in his cabin without looking at mine. A while later I saw smoke curl up out of the chimney.

I opened the door to find him there holding a six-pack. Amongst men, there are few better ways of indicating that conflict is not intended, at least not immediately.

'Where'd you go today?' I asked, when we sat in front of the fire.

'To a funeral.'

'Who?'

'Don. Guy who owns the bar up the road.'

'What happened to him?'

'He died.'

'So what happens to the bar?'

'It'll be closed tonight.'

'And then?'

'It will open again.'

'Who'll run it?'

He looked at me, as if to judge whether the inquiry was rhetorical. It was not, though a dim understanding was perhaps beginning to form. He shook his head. This was evidently a question I had to be able to answer for myself.

'You knew I'd come looking for my shells, didn't you?'

He nodded.

'And that I'd see what I saw.'

Nodded again.

'Why couldn't you have just told me?'

'You wouldn't have believed. The things people tell you, they never amount to much. People have to see stuff for themselves. Haven't you found that?'

'That doesn't mean I understand what I saw.'

'I've told you things. You've listened, but not said much back. I don't know anything about you.'

'I don't tell people much.'

'I get that. But it's why I mentioned the island in the first place.'

'And then let it drop,' I said, realizing that Ralph's method of dealing with me over the last weeks had been more subtle than I'd given him credit for.

'Right.'

'To let it work at me.'

'Which it did.'

'And you didn't do much to stop me going out yesterday either, did you, now I think about it.'

'It was going to happen. When it happened was your choice. I wasn't going to stand in the way.'

'You wanted to know what I'd see.'

'Yes.'

'Because that would tell you something that I had not.'

'Smart, aren't you?'

'Smart, but slow.'

'Slow gets you there eventually. And you're more likely to understand what you find, than if you get there fast.'

'And so what *did* I see?'

'You tell me.'

'Your wife,' I said. 'The woman on the island was your wife.'

'Sounds that way.'

'I know it was. I saw the picture in your cabin. The woman standing on the deck in the snow was your wife.'

'Okay.'

'But you said she was dead.'

He sat looking into the fire. 'She is.'

We drank a while. It became clear that the next person to speak was going to have to be me.

'Is she the only thing to see on the island?'

'No.'

'What else could it have been?'

THE BURNING WOODS

'I didn't know,' he said. 'That's why it had to happen the way it did. I was pretty sure already. I've been in your cabin before, couple weeks ago, when you were out walking.'

'Why?'

'To see what I could find.'

'And what did you find?'

'Shells, but no gun.'

'How do you know I don't have one stashed out in the woods somewhere?'

'Because you don't.'

'How do you know?'

'You're done with guns now.'

'Why do you even care?'

'I don't have much else to do. And if you had a gun here, it could have changed things, a little.'

'I don't.'

'I believed that. But the island made me sure.'

'What happened? Why is she there?'

He didn't speak for a long time.

I got more beers from the fridge. Then went outside for a cigarette. I smoked it on the deck, watching the snow come down, little drifting ghosts against a sea of black.

'It's hard watching someone die,' he said, when I sat back down in front of the fire.

'I imagine it must be.'

'I'd done it with my dad. Some with Granddad, too. But mainly I was kept away from that. My dad took a long time. And like I said, it was long, slow afternoons. There's a lot of waiting in any part of life. I get that. But most of it's going somewhere. Waiting for something new or better or at least not as bad. You wait for the girl to notice you. You wait for work to get easier. You wait for the spring. You wait for grief to fade.'

'Dying is different.'

He nodded. 'Dying is different. It's not going anywhere. It's time *itself* dying, minute by minute, hour by hour. My dad, he didn't mind too much. He'd always been a slow, tidal guy. Don't get me wrong—he did stuff. A lot of stuff. Never met a guy who could work so hard, for so long. But he had his own pace and it was timely and gracious and he was accustomed to things that took a while. She wasn't like that.'

'Your wife?'

'Always in motion. Doing this or that, moving something here or there, thinking about the next thing. But then all that was lost to her and she was just lying there day after day, nothing to do, nothing to move. And there *was* no next thing. Wasn't going to be. *Ever*. And she knew it.'

I knew what he meant. I had seen this. I had seen it in the mirror, for weeks and months and years.

'How did you do it?'

'A pillow. She was weak by then, but not as weak as I'd thought. She woke up.'

'Did she fight?'

He shrugged. 'I don't think so. But it took longer than I thought it would.' He looked wretched. 'We spoke before she went to sleep. We said nice things. I'd stopped trying to tell her she was going to get better, and that made it easier, because she'd known for a while already and you don't want to be sitting there lying to someone day after day, or to be the person listening to those lies. If you have loved and been loved for a long time, you do not want the last days between you to be nothing but untruths, however kind. I told her I loved her, just before she drifted off, and I told her again after she was asleep. I told her many times. So I thought it would be okay. I didn't do it for any bad reason. I didn't *want* her to go. I just didn't want either of us to have to keep waiting. Especially her. She was not a patient person. The waiting was killing her worse than the cancer. We'd talked, and I thought it might as well happen now. That it would be the best thing. The *kind* thing, for both of us. And maybe that made it okay.'

He lit a cigarette and smoked it right down before continuing.

'That next winter I was out on the lake. It hadn't snowed heavy yet and so it was bitter cold. There was icy drizzle coming down. Like being sandblasted.'

'So why did you go out?'

'I was beating myself up. I need to explain that?'

He did not.

'And after a couple hours I got lost out there, like you did, and a while later I saw the island too.'

'The same one?'

'I don't know. It didn't have a house on it. But the sides were steep, like you said, and one end jutted out over the water, looked kind of like a deck, so, I don't know. Maybe, maybe not.'

'And you saw her?'

He nodded.

'What did you do?'

'Tried to get to her, of course. Went round the island, twice, though by then my arms were dead. Couldn't find any place to land. Tried to tie up but the rope kept slipping off the rocks. Tried to throw myself onto the rock face, thought maybe I'd be able to climb it. But it didn't happen and that's for the best because the boat would have drifted away and my bones would be on that island right now.'

'Would they?'

'You know what I mean. Anyway in the end I gave up and paddled around the end and she was still there, looking out, and not at me. So I set for home.'

'You ever been back?'

'Nothing will have changed.'

'The other guys you mentioned. The ones you said disappeared out there on the lake.'

'They wouldn't have seen her,' he said. 'I can't know for sure, because I didn't get a chance to ask, but I know they didn't. They saw their own people. I figured that might happen to you, too, yesterday—if my guess about you was wrong. But I was right. You haven't killed nobody.'

I remained silent. He was correct but he wasn't right. He knew some things, but he didn't understand.

Or maybe he did, because then he looked up at me and smiled, sadly. 'On the other hand, here you are.'

12

Next afternoon I walked the three miles up the road. It took a while. The snow was deep and there were no tracks in it, suggesting Ralph hadn't done more yesterday than leave the resort and park up for a few hours, long enough to give me a chance to go look in his cabin.

Eventually I trudged up to the bar. From the outside it looked like it had been shut for several months but it had looked that way the other time too. There was nobody at any of the tables, but a man came from out back and stood behind the counter. His hair was white and his face blotchy but his eyes were clear and sharp. I ordered a beer and he set it down in front of me. I asked to see a menu.

'No food today.'

'How come?'

'It's made the night before.'

'And you were unavailable.'

He just looked at me.

'You're Don, right?'

He nodded. 'What's your name?'

'I don't know. Do you?'

He shook his head. 'We never met.'

I took the beer to a table in the corner, near the small fire he had going. After a while I got another. When I went up again he wasn't there and didn't come out. I left some money on the counter and poured myself a beer and drank it and did that a couple more times and then left.

It was snowing again and getting dark and after a while I fell over and found it hard to get back up, and in all honesty couldn't think of a particularly good reason for doing so.

After an indeterminate period of time I opened my eyes to see Ralph standing over me, his head a shadow against the falling snow.

I was still in no hurry to move. The snow was cold but comfortable. 'Got to stop meeting like this.'

He looked down at me with something like compassion and helped me up and led me back to the resort.

13

I was awake before the dawn. Packing my case did not take long. I left the couple remaining tins and boxes on the shelf in the kitchenette. There had been a few things there when I arrived. You pass it on.

THE BURNING WOODS

As soon as it was light I left the cabin. It was bright and crisp outside but I knew that would not last long. I did not stop by Ralph's cabin to tell him I was leaving. Once he'd got me back to mine the night before, he said goodnight and left. He did not come by later. He was done with me, and waiting for me to go.

Or so I thought, but then I found a note he'd left on the table. 'I'll be round tomorrow night,' it said. 'And you're going to tell me what you did.'

But I could not, and so I left.

I wish I'd known him better. I wish we had not lost touch. I know he did what he did for the right reasons. I knew that at the time, I think, or sensed it at least. I should not have let it come between us. Things might have turned out differently. I should not have allowed it to work at me until I came to wonder whether it was something you could do for yourself, like turning a broken machine off and on again.

But that's not his fault. Nobody lives your life but you, even if for much of the time you're just quoting the lives of others, walking tracks they cleared for you.

I didn't know what direction to go, but as I'd lain in bed in the small hours in the dark listening to echoes and wreathed again in the smell of burned timber, I'd come to suspect that was the point. That there are things you'll never find if you have a goal in mind. Any goal, however small. There are paths that only fall under the feet of those who are going nowhere, merely waiting. Staring into mirrors late at night, and seeing a stranger. Paddling, snow blind, with no direction home. That's why Ralph had never found it. He'd been looking too hard.

I walked a little way along the edge of the lake. I realized I'd been wrong about islands. You look at them and they seem separate. But *they do not float*. Every island drops beneath the surface, stretching down to the lake bottom. This continues in all directions, meeting the lower portions of other islands, joining them. It is all connected, beneath the surface. If you stand on one, you stand on them all. If you are one, you are all.

I looked back toward the resort, recognizing it now. It was a happy place, perhaps the last such recollection I carried of my childhood. The last vacation we took, the three of us, when my dad still laughed and my mother was still forever doing something, always planning the next thing, forever on the move. I was eight years old. We walked in the woods every day and kayaked and grilled up a storm.

Two weeks later we found out my mother had cancer. Nine months after that, my dad did what he did.

I didn't know about it at the time, of course. I just knew she had gone. And it's so long ago now that all I can get back of her with any clarity is that single image of her standing by the fence in front of our old house, arms folded, waiting for something she'd been expecting in the mail. Not waiting for me, nor my father. Nothing of substance. I don't remember her smiling at me or hugging me or making me a sandwich or singing me to sleep.

Just her standing at the fence, waiting for some dumb thing that was coming in the mail.

I walked. The snow was thick on the ground and it was cold and the sky frosted over and got lower and lower. At first I didn't notice because of the trees but the finally the snow started to come down and I looked up and knew it had settled in for the afternoon. I'd been going four or five hours then, half a day. I had changed directions several times, altering my course by a few degrees, one way or another, randomly.

Some are born with a destination. Some find one later in life, or else elect to designate some place or person to perform that function. Others merely wait the whole thing out, because that's what you do, one way or another.

But there are those who don't. Who can't.

Some drink themselves to death, like Don—my grandfather, who I never even met. He had his own method of making the waiting stop, by following the endless circular path of being drunk, hungover, getting drunk again, and it may have been witnessing this slow, sip-by-sip drowning that made my father do what he did to help my mother. The last time I saw my dad, twenty years ago, I think he tried to explain it to me. But I was pretty drunk myself at the time, and angry at him, or the world, or something, and I didn't hear.

I thought I was better than that. Better than him, better than his father. I thought I was the guy who'd find what we'd all been looking for, the path

THE BURNING WOODS

they'd both missed. I thought I had it all figured out. Or some of it, at least. I hadn't realized that the three of us were islands in the same water, our feet planted in the same lake bed, connected and surrounded by the same currents. Or maybe I never even got to be an island, never grew up that much.

Perhaps I was just a lost boy in a kayak, trying to find a route between those men who had come before me, but always in the dark, and forever running into them.

I kept walking, paying no attention to where I was going. Wherever there was a gap between trees was good enough. There is only a road to follow because one day someone put it there, and once it's there it looks like a path and so we assume it must go from one meaningful place to another. But it's not like that. Nowhere in the woods is more a place than any other, just as each of the moments that fall are going nowhere other than to rest upon all the others, to melt into what was, a cold mass of that-happened-but-now-is-gone.

I kept walking, a man trudging through deep forest in the snow, carrying a small suitcase.

Eventually I began to see a glow in the distance. It was pretty dark by then and so it was hard to tell how far it was. It didn't matter. I wasn't going back.

It took maybe another hour to get to where I could hear the crackling of the flames. The trees around me looked the same as they had all day. My father had been wrong about that, and his father before him. They weren't any special kind of trees, just more of the same.

They were on fire, though. I'll give them that.

I walked into the flames, deep into the burning woods. I walked until all around me was yellow-orange and searing and then I sat down on the forest floor, looking up at glowing embers as they tumbled out of the black sky.

The trees are on fire in the way it feels when a bullet carves into your brain. There are no pain receptors in there and so the fire is not that kind of pain. It is not physical. It is the righteous fire of the end of it all. It is the burning of permanent and irrevocable mistakes, of sailing off the edge of the world. It is the percussive echo of that last sound, the gunshot with which I ended it all.

And that's why I always leave before Ralph and I have that last beer together. How can I tell my father that's what I did? That the boy he used to kiss on the head, and lift up into the air, waited until his family was out of the house and then took his own life by blowing that same head to pieces? Even if it's maybe partly his fault, and his father's fault too, and so on back to the dawn of time.

Because it's not. I didn't know that then but I know it now. They didn't buy the gun or the shells. They didn't tell themselves that by ending the waiting by their own hand they were finally understanding and forgiving their father for what he'd done to help his wife, my mother, along; or that by doing it drunk—as I did—I felt I was honoring my grandfather's path too. It made sense at the time. Or seemed like it did.

I'm not sure I regret it, even now. And it's possible the wife and daughter I left behind don't regret it either. I have no idea how long it's been. Though I do not believe it was a conscious factor in the timing of my action, my daughter was eight years old when I left her life. I accept that is a curious coincidence. And I'm aware what shape an eight makes when turned on its side. I wonder if she still sings when she combs her hair after a shower. I hope so. I hope I didn't take that from her. I hope her mother found someone else.

Some men are destined to find the burning woods. I am one of them. I think my wife knew that by the end. It's better this way. Or if it's not, it doesn't matter. What's done is done.

And yes of course I know I'm dead, and I am fine with it. Being alive was worse. Alive is just an expression we use for those parts of being dead where it feels like you might be able to change something. You can't.

You're just waiting for the waiting to stop.

In a while I will stand and pick up my case and walk out the other side of the burning woods and keep on walking. I will eventually find a road on which it has not yet snowed, and head up it. I will buy beer and cigarettes at the store and continue on to the resort and my father will check me in and affect not to notice that I smell strongly of wood smoke.

This has not happened before. It's *always* happening, and it's only the fact every moment lasts for infinity that makes it feel like you're going around in circles. All paths seem straight while you're following them. It's only when

THE BURNING WOODS

you look back you see the curved line. You circle yourself and those who made you. You revolve around your point in time. You happen, and you will keep happening.

I will get up eventually, and happen again, or still.

But for now I will sit here and watch my woods burn.

SHIT **HAPPENS**

I was pretty drunk or maybe I'd've figured out what was happening a lot sooner. It'd been a hell of a day getting to Long Beach from the east coast, though, kicking off with a bleary-eyed hour in an Uber driven by a guy who ranted about politics the entire way, then two flights separated by a hefty layover because Shannon my PA is obsessed with saving every penny on travel despite—or because of—the fact she's not going to be the one spending hours wandering an anonymous concourse in the middle of the country, trying and ultimately failing to resist the temptation to kill the time in a bar. Once I'd had a couple/three beers there it seemed only sensible to keep the buzz going with complimentary liquor on the second flight, and so by the time the cab from LAX finally deposited me on the quay beside the boat I was already sailing more than a few sheets close to the wind.

When I say "boat" I mean "ship." The company conference this year was on the Queen Mary, historic Art Deco gem of British ocean liners and once host to everyone from Winston Churchill to Liberace, now several decades tethered to the dock in Long Beach and refitted as a hotel. I stood staring up at the epic size of the thing while I snatched a cigarette, then figured out where the stairs were to get up to the metal walkway that took you aboard. I hadn't even finished check-in before a guy I know a little from the London office strode up and said everyone was in the bar and it was happy hour for God's sake, so what the hell was I waiting for?

MICHAEL MARSHALL SMITH

I hurried my bag to my room and brushed my teeth and changed my shirt, taking a second to remind myself of the name of the British guy (Peter something-or-other, I evidently hadn't noted his surname) so I could hail him when I rocked up in the bar. See? Totally professional.

The bar turned out to be at the pointy end of the ship, and—wonder of wonders—featured an outside area which not only had a great view over the bay, but you were allowed to smoke there *while drinking*, which meant there was basically no good reason for me to leave it, ever, or at least for the duration of the conference. The bar wasn't even super-crowded, because the conference didn't start in earnest until the next day: I'd only arrived Thursday because Shannon had been able to shave a few bucks off the flights that way. Of course it meant paying for an extra night on the boat, but she assured me that was actually a good thing because of some unfeasibly complex points system she's got me locked into—and began explaining it in detail and cross-referencing it with her own plans for the weekend—but after a while I basically stopped listening.

Most of the guys and girls present were from outposts in Europe, arrived early to make a head-start on recovering from jetlag, which many seemed to believe involved the consumption of alcohol at a rate some might have considered injudiciously brisk. I knew most of them only by sight but when you work for the same multinational tech giant and have access to strong, relaxing beverages—and are all a little hyper as a result of being away from home and out of the normal grind—it's not hard to get along. Peter-from-London insisted on taking me on a tour of the boat to point out the curved metal and worn wooden paneling and general faded-grandeur of the whole deal (out of Brit pride, I suspect, and also to temporarily remove himself from the sight line of a freakishly tall woman from the Helsinki office whom he'd evidently slept with at the previous year's event, and who was drinking hard and fast with her colleagues and staring at Peter like she either wanted to bash his head in or else renew their acquaintance right away).

Aside from that I stuck to the bar—itself no slouch when it came to looking like the set from some glamorous black-and-white movie where people spoke in *bons mots* and drank cocktails and broke into dance every ten minutes. I was all too aware I had to give a gnarly and unpopular presentation

SHIT HAPPENS

explaining why the update to our flagship virtual networking module had been delayed *yet again*, but that wasn't until Saturday and hey, it isn't every evening you get to drink heavily on a damned great boat.

I drank. I chatted. I went out front to smoke and watch the sky darken and the lights from the city across the bay come on—and then gradually start to dwindle and fade, as a fog rolled in. I stuck to beer in the hope this might help the hangover remain dreadful rather than crushing, and after a while this started to catch up with my bladder. Luckily my earlier exploration of the boat with Peter (the Finnish woman was now hanging with our group, and it was becoming clear that the only vigorous acts on her mind were the kind that would have a bedstead banging against a cabin wall into the small hours) had included locating the nearest john.

It was down a narrow and windowless corridor that led down the middle of the boat and seemed to have escaped the attention of most of the guys, who instead marched off down one of the much wider walkways on the outer edges, to the main restroom mid-ship that—while significantly larger and nicer—was much further away. The closer one looked like it had been converted out of a far more lavish single toilet (there was still a lock on the outer door to the corridor, and the sink, two urinals, and stall retrofitted into the space were seriously cramped) but never let it be said that I can't make do with what's available, especially when I really do need to take a piss.

Coming from the sophisticated Old World as some of these people did, the proportion of tobacco users was higher than with an all-American crowd, and by nine o'clock over half of us were in permanent position out on the smokers' deck. Peter and the Finnish chick were nowhere to be seen, suggesting that a two-person tour of some low-lit and discreet corner of the boat might be under way. A few of the others had staggered away toward other regions of the boat, looking a little green around the gills though promising to come back once they'd had some air. The view had also disappeared, blotted out by a thick, chewy fog that was getting thicker and thicker and smelled very strongly of the ocean.

I headed indoors—accepting in passing the offer of yet another pint of the strong local IPA from some suave dude from the Madrid office—and wobbled off down the corridor. Two collisions with the wall en route made me realize I ought to slow the drinking down, and I promised my tomorrow-morning self to at least consider the idea.

When I got inside the gents' I saw the stall door was closed and felt the customary beat of gratitude for the fact that my digestive system decided long ago that one comprehensive defecation per day (early morning, in the comfort of my own home, right after my first coffee and cigarette) is all it needs. As I stood swaying in front of the urinal furthest from the stall (still almost within arm's reach) I glimpsed a pair of shoes planted on the floor within, dark slacks pooled on top, a couple inches of pale, hairy calves. I coughed as I began meeting my own needs, as is my practice, to let the guy in there know he was temporarily not alone.

Nonetheless, a moment later, there was a quiet but clear straining sound. I winced—it's bad enough knowing there's some dude nearby voiding ex-food out his ass, without getting auditory updates—and tried to hurry my business.

A moment later I heard another noise from the stall. This was more of a grunt. It was followed rapidly by another, broken in the middle by several panting intakes of breath. And then one more. Long, low and painful-sounding.

"Shit," the guy said, in a low voice. "Ah, fuck."

"You okay in there, pal?"

The words came out without conscious thought. There was silence from the stall, and I realized the guy maybe hadn't heard my warning cough earlier. Awkward.

But then he made a groaning noise again. It was five seconds before it tailed off this time.

"I'm sorry," he said, sounding wretched. "I'm sorry."

I was well-oiled enough to be breezy about the situation, and it was something of a relief to be talking to a fellow American after a couple hours parsing foreign accents. "No worries. I'm just glad I didn't have whatever you did. What was it? An entire bowl of jalapeños?"

"No."

"Hot sauce? Stick to the ones you know, is my advice. Some of those local-brand bad boys will put you in a world of sphincter-pain if you're not used to them. I've been there, trust me. Avoid anything with Ghost Chili in it, for sure."

"Nothing like that. Just…"

SHIT HAPPENS

There was a sudden and very loud growling sound, evidently from the guy's guts. Then a sploshing noise.

And then—wow.

I mean, *holy cow*. One of the worse stenches I'd ever experienced. Maybe *the* worst. There's that saying about how your own farts never smell as foul other people's, but seriously. This was *bad*.

I abruptly realized I'd finished pissing and there was no reason for me to be there anymore. I hooked myself back into my pants and muttered a "Good luck with that, buddy," farewell while I took the single step from the urinal to the washbasin—again realizing just how drunk I was, when I managed to bang my shoulder into the clearly visible corner wall. The smell had blossomed further and was so very bad that I considered going rogue and leaving without a hand-wash, but (though I won't spend the ten frickin' minutes some guys will, like they're about to perform heart surgery and have spent the last hour with their hand up a cow) the habit's too deeply ingrained.

I held my breath, did a water-only rinse and grabbed a paper towel. The guy groaned again as I was making a hash of drying my too-wet hands, the paper tearing into damp shreds. There was another growling sound and I flapped off the last remnants, knowing a similar noise had prefigured the smell last time and having no desire to experience the second wave.

Too late. This time the sploshing noise was shorter and louder and far more explosive. I had my hand on the handle to the outside door when I heard something else, however. It was quiet, a sound he'd tried his hardest to keep inside—a kind of focused, tearful gasp.

"Shit, dude," I said, stepping back from the door. "You don't sound good at all."

"Sorry," he said, quietly.

"Look, is there someone out there that I should tell... Like, a friend, or something? I could let them know you're having a moment, and will be back out in a while?"

"No," he said, quickly. He sniffed, hard. "I'm fine. I'm just...it feels *really* bad."

"Definitely not a chili-related malfunction?"

"Haven't eaten any in days. And it's not...look, it's not my actual asshole that hurts, okay? It's..."

He broke off, and groaned again.

The second wave of the smell had hit me now, and it was a struggle to speak in a non-strangulated tone. "Is it the Norovirus?" I'd endured that back when it was new and fashionable a decade ago, and it's not fun.

"I don't think so. I had that a few years ago. It's fast and liquid. And it sucks but it doesn't actually *hurt*."

"This hurts?"

"*Hell* yeah."

I couldn't believe I was having this conversation when there was a beer and convivial company waiting for me, but it would have felt rude to simply walk out. "Though not at the point where stuff, uh, exits?"

"No. Inside. Like there's a fist squeezing your fucking guts. And lets go, but then squeezes again, even harder."

"That doesn't sound good."

"It's really not. And it came on super-fast. I was hanging out in the bar, having a blast, and suddenly there's this searing pain. I got here just in time. Look, I'm Carl, by the way. Carl Hammick. From the Madison office."

"Rick Millerson,' I said. 'Boston."

"Oh, hey. Any update on the RX350i?"

"Still delayed."

"I figured."

"Keep that to yourself until Saturday, though. I'm doing an announcement thing on it."

"Sure. Rather you than me, pal."

"Tell me about it."

I was about to wish him well and get the hell out but it occurred to me that the guy could have touched a bunch of stuff on his way in. I'm never sure how communicable stomach bugs are, but—especially with the presentation to make—this guy's problem was one I really didn't want to have.

I stepped back to the sink and washed my hands properly, using plenty of soap. From now on I'd be making the longer trek to the other bathroom, too. While I did this there was a grunting sound from the stall, and a sharp intake of breath. I rolled my eyes. I'd really had enough of this scene now, especially the smell.

SHIT HAPPENS

"Another wave coming in?"

"I think so," he said, between gritted teeth. "Holy crap, this feels even fucking worse."

He made a non-verbal sound. This time it was an actual sob, hard, fast. Followed by another.

I was trying to work out what I could possibly say that would be reassuring but not too weird, when I realized my phone was buzzing. I pulled it out and saw Shannon's ID on the screen. I was torn between not wanting to answer—especially in these circumstance—and knowing I probably should. One of the reasons I tolerate Shannon's tight-fisted travel booking policy and pay her significantly more than I have to (and in fact stole her from another office, somewhat controversially) is she's the best PA I've ever had, or even heard of. That includes knowing how to deal when I'm out of the office. Reminders pre-set on my phone, remotely updated. Digest email of where I need to be and when, and with whom, and why, delivered to my inbox at 6:30 every morning. If necessary she'll send a brief text to alert me to late-breaking changes, but she won't call unless it's something I'd look dumb for not being right on top of—like some fresh disappointment in the slow-rolling train-wreck that is the fucking RX350i.

The guy in the stall grunted again, harsh and loud. There was a sudden bang on the door to the corridor. I flipped the lock before anybody could come in.

"Busy," I said, loudly.

Whoever was outside rattled the handle and banged on the door once more, but then seemed to go away. Shannon went away too, so I guess it hadn't been that important after all.

"Thanks, man," Carl said, between gritted teeth. "Bad enough having you in here. No offense. But I'm not selling fucking tickets for this."

"I hear you. And look, I'm going to leave you in peace, okay? When I'm gone... Maybe you could bunny hop out of there and lock the outer door? Give you some privacy, right?"

"Sure, if I ever get a chance to get my ass off this..."

He stopped talking suddenly, making a sound as if he'd been punched in the gut, and a moment later I heard that bad stomach-growling noise again. Shorter, but really loud.

"Christ," I said, reaching once more for the outer door—but my phone started ringing again. It was Shannon, again. If she was pinging me multiple times then I really had to engage. "Look, uh, Carl—I'm actually going to have to take this call, okay?"

"Sure. Whatever."

"Just try to..."

"Try to what?"

"I dunno. The smell, dude."

"I can't help it."

"I get that. But if you can hold it back for a couple minutes that'd be super-cool."

"I'll try." The last word was strangulated, and ended in a gasp.

I hit answer. "Rick?" Shannon said, immediately.

"Well, yeah, Shann, of course it is. This is my phone, right? Kind of caught up in something right now, though."

"Are you drunk?"

I hoped I'd hidden it better. "Shannon, Christ's sake, of course not. Well, a little, yes, obviously. Okay, I'm drunk. What's your point? And why are you calling me?"

"You need to leave."

"I need to what?"

"Didn't you *see my email?*"

"Email? No—when?"

"*Over an hour ago.*"

"Shannon, I'm *at the conference*. I'm talking to people. From, all over the place. London, Helsinki, uh, Wisconsin. I can't be checking my phone every ten minutes."

"Haven't you seen the TV?"

"The bar doesn't have a TV."

"*There's no TV?*"

'It's not that kind of bar."

"Rick—you need to get on land."

"I'm *on* land, Shannon—seriously, what the heck?"

"No, you're on a boat."

SHIT HAPPENS

"But it's *attached* to the land. By...walkway things."

"It's in the actual ocean, still, though, right?"

"I guess, *technically*, but..."

"On TV they said to stay away from the ocean. Any part of it. That everybody should *stay away from the ocean*."

"What are you *talking about?*"

Carl grunted again suddenly, far louder than before. This time the growling was coming up out of his mouth, like a long, rasping belch.

"Oh shit," he groaned, when it abated. "Oh Jesus fuck." He sounded confused and desperate.

"Shannon," I said. "Can you give me a simple, declarative sentence to respond to? Imagine you're texting me. Try that."

She said something but I couldn't hear it because of another sudden barrage of blows on the outer door. It wasn't the kind of sound you get from a person requesting entry. It sounded more like someone trying to break in.

"Busy in here," I shouted. There was a momentary pause, and then the banging sounds started up again, even harder.

"Tell them there's another restroom down the boat," Carl said. He sounded very tired. "My head really hurts. I can't take the banging noise."

I opened my mouth to do that but the banging suddenly stopped. There was silence.

Then what sounded like a scream.

I stared at the door.

"What...was that?" I'd forgotten I still had the phone pressed to my ear, and Shannon's voice startled me. It sounded as though she was right there, as if our heads were on pillows alongside each other. Which they never have been, though since my divorce she's the one woman who's seemed to give a damn, my mother being down in Florida and also the most foul-tempered and least maternal person I've ever met.

"I don't...know," I said.

"Was it a *scream?*"

"Kind of, yeah." She sounded panicky and I spoke as calmly as I could. 'Look. *Who* is saying *what* on TV?'

"It's on all the stations," she said. "And the Internet. Twitter's gone insane with it. A few hours ago people posting about odd things happening. Kind of, well, nobody really seems to know. Things going weird, near the coast. And not just in one place—everywhere. Not the lakes. Just the ocean. Something's wrong with the ocean."

"But *what?*"

"I don't *know*," she said. "A fog coming in."

"A fog," I said, remembering how it had been on the smokers' desk when I left it…what? Ten minutes ago? A dense sea fog. Getting thicker and thicker.

"Right. But then it started to snowball and now they're saying it's not the fog after all, or maybe that's part of it but not the main thing. But nobody *knows*."

"Stay on the line," I told her.

"Hell's going on?" Carl said. His voice sounded weak and strained.

"I have no idea," I said, flipping over to Twitter on my phone. All my follows and followers are business-related—tech rivals and bloggers and a bunch of "influencers" and "growth hackers" who are super-annoying but I nonetheless track in case they start trash-talking the company and in particular the fucking RX350i and why it's *still* not on the market. As a result my feed is usually crushingly dull.

One flick with my thumb showed this wasn't the case now. Nothing tech at all. A mass of retweets from news organizations and randomers, blurry footage of people running, others asking if the country was under terrorist attack—and yes, a consistent message urging people to get away from the coast.

"What are you *doing?*" Shannon asked.

"Looking at Twitter. It's a dumpster fire. What the fuck?"

I heard another scream from out in the corridor. This one approached like a siren and went past like one too, as though someone was sprinting down the corridor outside.

The sound suddenly cut off.

The silence afterward seemed so loud that I barely noticed the growling noise from the stall, followed by another explosive release of air and something splashing into the toilet bowl.

"Oh no," Carl said, very quietly. "That's…oh no."

"Who's that?" Shannon asked, sounding freaked. "I heard a voice your end."

SHIT HAPPENS

"I'm...in the restroom. It's a guy from the Boston office."

"Carl Hammick?"

"You *know* him?"

"Not in person. But it's my job to know—"

"Whatever. Shann, what *I* need to know is..."

I tailed off. I didn't know what I needed to know. My Twitter feed was still spooling down the screen, absurdly fast, showing more of the same. I flicked sideways to trending stories and saw identical retweets, the same information—or lack of it—being rotated very quickly.

Then one popped up that said: *Santa Monica to be evacuated?*

My heart was thumping now. It was impossible to believe this was real. But then there was a retweet of something that looked like a genuine news source. The problem with social media is it'll recycle bullshit without anybody stopping to check it has any basis in reality, but then—there it was: a different source saying the same thing.

This source was CNN. And regardless of the 45th president's views on the matter, I consider CNN to be real fucking news.

There was a thudding sound above me, then a heavy crash. I didn't know the boat well enough to know what would be on the next floor but it sounded like some large piece of furniture had been overturned. I hoped it was that, anyway—because if the noise had been caused by the collision of a *body* with something, the person could not have survived.

"Shannon," I said. "Where are you right now?"

"In the car," she said. "You're on speaker."

"Going where?"

"Wait..." She stopped talking, and I caught the faint sound of other voices in the background.

"Are you with someone?"

"No—it's the radio. There's some guy from the army saying they think *definitely* it's the water now."

"Not a terrorist thing? I saw—"

"No. They bailed on that idea half an hour ago. This isn't terrorists. It's *something in the water*."

"But what *kind* of thing?"

"They don't *know*. Just *get onto land*, Rick."

I heard another person run past in the corridor, this time shouting—a deep, tearing, guttural noise. It sounded like a man's voice, and he stopped to hammer on the door of the restroom with a truly terrifying degree of force, before running on. "That may not be a straightforward undertaking. Sounds like things are pretty fucked up out there."

"Rick—*get off the boat.*"

The smell was truly appalling now. I'd stopped noticing the warning sound of growling from the stall and further splashing sounds. The last couple of pints I'd drunk had come home to roost, too, and I felt muddle-headed, off-kilter, unprepared. *Really* drunk. So much that it took me a couple of seconds to get my head around the fact my phone was vibrating, again, and work out what that meant. Another incoming call.

The screen said: PETER ???—LONDON

"Hang on, Shann. Don't go away."

"What are you—"

I muted her and accepted the call. "Pete?"

"Where are you?" Pete said. He sounded terse and clipped and pretty drunk but a lot more together than I felt.

"The john."

"Which one?"

"The small one you showed me. Near the bar."

"Is the door locked?"

"Oh yes."

"Good. Keep it that way."

"What the hell's going on? Where are you?"

"Up on top. Of the boat. Came up here with Inka to... Doesn't matter."

"Is she there with you?"

"Not anymore. I pushed her down the stairs."

"You...*what?*"

"We left the bar because she was feeling queasy. I assumed it was just jetlag combined with a truly astonishing amount of vodka, and also perhaps she had something else in mind—but no, she genuinely wasn't feeling well. So I escorted her to the restroom. When she came back out she said she felt better and so we came up on the top deck for some air but then she started behaving *extremely* strangely and..."

SHIT HAPPENS

"Pete, wait one second. My PA's on the other line."

I flipped over and said: "Have you heard anything new?"

"No," Shannon said. "They're recycling the same clip."

"Are you still driving?"

"Yes. And Rick—"

I cut her off and flipped back to Pete. He'd evidently missed what I'd said and just kept talking in the meantime. "...blood dripping down my fucking cheek. I had no choice—she *was trying to bite my face off*."

"Christ," I said. "Is anybody else up there?"

"No. Hang on, shit. I can smell burning."

"What kind of burning?"

"The *burning* kind of burning, Rick. I...oh. In the fog...there's a glow. I think the burning smell's coming from the shore."

"Where the walkways are?"

"No. The other shore. Where *the city is*."

I abruptly remembered there was one thing at least that I could do to improve the situation. I pulled out my cigarettes and lit one.

"You can't smoke in here," Carl said, from the stall. His voice sounded weak.

"Seriously? Have you even been *listening*?"

"It's no-smoking in here."

"This room smells like I am literally *inside a turd*, Carl. That's on you. So deal with the fucking smoke."

"Who's that?" Peter said, in my ear.

"Carl. From Boston."

"I know Carl. But what was that about a smell?"

"He's... Carl's experiencing intestinal difficulties."

"Oh fucking hell. Get out of there," Peter said, very seriously. "Get the fuck out. Now."

"You told me to stay *in* here."

"Yes, but that's what happened with Inka. Weren't you *listening*?"

"I missed that part—I flipped across to my PA to check she was okay."

"Inka's stomach...it gave out. When we were up here. It growled and then there was a flood of—it was truly disgusting. But then she said "Oh, I feel a lot better now", and *that's* when she came at me and tried to bite my—"

"Carl," I said. "How're your guts feeling now?"

The answer came in the shape of a sound in the stall. Not a growl, but an explosive impact of something in water.

"Oh no," he said. "There's more blood in it."

"*More blood?*"

"It's everywhere."

I took a cautious step back from the cabin door. From this angle I could see a patch of the floor within the stall. It was liberally splattered with red. I looked up and saw there were splashes of blood all the way to the ceiling too.

"But...I feel better," Carl said. "A lot better."

I heard running feet again outside the cabin. More than one set. A distant shout, and broken, high-pitched laughter.

"I think it's over," Carl said. There was a strange, dreamy quality to his voice. "Yes. I feel fine."

I'd lowered the phone but I could hear Pete's voice from the speaker, still shouting at me to get out.

"Uh, maybe you should stay where you are," I told Carl. "And I'll go find a doctor or something."

"I'm good."

"There's *blood all over the place.*"

"That's okay. Honestly, Rick—it's all fine." His voice sounded normal. Strong, confident. "And thanks for being a pal. Is that Peter Stringer you're talking to? From London?"

Stringer, *that* was it. "Yes."

"He's a solid guy. We should go find him—and work out what the hell's going on out there."

I heard Carl sliding the latch on the stall door, and mainly I was thinking: *Yeah, that's an actual plan. Three of us, three guys together—that has to give us a decent chance against...whatever the hell is going on out there. Right?*

But then I saw that while Carl was approaching the door inside the stall, his pants were still down around his ankles. That seemed weird to me.

When he opened the door I semi-recognized him. We'd met before at some event or other. Though not like this. His lower half was naked and awash with red and brown liquids, and his eyes were bleeding down his face.

SHIT HAPPENS

"I'm hungry," he said, looking at my throat.

I kicked the stall door back at him as hard as I could.

He was knocked back into the stall, banging his head hard against the tiled wall. He stayed on his feet, however—slip-sliding in the confined space because of all the stuff on the floor, but remaining upright.

I heard Pete's voice shouting at me to tell him what was going on, and put the phone back to my ear.

"Carl's…I don't think he's okay anymore," I said.

"Knock him out," Pete said. "Do whatever it takes. Keep doing it until you're sure it's done. I had to kick Inka down the stairs three fucking times before she stayed down."

I realized Carl was coming at me again and I slammed my foot into the stall door even harder this time. He crashed back down into the narrow space between the toilet and the wall. Started to move again, but sluggishly. As he turned his head I saw that the back of it wasn't the normal shape. Impact with the wall had broken his skull.

He was still trying to get up, though, reaching out with hands that were trembling and shaking.

"Pete—what the hell are we going to do?"

"We've got to get off this boat," he said.

"*How?*"

"Come find me up top."

"Can't you come down here instead?"

"Look, mate, this ship is full of people trying to kill people. I'm up for working together on this but I'd be out of my fucking mind coming back down to where you are."

"Nice. Seems last year's team-building weekend was a waste of money, hey."

"There's no "i" in team, you twat, and *I* do not want to get *fucking killed.*"

"Wait a second."

Still keeping an eye on Carl—he'd managed to lever himself up halfway to his feet again, but was still trapped behind the cistern, one eye open, the other closed—I flipped to the other line on my phone. "Shannon?"

"I'm still here," she said. "What's going on?"

"Carl Hammick is trying to kill me."

"Because of the delay on the RX35oi?"

"*No*, Shann. Because *he's lost his fucking mind.*"

"Get out of there. I'll be as fast as I can."

"What are you talking about?"

"I'm coming to get you."

"You're... Shannon, it will take *days* to drive here from Boston."

"You don't listen to a single word I say, do you?"

"I do, but..."

"If you *had*, you'd have heard me saying earlier in the week that because you were going to be out of town, I'd decided to visit my mother in Las Vegas."

"You're in *Vegas?*"

"Not anymore. I'm... Oh, gosh."

'What?'

"Another accident. It's... God, that's horrible. There's dead...and people are... Eurgh. Everyone's driving like maniacs. Mainly going the other way."

"But you're..."

"Coming as fast as I can."

"But why would you even *do* that?"

"Because I'm your PA, you dick. It's my job."

"It's really *not*, Shannon. And Las Vegas is a very long way from Long Beach. I mean, like, hours and hours."

"Unless it gets much worse than this I think I can do it in five and I've been on the road nearly two hours already and I'm driving as fast as I can. I'm going to hang up now so I can focus on the road, okay? I'll call back in a while."

"But what about your mom? Will she be safe?"

"Nobody's affected in Vegas. It's a long way from the ocean. As a precaution they've made everyone stay indoors wherever they were when the news broke. My mom's locked inside the Flamingo with a hundred bucks in change and a long line of margaritas and literally could not be happier. Just get off the boat, Rick."

And then she was gone.

I turned just in time to see Carl had managed to haul himself to his feet again and was shambling in my direction, grasping hands outstretched toward me.

SHIT HAPPENS

I braced myself against the wall and kicked him in the chest as hard as I could. I didn't land my foot squarely, though, and so he spun lop-sidedly away, crashing into the urinal I'd used, slipping and smacking his face really hard into the metal fixture at the top.

The sound this made was bad and the way he crashed onto the ground looked extremely final and I realized with incredulous bafflement both that he'd looked exactly the way they made these things look on television and also that I'd just killed Carl Hammick from the Wisconsin office.

Except I hadn't. After maybe three seconds of stillness, his fingers started to twitch, and his shoulders bunched as some impulse deep inside pushed him toward movement again.

I remembered I'd left Peter hanging. I kept a close eye on Carl and flipped to the other line. "You still there?"

"Look, I'll meet you halfway," Pete said. "You're right. I can't expect you to come all the way up here, and anyway that's not how we're going to get off the boat."

"Deal."

"I'll meet you at reception. Where I saw you when you first arrived. That's where the main walkway is. Be as fast as you can, Rick. I'm not going to wait forever."

"Understood."

I ended the call and stowed my phone in my pocket. Carl was pushing himself up from the floor, slowly but irrevocably. I tried to think of something to say but couldn't imagine what it would be, and doubted he'd even understand it any more.

So I put my ear against the cabin door and listened. I could hear noises out there but they seemed distant and I couldn't tell what they were. The one lesson I learned from years of video games as a teenager is when you reach a new level you don't screw around. You get going immediately, before the situation has a chance to get worse.

I opened the door and stuck my head out.

The first thing I noticed was a long splash of blood on the opposite wall of the hallway. It was still dripping. There was another splash of something much darker and brown below it. It smelled bad and was still dripping too.

I glanced left, back toward the bar. Some of the sounds were coming from there. They weren't good sounds, and some of them were to do with the fact the place looked like it was on fire. An orange glow, crackling noises, the smell of smoke.

Nonetheless I started cautiously in that direction, as I recalled there was a lateral sub-corridor that would take me to the outer and much wider walkway, which I figured would be a faster and safer way to the stairs that'd take me down the single flight to the reception level.

I'd barely gone three yards before someone came lurching out of the sub-corridor. A waiter. One I'd been dealing with earlier, in fact—who'd put my Amex by the register so I could run a room tab. The card was still in there but I decided it was going to stay that way. The left side of the barman's face was raw and burned and he was missing an eye and most of one check and I could see his teeth through the hole. He was dragging one leg behind as he stumbled toward me, and leaving an unpleasant brown trail, but nonetheless closing in fast.

I swept my foot to hook out his good leg, and as he crashed to the ground I turned and ran back the other way.

The door to the toilets flew open as I got level, smacking me into the wall. Carl came staggering out, still with his pants around his ankles, still intent on getting his hands around my neck.

He managed it, too, but some instinctive memory triggered me to use the single piece of useful advice my mother ever gave me. Actually, it's more of a technique. I grabbed him by both ears and head-butted him on the bridge of the nose. It's because of the implications of nuggets of maternal wisdom like this that I've never blamed my father for leaving home in the dead of night when I was nine.

Carl collapsed to the ground and I ran.

It was plain sailing down to the open area where the expensive little wine and cosmetics concessions were. As I hurtled toward the grand staircase, however, jumping over the prone body of someone I'd been drinking with earlier, I saw a woman coming up to my level. She was completely naked and liberally splattered with blood and it was clear both that none of it was hers and that she was keen to add to her collection.

SHIT HAPPENS

She saw me and came running, and I didn't know for sure what language she was screaming in but I thought it was probably German, which would imply the Dusseldorf office. She was fast, and gleeful, and next thing I knew I was smashing backward into a curved glass cabinet that was probably eighty years old and quite valuable. Thankfully I hit it at an angle and the shattered glass didn't sever anything important but then the woman was straddling me and trying to stuff a thumb deep into each of my eyes.

Her breath smelt awful, the kind of stench Carl had been producing in the toilet, but coming up the other way, out of her mouth. My eyes started to sparkle and meanwhile she was feverishly trying to knee me in the balls so I gathered all the strength I could muster and planted both feet firmly on the ground and thrust upward, trying to buck her off.

It didn't work but for a moment she was off-balance at least and so I twisted sideways instead, managing to roll on top of her. I banged her head down onto the parquet flooring—very hard—and scrabbled to my feet. She was snarling and I could barely see anything because of the stars in my eyes but as she started to get up I sent a swinging kick at her head and managed to catch her in the jaw.

I didn't wait to see her land but sprinted the remaining yards to the stairs, leaping down most of the first flight in one jump. This meant I nearly went sprawling and bounced painfully into the wall on the next return, but thankfully I kept my feet and half-ran and half-fell down the next flight.

As I landed chaotically in the reception area I saw a group of people attacking each other. It was impossible to tell who was trying to kill who. It's possible everybody was trying at once. I also saw Peter, at the reception desk, repeatedly smacking someone's forehead down onto its polished walnut surface, lifting it up, and bringing it down again.

He saw me coming, whacked the person's head down one final time—there was enough of their face left for me to recognize him as the clerk who'd checked me in when I arrived—and turned to me, panting. His face and shirt were smeared with something brown. "You took your fucking time, mate."

I sniffed. "Are you covered in shit?"

"Yes."

"Why?"

"I thought it might help."

"Again—*why?*"

"When I came down the steps from the top deck I found out Inka was still alive, even though both her legs were broken. She grabbed my ankle and I fell down. We ended up rolling around in her, well, her *shit*, until I could get away from her again. I thought about wiping it off but then I wondered if maybe it'd help, if the smell would make these fucking loonies think I was one of them or something."

"Does it work?"

"Not even slightly. It was a bad idea."

"Hell yes."

As we ran to the walkway Pete dodged over to the souvenir store, undoing his shirt and throwing it to the ground. Grabbed a Queen Mary sweatshirt and pulled it on.

As he turned back he also picked up a souvenir coffee mug, shaped like one of the ship's funnels.

"Why the hell are you—"

I ducked just in time and the mug reached the target he'd intended—the head of the naked woman from upstairs, who'd come running up behind me. The mug smashed to pieces on her face and she fell like a sack of bricks.

"Dusseldorf?" I asked, as we looked down at her.

"No," he said. "Warsaw."

"Oh. Well, thanks anyway."

"You're welcome. Now let's get the fuck off this boat."

We ran through the doors and out into the fresh air, along the metal walkway toward the staircase that'd get us down to the parking lot. "Why are *we* okay, though? Why isn't this happening to us too?"

"Don't know, don't care," Pete said. "That is a problem for another time, if ever."

"Jesus—look at it back in there."

There were now forty people or more in the reception area—all tearing at each other—with others joining them from above and below. It was hard to tell who were victims and which were attackers, though I did spot

SHIT HAPPENS

the guy from Madrid who'd bought me a pint I never got to drink, and it seemed like he was trying to escape, rather than kill. "Do you think we should try to…"

"Fuck that," I said. "I'm not going in there."

"I'm of like mind," Peter admitted. "But then what the hell *are* we going to do?"

"Get off the boat. Properly. Onto dry land."

"Obviously," he said, "but look." He pointed down toward the dock area. Figures were running back and forth, screaming. Some had weapons. Others were attacking people with their bare hands. "It's no better down there."

"So we find somewhere to hole up."

"For how long? And *then* what?"

"My PA is coming."

"Shannon?"

"How the hell do you know who my PA is?"

"Seriously? Everybody knows you stole her from the Chicago office by doubling her salary. All the other PAs are seriously pissed off about it."

"Okay, well, maybe that wasn't such a bad decision, okay? She's on her way from Vegas right now to pick me up."

"That's an impressive level of dedication."

"This is my point."

"She may not make it here, you know that."

"I do. But I owe it to her to be ready and waiting if she does."

"Definitely." He reached into his jacket pocket, pulled out two small bottles, and handed one to me. "Here."

"Hell is it?"

"Jack Daniels," he said. "Stole them off the plane."

"You do good work, Pete."

"Cheers."

We knocked the drinks back in one, threw the bottles away and ran together to the stairwell and pattered down the three flights to ground level, pausing only to simultaneously kick a fat man who tried to throw himself down on us from the flight above, but thankfully missed us and instead landed with a bad-sounding crunch on the concrete landing.

At the bottom we stepped cautiously out into the parking lot. A car was on fire in the corner. In fact, every car I could see was in flames. The air was full of smoke and choked with the smell of burning tires and the sound of distant sirens. A helicopter flew fast and low over our heads but with no intention of stopping—instead heading out over the bay. When it was clear of land a soldier stuck a huge machine gun out of the side door and started firing down into the water.

"That doesn't seem like a positive development," Peter said.

"No. You figure something even worse is fixing to come out of the ocean?"

"Looks that way. Christ."

"We've got to get farther from the ocean—and fast. Over the causeway and onto the mainland."

"But how's Shannon going to know where to come?"

"She knows where the conference was. She'll have established the ways in and out. Knowing Shannon, she'll text me a map with estimated walking/running/fleeing times under post-apocalyptic conditions—and knowing her, they'll be right."

We headed across the parking lot toward the access road to the bridge back to the mainland. We both ran in a relaxed mode, keeping it loose, not knowing how far were going to have to go. Pete clocked my style and nodded approvingly. "You run?"

"Of course," I said. "Though only a 5k or so, couple-three times a week."

"Me too. I hope that'll be enough."

"You'll be fine. Your form's pretty good. You still stink of shit, though."

"*Everybody* does, Rick. I never realized the end times would smell this bad."

"And it's only going to get worse."

As we ran onto the bridge we watched a group of four women in the middle, as they took each other's hands, stepped up onto the ledge, and threw themselves silently into the bay.

"I fear you're right. But there's one thing at least."

"What's that?" I heard shouting behind and glanced back to see that a group of men were staggering out of the parking lot. Arms outstretched. Coming for us.

Peter saw them too, and picked up the pace. "Nobody's going to give a damn about the RX350i being late anymore."

Then both of us were laughing as we ran faster and faster, over the bridge and toward a city on fire.

ALWAYS

Jennifer stood, watching the steady drizzle, underneath the awning in front of the station entrance. She waited for the cab to arrive with something that was not quite impatience; there wasn't any real hurry, though she wanted to be with her father. It was just that the minutes were filled to bursting with an awful weight of unavoidable fact, and if she had to spend them anywhere, she would rather it were not under an awning, waiting for a cab.

The train journey down from Manchester had been worse. Far worse. Then she had felt a desperate unhappiness, a wild hatred of the journey and its slowness. She'd wanted to jig herself back and forwards on her seat like a child, to push the train faster down the tracks. The black outside the window had seemed very black, and she'd seen every streak of rain across the window. She'd stared out of it for most of the journey, her face sometimes slack with misery, sometimes rigid with the effort of not crying, of keeping her hands and body from twitching with horror. The harder she stared at the dark hedges in shadow fields, the further she tried to see, the closer the things she saw.

She saw her mother, standing at the door of the house, wrapped in a cardigan and smiling, happy to see her home. She saw the food parcels she'd prepared for Jennifer whenever she visited, bags of staple foods mixed with nuggets of gold, little things that only her mother had known that Jennifer liked. She saw her decorating the Christmas tree by herself in happy absorption, saw her in her chair by the fire, regal and round, talking fond nonsense to the utterly contented cat spread-eagled across her lap.

She tried to see, tried to understand, the fact that her mother was dead.

After her father phoned she'd moved quickly through the house, throwing things in a bag, locking up, driving with heavy care to the station. Then there had been things to do. Now there was nothing. Now was the beginning of a time when there was nothing to do, no way to escape, no means of undoing. In an instant the whole world had changed, switching from a home to a cold hard country where there was nothing but rain and minutes that stretched like railway tracks into the darkness.

At Crewe a man got on and sat opposite. He had tried to talk to her: to comfort her or to take advantage of her distress, it didn't matter which. She stared at him for a moment, then looked back out of the window. She judged all men by her father. If she could imagine them getting on with him, they were alright. If not, they didn't exist.

She tried to picture her father, alone in the house. How big it must feel, how hollow, how much like a foreign place, as the last of her mother's breaths dissipated in the air. Would he know which molecules had been inside her, cooling as they mixed with the rest? Knowing him, he might. When he'd called, the first thing, the *only* thing she could think was that she had to be near him, and as she waited out the minutes she tried to reach out with her mind, tried to picture him alone in a house where the woman he'd loved for thirty years had sat down to read a book by the fire and died of a brain hemorrhage while he was out of the room making her a cup of tea.

As long as Jennifer could remember there had been few family friends. No need for them. Her parents had been a world on their own, with no need for anyone else. So different, and yet the same person, moving in a slow comfortable symmetry. Her mother had been home, her father the magic that lit up the windows; her mother had been love, her father the spell that kept out the cold. She knew now why, as the years went on, her love for her parents had begun to stab her with something that was like cold terror: because some day she would be alone. Some day she would be taken in the night from the world she knew and abandoned in a place where there was no-one to call out to.

ALWAYS

And now, as she stood waiting for a cab in the town where she'd grown up, she numbly watched the drizzle as it fell on the distant shore of a far country on a planet the other side of the universe. The trees by the station road called out to her, pressing their twisted familiarity upon her, but her mind balked, refused to acknowledge them. This wasn't any world she knew. In three weeks it would be Christmas, and her mother was dead.

The cab arrived, and the driver tried to talk to her. She answered his questions brightly.

At the top of the drive she stood for a long moment, her throat spasming. Everything was different. All the trees, all the pots of plants her mother had tended, all the stones on the drive had moved a millimeter. The tiles had shifted infinitesimally on the roof, the paint faded a millionth of a shade. She had come home, but home wasn't there anymore.

Then the front door opened, spreading a patch of warmth onto the drive, and she fled into the arms of her father.

For a long time she hung there, cradled in his warmth. He was comfort, an end to suffering. It had been him who had talked her through her first boyfriend's abrupt departure, him who had held her hand after childish nightmares, him who had come to her when as a baby she had cried out in the night. Her mother had been everything for her in this world, but her father the one who stood between Jennifer and the worlds outside, in the way of any hurt.

After a while she looked up, and saw the living room door. It was shut, and it was then that finally she broke down.

Sitting in the kitchen in worn-out misery, she clutched the cup of tea her father had made, too numb to flinch from the pain that stabbed from every corner of her mother's kitchen. On the side was a jar of mincemeat, and a bag of flour. They would not be used. She tried to deflect her gaze, to find something neutral to focus on, but every single thing spoke of her mother: everything was something she wouldn't use again, something she'd liked, something that looked strange and forlorn without her mother holding it. All the objects looked random and meaningless without her mother to provide the context they made sense in, and she knew that if she could look at herself she would look the same. Her mother could never take her hand again, would never see her married or have children. And she would have been such a fantastic grandmother, the kind you only find in children's books.

On the kitchen table were some sheets of wrapping paper, and for a moment that made her wanly smile. It had always been her father that bought the wrapping paper, and in years of looking Jennifer had never been able to find paper anywhere near as beautiful. Marbled swirls of browns and golds, of greens and reds, muted bursts of life that had lain curled beneath the Christmas tree like an advert for the whole idea of color. The paper on the table was as nice as ever, some a warm russet, the rest a pale sea of shifting blue.

Every year, on Christmas morning, as she sat at her customary end of the sofa to begin unwrapping her presents, Jennifer had felt a warm thrill of wonder. She could remember as a young girl looking at the perfect oblongs of her presents and knowing that she was seeing magic at work. For her father would wrap the presents, and there were never any joins. She would hold the presents up, look at them every way she could, and still not find any Sellotape, or paper edges. However difficult the shape, it was as if the paper had formed itself round it like a second skin.

One evening every Christmas her father would disappear to do his wrapping; she had never seen him do it, and neither, she knew, had Mum. In more recent years Jennifer had found the joins, cleverly tucked and positioned so as almost to disappear, but that hadn't undone the magic. Indeed, in her heart of hearts she half-believed that her father had done it that way deliberately, letting her see the joins because she was too old now for a world where there could be none.

She could remember once, when she'd been a very little girl, asking her mother how Daddy did it. Her mother had told her that Dad's wrapping was his art, that when the King of the Fairies needed his presents wrapped he sent for her father to do it, and he went far off to a magic land to wrap his presents, and while he was away, he did theirs too. Her mother said it with a smile in her eyes, to show she was joking, but also with a small frown on her forehead, as if she wasn't entirely sure.

As Jennifer sat staring at the paper her father came back in. He seemed composed but a little shocked, as if he'd seen the neighbors dancing naked in their garden. He took her hand and they sat for a while, two of them where three should be.

And for a long time they talked, and remembered her. Already time seemed short, and Jennifer tried to remember everything she could, to mention every little detail, to write them in her mind so that they would still be there in the morning. Her father helped, mixing in his own memories, as she scrabbled and clutched, desperate to gather all the fallen leaves before the wind blew them away.

Looking up at the clock as she made another cup of tea, she saw that it was four o'clock, that it would soon be tomorrow, the day after her mother had died, and suddenly she slumped over, crying with the kettle in her hand. Because the day after that would be the day after that day, the week after the week after, next year the anniversary. It would never end. From now on all time was after time: no undoing, no last moment to snatch.

There would be so many days to come, and so many hours, and no matter how many times the phone rang, it would never be her mother.

Her father stood up and came to her. As she laid her head on his shoulder he finished making the tea, and then he tilted her head up to look at him. He looked at her for a long time, and she knew that he, and nobody else, could see inside her and know what she felt.

'Come on,' he said.

She watched as he walked to the table and picked up some of the wrapping paper.

'I'm going to show you a secret.'

'Will it help?' Susan felt like a little child, watching the big man, her father.

'It might.'

They stood for a moment outside the living room door. He didn't hurry her, but let her ready herself. She knew that she had to see her mother, couldn't just let her fade away behind a closed door. Finally she looked up at him, and he opened the door.

The room she walked into seemed huge, cavernous. Once cozy, the heart of the house, now it stretched like a black plain far out into the rain, the corners cold and dark. The dying fire flickered against the shadows, and as she stepped towards it Jennifer felt the room grow around her, bare and empty as the last inaudible echoes of her mother's life died away.

'Oh mum,' she said, 'oh mum.'

Sitting in her chair by the fire, she could almost have been asleep. She looked old, and tired, but comfortable, and it seemed that the chair where she sat was the center of the world. Jennifer reached out and touched her hand. Kissed by the embers of the fire, it was still warm, could still have reached out and touched her. Her father shut the door, closing the three of them in together, and Jennifer sat down by the fire, looking up at her mother's face. What had been between the lines was gone, but the lines were still there, and she looked at every one.

She looked up to see that her father had spread three sheets of the pink wrapping paper on the big table. He came and crouched down beside her and they held Mum's hand together, and Jennifer's heart ached to imagine what his life would be like without her, without his Queen. Together they kissed her hand, and said goodbye as best they could, but you can't say goodbye when you're never going to see someone again. It isn't possible.

That's not what goodbye means.

Her father straightened again, and with infinite tenderness picked his wife up in his arms. For a moment he cradled her, a groom on his wedding day holding the slender wand of his love at the beginning of their life together. Then slowly he bent, and to Jennifer's astonishment he laid her mother out on the wrapping paper.

'Dad...'

'Shh,' he said.

He picked up another couple of sheets of paper and laid them on top of her. His hands made a small folding movement where they joined, and suddenly there was only one long piece of wrapping paper. Jennifer's mouth dropped open like a child's.

'Dad, how...'

'Shh,'

He took the end of the sheet lying under her mother, and folded it over the top. Slowly he worked his way around the table, folding upwards with little movements of his hands. Like two gentle birds they slowly wove round

ALWAYS

each other, folding and smoothing. Jennifer watched silently, cradling her tea, at last seeing her father do his wrapping, and as he moved round the table the two sheets of paper were knitted together as if it were the way they'd always been.

After about fifteen minutes he paused, and she stepped closer to look. Only her mother's face was visible, peeking out of the top. It could have looked absurd, but it was her mother, and it didn't. The rest of her body was enveloped in a pink paper shroud that seamlessly held her close. Her father bent and kissed his wife briefly on the lips, and she bent too, and kissed her mother's forehead. Then he made another folding movement, brought the last edge of paper over and smoothed, and suddenly there was no gap, no join, just a large irregular paper parcel perfectly wrapped.

Her father moved to halfway down the table. He slid his arm under his wife's back, and gently brought it upwards. The paper creaked softly as he raised her body into a sitting position, and then further, until it was bent double. He made a few more smoothing motions and all Jennifer could do was stare, eyes wide. On the table was still a perfect parcel, but half as long. He slid his hand under again, and folded it in half again, then moved round, and folded it the other way, gentle and unhurried.

For ten minutes he folded and smoothed, tucked and folded, and the parcel grew smaller and smaller, until it was two feet square, two feet by one, six inches by nine. Then his concentration deepened further still, and as he folded he seemed to take especial care with the way the paper moved, and out of the irregular shape emerged corners and edges. And still the parcel grew smaller and smaller.

When finally he straightened there was on the table a tiny oblong, not much bigger than a matchbox, a perfect pink parcel. Jennifer moved closer to watch as he pulled a length of russet ribbon from his pocket, and painted a line first one way round, then the other to meet at the top. As he tied the bow she looked closely at the parcel and knew she'd been right all along, that she'd seen the truth as a child. There were no joins, none at all.

When he had finished her father held the little shape in his hands and looked at her, his face tired but composed. He reached out and touched her face, his fingers as warm as they'd always been, and in their touch was a blessing, a persistence of love. All the time she'd been on this planet they had been always there, her father and mother, someone to do the good things for, and to help the bad things go away.

'I can only give you one present this year,' he said, 'and it's something you've already got. This is only a reminder.'

He held up the parcel to her, and she took it. It felt warm and comforting, all her childhood, all her mother's love in a small oblong box. She felt she knew what she should do, and brought the present in close to her, and pressed it against her heart. As she shed her final tears her father held her close and wished her Happy Christmas, and when she took her hand away, the present was gone from her hand, and beat inside her.

The journey back to Manchester passed in a haze of recollection, and when she was back in her flat she walked slowly around, touching objects in the slanting haze of early morning light. She wished she could be with her father, but knew he was right to tell her to go back. As she sat in the hallway she listened to the beating of her heart, and as she looked at reminders of Mum she let herself feel glad. It would take time, but it was something she already had: she had her mother deep inside her, what she'd been, the love she'd given and felt. She was her mother's pride and joy, and while she still lived her mother lived too: her finest and favourite work, the living sum of her love and happiness. There would be no good-byes, because she could never really lose her. She could never speak to her again in words, but she would always hear her voice. She would always be inside her, helping her face the world, helping her to be herself.

And Jennifer thought about her father, and knew her heart would soon be fuller still. She knew it would not be many days before another parcel was delivered to her door, and that it too would be perfectly wrapped, its paper a pale sea of shifting blue.

BEST OF—**STORY NOTES**

Welcome to this part of the book.

At time of writing, in fact, as of yesterday, I've sold 96 short stories. We couldn't put them all in here, of course. That would be unwieldy to hold, and a 'Complete' rather than a 'Best Of'.

I didn't write any new stories for this collection. That's not out of laziness, but because of the 'Best Of' thing. I can't be objective about my own work (the Table of Contents here was largely chosen by the publisher, with a few tweaks from me) so unless a story has at least been accepted by an editor somewhere, it wouldn't seem right to give it that 'Best Of' badge. So these are a selection, a subset, of the stories I've written that have seen print. I'm slightly annoyed with myself for not having sold an even hundred, but there's still time. I hope I'll write a significant number more yet, and that at least some of them will be good.

This is a 'Best Of', for now.

It's also a deep dive into the past. The first story I ever wrote is in here, and that takes me back to 1987, the year I left university. The most recent included is from 2017—a neat and tidy thirty year span. Reading these stories, especially the ones from two or three decades ago, is time travel. Every single one brings back, with great clarity, some moment, situation or environment. Each has a part of me preserved in it, verbal insects trapped in the amber of the short story form complete with the DNA of the time when it was written, and the person I was then.

I've always enjoyed reading story notes by other authors (the first I remember were by Stephen King), possibly because when I was starting to write, they helped to make the creation of stories seem more possible. I hope there will be at least something of interest in what's to come. Caution: there will be spoilers, naturally. You'd be far better off reading the note after the story.

I've provided notes before, for some of these stories, but I haven't looked back in those cases to check what I said last time. The note for each story here is whatever it occurs to me to say about them now, as a man of fifty-four, living five thousand miles from where the earliest tales were written: a married man with a greying beard and a disconcertingly tall child; not that single guy, fresh out of college and wondering what the heck happens next.

That was then. And as the title of one of the stories says:

This is now.

The Handover

I've always been deeply touched by ruins.

I'm not talking here about ancient ones, though they're fascinating, but the more quotidian and recent. The tilting barn. The remains of an old road in the woods, superseded by a more modern route perhaps only fifty yards away, the original hard-fought track now pressed in by trees and cracking and letting through tufts of grass (I remember seeing one of these somewhere in America as a teenager, and can picture it now, as if it's in front of me). The boarded-up house a couple of turns away from downtown.

It's salutary how quickly something in use can come to feel disused. How long does it take for the leftovers on your plate to go from still-delicious to a sludge that looks cold and dead and wholly inedible? One of the things that distinguishes humankind is our constant efforts to change and refine the environment, to build places to live and be, forge ways of getting from A to B, or even just put up a structure for children to play on for a few afternoons. A friend of mine has the concrete remnants of what must have been quite an overkill swing base in his back yard. It's in the way, but would take a lot of effort and money to remove, so persists there like the ghost of long-ago afternoons. Just down the road from where I live is a house with the perilous remains of a semi-fancy side gate from the yard to the street, fashioned from old railway sleepers, which must have occupied quite a few afternoons of some dad's labor, but is now disused. I pass it several times a week, and seldom fail to see the shadow of that work in my mind's eye.

We create things, and make places, and for a while they are warm with our souls. But kids grow old, and people move, and towns die, and the inevitable structural decay that follows seems to strike at the heart of what we do, and thus who we are.

So I guess this story, which I wrote soon after a long vacation with my wife spent trawling some of the back highways of the western states of America, is about that.

Save As...

This is one of the few short stories I've written that revolves around a "science fictional" idea, in the sense of something that's not possible now, and would take a technical advance to be true. It's also, for my money, one of the most downright depressing and sad tales that I've ever committed to print.

I mean, Jesus.

Something that's striking and odd about putting together a career-spanning collection is the large periods of time involved (in human terms, anyway). THE MAN WHO DREW CATS, my first story, was written in 1987. This particular story comes from 1996—before I was married, and nearly ten years before I had a child. Time sure as hell passes. My son is now, as noted, noticeably taller than I am.

So in some of these stories I was reaching forward to how I believed I might feel in certain circumstances. For the most part I seem to have got the emotions pretty right, although—thank God—few of the circumstances involved have actually come to pass.

Science fiction is never really about the future. Not my version of it, anyway. It's pretty much always about now, seen through the prism of what-might-be. Given that humans have been functionally the same for many tens of thousands of years, all tech is new tech. Human nature is dogged. We change technologies, not the other way around.

Being Right

One of the benefits of being a writer is that, once in a while, you can indulge in a little speculative wish fulfillment. The idea of a Listening Angel was very much one of these.

One of the most real benefits of the job, however, is that writing a story around such an idea gives you the opportunity to think a little harder about it, to examine your motivations, and consider what the truth of the situation might be.

The idea of the Listening Angel was very much one of these, too.

Hell Hath Enlarged Herself

However long ago they were written, I can almost always remember the initial spark for a short story—the moment where the seed dropped into my mind. This one came from meeting the friend of a long-ago girlfriend. Despite an already long-term interest in the spooky and occult, I'd never taken the idea of mediums very seriously. Over the course of a long evening with this woman, however, I moved a few degrees closer to finding the whole idea somewhat credible. I can't remember exactly why, but that's not important. It was evidently enough to make me reconsider the notion long enough to conceive of this story.

In which, because that's what I'm like, I came up with the idea that yes, the dead do stick around, and may surround us all the time—though only the ones we never want to speak to again.

This story has stayed in my mind and life more than others from its period because it's been in semi-active film and television development for about fifteen years. It may even make it there, some day.

I just hope I'm not a ghost by then too.

BEST OF—STORY NOTES

More Tomorrow

Like others from an early period, this story strongly brings back elements of my life at the time. It features a fictionalized version of the office where I worked as a graphic designer for several years—way back in the very early days of the Internet.

From what I've gathered, it tends to be judged as one of my more harrowing stories. I guess I can see why.

Yes, the Internet has moved on since then. But not that much. And humans are still the same.

The Motel Business

Stories come to me in one of several ways. Sometimes the whole thing—or at least the main point, or key twist, whatever is the Big Thing about the idea—will drop into my head. At other times it's more of a mood, an atmosphere in search of a story.

Unusually, as in this case, it's a title—and merely that, with nothing else attached. The original title for this story was 'The Suicide Motel'. Those three words occurred to me, forcefully, and I wrote them down, waiting for a narrative to attach.

A year or two later this one arrived, but after it was written I changed the title, to avoid it being too much of a spoiler. I'm not done with the original title yet, as a result. I'm sure there's some other and possibly longer story waiting for it.

I'd had this story lying around on my hard disk for a while (I rarely write stories without a commission these days, but I'm always glad when I do), when someone approached me for a popular series of noir anthologies set in specific towns. In this case, Santa Cruz. I sent it to the editor. She came back saying that while she liked it, the female character wasn't empowered or strong enough, and didn't triumph in the end, and I should change that. I emailed back saying that though I was in firm agreement with the case for female empowerment in general, this particular character, in this particular story, wasn't that way: that her powerlessness and desperation and weakness was the backbone of the story, and characters of this type (of any gender) form part of the heart of 'noir'. That was not an acceptable answer for the editor, so I took the story back, without chagrin. This is the only time in my career I've thought: "I've been doing this a while. I said what I said. If you don't like the story, fine. But I ain't changing it."

A few months later, however, I showed it elsewhere in response to a request from a different editor, for another anthology. This editor liked the story but felt the ending was really very dark, and suggested another approach. I was happy to make the minor edit to align it in this case, as—while it became a slightly different thing—it remained consistent with the spirit of the story, and the change was interesting in its own right.

Here, the story is the way I wrote it. Sure, it's a little dark.

But this is what you came for, right?

Dear Alison

A lot of my stuff is firmly placed geographically. I've always believed the location of a story is as much a character as the humans (or in-humans) in it: playing a much bigger role than mere background detail. I can't write properly unless I have an extremely clear mental image of where I'm setting the action, even if that location is entirely fictional. I recently threw out the first five chapters of a novel because I realized I was faking the location, describing it rather than feeling it, and started again.

Almost all of my novels have been set in America. A lot of the short stories, however, were set in London; usually reflecting the parts I was living or working in. This is mainly a swathe of North London encompassing Finsbury Park to Hampstead, but most often Kentish Town, Tufnell Park and Camden.

This very melancholy story charts one route through some of that landscape, in effect an emotional map of where I spent the bulk of my late twenties and thirties. The weird thing is: as I'm writing this I've just realized that last year, on a vacation in London, when my wife and son and I spent a day revisiting some of our old London haunts, we effectively walked this route in reverse—exactly as the character in the story imagines doing.

I'm very, very thankful I did it under my circumstances, and not his. Taking my son back to the park where he and I spent many hours, while my wife, his mother, looked on, is one of the best memories I'll ever have.

The Man Who Drew Cats

Fate is weird, and it scares me.

Actually I'm not sure "fate" is the word I'm looking for. It often seems to be deployed by people looking for intelligent design in the world, a method of reconciling themselves to the way in which random events of the past have brought them to where they are. I guess what I mean instead is the way that when you look at your life, you realize that things which absolutely did not have to happen, that could so easily not have happened, have critically shaped your existence. 'The Man Who Drew Cats' enshrines the biggest example of this in my life. A whole massive list of them, in fact.

Bear with me: this will take a moment.

In 1987, I'd just finished college. I was waiting to hear whether I'd got a grant to start what I assumed I was doing next, a Ph.D. in Philosophy and Social Science. In the meantime I continued with what I'd spent far more time doing in the previous three years—comedy—in the shape of a three-month tour around the UK, with the Cambridge Footlights.

There's a lot of waiting around and killing time in the afternoons during such a tour. Luckily I had plenty to occupy myself, because during a long evening in the pub with my friend Howard, just before the tour, he'd convinced me to try a book by someone I'd obviously heard of but never read—Stephen King (in fact, King and Peter Straub: the novel was 'The Talisman'). I read this book, it flicked a switch in my brain, and I spent that Footlights tour reading everything of King's and Straub's that I could lay my hands on, becoming increasingly convinced that telling this kind of story was what I wanted to do with my life.

Then, one afternoon, during the final part of the tour (a three-week stint at the Edinburgh Fringe, during which me and my Cambridge pals were vilified on British TV for being too posh to be funny) I happened to be wandering by myself through the Princes Street area of the city. It was busy, as always during the Fringe. Some guy was earning a few coins from tourists by doing chalk drawings on the pavement. As I passed this I heard the sound of a child crying, somewhere out of sight. And bam: the idea for my first ever short story dropped straight into my head.

I didn't do anything about it immediately. But when I got home (at which point it turned out I hadn't got the grant to do the further degree, and needed to rethink), I wrote the story. It took about two days. I had no idea what to do with it, so I let it lie.

About a year later I wound up by accident working for a company involved in corporate video (having been mistakenly informed it was a real production company). I met a guy there called Nicholas Royle, who was already making headway in the genre by dint of his stunningly distinctive short stories. And who changed my life. We got on immediately, he encouraged me to keep writing, and gave me the contact information for an editor called Stephen Jones, who accepted the story—making my first-written story my first sale. When the anthology came out the story was well-received, earning (to my frank astonishment) awards for both Best Short Story and Best Newcomer in the British Fantasy Awards held in London in 1991. Emboldened by this, I asked Nick for the names of some editors. One of these was Jane Johnson at HarperCollins.

I sent Jane a letter asking if she'd be interested in publishing a book of stories. She wrote back, kindly explaining that a collection by an unknown young writer was not exactly financially viable, but inviting me to send her a novel if I wrote one—taking me seriously, at least in part, because she'd happened to be in the audience when I won those awards. I was, also by chance, about halfway through my first attempt at writing a novel. When I finished, I sent it to her. She'd accepted it by the following week.

And that is how my so-called career started.

The point of all this "too long, didn't read" back story is this. What if Jane hadn't been in the awards audience: would she still have been as open to me sending my novel? What if I hadn't had the extreme good fortune to meet Nicholas Royle, who was not only crucial in getting me to take my writing more seriously, and introduced me not just to Jane but other writers and other works, but became such a good friend that he—along with

Howard—was best man at my wedding? Speaking of Howard, what if he hadn't bullied me into reading that Stephen King book, without which I'd never have discovered the genre or wanted to try writing in it? What if on that random day I hadn't randomly decided to wander through Edinburgh, and seen and heard those things that led to the story?

I've spent the last thirty plus years as a writer because of all this. It'll be what I do until the day I die. My best friend is Stephen Jones, who accepted that first short story. I met my wife because, having failed to get into academia and having decided to be a writer instead, I wound up supporting myself as a graphic designer for a few years; this brought me into contact with Paula, who became my boss for a short period (who am I kidding: she's still my boss, just in a more informal way). Without all this I would have a different child, or none at all. I would live in a different place, and have done few or none of the things I've most enjoyed and valued down the years. Sure, I'd have a life and have done something—but it wouldn't be this.

And I like this, and I love all those people.

That's why I say fate, or whatever the real word is for that series of variables which shapes our lives, scares the crap out of me.

This is Now

Sometimes stories come not from an idea but a place—including the atmosphere a place enshrines. This is one of those, and dates from a period when my wife and I seemed to wind up always spending time in the Pacific Northwest of the United States.

It may be stretching the metaphor, but it probably comes from a 'place' in life, too: the early days of middle age, when you look at what you've done and wonder if it shouldn't be more.

To Receive is Better

Though toward the shorter end of the stories I write, 'To Receive is Better' has loomed large in my life.

The idea came straight out of a dream (as was the case with a number of early stories, including the first novel, 'Only Forward'). The dream was extremely short—merely a glimpse of a tunnel bathed in murky blue light, with figures lurching in it. From that came this story, and then ultimately my novel 'Spares'.

In a piece of good timing which is unique in my working life, 'Spares' was finished days before the announcement of the cloning of Dolly the sheep. It was quickly optioned by Stephen Spielberg's then recently-formed DreamWorks SKG—news that I received while out playing pool in a local pub, and yes, that was about as exciting (and bizarre) an event as it sounds.

I won't get into the ins and outs of what happened afterward: Google "Spares + The Island" and you'll get the top line.

Bottom line, the movie didn't happen. On the other hand, the sizable option was what enabled my wife and me to put a deposit down on our first house. And last week, twenty-five years later, someone approached me—not for the first time—about the idea of turning 'Spares' into a TV show. It's one of those projects that seems destined to keep rumbling on in the back of my life forever.

They Also Serve

I am on record with regard to my affection for cats. I am, truth be told, a cat fundamentalist.

Unusually, I have absolutely no recollection where the idea for this story came from. Possibly simply the notion that, should humankind head out into space, cats would be their ideal companions.

Except of course for the fact that they'd always want to be the other side of any given door, which might cause problems with regard to the external airlock.

The Scariest Thing in the World

Dating from 2017, this is relatively recent—written after attending the World Science Fiction Convention in Helsinki, Finland.

At least once a year my friend Stephen Jones will email saying 'Hey, I'm going to do an anthology about such and such. Write me something. Don't be late this time.' The two great things about these invitations are that Steve's a subtle editor, open to oblique takes; and also the subject of the book will often be right there in the title, which enables you to tackle a subject from the side.

That's how I ended up writing a barely-vampire story like 'Dear Alison' for The Mammoth Book of Vampires, a not-really-zombie story called 'Later' for The Mammoth Book of Zombies, the slightly Frankenstein-adjacent 'To Receive is Better' for the Mammoth Book of Franksteins, and so on, a list which happens to include many of the stories I've ended up most happy with, which is why they're in here.

This particular story came about as a result of Steve giving me a heads-up about 'The Mammoth Book of Halloween', and so, naturally, is only tangentially about Halloween. What it's more about, it seems to me upon re-reading, is how it can feel to have spent your life doing a thing—especially something creative—with its ups and downs, good years and bad.

How also it's the friends you make along the way that are most important, rather than the work.

I loved Finland—the people, the food, the countryside. It was also great to spend a few days in the company of old friends, and to see my son hanging out with them too. The convention itself, with its worthy panels and fizzy launches, the parties and readings and endless career and brand-building opportunities? I didn't really attend it. Thinking back, not a single panel.

That's not what I was there for.

The Seventeenth Kind

This is, I'll happily confess, a silly story. It came out of a period where my wife Paula and I would laze around in front of QVC, the shopping channel that made its way to the UK. Almost never buying anything, but enjoying the cheerful near-chaos.

It's almost unique amongst my short fiction for having humor as a dominant component. My first three novels (and a much more recent one, 'Hannah Green and her Unfeasibly Mundane Existence') have light-hearted and (hopefully) comedic elements, but that seldom seems to bleed through into the shorter work. I have no idea why.

MICHAEL MARSHALL SMITH

What You Make It

This story was born of two things. The first was my honeymoon—during which we went to (amongst other places) Disney World and Key West. The relevance of the former is pretty obvious. While in the latter, I read something written by someone who'd famously lived there—Ernest Hemingway. 'The Old Man And The Sea'.

In that novella he does something I'd never seen before, pulling focus horizontally across his cast, ending the story on a different character to the one he'd started with. I thought that was pretty cool, and tried it here in this story too.

The second impetus for the story was growing tired of cheap cynicism, of people who think it's cool and grown-up to second-guess and diminish the world and its simple pleasures. Disney World, for example. Of course it's fake and expensive and showing its age a little bit. But being there on honeymoon reminded me of the effect it'd had upon me as a child, when my family lived in Florida. Once you go through the gates, the outside world ceases to exist for a while. Sometimes that's what you need, and why we have books, too.

Not Waving

Some of these stories are even more like time capsules than usual. This is one. Though none of the events happened, obviously, pretty much everything in it reflects something of my life during that time.

In fact, more by luck than judgement, this and the following two stories encompass different sides of a similar period, how I was earning my living, the transition from one long-term relationship to another, and the places I lived during those years.

Later

As noted above, this is—however slightly—a 'zombie story'. At least it came from an invitation to write such a thing.

But...it's really not, except in trying to touch that most terrible heart of the zombie idea, the fear of losing someone to death, along with an instinctive understanding that there's nothing you can do about it, and—as in the classic story of The Monkey's Paw—you shouldn't even try.

Except the protagonist in this story does.

And it goes okay.

Walking Wounded

This was written (as is transparently obvious) in the throes of non-critical loss, having just moved from a fabulous flat in Belsize Park to a much less-fabulous one in Kentish Town.

Another grain of truth is that I really did break a couple of ribs during the process (in reality, as a result of slamming them down onto the hard, metal back of a car seat, while trying to warn my not-yet-wife that her car was about to get a parking ticket). It hurt like HELL, and took forever to stop hurting.

About ten years later I went on a damn-fool trip to Morocco with some old college pals and tried surfing. A couple of days of slamming my chest onto a board while wearing a heavy, crappy wet suit, followed by a calamitous afternoon at Banana Point from which the whole team limped away injured in one way or another, rebroke them, leading to another couple of months of discomfort.

The point of all this whining is to serve as a warning not to break your ribs. It's honestly no fun at all.

The Gist

I have written almost all my stories in a maximum of three days. Sometimes you can add a day or two to that, and perhaps a week of resting before a hard edit, but by and large I like to get shorts out fast: inhabiting the story for as long as it takes to get a first draft down, but no longer. I also try to get at least a first paragraph or even just a line down literally as soon as possible after I get the idea, to fix it. Otherwise it may just fly away.

The Gist was very different. It took, from start to finish, about ten years.

This isn't because it's a particularly long or complex story. It's because of what I wanted to do with it. Somehow I conceived the idea (and this is unlike me, because I'm generally a very straightforward writer) of coming up with a tale and getting it translated into another language. Then having this translation translated into a further language. And so on…before finally having the last iteration of the story translated from whatever language it had ended up in…back to English. The idea was that all these versions would then be published together in the same book, capped at either end by the two English versions. So readers could see how much, or little, it had changed in the meantime, and whether 'the gist' had survived.

Kind of a cool idea, right?

Just say 'yes'.

Getting the project set up was, of course, tough. I talked to some of the people who'd translated my novels for foreign publishers, and got them to talk to their friends and colleagues.

In the meantime I started the story, and for extra meta-narrative credit, I decided to write it about the process of translation. I made the prose deliberately challenging, too, by allowing myself a lot of very London vernacular in the dialogue, in terms of words and sentence structure and verbal rhythm—because I thought it'd be interesting to see what happened to that when it ended up in, say, Icelandic. (As I say, this level of artifice is utterly unlikely my usual work and ideas; I have no idea what came over me). It came slowly, and I got derailed from it onto writing an overdue novel, and then some screenwriting. Then another novel.

Years passed, with me adding a bit here and a bit there, but that was kind of okay because I was still laboriously piecing together the chain of translations. I had a beginning (my Italian translator) and an end—my friend Nicholas Royle (qv), whose work I've always admired, and whose French was good enough to bring the story home to English.

The steps in the middle? Dear lord. Part of the problem was the international publishing industry, which is dominated by the English language. As a result, there's a bunch of professionals able to translate a book in English into a wide range of other languages. There's a smaller, but still significant, number of people who can translate a book from those languages into English.

BEST OF—STORY NOTES

But finding people who can translate from Japanese into Polish? Good luck with that. It took me years to piece together a string of translations through six languages. I can't even recall what the final collection was, or in what order, though yes, it involved both Japanese and Polish (though not next to each other: in the end I had to jam some other language between them).

And so, the story itself finally finished, I triumphantly sent it to the first step in the chain.

And didn't hear back.

Years later I did manage to reconnect with the translator, and he'd been going through some stuff. But the result, despite regular and fairly patient reminders over the next months, and years, is that the project didn't get off the ground, hitting a wall at the very first step. And I gave up.

Then, a few years later, I happened to mention the project to Bill Schafer, who showed guarded interest. Realizing I'd better be more realistic this time, I settled for having it simply go from English to French (courtesy of Benoit Domis) and then back to English (by Nick Royle, as planned). Bill not only agreed to go ahead with the project, but let me design the entire thing too, inside and out. For reasons I can't quite recall but almost certainly extended no further than the fact I've always liked the look of it, I designed the book in a pretty specific Arts & Crafts style, even faking the look of the paper on the cover to look aged.

The book, when it came out, sold predictably badly. But I don't care. I'm proud of it, and extremely thankful to Bill for making it happen (and also for dealing kindly and patiently with me nearly fucking the whole thing up at one point). Bill is also the guy publishing the volume you hold in your hands, by the way. The reason why genre fiction has a past, and a future, is hardworking smaller press publishers like Bill, and Paul Miller at Earthling, and Brian Freeman at Cemetery Dance, and Pete and Nicky Crowther at PS Publishing, and editors like Stephen Jones and Ellen Datlow, and others.

People who hope to make a little money along the way, of course—but are mainly doing it just because they care.

MICHAEL MARSHALL SMITH

Author of the Death

This story is a function of a period when for one reason or another I seemed to wind up spending a few days a year, sometimes as much as a week, in New York City.

I would spend that time doing what I love to do in cities, which is walking. Manhattan is a fantastic place to do this, because—so long as you're prepared to walk up to a couple hundred blocks a day, which I absolutely am—there's a huge amount of variety and so much to see, so many styles and atmospheres to walk though (and, once in a while, a great bookstore to get lost in). One of my tactics for walking in the city is to halt as seldom as possible when on my way somewhere (however loosely defined the destination may be, for example "the next random thing I want to stop and look at"). If my way is temporarily barred by traffic lights, for example, I'll simply turn 90° and cross the other road instead. This can, if you're not careful, add twistiness and happenstance into your journey. I was, deliberately, not careful.

The story also references the fact that I've written under more than one name. In fact, every short story has been written as Michael Marshall Smith (though in one case, and it's one included in this volume, the story relates to a world I've written about under a different name). But I've published novels under Michael Marshall Smith, Michael Marshall, Michael M. Smith, and more recently as Michael Rutger.

I hope that's enough Michaels, but I guess we'll see.

The Dark Land

Another story that came out of a dream.

The first several pages are, in fact, simply a transcript of a particular type of dream I've had a few times in my life, which never fails to be intriguing: a dream in which I'm dreaming that I am where I actually am in reality. There's something very disconcerting about thinking you're in a place, then waking up and finding that you are, in fact, in that place.

This was the second story I ever sold, though it would end up being the first published, in 'Darklands', a volume edited and published by my ever-busy and ever-supportive friend, Nicholas Royle. Back in the old days, when we were doing it in the barn.

Different Now

There's not much to say about this story except that it's set in the first flat I rented in London, shared with a good friend from college, called Jane.

Reading it brings that house back with such clarity that I could model it in clay, life-size.

The Things He Said

This tale is based around the simple—and I believe correct—notion that a global apocalypse would make remarkably little difference to some people's lives…

…and for some, might even come as something of a relief.

The Window of Erich Zann

As noted above, a substantial portion of the stories in this volume wouldn't have come into existence were it not for an invitation from Stephen Jones. This is especially true of the last ten years, when my output in the form has dwindled. Steve's one of the very few people for whom I'll always make the time.

This story was written as the second in a series of contributions to Steve's 'Lovecraft Squad' series of shared-world narratives inspired by that Providence-based scribe's heady universe of cosmic horror. Steve's a master at giving you a brief while allowing you space to enjoy the process, and to create something that's truly your own. He suggested I base the stories around Santa Cruz, my new home, which gave me the opportunity and excuse to do some research and learn about some byways of local history (and Santa Cruz, for a non-huge city of about fifty-five thousand people, has a surprising amount of interesting and often dark back story).

For the first volume, I delved into the stories of a couple of significant local women. For the third, I touched on the area's ominous history of serial killers (you may recall the sign in The Lost Boys, which was set in Santa Cruz, dubbing it the 'Murder Capital of America': that's because at one point they had two serials killers operating at the same time). The idea for this middle tale came from the discovery about the forgotten skeletons of old sailing ships buried beneath the streets of San Francisco, just seventy miles up the coast—a story which is entirely true.

My original title for the story was 'Some Day I Will Sail Away', which I do prefer, but Steve wanted to change it for greater Lovecraftian resonance. I've long made a practice of doing what Steve tells me, and it's seldom steered me wrong.

Everything You Need

A story about loss, I suppose—but also about how, when you've loved and have been loved by someone, they never really go.

On a lighter note, the stuff about the filing cabinet makes me smile. Way, way back when I first started to work as a graphic designer, I ordered a filing cabinet from a catalogue (there was no 'online' in those days). It was, in fact, the filing cabinet described in the story, in precisely those colors.

After that, updated and unwanted catalogues would regularly arrive at the flat I was then living in, addressed to "The Office Furniture Buyer, Michael Smith Associates". There were no 'associates', of course. I just styled myself that way in the hope of looking like more than one scuffling and only semi-competent (and wholly untrained) freelance designer. There was most definitely no 'office furniture buyer', and the two guys I shared the flat with used to relentlessly mock me over this.

Nearly thirty years later, one of them still does.

But as a few eagle-eyed readers of my novels have noticed, I have ways of getting my own back.

What Happens When You Wake Up in the Night

This story does, of course, arise partly out of a weary frustration at a certain child's tendency to get out of bed in the night and—rather than trying to get back to sleep—coming and waking his parents. But a swelling love for your family is born of those hot crucible years of early parenting, and I guess that's what the tale is really about.

How much more there suddenly is to lose.

Failure

This is, I believe, the only time I've written a short story that ties in with one of the larger worlds I've written about in novels—in this case, the Straw Men "mythos" that underlay the first three novels I wrote under the name Michael Marshall (and also features in a fourth novel, which I won't spoil for you).

It's one of the first stories I set in the place which has become my home over the last decade, Santa Cruz, California.

It additionally reflects a growing awareness of the weight of responsibility involved in bringing up a child, and how that duty of care never ends.

Charms

Music has been important in my life. I learned classical piano for years, played the cello (not terribly well) in an orchestra, and the church organ, and still mess around on acoustic and electric guitar. I don't like music on the whole time, but that's because I can't ignore it. My brain seems unable to let music fade into the background. If it's playing, that's all I can hear. Which isn't always what you want.

Possibly because I spent so much of my childhood and teens learning to play, my favorite bands have tended to be pretty instrument-dominated (generally the guitar). Dire Straits. AC/DC. Eric Clapton. There have been others, though I'm struggling to bring them to mind at the moment (I'm crap at making lists). In the last few years, the band I've played by far the most often is My Chemical Romance. I'm sure those choices make me sound terribly male and white and boring. I don't care. One of the nice things about getting older is reaching a point where you genuinely don't give a damn what other people think of your tastes.

But if I had to pick the music that's meant the most to me, for the longest, from the first time I sat at a piano, aged about ten, right up to today? It'd be Bach. No question.

And this story is about Bach, I guess. Also about families, and love, and the passage of time, and how that can break things, and how sometimes they can maybe be repaired. Reading this old tale now, I'm also charmed (I hope you see what I did there) by the way in which a story about time has become its own time capsule: featuring CDs, and set in record stores. Both barely exist anymore.

But Bach carries on.

The Burning Woods

Several years ago I made a trip to Alaska with a college pal of mine (also present on the rib-cracking surfing trip mentioned in 'Walking Wounded' above). He emailed our group saying "Hey! Let's go snowmobiling in Alaska!" and we all said sure, cool, and then the time came, and the others backed out, it was just me and Will.

Flight into Anchorage.

Snow. Cold. Very Cold. Why am I doing this?

A two-hour drive out into the extra-wilds. A five-minute instruction course on how to pilot a snowmobile ("Sit on it; doing this makes it go faster; not doing that makes it go slower; are you ready?") then a descent down a vertiginous two-story slope onto a frozen river. In winter, rivers are the roads.

We were the only two people who'd turned up, it turned out, so it was just us and the guide.

Day one? Do this for fifty miles.

I won't lie: there were many times during the following four days where I was uncomfortable, unnerved, or utterly terrified. I'm not one of those men who are excited by the idea of piloting anything petrol-fueled, nor one who regards danger as inherently beguiling. I didn't enjoy the bits where the ice cracked, or when I understood I was the beta-boy of the team, nor the parts where my snowmobile seemed determined to pull to the left. It transpired that the latter was because of the moment I enjoyed least of all, when on the

BEST OF—STORY NOTES

very first day, already many miles from help, I rolled my snowmobile on an unexpected patch of ice just before a hard left turn up a slope, slapping me sideways onto the ground hard enough to knock a bolt out of my helmet and make me see stars.

The guide later admitted the incident could have gone badly.

As in, fatally badly.

But thankfully, apart from knocking the steering column out of true and giving me a very, very keen sense of the dangers involved, it didn't. The overall experience was cold, and scary, and I spent long periods muttering to myself: I fucking hate this.

But there were other parts, too.

Time spent speeding across mile after mile of frozen meadow, nothing but dark pines to navigate between, a snow-laden sky above.

Time spent drinking beer outside the empty lodge at night, knowing we were the only inhabitants, the nearest town a hundred miles away. And thinking: Will—I'm glad I know you.

The feeling, at the end of a long, cold, scary day of being intrepid and brave, of seeing the (genuinely tricky) upward approach to the lodge by the river, and knowing that—if I could just pilot the snowmobile successfully up it, and once more somehow not crash the thing—I wouldn't have to be intrepid and brave for a little while.

Most of all, the day when—after a morning of hacking along the river in a blizzard, and then a half hour of pretty intense back and forth through a very uneven forest (the sole environment where I had the advantage over Will, as my stomach is strong, whereas he wound up looking pretty green)—we arrived at a lake.

In the middle of nowhere.

Obscured by heavily-falling snow.

And yet there, up on the bank, a tiny cafe.

Inside it was warm and there were glowing lights. We ate, and talked, and warmed up. Bizarrely, in the hour and a half we were present, not one but two of the tiny number of guys lunatic enough to attempt the Iditarod without dogs, arrived, separately. They ate silently, by themselves, and then disappeared again into the snow.

Were it not for them, this place could have just been our dream.

Will and I lingered over sweet coffees, rich with cream, then doggedly pulled back on the multiple layers of clothing and gloves required, clambered back down to the river and onto our machines, and set off into the whiteness, across beaver dams in falling snow, leaving the cafe behind as if it had never existed.

And frankly, it still seems improbable that it ever did.

Strange, dreamlike, an experience that made all the terrifying bits worthwhile. It's that day, more than anything, that started this story seeping into my mind.

Shit Happens

This is one of those stories that just dropped straight into my head as if from nowhere. Not the soup-to-nuts of the plot, but the idea and the tone and a good sketch of how it would go.

I was, in point of fact, in the gents on the Queen Mary at the time, but that's possibly more information than you need. It's the only time I've tried to do horror and humor at the same time—it's a tricky balance to pull off—and yes, it's silly.

But I had fun writing it. In this case for Ellen Datlow, another of the very small number of editors who've made a huge difference, and for whom I'll always try to get something done.

Always

I said near the beginning of these notes that some stories contain events that I was describing before they happened. This is one. At the time I wrote it, my father and mother were alive and well and in their late fifties (not very much older than I am now, in fact). Now my father is in his eighties, and my mother is long gone. Or, at least, is less concerned about preserving a physical presence than she used to be.

Does this story capture the experience of that transition? I don't know. I expect it's different for everyone. But I do know that when I was looking

BEST OF—STORY NOTES

at the suggested table of contents for this collection, I decided this story should go last.

It's an early work, and it's not very long, but I think it's as good a thing as anything I've done, or will ever do.

COPYRIGHT INFORMATION

"The Handover" Copyright © 2000 by Michael Marshall Smith. First appeared in *Dark Terrors 5: The Gollancz Book of Horror*, edited by Stephen Jones, David Sutton.

"Save As..." Copyright © 1997 by Michael Marshall Smith. First appeared in *Interzone, #115*, January 1997, edited by David Pringle.

"Being Right" Copyright © 2003 by Michael Marshall Smith. First appeared in *More Tomorrow & Other Stories*.

"Hell Hath Enlarged Herself" Copyright © 1996 by Michael Marshall Smith. First appeared in *Dark Terrors 2: The Gollancz Book of Horror*, edited by Stephen Jones, David Sutton.

"More Tomorrow" Copyright © 1995 by Michael Marshall Smith. First appeared in *Dark Terrors: The Gollancz Book of Horror*, edited by Stephen Jones, David Sutton.

"The Motel Business" Copyright © 2018 by Michael Marshall Smith.

"Dear Alison" Copyright © 1997 by Michael Marshall Smith. First appeared in *The Mammoth Book of Dracula: Vampire Tales for the New Millennium*, edited by Stephen Jones.

MICHAEL MARSHALL SMITH

"The Man Who Drew Cats" Copyright © 1990 by Michael Marshall Smith. First appeared in *Dark Voices 2*, edited by Stephen Jones, David Sutton.

"This is Now" Copyright © 2005 by Michael Marshall Smith. First appeared in *The Mammoth Book of Best New Horror 16*, edited by Stephen Jones.

"To Receive is Better" Copyright © 1994 by Michael Marshall Smith. First appeared in *The Mammoth Book of Frankenstein*, edited by Stephen Jones.

"They Also Serve" Copyright © 2001 by Michael Marshall Smith. First appeared in *Cat Stories*.

"The Scariest Thing in the World" Copyright © 2018 by Michael Marshall Smith. First appeared in *The Mammoth Book of Halloween Stories*, edited by Stephen Jones.

"The Seventeenth King" Copyright © 2007 by Michael Marshall Smith. First appeared in *This Is Now*.

"What You Make It" Copyright © 1999 by Michael Marshall Smith. First appeared in *What You Make It*.

"Not Waving" Copyright © 1996 By Michael Marshall Smith. First appeared in *Twists of the Tale: Cat Horror Stories*, edited by Ellen Datlow.

"Later" Copyright © 1993 by Michael Marshall Smith. First appeared in *The Mammoth Book of Zombies*, edited by Stephen Jones.

"Walking Wounded" Copyright © 1997 by Michael Marshall Smith. First appeared in *Dark Terrors 3: The Gollancz Book of Horror*, edited by Stephen Jones, David Sutton.

"The Gist" Copyright © 2013 by Michael Marshall Smith. First appeared in *The Gist*.

"Author of the Death" Copyright © 2013 by Michael Marshall Smith. First appeared in *Everything You Need*.

"The Dark Land" Copyright © 1991 by Michael Marshall Smith. First appeared in *Darklands*, edited by Nicholas Royle.

COPYRIGHT INFORMATION

"Different Now" Copyright © 1997 by Michael Marshall Smith. First appeared in *Scaremongers*, edited by Andrew Haigh.

"The Things He Said" Copyright © 2007 by Michael Marshall Smith. First appeared in *Travellers in Darkness: The Souvenir Book of World Horror Convention 2007*, edited by Stephen Jones.

"The Window of Erich Zann" Copyright © 2018 by Michael Marshall Smith. First appeared in *The Lovecraft Squad: Dreaming*, edited by Stephen Jones.

"Everything You Need" Copyright © 2013 by Michael Marshall Smith. First appeared in *Everything You Need*.

"What Happens When You Wake Up in the Night" Copyright © 2009 by Michael Marshall Smith.

"Failure" Copyright © 2013 by Michael Marshall Smith. First appeared in *Psycho-Mania!*, edited by Stephen Jones.

"Charms" Copyright © 2000 by Michael Marshall Smith. First appeared in *Taps and Sighs*, edited by Peter Crowther.

"The Burning Woods" Copyright © 2018 by Michael Marshall Smith. First appeared in *I Am the Abyss*, edited by Chris Morey.

"Shit Happens" Copyright © 2018 by Michael Marshall Smith. First appeared in *The Devil and the Deep: Horror Stories of the Sea*, edited by Ellen Datlow.

"Always" Copyright © 1992 by Michael Marshall Smith. First appeared in *Darklands 2*, edited by Nicholas Royle.

Mount Laurel Library
100 Walt Whitman Avenue
Mount Laurel, NJ 08054-9539
856-234-7319
www.mountlaurellibrary.org